UNDER THE COLORS

BY MILOVAN DJILAS

The New Class

Land Without Justice

Conversations with Stalin

Montenegro

The Leper and Other Stories

Njegoš

The Unperfect Society: Beyond the New Class

Under the Colors

Milovan Djilas

UNDER THE COLORS

Translated by Lovett F. Edwards

HARCOURT BRACE JOVANOVICH, INC., NEW YORK

TO ŠTEFICA

for her love, constancy, and loyalty

*Note on the Spelling and Pronunciation
of Serbo-Croat
Words and Names*

s = s as in sink

š = sh as in shift

c = ts as in mats

č = ch as in charge

ć = similar to, but lighter than, č—as in arch

ž = j as in French *jour*

z = z as in zodiac

j = y as in yell

nj = ni as in minion

g = g as in go

dj = g as in George

lj = li as in million

CONTENTS

PART ONE

PRISONS AND CAVES

From Generation to Generation

Knez Anto Radak expected evil, could only expect evil.

Not that everyday evil to which he was accustomed in his dealing with the Turkish authorities and the begs—slipping them bribes or bringing them gifts, flattering and wheedling them, suffering oaths, threats, and scorn—but some exceptional evil, evil that raged like a plague, totally destroying human life.

Indeed, the Turkish authorities no longer imprisoned and tortured on a whim. They did not want to stir up a wasps' nest among the serf villages and the Serbs, who were tense and ready at any moment to involve themselves in a complicated Montenegrin-Turkish frontier dispute. Even into the most isolated villages the news had penetrated that the Great Powers last year, in 1878, at Berlin, had decided that the Moslem towns of Plav and Gusinje, near the Albanian border, should come under the rule of Montenegro, now recognized as an independent state, with its capital at Cetinje. The Ottoman Porte had agreed. But the Turkish chieftain begs of Plav and Gusinje, under their leader, Ali-beg of Gusinje, secretly supported by the Vali at Skadar, in Albania, and by the dignitaries of Albanian origin at Istanbul, whose countrymen and co-religionists had governed Plav and Gusinje through the centuries, had been unwilling to accept that decision.

It was reported that Ali-beg had said, when he heard of Istanbul's adhesion to the Berlin decision: "Let the Sultan whittle away what he is master of and what he has won by the sword. Miljan Vukov and I have shed our blood in these fields and

3

meadows for thirty years or more and with the Montenegrins for
fifty, and for what he cuts off with the knife may he be blessed
before God and before man!"

Both sides, Montenegrin and Turkish, had tried to avoid in-
tensifying the dispute and to prevent frontier incidents: Cetinje
in the hope that the Great Powers would force Istanbul to reduce
the defiant and obstinate begs of Plav and Gusinje to obedience;
and Istanbul with the idea that by relying on the resistance of
the local Moslem population it could postpone, and even prevent,
the cession of Plav and Gusinje.

This indecision and uncertainty restrained the local authorities
and the begs from rashness and gave their serfs a breathing space.
But Anto knew that it was only temporary. They would not—
they never had and never would—let wealth and power slip from
their hands without bloodshed. For the past fifty years peace had
meant only a respite in the killing and burning, and now, in
these days, even hours, the tension was building up over which
faith and what tribe would become masters of the plains around
the lake of Plav and the mountain pastures above them. The begs
and Moslem clans, wearied of the long bloodshed and the loss of
their lands, feigned innocence, even as the Orthodox clans and
the serfs nurtured the seductive hope of one more uprising, the
very last. So Anto was rightly uneasy when, on the eve of St. Peter's Day, the authorities lured him to Plav for a discussion about
tribute and feudal dues. They shut him up in the kula of the
fortress, without any sort of investigation or interrogation. From
the moment he heard the grinding of the key in the heavy padlock and the creaking of the bolt, he began to question himself
and to steel himself to endure the tortures he expected. Though he
was not yet fettered or bound, he sighed deeply as he looked
around at the gloomy arched cell, whose walls he could scarcely
discern by the light from the tiny window set high in the wall
and crossed by heavy bars.

Anto knew too much about prisons, though he had never been
in one, and the torturing of prisoners, though he had never been
put to torture. Others had told him—haiduks, rebels, monks,
wandering guslars, tellers of folk tales. What he had himself seen,
in war and in frontier raids, from his earliest youth—heads cut
off, horses killed, men maimed whose numbers he could not recall

4

and whose faces he did not remember—these things did not make him bat an eyelid. Men of his own Radak blood had been killed and tortured, even though, living on the fringes of the mass and power of the Serbs and among Moslem and Albanian clans, they had been forced to stand aside from the rebellions. Though they were convinced that their rights were better served by common sense and fair words than by sword and rifle, nonetheless the waves of war and of revolt had flooded over them and carried away one or another from the nest and from the flock.

When the Serbian leader Karageorge had laid waste Pešter, razed Senica, and smashed the Moslems and Albanians at Suvodol, sending his standards to the tribes around the Lim and Ibar as summons to revolt, the Turkish authorities had taken Radule, the brother of Anto's grandfather, to Peć and there tortured him to make him say from whom he had received the standards and where he had hidden them. In the end they had flung him on the hooks in the market place. Gypsies had drawn two butcher's hooks through his ribs, taking care not to touch any vital organs, and then had hoisted him and left him to hang for two long summer days, until his last breath, to terrify the people and to so serve as a lesson.

Radule had not implored or called for help; he had only moaned when his tortures racked him, cursed the Turks, and blessed all the men of Radak, the bones in the graveyards, the children in their swaddling clothes, all the Radak clan, alive and dead, their pastures and meadows, their waters and mountains.

And Radule's brother, Anto's grandfather, after whom Anto was named, had followed his son step by step, since he could not take his place. He had found Radule as he hung, wiped his forehead and moistened his lips, lightened his sufferings with spirit and reason, and in the end had taken his son's body on his back to the wasteland above the Patriarchate and placed him in his grave.

The Radaks had existed before then and after then, but Anto's earliest memory had been of the black and bloodstained hooks through Radule's ribs. It had been handed down among the Radak men that Radule had been outstanding, strong, and wise, such a man as had never before been born, or ever would be again, among the Radaks. Anto suspected that perhaps this was

5

not true, that Radule's fame had grown in the course of time because of his exceptional martyrdom. Perhaps, too, Radule, racked by his tortures, had only suffered on the hooks from noon until evening, as old men from other clans had said. It had then been early autumn, which alway smells of thirsty soil, of weddings and fruits and the fatness of the land, and Radule's wounded body must have started to decompose while he was alive. But of that no one ever said anything, and the tradition was suspect. The wary monks would not let him be buried in the graveyard, because he was a rebel, so his father had dug his grave in an isolated spot far from the Orthodox graveyard. But even in Anto's time, the men of Radak, returning from the markets or from bringing gifts to the Holy King at Dečani—whose vassals they had been right up to the Great Migration of the Patriarch Crnojević—visited Radule's grave, set a wall around it, decorated it with kerchiefs and apples, and kept alive the memory of his death and the recollection of his tortures. There was even talk of moving his bones to his own village, to his own graveyard, but this the Turkish authorities would not allow, lest the people gather there and be kindled into violence.

If Anto did not himself remember Radule, the most hallowed and immortalized in song of the Radak martyrs, he could remember the death of his uncle Arsenius, which had taken place roughly forty years before, when Miljan Vukov Vešović, voivode of the Vasojević clan, had raised a revolt and waged war for the first time on the begs of Plav and Gusinje. As Radule had done with the standards, Arsenius, with toasts at *slava*s and weddings, strove to inflame the men of Radak and the nearby clans to revolt. No one ever found out who had betrayed him, though the Radaks had searched for years, secretly promising a reward, in the hope of avenging his death on the informer or his kin.

Anto's simpleton uncle, Pavle, told how Radule had cried out from the hooks: "Someone of the Radak clan, one of my own brothers, betrayed me!" But the other Radak men kept silent and blamed this on Pavle's lack of understanding. The simpleton uncle also asserted that a member of the clan had betrayed Arsenius and that therefore the Radak men had never revealed the name of the traitor. Pavle had concluded: "The traitor and the hero came from the same womb; neither recognized the other for what he was." Anto did not believe the fantasies of Uncle Pavle, but held firm to the tradition that the men of Radak not only had never been traitors, but also had never been divided.

The story of Uncle Arsenius' death had with time been exaggerated and embellished. Even in Anto's own telling, and despite the certainty of his memory, everything had inevitably been changed. They had not tortured Arsenius; they had not had time in the victorious euphoria between two battles. In the raid on the rebellious village, they had taken him, with about a dozen other rebels, and had killed him on the bridge, on the east side of the Lim, below Jezero, where they were met on their victorious return by the hodžas, their priests, and the old men, the children and dogs, drums and fifes. Arsenius, who was only in his thirties, had hoped for death after his capture. At every bridge, at every crossroad, they had killed one or another of the prisoners. But him, their own serf and neighbor, known in the little town and in the nearby villages, they had reserved for the bridge over the Lim in order to foment bitterness and enthusiasm in the crowd. He had spoiled their victorious rejoicings by refusing to kneel, so that the Turkish soldiers had been compelled to beat him down by force, and tradition had not allowed his perhaps unuttered words to be forgotten: "My head does not bow before the sword!" In fact, his head, which was cut off during his struggle with the Turkish soldiers and should have been planted on the fortress walls, rolled away and was lost in the troubled river.

Arsenius was neither so wise nor so young or strong as the Radule of tradition. Yet in Anto's recollection—he had then been a young man—and in the tales about him, Arsenius, with his blond locks and pale Radak face, was as exalted as Radule and as incomparable. His body did not interest the Turks, since the head had been severed, and the following night the old men and women of the Radak clan had brought it back and buried it. His grave, though it did not become a shrine like Radule's, was tended and mentioned at *zadušnice,* the feasts when the dead are remembered. Even in death, those two remained set apart and unique; them no man could either avenge or revile.

Thus tortures were nothing new to Anto, even though he had

not himself suffered them. As with everything else pertaining to his clan, and as was the case with all clans, their tortures were his, too. They could be neither mitigated nor lessened; they could only purify, show the way to the unattainable. Time did not exist; everything was common to all, to the whole clan. The clan had existed since time out of mind, and even beyond time; whereas individuals were born and died.

Anto, there in the kula, knew that he would be tortured. Through the traditions of his clan, he was as sure of that as he was of sunrise and sunset. But his own apprehensions led him just as surely to the same conclusion. As a Serb, as one of the Orthodox faith, as a serf, he was guilty in the eyes of the authorities, no matter of what or why. He had felt this all his life whenever he had come into contact with the authorities, and as knez of his clan and of his village he had come into contact with them frequently. That long-repressed feeling of guilt had become more definite, firmer, more fateful, as he crossed the threshold of his cell. They would not have imprisoned him if they had not known something. Since the end of the war he had been so involved in plots and conspiracies, and there had been so much coming and going in the clan, that the authorities were sure to guess that something was afoot.

Anto knew that men can reveal everything, but that under torture they reveal more quickly and easily. And he was well acquainted with the man who would be his torturer, the *ćatib* Suljaga Hodžić, though he had never had any special dealings with him. It was said of Suljaga that he had only to look at a man and he at once knew with what questions and with what tortures to begin. Around him had risen an icy wall of terror, behind which he sat, with a smile on his lips, observing men and every living thing as if measuring their resistance, as if imagining real and irresistible tortures for them.

There were still further reasons for the forebodings of Anto Radak.

Ibrica Buljukbaša, a kinless and rootless extortioner, had once again begun to visit the serf villages, as always running after the women and girls, cursing the housewives if there was not enough honey in his gruel, complaining to the householder if a sucking

8

lamb was not killed for him, and demanding tooth money from the brides. The appearance of men like him had always been a portent that the Turkish authorities and Ali-beg's bravoes were cooking up something and that bloodshed had begun along the undemarcated Montenegrin-Turkish frontier. Grgur Radak, Anto's eldest son, had only recently returned to the village with horses laden with arms and munitions from Montenegro. From earlier dealings with Montenegrin rebels and messengers, Grgur knew, even by night, every gorge and goat path around the Lim. Night and day the men of Radak had watched the movements of the Turkish frontier guards, but nonetheless Grgur had unexpectedly come upon one of them at night, and the next day at dawn Ibrica Buljukbaša was in the Radak village, searching the houses and inquiring who was absent and why. Clearly Grgur had not yet been discovered or betrayed, but the authorities, already suspicious, were alert and angrier than ever. The most significant fact was that, two days before, policemen and soldiers had attacked the kula of the Albanian chieftain Bib Doda, Anto's blood brother, with whom the haiduks Vučeta and Tomica had taken refuge. Vučeta was the only brother of Anto's daughter-in-law Stanija, the wife of his second son, Akan, and Tomica was Vučeta's blood brother. It was through Anto that they had gotten in touch with Doda. Doda's messenger did not know exactly what had happened to the haiduks and to Stanija, who had chanced to be in Bib's kula, having brought her brother a change of clothing. The kula had been burned down. The messenger had seen dead men on the wasteland above the kula and three bound men, with one woman, unbound, on the road to Plav. The messenger had only just had time to slip out of Anto's village into the mountains when the two mounted policemen from Plav had burst out of the twilight and given Anto a summons to present himself in the morning to the Kajmekam, the district administrator, to discuss the unpaid portion of the tribute to the Sultan.

There was no kajmekam at Plav, and the turbulent and powerful begs of Plav and Gusinje had made no effort to have one appointed. But since conditions were abnormal and relations strained, the Peć Kajmekam frequently came to inspect the local and frontier administration. Then the higher authorities, in order to keep in touch with the village knezes, would summon them, individually and in groups, to threaten them and give them orders.

Being a knez, Anto was unable to escape; he must either go to the Kajmekam or flee with all his people from the Turkish lands and thus expose the Radak men to exile and their lands to devastation. Therefore, after the policemen's departure that night, he summoned the heads of households for a discussion. But they were divided, as they had been also in the discussions held in spring with Vučeta and Tomica; and close to midnight they ended by leaving the decision to him: "You are knez and it is your head that is in question." For Anto that was a hard and painful decision, and he, alone in the night, sought a solution until dawn.

On the excuse of shortages caused by the war, taxes, and imposts, the Radak clan for the past three years had given almost nothing to the begs or to the Sultan. Like the other Serb and Albanian clans, they had been almost on the point of rebellion, though they had taken no part in the Vasojević revolt, and they had sent no volunteers to the Montenegrin army. Nor had they been able to do so, being too near Plav, on the right bank of the Lim, and among Shquiptar clans hungry for land and every gift of God and only waiting to lay hands on their high but fertile meadows and pastures. The Radak men had been feuding with these Albanian clans from time immemorial, and now, although in wartime conditions blood feuds had been stilled and blood payments settled because both were at odds with the Turkish authorities, the concealed hatreds might at any moment once more burst into flame. In the expectation that they, with Plav and Gusinje, would belong to Montenegro, the Radak men could, by passivity or rebellion, decide, or destroy, the future of the whole district once and for all. The Turkish authorities knew that well and suffered their disobedience, and that of the Shquiptar clans, up to the point of open revolt.

Not to go to the Kajmekam in such circumstances was equivalent to rebellion. The Turks would attack, and a still more terrible Shquiptar foray from Albania would follow, and that might end, as so often happened with unsuccessful revolts, in the destruction of the clan and its expulsion from its lands. Nothing was ready for rebellion: there was no imminent expedition by the Montenegrin army to be expected; more distant villages and clans were not in favor; and the men of Radak themselves were not in agreement.

Even had he not been knez, Anto, as a Radak, would have been unable to rid himself of his outlook and his way of life. The Radak clan had lived in its village from time immemorial, perhaps even from the coming of the Slavs more than a thousand years before and the expulsion of the peoples who had lived in these lands. The origin of the Radak clan, and that of the other clans, was lost in the darkness of the past. But old parchments, royal bequests that had been preserved by the monks in the monasteries, confirmed that they had lived in the same village for more than five hundred years, and that they had been there in the time of Stefan Dečanski, to whose monastery they had been given in fief, and whose feast day they still kept.

Some power, independently, maintained their number at approximately the same level. Should they multiply, then epidemics and killings again reduced them, and after the plagues and massacres they would once again multiply vigorously. They were often killed in conflicts with neighboring clans. But so it had to be; so, too, did others live. Stubbornly persistent, they hallowed and preserved their lineage.

They had settled in the high mountain area and had remained the smallest of the clans, in all about thirty households, but were powerful in their unity and rooted to the soil and their ancestry.

No one could recall that the men of Radak had taken part in any rebellion, though individuals had run away to the forests and had joined neighboring revolts. Such men usually did not return to the clan. The Radaks had always been peaceable, taciturn, hard-working, unboastful; obedient, but made stubborn and rancorous by injustice. At least men like this were the majority, especially those who were leaders of the clan. It used to be said: hard-working as a Radak; but also: unforgiving as a Radak.

More than a hundred and fifty years had passed since the Plav begs had seized them from Dečani and extorted tribute from them. Yet they were still unreconciled—not so much because the gifts to Dečani and the forced labor had been less, but because the true and regular order of their lives had been destroyed. All those years had strengthened their resentment at their separation from the monastery. In peaceful years they sent small gifts of wine, honey, wax, and dried fish from the lake, and also sent some of their young men to serve in the monastery and get a little book learning.

Still more were the Radak men renowned for their integrity. They could not abide toadies and thieves; womanizers they despised. It was said that they had driven from the clan one thief, Simon, with his whole family; and it was kept silent, only whispered, that one Radak youth—whose name was not remembered —had perished without trace for having cast his eyes on a relative. Her name, too, had been forgotten, and she had had to marry the most insignificant and kinless pauper. Every Radak was first and foremost instructed in loyalty to his own kin. They had to stick together to preserve the regular order and community of kin if they wished to survive in a world of murder and rape, of disorder, hatred, and every kind of evil.

Radak men believed that everything was transitory but integrity; that men left nothing behind them except what others remembered of them; and that they were greater if their names lasted longer, serving others as an example. For that reason it was not easy to be the Radak knez. To be knez demanded, over and above all other qualities, an unspotted conscience—a clear sky and a shining sun. Everyone must be able to have trust in him, be able to confide a secret to him and to get justice from him.

Though from time to time the begs tried to impose their own choice of knez upon them, such a man could not last long. The Radak men listened only to him whom they themselves had chosen. And they chose him carefully, in protracted confidential discussions, in controversies and disputes at the meetings of the grown men. There had been knezes who had been weaklings or lickspittles. Certain times and conditions had brought such men. But for the most part the knezes had been wise and capable, and, since the Radak men had never chanced to be in a position to raise a rebellion, no single knez of theirs had ever been an insurgent. They did not, as a rule, change their knez until he was overcome by old age or illness, and they often then elected his eldest son, or some other son, to succeed him. Anto, for instance, had taken over the position of knez from his father, Grgur, who had grown too weak to continue. The clansmen might deviate from this rule if some other Radak had distinguished himself by common sense and uprightness—two qualities that were, for the men of Radak, more or less the same. A man of sense cannot be a man of no account; nor can a madman know what is required of a man.

The ninth year of his knezship had passed. Though he had not been in any way outstanding, no one had any reason to complain of him, and he had succeeded, even in these revolutionary times, in holding the clan together. He had prevented the Radak men from joining the insurgents, though his eldest son, whom he was preparing to be his successor, had shown a liking for them. But when the war was over and it was noised abroad that their village, together with Plav, should belong to Montenegro, he agreed, though the majority wavered, that the Radaks should arm themselves secretly and make ready. If they gave no account of themselves, they might be left under Turkish rule. Neighboring Veliko had become part of Montenegro just because its men had rebelled at the right moment, so that no one could dispute their right. The Radak men, too, must be ready for that; not to foresee the future is as great an evil as to lack faith in the present. So the Radak knez must take care that the Radak clan was not left out of the reckoning.

Grgur was dissatisfied with his father's attempt to get all to agree. He felt that that way everything might miscarry. On the other hand, Vojin Milunov, the son of Anto's cousin, feared that before they were ready the Radak men might be swept into a round dance for which they had neither the strength nor the understanding. Grgur had, naturally, the night before opposed his father's departure for Plav; it was putting his head into the noose! But for Vojin there was no question about it. "They are still the authority for us, whatever may be in the future, and we must work with them," he said.

Anto had learned from his father, and knew also from his own experience and that handed down to him from his ancestors, that time and human intelligence can find ways and means out of every difficulty. So he did not concern himself overmuch with these differences, significant though they were, when he was plunged from the pure mountain-summer morning into the gloom of the ground floor of the kula.

The prison imposed other, unknown, cares upon him. The clanking of the bolts and the creaking of the key made him realize that he was alone, alone as never before, alone with himself. This was not the loneliness felt under the stars, as when he as a boy had awakened among the herds on the mountain; nor was it the feeling of exaltation above the valleys, as when he sat in front of his house on a summer evening. Those kinds of loneliness had always been linked with space and in some way with things created within himself, but this was a sudden rude exclusion from the world, from his clan and his family, from his life until then, from everything except himself. It was even as if he had been separated from himself, and saw himself now with all the weaknesses and uncertainties, the fears and doubts that, except in rare moments, he had scarcely suspected.

He began at once to explore his place of residence, to keep from thinking about himself, though there was nothing upon which he could dwell for long. The cell was five paces long, and when he stretched out his arms he could touch the walls on both sides with his clenched fists. It must once have been part of a larger room; the right-hand wall was built more roughly, more carelessly, from uncut stone and still-undarkened mortar. The floor was of coarse pebbles. In the left-hand corner were three thick ax-hewn planks on roughly squared tree trunks, which served as a resting place for the prisoner, and on the right side behind the door a low tub for excreta and a dish for water. In the wall above the planks were two rings for fettering prisoners, but they had apparently not been used for a long time.

At first it seemed to him that he had plunged into a dead world, into dumb silence. But in such a silence no one was able to imprison him; he quickly was able to distinguish smothered and distant sounds, lowing and bleating and whinnying, even crowing and, in the evening, sometimes girls singing in the gardens. Always he was able to hear the gurgling of the stream, which, as he remembered, flowed through the town gardens and vegetable plots and then was smothered under the kula itself. Sometimes at night he could also hear the heavy, primeval, and unearthly

14

breathing of the lake. And never would he forget the muezzin's call from the minaret, in the early morning, at noon, in midafternoon, at dusk, and in the evening. "A foreign faith," so he said later, "yet I waited for him to summon the Moslems to prayer as a chilled man greets the sun; man takes joy in man."

Thus something was always happening, outside himself, reminding him painfully and sensibly that life and the world were going on without him.

When he had more or less come to terms with his imprisonment and had lain down on his jacket spread over the planks, he concluded, encouraged, that, when he did not return in the evening, the Radak men would know he had been thrown into prison. It might be of some direct advantage to the clan, would make them keep a close watch and be ready to defend themselves. But that realization did not, strange to say, bring him any joy. It was as if the Radaks had all at once become distant and unreal, making his loneliness more terrible, and revealing within himself a hitherto unknown and unforeseen selfishness. His thought was not of the advantage they might draw from the knowledge of his arrest, but of his own pleasure and hope.

He remembered that he must put his cell in order, for it was tormenting and unworthy to lie among such filth. The cell was a real pigsty, though he had not at first noticed it. Straw was scattered in all directions, as well as old shoes, scraps of sandals, torn slimy stockings, and rags of indistinguishable color and use. Dust and dirt were over everything, and the fleas seemed only to be waiting for him to keep still, to sit or to lie, before starting to leap on his neck and hands and burrow into his stockings and trousers.

He rose and knocked on the door. Though the whole kula echoed, it was long before anyone came. At last sandals clattered down the steps and along the coarse pebbles of the corridor. The bolt was drawn back slowly and creakingly, and the key turned angrily. In the half-opened doorway appeared the washed-out, bony, hangdog face of Abdulah Mekić, the same policeman who had locked him in when he had first arrived.

"What do you want?" asked Abdulah curtly, as if interrupted in some important task.

"I want nothing, but I would like to clean my room"—*room! As if this is a room!*—"and get some water."

15

Abdulah thought this over carefully, as if it were something important. "All right, if you must," he at last said, and added: "The others, all sorts of scum and riffraff, we have to force to clean out their cells, so the mud and insects don't eat them alive. Just wait until I've had my breakfast."

Anto was in no hurry. He cherished the hope, walking to and fro in his cell, that when the door was opened he would hear something about himself from the guard, and if they let him go to the stream to wash out the tub saturated with the stink of piss and get some water in the dish, he might see someone he knew, even someone of his own family. His daughter, Roksanda, had been married in Plav that spring, and his relative Mitar and Mitar's son, Mirko, were working there as wool carders. The Radak men, and others also, would come to know that he was imprisoned. This thought easily reawakened that selfish joy.

But when Anto, on Abdulah's return—he had stayed away a long time, much longer than he needed for his breakfast—began clearing his room, with intentional slowness, he did not overhear anyone mention his name. He knew that on the first floor of the kula were rooms in which judgment was given and interrogations carried out and that there, too, the Kajmekam received when he came to Plav, whereas on the second, and highest floor were the policemen's quarters. He could hear a door creaking open on the first floor, that floor which was so important for him, and someone walking laboriously, as if carrying a burden, along the corridor to another door. Then that door creaked, and there was silence once more. From the second floor, however, policemen came down or climbed up the worn blackened steps every few moments. They went circumspectly, as silently as they could, as if in the kula were some great and important man on the point of death. Anto concluded from that that the Kajmekam was there and that it was he, fat and heavy, who had just walked along the corridor. *They are debating something important. About me? About the Radak clan? Who can say what? Turkish methods!*

When he went out with Abdulah, the summer sun greeted him, as warm as at midday, blinding him with the freshness of greenery and mountain streams. But the isolation and the loneliness went on, as if they were independent of the dank stone and twilit gloom of his cell. Anto felt as if he were in some unknown coun-

16

try, though every gateway, every paling, was familiar to him. The children, halting in their ball games, and the merchants and artisans, breaking off their business or conversation over their open counters, watched him gloomily and timorously. So, too, had he watched prisoners, as men already guilty, condemned and isolated from the world. Now that he was one of them, he was in no way surprised or ashamed that others should do so.

Water was obtained from above the little town. He passed through the whole market place, there and back, with light, measured tread, and did not meet anyone he knew, much less any of his kin. His relations, Roksanda and Mitar, lived away from the center. Everyone steered clear of him with aversion, as though turning from the heat into cool shadows, looking at him with suspicion and seeing the last of him with relief. The thought of flight he rejected with his first steps into the town; that autumn he had completed his fifty-sixth year and, though still strong and agile, he would not be able to cross the open spaces to escape from the long-legged, thirty-year-old, and armed Abdulah, much less the horsemen who were always at the ready in Plav. Nor would there be any sense in running away, for he still knew nothing, not even why he had been arrested.

Plav was a little town of about a hundred stone houses, with balconies and gardens, with eaves, doorposts, and cornices of carved and colored stone, for the most part belonging to well-to-do families. The market place was large and irregular in shape, bright with the glitter of copper pans, filled with the busy tapping of the filigree workers' hammers and with tanned hides and sheepskins hanging odorously amid the clatter of mallets and smiths' anvils. From a distance, from the mountains, the houses, under darkening shingles, looked like a flock of wild geese just risen from the green meadows to swim in the waters of the lake; as he walked through it, it seemed like a toy, with its village plots and magic gardens, wooden huts and stone palaces, a place in which men did not live, but some other kind of beings, better or much worse, more beautiful or much uglier.

He returned, step by step, with the tub in his right hand and the dish in his left, while Abdulah, behind him, teased and admonished him. "You are looking around you in vain. No one can help you. Look how everyone turns away from you, as from a rebel. And a rebel you are, since you have raised your hand against the authorities, as if you were Allah himself. Be sensible! Help yourself. Bow your head, and the authorities and Allah will aid you. I do not know why you have been arrested; they told me nothing. But it was not for nothing. They keep no one here because they have black eyes or blue. But take care when they begin their interrogation; then we shall not allow you even to go and get water. That we do not permit, in case you should give a sign, and other guilty ones run away. We know all these serf and Serb tricks! Hurry up and get back to prison. You may cool your head there. As man to man: be sensible. The authorities will find a needle in a haystack or a snake in the grass."

Anto did not expect to be called that day. On his return to his cell, he dozed. It was past lunchtime—he had been given a round loaf of bread only and had eaten half of it, for he had brought nothing from home in case the authorities might think that he knew they would hold him—when the bar was drawn back slowly and cautiously, with a sound like the rasping of a gigantic snake among the rocks, and then the padlock was turned twice. Abdulah had been relieved by Meho, also from the Mekić clan, a tall, handsome youth with full ruddy lips and cheeks and eyes dewy and deep as wells. When he smiled, which he did often and without reason, his powerful teeth shone and revealed a wolfish savagery. Unlike Abdulah, Meho, in his smiling strength and beauty, talked all the time, meaninglessly. Both Mekići were close kinsmen of the refugees from Kolašin, and because the Montenegrins had taken their land from them, they had been granted for livelihood the harsh and unpleasant police service. There were many refugees in Plav, for the most part desperately embittered and fanatically harsh. This could be noticed both in the obscure and boastful words of Abdulah and in the gay, muted malignity of Meho. Both seemed to Anto so transparent in their malice that he would not have liked to fall into their hands, although Meho almost gaily called him to go for interrogation.

Unlike Abdulah, who, slouched and impatient, supervised him casually, Meho seized him by the right arm and went beside him.

"Why are you holding me?" asked Anto, offended by the pressure of Meho's grip.

Meho was silent for a moment, then broke out curtly: "That's the way it must be." He did not even loosen his grip going up the steps, but pulled Anto closer in the narrow space between the wall and the rail.

The kula was colder inside than the cell, and Anto's vitals were pierced by a chill emptiness.

The kula had been built forty years before, just at the time of the first Vasojević rebellion under Voivode Miljan Vukov. It had been erected by the rash and insubordinate beg of a small but warlike clan, which, like many others, had squabbled over leadership from time immemorial with the stronger clans, the Redžepagići and the Šabanagiči. Foreseeing a final and bloody settling of accounts, this beg had designed and built the kula, which had turned out a discordant mixture of fortress and comfortable house for a large and rich family. Its thick walls of massive, crudely wrought stone, its countless loopholes, and especially its prominent position on a bare hillock had made it a fortress that rivals could not breach. Only the Vizier's heavy guns, dragged with immense difficulty over mountains and gorges, were able to damage the kula, and on it could still be seen the holes made by them, repaired with a coarser, darker stone. The small clan was thus defeated, and its rivals consolidated their position the more easily because the Vasojevići, under Miljan Vukov, had risen against the begs and the Sultan and from their mountains began raiding the Lim Valley, taking village after village and clan after clan. It was no longer a matter of which chief or what Moslem family would gain superiority, but of whether Islam and the rule of the begs would endure.

With the change of rulers, the deserted and half-destroyed kula quickly assumed a different purpose. The fortress, once the pride of the begs, became a prison for serfs and the seat of the authorities. But within it little was changed. Even the ground floor, which had been built as a storehouse and powder magazine, did not need much alteration to make it suitable for cells. The guest rooms and the reception hall on the first floor were turned into offices for the mudir and the courts, and the harem on the second floor became the police quarters. So the kula remained, and grew as a symbol of power and injustice. Plav was a whole flock of kulas, square stone houses with loopholes. But only one of them, the old fortress, was referred to without mention of its owner.

As a youth, Anto had worked at *corvée* for the kula. He had driven his beasts there with cartloads of stone and sand from the Lim. There were few in the upper Lim district who had not contributed their stone and their sweat, little suspecting that they were thus building a prison for themselves. Anto, too, had not then suspected this, though the labor had seemed useless and backbreaking. But later, after the haymaking, when he was resting and looking out over the lake, and saw the kula, with its blackened shingles, standing out among the Plav houses like a swan's neck, it had occurred to him that by chance he might one day be imprisoned within its walls. Now, as Meho pulled him along, he recalled for the first time that distant inexplicable foreboding on the mountainside, as if he had always borne within him a premonition of the kula, of the prison.

When Meho brought him to the *ćatib* Suljaga Hodžić, who spoke to him of torture in a chilling and detached way, Anto was divided between a fear that he would not be able to endure and a firm conviction that he would never betray the Radak clan or do anything that might bring dishonor upon himself. His thoughts were evasions to the *ćatib*, to himself, as he avoided evil bitter words. *I feel weakened, advanced in years, a small, wretched human creature in chains before insatiable and overweening force. But how could I, as a traitor, look men in the face tomorrow, men who have opened their souls to me, have shared with me good and evil, bread and salt? What sort of Radak knez would I be? The Radak graves would open before me that the bones in them might curse me, and the fruit in the mothers' wombs would turn to stone at my glance. Help me, merciful and almighty God, to subdue my body that the Devil does not overcome me craftily by torture. I can neither endure nor betray. I know neither who I am nor what sort of man I am. How can I know when I have not yet experienced the mortal trial, when I have never had to choose between honor and life!*

At first the *ćatib*'s conciliatory attitude astonished him. Already awed and terrified, he realized that it was a snare. To the *ćatib*'s veiled, intentionally vague threats he replied cautiously, with considered cunning. *Who knows? Perhaps he will not torture me. It is better that I do not excite and provoke the authorities.* But as the conversation continued and the *ćatib*'s tone became harsher, Anto indirectly, but deliberately, betrayed his firmness.

Tugging at his sparse mustaches, so blond that they were almost white—he often tugged at his mustaches or his short-cut reddish beard, as a sign of reflection or satisfaction—Suljaga began: "We, so to speak, do not know one another. Yet we are near to one another—so to speak, neighbors. I know all about you. You are not afraid for yourself but, so to speak, for the men of Radak. For you, the Radaks are your life and your existence, everything. So it is with you from the clans. But it has never occurred to us to destroy the Radaks; we should, so to speak, destroy ourselves. For there are no better householders and more honest serfs than you are. Why should we massacre and disperse you, who are hardworking and skillful in everything, only to hand over your lands to Shquiptar lazybones and paupers who know nothing except how to decorate themselves with weapons and sing mad songs? Let us two come to an agreement and discuss: I, how to spare you and the Radak clan; and you, to confess everything about the rebellion, so that we may bridle and suppress it. That is, I to you, and you to me. Nothing in this world exists that cannot be changed for something else; good and evil are mingled, and one is transformed into the other. It is not possible for all to be good at all times and in all places. Let us, so to speak, talk a little so that I may gain something from you and you from me. So the world is arranged."

Suljaga fell silent, having enjoyed his own words, but watched Anto attentively. Anto shifted uncomfortably from foot to foot, realizing that the gray inquisitorial eyes of Suljaga were caressing his face, reading his every thought. "Aga, I do not understand you well." *I understand you, all right. I know what you want, you crafty old fox!* "I do not know what you want or what you are talking about. We men of Radak are peaceful and hard-working, as you yourself say. We are good subjects of the Sultan and obedient serfs. Sometimes it is not good to stir up a beehive; angry wasps may come out."

Suljaga peered at him and ceased stroking his beard.

I've made him angry. He's holding himself in. I must tell him to his face, from the very start; I must let him know that we men of Radak know how to explode. Let him bear in mind that the

21

Montenegrin army is not far away and that it is only two hours'
walk to liberated Veliko.

Suljaga banged his fist on the table and stood up. "We are the
rulers," he broke out curtly, facing Anto with suddenly narrowed
pupils in eyes now green and virulent. "The authorities do not
stir things up; they do their duty. If you serfs have grown horns,
we will beat them back into your heads. You put your trust in the
Montenegrins, for they have warfare in their veins. But they, too,
are satiated with other people's wrongs. Now they are squabbling
among themselves about chieftainship and the distribution of the
begs' villages, like everyone else who seizes power. Or perhaps
someone has filled your empty pumpkin heads with the tale that
we dare do nothing against you because of Europe and because
the French consul will come rushing from Skadar to help? No one
will move a finger for these bugs from the Lim! And what if they
should? We do not give up what Allah gave us and the Sultan
and our ghazis died for. It is not from yesterday that we have
lived by the sword and the rifle. When we are not cutting with
them or shooting with them, then we are sharpening them and
loading them, so that they may cut the better and hit the target
with more deadly aim. Rifle and sword will decide to whom this
district shall belong, and not you lousy serfs! Be reconciled as you
have been till now. For who has more right to judge than those to
whom Allah has given the power to judge?"

It seems he knows nothing. He is softer than he makes out. I
mustn't irritate him. "We, honored *ćatib,* are submissive to every
ruler. We give our tribute and pay out taxes and everything that
is asked of us. I do not say that everything is good and just, no; it
might be better and more just, that it might."

"So it has always been and always will be," the *ćatib* said, and
suddenly smiled. "Human life, so to speak, can never be so that it
could not be better and more just. But that is not the question,
that we, so to speak, might become wiser. Tell me, why are there
so many weapons all at once among you Radak men?"

Someone has betrayed us! Who? Or perhaps no one has be-
trayed us, and these are only his suspicions, his gropings. "We are
not forbidden to have small arms, *ćatib.* We must defend ourselves against wild beasts and Shquiptars."

"I know, I know. But this is too much: all at once five pistols in the village, as well as other things—rifles and boxes of ammunition."

"I know nothing about any rifles or ammunition."

"You know, you know, all right. But now it is I who am speaking, and you who are listening. We know what is cooking and who is the cook. But, so to speak, we would like to put an end to all this with as little harm as possible, both for you and for us. Therefore, for the moment we are not touching any of the other Radak men. We are trying to strike a bargain with you, by peace or by force. But we are well able to strike at them, too, and hand over everything, so to speak, to fire and sword. The arms you have received must be surrendered, and we will decide who may keep what. No one may keep even a skinning knife that we do not know about. You have heard; now be sensible!"

Suljaga had gone back to his table and was stroking his beard. His eyes, in the shadow, again were gray and distant, and his beard seemed thicker and darker. He changed like a cloud, like a rainy day.

"Someone has been telling lies about us. There are informers everywhere, anxious to get into your good graces, aga."

"I know, I know. But I take their lies with a pinch of salt. I know what I know. And you, too, know what you know. Therefore I order you: the arms must be surrendered. I assure you and I promise you on my head and on my honor—and if you do not believe me you can, so to speak, have a chat with the Kajmekam —that not a hair of the head of any of the men of Radak shall be harmed if you do so."

Suljaga fell silent, twisting his fingers in his beard. *Even if I should consent, who among the Radaks would give up the arms? It would only be the beginning of inquisitions and investigations.* "I cannot, ćatib, hand over what does not exist. That not even the Tsar could do."

But Suljaga was not listening; he went on with his argument. "I assure you that I will wring the truth out of you! What must be, must be. Whoever has fallen into my hands"—his hands were white and plump, but capable, terribly capable—"has never been able to stand up to me; no living man can ever resist the tortures that man can imagine. Listen, Radak, a man thinks out tortures for another man at his ease and in a thousand ways, and that man has only one body, one soul, to resist, burning in agony more terrible than any other. Don't think that you are Ilija Kuč. He was one in a hundred years and in a thousand cases, and he who tortured him was not Suljaga Hodžić. I am, so to speak, one in three hundred years and among thirty thousand torturers."

Menacing and bitter, he again stroked his beard, as if he were horrified at the skill of which he boasted. The sunlight lit up his brilliant new fez, with its black tassel, like a wild poppy. He wore it with a strange air of dandyism, cocked to the left, and not on the back of his head like other Moslems. He said: "I, too, do not like evil, but I do not forgo evil against those who, I say, raise their hands against the Sultan's rule and the faith of the Prophet and the authority of the begs. So it was and so it will be. Everyone defends himself and his, and the world has never been, and never will be, without tortured and torturers. My bread, too, is bitter, more bitter than yours. I am now the torturer, but tomorrow I, too, could be among the tortured. So it is for you, and for everyone else."

Suljaga spoke truths, truths well known from Radak serfdom, from Serb experience and tradition. But, expressed so baldly in the suffocating heat and scintillating brilliance, they sounded like a terrifying dream. "Every such thought is distant from me, from every Radak," Anto almost whispered, though it was not clear to him exactly what he meant.

Suljaga rose, and, though Anto knew him to be a shortish, rather fat fifty-year-old man, he suddenly seemed taller and thinner, more powerful, as if within him were some supple impetuous beast. He stood by the window, and it seemed as if the lake flooded over his shoulders, with waves changing color, like his eyes, from gray to green, while a boat with two rowers slowly and with effort fled from him behind the black frame of the window.

It is stuffy; the top of my head feels as if there were a weight on it. It would be good if it rained, good for the pastures and for the maize.

"I am a night worker, a bird of darkness," Suljaga continued. "It is not that we should be hidden or that I should conceal my work. Everyone knows what we in the kula do to rebels, those who are disobedient and those we dislike. But we like, I like, so to speak, no one to interrupt or hamper me. I wish to be alone with the guilty one, face to face, and then it is force and skill for me and spirit and strength for him."

For him, everything is ordinary. To probe, to interrogate, to torture—that is his job, just like any other, just like pulling up onions or driving a plow. Work is well done when one thinks of nothing else, when no one hinders.

Suljaga finished, lifting his hands as for an oath or a prayer: "You go now and think it over till this evening. No one will interrupt you. Search your soul. Every authority is merciful, but it is also heartless. The sword does not cut off the submissive head—that is a Serbian proverb. And make no mistake: what you do not give voluntarily we will take from you by force; we will make the mother's milk shriek within you. Don't torment both yourself and me. Be a man, Radak."

Anto was taken back to his cell. He did not know how he got there. He was trembling at the thought of the night, of the torture that menaced him. At the same time he questioned: What does Suljaga know? Who was the traitor?

Obviously, Suljaga knew something about the arms, but he could have guessed that, even if no one had told him anything. When, in the spring, Grgur had clashed with the watch or with an ambush on the Lim, the guards must have heard in which direction, toward the Radak village, the clinking of arms had died away. It occurred to Anto that someone from the Radak clan might have been the informer. That thought he would willingly have rejected, but it intruded more and more stubbornly. Though the Radaks had always been of one mind toward the Shquiptars and the Serb clans, about their relations with the begs and the Turkish authorities there had always been dissidents and waverers. No agent or traitor had ever been discovered, though more than once there had been suspicions, especially in the case of Arsenius. The times had then been unfavorable—Montenegro weak and distant, Serbia still more distant, and the Radaks, though more closely knit than now, had been backward, forgotten, and uninformed. But now that the hope of liberation had washed over Radak souls and homesteads, who could be so pusillanimous, much less a traitor? Yet reality was rich in treasonable opportunities and possible traitors.

Surely the Montenegrin haiduks Tomica and Vučeta, if they

had indeed been captured, would not, could not, have begun to sing at the first burn or blow? Both had acted heroically. But that was something else, something quite different, as Anto well knew, from the heroism of a man alone and helpless, bound and thrown within prison walls at the mercy of all-powerful executioners. There are men who grow so hot before battle that they fear no one, especially if at least two others are watching them, but afterward, when taken prisoner, show themselves weaklings and poor in spirit. Perhaps Vučeta and Tomica had been such men.

They had brought with them messages to go for the arms. Anto had feared most of all the arrival of the arms, for it could pitch the Radak clan into living fire before anything was ready. But they had had to take the arms; had they refused, the Montenegrin chiefs would not have understood, and also the frontiers might soon be completely closed. Tomica and Vučeta had begun to accuse the Radak men of being waverers and to sow discord among them, dividing them into heroes and cowards in accordance with Montenegrin custom.

Anto did not like the activities of the haiduks, even though Tomica and Vučeta were better than most. They were, for the most part, men without family, rash and insubordinate, and not workers. Among the Radaks, peaceful, home-loving, and steady, even the songs about the legendary haiduks were transformed. The haiduks seldom chose whom to rob and paid no heed to what sort of reprisals might fall upon the serfs and the poor Serbian people. There were among them those who died without a cry or a regret, on the stake or on the hooks, but there were also many who betrayed those who had sheltered them and pleaded for mercy from their executioners. The Radak men themselves had had bad experiences with the haiduks, which Anto still remembered. Many times they had plundered the tribute money and stock, even the coins in the girls' dowries and their bridal jewelry, and scarcely forty years ago some of the Vasojević haiduks, whom Anto's father had sheltered during the man hunt, betrayed him to the Turks as soon as they were taken prisoner.

Vučeta and Tomica were well known for their inseparable friendship and blood brotherhood; their names were always mentioned together. This was the more beautiful and unusual because they were from quite different classes and districts. Vučeta was from the pasturelands below the Kom mountains, whence Miljan Vukov had come and preached rebellion, though his homeland had been quite free for the last forty years. Tomica was from a little Kosovo town, from the land that two hundred years before had been overrun by Shquiptars, and where the Serbs, almost exterminated, held out, oppressed yet enduring, maintaining their faith and their language. There was nothing visible or comprehensible that could have linked these two men except the Serb ideal. But that was so powerful and burning within them that it consumed everything that might have turned them from one another. Though they were both already in their thirties, both were unmarried, as if they feared that women might either separate them or turn them from their goal.

Vučeta was all muscle, of medium height, with broad shoulders, thin, wiry legs, and dark-brown hair with reddish lights in it. He had a large mole on his left cheek, which he tried in vain to remove because it made him easily identifiable. Of the two, he instilled the greater confidence, the more so because he was, rare enough among Montenegrins, taciturn and not boastful. Anto had more trust in him, especially because they were related.

Tomica, also thickset, was smaller and darker, with delicate shining mustaches of which he was evidently proud; he twisted them upward carefully and tenderly. He, too, did not boast, despite his talkativeness and—a wonderful thing for a man who had forever forsaken house and land—his humor, though that was not without an undercurrent of melancholy and bitterness. He would sing willingly and beautifully to the gusle, and only then was he frankly melancholy. Singing to the gusle was a Montenegrin custom. The Radaks, except the younger ones, did not much enjoy doing it, for they were Serbs in a different, unimpulsive manner, tempered by suffering and inward, inconspicuous perseverance. Their songs, for the most part love songs and religious songs, were mainly sung by the girls and were full of passion, mourning, and faith in things beyond this world of men. There could be no gusle-playing or Serbian heroic ballads in Kosovo, Tomica's homeland. There no one dared even to mourn in Serbian. Tomica must have learned his gusle-playing and singing in Montenegro, in the long and tedious winters of sheltering from the man hunts. But in this he was un-Montenegrin: he did not halt, break off, preen himself like an eagle, cry out, and whisper. His song flowed strongly and evenly, like a lowland river. This merrymaker, filled with a dense, impenetrable melancholy, became different in every way from what he was in everyday life. Though he was no kin to them, in such moments he seemed nearer to the Radak men than Vučeta did.

Both of them, each in his own way, danced attendance on the Radak girls. That was what most displeased Anto and now, in prison, most aroused and strengthened his suspicion of the haiduks. The Radak men did not suffer loose-living in the clan. Theirs was not the harsh Montenegrin implacability; accustomed to evil, to searching for a balance, they looked upon adultery as an inescapable and a human sin. That sin was unforgivable only within the clan, like other sins against their blood and lineage. But because their women were exposed to Moslem oppressors and libertines, they judged forwardness and licentiousness the more severely when it came from the Serbs, their liberators. Vučeta was the more open, the more avid, in his attentions to the women, whereas Tomica approached them with that same pained seriousness he had when playing the gusle, as if drawing nearer to some sacred, holy act.

It so happened that the haiduks were staying with the Radak clan at the time of the wedding of Anto's only daughter, Roksanda. It was not the right season for weddings, but it was time for the girl to be married. Anto, foreseeing fighting and rebellion, was trying to muster the clan, and a girl ripe for marriage in the house is like an open fire. All the Radak women were collected in Anto's house, and Vučeta at once set his eyes on a muscular brunette, the widow Petrana, while around Tomica, luring him with her dark-green eyes, moved Stojna, a town woman from Kosovo and Roksanda's future mother-in-law, still light and young in features, with a good figure and quick unembarrassed seductiveness. There was something comic in the clumsiness with which Petrana fought to get next to Vučeta in the kolo, threw her broad, heavy red hand across his shoulders in the dance, and afterward lured him into the darkness, shamelessly, her big eyes squinting. And Stojna drew Tomica after her like a shadow, trembling, with tiny, mocking smiles on her lips, her eyes sparkling with golden flecks beneath heavy, dusty eyebrows. That evening, on his way to the spring above the house, Anto had over-heard Tomica imploring Stojna, who hid her face behind the branch of an apple tree just bursting into flower: "Have you no heart? Don't you know a man's, a haiduk's, heart?" When at last the wedding guests went away, late at night, the haiduks had gone to the cave above the house, and Stojna had gone to Pe-trana's, though there were beds enough in Anto's house. And Anto, who woke early, saw the haiduks as they made their way back from Petrana's house, slipping through the garden filled with roses and fruit blossoms.

Indeed, the presence of the haiduks at the wedding was impru-dent and ill considered. For some time now all kinds of rebels and unknowns had circulated among the villages, and not all the Radak men knew for sure who Tomica and Vučeta really were or why they had come. They looked on them as guests from a dis-tance, as kin in some way to the bride or casual newcomers. Pe-trana certainly knew, but she, distrustful and more fiercely in fa-vor of rebellion than any Radak, was not a talker. Yet what if Tomica had confided in her fiery and seductive friend? From these townswomen, who love to live well and comfortably and who easily make friends with the begs and the rich Moslem mer-chants, any man, especially a peasant, may expect disloyalty.

But there was nothing about Stojna that would lead Anto to think that she could have betrayed him. Not only was she now related to him, but she did not know anything about the arms. In truth, she was friendly with the *bule*, the Moslem townswomen, but so were other Serbian women in the towns. She was of an honest, though poor, family, which, furthermore, had suffered heavily from the Turkish authorities. Her husband, Simo, had even been forced to leave his house and workshop, seek refuge at Plav, and begin anew his life and his trade as a coppersmith.

Both he and his son, Kosta, Roksanda's bridegroom, were re-served, hard-working, and modest, and honest in their dealings. That winter, Kosta had spent a whole month in the Radak vil-lage with his father, tinkering and welding copper cooking pots. Both he and his father liked the tall, slender, fresh, green-eyed girl, with her ash-colored hair, full lips, and swelling breasts. And though town dwellers unwillingly took brides from the villages, Simo was not for a moment in doubt about asking for Roksanda's hand for his son. He, too, had been a peasant's son, and in many ways the men of Radak differed little from the small traders and craftsmen of Plav in matters of cooking, cleanliness, and not wearing out their women with hard work. But Anto would not have given his daughter had not she herself urged him. Spoiled, and used to a comfortable home life supported by her brothers and mother, she did not try to hide her wish to marry into the circle of townsfolk. Moreover, Kosta, pale and quiet, with smoldering and trembling devotion in his small black eyes under long lashes, pleased her. Anto thought it over and decided not to thwart his daughter's wish. It would do no harm if he were to have someone of his blood in the town, close to the authorities, the tradesmen and artisans.

He was much less satisfied with his daughter-in-law Stanija, the wife of his second son, Akan, and the sister of Vučeta. He had not been pleased when his son said that he wanted to marry a girl from Montenegro. He knew neither the girl nor her friends. But Akan, his most obedient child and the most practical in the family, was also in some matters the most stubborn of them all. Against his father's wishes, he had neglected his work on the land and devoted himself to trading in stock and goats. It soon became apparent that he, and not his father, was right; money began to pour into the house, and, with it, town goods and every sort of comfort, as well as land and small stock, over which Grgur, a born herdsman and husbandman, kept close watch. So Anto finally consented to his son's wish, the more easily because he considered that to have friends in Montenegro was an advantage not to be despised. It was obvious that the power of Montenegro was increasing. The new generation realized that more clearly and definitely than he did. He must make up his mind, as had his father and grandfather and all the Radak men of old times. There had been similar dissensions in Montenegro, in Stanija's family; they were unwilling to enter into kinship with outsiders, with serfs, Turkish *raja,* whom they considered lower than themselves, but, faced with the inevitability of their descent into the fertile valleys, they did not hesitate overmuch to give their daughter to a prosperous household of a distinguished line. Thus it came about that Akan married a Montenegrin.

From Generation to Generation

But it remained far from clear to Anto and to the other members of the family what it was in Stanija that attracted Akan. It was of some significance that she came from a chieftain's family, though from a poor and unimportant household, and displayed a devoted affection for her husband and her home. She was not ugly; indeed, it could be said that she was beautiful, though not according to Radak standards. The Radak men liked plump, rounded women, broad in the hips, mild and placid, whereas Stanija, like most Montenegrin women, was on the small side, overly thin and bony, white-skinned and black-eyed, with brown hair so long and thick that it seemed like a wreath about her head. She was as quick as a weasel, of uncompromising probity and views, wild and unbending in her moods. This was a drawback in a large, co-operative family. But it was perhaps just this fiery harshness that attracted Akan—a blond young man of the new generation, a little heavy and inclined to fat—and induced him to break with Radak tradition. Having given his consent to his son's marriage, Anto hoped that the crossing of two differing human types would produce a healthy and long-lived progeny. But this was not to be the case. In this crossing, this symbiosis, there was some lack of accord. Their children were weakly. Of three, born within five years, one small son alone survived, whom, according to ancient custom, they called Anto, after his grandfather, hoping that Anto would look more favorably both on the child and on the mother.

Though Stanija was neither quarrelsome nor a gossip, as Montenegrin women often are, from the very start nerves were strained to breaking point between her and Stamena, Grgur's wife. And her mother-in-law, Milena, Anto's wife, was not able to take to her, despite the fact that Stanija saved her a good deal of work. This discord did not stem from open quarrels or clashes about anything in particular. It was only that with Stanija something stubborn and harsh entered Anto's house, as if a keen razor had begun to slash through sorrow and joy, even through words and thoughts. She came from another, a different, world.

Anto's dissatisfaction with Stanija grew sharper now in his prison cell, as did every other dissatisfaction he recalled. But not for a second could he bring himself to believe that she could betray him to Suljaga. Furthermore, he was certain that she was the one being from whom no one could ever extract anything, not even if she were cut to pieces.

Anto could not be sure, either, that someone outside the Radak kin had betrayed him, for no one except the Radak men and one or two chieftains in Montenegro knew anything at all about Radak affairs. The idea that Radak men might be traitors Anto rejected almost at once, fearing that such a thought would humiliate and weaken him.

While he was pacing up and down and arguing with himself in the gloomy cell, the night rushed onward too quickly, and, with it, nightmares of treason and hallucinations of Suljaga's knowledge became more real, more tangible. They were transformed into a dark throng, blacker than the night, which whirled around him and swarmed in from all sides. Exhausted, Anto lay down in order to escape from the black throng of his fears. But then they became unbearable, and he leaped up again. There was nothing, nothing he could catch hold of, touch, except the rough chill of the walls. Only by pacing to and fro and listening for the silvery sound of the brook and the breathing of the lake, which grew louder at night, could he disperse and lessen and drive away these apparitions. He hummed a little song that he suddenly recollected from far-distant, evergreen youth: "O green apple!" Then he was once more alone, in the kula, in the cell, comprehensible and perceptible.

Calmed, washed clean like a mountain after a storm, he again began to pace up and down his cell. Nowhere was there a breath of air. The dark-blue sky was crisscrossed by the black grille. Then, suddenly, from the left-hand corner by the doorpost he noticed a star, the big one that flames in the west in the early evening and, as the daystar, appears in the east at early morning to herald the coming day.

He remembered that learned men affirmed something incredible: the stars were like the earth and revolved around one another, as the earth did around the sun. He did not believe in the traditional fairy tale that the stars were the souls of the just, whom God had illuminated and brought to joy for the instruction of the whole human race.

It was now a mournful thought that falling stars were not, as was believed, those who had escaped from prison. Stars, the heavens, were God's mysteries among so many other mysteries, but were certainly for the joy and the advantage of man. Anto knew how to find his way in the mountains by them in the depths of night. But here, in prison, one must keep vigil night after night to see some star framed in a scrap of sky. Nonetheless, that single star brought joy to him from the immeasurable bluish expanse. By it he could orient himself; to the right were the foothills of the Prokletije mountains, wonderful in their brutal bareness and height, and to the left were the men of Radak and his home.

Anto remembered his wife, Milena. *Shame on me! All this time I have been ransacking my memory and have not even thought of her.* It was the same moment here and at home. There, everything was calm; the men had gone to lie down and the children were asleep. It was the beginning of the silence of the night. Below the house, the dog yawned loudly, and in the forest above an owl hooted. Only Milena was still awake. There was always something else that had to be done after her daughters-in-law had retired to bed. Perhaps at this very moment she was clearing the hearth, the embers were slowly dying out, and she was thinking about him and weeping, about him alone, walled in with his worries and misfortunes.

He and Milena had lived together for thirty-four years, and, it was now clear to him, he might have been better and kinder to her; from time to time her pale-blue eyes would fill with tears, which rolled down her plump face, now soft and floury like dough, at his roughness and severity. *And now, it seems to me, she must be thinking about me.* But it had had to be so; such was life, bad and good, misery and joy. He had had to teach others, as well as his own children, how to keep a house and maintain a family; there had been no time left for tenderness toward Milena. So it had been right up to recent years, until the children were grown up, and in those years their passions, their fierce angers and sudden lusts, had been dulled. But he had lived with Milena in fullness and conformity, through births and deaths, marriages and partings, passionate nights in the storeroom and the more sober desires of mature husband and wife in the great room.

Now at last, here in prison, it was no longer shameful to speak soft words to her, to call her by name: *Milena, Milena, my dear one, my only one!* "So there you are; that is prison," he was to say later. For the first time, he thought without shame about his wife, desired her, and saw life without her as a desolation.

Suddenly, in the darkness, he became aware, as with the stream, and the star, of something else: the clink of fetters at the other end of the prison, from some sufferer like himself. *Who is it? Does he, too, see some star or, tortured and broken, search only for himself in the darkness? Does he hear the stream? Is there someone to care for him and who will watch for him evening and morning?* This stranger was dear to him, kin to him, in the desolation of night and prison. He wanted to make himself known to him, to offer him sympathy and affection. But he did not know how. There was no way.

As in the daylight hours, the guards clattered up and down the wooden stairs. But he could deduce nothing from that. Nonetheless, he seized on these sounds, absorbed them and was absorbed by them, escaping from darkness and dumbness, fixing the hour of the night by some word or by the clumping of those bringing tubs of food, by some cry or by the harsh rasp of iron spoons on the soldiers' tin plates—quite different from the soft, almost inaudible village mealtime sounds of wooden spoons on wooden or earthenware bowls. About suppertime the movement became brisker; he was not given any supper, for the Turks gave their prisoners only an oka of bread and water, and he had had his.

Right in the midst of this evening liveliness there was a coming and going of policemen, two or three from outside and another two within.

"Shove the swine in with that thief Bogdan." He could hear Suljaga's sibilant voice, suddenly heavy and hard, like the blow of the bronze clapper on a bell.

"Why with him, when there are empty cells?" asked a calm, mild, drowsy voice.

"Don't ask questions. Do as you're told!"

They began to kick, jostle, pummel someone, some swine, Christian, Serb. "Get along, you serf beast. Must we light candles for swine! Brigand—he makes out he's innocent. He'd drink our blood if he could."

"No, no, kind people. I am as innocent as a newborn babe," whined the persecuted man.

Anto recognized the voice of Nasto Radak. This was confirmed a moment later by an exchange in front of his door.

"What is your name?" Suljaga asked.

"Nasto, Nasto Radak, aga."

"When we've finished with you, you won't know who you are!"

"In God's name, aga!"

It was Nasto Radak, undoubtedly, the angry clank of fetters, the jostling and pummeling, the oaths, cries, and entreaties. Anto kept his ear to the door, trying to penetrate its thickness, though there were no holes or cracks. *What is happening? What is happening to the Radak men? What is Nasto's attitude toward the revolt? What does he know about the arms, about the haiduks, about the Radak negotiations?*

Had any other of the Radak men been in prison Anto might have been able to see some reason for it. But Nasto was the mildest, the most peaceable of the whole clan, and, furthermore, poor and burdened with six children in his dung-plastered cabin on the hillside. He did day laborer's work wherever he could find it, sometimes even on Anto's lands, but more frequently on the properties of the begs.

But what does he know? Was he at Roksanda's wedding, when Vučeta and Tomica were there? Clearly he felt himself to be innocent. He had probably been at the end of his tether even before they had begun to interrogate him, perhaps even before they had brought him to the kula. However much Anto tried to recollect, and he recalled even the smallest details, to his exasperation he could not be certain whether Nasto had been at the wedding. It was equally possible that he had or had not been, for the whole village had come. The sowing had been finished, and the harvesting, which would take the day laborers into other villages, had not yet begun. Nasto would not have been there had there been work. Reserved and abstemious, he avoided feasts and celebrations.

The fact that they had arrested him rather than anyone else made Anto feel more at ease. Nasto certainly knew less than the others, and they must have arrested him by chance, in Plav or

35

somewhere nearby. That meant that the authorities had not yet decided to strike at the clan. Nothing bad had so far happened to the Radak men; nor would anything have happened to Nasto had he been at the discussion last night or had he known of Anto's arrest. The Radak men had taken precautions. That night they had decided to strengthen their sentinels and even to resist should a larger body attack to arrest and plunder, and then, if needs be, to flee with the children and stock over the frontier to Veliko.

But who could be the traitor, and what does Suljaga know?

That black throng began to return and also the drumming and tension within him, which spread through his whole body, making him tremble, echoing through him and into the once-more limitless cell. Anto rubbed his body as he paced up and down, turning quickly when he reached the walls. That movement, that rubbing, any kind of action, eased him; at last it occurred to him to look once more for the star and even pray to God, whom he had not forgotten, but to whom he did not want to turn until still heavier, more unbearable torments assailed him.

But before he could find the star, there was an interruption. The tramping of guards down the staircase cut him short. "They are coming for me!" he cried out silently, even before they reached the pebbly corridor. He was filled with horror; sharp chills penetrated him.

The door opened with the usual, though louder, creaking of the bolts and rasping of the key. In the doorway, in the faint light of a lantern, stood two policemen, Shquiptars, Huso and Kolj. Anto knew them by sight. Kolj was a Catholic, and Huso a Moslem. With an uncertain emotion in his voice, Huso summoned him curtly: "Come along!" Kolj was swinging the lantern in his right hand, and, in the flickering darkness, he seemed to Anto taller and thinner than he really was, and dark rather than the reddish he in fact was. Such men are uncommon among the Shquiptars, who were, for the most part black-haired, white-skinned, and ruddy-complexioned. Huso, however, was a real Shquiptar, tall, long-headed, bony, with a narrow forehead and thin black mustaches. A recent scar shone on his left cheekbone, the result of a skirmish with the Vasojevići. Both were young, scarcely twenty-five, though they seemed to Anto older, especially

36

Huso, on whose ugly face, pitted with smallpox, countless dark scars could be seen in the lantern light. Anto slowly followed Huso, but Kolj did not take him by the arm, only mumbled as he followed them: "Come, brother Anto Radak! What sort of a mess have you got yourself into, Anto Radak?"

Anto was annoyed that he had shown Kolj that he was frightened, that he should seem a weakling before men with whose clans he had often been in vendetta and whose people esteemed heroism above all else, and he replied, almost angrily: "I have never feared anyone. What have I to be afraid of? My conscience is clear and my reason is sound."

Kolj did not reply, though it seemed to Anto, because of the tense silence, that he had something more he wanted to say. They made their way up the steps and along the corridor to Suljaga's room, which was at the end, on the right. Stopping before the door, Huso opened it and pushed Anto in ahead of him.

The room was too brightly lit for Anto's peasant ways, and for his eyes, which were blinded after the darkness. Two candlesticks with three candles each, one on the right-hand edge of Suljaga's table and the other on a small table in the left-hand corner of the room, lit up every detail as if it were noonday. But despite this clarity, or perhaps because of it, everything quivered in an icy hardness, as in a dream or a terrifying fairy tale.

"You summoned me, honored aga," Anto said to Suljaga, letting his hands droop, suddenly superfluous.

Suljaga did not stop smoothing his mustaches; nor did he respond. He stared fixedly at Anto.

Anto looked around him uncomfortably. Suljaga was not alone. On the table were lying two dried and plaited bull pizzles, crossed, three or four pincers of various kinds, saws, chains, and cords, all intended for torturing men. There were also two long greased grayish pouches filled with something hard and malleable. In the corner, beneath the candlestick, two gypsies were sitting on the floor, Smajo and his son, Džem. They killed and tortured at Suljaga's wish, on the orders of the Turkish authorities. Anto knew the two of them; it was also known to him, and indeed to the whole district, what their trade was. But whereas a wall of terror had arisen around Suljaga, men despised this pair and were sickened by them, both because of their calling and because they sold on market days, for the most part to distant Shquiptar herdsmen, the things they took from their victims, especially clothes. Smajo sat cross-legged, immobile and dumb, as if in a trance but with a tense expression on his bony face, with its long graying mustaches and glittering eyes beneath thick drooping brows. His face was marked with little black points, as if he had been occupied with charcoal-burning all his life. His son squatted, resting on his clenched fists, with raised head, shining dark skin, and fiery eyes, as if ready to pounce. Whereas Smajo had the calm and permanency of a tombstone, there was something canine in Džem, something both bloodthirsty and obsequious. Džem, too, did not move a muscle, but watched Suljaga attentively and obediently.

The silence went on interminably, and Suljaga's gaze remained fixed on Anto, embracing him, not only his bones and muscles, his throat and skull, but also deep within, his vitals and breath, his mind and his thoughts. Anto kept reminding himself that it was all-important for him to remain silent and seem unconcerned. He shifted from foot to foot, so that his bearing should not seem unnatural. It made no impression on Suljaga.

"Have you had a good look at them?" he asked, also feigning indifference.

But since he did not make it clear whether he was referring to the gypsies or to the tools of their trade, Anto intentionally asked: "What do you mean, *ćatib?*"

"Well," replied Suljaga, getting up from behind his table and pointing at the tools with his left hand and at the gypsies with his right, "these things on the table and those there." His hands remained outspread in expectation, palms upward, as though he were a man who of a sudden had decided to make a generous gift.

Anto wanted to reply: "Why must I look so carefully? I know what these things are and I know what those two are." But instead, the cry was forced from him: "I am innocent, aga!" and then, ashamed of his own cowardice and recalling Nasto's whining and Kolj's taunts, he added almost angrily: "And you, do what you have a mind to."

It did not anger Suljaga. It seemed that when he wanted something nothing could turn him from it. "We, too, think the same, since you will not be good or wise," he replied, and slammed his right hand on the table so sharply and suddenly that the candle flames leaped up as if in fright. Džem also leaped up, and Anto started and stiffened in fearful expectation.

But Džem stayed where he was, gazing at Suljaga. "Wait below, to fetter him," Suljaga ordered, "and take these away!" Smajo rose, almost noiselessly collected his tools, and, with his son, backed out of the room.

"Sit, Radak," Suljaga said, sitting down himself and plucking at his mustaches with the short thick fingers of his white puffy hands. "Sit down. I see that you have decided for the tortures."

I have not, Suljaga, decided on anything, but if I must I must. I would feel shame if I should begin to sing your tune when you have not even slapped me.

"Sit, Radak, so that we can chat, so to speak, as men, if I may talk with you thus."

Anto did not sit. There was neither chair nor stool, and he felt it would shame him to sit on the floor. "Sit on the divan," remarked Suljaga, pointing to the divan along the right-hand wall, spread with tufted carpets yellow as cowslips and green as clover. But Anto did not sit even there. It would be embarrassing for him, a serf, to sit in the presence of the authorities, especially where begs and gentry sat. "No matter, aga. I can stand."

"All right, if you prefer," Suljaga said, without insisting, and at once began again. "Both you and I know well that we belong to two different worlds, and that harmony, justice, and peace between us, so to speak, can never be. But bad weather brings together the eagle and the hen; so we, too, may see if we can both exist with as little evil as need be. You must know that I will beat you and torture you. You will entreat your God and my God to take your soul, and I will not listen to your entreaty but will tear the soul out of you until I have made you a beast. But do not pretend to yourself that I will do this to find out something from you. What you might be able to tell me I know already, more or less. But what I know, you must confirm, out of your own mouth. You have neither the power nor the right to set yourself up against the authorities."

You lie, aga. You don't know everything. Authority never knows and can never find out all that the guilty know. Neither to

39

the priest nor to God does man reveal everything. But I know, I understand what it is you want. It is not my secrets, but my submission, that you want, and that you will never achieve. After thinking it over, he nonetheless replied: "I am not setting myself against authority, aga. Even if you are not of my faith, you are from God, since he has given you the power and for as long as you hold that power."

"You lie, Radak, brutish swine; you do oppose the authorities. Perhaps you think that you are not against them, but you are against them because in your soul you have hidden something from them. But I will bring it to light. I will reveal it with bare hands, even if it be concealed under burning embers."

You, too, aga, are insurgents. You do not recognize your Sultan. He agreed to give your lands to Montenegro, and you have not submitted. You are worse rebels than we are. We ask only for the freedom that other Serbs already have; while you have risen against your own world, against your own tsar. You are no sort of authority, but you have the power, and we Radaks, we subject peoples, we raja, are still weak. "Everyone preserves his own," said Anto, "and I fear for the men of Radak. What I could tell you I dare not."

"I can read you, Radak, as a priest his gospel or a hodža his Koran. We are the authority. We have been and we still are, even though the Great Powers do not recognize us, even though, so to speak, no power on earth, no, not even the Sultan himself, does so. But they will and must recognize us, so long as we hold the power, so long as the men in our district remain submissive to us. So long as we hold something by the sword, we are the power! May Allah still support and preserve our right hand, and Stambul will embrace us eagerly as heroes and sons of the true faith."

But the sword is a small thing, aga. What is held by the sword alone does not long endure. Had our nobles, may their souls be accursed and no man know their graves, not feuded among themselves and become Turks, then the Turkish sword would never have subdued the Serbs. "I do not say that you are not the authority, never in God's name! I have not yet gone out of my mind."

"You do not say, you do not say, but you think: weak is the authority that is held only by the sword. So I, too, think. But we link power and human existence; by the sword we defend both human and heavenly truth, as the Prophet has revealed. For evil is your Serbdom—as also mine. I, too, until yesterday was a Serb. We separated life from eternity, faith from everyday life. We sang about a Kosovo that never was and never will be. We live, so to speak, from one day to the next; we squabble among ourselves, we hate, we rebel, and we rise against rebellion. Faith without power is sterile seed. When I say the sword, I mean justice and truth. Everything is vain if your sword be rusted and broken."

"I have no sword, aga, either rusted or broken; not even a stout knife with which to defend my life. But when the grass has grown green above us both, and even above Serb and Turkish rivalries, men will know what was justice and what injustice."

"And to blow the head, to open one's soul, to the new power?"

"That, too. And to believe that every power is only for a time."

"It is only for a time. But men would, so to speak, tear one another's eyes out and the human race would exterminate itself if there were no authority, no power."

"That is so, aga. Man cannot live without power and authority. They are from God, aga."

"But since they are from Allah, from God, one must submit to them, Radak."

"One must, aga."

"What must be needs be."

"But everything that must be need not be done. Power without faith, without truth, is short in term."

"Faith without power is sterile seed! If Mohammed had not linked faith with the sword nothing would have been known of Arabs or Turks; nor would the human race have tasted all the fruits of wisdom."

"That is so, aga. That may well be so for the Turks and for the Arabs. You know that, aga, for you have had schooling. But we Serbs differ: the sword is one thing; justice is another. We know that we cannot live without one and the other. We had no way out; we separated the sword and justice and renounced our lives. When the sword and justice are divided, then we snatch at justice and pay no heed to our lives. Our heads are beneath the sword."

"You talk much wisdom, Radak. The *raja* are growing wise. Every second serf could become a cadi. They learn from priests

41

and songs, and now there are even teachers. But it is all quite simple: you men of Radak and you, Knez Anto, will you or will you not submit to the authorities?"

"We would, aga. But it is hard, aga." *We will, we won't. Clever bastards.* Anto heard the words, which Suljaga had not uttered.

Without anger, Suljaga remarked: "What would you and what is hard for you, Radak?" He obviously liked to talk with his victim, to prove to him the superiority of his intelligence and his faith. But nothing had come of it except an empty contest of sophistry, and now in his face, with its suddenly drooping lips, could be read disgust and discontent. "You are a brigand, Radak. You are one of the blackest of those who seek to disturb the order that human power and divine justice have set up."

"I am no brigand, aga. I have not fouled anyone's water."

"Be quiet! You have fouled no one's water, but you have fouled the soul. You have lived separate and enclosed within your clan and you have fouled and undermined our empire."

It has undermined itself, like a pine tree that has grown too old. It is rotten wood, which we Radaks, we raja, eat away like worms. If it were not rotten, there would be no worms.

Suljaga again changed, becoming more serious and withdrawn, as if Anto were not there before him. Short and heavy, he paced the room, hands behind his back. The squeak of the boards mingled with the words he poured out uninterruptedly, passionately.

"Faith, justice! What sort of faith and what sort of justice, if there is not human life and all the sweetness of living?

"I know how much the Serbs hate me, and I can see that the Moslems, the Turks, too, have an aversion to me. They are horrified by my bloody, inhuman, yet most human trade. I, too, am horrified at it, but I take pride in it. I do my duty, not just because someone must in any case do it, but also because I know that without force, without oppression, without the torturing of men, it is not possible to keep order among them or teach them to behave as human beings. Without evil, no good can exist. Man is man, but he is also a beast. He must know fear, must observe discipline, if he wishes to remain a man."

Man is not a beast, Suljaga, but a creation of God. Beasts do not know justice and truth, but man does, as God does.

"The Moslems look on me as one who until yesterday was a

Serb, a man without name or lineage. The Serbs regard me as a renegade and an apostate. But who of our Moslems is not an Islamized Serb; were not all their forefathers Orthodox? The Šabanagići even boast of being descended from the Crnojević princes of Montenegro! They are proud that they were among the first, more than four hundred years ago, to accept Islam. Some earlier, some later. Why should I be ashamed that I belong to the Popović clan, am from a priestly family? My grandfather, may he rest in peace, when he accepted Islam took, either from pique or from honesty, the name Hodžić, though neither he nor anyone in my family has ever been a hodža. Now we Hodžići are Turks, more devout than any in Istanbul. That is the way with renegades: 'a Serb turned Turk is worse than any Turk,' as the Serbs say. But he who has not tried it does not know the sweetness of renunciation, the entry into a different world, a new life. He who does not renounce will never be born again, will never drag himself out of the stinking pigsty.

"Who does not renounce does not know the sweetness of power. Who does not renounce does not feel how sweet it is to tame man, to drive out his wild-boar nature and savagery. If there were no wind, the spiders would cover the heavens with their webs.

"Turkey defends itself, whether it be from Christian tsars or from its own *raja*, from the mud, from the lice, from the sickle and the hoe, from the worms that gnaw, gnaw, perfidious and unseen!

"No, no. It is better to die, finer to lose the empire by the sword than to become servants and *raja*.

"We do not give up our great houses and gardens, our *zurle* and hand drums, our chargers and our weapons, our great ladies and rich robes, the gardens of civilization which we have planted, the sweet serenity of our hearts and the contentment of our souls.

"There is no happiness or freedom except in peace and quiet.

"As soon as men think that they have rooted out one evil, then a still-worse one is born, and still-greater efforts are demanded. And so on, unceasingly. Even my desire for peace and quiet is a mirage; I strive for it through bloodshed and imprisonment, and as soon as I think I have reached it, then it begins all over again. But wretched man must seek after something, must believe in something.

"I do not lay a finger on the murderer and plunderer. Allah or the Devil has already punished them, since he has led them into that way of life. Such men are guilty only to those whom they have harmed. They are not criminals, but misguided souls. The real criminal is he who destroys the established order. Devils have entered his soul. He has risen against the ordinances of God. Every authority, every rule, will harry and persecute him.

"I will harry and persecute rebels, only sorry that Allah has not given them stronger bodies, so that their souls may agonize longer in torment, until I tear from them every vein and sinew of evil and devilry."

Both were silent.

Suljaga has been talking about himself and to himself. No sort of tortures can degrade a man who has renounced life. Who said that? Monks used to say it of saints. But man is sinful; can he resist torture? Yet man begins nothing and creates nothing if he does not renounce life and enjoyment. Man is always being tortured, if he wants to be a man. Suljaga lies, and yet he, too, is tormented. All that he says is to reassure himself. He, too, is sentenced to misfortune; else how can he defend his empire? Who is not tormented does not live.

The creaking of the floor ceased. Suljaga stopped pacing and looked through the window, yawning as if from fatigue or sleeplessness. Then he turned quickly and stood in front of Anto. He was a whole foot shorter, shorter than a man of average height. He took Anto by the jacket as a friend would. "This is a misfortune for both of us, each in his own way," he said, not looking Anto in the eyes. "Be a man, Radak."

"I am. I will be," Anto replied curtly, as he had already decided.

"Don't pretend that you do not understand me. Be a man for your own sake and mine, though that is not the same! Put yourself in my place. Listen! Show us the way to pacify the Radaks. We do not seek your blood and that of our true and loyal *raja*. I am not, we are not, against either the *raja* or your faith or your clan, but only against rebellion and disorder. Appease them and not a hair of any Radak man shall fall to the ground!"

To betray, by confessing, in order to save the Radaks! No, no, no! I cannot, even though for many of the Radaks it would not

*be betrayal. I am not all the Radak men. And yet I am; I alone
am all the Radak men until I abandon them and accept a strange
faith, a stranger's will, a stranger's fortune.* "I cannot, aga. My
honor is my life. I wish no man ill, but I do not give away the
good of the Radaks."

"The good of the Radaks! Blood and death, burned homes,
scattered fugitives, crushed old people—that is your good of the
Radaks! And your honor—the keeping of an empty oath and a
foolish trust they have in you!"

"I have spoken, aga."

"Spoken? Spoken? May God have mercy on you. I am not to
blame." Suljaga clapped his hands twice, at which the two
Shquiptars, Huso and Kolj, leaped up, alert and refreshed. "Take
him away. And you, Radak, think it over once again. Pray God
that he put some sense into you and change your destiny."

The gypsies, Smajo and Džem, were waiting, half asleep, in
Anto's cell. They had already prepared all that was necessary and
now fettered him with a speed that would have astonished him
had he not known that forging was their trade and that he was
not the first. They paid no attention when the anklets bruised his
legs as they riveted the nails. They fettered him as if shoeing a
horse or beating out a scythe—calmly, indifferently, impersonally.

Left alone, Anto tried to walk. The irons were heavy, twelve,
perhaps fifteen, okas. He could walk a little, with legs apart. He
thought of wrapping them in cloth, tearing up his shirt, as prisoners in fetters did, or so he had heard. That could wait for the
morrow. He was tired, exhausted, but he was pleased with himself; he had stood firm against threats and seductions. He remembered the star. But it was not there. It had gone on its way while
he had been uselessly bandying words with Suljaga. *Suljaga!
What was it he had said at the end? That I should pray to God!*
Anto knelt on the cold stone, calling on God to help him in his
misfortune, to save his reason in the tortures. The vault of the
cell did not open, nor did any sort of brilliance appear, as he had
heard happened when a man in misfortune prayed sincerely, but
he quickly fell into a sweet, heavy slumber.

He could not determine how long he had been asleep, but it
must have been before dawn when cries in the distance awoke

him. He recognized Nasto's entreaties as he rolled down the steps, landing on his back on the pebbles of the corridor. "What are you doing to me, good people? I am not guilty, I am not, I am not. Woe to me for this night. I can't, I can't, I can't, brothers!" They were not striking him, but dragging him along. He could not move; that was what he was shouting that he could not do.

For some time more, until the little window in the vault of the cell grew greenish-white with the false dawn, he heard Nasto's cries growing fainter and less frequent from a distant cell, more despairing. Awakened by Nasto's suffering, which now and again became one with his own, Anto could hear someone consoling him, almost certainly the thief Bogdan, with whom they had imprisoned him.

The cocks and the muezzin announced the day. Anto heard Suljaga, only now going out, give an order from the staircase to one of the guards. Suljaga went down wearily, slowly; Anto counted his steps as he descended. Others, too, went with him, tired from their night's work of human torture.

Anto's chill terror died away with the daylight, with the sight of the cell and the things in it. It was unbearable to hear, to listen, to know that someone near him was being tortured. It was more terrible than waiting, than anticipating, perhaps even than suffering, his own torture. When it was full day and the life of the guards and the prison had begun again, Anto, longing to move about and think everything over, got up. Only then did he notice that his fetters were bruising him. His skin was already lacerated. He looked back on his last night's conversation with Suljaga as a nightmare, but also as a terrible, unendurable enlightenment. In all that Suljaga had said there had been mockery of self, malevolence toward the serf, and, above all, revulsion from human destiny. But he had, in a way Anto found rather obscure, spoken attractive truths which it was impossible to resist by reason. Anto began to take off his shirt, in order to wrap it around his fetters. The men of Radak, by contrast to the Montenegrins, were to some degree skilled in women's work. But Anto was an exception. He measured and tore the linen cloth clumsily, that cloth his daughter-in-law Stamena had brought as part of her dowry and had woven and bleached more skillfully than the Radak women. He spent almost the entire morning binding the anklets, thinking: It is easier when a man has something to do, when he is not alone with himself.

About noon Abdulah, grumbling, handed him a bundle and a bag filled with food. "Your wife brought it. That is like our authorities: they show mercy to all, and you know well that you do not deserve it. But it is not my place to pass judgment. I only say what I think."

It was pleasant, more pleasant than the warmth and light that filled the cell with the coming of day, to know that Milena had not forgotten him. That she, grown heavy and elderly, had come proved that the Radak men were on the alert. Tenderness, dear memories, flooded over Anto when he received the food. There were all the dishes that he used to enjoy and all the little extras he might need: a bowl of clotted cream, a jar of honey, dried mutton. There was bread, a twist of salt, and even some garlic and paprikas. In a kerchief was a *pita* of minced meat and onion, which Stamena knew how to cook exceptionally well. In the bundle also were a change of clothing, two sheets and a pillow, two towels, and a cake of soap. It was as if a part of his home and his home life had come to him. How had he dared to think that his people, that Milena, could even for a single day leave him without care and attention?

He liked the food and took a little of everything, though each mouthful stuck in his throat and drove him to tears and lamentation. When he had finished, he carefully collected all the scraps of bread, wrapped the remaining food in the kerchief, and put it away in the brightly colored bag. Then, after knocking at the door, he asked Abdulah to bring him some water or allow him to go and get some. Abdulah bared his worn-down yellowed teeth in wonder. "Water! What water? We keep the law; whatever is allowed to be eaten or drunk is brought and is given. We cannot be servants of the prisoners, to bring them more water!"

It flashed across Anto's mind that they had tricked him, as they had so many others in tales, that they had given him salted food, from his own home at that, and then would not give him water. *They will first torture me by thirst. Yes, by thirst, that is how they will begin the torture, to weaken, to poison, to destroy a man's soul.* That very morning it should have been clear to him, from Abdulah's earlier unwillingness to take him to get water, that they were making ready a trap. All sorts of torments had come to his mind, those of which he had heard and those he himself had imagined, each more awful than the last, but torture by thirst—that he had not thought of.

At first he wanted to shout, to curse, to bang on the door. But he quickly changed his mind. To get water, to spare himself this torment, could only be achieved if he betrayed the Radaks, if he submitted to Suljaga's will and served him to crush the discontent of the *raja*. Milena's tenderness had turned to gall; it was in vain that he had been pleased with the food. He could not beg or entreat. They would interpret that as weakness and would mock him. There was no sense in swearing and cursing; that would be rebellion and, as such, a confirmation of the Radak plot.

All that was left to him was to suffer in patience. The tears rose to his eyes at his own helplessness and the injustice wrought on him, at the memory of his home and his grief for Milena, at his own credulity and stupidity. But he hid his tears and smothered his sobs that they not weaken him. He remembered, on calming down, that tears meant a loss of precious fluid. When he stopped, he was not only calmed, but also resigned to all that was to happen to him.

In that resignation, both then and for the whole term of his imprisonment, there was recognition of his own helplessness, an adjustment to the evil that had assailed him. He suspected, in a dumb, indeterminate manner, that this was the surest way to protect and defend himself, because in fact he was not fighting against Suljaga and the Turkish power but against himself, his own fears, doubts, wishes, and illusions. Nasto had been weakened by his tears. He had wept when they had broken down his confidence and his resistance. But for Anto his tears had washed away all his doubts and apprehensions.

Toward dusk it became hotter, more stifling. He felt it in his head and vitals, in his lacerated legs. He noticed that from time to time he was talking to himself. He hunted down the quivering of his lips, though his words were not coherent. He forgot his own words and thoughts the moment he had uttered them. They became intertwined and confused with what he had inherited, what he had learned in a long life of suffering, and what had happened within him. Above all, there remained in his memory the precepts he had handed on to his own sons and to the Radak men. *Good sense and reason are like honor, wise men say. But that is not so—at least not quite so, not always. There you are: my good sense has been clouded; they have given me too much to drink. But who, or what, can make a man's honor drunk? It is in vain that I defend myself from thirst. Suljaga will find a thousand thirsts; evil can always find a way. If my reason is made drunk, what honor will remain? It will; it won't. Then it will be all the same to me; I will not know what is honor and what is not honor. That is what I fear, lest honor be sapped by the weakening of my mind. Everything burns, and I burn in everything. Even the star burns. Perhaps it has already burned itself out. Why doesn't the kula burst into flames; why can't it be burned to ashes?*

How long can a man endure without water? They say three, perhaps four, days. Without food one can endure for long; twenty days, perhaps even more. In hunger the mind is sharpened; in thirst it is clouded. That is what Suljaga, that renegade, that accursed convert, has contrived. He wants to cloud my mind, drag out of me what they need, shame me before myself, before the people, before the Radaks, and then split the Radak clan, saying: "Your knez is not for the rebellion! Your own knez has betrayed you! What kind of wretch did you yourselves elect as your knez?"

It will soon be night. In this district, and especially by the lake, the nights are chilly and good for sleep. Everything now is hot and will be still more suffocating, and there is no sleep, only some kind of stupor. Whence? Why? From thirst? Thirst dulls the mind. And intoxicates it. Does it? Nothing can intoxicate human honor; it is from God. And reason, too, is from God. Who am I and where? Who is man, what does he want, where is he going, and where is his dwelling place? A straw that the wind blows, a grain of sand that imagines that in it is the whole world. Such is man, and his reason, too, is thus; as is the man, so is his reason. No! What is it that I want to say? Man is even as his honor! I must keep my reason. Honor and reason. Reason-honor.

Indeed, there were other thirstings in Suljaga. As soon as dusk came, after supper, they again took away Nasto and tortured him. The groans, the blows, seeped through the walls, which echoed back his more and more penetrating, more despairing cries. "Brothers, brothers, **don't** torture me! I am innocent!" Anto was less sorry for Nasto than on the night before, as if Nasto were no kin to him, not even an acquaintance. Let him, too, suffer his destiny!

The silence and the tense unbearable waiting lasted for about half an hour. Certainly they were conferring up there in Suljaga's room, chatting, perhaps drinking coffee. Then they had taken away the man in fetters and kept him there for long, very long, a whole two hours, as far as Anto was able to judge the time from the changes of guard in the kula. He had not been able to make out how they had tortured him; he could hear only cries and the movement of many feet. On the way back they had carried him; they had panted and stumbled while his fetters clinked lifelessly, mingled with painful, smothered sobbing.

Let them come as soon as possible! Lord God, let me meet the tortures that await me as soon as possible, that I may drink the cup prepared for me!

They came for him after they had rested for another half hour. The guards had been changed. Now they were the Shquiptar Kolj and the stupidly smiling Meho. A change could be noticed in Kolj. The lively redhead was withdrawn; a cloud was over his easygoing nature.

It was clear to Anto why they had not come for him at once after they had taken away the unknown man in fetters. Scraps of bread and *čevabčići*, sausages, in *kajmak*, cream, and a jar of honey just begun were on Suljaga's table alongside the instruments of torture, and Suljaga was wiping his lips with a towel. Anto took it all in and remembered every detail, though he had scarcely a moment to look.

Throwing aside the towel, Suljaga awaited him in the center of the room, with feet well apart to get a better purchase. He fell on Anto with a shower of blows, cursing his father and mother. At the same time, the gypsies, Smajo and Džem, caught hold of him and bound his hands behind his back. Meho, encouraged, struck him in the groin with his fists, saying: "There, that's what you deserve."

Winded, Anto could see before him the contorted face and protruding eyes of Suljaga. He did not understand what was required of him and was astonished at his reception. But he resisted the blows and the tearing hands.

"Ha, so you defend yourself, you scum! And this spring you could welcome haiduks, eh?" roared Suljaga, growing larger and larger and more violent.

He knows. What does he know? He knows about the haiduks who were there with us. But that he might have guessed as soon as he took Stanija prisoner. Well, let him know.

They bound his hands with chains, and Suljaga shouted: "Kneel, wolf!"

Anto knelt, bewildered. Smajo and Džem quickly passed the end of the chain through the binding around his hands and linked it with the chain that joined his ankle fetters, drawing it so tight that his fists were almost level with his heels, the soles of his feet drawn together, and his body stretched backward. Then they locked the chains, and Džem took off Anto's shoes, as skillfully as if from his own feet and as roughly as if from the feet of another. Before Anto realized what they were preparing him for, the exultant Meho pushed him over, so that his head and chest struck the floor. "There, that's what you deserve!"

"Be more careful," Anto heard Suljaga whisper. He was now once more in control of himself, incomprehensibly calm.

They consulted in whispers, probably also by gestures, over Anto, thrust face down to the floor, the soles of his feet turned upward.

"Bastinado?" he heard Džem ask softly and indifferently.

They whispered again. Then Smajo remarked to his son, instructing him: "By all means, let's begin with that. At one time it was called horseshoeing."

It was now clear to Anto that they would beat him with a bull's pizzle on the soles of his feet, a torture frequently used, very painful, but which did not kill. Džem sat on Anto's back and forced into his mouth a rag so filthy that he could taste dust and recently shed blood. *So that I don't yell. It would hinder them. And perhaps also that the people should not be horrified. Shall I yell, shall I be able to keep myself from yelling? Which is better? To yell or not to yell?*

Suljaga fiddled with the instruments on his table. "This one is already unraveled and in strips," he said reprovingly and commandingly.

Smajo justified himself. "I have fresh ones at home, honored aga. This other one will still serve well. But even bulls are not what they used to be. It is difficult to find good pizzles."

Someone—*Suljaga; probably it is Suljaga*—tried the pizzle, cutting the air with it and making it whistle. *Yes, yes, Suljaga is testing it. Suljaga will begin the whipping.*

Anto was astonished at the clarity with which he noticed every detail, distinguished even the softest sounds, a whisper, a footstep, things being moved on the table, even though he had nearly been knocked silly by the blows. While he was staggering he had seen drops and pools of blood, and, lying on his right side and looking in that direction, he could still see them, only from nearby they seemed larger and much redder. He recalled that in that shower of blows and curses Kolj had neither touched him nor said anything against him. He was a Shquiptar, and among the Shquiptars, as among the Montenegrins, the torture of men and the ill-treatment of the helpless were considered shameful.

There was silence, as before some great terrible ceremonial.

"Radak!" Suljaga called him in a changed, solemn, strident voice, and Džem at the same moment took the gag from his mouth. "I ask you for the last time: will you confess?"

Anto, now that he was no longer horrified at the torture, replied without hesitation: "I have nothing to confess."

There was a rustling and murmuring of cloth and silk. Suljaga had taken off his heavy surcoat. He lamented: "Let us begin."

"Yes, aga, let us begin," approved Smajo.

The blow was so unexpected and so painful, cutting into him from foot to head, cutting into his brain, that Anto emitted a mad, inhuman shriek, stifled by the gag. But before the next blow fell he decided to count the strokes, not for curiosity's sake, but in order to mask the pain and, especially, the expectation of the next stroke.

Panting, Suljaga struck without haste, shouting: "Confess, confess, my martyr!"

Anto went on counting to himself, answering each stroke with a stifled yell. But about the twentieth stroke he lost count, and even Suljaga began to grow tired.

"Give it to me, aga." Meho snatched at the pizzle.

"No, no. You have too heavy a hand. Let Smajo."

Smajo struck more weakly than Suljaga, but more painfully,

for he was more expert. Every blow was struck so that the end of the pizzle caught on the fleshy end and nail of one of his toes, and more often than not in the same place. Every time, Anto, awaiting a fresh blow, quivered painfully in the hope that it would not fall in the same place.

After every three or four blows Suljaga would shout: "Confess! Confess!" and Džem would remove the gag from Anto's mouth. But when Anto did not reply or moaned that he had nothing to confess, the beating was resumed.

They gave him another thirty or so strokes, and Suljaga knelt by his head imploring him. "Confess, heartless one. Have mercy on yourself and on me."

Anto, embittered and intentionally provocative, moaned: "I will not confess, I will not," astonished that his insolence did not anger Suljaga and that nothing terrible happened.

Suljaga, indeed, ordered: "Let's take a rest."

They left Anto on the floor, as if they had forgotten him. Suljaga ate, while Smajo turned over his implements. Džem went out, but came back soon and poured a warm, pleasant fluid from a jug over Anto's soles. Smajo, who obviously liked remembering old times and instructing his son, explained. "It's a wonder—how soon the skin dries and cracks from the blows. Now you must take care, so that there will be no scars."

During the course of the torture the relationship between Suljaga and the guards changed, at least judging from Meho's cheerful approval: "That's it! That's it!" and Suljaga's exhortations to him to eat. Even the relationship between Suljaga and the gypsies changed. He exhorted them, too, to eat. All accepted his offer but Kolj; taciturn and motionless, he stood aside. Whenever Anto pulled himself together, he thought: Where is Kolj? What will Kolj, the Shquiptar, think about my bearing? What does he think about all this?

Smajo reminisced between mouthfuls. "Everything has changed. I used to listen to my father, peace be on his soul. He, and his father before him, broke bones freely and tore pieces out of the living flesh. It was easy to work in the old times."

Suljaga said: "Yes, everything is bottoms up, so to speak. Then, they used to impale men on stakes, but since Sultan Abdul-Medjid issued his *Hatti-humayun* one must take care that the criminal is healthy and whole to appear before the cadi. The authorities have, so to speak, grown softer and the rebels harder and more cunning. That's the way it goes! Every ill has begun from the fact that foreign, Christian, powers have become involved in our affairs and that, so to speak, in Stambul they have begun to take them as an example. When we lived in our way and looked after our own affairs, the begs were more humble and more spiritual and the serfs more peaceful. Our sword flashed over the whole world. The sun did not set upon our empire; everything Turkish flourished and, so to speak, smelled of myrrh. Then there was more justice for the *raja,* though the punishments were more severe."

Suljaga and Smajo lamented the old days and recalled them for a full half hour, while Kolj still remained silent and Meho approved. Finally they finished eating. Suljaga drank up the hydromel and then remembered Anto, exclaiming, as much to himself as to the others: "The night is passing, and we sit chatting here!"

At once they became active, returning to their task with energy and deliberation. Once more Smajo began to whip and Suljaga to implore. At first Anto responded with stifled cries wrenched from him, but then, remembering Kolj and thinking that his yelling gave pleasure to Suljaga, he decided to clench his teeth and endure the pain without a cry. They struck him two or three more times, then cried out in alarm. "Look, he's fainted," said Suljaga in astonishment.

"Are you sure, Džem, that you didn't stop up his nose?" shouted Smajo reprovingly.

"Croaked? Fine! That's the way," said Meho, laughing.

Suljaga shouted at him: "Shut up, idiot!" Almost tenderly, he put his hand inside Anto's jacket, on the left side of his chest, and then, in the silence, confirmed: "He's all right. A momentary faint. It often happens. Džem, pour some water over his head."

"Take care, son," advised Smajo as Džem poured water over Anto's neck and head. "We, too, have been given great trust and responsibility."

Anto, however, had not been unconscious. He managed to seize two or three drops of water with the edges of his lips and tongue. He now realized that it was important to them that he remain conscious and not die under torture. *And I, fool that I was, was*

54

afraid of unconsciousness! What I say when I am not in command of my senses is of no use to them. That's the point! It was a valuable revelation to him; it almost wiped away his fears that he might let slip something in delirium, and at the same time it opened the one gate through which he could, if only for a moment, escape from his torment.

They gave him another fifteen strokes. He responded to them with groans carefully moderated, discreet, from his throat and chest and not from his whole body, in order not to reveal his ability to resist pain. In truth, these last blows hurt less than the first ones. The moderation of his cries, though intentional, appeared natural even to himself. But it was hard to deceive Suljaga, who ordered: "Enough for tonight; he is exhausted."

They untied him at once. He stretched out, tried to stand, but at once slipped to the ground, groaning. It was as if thousands of living, squirming thorns pierced his soles. Suljaga brushed away his sweat with a white palm, grinning. "Come along, come along, don't play-act," he said. Anto again made an effort, slipped once more, but remained on his feet, shuffling, trying to find, but not succeeding, a sound place on which he could stand. "Lead him," ordered Suljaga, sighing.

Anto went, forgetting his shoes, which Kolj picked up and stuffed under his left arm. Meho took him by the right arm, but without hatred or animosity; for the time being all was over. In general, their hatred for him, as his for them, had disappeared. There was only apathy and fatigue. Even when Suljaga gave the order "No sleeping! Two of you keep watch on him," he did so indifferently, as a matter of routine. Meho, too, seemed gloomy and depressed; he did not give his usual gay and thoughtless approval.

Anto's tears flowed. He wept and groaned; not from weakness or pain, but from wretchedness and humiliation. *They trod me down like a worm, like a beast.* Suddenly he was overcome by thirst and the stifling heat, which he had forgotten during the torture. He felt robbed of strength and clarity. *Whence these tears, since I have not drunk water?* When he reached the top of the steps, he remembered Nasto's groans and felt ashamed. Pulling himself together, he stumbled down the steps without a cry, in pain, on needles that pierced him from the soles of his feet to

the crown of his head. He hoped that it would be easier for him
on the pebbles, and hastened toward the corridor, shuddering at
every step. But when we got there, the pain, which on the stairs
had spread evenly over the soles of his feet, became concentrated
and thereby increased tenfold. It was clear to him why they had
pulled and kicked Nasto along the corridor. He had not been
able to walk. Anto clenched his teeth. *So what if Nasto does hear
me! But I will lessen his courage—I, the Radak knez!* So, as during the torture when he had refrained from crying out, he walked
along the corridor in silence, swaying slightly.

He hoped that there would be rest and liberation in his cell.
But the struggle between thirst and sleep began as soon as he lay
down on the planks.

Meho and Kolj sat on tree stumps on each side of the door.
Evidently they had been forbidden to talk, not only to him, but
also to one another. Even with them in the cell, Anto was alone
with himself. But as soon as he began to doze, or when he closed
his eyes for a little, Meho would jog him with a sharp flick on the
sole of his foot and shout: "No sleeping! No, no!" Though he,
too, was overcome with sleep and yawned noisily every few moments, he zealously and insistently stared at Anto's eyes. Once or
twice he dozed off, and then, starting up, horrified, he struck
Anto brutally on the sole of the foot. Kolj, however, remained
awake, withdrawn, every so often pulling his pipe out of his belt,
slowly filling the bowl with his right index finger, and smoking
some pleasant and—or so it seemed to Anto—irresistibly sleep-
provoking tobacco.

Neither then nor, still less, later could Anto recall what he had
thought about or what he had noticed. He remembered later that
he had hated Suljaga immeasurably. He invented tortures for
him, cutting him up piece by piece. Fear of what Suljaga knew
grew with thoughts of the tortures that Anto expected and that
Suljaga would be able to invent. He was worried about the
Radaks, especially his sons, Grgur, Akan, and Rade, the youngest,
because the Turks might trick them, arrest them, and lure them
to destruction. His tongue stuck to his gums, and his unmoistened
throat was dry and burning, as if he were swallowing quicklime.
The great fire within him became narcotic and the black throng
whirled and whirled. From time to time he could feel in his head

a beating till then unknown, terrible and inconsolable, destroying every effort of body and mind to concentrate on anything. Separate thoughts spawned and were extinguished, despite his will, like fireflies.

I will go mad. They want me to go mad, so that they can do with me whatever they want. But they can't make me mad. What good am I to them if I am mad? Nor will they kill me. I would be of no use to them dead. But madness! Only in that way can they break me, cheat me. But they can't. They can. Suljaga, not even to you do I wish evil, only leave me alone. Leave me in my wretchedness, in the fire. I will burn. Everything will burn.

Put out the fire in the house! Save them, save the children! I know what the Šala mother meant when she advised her son, whom the Vizier of Skadar threatened to kill before her eyes if she did not induce him to betray his comrades: "My son, keep your honor and reputation and do not regret the spoonful of blood which the Vizier will spill!" The Vizier killed him. He roasted him between two fires, and when he could not take away his honor, he killed him. Me, too, they will roast. Already they are roasting me, by thirst. But my reason, my honor, that they will not, cannot, take. Reason and honor together! Keep your reason, keep your honor, Anto Radak. Keep the Radaks.

Lord God, you see my torments. Preserve my reason. Do not quench your light within me.

Go, get thee behind me, Satan! The Devil will deceive me, will seduce me! The sweetness of life, of which Suljaga talks, it will seduce me. It is a fine life there with Milena; we are not so old, in the mountain katun *where one grows young again. And my grandchildren—I will tell them stories, teach them, live again in them. When I look out from the mountains, there is no end to the world, no end to man. Haymaking in the mountains . . .*

What is it that you want, Granddad Anto? Yes, indeed, Granddad. Now I really look like my grandfather after whom I was named. And Radule, his brother. Which Radule? That one they threw on the hooks? But you, Radule, are dead long ago. You breathed your last on the hooks. I know your grave; there, outside the graveyard. You say: I am dead, but I live on! How can that be—dead-alive? But there you are; it can. You say, Radule, that the wolves have attacked the sheep? Good, I run, since you can-

not, when the accursed Turks have mangled the soles of your feet. But I must take a pistol. Your pistol, Radule? But what a pistol! Everything breaks into pieces as soon as I take it in my hands. Do you see? Stock, barrel, spring, trigger! Who could mend it? There are wolves among my sheep! And you, give me your pistol. With the pieces I will defend the sheep from the wolves. Do not shout at me, do not scold me!

Kolj was standing over him in the pale morning light blended with the yellow gleam from the lantern; Kolj, ruddy and young, with reddish-golden hair and mustaches. "Anto Radak, come to yourself, wake up. Meho will soon be back with breakfast. Wake up, Radak, so that I do not lose my bread and life because of you!"

Kolj, Shquiptar man—he has let me sleep. Thank you, Kolj, heroic, noble seed! "Don't worry, Kolj. I would rather lose my life than let a hair of your head be harmed."

Because of that short sleep, even though it had merged into tormented wakefulness and visions, Anto had a quiet, bearable morning. *Broken weapons! Misfortune, death! But that pistol had not merely been broken; it had been shattered. That, too, was some kind of misfortune. I am breaking up!*

After breakfast the guard was changed: Huso and Abdulah. *They do not trust even their own men! They do not trust the Shquiptars—one Shquiptar and one Moslem Turk. The Shquiptars are mostly Moslems but do not consider themselves Turks. Only the Serb converts consider themselves Turks. Among us it is like that. A Serb converted is worse than a Turk!*

But the noonday heat again brought terror and foreboding. That immoderate, persistent throbbing of his heart and entrails spread through every pore, seeming to shake the walls of the cell and of the kula; the whole space around him, the whole world, shuddered and echoed to the throbbing of that racing, rebellious heart.

In the afternoon there was a downpour of rain. The streams around the kula began to rush and bring freshness to him. Calm and collected, he awaited the evening.

Night fell, and with it came a change of guard: Kolj and Meho. When the cackling of the poultry, the mooing of the cows and calves, the noise and clatter of the policemen's supper had died down, they took away that fettered wretch, only to bring him back two hours or more later. Neither from one side nor from the other did he hear any sound of life. His fetters clanked monotonously, emptily, mournfully.

Soon afterward they came for Nasto. Even before they took him away he began wailing. "Don't, don't have this sin on your souls! My children, my home! Woe, O mother mine!"

Anto too, remembered. *And I, sinful one, did not mention my mother. I don't remember her. She died giving birth to me. She gave her life for me. Perhaps the tortures overcame me so much that I could not even call upon her.* "Mother mine!"

Anto tried to listen for Nasto's torture, his return and his laments. But he heard nothing, though shortly afterward someone shouted from the top of the stairs: "Bring the knez!" Anto was almost pleased that they had called him that, though he had nothing to rejoice about, and even began to tremble, empty and chilled to the marrow, as Meho took his arm and Kolj lit the way with the lantern. Everything about him seemed to sway.

Nasto was seated on the floor, his hands bound below his knees and his head forced down between them. Above the ropes at his elbows and under his knees they had forced the handle of a billhook, the ends of which stuck out a good foot. He raised his sweaty, emaciated face, revealing bruised and bloody lips around which the sparse hairs of his mustaches and straggly beard stood out unnaturally. He was thin, small, and swarthy, burned and desiccated by the sun, hard work, and poverty. When he heard Suljaga mention Anto's name, asking him if he had yet come to his senses, he whimpered: "Brother Anto, help me! They have torn the heart out of me with their tortures, I who am not guilty and who know nothing! You know that I am not guilty of anything, even if others have stirred up something."

Anto stretched out a hand to him, to console him by word or touch, but he encountered the enraged face of Suljaga, who cut him short. "Here we are, torturing an innocent man, a member of your clan, and you keep silent! Do you want me to have his children on my soul? And you, Nasto, you know what you have confessed and what we agreed. Now hurry up and tell it to Anto, face to face."

Nasto remained bewildered, taking refuge in sobs and entreaties. "Don't torture me, who am innocent! Must I bring evil upon my brother?"

But Suljaga was harsh and intransigent, consumed with anger. He spoke cuttingly. "Don't drive us to drag the words out of you by force. We are in a hurry. Speak!"

"Anto, brother. They demand that I tell them all I know. But to my misfortune, I don't know anything! How could I know anything, working as a day laborer to fill my stomach? What could I do? I told them that two strangers were at your house on St. George's Day. I can't tell Suljaga if they were or were not haiduks, because I really don't know."

"They were, they were. I know that from another source. Listen! What will you do now, Anto?"

Anto was struck dumb, and he saw that the others, especially Suljaga, noticed his dumbness and bewilderment.

"You tell them, brother Anto, not to torture us, that we Radaks do not jump into the fire," Nasto said. "They swear that all they want to do is put down the revolt and that they will do nothing to the Radaks, that they will even forgive the guilty. They say: 'We understand. You are Serbs, serfs, and times are thus.' Do something, Anto; you are knez."

Anto was silent, embarrassed by the presence of Suljaga as a sullen observer, saddened by Nasto's cowardice, even if not betrayal. He was embittered against Nasto, ready even to spit upon him. But something in Nasto's desolation, some presentiment that it would be wiser if he remained calm, made him say, almost indifferently: "Those men, my poor Nasto, were casual guests from Donja Nahija. They were buying cattle. Now they have caused you to be put to the torture. I know nothing, Nasto; I can say nothing."

"How well he knows how to embroider and tell the tale! And why was your daughter-in-law with the haiduks?" Suljaga hissed in Anto's ear, gripping him by the neck.

"That she knows."

"She! You know it well, too. And you know it better still."

Nasto, encouraged, recovered himself. "Perhaps they *were* casual guests, honored aga. I did not see them myself; my wife told me. You, Anto brother, you are knez, you know what to do."

But before Nasto had finished speaking, Suljaga's heavy shoe was thrust into his face. It was more of a push than a blow, but was hard enough to turn Nasto over. He yelled, but it seemed to Anto that it was not from pain. "Brother Anto, forgive me! What did I know? What could I do? They broke me down, I who am innocent, with unheard-of tortures."

"Take that swine away!" shrieked Suljaga. "Now, all of a sudden, he doesn't know. His wife told him! Let the filthy water that brought him here take him away again. You two, Smajo and Džem, to work!"

While the guards dragged Nasto away, wailing and lamenting, Smajo and Džem threw themselves at Anto with all the intensity of the previous night. Rapidly, almost soundlessly, they bound him with chains while Suljaga stamped impatiently. Meho, too, joined in, pinching Anto's neck artery with fingers like a vise, pulling and twisting it. "That's it, that's the way!"

Anto remained calm; and it seemed as if his calm was transferred to them. They made him sit down and, as with Nasto, bound his hands around his knees, pushed a broomstick through the crook of his elbows and then lifted him on it, with his head hung downward and the soles of his feet upward. His weight increased threefold, concentrated on his wrists. They held him up, watching him carefully for several moments, then placed one end of the broomstick on Suljaga's table and the other on the little table, from which they removed the candlesticks. The floor and Anto's head suddenly were in shadow.

"Upside-down shoeing," Smajo explained, "which is now called upside-down bastinado."

This threefold increase in the weight of his body filled his head with molten lead but in no way lessened the tearing at his wrists. Džem seized him by the chin with his left hand and with his right pushed the gag into his mouth. Meho took over the job of bastinado.

The pain surprised Anto, not because pain is always a shock and not because Meho struck harder than the others, but because the blows were now on open wounds. There was no interval between pain and blow; the blows were only the high points of the same continuous sensation. Anto did not fight against the pain, but gave way to it, responding to the blows with racking shudders and stifled moans, which echoed from the walls of the room. Suddenly it seemed to him as if his entrails were gushing into his head in a dense felty heat, through which the blows could not break but which thickened more and more.

They cried out and rubbed his chest. Someone exclaimed: "Water, water!" and Anto, stretched out on the floor, awakened from unconsciousness, saw above him unknown persons and a blackened ceiling with thick beams.

"Let him rest," he heard a familiar voice say.

Suljaga. "Suljaga!"

"What is it, Radak? Is it hard for you? Have you reconsidered?" Suljaga urged him solicitiously, almost tenderly.

For tonight it is over. "I have nothing to reconsider. You cannot cloud my reason."

But Anto was mistaken. After they had ungagged him and decided that he had rested sufficiently, Suljaga ordered: "Smashing!"

They laid him face downward on the floor, with his arms still pinioned behind him. Džem sat on his back and stuffed the gag into his mouth, and Meho held down his legs. "This is still called as it used to be: smashing," the father explained to his son. "Only now it must be done more carefully, more humanely; he can rot, but he must not die."

Suljaga knelt by Anto's head. "Don't force us to injure you, Radak. Don't make me responsible for your soul. Be sensible. You have a family. It would still be nice to go on living. We do not want to harm you."

Anto remained silent, thinking it over, though already determined to endure the torture. He later said that the hardest part was waiting until they had arranged him in the most suitable position. Now, on the floor, pinned down, he reflected, almost by habit, on whether or not he would waver under this fresh misfortune.

"Did you say anything? Speak, you poor devil," urged Suljaga tenderly. And the gag, as before, was removed whenever Suljaga wanted him to speak.

"No. I have nothing to say."

Only when Smajo began to strike him with something soft and heavy on the small of the back did Anto realize for what those two long bags, which he had glimpsed on Suljaga's table two nights before, were intended. They were filled with sand for smashing the kidneys. He had often heard tell of them.

The pain grew imperceptibly, from limitless dark depths, and spread stealthily, ever more swiftly and powerfully, along hitherto unsuspected channels, right to the ends of his limbs. Soon he ceased to notice the external pressures of the blows; they struck him from within, seized on his internal parts to which he had never before paid any attention, though he knew that they existed, and which now, suddenly, through pain became life, existence, being, himself, with all his mind and all his desires. The pain was not so sharp, not even so painful, as that caused by the pizzles, and he did not feel it so acutely and intensely in his brain. But nonetheless, in its manner—every pain pains and every torture is a torture—it was more terrible, more painful and pervasive. Shooting through his whole body, it struck even at reason, leaving it fully conscious, making it clearer, even sharpening it. It was just that clarity of thought and that consciousness of self mingled with the pain that made it more terrible. *It is strange how my awareness returns so quickly! From these bags one rots inside and dies slowly. If they do not kill me now, they wish me to die like a dog.* "Monsters! Vampires!"

"What did you say? Do you want to confess?" Suljaga bent over him.

"I said: 'I will drink your blood.' "

"I know, I know," said Suljaga, smiling, and he added mockingly: "You can't expect us to fondle you while you cook up plots."

As Smajo continued with his regular and considered blows, Suljaga said, as if to himself, but perhaps also knowing that Anto heard every word: "Every authority and every rule has a right to defend itself against rebels. And each defends itself, finally, as best it knows and can. When it cannot do it by fair means, then it does it by foul. And I? By foul means.

"It is impossible without foul means, beatings! Your own proverb says so: Beatings are for the *raja*. And I am glad that it is I who give the beatings. Without me it is impossible. Without me there would be no world. The world changes, but I remain; only my hand is changed.

"Our new sultan, Abdul-Hamid, may Allah grant long life to

him and his empire, withholds the beatings, wants mildness and goodness to win and to adorn his rule. But we who are farther away, who live and fight against human passions and antagonisms, we know that mildness and goodness are not for all men and that good wishes and intentions must be supported by force.

"I wanted mildness and goodness to win with you, too, Radak, and began in that way, but if you won't—well, let be what will be. You, when you decided to keep your own path and your own side and to go against the authorities and the law, should not expect anything human from us."

Suljaga went on expounding what seemed to be irrefutable and horribly attractive truths. But Anto heard only words, which fell leadenly with the suddenly painless blows of Smajo. Shooting through him, the pain somehow seemed exquisite, inexorable.

Suljaga again said something. They loosed him, and someone— *Suljaga? He alone gives commands*—ordered him to get up. He stumbled, not because of his legs, but because of some twisting internal pain. "Human curses will not give you life," he shouted at Suljaga, who smiled self-confidently and indifferently.

The guards prodded him, dragged him, seized him by the arm, and struck him in the small of the back. Every movement, every blow intensified his pain a hundred times, and Anto did not make any attempt to hold back his sobs and cries.

Once back in his cell, he recalled, or there came to him, his native village. He was sitting in front of his house on a summer evening. From early youth he had loved nothing so much as sitting on that stone at the end of his garden near the stream. He loved that stone, whose rounded greenish top emerged from the depths of the earth into the sunlight, which welcomed a man in the warmth of the summer evening and seemed a part of him. To the right, down to the stream, and farther, down to the valley below, were his fields and meadows, which on the left bordered the gardens and properties of other Radaks. Except for the hayfields in the mountains, this was all his property, ten acres of pasture and about as much arable land, three times more than any other Radak had. The land was under the agas, but he and his sons had watered it with their sweat and nourished it with their skill. Seated thus he could see it all at a glance and caress it, but on some evenings it was necessary to consider how to cultivate it, how to irrigate it, and what to sow. Now, in delirium and fever, the property vanished, the boundaries disappeared, and its borders melted away into the bluish evening twilight. His lands now covered the whole valley down to the Lim, seductive and soft as the kiss of a young bride, of Milena. Even there across the river it was all his; as far as the rising crests of the Visitor mountains, as far as eye could see, and even beyond, to the end of the world, in the chill of the coming evening and over the soil of his ancestors, between heaven and earth. His years fell away from him; he was neither young nor old, nor did youth or age exist, only Anto Radak, only a man who worked and loved, was born and bred, to suffer and survive, who was living and looking at his world.

Morning began, mild and refreshing. Again someone called. *Good, heroic Kolj! He brings the good morning with him.* "Kolj!"

But it was not Kolj and already it was full day.

"Who are you?"

"I am Huso."

"Ah, Huso!" *Who would have thought that Huso, a Moslem, would have let me have my fill of sleep. Huso, whom the Montenegrins had wounded; the scar now shines red, but otherwise is white. But humanity is humanity, wounded or whole.*

"Wake up, brother Radak. Abdulah will soon be back from his sick wife, and I will be punished because of you."

"Not a hair of your head shall be harmed because of me, Huso."

"I would bring you some water, but they do not trust even us, and we have no water here."

Then came Abdulah, who could not refrain from whispering to him and prodding him. But Anto did not hear him or understand his words. That black swarm rushed at him again. It was white, black, red, changing every moment. He no longer cried for help or continued to defend himself. But, from somewhere or other, his mother appeared. He did not see her, but he knew that she was there. She watched him, opened wide to him the softness of her lap and arms. *Or was it Milena's lap and Milena's arms? No, it was my mother! What am I thinking of? It was Milena! Mother-Milena. Who? She? They? I am not a child, Mother. Do not fear for me. How can you, Milena, Milena? Would you have*

*married me if I had been a little boy? But you, who are you,
Mother or Milena? Or have you merged, become one to care for
me, to pour balm on my wounds? But you do not know if I am or
am not a little boy! You do not know if I still have a man's
strength. You know better, you know everything. To you I am
always a child, to you I am always a husband and the only male. I
will come to you. Wait for me, call me. No, my mother does not
die; no one's mother ever dies. And wives wait for their husbands,
ever since the world and the centuries began, until death!*
"Mother mine! Dear wife of mine!"

Later he did not remember when or how the day passed, or
whether in the evening he heard them take Nasto or the fettered
prisoner. He could not even recall when and how they took him.
Suddenly he was aware of Suljaga, the gypsies, and the guards,
Kolj and Meho.

Grinning reflectively, Suljaga said something to him. He heard
the words, but they made no sense; he could not connect them.
Then he replied to Suljaga; he knew what he wanted to say to
him, but the words came brokenly, one after the other, as strange
as Suljaga's had been.

Devils. The Devil. "Get thee behind me, unbelieving one,
infidel!" *Suljaga is the Devil. I am the dead, and the Devil is
interrogating me for my sins.* "No, I am not dead, but you are the
Devil. Satan!" *I thought I was not so sinful, but see how it has
turned out. How many, how heavy, are my sins? A man does not
know when he sins, and the sins—how they pile up! Then of a
sudden a hill, a mountain, of sins is revealed, heavy on earth,
strait in Heaven.* "Treason! A traitor!" *Had I not sinned there
would be no treason and no traitor.* "To a sinner everyone is a
traitor"—*who reveals his sins.* "Sinner and Satan! Together"—*I
and Suljaga*—"from the beginning to the Day of Judgment!"

Suljaga was saying something mild, sweet, almost weeping from
goodness and pity. But Anto continued saying his piece; his
stream rushed joyously and furiously, without impediment.

"Are you a devil, are you a man?" *Why do you torment my
soul?* "Rebel!" *No, I am a Radak.* "Anto Radak, knez." *I was,
and still am. I am knez. I am not Radule.* "What Radule?" *He
who died on the hooks.* "I have been on the hooks and shall be
again." *That I know.*

"Suljaga, Devil, you know my sins." *Why then do you torment me?*

Nor am I Arsenius. "I will not kneel." *Arsenius did not kneel.* "The sword—my head!

"I am Anto Radak." *There is but one Anto Radak.* "I have nothing to confess; nor will I confess anything.

"Milena!" *Milena? Who mentioned Milena?* "Surely you will not imprison and torture her?" *Let my mother alone, you swine! She is too old for you. And she knows nothing; she has long been dead.* "She brought food! The prodigal son has come." *To whom?* "To me." *To whom else?*

"Why are you grinning?" *Devil! I see nothing. I do not fear you, grinning or not grinning. I wish to die honorably! Nothing more! Nothing more! O mother-wife mine!*

Of a sudden he was wakeful, alert, wet. "Drink, though you don't deserve it," shouted Suljaga, neither craftily nor angrily.

Meho forced the dish between his teeth. "That's it, that's the way."

Feeling the freshness of the water in his red-hot entrails, Anto seized the dish with both hands, taking care not to spill a drop, and drank in energy and awareness—*they are giving me water because I am still necessary to them, to torture me*—calm and hope, which refreshed, fascinated, consoled.

The torture for that evening had not yet begun.

"Bring in that wolf," ordered Suljaga.

As was soon evident, he applied the term "wolf" to Vučeta, perhaps because his name derived from *vuk,* the word for the beast, but more likely because he recognized in him the indomitable and wily master of the forest. But is was not Vučeta they brought in. Kolj and Meho carried in something that was no longer the Vučeta Anto remembered, but a bundle of torn, swollen, and smashed flesh. Anto would not have recognized him if he had not been wearing the gold-embroidered Montenegrin jacket, now spattered with blood, which he had been wearing when he was with the Radaks on St. George's Day, peacocking before the young girls and the widow Petrana.

"Don't you know one another?" sneered Suljaga, but since neither Anto nor Vučeta replied, he went on: "Just as you like; you do, you don't. We have brought him here, the wolf, so that you,

Radak, should see him and take a good look at him. For him, for a haiduk, we are responsible to no one, so we have paid no special regard to him except insofar as we, so to speak, are obliged to as men. From now on we shall not pay much regard to you either; a rebel, so to speak, is worse than a haiduk! Look at him well; you are looking at yourself, Radak!"

Anto noticed, first of all, that Vučeta's teeth had been drawn and his nails torn out. Vučeta mouthed as if he wanted to say something, but that cavern of a mouth remained empty, without the pearls of words, without the brilliance of sound. He made a motion as if to stretch out his hands to Anto and then slowly withdrew them, deformed as pollarded trunks. His mustaches had been torn out. They had cut or burned off that mole on his left cheek, and in its place was a clotted scar like a wild pear. Instead of eyes he had swollen pits with a dull shine, and his right leg, the thigh bone crushed or sawn, hung twisted and motionless. At first Anto was not sure if Vučeta could still hear or see anything, and to the end he remained inarticulate, if he had anything to say; a painful gurgling came from him as they took him away. Nonetheless, he shook his head, to indicate that he did not recognize Anto, and where his eyes had once been there flashed for a moment a bluish light, and the swollen lips drew back in a monstrous, sinister, and yet pleasant smile.

"So!" concluded Suljaga. "Now take the wolf away."

"That's it, that's the way," remarked Meho, taking Vučeta by the arm. They did not lead him out, but carried him, dragged him, away.

"Well, Radak?" Suljaga asked. But Anto, stunned and yet somehow exalted by the horror of Vučeta's, of his own, destiny, did not utter a word.

He remained silent, moaning, even when they tugged at his teeth. They did not pull them out, although they broke some and loosened others, which later fell out. He thought to himself: They are only pulling those from the upper jaw, those nearest to the brain. Smajo had interpreted this torture also: "Tugging. But now we only pull at them; we must be careful." The eyeteeth pained him most; they tugged at his brain, and some forgotten, till then inviolate force twisted in his skull like a finger in a glove.

Thrown later into his cell, Anto heard from the depths of the kula a slow, regular clinking of fetters. He listened attentively. *Vučeta. Is that Vučeta?* He replied, equally softly, with his own fetters. The haiduk replied. He signaled again—*just so that you know, Vučeta, that I have heard and have understood.*

Meho did not notice this exchange, but Kolj seemed to; he smiled with melancholy comprehension.

The following evening Anto said nothing, and was not asked anything. It seemed that Suljaga had lost all desire to convince or to explain and was devoting himself entirely to torture. That night they forced wedges under Anto's nails, but did not set them alight, as in earlier times. He forgot which torture was on which night; he remembered them only by their nature and by the names that Smajo, instructing his son, called them.

And that night, too, Vučeta greeted him with his fetters, and Anto returned the greeting.

The night after the wedging, as Smajo called this torture, they let him sleep in peace. From that long, but clouded, broken sleep he awoke invigorated to a world that was somehow strange, as if even to himself he was in some way strange and unknown.

The awakening itself was terrifying, as if in a moment the frontier between sleep and waking had been torn down. In his sleep he had been conscious, or perhaps only dreamed he was, that he was in his cell in the kula, that he was lying on the planks, tortured and broken, and that peace and rest were more necessary to him than anything else.

Despite that longing, despite his weariness and the heat of the noonday, he felt that there in his cell was some unknown man. He felt his presence there even though he knew that the cell was locked and that no one could enter except the guards, Abdulah and Huso. Nonetheless, the unknown had crept in and was approaching him stealthily to attack him, to do something to him even more terrible than any torture he had been able to imagine. It was as if he were immaterial, though dressed in coarse black cloth and with white weak hands, like a monk, that were, Anto felt, inflexible as a vise. He tried to call for help, to stand and defend himself or to run away. But, just as in a dream, he could not move a finger or emit a cry, and he knew with terrible inevitability that he could not run away from his locked cell. Slowly that someone approached the boards malignantly and evilly and raised himself up on them as if to find a place alongside Anto. He began to strangle him and weigh upon him, though he had no weight and his hands were not sharp and hard. The pressure and the suffocation came more from Anto himself, from his helplessness, his immobility. Yet Anto knew that if he succeeded in shouting, in shaking his shoulders or pushing away the hands of the unknown, then everything would vanish. He began to pull himself together, to summon his breath and unknown, unsuspected forces. It would be a real solace and alleviation if he were to die, if he could succumb. He was seized by a terrible fear of the unknown man. This man was able to do something to him more terrible than death, to take from him his reason, his ancestors and kin, the Radak clan in him, and crush and destroy his soul. He succeeded at last in crying out and moving, and was wakened by his own cry and the summons of the unknown: "Anto, Radak, what have they done to you, poor wretch?"

It was at once clear to him not only where he was and what he had dreamed, but also that the man who was sitting by his legs was not that someone who had strangled him in his dream. This man was dark, bluish, with a cunning, broad face. His eyes were shifty, yellow and green. Anto later said that they were of different colors, the right one yellowish and the left green, which heightened the gay craftiness of his expression. He was of moderate height, thickset, and inclined to plumpness, though it could not be said that he was fat. His mustaches were sparse and blond, and between his thick moist lips, half-opened and ready for laughter and jest, shone healthy wide-spaced teeth. He had prominent jaws and Adam's apple, a beard divided in the middle, a rather low forehead, and darkish hair, with ruddy curls, intentionally allowed to hang over his neck and ears. He was unusually, almost comically, dressed, neither in town nor peasant style, and it might be guessed that he was a trader in livestock, a carter, or a market gardener. From his short, flexible limbs and especially from his hands, strong and beautiful, bronzed and a little coarsened, with overlong fingers and strong nails, it could be deduced that he was

not a nonworker, but that, on the other hand, he did not over-
burden himself with work. Anto felt that he had seen him somewhere or other, but thought that he might be one of those vagabonds of whom there are many in the world and who, at first
sight, all look more or less alike.

"I am Bogdan Hašanin," he began, as soon as he saw that Anto
had come to himself.

Anto went on looking at him questioningly, meaning: Where
do you come from? What do you want? What kind of man are
you?

"I am a thief," explained Bogdan, anticipating Anto's questions. "You have nothing to fear from me, except that you must
take care not to say anything in my hearing that I must not tell
others. As for beatings, I don't say that I cannot endure them, but
I will not, for my own sake. It's not worth it, and it is a sin to
torture one's own body. So revolts, plots, wars, rebellions, disor-
ders, riots, murders, and suicides—all these are things that do not
concern me. That is a fact.

"Nonetheless, I am not so evil as many good men. If I look
after myself alone—well, one only lives once. Indeed, you, too,
think that, but you reason otherwise. To you, life is not the greatest good; to me, it is the only one.

"I have nothing of my own, except this little grain of sense and
these fingers; even if my reason is not great, my fingers are skillful
and prefer night to day. I have no one belonging to me, neither
wife nor children. All women are mine who are willing, and if I
have children by those who are willing, God alone knows, if he
bothers himself about such matters. I have neither father nor
mother. That man begot me on woman can be seen because I
walk on two legs and know what is good and what is evil, even
though I pay little heed to it, but live as best I can and in the
way I know best, doing all I can to harm others as little as possible and to benefit myself as much as possible.

"I have neither name nor surname; my mother or my *kum,* my
kinsman, if I ever had one, called me Bogdan, for God gave me,
since I do not know who my father was. Hašanin I am from my
homeland, Haša, where, so they say, I was born, though for me
the only important thing is wandering about the world.

"So much you may know about me! Anything else you may make up for yourself."

"I seem to have seen you somewhere," remarked Anto, wondering at his changed voice and at the pain that words provoked in his twisted and shattered teeth.

"Maybe yes, maybe no. I have been in your village three times. Each time I stole a lamb and comforted a widow. But you did not see me there. From knezes and policemen, from monks and dervishes, I fly like the Devil from the cross; the former love to beat and the latter love to preach.

"Perhaps you met me somewhere on my way; all ways are mine. Or perhaps you met my brother. No one knows how many brothers I have. We are the most numerous clan in the world."

"And what are you doing here, Bogdan Hašanin?"

"For a sensible man, I have said enough. But since from my viewpoint you do not seem such, for I see that you enjoy it if they tear out your teeth and smash your kidneys to a pulp, I will add this: I find myself here with you much against my will. I had no wish to be thrown into the kula, and, once in it, I had no wish to be here with you. I do not enjoy getting mixed up with anyone's misfortunes. Rebels are as infectious as the plague, and I still want gaiety and life.

"But one cannot counter God's will. Suljaga threw me in here to find you in your misfortune. They have so worked on you that they have lacerated your feet, torn out your nails, and drawn your teeth, so that you cannot revolt, you cannot even take anything into your mouth, if you still call that gap a mouth. And since I see that you are your own worst enemy, I dare tell you that they gave me orders to let them know if you let anything slip. Since I am a Serb—and that is my folly, for it is neither easy nor wise to be a Serb—it would be best for you to take care what you say so that I need not become a traitor, so that I may tell Suljaga truthfully, and give my oath on it, that I have heard nothing. Though it is easier to lie, it is better to tell the truth—if all ends well. Because as soon as one hears, others may, too; since they first existed, walls have had ears. And beatings are the one food I cannot eat with pleasure; nor can I vomit them.

"I am one of those Serbs who do not choose between the grave and the slave. I am a slave and I live. Let the Montenegrins sing and exalt heroism to the skies as much as they like; I know what I know. Without such Serbs as I, Serbdom would cease to be. Who would till the fields and beget the children?

"You, I see, have convinced yourself in that head of yours, which was once a head, that you are not for this world, and you behave so, even if you remain without a head. But I say: He who is without a head is neither mad nor wise, neither good nor evil, neither Serb nor Turk. All lost heads are alike.

"Your kinsman Nasto they also placed with me, so that I would be at hand to win him over and tempt him. And I won him over; he was only waiting for someone to win him over. But it served him little, for he knew little. Perhaps he would not have let himself be persuaded had he known more. So he got plenty of beatings, all because of you and your reason. They have a simple but sure calculation: since the Radaks are one clan, he must know. But still he got off better than you did; he got out with a whole skin and a quiet conscience.

"I tell you truthfully that, as far as saving his skin is concerned, I understand him. Man has only one. As for his conscience—well, that is more doubtful. Conscience is a perishable good, even though everyone beats the big drum about it. I do not sell such goods, or boast about them, even were I able to steal them from another.

"Now I shall persuade you, too. Be good and reasonable, Anto Radak. Betray your blood brothers to the Turks. Don't be mad and keep your honor if your bottom suffers for it. Be a Branković, a traitor; that profits you, even if it is not soon forgotten. Have you heard and understood?"

Not knowing what to conclude, Anto smiled at this warm, springtime freshet of words.

Bogdan went on, as if from a pulpit. "You who raise revolt and seek for justice in a world so arranged that there can never be peace and justice, you are a nuisance to your brother Serbian thief. Your words are honey and your promises paradise; but give man something that later on cannot be beaten out of him with pizzles, or torn out with pincers, or burned out with fire.

"You are drunk with glory which you cannot achieve and with

73

life which will never come, while I and my brothers carry on as best we can, and what we cannot get our teeth into or set our eyes on we pay no heed to.

"Your Serbdom is thorny, and has been from time immemorial; your Serb faith delights in human renunciation. Whereas I live from day to day and take delight in our Serb songs and Serb sucking pigs and a good glass and a comely wench. I live as a Serb without shedding blood. I love a tender fowl, whether Serbian or Turkish, and a good supper as much as a faith."

Bogdan rose from time to time, stretched his still-young, carefree limbs, and then sat down again.

"Am I chattering too much?" he asked, and continued: "What else can I do? I am throwing off my burdens and amusing myself in this misery. What can man do if he does not talk? He can only burn himself up. If it is hard for you, then stuff up your ears, think of something else, tell me to shut up. They say that words are from the mouth, stones are from the hand. But my words do not wound, only entertain—firstly and foremostly myself, then anyone else who likes, and, finally, even those who do not like."

Up till then Anto had listened to him attentively, though with distrust. Now, of a sudden, he felt pleasure, not only because he would no longer be alone, but also because of Bogdan's intangible, shimmering moods. Yet he was also assailed by fear. He feared that it was not Bogdan Hašanin saying all this, but some apparition. Why was he, Anto, in prison? What for? Might it not be only a dream? Was there any sense, was it worth-while, to suffer torments for some, perhaps even nonexistent, Radaks?

It was as if he, Anto Radak, he as he had once been and as he knew himself to be, had vanished, as if he were two Antos at the same time—one who saw, realized, and understood everything, even more deeply and clearly than before, and another who accepted everything as strange and unreal, even himself and his thoughts. Whenever he tried by his own will to form a bridge between the two, this duality would reappear, final and inflexible, goading his consciousness and reason to prove to himself that it did not, could not, exist.

"I have gone mad! Everyone has betrayed me and abandoned me!" he cried out silently to himself in horror, while attentively, even smilingly, he listened to and watched Bogdan, replied to him, or questioned him.

It had chanced before that something or someone, perhaps he himself, had seemed strange and unknown, or unreal, as in a dream. That had happened, he knew, to others also, perhaps to everyone in moments of great emotion or too great concentration of thought. But it happened rarely, fleetingly, and the split between him and events, between him and objects, between him and himself, would again be bridged; his personality would be restored to reality and its own integrity. Now, that unreality became total and frequent, despite his will and his consciousness; someone else, some other Anto, lived and acted continually within him.

There, it has happened, what I was most afraid of. I have lost control, and now Suljaga will be able to do what he likes with me. But no! I have not lost control; I see, I hear, I understand. "They have tortured me, Bogdan, and they will go on torturing me." *Nonetheless, the tortures are not so terrible now that I know Suljaga will not be able to do what he likes with me, to shame me.* "Yet on you, I see, no one has laid a finger." *Now he will tell me that I am right in what I see and conclude—that no one has laid a finger on him.*

"Just so: no one has laid a finger on me," Bogdan replied calmly. "They know me as a bad penny; they gain nothing if they beat me, for I remain what I am. I promise them everything when they catch me and compel me, and it even seems to me then that I will keep my word. But as soon as I get a taste of freedom, I forget the prison, and the longing for theft and a wandering life seizes me so powerfully that I do not dream of resisting it. Now they no longer beat me; old wood breaks and cannot be made straight. Even Suljaga does not beat my sort. He is terrifying only to you and those like you."

That is his answer, just what I expected. It means I am sound. But perhaps he knows what I want and is sympathetic to me, is deceiving me, so that later on Suljaga can take me unawares and break me.

"Would you mind helping me to go to the tub?"

As Anto had expected, Bogdan took him by the elbow and

raised him easily enough. Though he was not tall, he was muscular and big-boned and enormously strong. "Eh, my Radak, my fine fellow, you could have spared yourself all this. You are in a pretty mess. Now you cannot do anything for yourself unless someone gives you a hand."

Anto heard and understood him. Though he needed to go to the tub, he felt the need to verify this action through Bogdan. From then on, he verified everything frequently, both insignificant details and important questions and events.

He verified it even further. *Eh, I am pissing blood! Is it really so, or does it only seem so? Has Bogdan seen that it is blood? Why is he silent so long?*

Bogdan remarked: "Blood is flowing from you, brother. You're not pissing as you should; doctors won't give you much help for that. But, you know, sometimes it goes away of itself, though it is very painful. You should have thought up some tale, if you didn't dare speak the truth, and not let them bring you to this pass. Pity everyone, but look after yourself. You've only got one head."

In whatever way Anto tested himself, laid traps for himself, whether through Bogdan or not, he learned, was forced to learn quickly, that everything turned out to be real, comprehensible, just as he had foreseen. But on whatever came into his mind or whatever happened would fall the shadow of alienation and the fearful suspicion that he was going mad. To think had become more painful than to live, broken, lacerated, torn.

In the cool of early evening and in the mild twilight, to some extent calm and reassured, he asked: "Bogdan, do you notice anything about me? Have I changed much?"

"Of course I noticed, by all the angels!"

There you are! Why did you not save me, O Lord, when I prayed to you so wholeheartedly? You preserve the reason of murderers and perjurers, of renegades and of the sacrilegious. "What did you notice, Bogdan?"

"Well, you are weaker—all skin and bone. If you go on in this way, the worms will curse you."

"Nothing else?"

"Nothing. You have wounds and bruises; soles ready to burst, nails torn out, gums full of wounds. You can see and feel for yourself. Had you had a little more sense in your head, you would have saved yourself from having to learn from an idiot like me."

Anto smiled, amused by Bogdan and his own foolishness. Then he burst out in anger at himself, that he had begun to like this thief and Turkish stooge. *But he, too, is a slave, as I am! And such a blessed, sunny nature.*

He exhorted him in the twilight. "Here, Bogdan, eat my slop. Don't worry. I can't eat it, with my broken teeth."

"I would have refused anything but that, even if I were to die like a beast. I have already had a look in your bag, a bag from a fine household and from a soul dear to you. I took nothing and would not; I do not steal from a fellow sufferer. I took only a look, just to refresh my eyes and nose. I say: Nothing that a man eats is bad; only what beasts eat is bad. Never, Knez Anto, have I been able to make up my mind, and no one has ever been able to tell me: which is the sweeter, a *pita* or a young girl?"

"Well," Anto started to reply, but undecided whether to say one or the other, he smiled, then found his answer and finally passed sentence: "That for which at that moment you feel the greater need."

"So I, too, say. And the best of all is *pita* with a young girl."

Anto supped from soup that Bogdan brought from the guards' cookhouse in a copper dish. Amused and served and reassured by Bogdan, he awaited the evening more confidently than he would have had he been alone. But only under torture did he finally confirm the significance and depth of the change that had taken place in him.

He walked on red-hot nails, and his lacerated entrails dragged after him, when Kolj and Meho pulled him along between them. He had expected that Bogdan, out of cunning and in order to curry favor with the guards, would see him off with "Be sensible!" or something of that nature. But it did not happen. Hašanin kept quiet, apparently occupied with the arrangement of the sleeping planks.

Suljaga looked him over attentively—*the swine knows that the pulling of teeth and uprooting of fingernails changes a human being*—but neither in his behavior nor in his words was there anything to indicate that he thought he was in the presence of a madman. Anyhow, Anto knew well that Suljaga would gain nothing from a madman and would not agree to work on one.

While they were making preparations to torture him, Anto went further in his conviction: Suljaga was not able to discern his madness—if indeed he was mad—and to profit by it. That was a great, a joyous revelation. If I am mad, then Suljaga will gain nothing by it.

Though on the other evenings he had become calmer as soon as the torture began, as if it were not a question of his own body, that evening he was flooded with a secret joy at his serene, almost complete bodilessness, the alienation of his thought from his body and everything connected with it. His body, his behavior, and all the things around him that he noticed and accepted seemed unreal and foreign to him, as if they were happening in some other world, from which his thoughts, mind, and feelings were entirely cut off; as if the unreal was the world and the only realities his reflections and feelings.

Now he knew in advance that no sort of skill or torture Suljaga could imagine would be able to break him. While his whole body, racked with fevers, convulsions, and shudderings, resisted pain and wounds, that other Anto not only remained inviolate, untouched, but even grew more resolute.

Neither then nor later was he able to explain what had happened to him or how it had come about. As a God-fearing man brought up in the beliefs of the Serb people, amassed and refined for hundreds of years by human multitudes and in mysterious ways, he believed and repeated to himself and others: "God had mercy on me in my tortures and separated my body from my soul, did not cloud my reason, and did not let me go mad. He kept every evil from me, left evil to the body and good to the soul and the mind. Doubts and disbelief tormented me, and I even revolted against God and all that is dear and holy, but when it came to the moment of test, to the loss of honor and to shame, my soul became as calm as a spring morning."

That other Anto, that incorporeal one, was Anto, too, stronger and more outstanding than anyone, even he himself, had been aware of; he loved and hated, dreamed and suffered. He even became furious, especially, Anto recalled, if Suljaga or any of the policemen humiliated him.

Though he concealed his new power from Suljaga, he could not refrain from shouting as they restored his elbow to its socket: "May you be accursed forever, Suljaga, as you indeed are. You have trampled underfoot all the laws of God and man!" And, at the end of his torture: "It is useless, Suljaga. Even your poisoned brain cannot imagine as much evil as I have honor in my healthy one."

Suljaga retorted: "You are wrong, Radak! There is no end to human reason. Could it be from God, and divine, if it had an end?"

Suljaga was obviously dissatisfied with the torture that evening. The extension, which Smajo and Džem carried out unskillfully with their hands, clearly could not replace the onetime rack.

"We have still to see, Radak, what is useless and for whom, what I am able to invent and you to endure. But there is one thing you must know: if you ever get out of here, you will not be as you were before."

And Anto, as they took him away, moaning to himself, concluded: "Suljaga knows, he knows what has happened to me!"

But Suljaga did not know everything; that, too, Anto concluded. He did not know, could not know, for he had not suffered such tortures, that a human being can conquer himself, his life and his death.

As the guards lowered Anto onto the planks, he was greeted by Vučeta's fetters, as dear as a friend from afar. With difficulty, he raised his untwisted leg and struck leg iron against leg iron, reawakening his pain, once, twice, thrice. And the haiduk replied three times.

"That's he; that's the haiduk Vučeta," Bogdan Hašanin, unseen and forgotten, announced from the darkness. "Poor devil, he was already sentenced before he was captured. All his madness has fallen upon his own head. But your nature is not a haiduk's; you are a householder, not mad, but reasonable and judicious. If you had less honor, you would have fared better—and with less misfortune."

Grumbling about heroes and honorable men, pointing out that evil would not exist if there were not heroes to fight against it, and how it was senseless to be honorable when it was never possible to be, Bogdan wet towel and kerchief and squeezed them into the tub. Then, carefully and tenderly, groping in the darkness, he wrapped Anto's dislocated joints and his head. "There will be swelling and fever from the dislocations. If only I were free, I could prepare poultices that would lessen the pain and quickly get you on your feet again. Wandering through this varied world a man learns every sort of filthiness, but a few good things, too."

The moisture revived Anto, and Bogdan's words comforted him. "Tell me something, Bogdan, something to distract me; you know how," Anto begged him.

So Bogdan told him how once in his random wanderings, in some village he had come across a silly but still-desirable widow and had come to an agreement to sleep with her for one or two nights, but he regretted the arrangement when her daughter-in-law began to flirt with him, so that he had had to pay a substitute to content the older woman while he himself enjoyed the younger one.

Anto did not listen to the tale and could not follow all Bogdan's sly embellishments. He fell into a deep sleep, in which his pain did not cease but did not waken him. Bogdan, sitting on a folded jacket, slept at his feet, hands crossed on the edge of the boards and head resting on them.

The next evening, they confronted Anto with his blood brother Bib Doda, the chieftain of the Albanian *fis,* or clan. Bib Doda looked as if he had come straight out of one of the Albanian heroic songs; he was straight, tall, and slender, and wore a new white kilted costume, black-piped and incomprehensibly clean, with a broad red belt, and a white skullcap on his thick black hair. It could be seen that no one had laid a finger on him. Anto concluded that the Turkish authorities were doing all they could to win over the Shquiptars, fearing their hostility on the eve of a possible Montenegrin attack and a revolt of the serfs. Robust and vigorous, Doda was aghast to see Anto crushed and twisted on the floor. It seemed to Anto, and he recalled his own meeting with the mutilated Vučeta, that Doda, though he at once recognized him, looked at him with horror and disbelief.

"Eh, brother, what have they done to you?" he cried out as he knelt beside Anto, tenderly taking Anto's hand in his. "Who allowed them to do this to you, Anto Radak?"

"Forget the keening, Doda," cut in Suljaga. "Tell him what he must do."

But Doda, as if he had not heard, went on with his lament and his tenderness.

They had sworn blood brotherhood quite recently, that spring, that their trust would be firmer and their love the more unselfish in their precautions against the Turkish authorities and in their defense against other clans. This was the moment of trial, of trust, of the love they had sworn, and Anto, realizing that Suljaga had deceived Doda, raised himself painfully and replied: "What could I do, Doda? I could not involve my brother and my friend, as you are to me."

Suljaga pulled Doda away and stood between him and Anto, but the Shquiptar leaped back to his place by Anto and, shaking his finger at him as if threatening, said: "You know better, Anto. They swore to me that they wished no harm either to you or your kin, and I thought that you would give them what they wanted, so that they would not torture you. But now I see to what a pass they have brought you—and what they ask of you."

"Get him out of my sight!" shouted Suljaga. "Take him away! He promised to persuade him, and he is even worse. They really are blood brothers—brigands, the pair of them."

But Bib Doda went on standing there, implacable, obviously aware that Suljaga did not dare use violence against him, furious at what he saw, and eager to say all that had boiled up within him. "They killed Tomica and my brother!" he shouted. "They took prisoner your daughter-in-law Stanija and her brother! They tried to deceive me! But all these evils are small things compared to your tortures. Forgive me, blood brother—what I wished for you God gave to me."

"Get out! Take him away, I tell you," Suljaga raged.

"Be quiet, scum!" Doda retorted. "You are a hero before a bound man, but if you met Anto Radak man to man in the mountains, your legs would take you away so quickly that you would not have time to dirty your bottom."

The guards pulled him away, but digging in his heels, he shouted from the door: "Good-by, Anto Radak!"

"Good-by, blood brother," Anto groaned, with pain, only sorry that he could not shout louder and more clearly.

That night, too, they tortured him. Quartering was on the program. This consisted in sawing the shinbone, sufficiently shallowly so that it would not be cut in two, but slowly, so that it would torture the more. This torture Suljaga and his assistants carried out easily and well, as if it were their only trade in life, and they did not give their victim a moment's respite or breathing space.

But Anto, despite the novelty and horror of the pain, was convinced that Suljaga was not able to invent anything new.

The next night he was even more sure of this. The torture was the boot, which they now performed by twisting a cord about his temples. Anto had inherited from his mother a tendency to headaches. While the torture lasted, he felt that his eyes were leaping out of his skull and were wandering around, goggling now at this, now at that. Some evil smile or enraged glance, some hand quivering in the candlelight, or some black rafter without beginning or end, his eyes remembered as a too strong light, as a vision from an immense and unknown world. So, too, strange, incoherent words were forced from him, leaping out from deaf and lacerated space like moths around a candle. But he knew, with a knowledge unconscious but sure, that he had not said what he should not have said, even though he cursed his mother that she had given him birth and moaned for her lap and her tenderness.

Then they left Anto in peace for two days. Scabs began to form quickly over his wounds, and bruises eased, though inside he was broken and he could not stand up. On the third day, about noon, they took him into the room opposite Suljaga's, a flower garden of rugs and cushions, rich scents and quiet softness. They took him there silently, carefully propped him up, and even placed a cushion behind his back. Anto looked around him and in the light, still too strong for his eyes, recognized the Kajmekam.

He had seen him before, when he had come to Plav in the spring to hold discussions with the village knezes. He was a real Turk, not from Asia, but from Macedonia, from Monastir, though the exigencies of the imperial service had brought him into the savagery and discomfort of Plav. He was of medium height, but broad, fat, and heavy, with a long shaved skull and already graying auburn mustaches arched over a thick-lipped mouth. His face was disfigured by deep Arab boil scars, and his yellowish eyes and inscrutable tense expression made one think somehow of the amber mouthpiece of his long silver-inlaid hookah. His body, as if suffering from some incurable disease, reminded one of the heavy, sour stink of death. Fatigue and boredom lay on his bluish, dewlapped cheeks. He looked fixedly at his interlocutor before he began to speak, as if making ready to fall angrily upon him with his tired, flabby body or to caress him lasciviously with his plump reddish fingers with long yellow nails.

It was said that few were able to withstand that look, partly because of his reputation and partly because of exhaustion. Anto Radak did not endure it either, but withdrew into his pain-filled loneliness and serene invulnerability.

The Kajmekam also made Anto feel embarrassed, because he was known to be a sodomite. For that reason he must have been repugnant to Suljaga, too, who lived a regular family life. In that district Moslems were as disgusted by sodomy as were Christians.

Whenever he set out on a journey, the Kajmekam took two horses with him, one white and the other black, which took turns carrying his heavy rigid body. He always had in his suite his favorite, Milenko, to whom someone in mockery had given a girl's name—Milka—which remained secretly in use among the people. It had been explained that it was impossible for the Kajmekam to bring his harem with him into this haiduk-ridden rebellious land, without roads or comforts. Since it was felt that so high an official and so great a gentleman had a right never to lack for anything and that nothing should ever disturb him in his important tasks, he could, without arousing great aversion, bring Milenko-Milka with him to look after his food and lodging. The disgust and contempt fell upon Milenko, a fattish young man, red and white, like a sucking pig, with softly budding lips under downy black mustaches.

No one knew exactly where Milenko-Milka had come from, and he always avoided saying. But there was no doubt that he was Orthodox and that he paid no attention to the Kajmekam, but went to church and to confession and kept the fasts. In the minds of the people, Milka was inseparable from the Kajmekam, and even better known as the Kajmekam's darling. And though Milka must have been conscious of the tormenting and prurient curiosity that followed his every step and enveloped him like a veil, he never showed this in any way, but was always courteous and smiled graciously. Contempt for him, mingled with resistance to the Kajmekam, assumed provocative and derisive forms: young townswomen and even girls approached him with feigned seductiveness and sent him billets-doux, knowing that he would ignore them. Small tradesmen, ruined begs, crafty monks, and all kinds of hangers-on, knowing that through Milka's good graces they could insinuate themselves into the favor of the Kajmekam, swarmed around him with petitions and gifts, justifying themselves derisively: poor fellow, he must make his living somehow.

Milenko-Milka, with a silk cummerbund about his waist, hands and arms laden with rings and bracelets, now withdrew into a corner, in the half-light by the door, following with devoted, lascivious, shining eyes under long lashes every move and gesture of the Kajmekam, in order to anticipate his wishes. Then, while the Kajmekam probed Anto with his bloodshot eyes, Milenko, almost unnoticed, approached in soft yellow slippers to fill and light the Kajmekam's pipe, and then brought coffee and placed it with the *fildžan,* the cup, on the little circular table before him. He silently filled the *fildžan* and again retreated into his corner, in humble vigil; and later, when the *fildžan* was empty, Milka would see, take it away, and fill it again. The Kajmekam, accustomed to such obsequiousness, did not even notice.

Strange, too, was the relationship between Suljaga and the Kajmekam. Anto had expected Suljaga to bow deeply before the Kajmekam, and indeed he did exaggerate his cordiality and humility. But all that was external, insincere; in everything that came within his sphere of duties, even in his duties as a torturer, he was not only inflexible but also commanding. By his attitude he showed that kajmekams and viziers, even sultans, came and went, while the Suljagas remained, indispensable for their torturing work in this insubordinate land, and that everywhere human moods must be subordinated to the true faith and its rule. Suljaga looked calmly at the Kajmekam's dreaded eyes, as if he were looking at the bowl of his pipe or the square green transparent stone in the ring on his right index finger. Furthermore, the Kajmekam felt a certain aversion to Suljaga, perhaps thinking that he might one day fall into his hands, and before saying anything he looked at Suljaga questioningly and attentively.

"Very well, Radak," the Kajmekam began, "as you see, the *ćatib* complains that you are rebellious and do not believe in the Sultan's authority."

Suljaga hastened to complete his meaning. "As for being rebellious, let him do what he will. We have a medicine for that. But, honored effendi, he does not believe our word when we say that his clan has nothing to fear from us."

"Well, Radak?"

Anto was silent for a moment, then moaned out: "I know nothing."

"What do you mean, my poor fellow? What is it that you don't know?" asked the Kajmekam with sly mockery.

Suljaga again broke in. "He intrigues and is evasive. The serfs have all gone to the bad, effendi, ever since we made, so to speak, equal laws for them. He wants to say: I do not believe you. He does not dare to say so openly, but wraps it up. He pretends not to know what we are talking about or what we want from him."

"So, so. What have you to say, Radak?"

"I will explain it to him, effendi. Here is the Kajmekam, a high official, who will promise you and give you his word that not a hair of any Radak head shall fall if you say what you should say and make your mark on what is required of you, that is if you help us pacify this discontent. Have you heard? And have you understood?"

"I have," Anto replied after long and obvious consideration.

"Well?" Suljaga urged.

"Nothing."

With intentional helplessness Suljaga spread out his hands.

The Kajmekam snapped out something curt in Turkish, some oath, and then went on mildly: "No one will touch you any more if you do what I tell you. We already know all that we need to know, but you, you must confirm it."

"Do you understand what the effendi is saying? You surely don't expect us to bring the Vali here; the Kajmekam-effendi would not be talking with you here had not his journey brought him to these parts, and he has a merciful heart. You must speak, you, you, you!"

Anto remained silent, as if he had not understood or had not heard. But in his invulnerability he had both heard and understood. "I no longer ask myself," he replied finally.

"And who then asks? Is not everyone his own keeper?" the Kajmekam retorted sharply.

Suljaga interpreted. "He, honored effendi, wishes to say that he cannot make any decision without his clan. But that is a lie! No one is meddling with his clan or village order; nor does he care a straw about it. All the evil is in him. Not only is he stubborn and disobedient, but there is some sort of devil in him which will not let him be open and frank."

Racked and twisted, Anto listened to the soft intransigent words of Suljaga and saw, behind the bare, shining skull of the Kajmekam, the stony hillsides cut off from the sky and the mountains by the frame of the window. He could not recognize for certain the rocks beyond the Kajmekam's head, though he remembered them as something he had looked at and rejoiced in all his life. He felt no wish to reply. Words hurt him. They were torn out of him and were incomprehensibly superfluous and could not be spoken; they tore from him something even more painful and precious than human flesh. So, in order not to be further tormented by those forgotten heights so dear to him, by long sessions and explanations, he groaned: "Suljaga knows."

"What does Suljaga know?" whipped back the Kajmekam, probing him with those glittering eyes. "Speak, speak for your own good and that of your clan."

But Anto remained silent, and Suljaga impatiently began to tap his feet behind the Kajmekam. "Why don't you talk, man without conscience?" he began, at last growing angry. Anto remained silent. Suljaga's anger changed quickly into equally convincing astonishment and amiability. "Can't you see, poor devil, who is talking to you? Ah, honored effendi, everything is clear to him, but he will not give way to harsh treatment, so how much less to good. It is kismet; from the *raja* evil cannot be uprooted by evil."

The Kajmekam frowned and drank his coffee, was concealed for a moment behind a cloud of smoke, and then reappeared with a clear countenance. "Come along, my dear fellow, tell Suljaga what you must and then go home at your ease; they are waiting for you at home. I give you my word. I will even give you my word before the Serb merchants! What about it?"

Suljaga agreed, turning as much to the Kajmekam as to Anto. "Have you heard? What else do you want? Who are you? Nothing and no one, so to speak."

The Kajmekam muttered: "It would be nice to have someone of your kin in service with me; I have heard that you are a handsome and hard-working clan." There was something almost entreating in his words, and his eyes seemed melancholy, rather than implacable, tired of the whole affair.

In the corrupt mind of the Kajmekam there could not have been a lust for Anto, now old and broken, akin to that he had for Milenko; but Anto was seized with the suspicion that the Kajmekam was suggesting something of the sort with one of the Radak youths. Milka's attitude confirmed his suspicion—his disturbed overturning of the *fildžan* and the restrained, yet bitter, jealousy in his eyes. Anto thought of rejecting the suggestion with scorn and disgust, but held himself back; he could not utter a word about it without humiliating the manly Radak line. Therefore, he considered his reply carefully. "The Radak men are unsuited to be either servants or masters." But he did not say even that, only: "I have said all I have to say."

All three fell silent. The only one to move was Milka, to pour out the Kajmekam's coffee.

"Cursed land and evil people," sighed the Kajmekam, and, since Suljaga made no comment, he went on, with outspread arms: "Well, since he won't speak . . ."

Suljaga finished his sentence for him: "We must do what we can."

Anto was convinced that he would be left that night in peace; the Kajmekam, the higher authority, would spare him for at least a short time after their meeting, and perhaps would even realize the senselessness of their demands and their continuance. Bogdan supported him; though more from a desire not to disillusion him than from conviction. "As you go higher," he said wisely, "you find that authority is both softer and harder. Softer because it is easier to come to an agreement with it, and harder because it is more difficult to make it desist from what it has already decided. The authorities never admit that they are in the wrong, and even when they do admit it, then the fault is not theirs. The Kajmekam did not summon you for nothing; he will make some concession. If only I had got as far as the Mudir! The policemen chased me away without asking me, even before I had set foot on the prison threshold. But that's the way of it; I am guilty because I stole a miserable lamb or a piece of cloth, whereas you showed your teeth and stood up against authority! You are of greater interest to the authorities, but—and that is how it must be—they are more severe toward you."

But Anto was mistaken, as always when he weighed Suljaga. That evening they took him and began a torture that, from the beginning, horrified even the Anto who already feared nothing and was horrified at nothing. They tied his hands behind him and stretched them upward by a rope passed over a beam. They did not quite raise him from the ground, and Smajo inserted a forked plowshare in his leg irons, so that his legs remained wide apart and just touching the floor. Then they rolled down his trousers and pants. They did all this without shame and at first as if preparing for something great and mysterious. Suljaga dissociated himself from this solemn portentousness by cracking coarse jokes, to which Meho responded with silly chuckles, Smajo and Džem with atonished grins, and Kolj with dumbness.

This time Smajo did not instruct his son, but Suljaga directed both of them. "Castration!" he shouted. But he did not explain what it had formerly been called, or how it was done, so that Anto was convinced that it was Suljaga's invention, if not the Kajmekam's.

Smajo attached a noose to Anto's scrotum and on its free end hung a metal plate from a weighing machine. Then Suljaga began to place weights on it, one after the other, at long, irregular intervals.

Anto was not able to see how big each weight was, nor was he able to assess their weight by the pain, for it quickly reached such an intensity that the addition of even an insignificant weight increased the pain tenfold and changed it at once into something new and unknown. This time they did not put a rag in his mouth, but left him to cry out, watching him attentively and whispering among themselves, discussing the proceeding.

"Why this?" Anto recalled shouting out. "Why this? I am old. I do not think of having any more children."

"Old or young," explained Suljaga, "it is a sorrow to everyone that his seed, so to speak, is destroyed in him. Even an old man does not want to be wholly impotent! Even a monk! A monk betrayed his brother to me when I tried this on him. Even men condemned to death, on the eve of death, betrayed their band to escape being castrated. I am in no hurry; you have time to think it over before we break the tendons."

The weights dragged Anto's entrails into an unseen gulf, and his mind was horrified by this undeserved and final ruin. Even the invulnerability of that second, disembodied, Anto could not resist this pain. It extended limitlessly, beyond death, beyond the destruction of the body. There was not only despair that his manliness was being destroyed within him, his virility, but also something fateful, incomprehensible, and superhuman. "Life was being dragged from me, torn from me, and they let me go on breathing," he said later.

He did not know how long it lasted. Bogdan told him that he had endured it for a good two hours. Time and even place were totally wiped out. He asked himself: "Where did this torture happen? Who thought of it? Who? Did it happen to me? Was that me?"

He yelled, whimpered, wept, cursed shamelessly and obscenely, forgetting the Radaks, his faith, and his Serbdom, his children, his duties, and his oath. He was a small, wretched piece of living weave shot through with pain and human desolation.

"I will. I will agree to everything!" he shrieked at one moment.

But his words, once spoken, once forced from him, awakened him. The moment they lightened the weights so that he could understand Suljaga's question and his own reply, there arose from his unplumbed gulf of pain that invulnerable Anto, maddened and lacerated, but conscious of his insubordinate rebellion. "No, no! I have said everything. I have nothing to say."

It was not clear to Anto if he actually saw Sujlaga, for he was in the shadow, or whether his consciousness was darkened by his pain, or both; but Suljaga stretched his soft white hands into the light, and Anto recognized them with horror. Those were the hands of that apparition in black peasant cloth which had threatened to strangle him in his dream.

"You said: 'I will admit everything,' " Suljaga's voice began seductively, as his white hands withdrew into the darkness. "It is only difficult the first time, till you have uttered the first few words, and later—later it is easy and pleasant. I, too, am a man like you; I do not want to destroy you. I want to help you to survive and to go on living. Are human torments a pleasure to me? Can it be dear to me to destroy the gifts of God?"

The hands once more emerged from the darkness, as soft as if boneless, ready to caress, to wipe away tears. But Anto shrieked: "Satan! Get thee behind me!"

The invulnerable Anto again won, bodiless and even blissful in the tortures which that other Anto endured. The torture went on in another world and among men whom he did not know.

Anto later came to himself out of the dark narcosis of delirium and dream, awaking fully in the mild morning light under the soft outpourings of Bogdan's lamentations. "I have traveled so much of the world and have seen everything, but nothing like this have I ever seen or heard of. What will man not think of against man! To destroy the human seed, to exterminate the human race in man!"

Anto did not remember when they had taken him back to his cell, nor when they had ceased to torture him. Only Bogdan's words recalled to him the previous night and the torture to which they had subjected him. His groin and entrails pained him and, still more, his memory of the torture. But he knew that he had resisted, and he wanted to pray to God in thanks.

Bogdan said: "I understand everything, but this, no; neither on your part nor on theirs. They have killed God in you!"

Immediately afterward, as Anto later told the Radaks, asking them to forgive him, Anto began to curse his own clan madly, the martyrs Radule and Arsenius, his tongue and his God, even his own kin and the moment he was conceived in his mother's womb. That, too, did not last long. He cursed his fill and lamented his fill, and quickly began to calm down, plunging into sleep and oblivion and into a silent prayer for forgiveness.

That day and evening and the next day and the next evening they did not touch him. He was unable, however, to drive away thoughts of his sons and grandchildren and, despite his shame and awkwardness, of Milena.

His youngest son, Rade, whom he loved most of all, was not yet married. It was time; marriages should be early, to save the family from revolts and wars and every kind of affliction. He recalled the close affection between Rade and Vojin's sister, Raduša, which might cause trouble. The youth and the girl, kinsmen, loved one another as brother and sister and were at the same time more desirous of each other than betrothed or lovers. Especially at the wedding of Roksanda, Anto had noticed how Rade and Raduša had clung together in the kolo, as though they were not related and yet, like brother and sister, exchanged petty, innocent caresses.

Anto, too, had been in love with a cousin, long ago, when he had been a youth like Rade. That love had begun to consume him and imperceptibly to wean him from the thought of marriage. It had developed in brotherly warmth and in the sweetness of memory. It might well be that there was something of the sort between Rade and Raduša. That must be stopped, discreetly and painlessly. It kept the boy from marriage and the girl from a husband. The Radaks did not marry young. But the times foreboded evil, and a man must forestall them. Therefore Anto had thought, and it had been decided, that Rade must marry in the autumn, even though he was only just eighteen.

Without mentioning Rade or his intentions, he said to Bogdan, the first evening after the castration, that in the present times a man should marry early and a girl have a husband young, as in Montenegro, and asked him why he had never married.

Bogdan agreed with him and said: "If I have ever made a mistake in my gay and sweet life, it has been that I have scattered my seed so that now I have neither sight nor sound of it. But a man cannot have two good things at once—the joy of wandering and the joy of family."

The next night, the second after the castration, Anto dreamed a dream that was linked with the dream in which his grandfather's brother Radule, he who had died on the hooks, had handed to him his shattered pistol.

He was standing in front of his cottage in the mountain *katun*, and everything around him was filled with a shimmering, quivering inner warmth. "Bring me something to drink! I am dying of thirst," he cried out to Milena, who rushed out of the cottage, both hands caked with dough. "Get it yourself, for Heaven's sake. Can't you see that I have my hands full?" She grew angry. In vain he tried to take the bung out of the barrel. He cried out: "Who has driven this bung in so tight? Am I to die of thirst with water right beside me?" Milena again appeared at the door, new, young, and with clean hands, holding out to him a silver-inlaid pistol. "Shoot at the barrel and let the water out, drink. The barrel does not matter, only that you be not thirsty." She called out to him persuasively and at the same time smiled that sly, seductive little smile which, when they were young, he had never been able to resist. How could he resist her, so young and so beautiful, when he loved her so much? He could resign himself to damaging the barrel, but the pistol! He took it timidly from her young hands, uncaressed, yet eager for caresses, remembering that recently a similar pistol had shattered into pieces. The weapon was quite new, the steel dark blue without a trace of rust, and the silver without the slightest tarnish. Still undecided, he aimed the pistol at the barrel, and, for a wonder, it fired at once.

A shot and a smell sharper than gunpowder aroused him from his dream. Bogdan, in the darkness, was tapping his pipe on the edge of the boards, and calling softly: "Anto, Anto, wake up!" When he answered, Bogdan added: "You have had a bad dream; you were struggling, sobbing."

"Yes, I was dreaming. It was a heavy sleep but not a nightmare. Give me some water, for God's sake, brother." Having drunk his fill, he asked: "Can't you sleep, either?"

"No. I, too, could not sleep."

In the silence could be heard the gurgling of the stream, like long-forgotten joys. It flowed unceasingly, tirelessly, sometimes with noisy gaiety.

Anto remembered Vučeta, whom he had forgotten in those two days of darkness, terror, and pain. "Did that haiduk make any sign when they brought me back the night before last?"

"Yes, he signaled. But you didn't hear him."

"And last night?"

"Yes. Last night, too."

"Did you reply?"

"Yes. Both nights."

"And tonight he has not signaled?"

"No. He will not signal."

Anto propped himself up on his sound elbow. "They took him away? They killed him?"

"They took him away. Early in the morning. I don't know for sure if it was today or yesterday, but it seemed to me that midnight had not yet passed. He signaled on leaving. You were sleeping and did not hear. I did not like to waken you. Why should I? I replied with your fetters, as I knew you would have done, and he would not know that it was not you who clanked."

Anto stroked Bogdan's hand in gratitude and wept unconstrainedly.

The next evening, the third after the castration, they took him early to Suljaga. Suljaga, who was walking up and down, said with real or feigned conviction: "All you have endured till now is a joke compared with what awaits you."

Anto did not believe him. The torturers' tools had disappeared from the table, but there was a brazier there on which water was boiling in a tin pot.

Smajo explained to Džem. "Slow fire. It has always been called so and still is now, and it is still done as it has been from time immemorial."

Only then did Anto notice that three or four eggs were cooking in the pot. It was at once clear to him what was going to happen, and he wondered that they had not inflicted this torture on him before. It was widely known from past times; it was, so they said, used in the Sultan's palaces and was regarded as one of the most terrible, though it did not leave any visible traces.

After they had bound him in the right way, they placed in his armpits eggs just taken from the boiling water, and then they gently pressed his arms against his body. His whole body seemed consumed from within, as though on a low, but unquenchable, constant fire, with shudders and vibrations unable to separate warp from woof, picking out separately every muscle, every pulse beat. The flickering fire was transmitted in shocks, in waves and tremors of his heart hitherto unknown and now unbearable. In the meantime his mind remained quite lucid, and he could hear and see and reply to every question clearly and comprehensibly.

But it was not his consciousness that was unusual; it was the inner trembling waves of burning, to which he could not forecast an end and which, although not stronger, became ever more unbearable, killing every wish for resistance and permitting no escape into the haven of unconsciousness.

His only hope was that the night had an end and that his torturers would grow tired. From time to time the torture was interrupted to give him a drink and to wipe away the sweat, to discuss and to take a breather.

It was with joy that, almost at the beginning, he overheard Smajo, who was taking away the second egg, which had cooled, and listening to his heart, say to Suljaga: "He's almost had it, effendi."

"Do you think so?" asked Suljaga.

"Try his pulse."

Suljaga tried his pulse. "Space them out. And take care. He mustn't die."

"As you say, effendi."

But that joyful realization did not strengthen his will to resist. Neither then nor later was Anto able to explain how he endured that torture, boundless in duration and horror. He remembered that he sweated more and more copiously, that he trembled more and more violently, and that thoughts of submission and betrayal, though they rose to his lips, did not have the force to take form in comprehensible sounds, in words. Only the seductive, unquenchable desire for death gave him strength and revealed his identity with that other, bodiless, Anto.

When they took him away, Suljaga burst out in fury: "The beggars and *raja* will honor him as a saint! He, this brigand, will boast: 'I have won!' Over whom? Suljaga. Suljaga Hodžić. Perhaps you have conquered Suljaga. Suljaga is not God, only a man; he cannot do everything. But you have not won. You have shattered yourself, but you have not saved the Radaks. And I? Let the Serbs and Turks say: 'Suljaga cannot do everything. Not even the power of the Sultan can do everything; it leaves rebels alive. So what can Suljaga do?' Cursed land, false people! It is hard for those who defend you and who rule you, and hardest of all for him who corrects and instructs you!"

In his anger he wrapped Anto's long black, silvery-peppered

mustache around his finger and tugged it out, first the right side and then the left. "At least you will not take these away with you whole; at least you will not play the hero with these!"

Anto realized that this was the end of his torments and tortures. Suljaga had humiliated himself in hatred and revenge, as if Anto had insulted him. And, since mustaches were a mark of honor and manly pride, an insult to them was not forgiven without blood. But Anto was not humiliated or offended, was even ready to say to Suljaga: "May God forgive you that and all else!" but shouted instead: "Be accursed! I would not deign even to drink your blood, lest I infect my soul and dishonor my family."

Suljaga, as if he had not heard or did not want to hear, burst out again: "What, he a martyr! I, I am the martyr. No one will recognize or forgive me."

Smajo, embarrassed, came to the staircase where the guards were carrying Anto down feet foremost, and, stumbling along beside him, carefully wiping the sweat from his forehead with his hand and greasy fez, whispered: "As far as I am guilty of your tortures and so far as I have wished harm to you or to any other human being, so may God do unto me."

Between the Past
and Hope for the Future

I t all seemed to begin with the Cave.

Taking refuge there on the day his father was arrested, Grgur Radak felt that he had withdrawn from life as it had been till then and had not yet found his place in a new one.

At first sight this change seemed insignificant. The Cave was about a gunshot's distance from the house, and from it he could not only see all that took place in the village, but also hear the crying of the children, the clucking of poultry, and the cutting of wood. He saw the Radaks and almost always some member of his household, if no one else than his first-born, Trifun, who was with him, as much to keep Grgur amused as to satisfy Trifun's childish curiosity.

But from the beginning the Cave was a point of no return. Imperceptibly, ever since he began to live there, he measured time, his own and that of the Radak clan.

It was, in fact, not really a cave, but a sort of cleft in the rock where the forest grew sparsely. Coarse grass sprang up, partially covering it, so that it looked like the head of a sleeping, almost forgotten, djin beneath a coarse coverlet, in spring dense green and in autumn yellow and red. One could approach the Cave by clambering over the stone from one side only, the western. Because it was low and close to the ground, the branches of the hornbeams hid it from sight, and from a distance even the stone did not stand out in the forest. There were few among the Radaks who knew of it, except the shepherd boys who sheltered in it from the rain. It was seldom mentioned, and the term "the Cave" became generally used only after Grgur had taken refuge there. Ten men could sit in it, but only three could lie down at full length; even then, their legs would get soaked by the rain if there was a wind from the north.

Grgur had known of the Cave since his boyhood. Looking after the stock, he had taken shelter there from the rain and from the intense heat. But from that time until he took refuge in it, it had had no special significance in his life. Nonetheless, the Cave was oppressive now, as if at any moment something unexpected and invincible might emerge from it.

Like his forefathers, his father, Anto, and most of the other Radaks, Grgur believed in premonitions. But whereas Anto and some of the other older men believed that evil and the powers of darkness ruled over men's bodies and fought in man with divine qualities, with goodness and reason, Grgur regarded them as something external, which a man might resist and avoid by bravery and intelligence. His father and his forefathers believed that the powers of darkness, like God, were present at all times and in everything, and that they not only followed man's footsteps from birth to death, but also were a part of his everyday existence. Grgur believed differently. Though he did not contest their beliefs, he thought that the powers of darkness showed themselves only at certain times and places and by night, especially in moments of doubt and tension, human sinfulness and temptation to sin. He did not know where this difference in belief came from, but he attributed it to the influence of the few educated men from Montenegro, and, still more, to the rebellions and wars which nakedly revealed and corroded old traditions and ancient beliefs by sword and gun, exile, rape, and fire.

But in the Cave not even the day was pure and undisturbed by fears. Day was little better than night. Doubts and exile from home and work on the property, from life itself, became by day more unbearable when Grgur was alone in the Cave.

He had no choice; he had to keep out of the way. And the Cave was the most suitable place, being near his house and the village, yet out of sight. When Knez Anto did not return from Plav, it was clear to Grgur and the Radaks—and later confirmed by a message from their kinsman Mitar Drndar—that he had been put in prison and that there might be more arrests and even a surprise attack on the village. The sudden attack on the Shquiptar Bib Doda and, before that, the presence of scouts and informers around the village, as well as reports of the activities of the brigand Ibrica Buljukbaša in the villages, all pointed to such a possibility. It was hard for anyone, especially Grgur, to suspect that Anto could betray or in any way provoke the Turks to attack the Radaks. But the haiduk Vučeta had also been captured, and soon after that Nasto Radak had been put in prison. Certainly Nasto knew little or nothing, but just for that reason his imprisonment was a sign that the authorities would arrest every Radak they could lay their hands on.

Therefore the Radak householders, as had always been the custom when they were without a knez, had gathered at dusk on the day Anto was arrested to discuss what to do. They met near the Cave. Without much argument or opposition, they decided to strengthen the guards and that the men of the clan should take up arms and stay in the forest.

As always, if they were attacked, the Radaks were unanimous in defense. But when it came to appointing a deputy knez, they accepted Grgur with so much dissension and ill will that he himself suggested they elect someone else. No one denied his common sense, initiative, and uprightness, but he was, and it had been noticed, a supporter of rebellion and of co-operation with Montenegro, and he could be violent and hotheaded in quarrel when he had once made a decision. But Grgur's kinsman Vojin Milunov, his huge fair eyebrows pulled together in a frown, so they almost covered his hard, slightly bulging green eyes, conciliated the disunion with reasonableness. The Radaks, he said, should not transfer the position of knez from Anto's household as long as Anto was alive, but two other Radaks should be elected to advise Grgur. These were Vojin and the old man Milija. It was something new, a sort of Shquiptar council among the Radaks. But times were unusual, not as they had been before, and the Radaks were divided.

The triumvirate consulted in the Cave, though Milija, the oldest of the three, otherwise seldom left his house, and Vojin for the most part stayed in his ramshackle cottage beside the stream that divided his property from Anto's. They came to see Grgur in the

Cave early in the morning, and also consulted with him during the day, when necessary, on whatever was to be done.

The Radaks kept the secret of the Cave. They approached it by roundabout goat paths hidden in the forest, and among themselves kept silent about it. But because the life of the clan and its links with other clans, with the Montenegrin authorities, with messengers and guards, all centered on the Cave, it slowly, imperceptibly, became a part of everyday life and permeated their habits, unspoken thoughts, and secret desires. It was the source and origin of secrecy, of anxiety and of hope, becoming a part of every individual and even entering into their relations with the women and children.

The old man Milija, burbling through the sparse white mustaches that hung over his lips untended and forgotten, used to say: "Thus it is when times change! My grandfather told me that it was like this in Karageorge's time, and it was like this when Miljan Vukov rebelled and roused the Vasojevići."

But Grgur knew that it had not been quite like this; he could remember the revolt and the forays of Miljan Vukov, and from the tales told by Grandfather Grgur, who had been born at the time of Karageorge's insurrection in Serbia and had heard much and even remembered a little from that time, it seemed that many things had been different. Old men—though their wisdom was irreplaceable, because it transmitted eternal and unchanging truths—nonetheless were sometimes mistaken, saying that this or that had happened before, or had never happened before. One had to listen to old men, Grgur knew, but he did not have to trust them; nor did he dare take their advice if he wanted to free the Radaks from the begs and get them, as Serbs, to join neighboring Montenegro. The Radaks had never rebelled before, or even dreamed of liberating themselves from the begs and from Turkish rule; the opportunity had never been within their reach. So there was no one among the older men who could say how a revolt began or what the overthrow of established order and the destruction of centuries of rule would be like.

The differences among the Radaks were not so much that some were for the revolt and some against it; they were one and all in favor of freeing themselves from the begs and the Turkish authorities. But they had different opinions on how this should be done and on the choice of a suitable moment to begin. Even in their efforts to save their knez, Anto Radak, they were not unanimous, though not one of them would have refused to sell his stock, and many would have sold their property, to obtain his freedom. They held that they should go to Plav and bargain, and there were some willing to offer themselves as hostages and guarantee, with their lives, freedom for their knez and peace within the clan. But as soon as the question was raised of exactly how and what to do for him, differences arose.

The day after Anto's arrest, on the eve of St. Peter's Day, when the Radaks usually went up to the mountain pastures, the three chosen Radak leaders discussed from early morning what to do, and in the evening, angry and tired, dispersed without having come to an agreement about anything. The dissensions in the clan, smoldering and long suppressed, had now come to the fore among these three, with their differing moods and points of view.

Their arguments were renewed that night in Grgur's mind, condensed and divorced from reality, but, for just that reason, more tormenting. The whole space before the Cave was white in the moonlight, and everything in it that had form, mountains and valleys, rocks and forests and meadows, vanished in a bluish misty expanse. Trifun, breathing scarcely audibly, had for long been sleeping a sweet childlike sleep, while Grgur, racked with sleeplessness, sat by the child's legs at the entrance to the Cave and turned over in his mind the events of the day.

He was quite alone, even though the being dearest to him was asleep beside him, that being who could prolong his life and who was unaware of his torments. Just as now in prison, languishing and writhing in torment, his father, Knez Anto Radak, looked for salvation to him, his deputy in the household and the clan. And it had been he, Grgur, because of the revolt, because of Serbdom, because of the future happiness of the Radaks, who had argued against sending representatives and hostages to the Turks.

The Cave that day had been filled with tension; words and thoughts had clashed with its harsh, rough stone, and the Radak chiefs had had to take care not to wave their hands or stand up suddenly, in order not to bark their knuckles or hit their heads.

Vojin had mostly remained silent, patient as always, but inscrutable. With him, silence was usually an indication that he was mulling over what should be said and what should be done; his words did not pour out before thought, as with Grgur. But that day it had been different; that day his silence was obstinate, full of smothered bitterness and resistance. He did not try to hide his mockery and anger from Grgur. And that day he could not forgive Grgur his talkativeness, his groping amid torrents of words for ways and means toward what must be done.

In the early evening some sluices hitherto unknown to Grgur, and perhaps even to himself, were opened in Vojin, as if he feared that his words might dry up and his thoughts wither. He began with feigned complaints about himself. "My head is too hard and my understanding too shallow to grasp all that is going on among us and around us, but I have no peace as long as Anto is in prison —as if I could see with my living eyes Radule on the hooks and Arsenius beneath the sword."

That was what he said, but Grgur was sure that he meant: "How can you, Grgur, see your father being tortured? Is there anything harder than watching a man, especially a relative, being tortured?" *As if I were not my father's son! As if I, too, were not standing in the shadow of the hooks and the raised sword!*

It was well known that Anto took special heed of his cousin Milun's son Vojin, and that Vojin's attitude toward Anto was that of a son to a father who never scolded him but offered him wise counsel and warm affections. Vojin's stressing of this relationship and of his debt to Anto seemed like a reproach to Grgur that he was not the son that he should have been to such a father.

The old man Milija, with the coarse simplicity of a woodcutter and logger and his old man's slowness of speech, said openly: "If my sons so burned for me, it would have been better if I had scattered my seed in the wasteland."

Grgur's little son Trifun had been listening to the whole conversation, unnoticed and forgotten. *What will he think of me? Surely some seed of doubt about the inhumanity of his father toward his grandfather will have been planted in his innocent soul. He begged to stay here with me, and I yearned for his presence, not to be alone in this stony solitude. Now it is on my conscience that I do not wound his soul, even as it is on my conscience that I do not remain ungrateful to my father for the life he has given me.*

Milija went to extremes in counseling submission to the authorities and preservation of the clan. He kept repeating: "Kiss the rod you cannot bend!" He waved his staff as if it contained some hidden wisdom. "The sword does not cut off the submissive head, and freedom is of no use to the dead." While Vojin was not against sending a messenger to Montenegro to ask for help, the old man would not hear of it. "Montenegro and the Montenegrins! Rubbish! When they take Plav and when the authority is theirs, then shall we go to them and join them. Is it dishonor to bow one's head to force for the salvation of one's line? Black and miserable is your freedom if the Radaks are scattered and destroyed! Whose is the land if there are no men in it? Without the Radaks, not even the sun would warm it."

Milija was not renowned among the Radaks for either his common sense or his probity, but for his diligence; he had cleared half of the meadows and mountain pastures in the course of his overlong working life, and for that reason the expansion of the clan on the land was linked with his name. It may well have been that he had not cleared the land for the clan, but for himself, eager for fertile land, of which there was not enough, and driven as by furies by the many children who arrived hungry and avid for every gift of God. But from his work he personally had had little benefit; either the begs took land he had cleared, if it was worth anything, and sold it or handed it over to some other serf or, as was most frequently the case, the land cleared of rock or undergrowth turned out to be shallow and too sandy for the plow. Yet he was too used to all that to make much fuss about it. The important thing was that the land had been cleared and that the Radaks had had some benefit from it. The creation of fertile land by clearing and irrigation had become the one supreme aim of his life, and when they chose him as third man in the knezship, the Radaks knew that they could rely on him as on their own land. Even as the clan remembered martyrs and wise men and relied upon its memories of them, it found in him, the insatiable clearer, its foundation and guiding mark. It did not confound Milija's virtues with martyrdom or wisdom, but it valued them almost as much.

Now seventy years old, thickset and flintlike, all sinews, knots, and muscles, Milija, now stricken with rheumatism, moved clum-

sily and with difficulty, sadly going the rounds of his, the Radaks',
clearings and reproving the younger men because they did not
pull weeds or grub out rocks. Ossified in thought, taciturn, and
undemonstrative, he represented the existence, the changeless-
ness, of the clan, the confirmed wisdom and recollection of its old
men, and also the uncontested fact of its centuries-old existence
on this soil.

But what was it that had estranged Vojin and even made him
oppose the revolt?

In his irritation, Grgur nearly said to him: "But you have no
children; what have you to lose? Surely you're not afraid for your
wife, Jelica? You look on her as though she were an ikon, as if
God had never created any other woman on earth." But he did
not say it, for his own sake, since he knew that it was not true,
and also for Jelica's, for he loved and respected her and was
ashamed of harsh words by which, even unintentionally, she
might be hurt.

Similar harsh words and evil thoughts crowded in on him all
the time they were talking, and, with them, the longing to spit at
Vojin's calm, reserved face and watchful eyes. But, feeling that he
must hold back, Grgur instead reproached Vojin indirectly with
what could touch him to the quick. "The hour of Serbdom has
struck. Whoever is late for it might just as well have betrayed
Serbdom!"

Vojin merely replied, without rancor: "Who knows? When it
comes to that, then every sacrifice will be small, even though men
live and die only once. I know what human life and Serbian life
is: honor and faith and our own language, and not selfishness or
fear."

Grgur restrained himself less when talking to Milija, and
openly shouted at him: "We do not live only from one day to the
next; nor are we Radaks only, but Serbs, Serbs!" But even less
should he reproach Milija in this way, Milija, who had spent his
entire life for the future of the Radaks and who lived and
breathed his Serb heritage and his faith without consciously
thinking of them. For him, the fact that a man was a Radak
meant that he was also a Serb, and everything that was good for
the Radaks was also good for Serbdom. For him, the clan was
faultless, natural, like breathing, like thinking. It was not only a

way of life; it was also life itself. Milija could live anywhere where there were Radaks, despite the fact that every member of his family would remain a poverty-stricken laborer who wrested land from the forest and the rock and for that labor would have to pay taxes and tribute to the Sultan.

Vojin was able to live even under the Turks, grumbling, resisting, complaining, jostling, but, still, living. It was as if he could not believe that life could be quite different, though he knew that under Montenegro he would have his own faith and language, if nothing more. For him, Serbdom was equivalent to the mild nurturing and development of the life of the Serbs, and recourse to force of arms was only justified and conceivable when it was necessary to defend that life from enemy force.

To Grgur, however, it was anguish, unbearable, for him to live while the Moslems still ruled and the Serbs had to live mingled with them. Radaks who were not also rebellious Serbs had become something strange and laughable to him.

That day he had shouted out: "I cannot and will not be a serf. The world has changed for me since I decided on revolt, and I can no longer live in it as it is, but only in that world which is to come!"

All this was clear. And now, from the limitless expanse, from the loneliness of the Cave, alongside Trifun's life, which was just beginning, and Anto's, which was breaking in the kula, in Grgur were born doubts, questions, uncertainties.

It was as though all three differing viewpoints on Serbdom were irrelevant, perhaps even pretexts and excuses. Until the spring, these same men had not differed from him in their enthusiasm for Serbdom, in their hatred for the Turks, or in their loyalty to the clan. Despite the insults and the pinpricks, it had nonetheless been easy and convenient that day to believe that it was Serbdom, or, rather, the means of realizing it, that had divided them and set them against one another. Now, in the shining void of the moonlight and the rough stoniness of the Cave, Grgur was frightened, yet fascinated, by the incomprehensible reasons for the Radak dissensions. Their differences, their various aims, became inexplicable, as also why men lived, loved, hated, worked the land, and multiplied. It was as if men, by countless circumstances, by the power of desire or hope, by wealth or poverty, by bitterness at injustice or patience in enduring it, by the force of belief and enthusiasm, and perhaps also by their own natures, were destined to be in favor of this or that, to destroy or establish empires or to nurture the quiet course of their everyday lives. It was as if only in this ordered immensity of light was there an answer, when a wretched human being would no longer be mortal, enchained and immured.

But greater than the chill aerial wilderness and harder than the harshness of the Cave, his remorse over his father spread within him and strangled him. Even now he was disturbed that he had rejected the suggestion to offer hostages to the Turks. It seemed to him that he could claim justification: why place new heads beneath the Turkish swords when that gave no assurance for Anto? Was it not better to rely on Montenegro and threaten the Turks with revolt if anything happened to him? Yet it was as if some conscience, till then unknown, was aroused in him, and was saying: "What use are revolt and freedom if one attains them through sin, through the abandonment of one's father to criminal tortures? Are Serbdom and Serb freedom never to be attained except by trampling on one's word and grinding one's humanity to dust?"

There was, however, no stopping after one had tasted a hope greater and finer than the past mere existence. His father himself would not forgive him, much less understand, if he should fail the Radaks and compromise their freedom for the sake of anything, anyone's life.

When Vojin and Milija had gone away at sunset, resentful and more confirmed in their beliefs, Grgur had taken his little son and rushed up the hillside, carried away by the wish at least to see the kula, to greet his father and, in his own heart, to talk with him. Engulfed in darkness, the valleys had swallowed up the foothills and the mountain shoulders, right up to their summits, which peered vainly into the splendor of the skies. On the shore of the lake, only the kula windows shone with red, glittering reflection. Trifun dreamed up plans to get his grandfather out of prison, while Grgur's thoughts ran on. *I saw the kula, Father, that accursed white tower by the green lake, bloody from the sun, from your blood, from human blood. Do you hear me, Father? I have walled myself up in stone harder than the kula and have put myself to the torture, for your line and mine, for I know not what, Father. Forgive me! You are suffering for what you are—for the Radaks, for human honor.*

The dusk rapidly swallowed the kula; in the twilight, only the silver plate of the lake was visible. Then everything was gradually soaked in the impersonal brilliance of the moonlight and sank into its chill immensity. Grgur found himself with his son under the open sky. He took Trifun on his back and hurried to the Cave.

Now the dumb, shining immensity came nearer, silently and imperceptibly, and the top of the hornbeam was covered with greenish-golden steely leaves. Sleeplessness, in which everything became clear and hard, spread and tiptoed to him, uneasy, shining, and cold. This was not new to Grgur, or exhausting, though he was afraid of it. It always assailed him at times of great emotion and before important decisions.

When the moonlight crept to the mouth of the Cave, Trifun suddenly awoke, frightened and lost.

"Papa, where are you?"

"I'm here. I'm sitting at your feet. Thinking and smoking."

"Why are you thinking? I'm scared, Papa. Come to me."

So that Trifun would go to sleep again, Grgur lay down beside him and hugged the small warm body which snuggled up to him. He began to feel sleepy himself, forgetting his father, with the shining expanse still in his memory and the stoniness of the Cave under his head.

After those fruitless discussions and Grgur's first solitary nights in the Cave, the Radaks had squabbled for two days about what they were to do, until at last, at the end of their tether, late at night in the forest clearing above Vojin's house, they had agreed to offer a bribe for Anto's ransom. Immediately after that, without asking Milija and the opponents of revolt, Grgur had sent to Montenegro Stojan Radak, an unmarried man skilled in spying and an expert on the passes and defiles around the Lim and in the mountains. Stojan returned ten days later with unfavorable news; because of the clashes around Plav and Gusinje, the Montenegrins were on bad terms with the Vali of Skadar and with the Plav and Gusinje begs. Stambul was too far away to do anything in time.

Later, when there was discussion among the Radaks about Stojan's trip, those who were not in favor of revolt were angry that
such an important move had been taken behind their backs, and
those who supported the revolt were angry with whoever had told
the opposing side, an anger almost as great as if he had betrayed
them to the Turks.

On the sixth day after Anto's arrest, when Stojan was still in
Montenegro, there arrived from Plav, about noon, Mitar Radak,
known as Drndar (the Carder), whom Grgur had ordered to
come as soon as possible so that, through him, they could get in
touch with the Turkish authorities and bribe whomever was necessary.

The village was almost deserted, because of the summer migration to the mountain pastures and because many were in hiding.
Therefore every movement, every appearance of anything new,
was noticeable, and it was easy for Grgur, keeping watch from the
mouth of the Cave, to recognize Mitar, bent and twisted, with
hands almost reaching his knees, as he waddled with tiny steps up
the meadows.

Grgur darted out and reached the garden of his house soon
after Mitar, who had already told Grgur's mother, Milena: "They
nearly arrested me, too, but Murat-beg said that there would be
nobody to card the wool and gave his word for me, and so they
left me in peace. They picked up Nasto from the plowing at Plav,
but he had no one to stand pledge for him. Suljaga is seething,
even at a Radak shadow."

Later, alone with Grgur in the garden, he told him that cries
had been heard from the kula after nightfall. Perhaps they were
torturing Anto and Nasto.

Grgur avoided mentioning Anto, for Grandfather Grgur,
Anto's father, dragged himself from the house, coughing and sur-
reptitiously brushing away tears from his reddened drooping eyelids. Tall and, for a wonder, still upright, he bent, withered and
trembling, over Mitar, embracing him warmly, not so much because he had not seen him for a long time, but because at the
sight of a kinsman from Plav he was overcome with sorrow for his
arrested son. "They have put my Anto into prison and my Grgur
they have taken away from me and all the others are in the
mountains. I am left here among the women," he wailed to

Mitar, who helped him to his chair, "as if it were the funeral of the Radaks."

Making himself comfortable, Grandfather Grgur carefully put his knez's staff, smooth and shiny from long use and transfer from knez to knez, between his knees. The staff was longer and the crook narrower than usual; it was cut from a single piece of sycamore, not twisted from a sapling. An unknown master had carved it, though now its colors and the edges of the carving were almost completely worn away. Anto did not use it except in circumstances when it was necessary to stress his rank, because the Radaks took great care of this staff and honored it, as men treasure ikons and every sort of symbol even after they have lost faith in their mysterious superhuman power. No one had ever believed in the power of the staff, but it was still cherished; it hung between the windows of the big room opposite the door. It was not quite clear to Grgur why, ever since Anto had been arrested, his grandfather held it in his hands or kept it beside him whenever anyone appeared who did not belong to the household. Perhaps it was in order to show his grief for his arrested son, the Knez, and perhaps he was afraid the staff would go from their family. Grandfather Grgur was more than eighty years old, though he still heard and saw well, but he suffered from trembling and weakness; his egotistical and childish obstinacy made him hold firm to anything he considered valuable or which his memory counseled him was important.

He planted the staff before him and leaned his head on his hands crossed over its crook, his long sparse white mustaches quivering. "They say there is no wedding without meat," he lamented. "I know, I know, so it always will be. But this is my flesh, Radak flesh. For me the sun does not shine without Anto here. Why has God no mercy on me, that I must see such sorrow? And the Radaks, too, are divided. I live to see more evil."

"We shall all be together, Grandfather, when the fateful hour strikes," Grgur said to console him, and he turned to Mitar, who completed his phrase with conviction: "As we have always been."

But they could not console him, and he had not ended his laments when, from the bushes, as if waiting for a suitable moment, Grandfather Pavle, Grandfather Grgur's brother, emerged, clamoring through his two remaining teeth and his disheveled, not quite white mustaches hanging over drooping lips: "Lies fly; to scare children and ware women! We Radaks have never been united against the authorities. We have always been avid for pleasure and leisure. Why did no one die alongside Arsenius? Why did we not avenge Radule on the hooks? Why have we squabbled for a century about his grave? So, too, for Anto; we hold meetings, creep and crawl and dither, till he, too, will lose his head."

Grandfather Pavle was in one of those fits when exaltation and despair, foolishness and wisdom, mingled in his knotted head, which was covered with curly red hair. In the oppressive heat that had lasted all morning, Heaven and earth, thoughts and words, had boiled together in the head of this crazed old man, so that now he could no longer check his loquacity before a newcomer, Mitar, especially when, directly behind him, Vojin and Milija burst unexpectedly into the garden. Trifun had rushed to tell them of Mitar's coming. Excited by the presence of so many people, Pavle turned and leaped among them, barefoot and wearing unbuttoned linen trousers and a shirt dirtied with earth and grass. Almost as tall as Grandfather Grgur and Anto, for tall men were common among the Radaks, but rather bowed, he was sinewy, with big hands and a prominent breastbone, like a chicken's. He was fifteen years younger than Grandfather Grgur. Once, long ago, he had been married, but his wife had left him. In manner he was usually mild and unassertive, but irascible. In rare moments he was conscious of his weak-mindedness and unfitness for life and put the blame on his elder brother for his own physical and mental failings. Now, too, he began with indirect but transparent attacks, with mocking glances which were only a prelude to further outbursts and revelations.

"Good people, we have outgrown fairy tales! Yet when we have to fight the Turks, then no one has the guts. How nicely we have lied and deceived ourselves about Radule and Arsenius! The Radak lies—they took and gave and lied and lied again."

Mitar, a little embarrassed that his presence had set Pavle off, felt obliged, as a distant relative and rare guest, to try to influence him. Still panting after his climb up the hillside, he tried to calm Pavle down, reproaching him. "Forget it, Granddad, for God's sake! We have not met here to listen to your blatherings, but to do something about Anto."

"No, no." Pavle would not give way, intoxicated by the torrent of his own words. "I will not stop. My blatherings, indeed!"

"Blatherings!"

"Fantasies! Fantasies about phantoms, but they hit the mark. Do you know whose fault it is that Anto is shut up in the kula? He, my brother—but no brother of mine. A fine brother, a fine fellow. He let him go. He drove him and urged him to go. Go, so that the clan will not be divided and scattered. Lies, false lies, to scare children and ware women! Even if he is his son, he has been torn out of my heart. For me, without Anto, the sun is veiled in black!"

Grandfather Pavle rubbed his reddened eyelids as if he yearned for tears, as if something was dried up and split within him under the hot gray cauldron of the sky. His words, sorrowful and embittered, clouded and clear, flowed like the tears down his earthy face, while everyone listened patiently and with embarrassment, knowing that he would soon calm down. "He, my brother, has destroyed me, too! He even snatched from me what God had intended for me; he sucked away everything that was worth anything in my mother's womb and left me the dishwater. Therefore my head is sick and empty—a horrible head. What luck if it had not been on my shoulders! He pushed me out among the sheep and cows and for himself he took the knez's staff in his hands and now he keeps his hands on it though he is no longer able to hold a pair of drawers. So he got me married; for himself the prettiest girl in three districts and for me a sterile birch left on the shelf, who from me, enchanted, would take no enchanted seed. As for Anto—he let Anto go, so that now even my eyes have nothing more to look at."

He calmed down suddenly, withdrew from the circle, and curled up like a lost dog on the bare earth under the apple tree and dozed.

Grandfather Grgur said sorrowfully: "I had hoped that with the years, even if he did not find understanding, he would at least find peace."

The Radaks continued their discussion as if all their storms had blown out. They agreed to try to do something with a bribe. It was only a question of how Mitar was to set about it. But traces of the recent disputes and disagreements still broke out. Milija and Grgur exchanged barbed words and allusions to concealed clashes. The women, Milena and Stamena, saw this and kept Vojin and Milija to lunch almost by force, in order to reconcile them after a meal together.

The men did not show much reluctance at spending the day in the village. The surroundings were clear and open below them for a long distance, and the guards frequently patrolled the hills above the village. Therefore they sat as if at a banquet around the table in the shade of the garden, under the open sky and above the village, with the mountaintops, grassy and stony, in a semicircle around them. Something in that clear expanse of space, something in the food and drink, something in their common worries and misfortunes, released the tension and even reawakened hope and joy.

Not even Grandfather Pavle, awakened to join them for lunch, was as lost and angry as before. As first, after rubbing his eyes and neck, he blurted out: "I said, I went! Bad beef, forever steer! But even a steer can revolt; when it bellows, there it follows," and he fled down the garden. But Stamena flattered him with sweet words, then grasped him tenderly but firmly, her arm about his waist, and pulled him back. "Won't you join us? I have prepared lunch. Mitar and Vojin are both here; you like both of them, I know."

"Let the Radaks stew in their own juice without me! Right-tight will turn out sowing-owing."

But Stamena would not give way. The younger Radak women were fond of Grandfather Pavle, for he was always ready to help them in their work and did as he was told; and they secretly enjoyed his disrespectful impudence, his crazy street-urchin tales and piquant couplets. He alone said openly everything that was kept hidden among the Radaks and about which they kept silent, especially before the young people and women. And he was easygoing and generous toward youth, especially the younger girls.

"Ah, you, Stamena, Grgur's little darling, little dove; he caresses his darling and his dove coos to him. You, little Stamena, would make an old man lusty, and you persuade me, I who am old and crazy."

Her arm about his waist, Stamena, a little embarrassed before the others, glanced smilingly at Grgur, who looked down, also smiling. Grandfather Pavle, strolling about, had come upon them making love in the hayloft that summer.

After lunch, sipping chilled mead and scratching with crooked fingers at his bony cheeks, Mitar, as though speaking to himself, but aloud, started talking about what he intended to do and what could be done. It seemed quite natural, and no one interrupted him, for he had not lived among the Radaks since his early youth, but had moved from one job to another in the villages and small towns along the Lim. Yet he had never cut himself off from the Radaks, often coming back to the village and receiving the villagers as guests in his little house at Plav. He knew the Radak misfortunes well, and also the men and conditions in Plav.

There were many possibilities; the begs and chieftains were avid for money. Used to luxury and plenty, they had now grown poor and were without any regular income. But Mitar did not mention a single name, being accustomed, under oppression and in continual fear, never to say what was not necessary or to whom it should not be said. Every time it was necessary to pass something over in silence, his sparse, silvered-black mustaches bristled over his full lips, and he would stop for a moment and then conclude, "as I have already said."

"We will pay with everything except our lives," Grandfather Grgur kept on repeating, supporting Mitar in his plans.

"And with our lives," added Grandfather Pavle.

Milena, although it was repugnant to her, as a woman, to break into the men's conversation, especially since it concerned her husband, muttered as though to herself: "If only he be spared torture."

The other Radaks for the most part remained silent, which meant that they agreed with everything that Mitar might do, though he put forward several possibilities without committing himself definitely to any one of them. The Radaks knew him from earlier misfortunes; he was indefinite, vague, and cautious, but also reliable.

Mitar went on sitting until it began to get chilly. Then Milena accompanied him to the end of the garden, whispering her troubles to him and promising him gifts. On her way back, she turned her head away from her daughters-in-law and the men as she wiped the tears from her plump worn face with the edge of her kerchief.

Later, other Radaks came to greet Milena, to hear the news and to encourage their hopes. Then they and the guests, calmed and reconciled, went their ways as if a storm, threatening in the tense, stuffy heat, had avoided the Lim Valley and broken in some other district, somewhere among the mountains to the east. It seemed to them that something united had at least been done, and the sky had become clearer.

Over the Radak village, beneath the bare and the grassy mountain heights, evening came slowly from the lowlands, with a breeze from the mountains. Grgur, too, moved more serenely toward the Cave, whence Trifun, who had returned from keeping watch on the hills above, welcomed him with a whistle which dispersed the gloomy fears and harsh loneliness of the Cave.

Stamena, not worrying about her mother-in-law or Grandfather Grgur, followed him down the path by the dried-up stream with uneasy persistence, as if afraid of the dusk thickening in the valleys, enveloping the copses, and shadowing the bare peaks. Never till then had she done anything of the sort. In public she was more modest and reserved than the Radak women. In truth, the Radak women, too, could go where they liked with their husbands, if they had the excuse of household tasks or if they happened to take the same path. But it must have been clear to Stamena that that evening, before Milena and Grandfather, there was no possible excuse, much less need. The relatives were still stunned by Anto's misfortune, and Grgur, burdened with duties and troubles, was distrait as a husband and useless as a mate. Yet she followed him, walked behind him as if bewitched, as if the misfortunes of the evening and her own desire had wiped out every shame.

Nonetheless it was flattering and enticing, all the time he was walking silently in front of her, especially when she stopped him in a little clearing, shut in on all sides by thickets and the dusk, to let him know that she had so persistently followed him. She wanted him as her husband, as her mate.

Full-bodied and rather sluggish in her desires, almost calculating, she rarely turned to him for love, but awaited his summons and gave herself to him silently, seemingly as a duty or an obligation. Sometimes she even protested, at night that he had awakened her, and by day that she was too busy to give way to his insistence suddenly and on no pretext. He would threaten her: "Woman, either you must change or I will change you!" But he knew that her reluctance was apparent, calculating, and not because she was angry with him or with herself, and that for her the act of love was something exceptional, solemn, hallowed, to which she must give herself with an almost religious languor, enjoying it with all her soul.

They, as did all the others, had to steal, to snatch, their moments of love in the crowded house, with due regard to the demands of modesty and the burden of daily tasks. She had always, even at the beginning, been worried that someone would hear them or come upon them. She was astonished, not feignedly but genuinely, at his shameless words, his male allusions, and even at his right hand, which he liked to put in her crotch. But in moments of ecstasy she forgot about everything and took pleasure in the most open, the most shameless, positions and endearments, urging her husband on.

Just because of her reserve and modesty until the act of love itself, Grgur understood that her coming into the forest with him was a sign of some unusual emotion in her, some unease that drove her to seek him even though she must know that misfortune and dissension had deadened his desire.

From the spring, from the time when, with a group of Radaks, he had decided to bring arms from Montenegro and prepare for a revolt, Stamena and his property, the mountains, his house, and his way of life had become commonplace, too well known and familiar, too unchanging. He had begun to take notice of and to desire other women, even Radak women, feeling that they would give him the charm of novelty and a sense of his own rejuvenation. Despite the realization that Stamena was devoted to him till death and that, reluctant and calculating as she was, she was still the sweetest and dearest of all women whom he would ever meet, whom he could even imagine, he could no longer be reconciled to the tedious, commonplace nature of his life with her. He feared that he might become a stranger to her, conscious that for him that would be an irreparable disaster; and yet from time to time he was seized with a mad lust for her body and her reserved yet shameless caresses. But from the time of his father's arrest that, too, had changed; his passions were quenched, and, suddenly, he saw in her a comrade in arms, obliged to follow him, though till then she had appeared only as an obedient and faithful wife.

"What do you want?" he asked, pretending not to understand her when she came close to him and stood before him in the clearing, and he pushed away her hands, which she had placed on his shoulders.

Her face, a little flushed from the climb, paled; her prominent cheekbones and the strong corners of her jaw were close to him, and her eyes, in the blue clarity of the sky, burned with some flame different from the evening glow behind the distant mountains and clouds, so well known to him but at the same time new and irresistible. Filled with anger, her eyes at the same time begged, implored, demanded, and ordered. Her forehead, flooded with that same heavenly radiance, contracted, as when she was worried, into deep wrinkles between her brows. Her pale lips parted; the lower, rounded and smaller than the upper, pursed slowly, quivering. Her right eyetooth, too, seemed to be imploring him; pressed by her other teeth, it jutted out like a tiny tusk, now moist with saliva, with passionate entreaty. He noticed that the freckles on her face were darker, filled with blood.

"Why do you ask?" she whispered, hugging him with arms that he knew were beautiful, rounded, white, and smooth, though now they were concealed above the elbows in wide woolen sleeves trimmed with red embroidery. When she bent his head to hers, she gasped hotly: "Why do you torture me?"

Her kerchief had fallen to her shoulders, and her ashen hair smelled strongly in the dusk of rain water and oil and some pleasant, unknown, yet familiar herb. Born in the fertile lands of the Donja Nahija, she came from a family of lesser reputation but well-to-do, and was clean and neat even by Radak standards of

115

cleanliness, though she never wore any sort of ornament. The Radak women made soap out of fat and lye, but Stamena added something to it, hiding even from Grgur the source of the mysterious perfume of her hair. Of moderate height, she did not rise above his shoulders, and Grgur had to bend down to kiss her face and lips. But because he did not do so at the moment she expected, she reproached him. "Why are you so stiff toward me? I came down from the mountain today to be able to stay the night here because of you—and for you."

"Well, you know," he began awkwardly, "I am upset, now that my father is in prison."

"Ah, and me? We might as well be dead! I want to live again, with you!"

He put his hand on her crotch. She was not ashamed and did not resist. He felt her heavy, still-firm breasts, which his hands searched for even in sleep, pressing against his ribs, and a well-known but no less sweet desire slowly began to sweep over him. Without waiting for a sign from him, she drew him down to the ground, into the pleats of her wide skirt and the firm softness of her hips, whose opening and expected, but always different, intoxicating depth he could not, even had he wished to, resist.

"But Trifun is alone; perhaps he will be scared," he said, still resisting, waiting for his desire to carry him away.

"He's a big boy now, and it's not quite dark," she said firmly and confidently, adding immediately afterward, languidly: "Come, my love."

She was again that well-known Stamena, waiting for him, almost motionless, fervent and dedicated. But now there was also in her warmth and impatience, as if in truth life were escaping from her grasp.

As always, after their ecstasy, she said: "If you only knew how dear you are to me!" and then at once added: "Who knows if I shall ever enjoy you again. Can't you see how everything is being turned upside down?"

For him, lying beside her, it was as if he had again found himself and that life which had been slipping away little by little. But his resistance to love continued, and he slowly but not loudly called up to Trifun. The child replied at once, from about a hundred paces above them, from the forest, from the mouth of the Cave.

"Wait a little longer," Stamena whispered, putting her arm around his waist and her head under his arm. "The little one can wait. Nothing will happen to him."

"I must . . . I must talk to Mother a little," Grgur called to Trifun, gently drawing his wife to him, his arm around her waist, while the child above called back impatiently: "I'm afraid, Papa. Hurry, hurry!"

Grgur waited for Stamena to ask him, What is going to happen, what will happen to us? But she, snuggling to him, almost commanded, in that same stubborn voice, sure and intransigent, with which she argued about household duties: "Don't stray from the path on which you have already set your foot."

Till then she had never interfered in his affairs outside the household and had never shown such eager and impatient affection. Slowly she turned him over on the grass. Suddenly he saw above him the first stars and her joyous eyes and face, as radiant and young as when she was a girl. Pressing on him with her breasts, peering into his face, her left hand smoothing his mustaches, while her right, thrust into his shirt, caressed the hair on his chest, she whispered loyally, cunningly, and exaltedly: "Let Vojin and Grandfather Grgur and all the other Radaks say what they like; you do what you have set your mind to. I married you because I knew that you were not like the others. Let us be ourselves, even if we are destroyed. You are sweeter than ever to me; I cannot live without you. But you seemed to have lost something, and were distant toward me."

She was new and enigmatic, flaring up for the revolt and shamelessly desirous of him. He knew her as cunning, but not out of malignity or stubbornness. Stamena had waited two years before Grgur had overcome his father's opposition and asked for her hand, and it did not worry her a bit that he was a widower—his first wife had died in childbirth—and was ten years older than she was. Now she was approaching her thirties, and he his forties. She did not love anyone else in the household, not even Anto or the grandfathers, and though she never wavered in her attentions to them, her respect was mingled with a chill reserve. Certainly

117

her upbringing played a part in that. She had grown up in a household and in a district in which, for a long time past, clan roots and relationships had grown weak or been broken. Anto's communal household had smothered her resistance and self-confident personality. She suffered, aware that everything in life could not be as she wished, but she was also implacable in changing and undermining clan traditions and relationships. She could not stand Grgur's brother's wife, Stanija, because she was slipshod and careless and, still more, because she had introduced Montenegrin exaltation into the household and had involved other Radaks in household secrets. Grgur's sister, Roksanda, she considered secretive and spoiled and, in recent times, inclined to license. Toward Akan, too, she was cold. She was intimate only with Rade, but even with him no more than with a younger brother who needed help and guidance. Grgur himself was not successful in molding and curbing her nature and moods. Their love, the union of these two beings, was one continual friction, now coming together and now drifting apart, a mutual clashing and respect. It was inconceivable to Grgur that she would ever permit him to beat her or insult her, and he never did; whenever in his anger he began to approach the frontiers of action, she would withdraw silently and resentfully.

As the eldest daughter-in-law she had slowly and surely taken over from her mother-in-law the keys and the stores and the ordering of household tasks. Thrifty, even miserly, she spent liberally only when honor or celebration demanded. Grgur and his father knew that in Stamena the household had an impeccable guardian and a vigilant chatelaine. Grgur, more and more taken up with the affairs of the clan and of the revolt, knew, even without Stamena's assurance, which, indeed, she never gave, that as long as she stood behind him, that other, everyday, side of his existence, without which no man can exist or undertake anything of importance, was based on the most solid and the wisest foundations.

Now she had revealed another side of her nature, which, in their intimate relationship, he alone had suspected. In truth, her caresses were not quite new to him, or her use of affection to induce him to do this or that through the influence of love and passion; like other women, she did not distinguish the marriage bed from other needs and intentions. Lying beside her, in her arms, he recalled that whenever it was a question of something that seemed important to her for the two of them or for the family, she would make allusions and try to coax him in the intervals of their unions, when he was soft and weak from passionate satiety. But now, that evening, it was not a question of petty needs or of squabbles with anyone in the household for which she needed to win over her husband with love. Her caresses were different, feverish and imperious, filled with some ultimate mortal surrender. Once more she drew him into the whirlpool of passion, cloudy and boiling, which rose in his body and became radiant in hers. Although Trifun, impatient and afraid up there in the Cave, was never far from his mind, this new, enigmatic Stamena, transformed into passion and desire, held him, as if he were united, finally, with that impersonal, motionless, and shining immensity that rose from the hills, from the sky, and from himself.

She was right; he could create nothing without revolt, without liberation from the begs and the Turks. He would be only one of a countless host of Radaks, one of those unknown and featureless serfs of whom there were millions in the empire; they existed, worked the land, and disappeared without trace, leaving nothing behind them but a nameless mound. Certainly she envisaged change, and his role was to insure the extension and liberation of his patrimony, which was impossible under the begs, and the future of their children, cloudy and obscure under the Turks; she would like them to be free on their own land. The revolt had now become a part of her, as if its advent were a matter of course, something that would not make life either happier or much better, as he hoped, but that would be measured in new meadows and fresh plowlands. But in urging her husband to suffering and death, she, too, felt some implacable, enigmatic longing to extend the bounds of life and no longer to submit to everyday, monotonous ways of living.

Because of her attitude toward the revolt, as well as his own, he could now scarcely recognize that immature girl who, on the great feast of the Virgin at Djurdjevi Stubovi, had openly and attentively summed up his strength as he leaped and threw the rock, and then with timid shame inquired of his relatives who he was and what his standing was. Then, she had been a twenty-two-year-old girl who, having broken off a betrothal concluded against her will, was uneasily awaiting the moment when she would go to a house of her own.

Then, her cheeks had been ruddy, and she herself budding with ripe, untouched fruitfulness. As she laughed with vague coquetry when she went off with a girl friend across the trampled field into the tumultuous crowd, that prominent eyetooth had etched itself on Grgur's memory, a symbol of her seemingly straightforward and down-to-earth personality, though he could not explain to himself why at first sight he had been so sure. He was sure of something else, too, as a peasant is sure when he treads a fruitful meadow—namely, that she was the woman who must bear his children. That assurance was the more strange in that he had already been married; it was now the third year since he had been a widower, and the secrets of married and other love were no mystery to him. But this was the one woman, found unexpectedly and at last, who really appealed to him and in whom alone he wished to plant his seed. Everything was now changed between them, but he had never lost his feeling that she was the one woman to bear his children, identifying her most frequently in his memory with the seductive fullness of her hips and her breasts.

The week after their meeting at Djurdjevi Stubovi, he had gone to her village to meet one of his friends. Stamena gaily joined him in the kolo, and when he danced the oro with her the aspers and thalers clinked gaily on her proud and provocative breasts. As if they were old acquaintances, they teased one another and flirted discreetly. She even asked him: "Why don't you marry?" And when he replied "And why have you never married?" she interrupted him roguishly and curtly: "I was waiting for you." After that she did not approach him in the kolo, which he took to be both an incitement and an estrangement.

On St. Demetrius' Day he again found himself in her village, and after some pushing and jostling they were again beside one another in the kolo. Her clear, laughing glances aroused in him a sweet, hot confusion, in which her body seemed to float, and later, in the darkness of the garden, he tried to kiss her. For a wonder, she did not resist. But she said to him: "Don't make any mistake. I like you, but I am an honest girl."

After that he had no other chance to meet her until he had induced his father to ask for her hand.

Working out for himself, later and again that evening, how it came about that he married her, Grgur concluded that she had consciously led him on, retreating and advancing, but that had been just what he wanted. He even reproached her jestingly: "You offered yourself, put yourself forward." But she never, not even when they were alone or in a passionate embrace, acknowledged this. It emerged as: "Everything was as it should have been. Seduction, too, is a part of love life."

In any case, she never admitted her mistakes; that was one of the reasons for their daily altercations. It did not mean that she was not aware of them; everything in her was banked down, silent and inflexible, and Grgur was accustomed to this. For him, the admission of mistakes was an act of purification and remission, a condition of life, so that it would go on smoothly and joyously. For her, however, it was as if confession were a defeat; all that had been no longer had any meaning and could only spoil the hope in what now was.

Her ruddy cheeks had paled and her hips softened after her first delivery. But it was evident to him that he had not been mistaken in that incomprehensible and exalted feeling that it was just this woman who must bear his children and that he must beget his children with her alone. She carried well and was fruitful; she would conceive through her pants, Grandfather Pavle used to say. She suffered in labor, but she kept her children, though her eldest daughter had been taken away by whooping cough. She was a severe and irascible mother, making sure that her children would grow up honest and capable, and they, despite the hard words and the switch with which, when angered, she would beat them till the blood came, always respected her. She loved them with the unbounded love of an animal, and was always ready to die for them and to do battle with any monster that threatened them.

Her body, however, growing slower and heavier, did not wither, but ripened, overwhelming Grgur with tiny, confidential sensualities, and it spread like a meadow, like a living weave, beneath his hands.

They continued lying there in the clearing, under the sky, already filled with stars, calling from time to time to the anxious boy above them in the Cave. Stamena, tired and languorous after that too sudden burst of passion, whispered: "If only I could spend my life in your arms!"

Grgur knew that she spoke this way because she felt so at that moment, and that as soon as she moved away from him she would return to her everyday trials and troubles. Despite that, he was sure that evening for the first time she had given him everything, to the roots of her being. He wanted to prolong her desire to spend her life in his arms and the moment of losing himself in her. He felt that nothing existed any longer outside her, that all of him and everything was a part of his or her hot quivering body. Nonetheless, he slowly withdrew his arm and, burying his face in her soft breasts, murmured: "With you beside me, all will be well, my love."

She held his head close to her breast, like that of a sucking child, and, filled with joy and pride, whispered: "My head, the head of a fighter!"

Then they separated, and Grgur, for the first time since he had taken refuge in the Cave, felt as if he were not alone. He had a snack with his son, and, curling around him, slept soundly.

He was awakened by the chill light of dawn, which the thrushes and robins welcomed with glad cries and the blackcaps with their chittering. It was as if the morning, despite the interlude of sleep, linked him with the night before, with Stamena.

Last night, for the first time since the Cave had imposed its stony emptiness upon him, he had not thought about anything. This morning his thoughts had awakened clear and definite, penetrating beyond the world in which he lived, and the life he lived in it, in smooth, unbroken ranks, like a flock of migrants on its way to known but distant lands.

There was no going back, either in words or in the clouds. *I will say to myself: "You cannot go back, to be shamed before Stamena, before a woman. You are a man." I will say to others: "I cannot betray the Radaks and Serbdom. All that I do, I do on my own and because I must. To leave a trace behind me! Together with Stamena!"*

It was all clear and simple in that dawn, growing lighter in the soft mists and the shimmering drops of dew on the clear-cut leaves of the hornbeam. He lay down and again fell asleep. When he awoke, the Cave and Vojin were there beside him, and as the day went on, everything was just as it had been before, involved, tedious, cut off from the past, and without hope. He would always remember that dawn, the transparency and ease with which his thoughts flowed and the resolution that arose from them.

Vojin, reserved and attentive, intransigent in his probity and caution and devotion to the clan, had come without any special purpose, but as a duty, in case anything was needed. He played and joked with Trifun. He married him off to little girls from the next clan, at which the boy grew angry, but not overmuch, because he was curious to know what it was like when people got married and why they did.

"First of all, Papa and I must ask for her hand," Vojin explained, "and then comes the wedding and the marriage ceremony and lastly the most important of all: you must go and sleep with the bride."

"I don't want to sleep with her," the boy protested. "I sleep with Father; I keep his back warm."

Grgur recalled with sorrow Stamena and the dawn, while Vojin assured the boy. "You must; without that, there is no marriage."

"Why?"

"So. If you do not breathe into the bride's soul, then the child cannot be born."

There was no end to Trifun's questions and to the patient, discreet, and serious explanations of Vojin till the sun, rising slowly, cast shadows over the Cave. The heat again began to shimmer on the stony slopes, and through it floated Stamena in a white shift, spreading a red bedspread on the drying rack at the top of the garden, an agreed-on signal to Grgur and the others to come down. Milena had brought out the table, and in the garden they were keeping watch for newcomers.

"What does that mean? Who has come?" Vojin asked.

"By God, someone will pay for it if we have to go back in this heat," Grgur said, coming out of the Cave into the burning heat of the bare stone.

They went down, summoning old Milija, who was dozing under the hornbeam, then silently went on their way to the house, accompanied by the boy, for whom the Cave lost its fascination as soon as his father was no longer there.

Majstor Simo, Roksanda's father-in-law, was already seated at the table, opposite Grandfather Grgur, in the garden under the shady apple tree. But the garden, the kitchen, and the path between them seemed filled with women running to and fro, like a whole flock of flurried hens, and with the cackling of Simo's wife, Stojna. "I'll die of this heat," she cooed, cooling her reddened neck with a folded kerchief, as she ran to meet Grgur. "If I had only known how far it was in this heat. I wouldn't have stirred. But I'm not sorry I came, for Anto's sake. And you, Grgur's little curly-headed one, have you, too, run away into the forest?"

She did not even leave them in peace after they had sat down and begun their conversation with Simo, but ran in and out of the kitchen, where Milena was preparing drinks and snacks. Stamena had gone up to the mountain early. As Majstor Simo, small, yellow, dried-up, weaving his words carefully through his sparse graying mustaches, tried to explain the reasons for his coming, she interrupted: "I have already told them." And then to Grandfather Grgur and Simo, she said: "Don't waste a moment, since there is a chance! Simka Dimčova—you know her well—even though she's not worth anything in other matters, would not tell lies or steal. She rushed in last night and said: 'I can place the bribe through Smail-beg and so save Anto's life.' So we got up very early. We would have come last night, but you know what times are like now; even by day they eat men, so how much more by night!"

"Good wife," Simo said, putting his pipe aside, "you've said your say. Now let me explain to them."

"In God's name, I'm not stopping you, but you are frozen—and in this heat, too. You're a time-waster, and this is a question of Anto's life. I am going with Milena, on woman's business. You do as you think best, but you must save Anto."

But she did not stay long in the kitchen; she came back just in time to correct her husband, to guide and enliven the conversation.

The Radaks were accustomed to her and to her husband's patience with her, since he trembled more at making a mistake before her than before his own conscience, but now, despite the fact that it was a question of their own knez, they listened attentively to the two rivals, though more to her than to him.

Actually, none of the Radaks knew Simka Dimčova, the gun-smith's wife, whom Stojna had mentioned. Only Grgur and Vojin, who went more often to Plav, had heard tell of her as a loose woman and a light of love among the begs. But none of them were enthusiastic about having Stojna and her intervene, and still less that the bribe should pass through so many hands and become known before it reached its destination. It was hard for Grgur to think that his father, the Radak Knez, should owe his life to a Turkish whore. It seemed to him only too true that nothing good or beautiful could be done without evil and shame, and Vojin, suspecting what he was thinking, cut in, knocking out his pipe on the heel of his sandal: "Now everything else is of no importance. We must ransom him, even if each one of us must beg his bread."

The sun rose higher, sweeping away the shade, confusing the thoughts and reviving the dissensions among the Radaks. But, though no agreement had been reached, to none of them, not even to the child Trifun, did it occur to mention Mitar Drndar or anything about what he had undertaken to do, and, even more especially, anything about the Cave and the flight of the Radaks. Not that they suspected Stojna and her husband, for there was no serious reason to believe that they might be Turkish informers. The Radaks were accustomed to keep silent and conceal their intentions, even more unanimously before people not of their clan. Nonetheless, knowing that Mitar's connections were weaker and that there was a possibility that Stojna and Simo could find out how matters stood and how big a sum would be needed, they agreed to their trying.

As they went away, about noon, Vojin remarked to Grgur, who was accompanying him and Milija as far as the stream: "Something will come of this, as soon as we and the Turks come to the same opinion."

Grgur wanted to say to him: "There will; something will come of it, but hatred of the Turks will remain. Fire and water will not mix, nor will the mountains Kom and Prokletije meet, before we and they." But Vojin did not like big words, and after last night with Stamena they now seemed superfluous; the revolt had become Grgur's existence. "There will," he agreed. "Something will happen, as soon as good and evil agree."

But a week passed, and the Radaks got no news, either from Mitar or from Stojna, as if before anything could happen, Suljaga and the authorities had to vent their fury on Anto.

Then two messages arrived on the same day, one from Mitar Drndar, through his son, Mirko, an eighteen-year-old youth, and the other from Stojna, through her son, Kosta, Roksanda's husband. Both agreed; the Radaks had to find two hundred ducats and gifts for the intermediaries in the course of three weeks. But Mitar at the same time admonished them: "We could have got away with half that sum if other people had not mixed themselves up in this affair—Selim-beg and Simka Dimčova."

It was recalled that other clans had paid ransoms in the past, and bribery was unavoidable in daily dealings with the Turkish authorities. So great a bribe the Radaks regarded as legendary, even as everything else that had happened among them seemed to have come from the shadows of the past. The custom of ransom had been abolished by law, but this had not affected the realities under which they lived.

Anto's family group did not have much ready gold. The sum had to be collected by the sale of stock. No one was forced to give of his insufficiency, but it was thought that everyone should renounce something for the Knez of the clan. Anto's household, naturally, had to bear the brunt, but the other Radaks—perhaps just because they were in conflict—were far from miserly. Everyone gave, no one held back, whether for the past or for the future, and Grgur, moved by their sacrifice, forgot the terrible reality that had divided them and set them at odds, and even nourished the hope that the unbreakable Radak unity of tradition would be preserved, together with the Radak line itself.

The moment was exceptional, so he and Vojin made their way up the mountain to the Radak *katun* to collect and accompany the stock. Only that morning, when parting with the stock was immediate and inevitable, did Grgur realize the painful wonder of the Radak sacrifice.

With the first rays of the sun, all sorts of animals, suspecting departure from their familiar meadows and their herds, crowded around Anto's hut bellowing, mooing, and bleating, shaking the mountain to its foundations and splitting the cloudy sky, while the shepherds and herd girls silently brushed away their tears. Stamena, too, wept; her nose and lips became swollen. Hands on hips, looking at the frantic and uneasy herd, at the devastation of the Radak way of life and of her own, she did not notice her little daughter, Vasa, who was crawling on the manure-littered field among the trampling hoofs.

Grgur shouted at her from the door of the hut, as if from a great distance: "Watch the child, you stupid woman, the child!"

Stamena, blinded by tears and stupefied by grief, looked around her, but even then did not realize what was happening. She sobbed: "Better I had not been born, when all our livelihood is thus scattered."

Grgur rushed out, grabbed the little girl, who only then began to cry, and went toward Stamena. "Don't take it out on the children, wretch!"

The youngest brother, Radule, known as Rade, was leaning on the paling of the pound, wiping away the tears from his eyes and whispering something inaudible and inarticulate. Stamena took the little girl on her lap and began soothing her, pretending nothing had happened. Grgur went up to his brother, shook him, and shouted at him with bitter mockery: "Come on, my fine ram, why are you sorry for the other rams?"

"I don't regret the rams," the young man said gloomily, "but this will lay waste the mountain, the *katun,* and the huts, as well as us."

Rade, too, was tall, but too slender, unformed, with limbs still bony. His face was long and pale, soft and rounded like a girl's, framed in silky ringlets of chestnut hair. But despite this immature softness, there were signs of bitterness and too early maturity in the deep clefts above his mouth and around his thin-drawn red lips. He, too, had not noticed his favorite, his five-year-old nephew, Todor, who was tugging at his trouser leg and crying, for his uncle and his mother were weeping amid the complaints of the countless cows, calves, lambs, and sheep. This emotion suddenly overcame Grgur, too.

The stock must first be driven into the pounds, each to its own, and there numbered and selected, and he began to drive the calves into the pound set aside for the sheep. The middle brother,

Akan, thickset, red-faced, and also with curly, but fairer, hair and thin grayish mustaches, kept his left hand on the fence around the enclosure and went on numbering and separating the lambs as if nothing special were happening. He kept in mind the hot, sultry day on the bare heights and in the ravines through which he would have to drive the stock for sale, at a bad time for marketing. He did not complain, but went on slowly and unerringly checking the lambs, one after the other, which he would need for his journey. Engrossed in his work, he did not look at his six-year-old son, Anto, who was playing near him with a black-eared lamb.

The *katun* was divided by a stream, whose farther, eastern, side was still in chill dark shadow. Into the full glare of the sunlight and the uneasy milling of the stock, Vojin and his wife, Jelica, came, driving their stock, sheep and cattle together. They were the last to bring their contribution, about fifty sheep, with the bellwether, both their oxen, and about a dozen cows and horses. That was all they had, except for one cow.

"Take back an ox, the bellwether, and five or six sheep," Grgur shouted, angry at himself. "So at least you can build up again, and the seed from your herd is not destroyed."

"I take back nothing!" Vojin retorted unreasonably, and at once, contrary to his custom, began to explain at length. "While there is a cow, there will be a calf. I am only sorry that I have no more; I would give them, too. But if this does not suffice, I will give the little there is left. It is only human lives that cannot be replaced."

"And how will you satisfy the aga and pay the tribute?"

"It will breed! I will content him with wheat, fat, fruit. And if it does not breed, then I will work off my debt, will borrow, will sell my meadow and my plot."

Jelica did not weep. Her long pale face, with black, shining arched eyebrows and lashes so long that they shaded her cheeks, was tense, and her full, rather swollen, lips, blue with the morning cold, were open and dumb, in contrast to Stamena, who was bitter and angry. In moments of stress she gave the impression of icy, final resignation. As always, slightly swaying in her walk, her well-formed slim body as supple as a salmon's, her maidenly breasts firm, she went over to Stamena, threw her slender right

128

arm around her shoulder, and, catching hold of the little boy
Todor as she went, led her to the hut, quietly consoling her.
"Don't, don't take on so. Everything will be won back again!"

The Radaks had agreed to send Akan with the stock to Peć,
because he was a skilled trader and knew the prices and the merchants there. He was also to visit Dečani and make a gift to the
Holy King, to see if the monks could protect them or even restore
them to the monastery patrimony. Grgur was not wholly in favor
of this idea. "They are all the same," he said, "christened, or un-
christened begs!" But he gave way. Vojin's viewpoint won him
over, though he, too, had little hope of success. "There's no harm
in trying. You can at least argue with men of your own faith." So
Vojin had begun to load gifts for the monastery on the horses in
front of Anto's hut: wool, honey, and wax, packed in goatskins.

Akan soon finished checking the stock, and the herdsmen divided them, sheep and goats separately and cattle and horses separately, in the clearing above the huts. The shaggy sheepdogs
were already on guard and roved around, driving back disobedient and wayward animals. Everything was ready, even Akan's
white horse, saddled and tethered to a post; Akan had to ride a
white horse for the sake of dignity, and was not to sell it except as
a last recourse.

Akan shouted to the drovers to get going. But he himself did
not move off; he wanted to calculate everything once more, in
Grgur's and Vojin's presence.

Taking into account losses because of the thinness of the animals and because it was not the right season for marketing, he
had, the night before, reckoned up with his brother that it would
not suffice even if they got all the animals the other Radak householders had promised. But Vojin's contribution, which he had
discussed with Jelica overnight and increased several times,
nearly tipped the scale, and Akan concluded unemotionally: "So,
there you are. We're short twelve ducats."

"Take all the rest of the stock," Grgur said, and waved his
hand as if he were cutting short a life dear to him.

"We've already taken them. You know that yourself; we have
left only one cow for milking and five or six thin ones for stud. In
any case, they would not stand the journey."

"And the fat?"

"Everything is ready. And there's not so much—six tubs. And we have loaded all the wool."

They were silent, helpless and hopeless, as though in fetters.

"I will give ducats, ten ducats," announced Jelica from the hut, in a calm, soft, throaty voice. She looked out of the little door, too low even for a small woman, tugging at her waistband and unfastening her necklace. Only now Grgur noticed that she had brought it with her, as if for a rare occasion, and the ducats were glittering on her firm breasts. After removing the necklace, she slipped her embroided kerchief off, wrapped the ducats in it, and handed the bundle to Grgur. "Take it, *djever!*"

The young Radak women called all the younger Radak men *"djever,"* or brother-in-law, though the men did not call them "sister-in-law." It was an old custom, which the women kept out of respect, and the men let them do so out of consideration. A barren woman, already in her thirties, Jelica had been the most beautiful of the Radak brides, and Grgur was sorry to leave her without her ornaments, because her beauty was the pride of the clan and because he had always felt a special tenderness for her, now in one way and now in another, ever since she had first been brought to her husband's house.

"How can I take your beauty, my Radak pride?" retorted Grgur jestingly, but deeply moved.

"Take it," Vojin said curtly. "What is pride, what is money, when a man's life is at stake?"

"You are a man, a hero, and a comrade." Grgur turned to Vojin, suddenly moved by the beauty of this sacrifice and feeling fine words rising within him.

Just like Vojin, ready to give up his life, his honor, for his kin. And Jelica! I could draw blood from her throat, and she would not even say: "Oh!" To Stamena, too, she is dear; only of Jelica is she not jealous, though she knows that I like her and in some mad nights have desired her and wanted to go to her. And Vojin, too, knows. He suspects and laughs, as at a dream for which a man is not responsible. Jelica, too, knows, though I have never said anything to her. And I will not, I cannot, after all that has happened. She has renounced everything without a word! I could kiss them both. And I wailed for the herds, for myself, and for my father, for the desolate mountainside. Only yesterday I would not have expected this of Vojin. A man is always making mistakes about everything, especially about men and about himself.

With bent head, as always when she was embarrassed, and looking up at him with eyes washed by the sun and shadowed by her long lashes, Jelica begged him: "Take it, for my sake."

"No, no, I cannot. I will not. I would rather give myself in pledge."

But Akan, shuffling from one foot to the other, looking at the herds as if numbering them at a glance, said: "We shall need more money."

Vojin took the kerchief from Grgur's uncertain grasp and handed it to Akan, who unwrapped it, weighed the necklace in his left hand, then pulled out the thread and, muttering, began to throw the coins, ducat by ducat, clinking softly, from one hand to the other. As he threw the last ducat, he said in a dispassionate, unemotional tone: "Exactly ten. If we're short, we will borrow from some friends."

He handed the money back to Grgur, but Grgur pushed his hand away. "You keep them. The whole thing is now in your hands anyway."

Akan silently took out of a pocket sewn into the lining of his jacket a leather purse, put the money in it, and returned the kerchief to Jelica. Stamena, standing beside Jelica in the doorway, had been watching the whole scene and now, stepping over the threshold, picked the thread of the necklace from the ground and, rubbing her eyes with her fists, sobbed loudly and fled back into the hut.

Bewildered by unknown paths, confused by mixing with strange stock, the herd calmed down as soon as it left the *katun;* the horses and cattle went first, then the sheep and goats. Only the lambs and calves left for stud bleated and mooed despairingly, while their mothers answered their calls helplessly and vainly as they disappeared into the forest above the *katun.*

Akan said farewell to his brother and Vojin and jumped on his horse. Then, suddenly, he turned it, picked up his little son, Anto, and kissed him. He put him down again in embarrassment. "Look after him!" he shouted to Grgur, without referring to his wife, in prison, though Grgur knew that at that moment he was thinking of her.

Akan spurred his horse and, without another word, hastened after the herd. The women sobbed and wailed aloud, and the men fled into the huts in order not to hear them or see them and took refuge in the darkness. Stamena brought out a wooden trough and began angrily to smash it against the corner of the hut, and a toothless old woman from the *katun* cursed in a phrase from the still-living, yet traditional, past: "O Turks, Turks, may God send that no one know where your carrion may be! May God grant your mothers call you and call for you in vain!"

To Grgur, it seemed that the mountain, on which he had been brought up and in which he used to rejoice as in a fresh, new world, azure and immeasurable, had died; he sat at the threshold of his hut and wept, not trying to check Stamena's savage anger.

Tormented, yet calmed, he went, after lunch, with Jelica to the village. She was hurrying down there to harvest the overripe barley, but at the same time, like him, was running away from the inactivity and depression of the desolate and now hateful *katun*.

Now Vojin, too, had to work to make some money. A skillful wood carver, he remained in the *katun* to cut some yew, of which there was none near the village. Its sweet-smelling wood, it was believed, endowed vessels and staves with a healing force and protected their owners from sorcery. Stamena had to remain for two or three days to see to things before returning to the village. Vojin's sister, Raduša, stayed to look after Vojin and milk the Radak cow, for it had to stay on the mountain to help Vojin in his work and to carry the haycocks for the mowers.

Grgur wanted to go with Jelica. After the desolation and misfortune, he longed to be near her. Considerate and consoling, not generally talkative, she always had something wise and at the same time tender to say, which, if it did not drive away difficulties and despair, at least modified them and reconciled a man to them. Perhaps because of that and because of her beauty, of which he could never see enough, she now seemed like a prayer, like a cool spring. He was convinced that he had been purified and strengthened, by the Cave and the thought of revolt, by his father's misfortune, by his reawakened love for Stamena, and, that morning, by Vojin's loyalty and by Jelica's sacrifice. Walking with Jelica foreshadowed a clear tranquillity and a still-deeper and friendlier warmth. Even Stamena, venting her fury in violence and tears, suspected that and urged him: "Get out of this house of ruin; go and talk with Jelica."

The way to the village was downhill and took less than two hours. But, though supposedly in a hurry, they walked slowly, resting beside every spring, stopping at every clearing, to look down on the valley and plain below them, over the outstretched carpets of ripe wheat garlanded with the green dolmans of the maize, finding themselves at one in their feelings and in the beauty unveiled before them.

He had often been alone with Jelica; he and Vojin were as close as if they belonged to the same household. But till now he had never walked with her from the mountain, through the moist forest-covered solitudes, sultry with the air from the valley, and across the pastures and hayfields, rich in scents, sun, and wild flowers. Today, because his feelings for her were so conscious and lasting, and unconcealed from the others, he moved beside her calmly and almost joyously, without consciously recalling her much-praised beauty, her heavy black hair, over a smooth radiant forehead, her pale pure face, straight nose, with wide quivering nostrils, and eyes that shone mildly from beneath the shadow of her lashes with measured seriouness, perhaps stricter with herself than with others.

He had burned for her for years. As soon as he felt free from his longing for her and had assured himself that everything was over, desire would burst forth again unexpectedly with greater, more obscure force. In no way did she ever stimulate his desire. But she never quenched it. She was a woman; it pleased her to notice men's glances and to remember words other than commonplaces that had been said to her. Grgur had noticed that she looked on him differently from others, because of his quickness of mind and courage, because of his present and future reputation, and especially because of his boldness and vigorous and mature manliness. At night, when sleepless, he realized the intangible, instinctive ties that bound them, secure in the belief that she was thinking of him, perhaps at that minute, not only as an unattainable delight, but also as something that should not be attained, in order to preserve it in its pure, incorporeal yearning and beauty. But when with him she never went beyond cordial greeting and pleasant conversation. She trembled, more aware than he that if she took a step too far, it would wither the close intimacy among the four of them, Vojin and him, Stamena and her.

Tormenting himself to drive out her magical beauty, her fascination, and her intelligent subtlety, and because of his realization of sin against the clan and, still more, against Vojin, his relative and almost his brother, he brought her presents whenever he gave presents to Stamena and fostered a new intimacy with Vojin, perhaps not so much brotherly, as more serious, more fundamental. But this did not stifle his personal alienation from the clan, no less painful and sinful, even more primordial and vital than was his love for her. The growing strength of his longing for her was involved, even if it did not coincide, with the withering of the clan feeling within him. With horror and a sort of joy he began to realize that he was not merely a Radak, but that in himself were desires that were outside time and outside the clan, outside humanity itself. He did not know the reason for this estrangement, or whence it arose, whether the longing from the estrangement or the estrangement from the longing, or both of them from something unknown and incomprehensible.

He remembered, and would always remember, his first realization of her beauty. One fresh winter's morning, a year after Jelica had first been brought there, he had burst into Vojin's house, for what reason, he had forgotten. She was sitting by the hearth combing her long wavy hair and did not notice him at first. He stood in the doorway, bathed in the dark waves of her hair and dazzled by the whiteness of her neck, fascinated by the slenderness of her hand and the agility of her fingers. She noticed the darkening of the doorway and pushed back her hair with both hands. Her face, smiling and embarrassed, shone like silver on velvet, and because it was not proper for a woman to comb her hair before men, except those closest in kin to her, she whispered, "Excuse me" and, with a toss of her hair, ran toward the storeroom and paid no heed to his shout: "Don't worry. It doesn't matter. We are kin!" Waiting till she had arranged her hair, he withdrew to the front of the house. The Radak houses, all of wood, darkened by age and bad weather, clustered around Anto's, looking, in the whiteness of the snow, like a flock of ravens. Vojin's house was at the beginning of the ravine, to the south. Whether from the sun, the glare of the snow, or the mist that hovered in the ravine, or from the unexpected beauty of Jelica, the whole expanse seemed to Grgur to tremble, writhe, and disintegrate. He had to shake his head to hold the sky and the land firm in his vision. And suddenly, because Vojin's house was a little aside, it seemed no longer to belong to the village, and between him and Vojin, second cousins, there seemed no longer any relationship. He asked himself: "How do people live who pay no heed to tribes or clans? Would the Radaks hold together if they were not forced to do so by evil, by serfdom, by the Shquiptars, by other clans, even by the snows and the forest? Where does sin against the clan begin, and where does it end?" But she cut short his reverie, coming out of the storeroom, her face still embarrassed, fresh as a dew-washed rose. She called him in and put a stool in front of the fire. "It must be the sirocco," she said, waving at the smoke, which billowed low. "It must be," he agreed, thinking of the un-dimmed, though now transformed, charm of her beauty. Pulling himself together, he added: "But it won't thaw. The sun is too hot here on the heights and will draw the colder mists from below." And everything was once more as it had been before this meeting. She poured out plum brandy for him, yellow and shining, which scented the whole house, driving away her transparent, delicate perfume—an unknown perfume, which inevitably faded.

It was about then that dissensions arose among the Radaks. Their traditions and legends clashed with reality, with Grgur's experiences and beliefs. Even the Radak lands, waters, pastures, meadows, and forests, though familiar, began to reveal their inhospitable side; there was scarcity and harshness, great snows and isolation from the world and its comforts. Within Grgur, the Radak springs dried up, the woods were transformed into bare coverts, the hayfields into thorny wastes, while he swore to himself and before others that he would never renounce his kin, his Radak blood, for anyone or anything—as if he could go on living without the warmth of the clan and the homeland!

Those feelings had lasted long, for years, and it seemed as if, at the close of the Montenegrin-Turkish wars, everything would begin to settle down and return to accustomed, unchanged ways.

But it turned out otherwise; at the end of the wars, which offered hope of liberation, the differences and dissensions revived, and also the bitterness of his longing for Jelica.

That morning, in the *katun,* everything had again changed, had been exalted to unsuspected purity and spirituality. But his desire burst out more intensely and more bewilderingly as soon as he found himself alone with Jelica, and he was consumed by fear at being so long alone with her in the lonely mountains. It was no longer of any importance that she was a woman of his kin, who only that morning had sacrificed so much, all that she could and had, to save his father's life. Even Vojin's sacrifice began to seem distorted. Had he not done that only to suppress the revolt and to break Grgur, overconscientious and beginning to waver, and estrange him from Jelica? How well Vojin knew him! To Vojin, Grgur's feelings for Jelica were plain; he even knew how to make fun of them, sure of his relative and no less sure of his wife. Jelica's gift of the necklace that morning, though it cemented forever her relations with Grgur, began to destroy the barriers of kinship that encircled them and that prolonged into infinity the countless ways to her. Every step that day seemed to Grgur to lessen the impediments that stood between them; it was as if they were hastening toward what they had for years resisted and succeeded in avoiding. The fires of their desire, once kindled, were only banked down, and every chance detail, every word, and every stumble, look, and touch stirred up those fires on this sultry, perfumed day filled with sacrifice and longing.

Just below the *katun* the path entered the forest, dark and silent, and emerged about half an hour's walk later into the open brilliance of the mountain pastures. Another half hour's walk and the hayfields and pastures were interspersed with thickets and dried-up stream beds. To the east the pastures rode like horses over the bare heights, the gray stone crests, and to the west the view opened over the villages in the Lim Valley and the mountains beyond. Thence for almost an hour the path wandered over bare hills and little streams until it broke out into the heights just above the village. The view over the valley kept opening and disappearing again. There was another and easier way, shorter though steeper, through the forest. But these two, without a word, set out along the first one, for the sake of the view and because it was longer.

Tormented by desire and torn by remorse, Grgur felt apprehensive of the dank, gloomy woods below the *katun*. And as soon as they stepped into the forest, it seemed to him that Jelica slackened her pace, as if by secret agreement, in the half-light and at a spot so unknown that they could feel completely at ease. No one could either hear them or see them, and he had no reason to expect any resistance from Jelica. Even if she did not consent, she would not betray him, and even if she should betray him, it would only intensify the already inevitable separation between him and Vojin in the affairs of the clan. *And I would never confess anything of the sort! I would say: "She lies, the whore. She offered herself to me, and I would not consent. She thought this up to compromise me!"*

All that had held him back from her was transformed into a feeling that seemed to be not his own but that of some other man, and he trembled with passion and apprehension. What was more, by some sense, some intuition, he knew that something similar was taking place in her; a gulf separated them, but through her he realized that they were united by countless and invisible bonds. *No! She will not betray me! She would never do that, never cause discord between me and Vojin. I know her well! And could I really say that she threw herself at me? No one would believe me. She is regarded as a respectable woman, as indeed she is. What? A respectable woman! What is a respectable and a disreputable woman if I am dear to her, if she wants me? And am I an honest man? Am I really, with these desires tormenting me while my father is being tortured in prison and all Radak life is disintegrating around me? All that comes from the Cave, from this terrible forest; all men and everything manly in me have disappeared! Everything. Except this love for her.*

She was walking behind him, and, as if by chance, he kept turning back to look at her; he saw her reserved, submissive expression and the tense expectation in her pale face, her lips bloodless and quivering. Everything seemed simple and easy. But it was he who must begin, must find words that did not frighten or insult her, that she could understand in their true meaning but that, should she feel insulted, he could explain by saying that she had not understood him. Such words, if there were any, he could not find. He was filled with indecision, uncertainty. *Words for what? Could I, after what Vojin did this morning, do anything to humiliate him, to shatter his peaceful, regular existence? Well, let us assume that she consents. She will consent, she will not resist strongly; that can be seen from the trepidation with which she follows me and marks my every movement. So? We shall enjoy today, tonight, perhaps occasionally now and again— but it would destroy her and Vojin's lasting happiness. Something incomprehensible, some terrible renunciation, must keep those two together. She is barren, and he has never suggested driving her away and taking another. There is something great between them. And in me, too, there is something terrible and great. I might be able to suppress my longing, but . . . I must once and for all break with the clan, with Vojin, with myself. How all this has changed and been turned upside down! How perverse and complicated is man! I do not want Stamena, thus weighed down with misfortunes and ill luck. And her . . . I am confused! Father and the Cave!*

They reached level ground and suddenly they could no longer hear the gurgling and murmuring of the stream whose waters welled up below the *katun* and coursed down its stone channel through the coltsfoot and coarse grasses that carpeted the forest. They were in the moist green silence, where not a leaf, not a beetle, made a sound. Fascinated and numbed by silence and desire, Grgur asked Jelica, not daring to turn around: "Are you afraid, Jelica?"

She did not reply, and it seemed to him that he could hear her thoughts and how she searched for words that would not invite him or totally reject him. "What should I be afraid of," she said finally, aloud, as if to encourage herself, "with you?"

He guessed her thoughts and even the timid undercurrent of her words, and that emboldened him. "And of me? Aren't you afraid of me?"

She was silent once more. Again he seemed to hear her thoughts, though now, trembling in expectation, he did not clearly understand them. "With you, I am afraid of nothing," she said, though not so loudly. "You can only do good to me."

138

She was as she had always been; she repulsed him, but in a manner that drew them still closer. He stopped and turned around boldly to her. But she, as if she had guessed that he would do so, stepped onward lightly, looking in front of her, her lips slightly parted and with quickened heartbeats in her smooth white throat.

"Jelica!" he called, so loudly that he startled himself. "We are alone. Nobody but God can hear us." *Who knows, perhaps the Devil is listening to me now and driving me on in this terrible silence.* "Tell me, is there anything you would refuse me?" He looked straight at her, but she did not raise her eyes, suddenly mysterious and enigmatic. "You know that we are not like the others," and there burst from him an unexpected torrent of words. "We are closer, we love one another, we wait only to see one another. Why don't you answer? I myself do not know what is the matter with me today, but I have been waiting for years to tell you, so that you know. No one has ever been as dear to me as you are! You yourself know that well. Don't you see with what terror we Radaks have set one foot on the ford; we shall talk and discuss, and you and I shall not know what we have longed for, what we could be to each other. Answer me! Why are you so silent, now that you have nothing to fear or be ashamed of?"

She lightly shrugged her shoulders and glanced at him so fleetingly that he could not manage to interpret her glance. Then she lowered her eyes and murmured: "I have already said."

"What have you said? What I already know and have heard a thousand times!"

"I can deny you nothing. And you will not ask anything of me that could spoil our affection."

Clearly she was not able, did not want, to tear herself away from her indecision, her tress of unconscious longings, kinship, maidenly shame, and intimacy. She stood before him with arms lowered, pale and subdued, as if she wished nothing but was not able to resist anything. He, too, was unable to do anything. The silence brooded over the forest, but now it aroused a mild sorrow both for himself and for her. "You have no need to be afraid of me," he said, and went on his way. "I mean you no harm. But a man does not always know how to separate evil from good. And sometimes I am so lonely and unhappy; because of these dissensions, because of my father, because of the destruction of the Radaks, because of us two."

She was silent, and he talked and talked, not considering his words and at times even forgetting what he had said, inarticulately justifying his longing for her.

Again they began to go down the steep slope, taking care not to stumble over the beech roots or slither on the damp leaves. Once more the stream appeared in silvery necklaces in the breaks in the dense greenery about it. But she was still silent, enigmatic, neither more joyful nor more courageous because of the breaking of the silence and the greenness of the sunny meadows shining between the treetops below them on the far side of the valley. Leaping over the rushing stream from stone to stone, they reached the rocky outcrops above the meadows. They went onward in silence, panting from fatigue and the damp heat. When at last they emerged from the green forest twilight, from the sultriness of their desires and their intents, Jelica burst out in childish rejoicing: "As if it were day once more!"

Quickly their mood blended with the purity of meadows and sun, and Grgur, with regret, remarked: "The hay cutting is almost over. It is terrible to sit about with nothing to do. This year neither you nor I will spend the summer at haymaking."

They went on for another two or three hundred paces, absorbed in their own thoughts, till they reached the spring, which seemed to be inviting them to halt. There, once more serene, they turned to one another. Grgur threw himself down under a beech, took off his cap as though tired out, and shouted joyfully: "Let's take a rest!"

But Jelica stood, nibbling at a leaf with white teeth, whose irregularity gave life to her pale, cold, expressionless face.

"Why don't you rest a bit?" he asked.

"I'm not tired."

"Nor am I. But let's sit for a moment."

"I'm all right as I am," she said, as if there had never been any conversation between them.

"Good. Just as you like. We might as well go on," he remarked, almost curtly.

He leaned over to drink from the spring, though he was not thirsty, irritated by her defensive, self-contained reserve, by his own lack of decision in the forest. He drank the icy water eagerly, because it seemed to him that it would cool him, calm him. Straightening up, head and neck flushed, he saw her face above him, as in the forest, tense and watchful. Her eyes had something pleading in their timid brilliance, and her lips were pale from desperate contraction. Now she was again enigmatic. He was angry with himself for his recent irritation and felt a fresh, pleasant desire. In order to pull himself together, he again leaned down to the spring, to bathe his face and neck.

When he had finished, without knowing why, but carried away by a meaningless joy, as in a game, he took some of the water in his palms and, standing up, splashed it over her face. She flushed scarcely perceptibly. Her eyes forgave him joyously, and her lips parted in a caressing whisper. "Don't!" She did not now, nor had she in the forest, address him as *djever*, though she did so on other occasions.

"Why, why not?" he asked.

"It's not right. For us, it is not a game."

"Why not? Didn't you tell me a short while ago you couldn't refuse me anything? Why shouldn't we play? We are not old; you are in the prime of life for a woman."

"But not that! You know everything, as I do, too. Even though I am not of Radak blood, it is now as if I were. I am a Radak woman, like all your kin."

She still refused him, however unwillingly and inarticulately; yet, submissive and intimate, she deferred to him and his decision. Had she done anything else—had she refused outright, had she been forward, had she played a game—he could easily have decided. In this way nothing had changed; everything was as it had been before, the sinfulness of sweet desire, abnegation, and renunciation in the name of the clan, of friendship, and of honor. Balanced between two extremes, he now found it harder, in the purity of the meadows and their clear revelation, to slip either to one or to the other side.

They again started out, as if they had not openly and finally renounced one another. They walked side by side, she on the left, he on the right, of the worn path. The desire to tease her seized Grgur once more. But there was no excuse and no way to do so, and he at last found words, as if he had seen them in the yellow-

141

ing hollows around the Lim or gathered them from the grasses, with their scented juices and shining pollen, which brushed against his legs. "Tell me, my beauty, does it sometimes happen that a man pleases you, so that you are wakeful at night and cannot sleep?" But when she, smiling, did not reply, he went on, questioning both her and himself. "You are in the prime of life, beautiful as the sun, and you have no children; might it not be that you would like someone other than Vojin? I am not saying that you would want to sin, but just so; he pleases you, your heart beats when you meet, and he is before your eyes when you are alone?"

"No, nothing of that sort has ever happened to me," she replied with intentional resolve, which he understood to be directed against him alone.

"Not toward anyone?"

She was again silent, with downcast eyes and half-open quivering lips.

"Not toward me?"

It was as if the ground shook beneath him or as if they had run into a wall. They stood, one beside the other, and she raised her eyes to him, filled with sun and tears. "Don't torment me, *djever,* today. We must not spoil, must not renounce, the love among us four."

Agitated and frightened, she hurried on. It was beautiful, sad, and irrevocable, as in a dream—a dream he could not dispel. He could not cloud her inward peace, splendid and enchanted, destroy her belief in him, his own belief in himself.

At last it was irrefutably clear to him that he would never do anything to her and nothing would ever happen between them. That love, that longing, would increase even more in him than in her, hateful and splendid, yet unattainable. *We Radaks are like that—too much conscience and too much empty longing! We are wrestling with ourselves, with some sort of devil within us. Perhaps it is more beautiful so; our love will never turn to disgust, will never be quenched. We shall always remember and regret it.*

He no longer looked at her. He was aware of her legs swaying through the grasses, and that was enough. And she no longer walked with downcast eyes, which had made her stumble once or twice. What was it she was looking at? What was she thinking? The fields were golden and the grasses bluish, and the valley spread out below her, soft and mild as far as eye could see. Nonetheless, her thoughts were far from him. She was withdrawing, melancholy and unreal with the slackening of desire, amid the welcoming foothills.

"They've cut a lot already," he said, breaking the silence and the indecision as they came out onto the stretch from which they could look down at the village.

"It's high time," she retorted. "More than overdue. I shall have to get some more cut tomorrow."

"Good," he said, continuing the train of thought that her words and the sight of the cutting had deflected. "It's never clear to me how you women manage to do everything, even now when we are abandoning homes and property. Whatever we ask, you have already done; whatever we ask, we get! You could, like the bees, live without us, were there only someone to beget the children."

As he spoke, he remembered that he should not have mentioned children, more especially the sterility of the worker bees, to her, a barren woman. She made no sign, or perhaps suppressed any sign, of indignation, but explained to him gaily: "I myself don't know how we do it. We go to bed late, get up early, doze standing or sitting, yet a house is a cave without a man in it."

"And it is black for us without you. One does not make a home out of a cave."

Thus they reached the village, serious and intimate.

At the house, Stojan Radak was waiting for him. He had just returned from Montenegro, by byways known only to him.

Grgur always remembered that Stojan had returned on the same day he had come down from the mountain with Jelica. His memory stressed with spiteful malignity the link between these two events, for it seemed to him that Stojan, chatting with him about his indiscretions with the Radak widow Petrana and asking for his advice on what to do, was in fact speaking of him, his only just tranquilized desires and intentions toward Jelica. It was as if that day, from dawn until sunset, had set out to torment and tempt him. But after the sultry heat of the day, the evening freshness was pleasant, and eyes and thoughts were calmed in the bluish depths before them and in the distant peace.

As they were walking in the garden, looking at the yield of the fruit trees, Stojan told him about his trip. He had not in fact been in old Montenegro, but in the Vasojević district, with the Vasojević leaders, who had transmitted the Radaks' desires and misfortunes to Cetinje, while he waited for a reply in Lijeva Rijeka.

Bony, fairly tall, long-legged and bull-necked, with long sinewy hands and graying red hair, Stojan moved easily and vigorously, almost inaudibly, with his head always thrust a little forward, by day on the plain and at night in the precipitous ravines, as if it were his feet that saw the earth beneath him. Even now he did not look tired, only unshaven.

A hunter, he was sparing of words. He knew how to condense and draw out the essence of a conversation, leaving his interlocutor to work out for himself the inessentials and the possibilities. Lisping beneath sparse reddish mustaches, he said at once that he had not been able to do anything in Montenegro. He had seen both voivodes at Bukovo Polje, Miljan Vukov and his son Todor. They had done what they could. They had at once sent a messenger to the Prince at Cetinje, and to Voivode Marko Miljanov in case he, through his links with the European consuls at Skadar, could undertake anything. They had promised to do everything they could but, as the Radaks had foreseen, they had little hope, for the Vali of Skadar himself was instigating and supporting the Plav and Gusinje begs to do exactly what they were doing. Stambul was too far away and too high and mighty for the arrest of one village knez to be regarded as of any importance. However, the Vasojević leaders had warned the authorities at Plav to take care what they were doing, threatening that they would pay for Anto's life with their own lives if a hair of his head was touched.

Stojan and Grgur had become intimate only when the revolt had come to the fore, but for that very reason their friendship was both warm and all-embracing. Leaning against an apple tree, Stojan began to tug at his mustaches, and Grgur suspected that he had not told all.

"What else? What about the army? Will the Montenegrin army strike soon?"

"In Montenegro, too, the news is bad. The leading warriors and insurgents—the Sirdar Jole Piletić, Peko Pavlović, and, it seems, even Marko Miljanov—are out of favor with the Prince. It is even said that everything is not at it should be with Todor and his father, Miljan."

Grgur seized his head as if to tear his hair out or to wrench it from his shoulders, or as if to revive in the darkness the ancient songs and stories of the Serbian past, disunion and treachery, the promise of sufferings and struggle continuing from generation to generation, as long as the name and race of Serb should exist. He almost yelled: "In what have we put our trust? What can we do? What is left for us?"

But he was a resilient man, especially if anyone reproved him for faintheartedness or he himself became conscious of it, and that Stojan knew well. "There's no use moaning about it; leave that to the women!" he said.

"Who's moaning?" Grgur shouted, and then pulled himself together. "Yes, I'm moaning! And I've good reason—for the Radaks, for Serbdom."

Stojan pretended not to have heard him. "Now we have no other way, and we cannot invent better Serbian leaders."

"Am I inventing them? Have I, Stojan, lost my senses to turn back on a path from which there is no return? I, like you and many others, foolishly thought that Serbdom would be purified by blood and suffering."

"Since the world and the centuries began, leaders have squabbled, and they will go on squabbling while the world and the centuries exist. I did not take that so hard; little by little I realized it, since I had plenty of time for thinking on my way back here. There, in Montenegro, things look different; for them, the fighting is over. So now they quarrel about properties and leadership and precedence in honors and services. From over there, despite our troubles and misfortunes, it looks as if earth has rejected us and Heaven will not accept us."

"I know that is so," Grgur said, consolingly, placing his hand on Stojan's shoulder to encourage him and calm him. "One witches' sabbath is not yet over, and another one begins. But it is better for a man to let himself go sometimes; he cannot begin again without that."

Stojan remarked with a grin: "I seem to be piling evil upon evil. There is no talk about mustering the army. There is a guard on the frontier, but then, there are always guards on the frontiers! The men are dispersing. They have come back from the war and are going home; some to reap their harvests, others to trade, others to make love to their wives."

Grgur began thinking aloud, striding from fruit tree to fruit tree. "Very well, then. So let it be! We will leave our houses. First of all, I will raze my own. We've begun already. Today Akan broke all the Radak sheep bells, and tomorrow I will quench the hearths. But so it must be; there is no longer room for both us and the Turks! And since that is so, our hour will come, and we will find some way to get rid of them."

Making their way toward the stream, toward Vojin's house, they saw Jelica returning downhill from the spring with a trough on her head and a pail in her hand, the wide white sleeves of her dress fluttering around her like a butterfly's wings. In the clear twilight those white wings were in strange contrast with her body, bent under its burden, as if carved in stone. But in that incongruity was also everything else: the revolt and the news from Montenegro, the dissensions among the Radaks, Grgur at odds with himself, the darkening earth and the clarity of the sky. They halted in the dried-up bed of the stream, and Grgur whispered softly: "Don't speak of this to anyone."

"Not to Vojin?"

"Not even to him. Above all, not to him."

"So I, too, thought. But perhaps we could to him."

"No, no! He is too—how can I put it?—too upright; he could not keep it to himself, but would trumpet it to the whole clan." Then he added, biting his lips: "It's not to hide it from the clan, but—they would be bewildered and lose heart. We must wait."

"Wait, do you say?"

"And make ready. No one knows what the day will bring, and what the night. There are not many of us. All the Radaks able to carry a rifle number scarcely fifty. And we are alone among enemies and more powerful clans—a candle in a storm. We cannot go back and dare not go forward. We must wrestle for a fall."

"If we few take the risk . . ." Stojan began reflectively.

"First let's get some supper, and you must get some rest," Grgur interrupted him, setting out on the goat path to the Cave.

Stojan protested. He agreed only to have some supper. Grgur

interpreted this as a desire to continue their conversation; perhaps something was still worrying him. With reserved men there is always something that remains unsaid.

They went slowly uphill.

Grgur began to regret that he had, for the first time in his life, decided to conceal something vitally important to the clan, and had even urged a member of the clan to conceal it. Sin was piled upon sin; first his lust for Jelica, which he had suppressed more out of consideration for her than because of her kinship with him, and now this reserve toward the clan. "Some things have to be kept back," he began to explain, feeling pleased that because of the narrowness of the path he did not have to look at Stojan. "For it might happen that even those who are most eager would cool off and lose faith."

"I know," said Stojan. "It occurred to me also, in Montenegro. When men do not agree, nothing can be done in an open and honest manner."

Stojan was reliable, as he had always been, and so, too, was Stamena, though in a different way. That encouraged him and made him feel proud, as on that evening when she had given herself to him so unrestrainedly, there, up there in the clearing, which they had now almost reached.

He began thinking about Stojan, who walked behind him without a word, almost noiselessly. What had driven him, a man without a family, to revolt? He could only lose by it; where else could he find such mountains and waters, such abundance of every kind of game and such companionship of hunters?

Stojan was two or three years older than Grgur. Nearly forty and still unmarried, he lived in a ramshackle house on a neglected plot. But for a long time past he had not, even in jest, repeated his favorite proverb: If it is a good thing to have a house, then a wolf would have one. From his earliest youth he had passed days and nights, sometimes weeks, in hunting, frequently in the company of Izet-beg of Plav, who was also a bachelor. But to Izet-beg hunting was an enjoyment and a pastime, while to Stojan it was a profession. He hunted everything: wild goats on the Prokletije, bears on the Djeravica, martens on Visitor, partridges in the meadows, otters, ducks, and larks around the lake and all kinds of fish in it, in its tributary the Ljuča and in the Lim, which flowed out of it. He lived for hunting, abandoning his land, living as a lodger with the more prosperous Radaks, most frequently with Vojin. But time was taking its revenge; on becoming intimate with Stojan, Grgur noticed that he was longing for a home, for affection, for children.

As they were sitting at the entrance to the Cave, facing the heights lit up by the brilliance of the sunset, Stojan, lisping and hesitating, began. "You know, I can, I must, tell you: I am living secretly with Petrana. I am alone, without anyone, no one to do my darning or my washing, not to speak of anything else, and she, too, is alone. So, there you are."

"I guessed it; recently you have preferred to sleep in her house," Grgur replied without surprise, and thought of adding: "But I had hoped there was nothing more to it, even though you and her husband were only distant kin." However, he did not say it, recalling his unquenched longing for Jelica. Suddenly, as when a flash of lightning reveals a scene, he understood the terrible truth: blood, kinship, community, living, and existence draw one into sin, into mortal, forbidden love, sweeter than any other. In that only does a man drink passion and sin to the full, mingled together—against environment, custom, existence, against God and against man. Instead, seeking solace and tranquillity in those distant peaks, were it only for a moment, he replied to Stojan: "It would be awkward if it gets around, especially now."

"It is awkward. That's why I'm telling you."

When did it begin? She had had her eye on the haiduk Vučeta; he had spent the night with her at the time of Roksanda's wedding. Does Stojan know? "So this is the same story, like the revolt; push on till someone catches you," Grgur jested, with constraint. "How did she get hold of you?"

Stojan told him: "It just happened. The Devil knows how; I don't myself. It was in winter last year, when it was snowing hard. I was taking a marten from the hollow tree, up there above the village, and she, Petrana, appeared from God knows where, collecting wood. There was no one to cut it for her, and I thought it would be a good chance for me, on the excuse of helping her. She stood and watched me, to see if the marten would come out when I had cut down the tree. When it was down, she rushed forward

148

and put her hand into the hollow to pull out the marten. 'No, you fool woman,' I shouted. 'It will bite, tear out your eyes; it's a fierce little beast.' I pulled her away, but she resisted and laughed. 'I'm afraid of nothing but loneliness and boredom.' We struggled; Petrana pulled me, and the marten might have escaped at any moment. I said to myself: 'Petrana has nowhere to go.' I put a glove on my hand and somehow or other pulled out the marten. I wanted to wring its neck, but she said: 'Don't. It's pretty. Aren't you sorry for it?'

"I stuffed the marten into my bag and—her hand in mine. Somehow she seemed beautiful to me then, radiant and dark, like a forest! She enchanted me, and I found myself on her, behind the cut tree stump. We paid no heed to the snow and the frost. 'God must have made you all wrong,' she said, 'that you can live without a woman.' I felt ashamed. I am a man, but I swore she would be the first and the last.

"But women are a perverse habit. I spent one night with her, then another—and I got used to it. Those two children of hers made much of me, and I of them. They were always waiting for me to come and bring them presents.

"I heard that the bitch was unfaithful to me on St. George's Day with Vučeta. I thought of killing her, but reconsidered when I went to her house; it would be enough if I gave her a good beating.

"But—what will you! She is strong and not afraid; she was not even afraid of her husband. 'Come on, you beast, sit down and have your supper, then get out or—let's go to bed,' she said. I was petrified, and she put out her tongue at me. 'Aren't I my own master? Are you my husband? You range about at your own sweet will and eye every skirt you see, and then ask to see my permit to hunt such a falcon as Vučeta.' I laughed at her scolding, but thought it over, had my supper, and we went to bed, still scolding each other.

"That was the best night I ever had with her. She opened her soul to me; she knows how to be a dove when she wants to. Then she wept and said: 'You think I am pleased because I deceived you. I did it because I was tormented and angry that you are always leaving me and peering under someone else's skirts.' I said to her: 'I am a man, and it is different when a wife is unfaithful.'

149

'Yes,' she said, 'it is different, but I am not your wife. I never swore to you at the altar.' Then I said to her, thinking of the Radaks: 'We are committing a sin, Petrana.' 'It is a sin,' she agreed, 'but not a big one; any priest would marry us. It is only a sin because we are unmarried. And it's sweeter in sin; let's pray to God, and he will see our trouble and forgive us.'

"Then I thought and thought again. I am already well on in years. I cannot find a better or a prettier wife; I have no one to darn for me or wash for me, and old age is drawing near. I must share misfortunes with someone."

Grgur listened, pensive and amused. He recalled his brother Rade. He might be on the brink of still-greater sin. That wedding night, after Stojna's dance, Raduša had taken Rade with sweet words into the flower-covered garden. Perhaps even tomorrow Grgur would have to help his brother quench an unquenchable fire. It was as if there were a curse on them—everything centered around Vojin's house, around his womenfolk. One brother lusted for his wife and another, for his sister, even more closely akin. "Keep it hidden, Stojan, as a snake its legs!" he counseled after Stojan had finished.

"I am ashamed; before myself, before you, before everyone. I lie to my blood; I destroy my birth and my death."

"Hide it—at least until the more important matter is disentangled."

"Shall I fly with her into the wide world, till all trace of us is lost? There is no end to the world."

"And the revolt! You still need something more important than self, than the Radaks. Hide it!"

Stojan shrugged his shoulders in unwilling assent.

"Perhaps we are deceiving the clan," Grgur finally said, expressing his thought. "But we do not do so from ill will or for our own profit. Sins and misfortunes have set the clan, the revolt, and Serbdom at odds—and us, too."

They were glad that Trifun's little voice came to them from the blue twilight and drove away the cares and misfortunes that had closed in upon them like the jaws of the Cave. "Papa, papa, come and meet me! I'm bringing supper. Supper!"

Stojan leaped up swiftly and ran across the rocks. They ate their supper in silence, and later Stojan, after caressing the child, left. The stifling darkness swallowed him as soon as he went out of the Cave, and all that was left were the stars and the hooting of owls.

"I'm afraid of the owls," said Trifun from the darkness of the Cave.

"They won't hurt children."

"Why do they hoot?"

"To frighten birds, to make them move, and then they'll snatch at the chickens."

"Do they move? Why do they move, if they know?"

"There are timid ones, which move even though they know."

The child sat beside his father and snuggled up to him. "And the stars? Are they good souls? I am less frightened when there are stars."

"Did Grandfather tell you that? Probably they are good souls."

"And will my soul be in the sky?"

"You've still a long time to live, son."

"I don't know. I will not—sometimes I want to die, so much."

"Why?"

"To see how much you would grieve for me."

His father hugged him and, groping along the sharp-toothed walls, put him to bed.

Grgur, too, slept, though the troublous, passionate, and terrifying day had not yet settled within him. He fell into a heavy and uneasy sleep. And he dreamed a strange dream; he was quite sure that it was that night he dreamed it, a thin, pale, yet purified continuation of the thoughts and events of the day.

He was in the hayfields, those same hayfields through which he had walked that day, or some long time ago, with Jelica. But the fields were slippery, steep, like slides; he kept slipping on their moist greenness and falling against Jelica, against her unexpectedly soft, warm body. She moved away, but smiled coquettishly. Neither sun nor moon was to be seen, but the meadows shone with their own green and glassy radiance. As soon as they reached the spring—now with more abundant water than there had been in reality; the whole stream was boiling and bubbling—Jelica stepped into it, her legs bare to the knee, with shining slender calves, and her black hair loose over her warm firm shoulders, and her breasts incomprehensibly full and heavy. How was it that he hadn't noticed that she was barefoot and in her shift? Had she undressed a moment earlier? She sprinkled her face and neck and smiled at him without restraint, seductively, and her teeth seemed to him sharper and stronger than he remembered them. "Fool," she said through the water, smiling, "so you thought you were not dear to me?" "No, I never thought that," Grgur answered, justifying himself. "It was because of Vojin. I was ashamed because of him." "What Vojin? There's no more Vojin; he died long ago." "Yes, so he did," Grgur agreed, "but I was never able to understand how I did not know earlier." How had it happened that he did not know? Vojin was as dear to him as a blood brother, and they were together every day. But the strangest thing of all was that he did not regret Vojin, that secretly he was glad to know of his death, though he was dear to him, though that was neither fair nor right. And Jelica, somehow knowing what was troubling him, smiled, sitting beside him in the meadow, all wet and cold from the mountain stream and yet hot from her young blood, and said: "But now you know." And he seized her by the waist and under her knees, her body supple and yielding, but strangely and scarcely perceptibly she turned into Stamena, with her full hips and pear-shaped breasts and that prominent eyetooth, which fixed itself in his neck.

When he awoke he felt clearheaded and refreshed. The robins were welcoming the dawn, already sunny on the joyous mountaintops. It was the fifteenth morning since Anto's arrest.

But the morning sun was darkened and the bird song dulled by the unexpected keening of his sister-in-law Stanija, sister of Vučeta, which reached as far as the Cave in thin and terrifying waves.

As soon as she came out of the forest, out of the pathlessness above the Radak houses, she began lamenting, and a mournful terror spread through the leaves, dispelling the dream from which Grgur had scarcely awakened. He at once recognized her voice and, wrenched from the stony realities of the Cave, leaped up and hurried toward the dark course of the lament.

Stanija was squatting by the spring above the house, like a black bird, and, wailing incessantly, was washing something. From a distance Grgur saw a man's head in her hands and felt

sure that it must be Vučeta's, though it was smashed and mutilated and strangely reduced in size.

He ran toward her, and she, seeing him, cut short her keening
and, holding out the head to him, whimpered: "Here, brother, I
have brought black misfortune on the house."

Though she had always been bony, Stanija seemed thinner.
Her dark eyes flashed with madness and her cracked lips were
bloody. Grgur, without speaking, took the head in his hands and,
though it had already been washed, went on washing it.

The Radaks, unlike the Montenegrins, did not keen over their
dead, and did not regard the head as anything especially hallowed or the seat of honor. But under the influence of their Montenegrin neighbors and, most of all, of song and legend, they had
acquired respect for cut-off heads.

Grgur did not know what he should do with the head, but he
had heard that the Montenegrins combed, washed, and twisted
the mustaches even of enemy heads and put them in a place of
honor, and that the men of Plav and Gusinje did likewise. Influ-
enced still more by his own sense of what was proper, he combed
the head's long, curly chestnut hair, whose shine was already
dulled, with his fingers, and he smoothed out the long, partly
torn-out mustaches.

"Let's go home," he said to Stanija, and set out holding the
head before him in his hands and walking slowly, like a priest in
church with the chalice. Only then did he notice Trifun, rigid
and horror-stricken, on the path. Though at first he thought that
the child should be taken away, he then thought that this way
was better. *Let him learn, from childhood, since it has already
happened, that such things can and do happen!*

As soon as he started, Stanija again began to wail, following
him with measured steps, recalling the live Radaks and their
martyrs Radule and Arsenius and the heroes of their kin, bewailing the darkened sun, the wounds of her brother, Vučeta, and the
tortures of her father-in-law, Anto.

Her lament spread the news of the misfortune swiftly and certainly. Before Anto's house the Radak women were already waiting for them, some terrified, others weeping softly, and others sobbing. Jelica hurried across the meadow, from the stream to the

garden, a forgotten sickle in her hand, while Petrana, from the other side, leaned against the plum tree with tears pouring down her plump red cheeks.

Many of the Radaks were still on the mountain, but the men who were not came, too, worried and serious, subdued and reserved in their movements. In a few moments half the village was gathered in the garden. Milena spread a cloth on the tree stump, and Grgur, till then stiffly holding the head in front of him and displaying it to the Radaks, placed it on the cloth, crossed himself, and kissed it on the forehead.

Grandfather Grgur muttered, setting the staff before him: "The martyr is taking his rest. Would that Anto, too, could take his rest."

But he did not kiss the head; only Stojan and three or four others did. The women, Jelica among them, also refrained from kissing it; not from revulsion, for the kissing of the dead was a Radak custom, but from fear of the authorities. This was a haiduk's head.

Grgur shouted angrily: "Kiss the Serb, the hero!"

There were few to obey. Then Stanija began to shriek, tearing at her face with her nails and beating her breast, until Jelica took her by the waist and led her back to the house like a child.

From somewhere Grandfather Pavle, bareheaded and in tattered shirt, burst among them. He wiped his red eyelids and began to keen like a woman. "Well, come, O better come. Wings broken, the land shrouded in black. The heroic breast is not for the heart to beat within it, that I may kiss that, too! Where are the hands that broke the swords, where are the feet that moved so swiftly, the manly strength, the knife and the rifle? The sun's light is darkened; our hopes are quenched. The sun's light will warm us once again, but our hopes will shine no more. The Turks lie that they cut you down; they could never cut you down. Vain is their torture and their hope! The hero falls, but the standard is still upright!"

The old man Milija cut him short, angrily striking him on the throat with his stick. "Quiet, you dreamer of dreams. We are not here to listen to your dirges, but to see what we must do. We have a haiduk's head among us."

"A hero's head, a Serb head!" Grgur interrupted him with an

angry cry, seizing the staff from Grandfather Grgur's hands and leaning it against the stump by the head. Trifun ran up with a leafy beech twig and began to drive the flies away from the head.

Grgur's words flowed out with the impetus of emotion and haste, overwhelming him, but because of the uselessness of arguing with the hardheaded, slow-witted old man Milija, he checked his outpourings and shouted to Stojan: "You are the swiftest among us. Run up the mountain and fetch Vojin and the other Radaks, so that we may bury Vučeta's head and consult. There is no time to lose; the head is already stinking." He added, with curt disdain: "And you, Uncle Milija, had better look to the sentries; they are sleeping."

He remembered that he had not talked with Stanija. He had not consoled her in her grief, had not heard from her what had happened and how, had not even asked her about his father.

In the storeroom, instead of kissing her *djever's* hand, she threw herself into his arms. "I, the black coward, the sister without a brother."

Jelica was standing against the window in pale, mute rigidity. Bewilderment and sorrow made her beauty seem more incorporeal, more unreal, than in his dream. Grgur tenderly took Stanija's right hand and led her toward the coffer, consoling her. "Be calm! Don't presage evil for a man's house and a man's kin. Man is born to die."

Only when Jelica moved away from the window and, shadowy and unheard, slipped out of the room did he notice, by the greenish light that filtered in from the plum orchard, that it was not so much that Stanija had grown thinner, as that she was exhausted, burned out by inner fires, and that both her cheeks, from the eyes down to the chin, were lacerated by three red and bloody furrows.

She began to speak brokenly, feverishly, mixing oaths and dirges, filled with worries about her home, her husband, her son. What was happening around her mingled with all that *had* happened and her own troubles. "Who can drink up the sea and number the stars, or tell a sister's woes?" she began, as if in a song, and then, pulling herself together, went on: "As you know, I was going to Doda's to take a change of clothing for Vučeta and to tell him that you had distributed the arms . . . that his sister make him happy and bring to her house his mangled head! Of

155

Father-in-law Anto I know nothing except that they are torturing him with iron tortures. And is my child alive and well? From Vučeta not a chicken remains to rejoice me with its cry or shelter me with its wings! You have dispersed the stock; well, let it be. It will cause the children much sorrow. The land will become heavy, and the heavens burdened with its mourning. Only that your house, *djever*, be not destined to an ill fate."

From what he heard later from others, but mainly from Stanija that day, from her moaning and wailing, but also from her trenchant and accurate account, he built up a picture of what had happened to the haiduks Vučeta and Tomica in the kula of the Shquiptar Bib Doda.

Stanija had gone to see her brother and to spend the day at Bib Doda's. But she did not know the way and was accompanied by a Shquiptar, who stopped to see to his own affairs, so she had arrived late and been forced to spend the night in Bib's house. She had worried that those at home might be concerned about her, but was glad that she could be with her brother.

Mrika, Bib's wife, received her with open arms and suppressed curiosity, because she was the first Serbian woman to have entered the house; and Stanija felt as though she were in the house of a *kum*. In the evening, the Dodas gathered there, sat around the food, and engaged in conversation about heroes and their deeds. She did not have much chance to see her brother, for eager rivals contended for his time. A hero is no hero to his own kin and does not belong to them alone.

Everything in Bib's house that night was openhearted and courteous—words, food, drink, and jests. Stanija felt ashamed of taking part in the men's conversation and helped Mrika; Shquiptar women do not know even as much as Montenegrin women, but Stanija had already learned much in Anto's house. It was lovely, as in a song or in memory, as before death or fate.

It was late at night when the relatives left, and the haiduks and Bib and his younger brother, an unmarried youth, lay down, heavy with food and drink, untroubled and gay from talking and many toasts. Mrika and Stanija went on cleaning up the house. Suddenly the watchdog began to leap about angrily. It was a night for wolves, dark and rainy, but over and above the gurgling of the spring, the whisper of the grasses in the meadow in front of the house, and the stirring of birds on the branches, Mrika heard a far-off noise, like the approach of many men. "They are soldiers; they don't come without evil intent!" she shouted, and ran to waken Bib.

The men woke but not in time to seize their arms and rush outside. Still drowsy, they remained irresolute—is it or isn't it? Tomica even teased Bib. "Let's see if you are a *trim*, a hero, Doda." Bib was the first to make a move. But his brother forestalled him; he grabbed a gun and rushed to the door. From the darkness outside a volley of shots pierced the door and Bib's brother, riddled with shots, fell groaning across the threshold. Bib did not shed a single tear for his brother, lest the Serbs reproach him or the Turks mock him. He said: "It was his time to die. Let us at least take his place worthily."

They began to discuss the situation. Perhaps they should rush the door; some might die and others remain. But there was no time for that. The dawn was already seeping into the kula more and more brightly, more terrible than the night.

Bib's kula was of two floors, with loopholes and narrow windows, but roofed with shingles. It was at the top end of the village, on an open space about a hundred paces long and broad, on the rocky hillside dotted with lopped and gnarled oak and hornbeam. "My grandfather sited his kula badly," Bib complained. "It is always thus when one wants the best of two worlds: solitude and security. From the cover of those rocks they will not let us open an eye. It is not good when our fathers build houses as if soldiers would never attack them." Nonetheless, Bib and the haiduks reckoned they would be able to hold the kula for a long time if only the policemen and the Moslem irregulars did not succeed in setting fire to the roof.

The attackers, too, were waiting for something, peering from behind the rocks in their red fezes, their gun barrels glinting in the sunlight, dewy and gay after the rain. The defenders took advantage of this lull to bar and strengthen the door and, more important, to fix parapets of wool sacks, mattresses, and wine tubs on the roof. The haiduks manned the two sides of the roof facing the Turks, and Doda the two that looked toward the village. If it happened that someone in the village were killed by a stray shot, then it would be Doda's, and the clan could not demand blood ransom, as they would if the shot came from a Serb. Tomica said: "If we two have to die, then at least we shall not die stained with innocent blood."

When they had taken up their positions, Doda began to shout to the Plav leaders and to threaten them that he would avenge his brother and this attack on his house and his honor. But no one replied, by either word or shot, and the sun rose from the dewy mists, and hope began to grow that everything would turn out well. "Perhaps the Dodas or some neighboring clan have armed and shown their teeth," Bib reflected aloud, though Tomica assured him: "No. They're thinking up some deviltry. I know the Turks!"

Vučeta, meanwhile, though overwrought, kept looking around at his sister. "I fear for you; I would like some friend of mine to know where we are and how we died."

Through the lower loopholes they could see parts of the village and the surrounding countryside. The cattle lowed in the morning pastures, and the children, frightened and unfed, wept. This waiting was tedious to the defenders, and, as if by chance, they all gathered in the large room on the second floor.

Vučeta said: "Bib Doda, it would be a pity for you and the Dodas and the revolt if you should die. Surrender to the Turks, and as for us, may God forgive you a hundred times."

And Tomica agreed. "You have shed your blood. Save yourself for the good of the clan and the revolt, and we will put our heads in the bag, since they have already caught us."

Bib Doda answered: "There are some things that cannot be measured and that have no price. What do the Dodas and the revolt mean if one's honor has been blackened?" He was angry. "Even if the Malesia and the Malezez depended on me, I cannot tread my *bes,* my given word, underfoot. My honor would never be clean again, even to the ninth generation."

They took oath on a loyalty that not one of them had ever doubted, pardoned insults that were not meant as offense, and kissed one another as brothers, as heroes who say farewell to life. Stanija overheard them discussing who could be the traitor, for it was clear that the men of Plav had not come by chance. But though they searched for the traitor among the Dodas and the Radaks, they could not agree with certainty upon anyone.

The cattle had already returned from their morning pasture when a call was heard from the lower side of the house, an old man's voice. "Bib! Bib! It is I who am calling, I, Mark Doda, of your kin, your uncle."

Bib replied, and his uncle—who was not really his uncle, but a cousin—went on: "The Mudir of Plav is here, Isa-beg, and the *ćatib,* Suljaga Hodžić; they have guarded us with soldiers and will not allow a living soul to move. They demand that you surrender certain haiduks, and say that they will do nothing to you or the Dodas. That they say and seek. As for you, do as seems best to you and as befits your honor."

This explained why the men of Plav had not attacked at once. Now they heard the Turks curse Uncle Mark because Bib did not answer, while Bib grinned at his companions. "They have found the most upright and most sensible among the Dodas, or it may be that the Dodas chose him themselves." Then he shouted: "Uncle Mark, let one of the Turkish leaders come forward so that I may speak with him, and we can discuss."

But the Turkish leaders would not let themselves be caught in a trap. They beat and belabored the barefoot, bareheaded, tall old man into the open again. Under his unbuttoned jacket, Uncle Mark's bony chest shone white, with tufts of gray hair.

"You see, I have come out again, I, Uncle Mark," he began, "in case at first you heard me well but did not understand me. The Turkish leaders will not come out; they do not trust you, and much less those they say you have with you. They demand that you surrender and give up, they say, some haiduks. They say that they will do nothing to you. Now you have heard. So answer. It is hateful to me to be another's tongue and ears."

Bib replied: "Let them drive me from my house and smirch my honor; as for my brother, I will settle accounts with them later."

Till then, the haiduks had taken care that the attackers should not hear them, but Vučeta could no longer hold himself in and shouted: "Let us send out Doda's wife and children and a young woman who was staying here for the night."

The old man went back again and began talking with someone around the corner of a nearby kula. He soon came back. "They will let no one out if Bib and his band do not surrender."

"Talk with them some more!" shouted Vučeta.

"I will, I will talk with them. But it is useless. They don't care about the shame of burning women and children."

Finally the Plav men agreed that Stanija and Mrika and her two children—the younger son was still at the breast—could come out. But Stanija would not go. She hoped, she told Grgur later, that she would be killed with the men.

But the Turks were still hesitant, and the attack began only about noon, under a hot mountain sun. They came from the village, rolling bundles of reeds, which protected them from bullets. They shot at the kula from all sides, so that scattered shots and bits of stone were flying everywhere, and the smoke from the defenders' guns and the dust clouded and smothered the kula.

The defenders shot rarely, though they had no reason to save ammunition. They aimed carefully at hands that showed impatiently through the sheaves and at heads that, from need or curiosity, stuck out from behind them. But there were too few of them; two or three muskets could not prevent the attackers' approach, even had they not insured themselves by carrying the sheaves.

Stanija was everywhere at once, to be with each of the three, peering through the loopholes and loading the guns. But she had only one head, two hands, two feet—and one heart. Most frequently she stayed with her brother.

The number of casualties could not be guessed with certainty through the loopholes and the slits in the roof. But they saw one sheaf break up, from either a shot or a sharp stone that had cut its binding. Behind it appeared a thin peasant in a tarry fez with a bundle of reeds in his hands, of two minds where to seek refuge. That gave Vučeta a chance to shoot. The peasant tried to get back under cover of the sheaf, but, instead, stumbled on numbed legs, scattering the reeds, then shrieked, holding his hands to his stomach. Finally he spun around and fell in the open space.

"Got one!" shouted Vučeta.

"Fine! Finish him off. Don't let him suffer," Bib replied.

"No, no. Let him feel a bit, too; let them be a bit scared."

"He's yours; do as you like," Bib assented.

"They've broken through!" Tomica shouted. "You hold the lower floor, so they don't break down the door and the windows, and I'll go up to the roof."

Bib and Vučeta rushed down the stairs. They could hear the blows of two axes on the not overthick but strong oak door. They fired almost simultaneously at the door. An ax rang on stone, and a hoarse voice cried out, cursing. The second ax was silent.

Standing still in the center of the attic, Tomica, through the shouting and the uproar, listened and was able to distinguish sounds accessible and intelligible only to him. Stanija brought him soured milk to give him strength, but he signed to her to squat down and listen. She heard something like an enormous snake crawling up the wall. Tomica approached the upper eave on all fours, thrust his head between the rafters and the outer wall, and fired downward. Someone yelled and scrabbled at the wall, but could not reach the ground and wailed: "Take me down from this ladder, brothers, so that I may die on the solid earth, as a man should!"

Tomica grinned savagely and shouted to Stanija: "Now give me the milk. I've given that fellow all the food and drink he'll ever need!"

No one helped the unfortunate man down from the ladder, though he went on moaning and calling for help. Everyone was busy, or perhaps afraid to go near him. Tomica shouted at Stanija: "Lie down, lie down, or run downstairs!" Only then did she notice that clusters of bullets had broken away the shingles in many places, revealing shining eyes from which it was impossible to take cover among the rafters. But, either because she did not realize the danger or because she believed that guns were meant only for men and that her luck would hold, she remained standing until Tomica seized her by the shoulders and dragged her down the stairs, shouting to those below: "I have given one of them absolution!" Then he whispered to himself and to her: "Now the boot is on the other foot. The more we kill now, the better for us."

Soon there came a lull, complete and terrifying, such as can happen only in the heat of a battle. The man in the open space was silent. The entreaties of the wounded man on the ladder, which alone could be heard, became more hopeless and despairing. The defenders were unable to guess what the attackers were doing, and Tomica, sitting on the stairs, filled and lit his pipe, listening attentively. Stanija, too, listened.

"You bastards!" came Uncle Mark's voice. "The roof, the roof, the roof!"

Crawling, but with his pipe still in his hand, Tomica went up under the rafters again. Bullets struck like hail, breaking away tiny splinters and opening shining holes in the roof, which looked more and more like an irregularly pierced sieve. "Bib's house will let the rain in," Tomica said, laughing, to Stanija, who had crawled beside him, so excited and upset that she had almost ceased to distinguish him from her brother.

Outside, the sheaf-bearers, dragging ladders after them, moved toward the kula from all sides. Stanija and Tomica could not see this, but guessed what was happening. He whispered to her: "Run. Get them all up here. The roof, the roof is now what matters." Along three of the walls yells and scrabbling could be heard. Some of those climbing fell back, struck by bullets, their ladders falling with them. But from a ladder on the fourth side, a man threw a tar-soaked rag. At first, they noticed the smell, and then the moistened shingles began to crackle, and suddenly a flame burst out, welcomed by the attackers with a joyous cry.

"Axes, axes!" Tomica shouted. "I have saved myself twice with axes."

Bib and Stanija came running with tools they found on the ground floor—a mallet, an ax, a hatchet, and a crowbar. Flames had already burst out. Tomica grabbed the mallet and began, as if playing a game, to break away the shingles. Then fire appeared on the opposite side, and another ladder was set up. Bib, Vučeta, and Stanija also grabbed tools.

"The dog has bitten me!" Tomica cried out, and dropped the mallet.

In the smoke and the heat, Stanija did not hear the shots and did not notice the fresh holes in the roof. She went on smashing the shingles, while Bib and Vučeta went on shooting from behind cover. Soon whole windows were opened in the roof, on both sides.

Till then, Stanija said, they did not shoot at her, and even then, when they could see her, they were ashamed to shoot lest the Shquiptars and Montenegrins mock them in their songs as killers of women.

Though the situation of the defenders was no better, they were filled with joy at their momentary victory. They had repulsed the attack on the roof and thereby saved themselves from being burned alive. Even Tomica, his right arm broken, took his part in the rejoicing. "What luck! I'm left-handed," he mocked, suppressing his moans as Stanija bandaged him.

Vučeta consoled him. "It'll mend; it's not the first time. Now you're like Lazar Pecirep. He was maimed in his right arm; so when he wanted to aim he fixed a twig to the toe of his sandal and rested his gun on it, and then shot with his whole arm. Just remember that!"

Bib, too, jested, bitterly and harshly. "They want to make torches out of us, and there's not enough sun for them now, at noon."

Twice more the men of Plav tried, though without much enthusiasm, to set fire to the roof. Then, except for an occasional shot, they began swearing at the defenders. In this they got as good as they gave, especially from the haiduks.

"Isa-beg," Doda called out to the Mudir, "number your dead and see how dearly you pay for attacking my house."

"Pay or not pay; we will take it if we have to chew off the corners with our teeth," a strident voice replied.

"Your teeth are too soft and too rotten, Turk!" Vučeta mocked him.

"Then we will beat our way through your walls with our heads!" answered the strident voice.

"Have you had lunch?" Bib pretended to be concerned, and added: "Thank God, we have prepared enough meat for you."

"You will pay for this with your hides!" threatened a soft, sickly sweet voice.

"You know that soon, perhaps even tomorrow, Plav will be Montenegrin?" Vučeta mocked them.

"We know, we know," the sickly sweet voice replied, seemingly indifferent, "but first we will plant your heads on the Plav ramparts."

"While you are playing the fool here," the wounded Tomica mocked them, "some guttersnipe is making love to your *hanum.*"

A third voice, harsh and angry, called: "Your mother . . ."

"I have no mother."

"Then your sister."

163

"I have no sisters, no wives. I have no one."

"Well then, your virgin."

Stanija, too, broke in. "We will send you an ox yoke to take the place of your standard!"

"We regret having to sully our swords. We will tear out your tongue, wasp," the sickly sweet voice replied.

"Your swords! You are more suited to distaffs."

"Tongue, tongue! May it hang out of your jaws!"

"Then it will bark at you."

Battles can and must have an end, but there is no end to a battle of words. Unable to better Stanija's mockery, the attackers were silent for a time.

The day drew to a close; the shadow of the kula crept over the open space in front of the village. The defenders sat down to a meal. They hoped, in the sultriness and the torpor after food, that the fighting might take a turn for the better, if they could only wait for the night.

They were still sitting in the big room when it seemed to them that lightning struck, with a yellow flash and a deafening roar. They lost sight of one another, became invisible in the chalky dust and smoke, amid the smell of gunpowder. They called as the stonework of the kula crashed about them. The Turks had laid a mine. One wall collapsed to ground-floor level, the window and door frames were blown out, the floors sagged, and the stairs were torn away. But, thrown to the ground and stunned, they could not see all this, or the police and the Moslem irregulars who rushed in a horde through the ruined walls. Not one of the defenders had expected anything like this. The first to recover was Tomica, who groped for the door through the smoke and dust, with a yataghan in his left hand. The attackers had already rushed up the stairs and surrounded him with a flock of swords. They cut off his left arm and slit open his liver. He dragged his entrails after him down the stairs. At the doorway he stumbled, and someone cut off his head. His body fell across the threshold, and his head fell into the courtyard. But Stanija did not see that, or how they surrounded and bound Vučeta and Doda before they came to. She had been stunned. When she came to her senses, she found that someone's arm was dragging her down the stairs, shouting: "Here's the big-mouth!"

Isa-beg, tall, graying blond, fifty years old, with a long nose and thin upturned mustaches, came out of the kula behind the bound Doda and Vučeta and kicked Tomica's head aside. "Who's this?" he asked.

No one answered him. At that moment Suljaga came from behind a corner, smiling and stroking his beard, and with the toe of his boot stopped the head, which was rolling down the slope toward him. He turned to Vučeta and asked, in that sickly sweet and indifferent voice that Stanija had already heard: "And you, who are you?"

"Vučeta."

"Then this is Tomica," concluded Suljaga. "Good hunting— but costly. There was no other way. Throw his head where even the ravens will never find it. It's still too early to know what sort of a bag we've got."

They laid out the casualties on the open space before the house —five dead. While they were doing this, Suljaga went up to Stanija and looked her over from top to toe with his mocking and penetrating blue eyes, as if he were buying her, and asked softly: "And you, who are you?"

She did not reply, only turned her head away and gathered her disheveled hair under her kerchief.

"No matter, my beauty," he concluded. "At Plav there is a kula stronger than this one, and somehow or other we shall get to know everything."

In the prison they did not torture Stanija. Suljaga took the view that nothing could be learned from her, and the authorities were anxious to avoid the shame of torturing a woman to no effect. They found out the same day who she was and where she came from; there was a policeman who had been to the Radak village and had seen her in Anto's house. She had been put in solitary confinement and had learned almost nothing at all. But during her sleepless nights she had heard the cries of men who were being tortured and had come to know something from the gossip of the guards who washed the human blood out of the torture chambers.

In her tale, that place of tears, the Plav kula, with its madness and terror, its torture and human blood, including her brother's and her father-in-law's, was even more horrible and unbearable than Grgur imagined it later from Anto's account. According to her, Suljaga and his assistants took no heed of day or night; their minds and bodies were overtaxed by what they planned by day and put into practice by night.

They had released her the day before, about noon, and she had heard that they would soon release Nasto, too, and that he was weak from torture. She had been a continual source of annoyance to the Turkish authorities. "I bayed at them, swore at them, reminded them of all their misdeeds."

In the little town, at Roksanda's, she had found out that on that same day, early in the morning, they had executed a haiduk. She had hastened to the town walls, and on the parapet had recognized her brother's head.

"I walked, and Plav was a desert for me," she said. "I could see nothing but my brother's head, though I would not have recognized it had it not been for his blond hair. I hardened my heart and hid myself in the wheat, and when everything was quiet that evening I stole the head from the parapet, so that the Turks could not mock it and so that I would have something to mourn over."

From her despair, as she was finishing her story, rose a quiet, immeasurable sorrow. "I, too, searched for his murderer, but his tortures and his sister's sufferings no man can avenge or forget."

"Shut your eyes and rest," Grgur advised her, "even if you cannot sleep."

She obeyed him like a child, curled up on the bed, and shut her eyes, suddenly pacified, yet desolate.

"And you never found out who betrayed them?"

She opened her eyes, troubled and lost. "No, I did not find out. Nothing went well for him."

Grgur slipped out quietly. Jelica was waiting for him in the yard, her gaze glassy and bewildered. "How can I help her?"

"See that no one wakes her. Let her sleep, and at least for a moment forget."

Vojin and the other Radaks from the mountain, and Nasto Radak from prison, arrived immediately after lunch in a flame of tension and anger. Vojin had only just come, and was asking with feigned calmness what had happened, when Nasto's indignant and bewailing outcry filled the garden. "The head indeed! Have you thought what that means? Don't you know, or are you fools not to know, that the authorities will burn everything to ashes because of it?"

He walked haltingly and gropingly, leaning on a stick and screwing up his face as if ready to cry out at every movement. His arrival troubled the Radaks even more than that of the head, and they crowded around him to ask about the prison and about Anto's and his tortures. But Grgur, after all that he had heard from Stanija, was angered, lest Nasto should instill more fear into them, and shouted: "Our Serb name and our Serb honor they cannot burn! They burned the Vasojevići three times and Veliko twice—yet today they are free!"

The Radaks were quiet for a moment. Grgur easily lost his temper if anyone insulted Serbdom or its pride.

Stojan rarely took part in Radak dissensions, but now, sitting on the stump of an apple tree, he threw his cap down beside him and remarked: "Let them burn all your fleas and bugs!"

Vojin tried to introduce a little reason. "The Serb name and honor are one thing, but the roasting of Radaks, if we can avoid it, is another."

"No, no. It is all the same!" Grgur stormed. "Enough of this shilly-shallying. The Radaks and Serbdom! Who is not a Serb is not a Radak!"

There was another hush. No one in the depths of his being thought that the Radaks were not Serbs, but most felt that Grgur's exhortations were leading somewhere. Vojin smiled with tired resignation. "A strange sort of Serbdom—fire, suffering, and death."

Encouraged by Vojin's opposition and the wavering and uncertainty, Nasto went on, controlling himself: "We are all Serbs and we are all Radaks. As far as I am concerned, they have nothing to burn. But I saw and suffered all I could, and I have heard what they intend to do: the Radak nest will be destroyed till not a straw or a feather remains! I work for daily hire, from *čitluk* to *čitluk,* but my Radak blood is sacred, and I will not see its nest destroyed. Can we not live peacefully and in unison, as we have always done since there was any trace of us, and even before that?"

"Blood is not water," Grandfather Grgur said in agreement.

"That is to die like an animal and not to live!" shouted Grgur.

"As if the Turks had placed you on the stake," Stojan remarked bitterly to Nasto, and leaped to his feet. But, having forgotten his cap, he sat down again and groped for it in the grass. "Turks, too, are men, some good, some bad; even the fingers of one's hand are not the same. With wolves a man can howl. But there is no unity or peace with bloodthirsty men—not for a Radak, not for a Serb, not for any man!"

Tumult broke out. They shouted, swore at one another, raked up long-forgotten disputes about landmarks, pasture rights, ancestors, women. Vojin rose, making a sign for order with his hand. Then, calmly, he turned to Grgur. "It was not a wise thing to bring the head here."

"And stolen from the authorities," Nasto intervened, sobbing softly because of the pain in his feet when he stamped on the ground.

"Brothers, children." In vain did Grandfather Grgur raise the staff.

"To be burned, to be made homeless, for a dead man's head," wailed the old man Milija. "Better one dead than a hundred dead."

"It doesn't talk, it doesn't walk, and yet it's not dead," broke in Grandfather Pavle, coming out of the storeroom, and he added to Milija scornfully: "It is your lips that are dead, by God in Heaven! And they all say, here below and on high: 'Better one to die than a thousand who stuff themselves like cattle.' You will never satisfy the Turks; the better you, the worse they! Worse than last year, better than next year."

"You must think of something, Grgur—think!" Vojin shouted.

Grgur heard him but went on with his own train of thought: "It is not always the time for common sense. All you Radaks, as many of you as are dead or alive or yet unborn, will come from the earth and return to the earth, to be transformed in its entrails. The head will be buried in our graveyard, in the Radak graveyard."

Shouts burst out; passions flashed like drawn knives.

"The graveyard is not for haiduks, but for Radaks!" "The eternal resting place for Radaks!" "The Turks would never let themselves be made fools of!" "It was sent here to arouse discord

among us!" "The graveyard is not Grgur's garden!" "I, too, have
my share in it!" "The graveyard belongs to no one!" "It is no
one's. Lord have mercy on us!" "In Arsenius' grave—that's the
best place!" "He hasn't got a head anyway!" "Arsenius belongs to
us all!" "To some living, to others dead. Bury it, feed it, the
upper part with us and the lower part with the Turks!" "Shut up,
fool. I will take the staff to you!" "You and your staff—like a
Turkish woman with her breeches!" "We'll spread them out!"
"This is not wasteland, but living people!" "How can you bury
it, when there is no one to sing the service?" "It will sing its own
requiem." "It stinks already." "Each to his own view. To some it
is perfume." "Children, brothers!"

No one had had any lunch, and because Grgur had ordered
that plum brandy be served, as at the burial of one of his own
kin, the discord, added to the stifling heat and the strong drink,
made them angry and quarrelsome.

The women began to pacify them. As if by order, they stopped
pouring plum brandy. And having given vent to their banked-up
fury, troubles, and fears, the men became quieter as the day grew
cooler. They were ashamed of themselves. They became more or-
derly, ceased to interrupt one another, and even those who had
been the harshest and most outspoken began to listen carefully.

"First, let's listen to Nasto; he has come back from the torture,"
said Milija.

Nasto spoke slowly, in considered words, taking care not to
offend or contradict anyone. He turned and twisted, became
prolix and vague, so that no one, not even Grgur, remembered
his actual words, only his general meaning.

"It is my duty to talk, since most of the brothers wish it so. I
come from the torture chamber, Radaks, but my tortures are a
small thing compared with these problems. When we were both
being tortured, I said to Anto: 'First, save the Radaks!' Serbdom
is an empty word if we are all to be dispersed and exterminated.
The world is strait and is a desert without brothers, without kin,
without life. Our empire was destroyed at Kosovo, and yet we
Serbs still hold fast to our faith and our language. Were it for
Kosovo, then let us die, too! But that we be exterminated because
today, rather than tomorrow, we move from under the Sultan to
be under the Prince of Montenegro is a risk that even a blind

169

Radak should not take. We are toilers and laborers, more for others than for ourselves. Let us at least remain where our roots are. The people of Plav are determined to destroy themselves. They have something to fight for—their own lordship. But we must live, we must survive to keep that for which our grandfathers and great-grandfathers lived and died. Think of Anto and his tortures. We have too many martyrs. Their shadows weigh upon us, so we are unable to rejoice in them. I have told you little about my tortures in the kula; yet they were child's play compared with Anto's. Do not barter the living head of the Radak Knez—for you elected him—for the dead head of a stranger, even though it be a Serb's. I am not, may God and my tortures bear witness, against Serb freedom, or even against the revolt. When the hour strikes, there will be no way back for Plav or for the Turks. But when? We are too weak and too isolated. Not even Anto would agree to revolt now, when we are foolish and disunited! Man lives while he lives; then he belongs to mankind, and later he belongs to death—to God or to Satan. We must preserve ourselves and save Anto while he still lives, but first of all from himself, from those Radaks in whom the fury of impatience and intolerance strikes home. Let us measure our every step, to know where we stand. Wisely and patiently! Deceive the enemy and wait till he makes a false move. No one and nothing drives us to choose between death and life, between honor and shame. Let the head go to those who cut it off and to the place ordained for it! Shall we, for the sake of some bones, even though they be hallowed and heroic, give up our young men and our unborn children? Let the living live and let the dead be buried."

It seemed to Grgur that Nasto's eloquence made many of the Radaks waver, even some of those who had supported him. Stojan and his closest, most loyal adherents began to cast glances at him. He still had not raised himself above anger and misery; or perhaps his anger and misery had not yet reached the point where he could display and justify them before the clan. Luckily, the majority of the Radaks had not yet demanded that he speak. They wanted purer, more straightforward, words. They asked Vojin to speak.

Vojin came into the center, looked at all of them, and then, as always, spoke reasonably, as much to himself as to those present. But the sense of his speech was clear and memorable.

"I am no chronicler; still less am I eloquent, even less do I look for the easy way out. I do not underestimate life and reputation —there is no ducat without two faces. Reputation without life is dead, life without reputation is sorrowful. A man who does not smirch his honor lives even after his death. A man with unsullied honor fears neither God nor Satan; by living thus he builds himself a solid and eternal foundation. In this, all men are equal, rich and poor, all faiths and all peoples. We cannot give back the head to the Turks; other clans would call us Turkish toadies, and our descendants for generations would be ashamed of what we had done. Nor can we bury it in the graveyard; it is not of our blood, and we might, in these evil times, bring the Turkish oppressors about our ears. I do not know what else to do than to bury the head somewhere secretly, to await the time for both the head and ourselves. Or, still better, send it to Montenegro, whence it came. In everything that we do, Anto must still be in our minds. Our clan and all Serbdom and each one of us are with him in his tortures. If we abandon Anto thoughtlessly and shamefully, there will be no end to our torments. We will suffer in honor, in memory, and in recollection, and to such suffering there is no measure and no end! Every bird returns finally to its nest, and it would be best for Stanija, accompanied by Stojan, who knows the passes and the lonely ways, to take the head to its own kin. In truth, it is far and it is hot, but there the head will be welcomed and will rest in peace. There is no scale to judge how much each man is a Serb and how much a Radak, even as there is no measure for life or death. Serbdom is our hope and Radak is our way of life; there is no hope without life and no life without hope. Between these two there is no choice! For each of these a measure must be found at any moment. That is hard, the hardest thing of all—as life and death. But so it must be. Why are we men? Whoever knows how to judge and to measure is a man. Let the free Serb head go to the free Serb land! Why should there be the shadow of slavery and dissension over its martyrdom? The measure is all men—we who are here now, those who were here before, and those who will be here after us. We should, we must,

171

be united. If we cannot do better, then let us do what has for ages past been agreed—that is, to follow the reason and the will of the majority. Reason and will alone are what we have freely from God."

Listening to Vojin's speech, Grgur noticed how many of those who had wavered at Nasto's words, those whom until then he had regarded as supporters of the revolt, now smiled joyously. Something in that, something of Vojin's reasoned balance, and, most of all, the need to declare himself openly to those who believed in him helped him to calm down and to give form to his thoughts.

"It is true—everything has its measure. But men and measures change, now this way, now that. What was true yesterday is not so today and is still less so tomorrow. Today Serbdom is the measure for all. It is life, it is honor, it is existence, it is hope! For all these things Serbdom is today the measure. Without Serbdom we cannot appear before God, and, may God forgive me, perhaps it alone today is able to defend us against Satan. We Radaks have been given a chance such as no one else has: to preserve the head of a Serb hero and martyr. For that, we shall now, and always, be linked with Serbdom. But with what Serbdom? Not merely with faith and language and Serbian hopes, but with Serbdom that sheds its blood and burns in the flames. Human life is filled with suffering. A man lives as long as he endures in death, as long as his deeds are remembered and recounted. You mention my father; you burden my conscience with him. And you have no idea with what pain I bear his tortures! But if my father bound my eyes with the black kerchief of shame, then he would not be my father, and all his tortures would have been in vain. Should my brother or my son do the like, then he is no longer my brother or my son! But my father will not do this; he will never betray Serbdom and the Radaks. Let the Turks grind him to powder; every pinch of it will be he. Even in madness he will be a Serb and a Radak—manly honor driven mad. I know my father. His heart would break if I could not unite the Radaks. But what can I do and how shall I do it when some choose between Serbdom and life, Serbdom and the Radaks? The Serbdom of my father is from ages past; for him the seed of Serb and of Radak is one and the same. That sustains him among men and amid torture. And my Serbdom, too, is a need and a hope. The Serb seed is deeper within me than the Radak! And what is there to support me? Am I not rending myself in pieces? Is it easy to resign oneself to a father being tortured for delusive hopes and unknown destinies? But my Serb conscience is able to support both my own and his tortures, even if never again shall I find absolution and peace. When life has become a dueling ground and a battlefield—and so it is for me and for most of us—then for that alone one exists and thinks and believes. But do not call on the majority and its wishes and its reasons, do not drive both yourself and the majority to madness. If I did not believe that what I have in my mind is good for the majority, for all the Radaks, I, too, would shout: 'Majority, majority, majority!' Was there at first a majority to support Miljan Vukov and Marko Miljanov? Only a handful of madmen and rebels—those were all who rallied to them! The majority is those who build the world and change it. The bones of our ancestors, shamed by servitude, call us to battle and to hatred! The children call us, that they will not stammer their first words in gloom and darkness! Our seed calls from loins and wombs, that it need not fear the day and the earth on which it will fall! You say evil is everywhere; on this side agas and on that chieftains. Without evil a man does not live. I, too, know that. But also I cannot live without good men. Ever since there have been men, there have been fighters for justice and for freedom. And the immortal dead, too, live. The head lives; it fell for what does not pass away —for Serbdom, for life, for men. It was but one, yet from it shall arise a hundred still finer and more heroic. I have thought about his life. Vučeta was a haiduk, a weathercock, good only for killing and plundering Turks. But he has ransomed his sins by his martyr's death and has surpassed his human weaknesses. Serbdom is too narrow for such a head. The world is space enough for it. Let no man speak of Kosovo to whom it is not present every day and every moment! Let us link the head with Arsenius; let us comfort the past with our Serbian hope. A man becomes a hero by heroic deeds. With the head rooted among us, there is no one who can root us out. It will send out branches, and from those branches flowers will blossom!"

Intoxicated by his words, spoken and unspoken, and by his thoughts, uttered and unuttered, Grgur picked up the head, together with the cloth, and raised it above the heads of the Radaks. "Who is willing, let him come with me to bury it! If the living wish to live, then the dead, too, have the right not to be kept waiting!"

The cloth covered his arms to the elbows, so that it seemed, as he walked down the garden paying no heed to the men around him, to their discontent or their approval, as if the head were leading him. He walked carefully; the head prevented him from seeing the path before him. But in the valley below him he vaguely saw the graveyard, looking like a flock of tired birds around the green pine planted in far-off days, perhaps at the time of the first Radak grave. The head already stank unbearably, but he went on, growing accustomed to the nausea, as if it were hallowed.

Only when he went down from the meadow to the road that led downward into the valley, did Grgur notice that the commotion among the Radaks had ceased. About a third of the men had followed him, as well as women and children. Nearest to him, as he had expected, was Stojan, with Petrana, sullen and almost angry. Each was leading a child. After them followed others, among them Grandfather Pavle, bareheaded and bare-breasted, moving like a sleepwalker. Vojin, too, had come. But he had halted at the end of the garden, open-mouthed, bewildered, his broad arms dangling as if no longer part of his body. Jelica stood beside him, pale, rigid, stunned. There, too, was Grandfather Grgur, with his inevitable staff, made stupid by old age, melancholy, and lack of understanding. Higher up, at the top of the garden, Nasto had risen and, waving his arms, was proving something to the hesitant, wavering Radaks. The old man Milija, standing beside him, approved what he was saying and struck the earth with his cudgel. Between the fruit trees and the petrified ranks of the Radaks, Stamena was moving toward him. She had only just come down from the mountain with the children, and Grgur had not been able to exchange a word with her. She had her arm around Stanija's waist and was leading little Anto by the hand. Though the two women normally could not stand one another, in moments of great misfortune and sacrifice Stamena suppressed her aversions as if they did not exist. Behind her came Trifun, leading his younger brother, Todor, tired and querulous from drowsiness and the long walk.

Grandfather Pavle, suddenly alive to the situation, shouted to Stanija: "Mourn, poor soul! No task should be without a song." Stanija roused herself, shook loose from Stamena's arm, and gathered the ends of the kerchief on her head. In a bitter, angry voice, ringing yet tired, she began to compare her dead brother to the sun, to a sword, to an eagle, and the earth to a darkness and a curse, casting scorn on Radak cowardice and exalting Radak heroism.

The head and its burial divided and distributed the Radaks to such an extent that those who had listened to Nasto ceased to go on guard duty, and even began to collect and store a certain amount of tribute and taxes, though it was not time for either. On the other hand, those opposed to them, Grgur and his supporters, did not want to celebrate the Radak *slava*, for St. Ilija, out of respect and grief for Anto.

The Radaks began to call one another by names that till then they had called only their worst enemies, men of foreign faiths and tribes: toady, turncoat, lickspittle, yellow belly, outsider, infidel, bastard, renegade. With that began mutual exaggeration of one another's vices and virtues. Grgur's supporters began to look on Nasto as a Turkish informer and to conceal from Vojin, who had not broken with Nasto, even things of no significance either for them or for the revolt, for—who knows?—today it is not important, but tomorrow it might be! Grgur began to treat Grandfather Grgur as if he were in his second childhood, while with the simpleton, Grandfather Pavle, he noted only his remarkable perspicacity. Everything was confused and out of joint. Time began to be reckoned as "before the head" or "after the head," which was either cursed or exalted, a symbol of either fate or revelation. The Radak council broke up. When Grgur was present, Vojin and Milija were silent or discussed matters of no importance, such as damage caused by cattle. Intolerance and suspicion grew to such an extent that Grgur began to be haunted by the thought that Vojin's frankness and indecision showed a cunning and selfish ambition to win the Radaks over to himself. All the Radaks felt as if under a curse, and could find neither refuge nor resting place.

But the strangest change of all, to Grgur and the other Radaks, took place in Stanija.

When Arsenius' tomb was opened, the head placed there, and the stone replaced, she took Grgur's little knife and, as a sign of mourning, cut off her heavy black plaits and laid them lengthwise on the grave. From that moment, she no longer keened or lamented; she seemed filled with peace and calm, bound finally to her home and to Grgur. She became more devoted to household tasks, and even to Stamena. She continued to mourn for her brother, but she did so with quiet tears and a stifled yet unquenchable longing for vengeance. It was as if she had realized the finality of Vučeta's death and that with the cutting of her hair, she had cut away her past, the living threads that bound her to her kin. She became more reserved, sometimes whispering softly to herself, looking with inflexible, avid gaze into some gloomy depths known to her alone.

Akan, her husband, possibly under her influence, revealed to Grgur sides of his character hitherto unknown; his skill as a trader was transformed into a no less considered but silent determination for a settling of accounts with the Turks. He suggested to Grgur that he might abandon his home and the clan and settle in Montenegro if revolt and liberation did not come. He had managed to get enough money for the bribe from the sale of the stock, but he had returned disillusioned with the monks of Dečani; half of them were fattened by good living and the other half played hermit in the caves. They felt that if they preserved the shrine and its beauty from plunderers, they had done enough for Serbdom.

Akan's determination for revolt, till then scarcely perceptible, and his personality, till then overshadowed by his elder brother's, burst out with unsuspected sharpness when Roksanda and her mother-in-law, Stojna, came from Plav one morning before Assumption to get the bribe money.

At first the brothers wondered at Roksanda's coming, but were glad of it. The troubles had prevented them from making the formal visit due to her as a young bride, and she had not before been to visit them. Though Plav was near, all sorts of bandits and evildoers infested the roads, so that it was dangerous even for older women to pass. Nonetheless, her dress astonished and offended them, though they knew that, according to the custom of the townspeople, she wore the costume of a Turkish woman.

Stamena and Stanija, who did not like Roksanda, mocked and jeered at her when they saw her wrapped in a black cloak and covered by a veil.

Stojna hastened to explain everything. She had brought Roksanda with her specially, so that none of the Radaks would doubt where the Radak money was going. And they had been accompanied to the borders of the Radak lands by the servants of Smail-beg. Indeed, the brothers had noticed, and kept an eye on, three armed Moslems waiting in the shade by the graveyard. Stojna also pointed out that the costume of the Turkish women was more beautiful than the heavy blouses and coarse skirts of the peasants.

Peering continually, her big green eyes darkened by the gloom of the storeroom, Roksanda complained, and boasted to her ill-humored brothers: "I myself will take the bribe to Smail-beg."

"Why you?" Grgur burst out. "What have you to do with the Turks and with Smail-beg?"

"That's the way it must be. Mother Stojna says so. It may be that they will not admit Simka Dimčova if I don't bring it."

"Does your husband know of this?"

"Well—yes, he knows."

"What do you mean 'well'?"

"He knows."

"And he says nothing?"

"Well—he says nothing. He doesn't like it. But Aunt Simka says: 'It must be this way. Everyone goes to Smail-beg.' "

Akan, till then silent and motionless, leaning against the door, moved slowly and remarked sarcastically: " 'Everyone'! But you aren't everyone. You are our sister, Anto's daughter, a Radak girl, and a Serb."

Roksanda said nothing, her pale, gold-flecked lashes veiling her green eyes, which changed quickly and easily from one expression to another, from joy to sorrow. She was now, as a bride, prettier than she had been as a girl. She had inherited chestnut hair and green eyes with tiny flecks in them from her uncle, and from Anto her slender figure, long limbs, and pale face, which had only a touch of color on the cheekbones. This gave a sense of breeding to her rounded, not bony, fragility. She was conscious of her unpeasant-like beauty and now paid heed to her every movement, every

177

word, as if she were afraid to blemish the order she had established and controlled. She was still the same Roksanda, accustomed only to household duties, the one girl in the family, spoiled by her father, brothers, uncle, grandfathers, the whole clan, because of her beauty and the richness and sensitivity of her singing. Like her father and Grgur, she was obstinate and unyielding in whatever she made up her mind to do, and was inclined to sudden violent outbreaks of fury, followed by sullen reconciliations. It seemed to Grgur as if he were speaking to another self. Yet she had changed; she used town words and spoke in a modulated voice, holding in her hands an embroidered kerchief. She had even acquired a strange habit of licking her soft, fresh lips with the tip of her tongue as she spoke.

He burst out: "Don't you know why Smail-beg demands that you and only you bring him the money? Don't you know who he is and what sort of man he is?"

She said nothing, obstinately looking aside, away from her brothers.

"Smail-beg is a profligate, a spendthrift. That is why he calls you; he wants both you and the money," Akan explained maliciously.

"You're not to go," Grgur shouted, jumping up from his stool and striding about the little room. "You're not to go. Even if our father never gets out alive! My sister to become a plaything of the begs to save Radak lives! No, no, and no!"

She still kept silent, not because she was thinking it over, but from obstinacy, from, Grgur knew, some final conviction of her own.

"Why don't you say something? You heard what I said!"

"What can she say—except to her own shame?" Akan interjected.

Later on, Stojna, by her flow of words and worldly experience, to some extent pacified and calmed down the implacability of the brothers. Smail-beg, from one of the richest and most influential families in Plav, was not a bored and lustful libertine, as were many others from the wealthy and wanton houses of the Plav and Gusinje begs, but a skillful and cunning go-between. He did not abduct girls or play about with peasant women. Instead, he squandered huge sums of money on pretty gypsies and chased after handsome dancers as far as Skopje and Bitola. He was a connoisseur of horses and harness, of fine clothes and parties which sometimes lasted several days. Youths got their first taste of life and love from Smail-beg among picked company, and women sang the praises of his beauty and skill in song, dance, and hospitality. It was through him that young men acquired reputation and refinement and the marks of good breeding. Nor was Simka Dimčova, wealthy and skilled in business, a woman of easy virtue whom all might buy, but a townswoman with a taste for the most refined pleasures and entertainments, who attracted young men and ne'er-do-wells, who courted her and sang songs about her. Only rarely and by stealth did she grant her favors, and then only to those who could further her reputation by their ardor, their good looks and openhandedness, and who were at the same time honorable men who would never boast of their success. It was through Simka that one entered the society of the Turkish ladies and learned the most refined and leisured ways of life, ways in which the Radaks, insofar as they knew anything about them, could see only profligacy and sloth.

But at that moment the brothers knew only the shameful and evil aspect of Smail-beg and Simka Dimčova and held to their irrational and intolerant attitude. Finally, Roksanda replied softly but obstinately: "You're talking hearsay. They live differently down there and look on things differently. And the money does not go to Smail-beg."

"But you are going!" hissed Grgur.

"Don't talk rubbish," Akan broke in. "He's after you, all right. He has wasted his inheritance on gypsies and whores and is ready for pretty women. He is sated, and his corrupt heart craves peasant modesty and simplicity."

As if she heard only a part of what her brothers said, Roksanda went on: "The money goes to someone above Smail-beg and Suljaga—perhaps to the Kajmekam. Only, that not even the black earth must know."

"The black earth! Better it swallowed you up! To the Kajmekam the money and to Smail-beg—my sister!" Grgur strode up and down.

Her *dimije* rustling, Roksanda went out crying. "And my father is in prison! And I must live like other women!"

"You're not worrying overmuch about your father," Grgur shouted after her.

Akan spread out his arms. "It's all useless! She's made up her mind; she'll go to Smail-beg with or without the bribe. The town Serbs have lived too long with the Turks, and the life there has seduced her—parties and every kind of amusement."

"She has disgraced us!" groaned Grgur, and then called out: "Eh, Anto Radak, if you only knew how and by what means we are saving you!"

Stojna clattered into the storeroom, overwhelming them with her words. "You thought the worst at once and have all set upon my Rosa! Why, in God's name? Forgive me, God, my sinful words! Would I take my own daughter-in-law to another man? No, no. So it must be, so it has to be! Even greater and richer men go to Smail-beg for aid and service, both Serbs and Turks. It is an honor! It is not as if anyone were asking him, or entreating him, or bringing him presents; he will have mercy on her youth, her beauty, and her sorrow. And she will not go alone. One of us, Simka or I, will go with her. So make ready the money. We are late, and they are waiting for us."

She sat down on a cushion, tucking her feet under her, and explained to them who and what Smail-beg and Simka Dimčova were, concluding mildly: "You are still barbarians."

Though they were not convinced by her account and her conclusions, the brothers were reconciled; there was no other way. But their anger and bitterness again broke out when they remained alone to count out the money. They cursed their sister, swore at Stojna's lies and volubility, and resolved never to cross Roksanda's threshold.

"She has made up her mind to dishonor us," Grgur concluded when they had finished the counting.

Akan did not reply but, thrusting a handful of gold coins into a purse, which he put in his jacket, whispered, winking: "There's some left over. Let them find it."

Grgur was astonished at Stamena's acceptance of Roksanda's decision. Accompanying him in the evening to the cave, she, as had now become their custom, halted him in the place of their St. Peter's Day passion and, opening his jacket to bury her face in the scent and hair of his chest, whispered, without mentioning Roksanda's name: "How do we know in this desert how she lives and what she does?"

Grgur, taking her by the waist and leaning over her, did not waver in his opinion. "Let her live as she likes and how she likes! But my life will never again be mixed with hers."

The irreparable loss of Roksanda pained him. He used to caress her, do small favors for her, but, little by little, memory by memory, the past fell away, driven out by pain and heaviness. He knew, in advance, that because of her he would have to turn his eyes away from the Radaks, especially from Vojin, who would pretend to know nothing but whose silence would reproach him for what was happening and for the way in which the Radak Knez was being ransomed. Suspecting his bitterness, Stamena kissed him and slipped under him, murmuring: "Let them all abandon us. We still have each other."

The Radaks began the waiting for Anto's return, a monotony filled with uncertainty, doubt, and bitterness. Forgetting their differences and dissensions, they began to look forward to his return and to place all their hopes in him.

On Nativity Day, in formal dress, in harmony with the autumn morning, which was rich in gold and silver, the Radaks, young and old, gathered in the valley by the graveyard to welcome their knez. The day before, still suspicious of the Turkish authorities, they had sent to Plav only the old man Milija and Grandfather Pavle, who were to get Anto at Mitar Drndar's. But because Anto could not sit on a horse, the old men had to wait until a litter was made ready and porters hired. Their procession came out of the mouth of the gorge into the open valley only about noon. The whole clan went wild; they wept, laughed, yelled, and exulted.

Although almost blinded by his meeting with the clan, by the sun, and by the sight of his own land, Anto managed to find a fine, encouraging word for every Radak. He looked around at the peaks, the streams, the ravines, and the copses, calling each of them, as each Radak, by name. Reawakening from his battered, darkened memory, each became young again through his tears and his exaltation. They played joyously, yet bent toward him solicitously and with sorrow. For them, too, Anto found welcoming words; for the copses turning yellow, the orchards heavy with fruit, the undergrowth burgeoning, the brooks lamenting, the peaks towering above him. Men and lands and trees and waters were transformed and interwoven, and he mixed them all together, unable and unwilling to hold back his words, smiles, and tears.

"It was worth passing through all the tortures for this," he mumbled, embracing with arms widespread both people and the chalice of the valley. They set him down by the graveyard to look at him, to embrace him and to share his sorrow. One after the other they fell upon their knez, who was inhumanly emaciated and had a transparent pallor and livid scars on his cheeks and his blue lips. They kissed him on face, breast, or hands.

"I was afraid for you—I know you," he told Grgur tenderly, as he kissed him on cheek and hand, "in case you did something rash."

Vojin, however, he clasped to his breast, and he raised his voice so that all could hear him. "And you, Vojin, my son, I relied upon you when I was there in the kula. I relied on your good sense."

He caressed his grandsons—Trifun, Todor, and Anto—and spoke gently to them. "How you have grown, my little pine trees."

With Stojan he joked. "Have more game fallen to your bullets and more women to your strength?"

When his father, Grandfather Grgur, tearfully clasped him to his breast, Anto placed a hand on his head, caressing him like a child.

He hugged his wife, Milena, and said, without embarrassment, before all who were there: "Of you I thought most of all; I owe most to you."

He let Nasto kiss him, and was mildly reproachful: "Every man is weak; some in one way, some in another."

After he had greeted all of them and they had sympathized with him and expressed their joy at his return, the Radaks lifted the litter and carried their knez carefully and slowly, as if they were carrying a reliquary, pressing silently around him lest they lose any word or movement of his.

Anto, though leaning back on a cushion and lifted and carried onward by their enthusiasm, spoke to them in a weak and faltering voice, as if something had moved him, or as if he had just recollected something. The Radaks long recalled, but variously repeated and still more variously interpreted, his words, both said and unsaid.

"Everything by which men are exalted and in which they must place their trust cannot compensate for even a hundredth part of the tortures which all men must undergo. As long as a man believes and hopes, not even torture is too hard for him. Revolts, weapons, spilling human blood, and rebellion are great evils. One must pray to God and keep one's weapons ready. In an evil world there is no other way to defend one's life and honor from evil men. A drop of human blood is worth more than the whole world, and for spilling it there is no absolution. Forgiveness is peace and serenity. We must forgive our enemies and our torturers, but we must not deny our God and we must not betray all that we long for. Eloquence and power are in hatred; when they are extinguished then life and reason, too, are extinguished. They have trodden underfoot our martyrs and justice, both human and divine. We cannot meet with them again except through massacre and death. We cannot be other than Radaks and Serbs; without that we should not exist. Happiness and peace lie in love and forgiveness; yet faith and progress lie in hatred and war. Without justice and manly honor, man and existence cannot be and the struggle is difficult, inhuman, and unjust. Forgiveness heals all wounds, though evil drives out evil. It cannot be otherwise—love and hatred, forgiveness and vengeance."

Despite his yearning for his father and his emotion at the thought of his torture, Grgur was not interested in his father's thoughts. It seemed to him that were he to accept them, despite their cobwebbed and varied threads, he would never be able to control the underlying Radak conflicts and bitterness. The old man Milija, as they moved away from the graveyard, waved his stick and shouted: "He has spoken! No dead head is worth harsh words; how much less quarrels among brothers!" To this, Stojan retorted still louder and in a jeering voice: "You forget what Knez Anto said a while before at the graveyard: there is a link between heroism and honor, Serbdom and the Radaks, Vučeta and Arsenius!"

Grgur's uncertainty and confusion were increased because the faces of the Radaks, according to what pleased each of them in Anto's words, were bathed in victorious joy and radiance. Each took from Anto's speech and reflections whatever pleased him most and whatever could not support the views and attitudes of the opposing faction. It was as if from that expanse, from the chalice out of which they moved slowly toward the clear skies above them, they drank in also the intoxicating sweetness of his words and thoughts.

Nasto, before he turned off the road to his cottage, forced his way through the throng toward Anto, chattering and leaping about with excitement, which for a moment flooded over him. But Stojan was waiting for him, and whenever he caught something that pleased him would smile victoriously, raise his head, with its pointed nose, and look from right to left as if to say: "Aha, did you hear that?"

Only for Vojin did it seem as if nothing had changed. He walked as always, with heavy, measured tread, upright, his head slightly raised, and with an enigmatic, scarcely perceptible smile.

Jelica, too, walked with unchanged gait, smooth and easy as a deer, touching the ground carefully, in order not to offend it, her slender body swaying, her small pointed breasts quivering.

Exalted and smiling to herself, Stanija kept one hand on Anto's litter, as if she alone had the right to do so, as if she feared that it, with its precious, hallowed burden, might escape her.

All of them paid heed only to Anto, carefully identifying themselves with him, as though to equate their own consciousness, their own deeds, with his words and thoughts. Grgur's eyes met Stamena's. She looked toward him, with slightly narrowed eyes in a serious and clouded face, but with a sly, mocking quiver of her upper lip. *Do you see what is happening? Do you see what has happened to us?* Her eyes spoke to him, only to him, in no way frightened or bewildered, on the frontiers of grief and laughter. When the procession turned into the meadow and broke up amid the hedges, the blackthorn, and the dog roses, she left the women who had been walking behind the litter and, scarcely touching the coarse grasses with the tips of her sandals, her skirt swishing through the thorns, came up behind Grgur and whispered: "He is not what he used to be!"

Grgur whispered back to her, seriously and secretly, as if revealing a great and terrible truth: "He is the same. I know him well. Only he has in some ways fallen to pieces since he was in prison. Now one side of him speaks and now another."

PART TWO

BEGS AND SERFS

Bitter Sherbet

Muna was afraid of the dark, and Nura had to snuggle up close to her and whisper something nice, or anything at all, to help her go to sleep. Muna knew that Nura, too, was afraid, and that she drove away her troubles and slowly fell asleep by taking Muna in her arms and telling her stories. But both behaved as though it were Nura who was the brave one. She was certainly the bolder; she made up her mind to go without hesitation to the corner by the door to drink water and, in the evening, to go down the dark, narrow stairs without a candle into the courtyard, into the kitchen, to see Kara-Djula.

These night fears of the twin sisters had existed for some time. They had begun a year, perhaps eighteen months, before, after the fighting with Montenegro was over, but they had grown less since the spring, since the time when their father, Omer-beg, had brought his second wife, Bulbul, from Salonika. Though the two facts—the fear of the dark and Bulbul—had no connection with one another, or at least the sisters were unable to see one, they linked the lessening of their fears with the arrival of Bulbul, with their hatred for her and with the unhappiness of their mother, Biba.

At that time, four or five months after the fighting had ceased, Muna and Nura were just fourteen; their breasts had begun to swell, their arms and legs to grow longer, and shining golden lights to appear in their hair. Grandfather Murat-beg and the other members of the household had come to the conclusion that

189

they were now young women; young men's eyes rested on them and theirs on young men. So they were shut up behind walls and lattices. From that time they could go out, usually on visits to relatives, only with faces covered and accompanied by one of the older servants.

But the ceremony of their entry into womanhood was postponed for a whole year, because it was not known to whom Plav and Gusinje were to belong, and the fighting with the Montenegrins might break out again at any time. And their father did not want to admit that his marriage with Bulbul had embittered his first wife, their mother. Perhaps Grandfather Murat-beg did not want to give two banquets, for in the household they were economizing greatly on everything. Only about a score of his many serf villages remained to him, and they were ripe for revolt. Nonetheless, friends and relations had congratulated Nura and Muna on their entry into womanhood and at the same time had offered congratulations on the arrival of Bulbul. For the sisters, this was neither just nor pleasant. But they kept silent about it, betraying their thoughts to each other by glances.

Bulbul was a foreigner, a beastly Asiatic Turk who did not know how to speak Bosnian, or show any desire to learn it, as she should have. But the most painful thing, and one they could not forget, was that their mother, made bitter by the coming of this second wife, did not rejoice at her daughters' entry into womanhood.

Muna's and Nura's own joy at entering womanhood, their trepidation concerning love and passion and the expectation of a bridegroom in two or three years, was darkened by the fear of fresh fighting or, much worse, a revolt of the serfs in the nearby villages and an attack by the Montenegrins on Plav itself. That was a continual, ever-present fear. It was as if the Visitor mountains, whose tremendous mass could be seen at a glance, might fall upon the town and the fields and waters around it, and they were only awaiting the day and the moment when it would take place.

In the little town, and especially in their household, everyone knew what fighting meant, what it was like. All of them had lost brothers, fathers, or other relatives; everyone had someone who had fled from deserted towns and villages; and everyone remembered or knew how, twenty years before, Kolašin had been burned to the ground. In its strong stone kulas six hundred souls, for the most part women and children, had been burned, while every man capable of holding a rifle had been killed.

Under the pressure of the Great Powers, the voivode Miljan Vukov had been compelled quickly to evacuate Kolašin. He had taken it, in a surprise attack, on the day of St. Ilija, the fiery saint, and when he left, it was as if he had relied on the Saint's help in setting fire to the city. The Moslems, among them the twins' uncle Ahmet-beg, had returned to the devastated town. Now, after so many years and all the stories, it was not possible to determine what had been the most terrible: the white Kolašin kulas burning like torches among the green hills, with the heart-rending screams of women and children rising, with their smoke, to the heavens; or Kolašin in ashes and ruins, with headless corpses in the wastelands, the fruit trees burned or cut down, the mothers scrabbling in the embers for the bones of their children, the sur-viving children begging for a crust of bread, the unforgettable sour stink of burned and rotting human flesh.

The razing of Kolašin was perhaps the first story the twins re-membered. And its impression had not grown dim; the smoke, the flames, the cries, had not lessened in the telling, and in their memory still smoldered the horrifying tales of Uncle Ahmet-beg.

On the eve of the attack, Ahmet-beg had been assigned to the kula of Zeko Martinović. This was the strongest place after the Mušović inn, which, surrounded by walls, rose above the steep banks of the Pažnja. After watching Kolašin burn, he and his friends had been able to slip out in the evening and escape. The Mušović inn was burned, too, and, about noon, his own house, beside the little Svinjača River, with his family in it.

Afterward, Grandfather Murat-beg had helped this son-in-law to settle in Plav, and gave him his niece in marriage to console him. Murat-beg also wanted to continue to be kin to the famous Kapetanović line, to which Ahmet-beg belonged. Rash, embit-tered, and impetuous, Ahmet-beg had started life anew at Plav, and it was there that his son, Arslan, now eighteen and studying at Stambul, was born.

Ahmet-beg was now in his fifties. His coarse black hair was just beginning to gray at the temples, and an occasional silver hair could be seen in the glistening black of his long mustaches. He was a fine figure of a man, tall, slender, and still vigorous. But his thin, yellowed face and compressed lips, and especially his sinewy hands, whose thin fingers and long nails betrayed his noble breeding, quivered and twisted without reason, unexpectedly, and made him look tortured, worn out, and lost. He walked jerkily, with steps too tiny for his long, thin legs, and talked in shrill bursts, suddenly breaking off.

Muna and Nura were afraid, at every meeting with him, that as soon as he opened his mouth something terrible would come from his quivering lips and the black hole of his small mouth. In his tales, not only were children transformed into fiery shrieks and women into lighted torches, but also it seemed that this might happen, at Plav, to known and dear persons, even to them. But despite their chill apprehension, there was an irresistible curiosity that drew the twins to him. Why do men die? they wanted to know. Why do they hate one another like demons and fight with one another? The Montenegrins and the serfs—those bedraggled, dirty, simple, good-natured, talkative, and courteous peasants, who in the autumn brought tribute of wheat and fruit and wooden vessels of honey and cream, and in the spring young lambs and fresh cheeses—would they attack, demolish, and consign to the flames the white kulas and slender summerhouses, and kill bold and strong young men?

Ahmet-beg's eyes, shining feverishly and dark as wells in which the water is always disturbed, both frightened and attracted Muna and Nura as they submitted docilely to the caresses of his cold, bony fingers on their cheeks and heads, shuddering at his ill-omened words: "Grow, flourish, become more beautiful—to your and our sorrow!" They did not know, and could not imagine, a world without hatred, oppression, wars, and burnings. It was as if people were only distinguishable by how they imagined evil and defended themselves from evil.

Like everybody else, Grandfather Murat-beg hated the Montenegrins like the plague, like devils, but marveled secretly at their heroism and the ability of their leader, Miljan Vukov. The serfs, however, he hated in a different way. A number of serf villages, among them some of his, had broken away during the last war and were already united to Montenegro. So his hatred of the serfs was open and scornful, without a trace of admiration, as toward riffraff or scum who had only been waiting to show their ingratitude for the good done them for ages past. Those who had not yet been taken from him he regarded in a different light. He was uncertain whether to be severe or lenient, ruthless or merciful. One day he would say: "Give a serf an inch and he will take an ell!" and on another: "Had we behaved better toward them they would not have raised a hand against us!" But he was not horrified by massacres and burnings. It was as if the world could not exist without them, as if they were something self-evident, which arose naturally between Moslems and Orthodox or, as he put it, between Turks and Serbs. "Either the Serb must be submissive or the Turk must be exterminated."

Their father, Omer-beg, hated the Montenegrins and the serfs, too, with a sullen, deep-rooted, and callous hatred. Perhaps the reason for this was that he, realizing for some time that there was no hope of pacifying the serfs, had turned to trade, an occupation that their grandfather did not consider quite worthy of his family and reputation. Obviously, it was not all the same to their father if the Montenegrins came, but he considered that, fortified by his faith, his pleasures, and his disdain, it would be possible to live and to go on living without serfs, and perhaps even under Montenegrin rule.

The attitude of their uncles Izet-beg and Smail-beg was quite different, too.

Smail-beg hated, but with a cunning, concealed hatred. He was determined to die for his faith and his leisured way of life. He was so devoted to parties, to horses, and to flirtations that no other way of life was conceivable to him. Though he was nearing his fifties, his taste for luxury and refinement had become more confirmed, and his uncontrolled passions broke out more openly and crudely. He was unmarried; when he was a young man, his father had arranged a marriage for him, but he had emancipated himself and driven away his wife. That had strengthened him even more in his devil-may-care attitude and profligacy. He went to war gladly, looking on it as on a party or a picnic.

Only Izet-beg, wrapped up in himself, in his hunting, his dogs, and his guns, did not seem to know how to hate, though in battle he was courageous and full of initiative. Whenever arguments flared up about the Montenegrins, he would keep silent, usually playing with the bare, double-edged knife he always wore across his stomach, fastened to his belt by a little silver chain. Taciturn, almost unnoticed, he would quickly and quietly withdraw from the conversation, putting his knife once more in its filigreed sheath.

For the twins, all hatreds were measured by that of Ahmet-beg. In its vivid intensity, its bitterness and fire, it embraced and consumed almost every other feeling, every other thought. The horror of that hatred was that Ahmet-beg believed in the inevitability of Turkish—that is to say, his own—annihilation. But his desire to fight, to exterminate the Montenegrins and all the Christians and serfs, burned the fiercer, though even he knew that the lordship of the begs and the power of the Turkish Empire was founded upon them. He had spent a full twenty years in ambushing, burning, plundering, and killing. Peace meant nothing to him, except in the winter months or while his wounds healed. For him, those Montenegrins who, from generation to generation, had inherited and extended the never-ending, senseless war against everything Turkish and Islamic were inescapable. For them, war had become their principal task, by which they obtained food, land, joy, and material for their heroic songs. The disquiet of Ahmet-beg's shifting eyes proclaimed their unforgotten assault on the white city of Kolašin. The women and men and youths from the interminable black mountains, with axes and staves, with dry branches, straw, and lighted torches, where did they all come from, as if war, hunger, and disease had multiplied them?

Puffing smoke from his short pipe, with its amber mouthpiece, Ahmet-beg would say with strangled impatience: "They will win. They will annihilate us. But until that happens we will make mincemeat of plenty of them!" It seemed as if he did not believe that anyone could dare to be joyful. Even when he plunged into his icy depression, with drawn lips and eyes gleaming sullenly, the memory of his burning kula, his sons, his mother, and his wife shrieking for him in vain was never extinguished.

Below that kula, the shrunken Svinjača had flowed over pebbles, while flames and cries burst out among the gardens. Ahmet-beg's six-year-old son, Arslan, fleeing from the flames, with fiery wings on his shoulders, had jumped into one of its deeper pools,

just below the kula, and had quickly sunk. A huge, powerful
Montenegrin had leaped from behind the burning kula, torn off
his shoes, and hurriedly unbuttoned his white cloth gaiters; they
had countless clasps, a whole eternity of them. Then he had
plunged into the swirling waters and fished around for the boy
with a paling torn from the broken garden fence. Until then it
had not been clear to Ahmet what the Montenegrin was trying to
do—save the boy or take his head. But he had seized the boy by
the hand and, forgetting his shoes on the bank, carried him in his
arms and laid him down in an open space above the stream.
There he had tried to revive him, first placing him across his
knees to let the water run out, and then raising and lowering his
arms. But it had been too late and in vain; Arslan had remained
motionless. The Montenegrin, whom his comrades were calling,
either to battle or to food, had gone to the riverbank, his arms
dangling, and slowly, as if spellbound, put on his shoes.

The big Montenegrin was not clear in Ahmet-beg's memory, or
even the shadowy figure of the dead boy on the bank; only the
flames over the river and the leap of the burning boy into the
dark stony pool remained. The Montenegrin, though a merciful
man, had long ago become superfluous; perhaps Ahmet-beg had
even killed him himself in one of his many raids. And the little
boy, though not forgotten, had faded into the background of
Ahmet-beg's mind; his terrible death had more meaning than
anything else about him.

Only Ahmet-beg's love for his one living son was free from his
lethargy and bitterness. To that son he had given the name of the
burned, drowned Kolašin child. What was it he wanted by re-
newing that name—to keep the remembrance alive and to revive
the memory of the child's terrible death, or to spite the Montenegrins with a life renewed? That no one could know, for he explained it now by one of these and now by other reasons. And
though no one could know what sort of man the drowned Arslan
would have become, Ahmet-beg was quite sure that he would
have become what his name, Arslan (Lion), signified: angry,
powerful, and swift. It was not clear why he imagined this, unless
it was as a contrast to the living Arslan, who was mild, wise, and a
little slow. Ahmet-beg had gone so far in his imagination and his
resurrection of the drowned boy that he described him as a

slender, dark, and strong young man. The dead Arslan, he said, looked like he did, but was stronger, more ingenious, and more mature than he, Ahmet-beg, had been at that age. The living Arslan was quite different in appearance, and he seemed to Muna and Nura, though they spoke of it to no one, more handsome than that imagined Arslan. He was a chestnut blond, ruddy, with powerful muscles, slender limbs, and a well-built, but not overtall body.

It seemed that in the drowned Arslan Ahmet-beg had lost a warrior and a famous scion. But though the second Arslan did not entirely accord to the wish and imagination of his father, Ahmet-beg did not love him the less. He leaned, trembling, over him when he was asleep and, because he himself was not educated, was eager and attentive to the boy's schooling. Arslan was the only being for whom he did not foretell evil, at least aloud; he feared that he might cast a spell on him. It was no cause for wonder, therefore, that he, the merciless and tireless warrior, should wean his own son from battle and give him to knowledge, so that, as a cadi, he would keep away not only from the killing, but also from this district, which was plunged in hatreds and inflammable vengeance.

The twins came to realize that friends and acquaintances were being killed around them, and in the last war they were most frequently young men who seemed to them to radiate ingenuous beauty and youthful vigor. It had not been much better before, according to the stories of the old men; men had always died, fighting against the Venetians and the Austrians, against the insurgent Serbs, somewhere at the ends of the world against the Muscovites and the Arabs in Egypt. But, for these two, those had been far-off deaths, unremembered and incomprehensible. Now war and killing were everyday affairs, were life itself; for thirty years, night and day, almost on their own doorstep, death had kept watch and heads had fallen. They saw the shadow of death on every man who was handsome or dear to them, and, alone at night, they tried to guess who would be the next to die and then reproached one another for their evil presentiments.

In fact, no one from their own household had been killed in this last war. Grandfather was too old and too heavy and had taken no part in it. Father supplied the army with cattle and flour. Each uncle acted according to his nature: Smail-beg went with Mehmed Ali-pasha, to arrange banquets for him and to obtain musicians and dancers, so that the fighting would be more comfortable—a task not overdignified for a beg of ancient lineage; Izet-beg acted as guide and leader for raids behind the Montenegrin lines.

Muna and Nura could not remember their relatives who had fallen in earlier wars, but these men, proud and pure, went on living and dying in the heroic stories. Grandfather's brothers had died in the battle in the Lim Valley. The flight of the brothers Džidić on their fiery chargers still lived, unchallenged, in the imagination of the twins, though it was known that for one the flight had ended in the meadows by the Lim, red with blood and white with drifted snow, and for the other in the desolate, snow-covered mountains.

Miljan Vukov, whom, the Plav hodža claimed, the devils of the Kom mountains had begotten of a witch, and with whom the Turkish women of Plav still frightened their children, had descended on Plav. It had seemed that nothing could check the rebels, thirsty for Moslem blood, hungry for the plains, eager for the fruitful and fertile lands, blissful in death if they had wiped out one of the faith of the Prophet. Nonetheless, that time, the Montenegrin attack had been checked.

The Plav and Gusinje contingents used chargers, mainly of the small, tough local breed, and the begs used Arab stallions and mares. Moslems from the two small towns and the plain around made up the cavalry, while the Shquiptars from the hills made up most of the infantry. The long wars and the frequent attacks of the enemy had made the cavalry mobile and experienced. It could muster in a moment at the rumble of the gun at the Plav fortress, the gun that also served to announce important news and, in the evenings of Ramazan, the break in the fast.

The self-styled Voivode especially feared the horsemen, for he had none; nor could he have from the *raja* or the poverty-stricken hill villages. They charged like the wrath of Allah and surrounded their enemy like swift waters, clearing the plains of rebels and riffraff. Therefore it occurred to the Voivode, for his mind

was filled with every kind of deviltry and evil, to block the paths
and the gullies in the plain with tree trunks. By this means, he
slowly came nearer and finally reached the outskirts of Plav.

But that time his own cunning played him false. The Plav
horsemen had made their way by night through the thick undergrowth along the Lim. Miljan's sentries could not hear them because of the roar of the river, and early in the morning they had
crossed below the Montenegrins and attacked in the rear. Surprised and decimated, Miljan's army did not have time and also
was afraid to retreat up the mountains in the blizzards and snowdrifts. It broke into small bands, which took up positions against
the cavalry. Then the Moslem infantry rushed in. They drove the
leaderless and astonished rebels out from under the trees and
mustered them on the roads to number and identify them. Miljan, defending himself vigorously, fled on horseback into the
Zeletin mountains with his personal guard. Though he had lost
his army, he did not that time lose his life.

Grandfather's brothers had been killed in the cavalry charge.
One of them died just where the hills met the plain. He was the
standard-bearer, and when the green standard with the crescent
wavered in his dead hand and its peak plunged into a snowdrift,
an evil omen, the second brother leaped forward and raised it
once more in a fresh and still-fiercer charge, paying no heed to his
brother. Hatred and grief carried him up into the mountain and
to death. He fell near the stones, which could be seen from Plav,
piercing the skies at the summit. With the death of the second
brother, the battle had ended, though afterward the Gusinje
leader, Ali-beg Šabanagić, had narrowly escaped being killed.
They cut off the heads of all the Montenegrin prisoners and dead,
and a hundred and twenty of them adorned the walls of the Plav
fortress. There was a memorable celebration, though mingled
with sorrow in Grandfather's house.

The people of Plav remembered Grandfather's brothers because of their death, while to the twins the stone at which the
second brother fell, always in their sight, was a living and dear
being of their blood, like Grandfather, like Uncle Izet-beg. So
grief for Grandfather's brothers lasted eternally in the household.

There were no longer any such heroes as Grandfather's brothers, or any army so valiant as that whose standard they bore. Since

then, all had changed; all that the twins saw and experienced was uglier, valueless. The last war had been different; or perhaps everything ugly in earlier wars had been forgotten.

The dirty, worn-out, scabby Shquiptars, with the white skull-caps from which their pigtails dangled, their ragged, once-white trousers, and darned and stinking shirts, begging with lackluster eyes and giving thanks with piteous words for a scrap of maize bread or hard cheese, had little heart for battle, went into it un-willingly, and returned from it angry and embittered. Their horses, too, which carried their miserable provisions and sparse munitions, thin and with mangy hides and purulent saddlesores, had terrible, measureless sadness in their dark eyes, worse because they were not able to express it. Goaded by their drivers from the grassy and well-watered plain into the bare hills and waterless gullies, the horses as they walked tore off with prominent yellow teeth the dried tufts of coarse grass beside the paths, in a naked, insatiable hunger which abolished every sense of life except this frenzied snatching.

Whereas the Shquiptars and the Moslem irregulars were ashamed of their nakedness and hunger and left the women in peace, the Sultan's nizams, recruited from every corner of the widespread empire, of every language and every color, did not stop at anything. If they had any faith or honor, they felt they no longer had need of either when at war in a foreign land. They plundered everything they could lay hands on, poultry, cattle, bedclothes, and even things of which they could have no possible need—plowshares and washtubs and children's dresses—perhaps in the hope of selling them at the next burned-out and plundered village. They cut down fruit trees, burned carts and troughs, tore down and scattered haystacks to feed a few horses or prepare beds for a few men. They rushed at the women, and it was said that they even violated the female stock. They stripped shamelessly by the little river near Plav to wash their bodies, disfigured by scabs and eczema. They deloused their shirts in the middle of the market place and draped their sweaty and purulent rags and muddy foot wrappings over the stall counters.

It was incomprehensible to the twins why these foreigners went to war. But that, though no one explained it, seemed quite clear and natural to the grownups. They accepted the violence and insolence of the soldiers as something normal, something they could not prevent. What is more, some of them repeated with obvious enjoyment how at Rudo Polje, near Plav, four nizams had violated an old, mad servant woman, adding with malicious jest: "Well, so someone at last had mercy on her!"

It was not quite clear, though, why the Shquiptars and the Moslems of Bosnian-Serbian speech went to war. It was known, of course, that they feared for their lands and properties, but it was now noised abroad that the Montenegrins were no longer driving every Moslem from his homestead and did not meddle with any-one's faith. Authority certainly drove them into war. But who drove the authorities? Who drove them all, as if deaf and blind, submissive to some terrible power that seemed stronger than any external pressure?

And it was not even clear why the Montenegrins and the begs went to war, though it was known that what the one side de-manded the other would not give. Both seemed consumed by some terrible frenzy, some longing for a world of their imagina-tion. War, death, and oppression, plunder and evildoing had be-come a necessity, like other needs of existence—food, children, ceremony, and song. The begs and even the old men were seized by a deliberate, chill circumspection.

The children, for the most part, were excited by what excited the grownups—the ceremonial greetings to those who had cut off heads, the placing of enemy heads on the fortress walls, and, espe-cially, the lamentations for those of their own kin who had fallen, which darkened the reason and aroused longings for vengeance. Everyone hated and cursed war, but everyone glowed with a hid-den longing for it; if it was to be, then it must be, and so it must be.

Not only did this war and these warriors seem different from the wars in the stories, but it seemed that those who had taken part in the war of Grandfather's brothers were different from those who took part in this war, even though many of them were the same men grown older.

Grandfather Murat-beg was not so famous that songs were sung or stories told about him, though in earlier wars he might have been different, more active, bolder, exalted by something great, beautiful, and clear. In this war he had been a failing, slow, and taciturn old man. He had not taken a prominent part. He had ridden about the plain, keeping his eye on the serf villages, and, with his band, had guarded the main road along the Lim against haiduks and irregulars.

Not only Grandfather, but even the famous Ali-beg Šabanagić was no longer he of whom the stories told. One of Grandfather's brothers had married a Šabanagić, and Ali-beg, though he rarely visited them, was considered, insofar as so famous a personality could be so considered, a member of Grandfather's household.

Ali-beg had inherited the leadership of the district from his father, Djul-beg. But that was not enough. He had had to establish it, to seize it once again from the chiefs of rival clans, and to contest with Miljan Vukov and his captains, from whom he had more to fear in times of peace than in war. They would disguise their haiduks as begging monks or gypsy bear-leaders, even as dervishes, in order to get near him to assassinate him.

It so happened that it was Miljan Vukov who had removed Ali-beg's most dangerous rival, Pašo Šehović, when the three of them were still young and at the beginning of their fighting careers. Muna and Nura knew from tales how this had happened. Miljan and his band had withdrawn through Šekular, and in the Mokro mountains had waited to ambush a group of Turkish merchants. A band of horsemen had appeared and, not knowing who they were, Miljan and his men opened fire. Most of the horsemen escaped, but Miljan rushed across the meadow to the wounded ghazi, who was Pašo Šehović, a Plav leader, renowned throughout the region. When Miljan reached him, Pašo said: "Strike, Vlach, like a hero, as I would you!" Miljan took Pašo's head to Prince Danilo at Cetinje. The words of Stevan Perkov, the Montenegrin counselor, were repeated even as far as Plav. "Never have I seen two finer heads: the dead Pašo's and the living Miljan's!" The Šehovići had never risen again. That was the turning point for Plav, the weakening of Plav power and the rise of the poor but warlike Gusinje begs.

But the Redžepagići of Plav, relying on the Shquiptar clans, even now contested Ali-beg's leadership. Osman-beg Redžepagić shared with Ali-beg the control of the serf villages and also of the army. He led most of the men from Plav, and Ali-beg led those from Gusinje. Although it was necessary that they be subordinate to Ali-beg, the men of Plav often acted on their own initiative, as if they rejoiced in the misfortunes and failures of the Šabanagići almost as much as in those of the Montenegrins.

In earlier times, the rivalries of the begs had often developed into armed contests, which the valis had to suppress by force. The memory of these still rankled, and Ali-beg seldom and unwillingly went to Plav, fearing that some hidden assassin would kill him from a kula or balcony. When he did go, he stayed by preference with Grandfather, for Grandfather's clan was in conflict with the more powerful Plav houses. Thus, in the center of Plav, Grandfather Murat-beg supported Ali-beg's faction, and in his family and in the town itself this was considered as showing courage almost as great as if his household were surrounded by Montenegrins.

One of the famous brothers of Grandfather had killed a youth from another clan, and Grandfather had not dared to stir out of his house for seven years, until, during a fresh war with the Montenegrins, Ali-beg and Osman-beg, in a moment of union in the face of common danger, had imposed peace upon the two factions. Grandfather had paid blood money, and by that all had been forgotten. Muna and Nura would never have known about this vendetta if it had not been preserved in stories, especially those of the maidservant Kara-Djula, who was determined that they should never be forgotten as long as she lived and that all the misfortunes and misdeeds of the family should be recorded and remembered.

Ali-beg was now in his sixties, and though, especially on horseback, he was still upright and energetic, it was remarked when the war ended that he was beginning to show signs of weakening, as if that exalted and enthusiastic spirit that he, and with him the entire district, had displayed throughout thirty years of war was beginning to die out.

Muna and Nura could never forget the one time they saw Ali-beg at the height of his powers. That had been at the beginning of the last war.

The little town and the green expanse of the lake, round and shining like a silver tray, had quivered in the afternoon heat and from the hoofbeats of hundreds of horses. On a thin-legged white stallion with a long and shining tail and arched neck, Ali-beg, in a gold-embroidered green dolman, entered Plav at the head of the Gusinje calvary. They looked so fine, so clean and well set up, that no one would have recognized in them the familiar plowmen and herdsmen. They rode in file, first those on black horses, then those on white horses, then the bays and the dapples. The leaders were for the most part in green felt dolmans and red breeches, while the ordinary horsemen wore black cloaks bordered with red braid and tight white cloth trousers piped in black, the national costume of the district, clean and new, as if for a festival. Despite the restlessness of the horses, well fed and well rested, snorting and rearing, still unreconciled to the bit, the order and discipline filled the little town with a sense of savage power and aroused enthusiasm even among the people of Plav who could not endure Ali-beg. Ali-beg halted in the center of the town, under Osman-beg's high, gloomy balcony, reining in his trembling charger and waiting until first the black and then the white stream of horsemen came up. When the beat of their hoofs had grown quiet and the dust had settled in the trampled space around him, he shouted loudly, emphasizing his words with a thin whip: "They have taken Sutjeska! They have got us by the throat while you men of Plav philander with your wives! That is not the way to wage war, Osman-beg!" For a long time no one replied from the balcony. At last, from above, the calm voice of Osman-beg replied, deep and mocking: "Let the men of Gusinje go where they have a mind to. No one is ever in front of the men of Plav when there is blood to be spilled!" But Ali-beg's anger did not leave him; it was not the anger of every day, but a sort of exaltation and reproach, a forgetfulness of self. Paying no attention to Osman-beg, he went on shouting. "Alarm, alarm! Miljan Vukov will not wait till you have eaten your fill and made love to your lady!" Slicing the sky with his whip, from one mountain to the other, he spurred his horse, who needed only a loose rein to become transformed into a white storm of flight. The charger reared and bore Ali-beg through the stream of black and white horsemen, which opened smoothly to let him pass and then quickly followed him. Throughout the town sounded a sullen roll of drums, as from the depths of the earth, and the despairing wail of the *zurle* called the men of Plav onto the road to the skies.

It was a fine beginning to the war. And in that beginning Ali-beg was fine, too, as in the songs. It was evident to the twins why no one had ever succeeded in usurping or weakening his leadership, not even the prudent, wealthy, and brave Osman-beg. Ali-beg not only believed in his faith with his whole heart, but he lived for it, was ready always to die for it, was never deflected by pleasure and luxury despite the many serf villages he still possessed.

It was a sin to compare Ali-beg Šabanagić with the infidel Miljan Vukov, but the comparison forced itself upon them. Miljan, too, lived ascetically, despite his properties, purchased or seized from the begs, for he, too, believed intensely in his faith and practiced it. He, too, accumulated wealth not for the sake of enjoyment, but for the sake of power, and was ready to use all his goods for the cross and for Serbdom. Of him, as of Ali-beg, men said: "Everything is good and fine for him, but whoever stands in his way he will put six feet under the sod if he can." It was even said that Miljan and Ali-beg were similar in face and figure, as if some evil destiny had nurtured and raised them, one against the other, in order to take pleasure in their mutual annihilation. Grandfather Murat-beg, who knew Miljan Vukov well, said that Miljan was broader in the chest and had stronger hands, fitted for the plow and the scythe. But he was of deliberate enthusiasm and moderated violence.

Theirs was a battle between valley and mountain, fertile land and wilderness, men of noble stock and upstarts, an ancient empire and a new state, and, above all, between two faiths and two leaders—Ali-beg, who traced his ancestry, as the old men of his family boasted, from the Islamized Crnojević princes of Zeta, and the rootless Miljan.

Ali-beg's return from the war was miserable. Muna and Nura did not see him when he came back, but they saw his army. The armistice disbanded the army more quickly than the war had mustered it, but nonetheless the men camped around Plav for weeks, ragged, hungry, and inconsiderate. The strangest thing was that now no one was frightened of them, despite their excesses. Perhaps the townspeople had become accustomed to violence, shame, purulent wounds, maimed limbs, and gouged-out eyes, even to death itself.

Only Ali-beg's horsemen, though their horses were thin and

spiritless, their cloaks ragged, and their trousers yellowed and tattered, came and went through Plav in good order. They were noticeably discouraged and sullen, but, as if to spite the people of Plav, still unbroken. In truth, they were no longer heroes from the tales and ballads. These men of Gusinje again looked like what they were: plowmen, herdsmen, and minor agas such as could be seen daily on the pasture lands, in the inns, and on the roads.

Ali-beg was no longer what he had been, though his clothing and arms glittered with fresh, untarnished colors, and the charger under him was well groomed and fiery. At first sight he did not look any older or more exhausted, but, always taciturn, he had grown chill and silent, and the fatigue and bitterness he could no longer conceal were evident in his words and movements. Pressing his white, wrinkled hand to his belt, as if to soothe some pain, he walked up and down Grandfather's reception room and complained about the wavering of the Vali, the pusillanimity of Stambul, the arrogance of Osman-beg, the disobedience of the Albanians—in fact, about everything except Miljan Vukov and his own men from Gusinje.

Had it not been for his fame, which Muna and Nura had heard of ever since they had been able to crawl, they would not have known that this was the man told of in the songs or the man they had seen at the beginning of the war scolding the men of Plav for their indolence, molded with his horse into a single body and a single movement, launched toward lands and times unattainable by other men. There was nothing now to show that he would lead the men of Plav and Gusinje in their last combat, even though everyone knew that only he could do so. Muna and Nura were not able to feel the greatness of the moment when Ali-beg, on his arrival, had caressed their blond heads and red cheeks and given a ducat to each of them, a ducat that was a talisman. His fingers were cold and bony, like those of every old man, and a servant held his horse as he, broken and stiff, mounted.

If Ali-beg was at once commonplace and legendary, the Montenegrins remained, to the twins, enigmatic and unreal, even though during the war they had several times come so near that the sound of shots could be heard and there were rumors that they might attack at any moment.

Though it was not recalled that they had ever taken people away into slavery, the cry "They will enslave us!" was constantly to be heard. The words "slave," "slavery," "enslavement," "servitude" the twins had learned in earliest childhood, with their first fears, their first apprehensions, their first words. They were living words to them, though their original meaning and significance had become blurred. Now they no longer meant being taken away from one's own people and bound to unquestioning obedience to foreign people and ways, but something no less terrible—being taken away from the life in which they themselves lived and being cast into unknown and inconceivable circumstances.

Thus pike and trout were taken from the lake, and salmon and roach from the Lim. But though they were in torture on dry land, fish were not men and could not know what was happening to them. An unknown power had suddenly taken their breath from them, and they could no longer breathe despite all their threshing. Luckily, they died quickly, even when the fishermen did not bash their heads on the gunwales of the boat or on a stone.

Uncle Izet-beg had once brought home a marten in a cage; the serf Stojan Radak had caught it and given it to him as a present. The marvelous and fearless little beast had blunted his teeth and nails on the wire netting. It must have known that it had fallen into slavery. Not for a moment was it reconciled to finding itself suddenly in a space from which there was no way out. It would not take any kind of food, and quickly wasted away. It did not want to be, could not be, a slave. A man could be a slave. Caught and enslaved, he did not know how to die, but worked, conscious that he was irretrievably pulled out of his water, out of his den, out of his life.

Thus it was that Muna and Nura imagined and understood slavery. Arslan explained it to them in a fine but complicated fashion: to live and to have no life, to wish to be a thing and not be able to. The girls could not, and did not want to, reason so minutely, to explain the changing sense of words. Arslan had been to school and had learned to read books and to write. They looked on the matter more simply: their life and their faith would be enslaved, even if they themselves were not taken away in chains and fetters.

The Montenegrins, and the serfs who associated with them in

disobedience and revolt, were not only an ever-present fear, but also a destiny which kept vigil and inevitably awaited all Moslems in the district. Every evil, everything that destroyed Moslem life and threatened Moslem existence, was in some strange way tied up with the Montenegrins. Many likened them to hail and frost: "The Montenegrins are passing through the fields!" "The Montenegrins have touched the fruit!" "The Montenegrin shadow is over the harvest!" They called them wolves and werewolves; and of the spendthrift, licentious, and violent begs they said: "They are just like the Montenegrins." It was said of householders who cheated and defrauded the taxgatherers and begs, and of the taxgatherers who defrauded everybody, that they had learned cunning and greed from the Montenegrins. Grandfather Murat-beg was in the habit of saying: "Death will not get you, but a Montenegrin will!"

But nothing, not even the Montenegrins and their shadow, could altogether destroy for the twins the many everyday joys: the burbling of the brook at the end of the garden, fragrant and delicate; Arslan's visits, awaited tremulously and welcomed with joy; singing in the evening in the garden; the weaving of rosy dreams into their embroidery; consoling their mother and reconciling her to her life.

The garden was a joy to all, especially in summer, though since Bulbul had begun living in the summerhouse, it was only Grandfather who, by habit, willingly spent his evenings there. In the daytime Muna and Nura withdrew from the garden into the house, into their mother's or their uncle's room. That, too, could be wonderful.

A heavy stone wall surrounded the front part of the house, which was also built of stone, for defense. The courtyard in front was paved with flagstones, between which grass forced its way and, in the spring, dandelions, with their weak stems and shaggy golden heads. The gateway leading to the narrow street had thick oak panels studded with large-headed forged nails. It was always barred, so that no one could enter uninvited and take the womenfolk by surprise. To the left of the gateway were the stables and to the right the kitchen; behind, the stone wall had been extended and turned in a right angle to wall off the house from the garden. A little doorway, five or six paces from the house, led into the garden, which was encircled by a thick acacia hedge and lilac bushes, and stretched for a full two hundred paces down to the stream. Above the stream, the garden dipped steeply, and on the top of this slope, under an old pear tree, Grandfather Murat-beg liked to sit in the summer dusk, cross-legged on a shaggy rug, smoking his nargileh, talking, and sipping coffee with his friends. Just at this point, the stream joined the lake and, because the hedge along it was kept continually trimmed, the view was clear across the dark blue-greenness of the lake to the massive outcrops and white summits of the Prokletije and the broad grassy shoulders of the Visitor. There was nothing to check the cool, pure breath of the waters and the heights. Grandfather took his rest there, from his years and his memories, grew younger for a few moments, and collected his thoughts.

When, from the wooden minaret, the muezzin called for the evening prayer, and the twilight began to thicken and envelop everything in blue haze, Grandfather would call Muna and Nura to come and sing to him. He urged them to sing the old-time songs, now rarely sung, but which, because of their timelessness, were more melancholy or more joyful than newer ones. Grandfather's sorrow could be seen; he would cease smoking and, while the moon's radiance slipped across the fields and into the lake, would bow his head and whisper silently into his straggly white beard. Recently, however, Grandfather had seldom summoned Muna and Nura; he had noticed that they did not come willingly to sing there under Bulbul's windows, lest they gladden her heart.

A little away from Grandfather's pear tree rose the *čardak,* the summerhouse, a low building of rough, squared logs facing the lake. The lower story, half buried in the earth, was given over to storerooms; the upper story, divided by a wide passage, contained two rooms. Until Bulbul's arrival, their father and mother had lived in summer in the right-hand room and Muna and Nura in the left-hand one. When the weather was rainy, Grandfather would sit in the open passage, with a brazier at his feet, wrapped in a dark overcoat lined with otter fur. Uncle Izet-beg, if he chanced to be at home and not on one of his hunting expeditions, would come to sit there, too, silent and smiling to himself. Even Omer-beg, who never sat in the garden, would keep Grandfather and Izet-beg company there when he was not busy. If there were no strange men present, Biba would bring Grandfather coffee, which he kept hot on the brazier in a copper *džezva* and drank slowly from a white *fildžan* decorated with a gold crescent moon and star. In the *čardak* there had been quiet, incomparable beauty, and joy. In it, in contrast to the spacious, many-chambered, but gloomy and stifling kula, with its tiny windows and countless loopholes, the feeling of community, of closeness, between the twins and their parents had grown and been refreshed, as had that between their father and mother.

Although it was no more than a stone's throw from the house to the *čardak*, the change from one to the other had been much greater, as if they had suddenly moved into a new district. All the household and the servants lived in the kula, and there Muna's and Nura's room was far from the room where their father and mother slept. Also, their father was often away in autumn and springtime on visits to the serf villages or on distant winter trading trips. Only in the *čardak* had the family been near and intimate. Muna's and Nura's girl friends had come gladly to the *čardak* to work at their embroidery and amuse themselves, and the Turkish ladies of Plav visited Biba. The *čardak* had aroused Muna's and Nura's enthusiasm for childish tales and also the first whisperings of love.

But life in the *čardak* had been disorganized by the coming of Bulbul, the second wife. Now she lived there, while Biba remained in the house. This summer, Muna and Nura, sorry for their mother's evident desperate loneliness, had stayed with her more and more often, until finally they returned to the kula, leaving their father alone with his new wife. Overcome by a passion he could not resist but was ashamed of before them, he avoided their less and less frequent caresses and showered them with richer and more frequent gifts. Thus the *čardak* became alien, was transformed into a lost charm and enchantment, inexplicable, beautiful, and dear to them.

Almost overnight, with their entry into womanhood and their concealment behind lattices and veils and *feredžas*, they had become involved in the secret enthusiasms of love. The Serb townswomen Muna and Nura sometimes met at parties, though they, too, went covered in the streets for fear of violence, could not imagine the tender longings and the expectations that existed among the Moslem girls. Just because of their concealment and the prohibitions surrounding them, a song excited them like an embrace and a glance quickened their senses like a kiss; everywhere and in everything lurked joys incomprehensibly and mysteriously male. The Serb girl usually knew her bridegroom before marriage, but the Moslem girl knew him only through the tales of go-betweens and marriage brokers, unless, at mortal risk to herself and to him, she managed to meet him secretly or see him, supposedly by accident, in the narrow streets.

The most wonderful and exciting thing was that the young men knew, in spite of the wide folds of the *peča* and the Turkish trousers, how to differentiate by the shining warmth of their eyes, not only older women from younger, but also girls ripe for marriage from young girls. Their glances struck into the heart and into every crevice of the inexperienced, untouched maiden soul the more surely and sharply the more they thought that they were totally concealed. But in the same way, older men, those known as drunkards and profligates, knew at first sight how to distinguish a young *bula* and, screwing up their eyes and opening their lips a trifle, how to measure her from top to toe with a slow glance, so that she felt as if her clothing were falling from her piece by piece, from her bared face to her naked feet.

All this Muna would tell to Nura in bed in the evenings, in no way ashamed of the sweet lascivious thoughts that gripped her, while her sister, also secretly excited, whispered: "I'm not surprised; how quickly your breasts are swelling, while mine are still scarcely noticeable."

Muna was always falling in love, whenever she saw a handsome youth or heard talk of one. She was annoyed that Nura always knew and never failed to tell her that these were not true loves and that such love had still to come.

Nura faced all difficulties more calmly, even the arrest of the Radak Knez, which had aroused uneasiness, although for Muna and Nura it was not a matter of immediate importance. That day Muna had rushed into her mother's room late in the afternoon and stuttered excitedly: "Yesterday they arrested some Radak knez. He was planning a revolt. Ahmet-beg told Grandfather in the garden. That's terribly, terribly important."

It was dusk, and since their mother could not endure a light, Muna could not make out the expression on her face. Exhausted by the sultry heat, Biba was lying near the open window on a divan, half-clothed, her head resting on her hand, pale and delicate in the half-light, while Nura, slowly and quietly, was telling her a story about a cow that had gored the boorish servant Bešir and overturned Kara-Djula's milking pail.

"What if they have arrested him?" said Nura. "Is that so important that you must rush in here like a mad thing and interrupt me?"

"But it is important, terribly important," Muna insisted.

Nura was waiting to catch her for her inability to give any reason for her excitement. "Tell me, just tell me, why?"

"Oh, I don't really know. But it is important! Certainly it's important when Grandfather talks so much about it, and Ahmet-beg is so pleased about it."

Mother smiled vaguely. "Calm down, my little one. Why should it be of any importance to us if they arrest a serf?"

"But he's a knez."

"For us, it is neither here nor there," said their mother wearily. "But you two look after supper; Kara-Djula will be out of temper again!"

The twins rushed out into the gloom of the passage, lit only by a stray beam from the sun, setting behind the mountains. The courtyard was fresh and warm, filled with a reddish glow. Muna put her arms around her sister's waist. "It is important. They will torture him. Ahmet-beg says that they will torture him."

"Well, let them torture him." Nura wriggled out of her sister's arms, disregarding her tremulous whisper.

"So they will torture us, too, in the same way when they enslave us."

"They won't enslave us—at least, not alive."

"They will. Not everyone will die. There's no need for everyone to die."

"Don't be silly!" Nura retorted angrily, shaking her sister. "They're quite right to torture him. A serf is stubborn and perverse. How could we get to know the serfs' secrets if we did not torture them?"

Muna, frightened and disconsolate, was silent. *Certainly, they ought to torture him. They are quite right, since he refuses to disclose secrets. But haven't I—and Nura—haven't we got secrets, too? But our secrets are not worth torture. I'm afraid and get shaky; I can't even look when they're killing a chicken. Nura can; Nura can do anything, even though she is afraid, too.* "I couldn't torture anyone, not even Miljan Vukov."

"I could. If I had to, I could," said Nura disdainfully, not looking at her sister.

"You're lying, Nura. You couldn't either. But then, perhaps you could, if it was necessary."

In the kitchen, lit by high flames, the omniscient and all-powerful Kara-Djula was standing over the fire. She said, just as if she knew what the girls had been talking about a minute before: "So. In the garden they are pleased about the serfs' sufferings. But there'll be worse to come. They've only themselves to blame if the Montenegrins and the serfs pay them back in their own coin!" As always, Kara-Djula vented her anger on inanimate things; while she was speaking she was banging the ladle about, slopping the food intended for Bulbul into the dishes.

That evening the twins had to take the second wife her supper; their mother had sent them, though she had not said so in so many words, in order not to have to pronounce Bulbul's name. Kara-Djula had quarreled with Bulbul the third day after Bulbul's arrival, supposedly because of her incomprehensible Turkish language and spoiled exclusiveness, but in reality because she could not bear strangers and felt sorry for Biba. So that the twins would not have to work, Kara-Djula grudgingly continued to prepare Bulbul's dinner, growling and grumbling as she set aside the food. "May she choke! May leprosy eat her up! She who has changed nine homes in one shirt!" But Muna and Nura had to carry it to Bulbul, in little bowls and dishes on a square wooden tray, taking care not to catch its corners on the gateposts or the tree stumps in the garden.

Usually Nura went first, coarsening her voice to make it sound like Kara-Djula's and repeating Kara-Djula's curses and maledictions, while Muna, usually the more talkative, walked silently, balancing the tray, testing every step and trying to imagine Kara-Djula's and her sister's curses taking effect: the silk of Bulbul's trousers, rustling like distant rain, transformed into a beggar woman's rags; in place of the green, slightly oblique eyes, bleary, suppurating holes; her long white teeth rotten and yellow, her dark, olive skin flaking in scabs, and the heavy black wave of her hair fallen into the mud, leaving her scalp naked to the bone. But she knew that Nura, in jesting words, really wanted evil to befall Bulbul, whereas she only copied her sister's words. Nura, her eyes hard and her lips compressed into a tight line, had hissed to Muna in the garden: "She should be killed like a bitch, for a bitch she is. It is not for us to wait upon her."

Muna, too, hated Bulbul, though in a different way. She did not want to kill her or to do her any harm, but wanted to wear her down with chill and disdain. Whereas Nura simply hated her existence, Muna noted and remembered all her most insignificant faults and failings, to recount them and exaggerate them later to her sister or to Kara-Djula.

But the trouble was that Bulbul had few failings. She was a Turkish, or, more likely, a Tatar, woman of unknown past and origin. Omer-beg asserted that she came from a distinguished but poor family, but no one believed him. Everyone believed that he had bought her from her father or owner and that she had been a dancer or something similar in some great harem, or had been a member of a troupe of acrobats. In truth, she had something of the acrobat about her. In the morning, the sisters often came upon her twisting and turning on a rug, touching her heels to the back of her head, wrapping her legs around her neck, and even walking on her hands. Once they found her in the garden displaying her skill by hanging from the smooth branch of an apple tree. That had angered Grandfather, and Kara-Djula had jeered at the little monkey from God knows where. Bulbul soon withdrew entirely into her room.

She always withdrew whenever she met resistance or lack of understanding, though she never entreated or wept. On the day of her arrival, she tried to be friendly with Biba, displaying toward her, as the elder wife, a respect more obedient than cordial, filled with stiff, artificial courtesy and smiles. But Biba had remained impassive, unapproachable, smoldering with resentment, outraged by the fact that Omer-beg had not been able to find a wife in his own country but had brought some woman from the world outside to live with her.

Muna had, from her window, overheard Biba complaining to her *djever*, Izet-beg; only to him did she confide anything. If only Omer-beg had brought a wife from some well-known local family to bear his children! Muna had not been able to hear all her mother's complaints; Nura had called her for something. But a little later she met Izet-beg and her mother as they came out of the glare of the sun and entered the darkness of the kula. It had been, she remembered, in the heat of the morning. Izet-beg had just returned from hunting, wet to the knees with dew, and a spotted, pregnant bitch had rushed out of the kennel to welcome him, yapping and leaping around him with difficulty, overjoyed at seeing him but regretful that she had not been taken hunting. Muna had tried to hide, not wishing to be seen, overcome by a vague, uneasy embarrassment. But they did not even see her, and Izet-beg, letting Biba go first up the steps, gently placed his bony bronzed hand on her shoulder.

It was not proper for men to weep, except for a brother or son or if some close relative died or was killed. And Izet-beg did not weep except when he was saddened by a misfortune that befell Biba. Muna and Nura had seen that twice. The first time had been ten years before, when Biba had given birth to a premature, stillborn boy, and the second time had been on the eve of the war when news came of the death of Uncle Selim, Biba's only brother. Each time Izet-beg had wept in the same manly manner, soundlessly, as though embarrassed, wiping his eyes by slowly drawing his palm across them.

Biba, however, did not weep when she heard of her brother's death. She leaned, as if mown down, on her *djever*'s shoulder; she would certainly have fallen if he had not supported her tenderly in his arms. It was Izet-beg who wept; she had dry, staring, and wide-open eyes. Muna remembered that her eyes had been like that when they had told her, suffering and racked with pain, that she had given birth to a dead son.

As their mother's closeness to Izet-beg became more and more apparent, so did she conceal her feelings more and more, especially from their father. She did not reject Bulbul roughly or openly; she simply did not want to have any contact with her, or even see her. She withdrew into her own room, into isolation and sorrow, which she was not able to conceal from her daughters and did not trouble to do from Izet-beg.

Izet-beg had no contact with Bulbul; he had met her only a few times. She would not have existed for him had she not been the herald and the cause of Biba's inconsolable unhappiness and the disturbance of the regular routine of the household. When he did meet her and she asked him something, he would reply curtly and coldly and then slip away quickly, though he had a good knowledge of Turkish and otherwise willingly made use of it.

Bulbul's attempt to become intimate with the twins had been the most disastrous of all. From the first day, Nura had refused to exchange a word with her and, noticing Muna's spirit of conciliation, she had done all she could to increase her harshness and spite. That had caused the first serious and long-lasting conflict between the twins. Nura began to watch Muna and her behavior, so that Muna, too, changed her manner toward Bulbul, treating her with a cold and deliberate reserve, bringing her food and obeying her only when their father so ordered.

Thus Bulbul, despite her efforts, found herself lonelier than Biba. But nothing of that could be noticed in her, no ill will or sadness because of it. It was as if she were accustomed to living alone, to waiting for her husband, to providing him with the fullest enjoyment. She had, it seemed, the art of being self-sufficient. Except for her morning acrobatics and her careful evening anointing of herself with creams and perfumes, she passed her time embroidering or strumming on the *šarkija* and humming in an almost male voice, throaty and nasal, songs that were melancholy and as long-drawn-out as distant journeys in boundless, empty expanses. Only Muna's ear, keener and more attentive, was able to distinguish one song from another and one way of singing from another. Nura did not try to distinguish them, and forced herself not to listen, trying to prove that they were not songs, but only a monotonous and senseless howling. Muna objected, had to object, for in singing she had always surpassed her sister. Bulbul's singing pierced the heart. Although the words were incomprehensible, the sound was sometimes sad, sad unto despair, though her eyes never filled with tears, and sadness never cast its shadow on her face.

Muna also had to keep a strict rein on herself not to show Bulbul the curiosity and, in time, the enthusiasm that Bulbul's embroideries aroused in her. They were all different, but made up of such complex angles, corners, circles, and colors that they gave the impression of an intricate and reasoned, yet at the same time free, interplay of imagination. And for Bulbul, embroidery was neither a task nor an obligation, but more a way of singing to herself.

Despite Bulbul's unusual beauty, Muna and Nura were unable to understand why their father had brought her. Kara-Djula explained that the Džidići, Grandfather Murat-beg and his line, had poisoned blood and were avid for women's beauty. In truth, their elder uncle, Smail, was notorious for his licentiousness, and was not cordially welcomed in their house. There were quite a number of begs like him in and around Plav. But their father had not been that way before his fortieth year, right up to the coming of Bulbul, and Uncle Izet-beg had not even married. Kara-Djula explained that, too, ruthlessly: the time had come for Omer-beg, his poisoned blood had caught up with him, whereas Izet-beg was like a monk, though it was hunting that had broken him, rather than fasts. Thus Bulbul's sudden arrival harshly revealed to the twins the vague, secret weaknesses of passion and sin in the family.

That evening, as they took Bulbul her food, crossing the courtyard and entering the garden, which sprinkled them with freshness and scented warmth and moisture, Nura did not repeat Kara-Djula's curses on the second wife, but teased Muna. "You would even weep for the serfs! They aren't chickens! Don't you think they would do to us what they have learned from us? Cry, cry, crybaby. There'll never be an end of crying."

Muna listened to her sister, torn between different feelings and desires. Secretly, she was looking forward to meeting Bulbul, though with apprehension and curiosity. But she continued to show indifference, for this evening, too, she knew in advance that Nura would not help her carry the tray up to the *čardak*. Nura did not want to meet Bulbul and always sent her on alone with the tray, while she waited in the garden. The tray was light, but a whole arm's-length wide, with a dozen dishes and bowls covered by napkins. It was far from convenient to carry. Though Bulbul ate little, she liked to have a number of dishes before her, to taste and dip into. Still, Muna was quite able to carry the tray on her head. She would not agree to do the whole task alone, not because the tray was too heavy, but so that her sister would not tease her afterward. Nura's waiting, it seemed, was a sort of surveillance of Muna, to see that she did not stay too long with Bulbul. It would be followed by a deliberately malicious questioning on her return —hadn't some harm come to the second wife?

When they reached the *čardak*, Nura turned and without a word pushed her side of the tray into Muna's hands and then helped her put it on her head.

"Why me? Why not you?" Muna protested.

But Nura, who always behaved as if she were the elder, did not reply, clearly intent on having her own way. "Take care!" she shouted at Muna, almost pushing her across the threshold.

So Muna went up the steps, testing each one with her foot. Her awe and curiosity grew with every cautious step upward.

Bulbul's exceptional beauty and Biba's unhappiness had driven out the twins' hopeless attempt, soon after Bulbul's arrival, to make a comparison between them. Biba, it was now evident to them, had never been an especially beautiful woman, though even now no one could call her ugly. Perhaps her girlish freshness had been attractive, but now, in her fortieth year, she was flabby and faded; her dark hair had lost its sheen and was beginning to get gray. Her thin lips were wrinkled and colorless, and her slightly protuberant brown eyes had acquired a fixed, glassy stare. She was not ill, but was consumed by despair that she could no longer bear children and that therefore her husband had a certain right to neglect her. Her left eyelid twitched more and more frequently, and she suffered from prolonged, painful, and incurable headaches. Even before Bulbul's arrival, she, desperate and tormented, would one day urge their father to marry again, so as not to remain without sons and extinguish his line, and the next, certain he was looking for another wife and was amusing himself with other women, would reproach him for coming home late and neglecting her.

Though older than she, Omer-beg looked younger and better-preserved. Unlike Izet-beg and Smail-beg, both of whom were tall, dark, bony men, he was of moderate height, fair, and with a tendency to be fat. His carefully tended beard was still shot with youthful fires, and his curly silken hair receded only at the

217

temples, giving a youthful appearance to his full reddish face. He greatly enjoyed food and drink, and concerned himself only with his estates, his serfs, and his trading, which attracted him more and more and took him on distant journeys. In all else he was patient, reserved, good-humored.

All Plav was astonished when he brought Bulbul back, without asking the advice of either his father or his brothers. Yet, faced by opposition from both family and friends, torn between conscience and desire, he simply hunched his powerful head into his broad shoulders and decided, without explanation, to pay no attention to anyone, but to live as he pleased.

The more well-to-do Moslems often had two or three wives, since it was not forbidden by their faith. But there always had to be some good reason: the first wife was either ill or barren or too old. Otherwise, to have many wives, though not uncommon, was regarded as profligate and as a weakening of clan and family ties. The men of Plav, like other Moslems of Serb origin, were more inclined to condone womanizing than the bringing of a second wife into the home.

Omer-beg knew that well and, seeking a middle way, reckoned that Bulbul would be regarded more as a mistress than as a wife. Yet, though almost everyone did so regard her, there were few who approved. Biba was well known for her virtues, even if fate had closed her womb. Omer-beg had the right to look only for a more fertile womb to replace hers. No one could possibly have known whether Bulbul was barren, but all who saw her were convinced of it. Her body, without wrinkles and without fat, smooth and supple as an eel's, gave no promise of childbearing, but only of enjoyment. Furthermore, she was without kin and without a past and not much younger than Biba, despite her well-preserved and agile body.

There were few who openly condemned Omer-beg, but it was a good occasion to impress on him that he should take some girl or young widow of a good house and of Bosnian speech who would bear him sons, so that the line of the Džidići would not be extinguished. And since their father was a mild-mannered man, Muna and Nura were sure that sooner or later he would agree. Kara-Djula, who in this matter also knew everything before anyone else, confirmed that a girl had been set aside for him—Fatka, the daughter of Hodža Muharem. She was, actually, too young for him; she had just completed her seventeenth year. But because Muharem belonged to the Kaljević clan from Kolašin, once distinguished and strong, though now scattered and devastated by the wars, the marriage of his daughter to the wealthy, though elderly, Omer-beg offered prospects for a revival of the power and wealth of the family. Such a marriage would also make a reconciliation easier between the Kapetanovići and the Kaljevići, between Ahmet-beg and Muharem. For a long time there had been unransomed blood between them, and Ahmet-beg had been first married to Omer-beg's sister. Kara-Djula knew that Ahmet-beg did not look on this marriage with displeasure, since it would be a good excuse after so long a time of common devastation to forgive blood debts.

The whispers and gossip about Omer-beg's third marriage became more and more widespread. Though it was inconceivable to the twins that they would marry someone they did not love, they were accustomed to hearing, in connection with marriage, discussions about wealth, authority, and reputation. But they knew something that no one else, not even Kara-Djula, knew. Arslan, Ahmet-beg's son, loved Fatka with an unbounded love, beyond reason and dreams, yet a despairing love, because they were separated by blood unavenged. Arslan had confided this to them.

Muna and Nura had sworn to one another that they would say nothing to Arslan about the possibility of Fatka's marriage to their father. For the moment it had not gone farther than secret talks between Grandfather and Ahmet-beg and the grumbling of the omniscient Kara-Djula. It was inconceivable that they could sadden that dear and clever young man who was closer to them and perhaps dearer even than Uncle Izet-beg.

But Muna revealed to her sister another, and more important, reason for silence. The night after Kara-Djula's chatter about their father's marriage to Fatka, Muna had dreamed that she was riding an unsaddled and unbridled young yellow stallion. She was almost naked, in a short jacket, which the wind did not allow her to button, and in Turkish trousers, which were stripped from her even though she was sitting firmly on the horse's warm back. It was just as in her childhood when Izet-beg, back from watering his bay, had put her on its broad back. Then, she sat with the fingers of both hands feverishly twisted in its mane, quivering with fright and joy that she was so high and on such a horse, and her uncle ran alongside, holding the reins in his hands and urging on the bay. But the horse and the man could not keep in step, and Izet-beg leaped on the horse's back and put his arm around his niece. The bay, as if waiting to feel its master on its back, broke into a wild race across the fields. Muna, as now in her dream, had caught her breath in sweet terror, closely embraced by the huge man's arms and gripping the quivering flesh of the marvelous leaping wonder, in a whirl of wind and color, in the clash between desire that the race would never end and fear of its continuing. That same feeling of vague passion and awe she now felt in her dream. But now it was not her uncle, and the stallion was young and unsaddled and bore her through unmown meadows she had never seen before and yet which seemed strangely familiar, green and rich as those beside the Lim, toward the steep banks, deep and precipitous. Just as she was hoping and fearing that it would never end, the horse reared and plunged into the abyss. It did not swerve, but flew to the depths of that unknown abyss, threshing with its legs, as if swimming in deep and peaceful water, while she firmly gripped its mane and pressed with hot and sweating legs that seemed to be part of the stallion's body, so that somewhere, far off and deep in herself, she could feel the pounding of its powerful heart.

She awoke and was frightened by the clarity and the changed appearance of things; the moonlight entered the room and flooded everything with its pale, unreal brilliance. Nura, her face framed by hair as soft as flax and pale as new gold, was lying wakeful and tense in the bluish radiance, stiff and cold, as if carved in stone. Muna could see every detail of her sister's face, a mole on the left cheek, freckles on the nose, and a dimple in the middle of her short, rounded chin. But she could not see Nura's eyelids quiver, her eyes, darker than by day, like whirlpools in the shadow of willows, gazing fixedly at the ceiling under curved dark brows. At first glance, her sister's face seemed to Muna unknown, and she almost cried out: "How strange that high forehead and those strongly marked cheekbones, and yet, how lovely my sister is!" But she gave a start and realized that she herself looked just so, strange and terrifying. She hid her fears and calmed down.

Nura said: "You were sleeping so uneasily and crying out. Certainly you were dreaming of him."

She did not say his name, but Muna knew that she meant Arslan, and it at once struck her that Nura spoke the truth, that in some way the dream had been about Arslan. Still sharper was the realization that Nura had been lying awake and thinking of Arslan. "No! Not really." Muna replied in embarrassment. "I wasn't dreaming of him."

"Then of what, of whom, were you dreaming?" her sister insisted, turning gently toward Muna, her eyes emerging from the shadow, suddenly cold and unwavering.

"I don't really know. How can I tell you? I fell into an abyss."

Nura smiled gloomily, maliciously. "An abyss? We shall all fall into an abyss."

Nura was like that, seemingly fearless, but filled with evil presentiments when left alone and dependent only on herself. Muna hugged her, to drive away the last shadows of fear and to repress the pangs of remorse from her own lack of frankness. Nura accepted her embrace grudgingly. "And I thought you had been dreaming of him. You are more his type, more tender and more modest," she whispered, and Muna felt the warm tears from her sister's eyes on her face.

She snuggled closer, and suddenly sobbed: "No, Nura, foolish one, mad one. We are the same, the same in everything."

They went to sleep in each other's arms, weeping tears for which they could not have given a reason. When they awoke, the sun was streaming over the green slopes of the mountains, and they felt embarrassed before one another.

From then on they did not utter a word about their father's marriage to Fatka, or of their first, awakened love for Arslan. But unspoken love was smoldering, in the radiance that flooded everything and trembled around them, in the warmth that bathed everything, every thought, every being, in the whole expanse from the green valleys and clear waters to the stony heights. Everything that happened, and there was always something happening, reawakened Muna's trembling. And she was almost sure that Nura, too, was calling on Arslan with all her emotions, despite her unnaturally harsh manner and her proud nature. What was more, Muna suspected that Nura's angry malevolence toward

Bulbul and her eagerness to know if Bulbul was aware of the preparations for Fatka's marriage to their father hid an inarticulate but undoubted approach to Arslan.

Therefore it was not hard for her that evening to understand her sister's words, whispered on the threshold of the *čardak:* "Keep your eyes open!" Muna herself had kept a close watch on Bulbul after the night of the dream, though she was sure she would notice nothing. One could come to an understanding with Bulbul only about food and drink. Her smooth face, with slanted greenish eyes, prominent cheekbones, short, cleft chin, and firm, slightly upturned lips, seemed unable to express either joy or sorrow. Perhaps Bulbul, solitary and self-sufficient, confident of their father's enslavement to her secrets of bodily love, did not regard it as strange or superfluous that he should bring home a third wife. Was she not from another, a strange and mysterious, world, in which love itself was different? It was as if Bulbul were not a human being and a woman.

That evening her song, dark and mysterious, punctuated by the quivering strings of the *šarkija,* like flashes in the clear night, penetrated, with the flickering of the candle, through the open door of her room. Muna entered, serious and expressionless, and, after putting the tray down on the table, slid hesitantly toward the door.

Bulbul was sitting on the wide divan, with the *šarkija* between her crossed bare legs, her black plaits hanging down over her breasts. In this position, she seemed much smaller, and almost the same age as Muna. In a single supple movement, without touching the divan with her hands, she leaped to the floor. Silently, like a cat, she came over to Muna and took her by the hand.

Muna had never found herself so close to Bulbul, nor had she ever touched her. The sudden nearness embarrassed and frightened her. Bulbul was more fragile, even smaller, than when seen from a distance; close up, her smooth and slender figure was transformed into the thinness of age. It had been an illusion. Muna noticed the thin lines of her neck tendons, and, even more remarkable, that Bulbul had dry, withered skin; its apparent sheen was clearly due to unguents. There was something old about her dark eye sockets and her thin, pale lips, that evening unrouged. She smiled, strangely tender and almost imploring. Her

teeth were blackish, bad, and though she smoked, some other
scent, sour and stale, mingled with the smell of the tobacco. In
her youth Bulbul must have been of incredible beauty, and beautiful she still was, but her youth had passed, and her beauty and
strength were evidently maintained by that skill and incessant
care with which, it was said, only women from the East were acquainted. In the room, airless in the oppressive heat, Muna felt in
her hand the hard, uneasy chill of Bulbul's bony fingers.

Then, to her complete bewilderment, Bulbul said to her: "Sit!"
Everything was complicated by her sister's waiting and the inevitable interrogation. "I can't," Muna replied, slowly withdrawing her hand. "I haven't the time. My sister is waiting for me."

But Bulbul either did not understand or did not hear. Her
forehead began to wrinkle. She was concentrating, searching for
recently learned and already forgotten words. Finally, in her
deep, almost masculine voice, she spoke in a language whose
sound was not altogether strange, but of which Muna understood
only an occasional word, all the while drawing Muna gently to
the divan.

Muna thought: Bulbul is a flower picked long ago, and which
has a strong scent only because it is fading. She longed to ask
aloud, though she knew that Bulbul would not understand:
"What will you do, without fruit and without root, when you
wither altogether?" But as soon as she thought this and found the
words, it seemed wrong, because those words were not really her
own, but had been borrowed from Arslan's songs. Remembering
Arslan and his songs, she began to be angry at Bulbul and at
herself. To think of a song about Bulbul, and one learned from
Arslan, at that! About Bulbul, who wormed her way into another's life like a sorrow, a poison, a death.

Bulbul was smiling, holding her gently by the hand; in her
expression there was something sisterly, imploring, and compassionate. Muna could learn much from her, perhaps how to win
and hold him whom she would love, whom perhaps she already
secretly loved. But she felt bound, under an obligation to her
sister and to her mother, to hate Bulbul. "Let me go," she said
harshly, tugging at her hand. "What do you want from me?"

Bulbul held on to her hand and kept on smiling imploringly.
Filled with horror at the thought that she and Bulbul were

touching one another while her sister was waiting below, Muna cried out: "Let me go, for God's sake, Bulbul! How can I help you?"

But they could find no way to understand one another. Bulbul gently pulled her down onto the divan. Muna sat on the edge, ready to leap up at any moment. Bulbul, without noticing, curled up beside her, took the *šarkija*, and seized Muna's hand. She guided her hand, which was soon holding the plectrum and plucking at the strings, and Muna could not even guess how it came to be between her fingers. Before Muna had made up her mind what to say or do, Bulbul pointed to her little red tongue and then to Muna's lips and said, laughing: "You teach me the tongue and I teach you the play."

"No, no," shouted Muna, leaping up and forcing herself to be angry. "No, for God's sake! Oh, Bulbul! I can't, I dare not. They would hate me because of you. And what are you to me? No, I won't, I won't."

Her determined withdrawal revealed to Bulbul the uselessness of her efforts. She understood, too, the often-repeated words "no, no, I won't, I won't." Refusals, like prohibitions, are learned first and most easily. She ran to the right-hand corner by the door and from the carved chest drew out a piece of silk embroidery. Muna blushed. How had Bulbul known that it was just that piece of embroidery which had pleased her most of all? Before she could recover herself, Bulbul had pressed it into her hand, bowing, with a smile of beseeching generosity; then she gaily took her by the shoulders and pulled her close. Muna, with joyous quivering and icy terror, felt the fragile trembling of the slight, strange body against hers. When Bulbul drew back, still keeping her hands on Muna's shoulders, two big tears trembled in her glittering eyes.

Muna did not know what to do. Aware of the blush on her own face, embarrassed and confused, she turned and rushed out, almost blindly. On the first step, in the fresh air from the garden, she realized that Bulbul's embroidery was still in her sweaty hand. She quickly pushed it into the neck of her dress and slowly began to descend.

"Where have you been?" Nura, scarcely perceptible in the darkness, awaited her implacably.

"Where? As usual."

"I know, but why did you stay so long?"

"I don't know myself. Bulbul took a long time looking at all the dishes and tasting them."

"All you know how to say is 'I know nothing.' I wouldn't have given her that much pleasure. I'd have slapped them down in front of her and gone out." Nura coughed, but not from the cold; with her, that was a sign of reproach. "And what about her? Does she know about Fatka?"

Muna blurted out, as if she had her answer ready: "Nothing. As always. She never gives any sign."

"She is as hard as a rock. Her heart is a stone."

But Muna did not reply; those words, in any case, did not call for a reply. She slowly followed her sister across the garden to the wicket gate.

Faced by the huge stone house, whose unlighted windows and loopholes yawned like gouged-out eyes, they stood as if caught in something shameful. Their mother still lived up there, lonely and desolate, as if immured, and Uncle Izet-beg had not yet come home from hunting. It seemed, too, that Arslan had forgotten them that evening; he was probably busy telling stories to the youth of the town about the great world, or composing songs to Fatka or about Fatka.

"No matter. Let's wait for Uncle," said Muna, sighing.

"All right, let's wait. He'll be here any moment," Nura agreed, and sat down on a flagstone by the doorway, leaning against the wall of the house. Several flagstones on a low wall along the house served as seats for Grandfather and his friends when the earth was damp and the weather hot. From some garden in the upper part of the town drifted the song of girls, punctuated by the clatter of dishes in the kitchen and the champing and stamping of the horses in the stables.

Muna stood facing her sister, who had stretched out her legs in front of her, as Grandfather did, and, after a moment's silence, asked: "Why has Uncle never married?"

"Silly question," said Nura sourly. "As if the whole world does not know and as if you have not heard a thousand times—the chase."

"Yes, but . . ." Muna commented, without finishing.

"But, but . . . hunting, hunting!"

"But he could still hunt, even if he had a wife."

A shooting star streaked across the sky above the Visitor and burst into sparks. Muna did not know what to say, though Nura's explanation did not satisfy her. Nor did she say anything about the star, because, according to belief, some slave had escaped from prison and would be caught again if anyone said "A star is falling!" She wanted to say: "Uncle Izet-beg is something like that star that flies across the skies and wastes its splendor." But she said nothing, for anything of that sort could be said only by Arslan, in his songs. And if said aloud, such words might also portend some harm to her uncle, under whose gentle guidance they had become acquainted with flowers and animals, with mountains, waters, and skies, and without whose presence their own home might repel them with its chill, its terrors, and its misfortune. "I love Uncle terribly," Muna burst out enthusiastically. "More than Father, more than anyone else!"

"Terribly, more—what do you mean? You are all superlatives today. How can you apportion love? How can you measure it?"

"I don't know. I am mad tonight! But I have always loved Uncle very much."

Before they had been regarded as young women, Izet-beg had often taken them hunting with him and had even allowed Nura to shoot at wild duck and hares with his gun. To Muna, shooting seemed cruel, and, though she was not horrified by dead game, she could not bear the thought of a hare wounded by her hand turning and twisting about its little white tail or a duck hidden in the ferns peering at her with its round black eyes. But she was not horrified at pulling fish from the Lim or the lake, on the night lines laid by her uncle or Stojan Radak or with the rod and line her uncle had made for her. Fish were something different; they lived in an incomprehensible and inexplicable world. Uncle had taken Nura first, when she was just six years old, to see the flight of the wild ducks in the evening, and then Muna, envious of her sister, to night fishing, taking trout and pike from the lake.

Those first hunting expeditions remained moving and unforgettable, their first meeting with that strange and wild, not human, world. And they were all the more thrilling because it was regarded as unusual, even immodest, for women to go hunt-

ing or fishing. But revelation of this new world had begun long
before, with Izet-beg's tales about hunting, about flowers and animals. Arslan, though he did not like hunting, loved these stories
and explained them: "They, too, reveal a secret of human life—
man's bond with the world about him and the passion of his struggle with it."

There would not have been so much interest and excitement in
the tales if their uncle had not been so good at telling stories.
Stojan Radak, the serf, Izet-beg's boon companion on his hunting
trips, a hunter perhaps even more skillful, could not describe
things so well. A hunting incident heard from his lips at once
became dead and colorless; whereas when their uncle told it, it
became more alive and more beautiful than reality. These epi-
sodes became, in the telling, marvelous, faultless, and complete,
like the stories of the heroes in the national ballads.

Arslan explained it thus: "Men cannot live without song and
faith, even as they cannot live without bread. All these things
come to them from God, though they do not think of them so.
Without bread, they would not be able to live, even as without
faith they would have nothing to hope for, but would live like
mindless cattle. And without songs, existence would become ugly
and transient." This was too obscure for them. They were unedu-
cated, even though Arslan talked much to them and often read to
them from books, and Muharem gave them instruction in their
faith. They could not understand.

And Arslan did not understand hunting, though in his own
way he enjoyed flowers and animals, sunshine and water and
mountains. He said that hunting was a blood lust, which remained in man from the animal still alive in him. But how could
Uncle Izet-beg or Stojan Radak be called bloodthirsty when the
former knew how to bandage a man's wounds like balm and the
latter was good-humored and merry, as though he were not a serf,
and always gentle and considerate?

Hunting was not merely a pastime, though there was enjoyment in the twilights and dawns, in the heavy stifling scent of the
powder and the maddening, primitive croaking of the frogs, in
the strenuous effort, which was a restorative for the body and
cleared the mind of everyday needs and worries. No one was able

to say exactly what hunting meant, not even Uncle Izet-beg. He used to say: "Everybody loves something; everyone gives more to something than to anything else."

After they became young women, all that was left to the sisters were the tales of Izet-beg. These were the more pleasant and necessary to them because they were interwoven with hunting, that life they could no longer live.

Izet-beg recounted, step by step, how he went hunting: at first, briefly, the preparation of his clothes, his shoes, his guns, and his dogs, his hunting companions, and the game he intended to hunt; then, in greater detail, the stalking, the reading of the spoor, the catching of the scent, the examination and priming of his gun; and finally, most detailed of all, the unexpected appearance of the game, the gun at his shoulder, his finger on the trigger while he held his breath. But no, the end was never reached as quickly as that. Izet-beg only then began in detail to picture the surroundings, the game, himself. The end of the story and the shot came without haste and without shock; it followed naturally from all that had happened and the conditions of the chase.

Never did one tale resemble another; it was as if every hunt was different. Nothing was repeated, even though everything seemed as if it had been told a hundred times and had happened a thousand times. The words were naturally the most important things, for it was a tale that was being told and not an embroidery worked or a stone carved or a drum beaten. The words themselves were familiar and commonplace, but always differently arranged and selected. In addition, Uncle Izet-beg did not merely tell stories in words, but added much by the tones of his voice, which continually changed, becoming smooth and even when describing something well known and then changing to a whisper or a cry, cut short with an invisible knife sharper than a razor or made to dwindle away like a fine silken thread. His face changed, too; bony, hard, and bronzed, it achieved, when necessary, a youthful softness and freshness, or became desolate and rigid, like a corpse's. His whole body told the stories, seeming to grow tense and knotted or to stretch out and rise from the marshes and reeds around the lake or on rocky Prokletije.

But ever since Bulbul had come, Uncle Izet-beg had been unwilling to tell his stories. The unhappiness of Biba and the lack of peace in the household moved him deeply. He was also sad because in the last few weeks Stojan Radak had not been able to go hunting with him. He said nothing of this; it would not have been becoming for a beg publicly to desire the presence of a serf. But it could be seen from his behavior; he kept asking if anyone had come to look for him, and frequently in the early morning would walk along the Lim with his gun in the direction of Stojan's village, though there was almost nothing for him to hunt there.

Stojan was not a better shot than Izet-beg, but he knew the mountains better and was more expert in knowing where to find game. He could take Izet-beg with complete certainty to the wild goats in the mountains or to the bears in the dense oak thickets. He knew which routes were passable and where it was wise to withdraw. He listened, kept watch, and smelled out the game. And there was something else that bound them together, that swept away all distinctions between beg and serf: a life that was theirs alone.

By his continual associations with their uncle, Stojan had become almost a member of the household staff. In the lives and memories of the twins he had always been there, much more than a serf, even for Nura, though she would never have admitted it, especially since the news of the Radak discontent. The people of Plav and of the household had called him Dogandžija—Stojan Dogandžija, a word that meant falconer—since the time he had trained a falcon as a gift for Izet-beg. That sort of hunting had not been used for many years, but Stojan's maternal grandfather had still been alive then and had inherited from his ancestors the skill of training falcons for the chase. Stojan had learned to work with the bird, had presented it to Izet-beg, and had flown it for him, to the delight of the skeptical townspeople. And Izet-beg, as a return gift, had given him a short knife with a chased silver handle.

The falcon now lived on a beam in the stables. But there was no falconer. Izet-beg could not use the falcon without Stojan Dogandžija; nor would the falcon obey him.

At the beginning of summer, Izet-beg vainly waited for Stojan to come hunting deer with him around Kopiljača. In the late afternoon one day, out of boredom he rowed out into the reed beds on the lake. When he returned, Kara-Djula snapped at him: "Give it up. I know whom you are waiting for. The Radaks are rebelling!" He was silent, discouraged, and pulled the ducks from his gamebag, first a drake with a white neck and yellow legs, then two gray, dark-legged teals, threw them down in front of Kara-Djula, and said, sighing: "And he, too, rebels!"

"He's not a fool to show himself now in Plav!" Kara-Djula burst out, and, as always, snarled at the game. "How long must I go on plucking those beastly ducks. I am wearing my fingers to the bone. It's not as if you had nothing to eat. If that were the case, it wouldn't surprise me if everyone yearned for rotten game as if it were manna from Heaven."

Muna knew that Kara-Djula only talked that way; she was an expert in preparing game and willingly accepted the advice and experience of hunters and hunters' wives. There was no need to pay any attention to her grumblings when they referred to persons and things dear to her. But, linking that summer conversation between her uncle and Kara-Djula with what she had heard in the garden about the arrest of the Radak Knez, Muna, waiting with her sister for her uncle there in front of the house, concluded that her uncle and Kara-Djula had already known something about the Radak trouble. Though there had been much talk about discontent among the serfs, up to that evening the Radaks had not been mentioned. And Muna thought: Uncle will be sorry when he hears of the arrest of the Radak Knez. Certainly not because of the Knez himself, but because Stojan cannot, dare not, come to him.

Suddenly another falling star flashed through the arch above them. Its strong, shimmering brilliance lit up the mountains, and Nura, startled, continued the long-interrupted conversation. "You say that you love Uncle. Who doesn't? But tell me, do you love him better—than Arslan?"

As if caught out in something shameful, Muna, stung by Nura's repeated questioning, retorted angrily: "Can you measure love? That . . . that is different."

"What is different? Do you love Arslan differently from Uncle?"

"No, I didn't mean that! Yet, perhaps I did. I don't know. Why do you ask me?"

"You know very well!" Nura replied sharply. "But you're wrong if you think I'm jealous of you. I am only sorry that we have secrets from one another."

Before Muna had made up her mind what to reply to Nura, whose words had revealed truths she had never admitted even to herself, Kara-Djula came out of the kitchen with a small wooden tray on her hip, clacking and clopping in her slippers. "I am taking supper to that unfortunate one, but it's a waste of time. It eats her, rather than she it," she said, halting by the twins, and added sourly: "It's time for you two to have your supper. You're surely not going to count stars all night!"

"We're coming at once," said Nura. "We were waiting for Uncle."

"Don't bother. The begs will be talking all night, and those not talking will be mounting guard. Wartime conditions—it's a wonder that they ever stopped."

Kara-Djula clattered away into the house, and Nura sighed. "It's strange and terrible, but it's only when I think that Uncle and Arslan might be killed that I realize how much I love them."

"Really terrible when you consider that neither Uncle nor Arslan likes war."

"Who does like it? But still—they go to war!" Nura shouted with unreasonable irritation.

Though Izet-beg was always courageous, it could be concluded from his talk about fighting, brief and colorless, that he accepted war only as a man accepts storm or hail, from which he is bound to defend himself and his property by every means in his power. Even now, he did not seem to be worried about the serfs' revolt or an attack by the Montenegrins. He was engrossed in his hunting, in the silence and mystery of woods and waters.

Arslan, on the other hand, was hurt and unhappy about any kind of harshness or brutality, and especially about men killing one another. For him, war was an evil and a fury which men had invented for themselves and for which they alone were responsible. Nonetheless, he stressed that he, too, would take his part in the war, as an obligation to his clan, to his faith and his ancestors. When Muna, after a conversation with him about war and his part in it, whispered with horror to her sister that he might be killed, Nura, though she was no less anxious about him, cried out proudly and fiercely: "He is a man—and must act like a hero!"

It was inconceivable that Uncle, as little malicious as a man could be, divorced from all human problems, and a part of the twins' life from their earliest recollection, could suddenly disappear, die. To them, he seemed immortal, though they knew that he, like every other man, must die one day. But Arslan, who had only just entered their lives, could easily disappear, be killed. Despite this difference, Muna could not, in her ill-omened presentiments, decide which sorrow would be the greater: her sorrow for her uncle and his life, which was closing, or her sorrow for Arslan, with his whole life before him. Nor could she decide whose sorrow would be the greater: her own, mourning and unconcealed, or Nura's, proud and suppressed.

Muna and Nura did not at first think much about Arslan's regular daily visits. It was in the nature of things, since they were related. Even his discreet efforts to instruct them and acquaint them with the world by his tales, they accepted as something natural. What else should a learned man do for his relatives? Everything had glided along smoothly until, at the beginning of summer, immediately after his return from Stambul, he had asked Nura to take a love letter to Fatka.

By that the twins came to know that Arslan and Fatka had, even while they were still children, been in love with one another and had secretly exchanged love tokens every summer through Fatka's aunt, who had kept house for Fatka's father. But she had died during the past winter. Fatka was the only literate girl in Plav; her father had taught her Arabic script and to some extent the Arabic and Turkish languages. She and Arslan had corresponded by translating their own language into Arabic letters, strange designs, like the marks of sparrows or wagtails in virgin snow.

Nura had carried out her task and handed over the letter with strict and self-sacrificing conscientiousness. On her return, she almost virulently informed her sister: "He only comes to see us so that we can carry his messages!"

Muna noticed her sister's bitterness, the reason for which was still not clear to either of them. Arslan had visited them the day before and the day before that, and they had taken no messages to

Fatka and had only guessed at his and Fatka's love. "Don't be unjust, when you know that it isn't true," Muna protested. "We have no brother of our own, and we are in duty bound to help him."

But Nura would never take advice, and went on with her thought. "He has been taken in by Fatka's beauty. She has won him over to the enemy's camp!" She said this as if she did not see Fatka every day, and as if all Plav were not talking about Fatka's beauty.

Yet she went on carrying letters and messages, and her first bitterness against Arslan was no longer evident. Muna suspected what was smoldering in her sister, for she felt it in herself also. And the unusual, inconceivable beauty of Fatka overwhelmed her.

According to the stories current, every action of Fatka's was bound to be as lovely, as harmonious, as she was as a whole. In fact, her brown hair was too coarse and too curly, her skin rather too dark, her nose freckled, her hazel eyes somewhat prominent, her cheekbones high, and her lips too thin. Her waist was too small for her strong hips and overheavy breasts, and her legs too long in relation to her short, heavily built body. No one part of Fatka, taken by itself, was particularly beautiful, but the whole formed a harmony of beauty worthy of the tales told of her and the songs sung about her.

After Nura's first commission to take Arslan's letter, Muna began to compare her sister with Fatka, without admitting that the comparison referred to her as well. Her sister was more harmonious; every part of her, when compared with Fatka, was more beautiful. Nura was younger, was still growing and developing; she gave promise of becoming still more attractive. But she did not have that incomparable seductive fusion of burgeoning, voluptuous womanhood and youthful modesty and grace, which was not made up merely of swelling breasts and slender waist, rounded arms and long delicate hands, but also of dovelike and caressing, harsh and stern gradations of voice, scarcely perceptible quiverings of full, always slightly parted lips, and expressions in the eyes between offering and rejection, between fiery passion and restrained seductiveness. It was only necessary to forget some one part of Fatka to make her beauty wither and fade. Her beauty was a merging of contrasts, the inseparableness of conscious passion and ingenuous modesty.

Even when they began to suspect Arslan's love for Fatka, and when they became conscious of their own affection for Arslan, the twins never felt a trace of hatred toward Fatka. Not even Nura, always harsh and unyielding toward anything that crossed her wishes, ever let fall a rough or coarse word about the hodža's daughter. This was not because there was little or nothing to criticize in Fatka; as the elder, she was always kind and considerate toward them. Nor was it due to the resignation of Moslem women, accustomed to sharing their love with other women. Tolerance toward second wives and rivals was more usual and natural than jealousy. But Fatka was not a rival; the love between her and Arslan had been conceived before the twins had begun to dream about love or about Arslan. More important—Nura, the wise one, had been the first to notice—there was something similar and inevitable in the destinies of Fatka and the twins. As Arslan's father, and certainly Fatka's, would never have consented to become allied with a family with which he was in vendetta, so, too, their father would never have consented that they marry into a branch of their own family.

The situation, as always, had many facets. Arslan, it seemed, neither knew nor suspected the affection of the twins for him, for something that neither the proud Nura nor the oversensitive Muna could easily make known to him, still less speak of. That would have been a betrayal of him and his openness toward them. In their modesty and in the difficult conditions, they would never have dreamed of Arslan's marriage to them. Though such a thought was difficult to reject, there was an immeasurable, inevitable sweetness in the wish that they, conceived together in the same womb and indivisible, could share the same man. They kept silent about it, even between themselves, each one conscious of what burdened and oppressed the other.

Sometimes it seemed to them that without Fatka there would be no Arslan as they now loved him, with the songs and daydreams that were his existence and his life. That identification of Fatka with Arslan's songs was so powerful and complete that Muna, after Arslan's assertion a few evenings before of his intention, incomprehensible to them, to blend the voluptuousness of Arab, oriental song with their own reserved emotion, said to her sister as they were undressing to go to bed: "Fatka, too, is some sort of link; since she is so beautiful." To which Nura responded, sadly, with a long, pensive glance, but found nothing to say.

Any thought of Fatka's beauty as a link between the different worlds of which he had spoken had not yet occurred to Arslan. He had thought of this bond and reconciliation in a different way: as the interweaving of his inheritance with the intricate Turkish and Arabic songs, as the blend of oriental wisdom with the long suffering of his people, as the fusion of the green and shimmering mountains and waters that were a part of his blood with the dry, sun-scorched soil of Arabia and the fiery azure of the Bosporus, as the reconciliation of his people's inconceivable lack of everything, their proud rejection of everything, with the incredible luxury and dedicated enjoyments of the East. It would have seemed senseless and even insulting to him had anyone told him that his love of peace, his conviction that it would be possible to reconcile begs and serfs, Moslems and Montenegrins, for the sake of a better life and a more tolerant sense of humanity, had its origins in Fatka's incredible beauty and in his longing for her.

Arslan did not see Fatka as merely the union of various beauties or as a plaything of the harem, for passion and enjoyment and the raising of healthy children, but as a being equal to himself who must share everything with him, every thought and every hope. Fatka had become a part of the thoughts he confided to the twins, thoughts so madly rash and new that they, though they listened eagerly, did not dare to repeat: "The time will come when our women will not be hidden, when men will not be divided by faith and inheritance, but only by what each man is worth."

Arslan also revealed to them the difference between the men of Plav and the Montenegrins. Both sides preached that evil was unavoidable and that men could, and must, fight against one another. But the men of Plav considered that the Montenegrins were the evil that must be rooted out and destroyed, and the Montenegrins held the same view about the men of Plav. Montenegrin good was Plav evil, and the other way around. One could not exist alongside the other, and did not wish to. Therefore,

Arslan was eager to reveal what might be considered common to them; both wanted good and believed in it, yearned for a peaceful life and struggled for it.

In truth, there were evident differences between the men of Plav and the Montenegrins, between the Moslem hodžas and the Serbian priests. For the men of Plav and for the hodžas, existence and the body were not merely for suffering and misfortune, but also for joy and beauty. If one behaved justly and reasonably and fought fearlessly for the faith of the Prophet, he would find houris, rivers of enjoyment, and endless flowering fields under eternal light upon the earth, not just in paradise. They did not, as did the Montenegrins and their priests, differentiate body from soul, and ascetism and suffering in this world were not necessary preparation for eternal spiritual peace in the world to come.

Evil, for Arslan, was not inevitable, but arose from bad human laws, from unjust human relations. He was imbued not only with the joyful Islamic attitude toward the body and pleasure, but also with the Serbian idea of the renunciation of the worldly and the transient whenever it came into conflict with the imperishable, with justice and truth. War and evil between men would no longer be if they could peaceably with good will harmonize their passions with reason, their enjoyment with uprightness.

The men of Plav would never have heeded such lessons, even if Arslan had preached them loudly and importunately. For Fatka's father, they were a good excuse to mock the young savant from the vendetta clan. He had read too much! In the world everything that was and was to be had already been—although a trifle different, as Allah had ordered, so that man did not bore man and the world grow tedious. The gap between common sense and madness, between enjoyment and uprightness, between justice and injustice, between good and evil, came because each man considered his own faith and his own existence as true and just.

For the twins, Arslan, like Uncle Izet-beg, provided an escape from the desolate Plav savagery and the monotony of harem isolation into a new world, untried, perhaps even imaginary, but more beautiful and more just, without that continual bloody and destructive contest between their own good and another's evil. They were his most attentive listeners in Plav. He had grown up in Grandfather's house until Ahmet-beg had found a home for himself. The father of his dead mother had been one of Grandfather's slaughtered brothers, and Grandfather had taken the place of a father; their own father and uncles had replaced the brothers he did not have. Out of the ordinary, fresh and pure as the dew, open and transparent as the lake, so that everything in him was frank and clear, Arslan was still more dear to the twins because he had grown up in their own nest.

They waited for him even when they knew he would not come. Every moment without him was long and tedious, and time spent with him slipped past unnoticed in a warm, quivering light. They were terrified by the nearness and the inevitability of autumn, which would bear him away with the swallows and the first falling leaves.

That evening, though they mentioned their uncle only, they were also waiting for Arslan, under the stars, which plunged from the blue shining immensity above them into the gloomy Plav darkness. But the implacable Kara-Djula, returning from their mother, drove them in to supper and bed.

He came almost a week later, on the fourth day after Muna had come to know of the arrest of the Radak Knez, in the evening twilight, in one of those mountain mists that veiled and stifled space and cut short the daylight, hiding hills and homes and people, and crept into everything, into rooms, into thoughts, and into longings. Muna and Nura were sitting with their mother in their room, busy with their embroidery. When Arslan entered, their mother went into her own room, taking with her the rustle of her silken *dimije* and the scent of withered quinces. Recently, though she was regarded as a sick woman, the more seriously because she felt no pain, she had taken to wearing her festival clothes, dressing as richly as she could, powdering her face, and lacquering her nails.

"Where have you been all this time?" Nura asked Arslan, while he, kneeling, held his hands over the brazier.

Muna knew that her sister's indifference was assumed, forced, from the way in which Nura asked this question, not raising her eyes from her embroidery, restraining her voice. And for the first time there flashed the realization, final and irrevocable, that something had changed, not only between them and Arslan, but also between her and Nura. She, too, irritated with herself, repeated in a supposedly calm voice, raising her eyes from her needle in the silken border: "Really, where have you been?" She at once added reproachfully, so that he would notice her: "Today is the eighth day since we've seen you."

"It's nice here with you, warm and comforting," he remarked, rubbing his hands. Then after a short silence he replied: "I have been everywhere—and nowhere. I had—perhaps you won't believe me, but don't tell anyone—to go as far as Skadar. The Vali does not know Serbian, and I acted as interpreter for the Plav and Gusinje envoys. The dispute with Montenegro is getting sharper and more confused, and there is less hope that it will end well."

It was not the habit of the twins to question him; he always told them what they ought to know. Nonetheless Muna remarked distantly: "Here, too, five or six days ago, they arrested some knez or other. They say he knows much but will not reveal anything."

"I heard that on my return. That is not the right way. It is like pouring oil on fire! I heard, too, that they are torturing him. Suljaga hopes to get something of value from him. The law forbids torture, and anyway anything extracted by torture is of little value. It is a bad thing that they are torturing him. It makes a martyr of him, becomes exaggerated, and embitters them. Later, we shall have no right to expect anything better ourselves. Evil is worse for him who does it than for him to whom it is done."

There was something despondent in the young man's words. Suddenly he seemed mature, experienced, and worried. His beard and mustaches, golden, curled, and still sparse, were so much in contrast to his mature speech and thought that they stressed his youth even more. It could be seen that he was suffering from lack of sleep; there were dark rings under his eyes, and his eyelids were red. But his slightly prominent blue eyes were clear and his clean-cut mouth was firm and ruddy, smiling a little, as always. His white hands, with fine golden hairs on the fingers and the outer edges, hovered quietly over the embers. His whole appearance, despite his fatigue, his worry and despondency, showed his usual assurance and serenity.

"We are women and young," remarked Nura, "and it is not up to us to judge and worry our heads about such things. But it seems to me that it serves no purpose to torture him; though he is an enemy, he is not an animal. It is not even good to torture an animal."

Muna stopped embroidering and looked at her sister with astonishment. It was incomprehensible that Nura, who only yesterday had said it was a good thing that the Radak Knez was being tortured, had not only changed her mind so quickly, but had also begun to attack what yesterday she had upheld. For the first time, and certainly because of Arslan, she had obediently accepted someone else's opinion. But perhaps not; perhaps Nura had turned everything over in that astute head of hers and had decided to seem to change her mind. Perplexed but impatient to take part in the conversation and thereby feel nearer to Arslan, Muna said: "You don't drink and don't smoke. Let me find something sweet for you."

"All that you give to your slave," Arslan replied jestingly, putting his hand on his heart and bowing, "he will be grateful for. But I am not a lover of sweetmeats."

Filled with anger at herself, Muna remembered; he did not like sweetmeats, and it was she, just she, who had forgotten. In everything, he was different for the twins, for her, different from others. No one in the whole world had such white skin or such silken hair, which fell behind his small ears to the middle of his bronzed, rather short neck. She had never noticed before how strong he was, so broad-chested and strong-limbed, and, at the same time, so noble and so considerate. Then, remembering that he loved fruit, she hurried out to get some for him.

Returning with a dish of strawberries and cream, Muna, with amazement, overheard Nura's question: "She showed herself to you? What do you mean—showed herself?" and the continuation of Arslan's account: "Just so, she showed herself. I am ashamed to repeat it. She took off all her clothes, till she was as naked as the day she was born, and showed herself to me from all sides."

The young man stood up, took the bowl from Muna's hands, went slowly over to the divan, sat down with the bowl between his knees, and then forgot all about it. The sisters were silent, glancing around stealthily, not looking at Arslan or each other.

"I don't know what Fatka meant by that. Perhaps to put me under an obligation, as if by doing that I had become her lover, or else to show me all her beauties and thus bind me to her even more closely. She knows that I know what she is like, even though I have never seen her thus—naked. And as she did it, she was wiping away tears. No, I am not imagining; she was wiping away tears with the tips of her fingers. She was so sad. What had made her so sad? What could have made her weep?"

Hodža Muharem had kept strict watch on his daughter, and Arslan had not been able to meet her, but from the house of one of his friends he had been able, late at night, to see Fatka's face when she stealthily took the lattice from her window. They could not talk at that distance, only see one another vaguely in the moonlight and exchange signs of love. But it was not important how he had been able to see her undress last night and see her wipe away her tears; once Arslan said anything, it meant that it had happened, and from Nura's reply it was at once clear why he had told her. "But certainly I will; I will take the letter at once!"

"Take care you are not caught. She showed me by signs toward her father's room that she was threatened."

"Don't worry," Nura said, getting ready quickly. "I will say that I have come for her to start some new embroidery for me. Shall I wait for an answer?"

"Wait, wait, by all means. If she cannot write, let her tell you by word of mouth. Let her tell you everything."

Muna and Arslan were silent, listening to the clattering of Nura's wooden pattens as she went down the stairs and across the courtyard and banged the knocker on the gate. Even without Nura's significant glance, it was clear to Muna from Arslan's account that Hodža Muharem had mentioned to his daughter the possibility of her marriage to Omer-beg. The skein had become twisted and tangled.

What would Arslan do? What would Arslan think of them, since it would be difficult for them to dissemble? Despite her wish not to intrude, but believing that it was somehow important for them, Muna asked: "Are you sure? Perhaps it only seemed like that to you, in the darkness?"

"Don't be silly! What darkness? It was a cloudy but moonlit night; one could see and yet not see, as if between waking and dreaming. She took down the lattice, then brought two candles and put them on the coffer, and—I am ashamed to speak of it, but her misfortune is stronger than I am—took off all her clothes, one by one, turning slowly so that I could see everything clearly. She was twisting painfully, as if she wished to say: 'All this, all this, is yours and will not be yours. Do not give me up, save me, take me away, my darling!' "

The young man rose and paced up and down. Both he and Muna had forgotten the strawberries. "I simply cannot imagine what it is all about," he said. "Why, all of a sudden, this—how shall I put it?—modest lasciviousness, this passion of despair, this call and these tears? I am thinking of talking with Father, or with Omer-beg and Izet-beg."

"Better with Uncle Izet-beg," Muna said, interrupting Arslan.

"If I talk with Father, there's that cursed blood feud—I don't know whose or why. Why don't we wipe it out once and for all, especially now, when destruction threatens all of us! At least as far as I am concerned, who only long for humanity and peace in this world, since destiny has put me in it."

Never had he been so agitated, so determined. His smooth, honeyed words, his clear pensiveness were replaced by a premonition of harshness and anger.

"Calm down," Muna implored him, thinking that it would now be necessary to tell him everything. But she held back, hoping that nothing was yet decided and that, perhaps, everything might still turn out well. Noticing the strawberries, she offered them to him with outstretched hands. "Have some strawberries. We forgot all about them."

He sat down again and put the bowl between his knees. But he still did not eat. Muna squatted by his knee, ready to put her head in his lap, to caress him, implore him, as her mother used to do when she was a small girl. "Take some. Eat. It will pass. So Mother says, and it is not easy for her either. Everything passes."

Arslan smiled and tasted the strawberries and cream. "You know that I don't like strawberries when they are all squashed, and you brought them to me just as I like them. You two know everything that I like and look after me better than if you were my born sisters."

The comparison with sisters put Muna out of countenance a little, but gave her courage to say: "You are one of us. We have no brother; we have no one closer than you." Then, uncertain how to get nearer to him, she added: "Have you any new poems to read to me before Nura comes? That will help to lift your worries and mine."

He ate slowly, talking between mouthfuls. "No, I have nothing new. In fact, I have, but only in my mind. I haven't written it down yet. Before I can write anything, I lose interest and can no longer put it on paper. As if I had then revealed all its nakedness; nothing is left except the nakedness."

"Will you write a poem about that, about Fatka undressing?" Muna asked, blushing at the immodesty of her thoughts.

"I hadn't thought of that. Some time must pass before one can write a poem about anything. It is still not clear to me why she did it. I feel astonished and uneasy."

Pretending to think it over, Muna said: "Perhaps they want to give her to someone else, to someone she does not like?"

"I, too, thought of that. But there has been no indication."

Muna was silent, once more considering. Then she asked suddenly: "Is Skadar a fine city?"

"No, it's not. I was surprised. There is not a single beautiful or noteworthy building in it. Even the fortress is small and ugly. And all around it are bare mountains."

"In the songs it is beautiful."

"Everything is beautiful in the songs. It would not be a song if everything in it were not beautiful. Even the ugly is beautiful in song."

"What do you mean: the ugly is beautiful?"

"So it is. If there is something ugly in life, it becomes beautiful in song—old men, illness, war." He fell silent, considering. "But song, poetry, is not beauty alone. It is also truth. And something more: it is a new life, a new world."

"I am sorry that Uncle Izet-beg is not a poet," Muna observed. "He would have something to sing about; he has seen so many mountains and waters, battles and hunts."

Arslan stood up, put the uneaten strawberries on a shelf behind the door, and stood facing Muna. "He, too, is a poet. He talks about hunting as if he were singing. Hunting is singing for him; he has fled into hunting from life and thinks about everything that takes place before his eyes. Everyone flees like that; everyone conceals himself in something."

"That is so. And if he has nowhere to hide, then he hides in himself. But there is no profit in that. Nor is there any profit in Uncle's hunting."

"Well, that depends on how you look at it. There is some profit in his hunting. The hunters who come after Izet-beg will learn from him. Nothing that man creates dies; it is later handed on to others."

"But that is not the same as song. You said: song endures, poets die."

"That is true. But there is one great difference. No one knows what it is except the poet, or the mason, or even the needle-woman, such as you; they draw from themselves something no one has ever seen or heard before and yet seems known to all, something that is theirs. Something more beautiful than anything that exists, than anything that can be imagined! Something—no one knows what!"

"Listen," Muna broke in suddenly, "would you like to see something? If you promise me to tell no one, especially not her, not Nura."

"All right," Arslan said, smiling.

Muna began to rummage in her coffer. "You know, I hide nothing from Nura, but—she would not understand. Three or four nights ago, Bulbul pressed on me, almost by force, an embroidery that had pleased me. I want you to tell me—you understand such things—is it beautiful? I like it very much. And I will confess to you: Bulbul does not seem so evil to me. We just cannot understand one another. She has been wandering in strange lands and hoped that she would be accepted here and that she would not be only a concubine."

She spread out the square cloth with golden edges, about a span long, on which golden shapes, similar to the cupolas of mosques, were interwoven with multicolored silk threads in designs with no resemblance to anything. But in those designs, if one looked long enough, it was possible to find all sorts of things —parts of unusual buildings and harmonious forms, flowers, leaping animals, flying birds.

Twilight was falling, but neither of them noticed it. In the half-light, and with Arslan, it seemed to Muna that the embroidery was even more beautiful, as though she had never seen it before. Every time, it revealed something different, as if it were alive and thus ever-changing. The multicolored threads did not stand out, but through their harmony of shape and color were transformed into a living dance, gay and yet, because of the darker shades, also a little melancholy. The twilight intensified that melancholy.

"It's like, it's like . . . wait a moment, what is it like?" Arslan said with enthusiasm. "Ah, I can't remember. Perhaps it is not like anything that I have seen, but it is wonderful."

"It seemed beautiful to me," Muna said, encouraged, folding up the embroidery. While she was carefully closing her chest, with its scents of quince and pine, Arslan asked: "Would you be able to embroider anything like that? Could Nura?"

Muna knew that Nura would not be able to. Nura was skillful only in making cakes and concocting sauces and dishes. But Muna was not sure she herself could create anything of the sort. Yet she replied: "Well, yes, I could—we could. Perhaps not at once, but if someone showed us."

"Yes, it must be learned," agreed Arslan. "But one must have a gift." Then he added, suddenly serious: "Anyone who could make a thing like that could not hate."

Muna was standing in front of him. "Do you mean Bulbul? A dancer, a čoček, a foreigner from the outside world. How could she not hate us, Mother and us two?"

"I don't know. I thought to myself, looking at it: She does not hate you. She, you can see for yourself, has been wandering. Who knows why? She has been hiding from something. How do you know she was a čoček? There, in Asia, many women from the harem know how to dance. They even learn before marriage."

"Why?"

"To become sweeter, more attractive."

"Isn't a woman—how can I put it?—sweet even without that?"

"She is. But that is a cajolery, a foretaste."

"A foretaste of what?"

"Of making love, of love's sweetness."

"I think that a woman can caress and be caressed in other ways. Not even Fatka knows how to dance."

"She doesn't know."

"And yet you love her?"

"Yes, I love her."

"Does she know how to caress in other ways?"

"She knows."

"Fatka is good. Fatka is beautiful."

"She is. Good and beautiful. To me."

She wanted to say to him: "I, too, we, too, would be good, and we are not ugly." But he was melancholy because of Fatka, and she remaked: "Bulbul, too, is beautiful."

"I haven't seen her. She covers herself before me. I am no kin to her."

"But you are no more kin to Mother than to her, yet she does not veil before you."

"But she practically brought me up. I have known her since I was a child. Bulbul has only just come, and I am now a young man."

"And I, and we two, Nura and I, aren't we already young women?"

Arslan was silent at that, measuring Muna with a serious glance, which told her: "Yes! And only now have I noticed it!" Embarrassed by a sweet shame and her boldness, she went on: "Bulbul is beautiful. But she is beginning to fade."

"Everyone must fade sometime. That comes with the years."

"But one only sees it in her when one is near her."

"She takes care, evidently. And she is of another race."

"Than my mother, do you mean?"

"I wasn't thinking specially of Biba, but of all our women. Our women grow old slowly, but one can see the process in them. Among the Turkish and Tatar women it is not seen; they become old all at once. Bulbul, too, will become old all of a sudden."

"Will Father drive her away then?"

"I don't think so. He, too, is no longer young. And where would she go?"

"Father would find another. She is barren."

"Perhaps so. He will enjoy her to the full and then find another. There are always more women than men. Wars always cut down men."

They stood, one facing the other, still beside the chest. In the twilight she noticed the enigmatic expression on his face. The half-light was pleasant; it filled her with courage and hope. Nonetheless, she asked: "Shall I light a candle?"

"As you like. I like it like this. We will wait in the twilight."

He sat on the divan, and Muna squatted down beside him.

"Why are you squatting there, like a slave girl? Sit up here beside me."

A chance courage took form within her, hardened. She longed to say to him: "What if I should like to be your slave?" But that would sound ugly, especially now, when he was worried because of Fatka, and when nothing had been disentangled concerning her father's marriage. She sighed, got up slowly, and sat on his left, feeling the pressure of his leg against hers, her first distant contact with a male body, which aroused a light trembling within her. For a moment she was afraid the trembling would be noticed, and ashamed in case that contact might in some way betray Nura and take for herself something to which her sister, too, had a right. But she did not withdraw her leg; that trembling was seductive, sweet, the more powerful, the more the feeling of shame became stronger. She did not know what she should do, but was ready to submit to anything he said or did. But it was obvious that, concerned about Fatka and her misfortune, it would not occur to him that she felt anything special for him.

"I—we two—Nura and I, love Fatka and you. We would do anything for you," she said at last, pensively, searching for the right words. But he did not reply, as if he had expected such words, as if she and Nura said them to him every day.

Muna suddenly felt overcome by shame. Everything seemed to her immodest—words, thoughts, and especially that distant contact. Nura would never have gone so far. But at the same time she inwardly reproached him. How was it that he, so clever and so sensitive, had not understood her desire, her allusions, her torment? Why did he see in her and in Nura, in her even more than in Nura, only sweet little relatives?

He turned fully around to her, and their legs touched. "And you, you and Nura, seem as if you are hiding something from me."

She could not imagine what to reply. But she was sure that it should be something that would make him understand, make him do what she wished, though she herself did not know what it was she wished. At that moment there was a bang on the knocker, and the gate squeaked and shook. There was another rap on the knocker, and then, immediately after, the sound of bare feet and the clatter of Nura's pattens.

"Nura!" Muna whispered, embarrassed, and at once ran to the window, opened the lattice, and called out: "Nura, Nura, on your way up bring a light for the candle. I was just going to get one."

Nura answered something, but without her usual contentiousness, and Muna slowly closed the window and stood there, leaning, with her hands behind her, on the sill. Arslan remained seated, motionless, pensive in the half-darkness. It seemed to Muna that she knew what he was thinking; at last he must realize, even if unclearly, that she, she and Nura, loved him as—as girls love young men. She was sure that something had happened between them and that everything would have been quickly and easily explained had it not been for Fatka, and all those unfortunate complications about her.

As if he discerned her thoughts, he turned toward her and said, softly and sadly: "Even if I wished, I could not leave Fatka now."

Nura, with a lighted splinter, brought with her the scent of pine, smoke, and damp. She lit a candle and placed it on a shelf in the corner, then carefully crossed the room, holding her hand under the splinter so that sparks would not fall on the carpets, and lit a candle in the other corner. Everything in the room became visible. The expressions of all three changed. Arslan looked questioningly at Nura, on whose tense, pale face only Muna could read the worst. Nura extinguished the splinter in the brazier and, as the thin wisp of smoke rose from the ashes, said: "What we two have suspected has just happened. Her father wants to marry Fatka to our father."

Arslan, thunderstruck, threw back his head and asked with trembling lips: "What father? Whose father?"

"Our father—mine and Muna's. Omer-beg, son of Murat-beg Džidić," Nura replied, curtly and clearly, as if she felt a chill joy in her own anger and brusqueness.

Arslan, his face flushed, stood up, thrust his hands into the pockets of his green trousers, then took them out again, fists clenched. "How can that be? Why, all of a sudden, Omer-beg?"

"Anything can be! Why shouldn't it?" retorted Nura, with intentional spite. "Your father is at blood feud with her father; her father is poor and so is yours; my father is rich, and my father's father wants his son to be the father of future sons and fathers. One buys a heifer for a bull wherever it is cheapest. That is all!"

"Oh, Nura, how wonderful you are!" Muna burst out, and hugged her impulsively.

Nura smiled. "Now this silly one! As if I needed tears, since only a while ago Fatka almost bathed me in them! But they mustn't count their chickens; it's not all over yet. Fatka refuses; she will kill herself before consenting. I called her down, and now she isn't thinking about that—girlish exaggeration and nothing more. But let us see; what is to be done and where can we find help?"

Through her tears, Muna saw Arslan's face filled with a shining disbelief instead of astonishment and anger. He hugged Nura, and Muna saw her sister blush furiously and the tide of red run slowly down to her throat. He cried out: "I really don't know how to thank you! Now it is all clear to me; you knew everything but didn't want to sadden me. I could see that you were hiding something from me. Only I don't know what to do and how to do it—my father and her father . . ."

Nura cut him short. "Let's forget about fathers. Sit here, closer; we will all get warm, though none of us is cold."

They squatted around the brazier, and Nura whispered significantly: "Uncle! We must tell everything to Uncle Izet-beg. He's the only one who can help us."

That night the three of them talked with Uncle Izet-beg, and he agreed—reluctantly, it seemed to Arslan, but as the twins expected—to put everything before his brother and ask him to abandon the idea of marriage to Fatka. The twins assured Arslan that their uncle was like that; he never promised much, but once he had made up his mind he did not weaken.

The weather cleared next day, and Grandfather again began his evening sessions in the garden. A whole week passed, and Uncle Izet-beg gave no sign that he had done anything. It seemed as if he were avoiding the sisters and Arslan, and the expression of grave concern did not leave his face. Every dawn and every evening he went out hunting or walked around Plav. Nothing seemed to have changed in his usual way of life. For the first time, he became enigmatic to Muna and Nura, even distant.

Then unexpectedly, on a Friday, the day on which relatives and friends usually gathered at Murat-beg's, Izet-beg did not go on his evening hunt, though the golden retriever leaped and gamboled about him, barking and reminding him that he should not let slip an unsurpassable joy for the sake of human trifles. Accustomed to Izet-beg's absences, everyone was astonished when he appeared. But no one expected him to create any sort of trouble, still less oppose the intentions of his father, Murat-beg.

Serving them continually with coffee and tobacco and lighting their pipes, the twins followed the conversation in snatches.

First of all, Ahmet-beg Kapetanović, though he had been the last to come, reported some news that affected them all, especially Murat-beg: the sword of Mahmut-pasha Bušatlija, the Vizier of Skadar, whom the Montenegrins had killed eighty-three years before, at the Battle of Krusi, had fallen at last into the hands of the enemy, the usurper and self-styled voivode Miljan Vukov.

Muna noticed that when the news was given, the dark shadow of the pear tree already lay across the stream; the garden was filled with a bluish evening light, and the stream gurgled uneasily. The men, till then good-humored and talkative, withdrew into dark forebodings.

The sword of Mahmut-pasha, by tradition, had belonged to Staniša, the Islamized son of the Montenegrin prince Ivan Crnojević, from whom the Bušatliji, the hereditary viziers of Skadar, and also the Gusinje begs of the Šabanagić clan, traced their origin. It was said that Staniša, the Turkish convert, had received the sword from Sultan Mehmet, with the rank of begler-beg over Zeta and Montenegro. The sword had passed from generation to generation as a symbol of glory and lordship. Mahmut-pasha had defended it at Krusi until the Montenegrins had taken it, and his life. From that time, the sword had been preserved in the Cetinje monastery as a holy relic, until the Montenegrin Prince Danilo had given it to the Sirdar Kusovac for his services at the Battle of Grahovo. But because Kusovac had died shortly after, the sword had been restored to the monastery. In the course of twenty years no one had been found in Montenegro worthy of wearing it—until now. The Montenegrin Prince Nikola had, as a sign of special favor, given it to Voivode Miljan Vukov.

The death of Mahmut-pasha and the loss of the sword had been regarded as an omen of Turkish decadence, and, in fact, from that time onward everything had been worse for the Turks in their struggle against Montenegro. Now the transfer of the sword into the hands of Miljan might mean that Cetinje had attributed to him some special role, which could only be the solution by force of arms of the problem of Plav and Gusinje.

Grandfather Murat-beg thought less of the possibility and the danger of war than of the sword itself, which, by the fact that it remained in his mind and memory, once more became the symbol of Turkish misfortune. "Ever since we lost it," he said gloomily, "it has brought death to us and victory to the Montenegrins."

Omer-beg shared Grandfather's presentiments with evident anxiety, but nothing was to be read on Izet-beg's face, though he, too, shook his head. Ahmet-beg was even more embittered and anxious than Grandfather. "Had it only fallen to someone else, and not to Voivode Miljan! Even when he is asleep he is thinking what evil to do the Turks." Once they had regretted its loss and prognosticated over the evil omen, there was little more to be said about the sword. But it hovered over them, influencing all that they said and did and all that they wanted.

Evidently the discussion had moved on to other topics, for when the twins brought in the *džezva*s with the first coffee, they found everything changed in both the men and their words. What was strangest, though hoped for and welcome, was the change in the usually tolerant and reserved Izet-beg. He was shouting at his brother Omer-beg, at Ahmet-beg, and even at his own father. "I will not permit it while I am alive, while I have any part in this household! Take whomever you like, but I will not permit you to take Fatka, Muharem's daughter. The day the bridal messengers cross the threshold of Muharem's house, I and Muna and Nura will leave the house forever!"

Everyone was astonished at his opposition; they had never expected anything of the sort from him, and they could not begin to guess his reasons. They kept silent, looking at Izet-beg with suspicion. Grandfather Murat-beg, who inflexibly demanded from his sons, as from all other members of the household, outward and slavelike submission, was totally unable to find words.

At last Ahmet-beg began, in a conciliatory tone: "To tell the truth, your kinship with my blood enemy was never very pleasant to me. But I did not want to insist on it; I had made up my mind to put up with it. And I was not pleased that Omer-beg should marry until it was clear if there would or would not be war. But nonetheless, I say one must take thought how to keep one's line alive."

"War or no war, maintaining the line or not, one way or another, Fatka will not come into this house!" Izet-beg broke in sharply.

Omer-beg, who had taken no part in the conversation, but had sat twisting and biting his reddish beard, unexpectedly and maliciously taunted his brother. "Perhaps you have an eye on her yourself!"

"I implore you, stop," shouted Grandfather, leaning on his clenched fingers and trying to rise.

Izet-beg leaped up. "I have said what I have to say. As for you, brother or not, I tell you: Were it not for the disgrace, since you are my brother, though you have never acted so toward me, we would already have settled our differences with swords, once and for all!"

Ahmet-beg had also risen and, taking Izet-beg's left arm, tried to make him sit down. He begged: "I implore you as a dear brother, on our love!"

Omer-beg noticed the twins and shouted: "You are listening to every word, little monsters! Get out of my sight!"

Muna and Nura fled from the words and the glance, which hurt and flashed like knives in the dark, gentle garden. Muna whispered: "Uncle is wonderful! But what will happen? What do those words mean?"

"How should I know, silly one?" Nura shouted, slamming the gate behind her.

In the kitchen, Kara-Djula was salting fresh cottage cheese for Grandfather. When they told her what they had heard and all that had happened, she calmly gave judgment. "It would have been better if you had not overheard. Then you would not know. And Izet-beg might have said even worse things to him—that is so! But did you ask if they would all have supper together? If so, I shall have to prepare something better."

The twins had not asked that, and now did not dare to appear before their father and grandfather again so soon. So Kara-Djula went herself, striding firmly on her powerful, stumpy legs.

Muna and Nura had thought that they knew the past of all the members of the household, as of the house itself. They knew when everyone had been born and when they died, whom they had married and from which clan, and who their children had been. Their ancestors were known to the tenth generation, even before their conversion to Islam, and they knew who had obtained everything in the house and when, who had planted every tree, and who had fashioned and laid every stone. But obviously there existed another life of the household, even of the things in the household, which from time to time, either through family squabbles or quarrels with other clans, and sometimes even through the overtruthful lips of Kara-Djula, came to light, appearing far more real and more monstrous than what was told openly. At any moment someone might mention forced labor on the kula or in the stables, serfs beaten, serf girls raped; or leaders and young men from other clans killed in vendettas, minor wars between the begs, revolts against the Vizier at Skadar, even against the Sultan himself; the seizure by agas and begs of serf villages from kmets and feudal lords and smallholders. But all that was as if it had happened in another world, intruding upon their kin and their household only at rare moments, fragmentary and incomplete.

"We know so little that we know nothing," said Nura bitterly, as if she and Muna were guilty. "We do not even know who Kara-Djula is, and she knows everything."

Ever since they could remember, Kara-Djula had been a servant, but also the housekeeper who had the final word about everything and did not allow anyone to contradict her. They suspected that she was by origin a Montenegrin, either a refugee or a slave, and they had noticed her special power over Grandfather. Dark, bony, compact despite her corpulence, fairly tall, she must once have been, if not a beauty, handsome and attractive, with her barbaric, virile, savage energy. Though she was now nearly sixty, her cheeks were bursting with health, and work always seemed to make her stronger and more robust. She moved slowly but easily, like a ship, and she did all her work at the same measured pace, effortlessly. She was curt and harsh toward the serf men and women when they brought tribute and gifts or came to lend a hand at some job, but she never swore at them, still less beat them. She behaved in the same way to others, even to members of the household. She never talked about herself, and everything she said, even if it were not the whole truth—for some things she always passed over in silence—was an essential part of the truth, just as a piece taken away from a stone still remains stone. She never wept or laughed. She would sometimes smile when she was mocking someone, as if she lived outside everyday joys and hatreds, outside human misfortunes and achievements.

Life with Kara-Djula was simple and easygoing, and Muna worriedly asked her sister: "What should we know about her? She, at least, is straightforward, like beans, like an open book."

"That's what everyone says. Yet no one is straightforward. I *must* know. We cannot be of any help to Arslan, or to ourselves, or to Mother and Uncle, if we do not know. Don't you see what a hole we've fallen into, we two and Arslan? And what about Uncle and Mother? Aren't you scared, Muna?"

"Yes, I'm scared, and I don't know why."

"I know. You are afraid of finding out. You would like everything to be fine and good and everyone comfortable and gay. Yet you must do evil and all sorts of beastliness, cause trouble and misfortune to yourself and others, if you want to live and to survive. You'll destroy yourself if you ever leave me."

"Perhaps I will. Certainly I would destroy myself without you. But let it be! How can I help it if I am like that?"

"But I won't let you! You are more to me than a sister. We came from the same bed. When Uncle and Mother and Kara-Djula are gone, we shall have no one left except one another."

Not for a long time had Nura been so tender, or so resolute. She no longer resisted her sister's embrace, and Muna's eyes filled with tears. "I really am silly—and lost. And you, Nura, are so good, and so strong."

Kara-Djula swayed up to them, pattens clattering, and, blocking the kitchen door with her body, shut out the evening glow. "Everything is quiet," she said mockingly. "The brothers have blunted their teeth. Now you can take them some more coffee and tobacco—till they sharpen their teeth once more. We will not take supper to anyone, except that witch up there in the *čardak*. As for the others, anyone who comes to the kitchen may grab what he can find."

The twins came upon Ahmet-beg standing with raised arms. Against the pale evening sky he seemed still taller and bonier than he really was, and more bitter and angry than when he was talking about the Montenegrins. He was shouting loud enough to be heard three gardens away: "My son! A Kapetanović! To marry into a blood-guilty house! Why, half Plav would spit at me, and the Kapetanovići would turn in their graves! Doesn't he know that we have held two captaincies for two hundred years and more? With a blood enemy one can come to terms, but one cannot enter his house and mingle his blood with ours. Arslan is everything to me, but honor and my good name are also everything to me. Not her—even if he never marries! If it is written that I leave no grandsons behind me, well, let it be so! But let my honor and my name remain unsullied."

"He will marry her, like it or not! With honor or without honor, as he wishes," Izet-beg broke in, mocking and intransigent.

"Who are you to judge my house and my family?" burst out Ahmet-beg.

"Whoever I am, that's the way it will be. I will give them horses and money, and I will ride with them. Then let them go out into the wide world, if there is no other way. If you cannot live without the past, Arslan, at least, has a right to the future. What stupid and heartless men our leaders are to have brought our land to this."

"Ha, ha, ha," croaked Omer-beg. "My brother Izet-beg sits in judgment on those whom no man has judged."

"Indeed, son, you have harrowed deep, first your brother and now your brother-in-law. I ask myself if anyone will be left in my household." Murat-beg shook his long white beard.

"You, old man, ask too much," Izet-beg replied heatedly. "But you, too, must be just if you want me to be your son, your servant, and your slave."

"Who asks for justice must first bring it himself," mocked Omer-beg. "You estrange his children from your brother and your brother-in-law."

Izet-beg paid no further attention to his brother, but turned only to his brother-in-law, Ahmet-beg, and his father. "Can't you see that everything has changed? You will take your family and your faith to the grave with you."

"If it were not for Murat-beg's honor and the bread with which you supported me, and if you were not to me what you are," broke in Ahmet-beg, as if afraid that he had not been fierce enough and that he would leave something unsaid, "I would settle accounts with you in quite another way."

"You have the place and you have the sword," Izet-beg cut in. "Up till now I have never wiped out anyone," and he added, with a sarcastic laugh: "But first I will see Arslan married."

"By Allah! He is out of his senses." Murat-beg raised his hands to Heaven. "Don't try to understand him."

"Get out, hags!" Omer-beg shouted suddenly at the twins, and threw at them the handful of earth he had been fingering.

The twins fled into the darkness of the garden. Muna could vaguely see her sister's white sleeves, which hovered among the fireflies like the wings of some strange night bird. "Uncle is a marvel, Nura! He will succeed in everything; he must succeed—he is afraid of nothing."

"Yes, he really is," Nura agreed, raising the latch of the side gate. "But I am not sure that he will succeed. This is a madhouse."

The begs soon dispersed, each going his own way, bitter and angry. None of them asked for supper, and Kara-Djula had not prepared anything, as if she had been sure what would happen. In the house and in the courtyard there was a tension almost tangible, a gloomy and stifling oppression, broken from time to time only by the stamping of the horses in the stables and the clatter of Kara-Djula's dishes in the kitchen.

Nor did the twins have any supper. At the open window of their room, pressed together as if to give each other courage in the cool of the night, they waited silently; they did not know for what. The clatter in the kitchen died down at last, the fire, which Kara-Djula had banked down, went out, and her heavy tread and continual grumbling could be heard under the window.

"I'm scared," Muna whispered.

"And I am no longer afraid of anything. Now, I would even spend the night alone in the graveyard."

"Yes, you are like that. You, Nura, are like a man. The summer night is long, with all this evil and anxiety about. What do you think? Let's go and talk to Kara-Djula, so that we do not torment ourselves. She is as strong as a mountain and will probably know how to calm us; she can explain everything."

Sighing, Nura took her sister by the arm and led her toward the door. "I, little Muna, am a woman like you. I, too, am afraid, but I keep my fear clamped down. I know how to restrain myself; I know that I must. You, Muna, are better than I am. You will be unhappy. All who are good are unhappy. See how unhappy Uncle is."

"Yes, somehow he is. When he is talking it seems that he is not unhappy; yet in fact he is. Father, too."

"I hate Father! I have never loved him very much. But I did not know it."

"Don't, Nura, I beg you. He is your father. And he, too, is unhappy, Nura."

"Perhaps. But he is bad. Spiteful and a weakling."

"Unhappy."

"That, too. Unhappiness has made Uncle good, but him bad."

Kara-Djula's little room was on the ground floor, in the corner to the right of the steps. On the opposite side was Murat-beg's room. At one time he had had a room on the first floor, the room that was now Biba's, but some five or six years before, since it had become harder for him to go up stairs, he had come down, driving the servants to live in the outhouses by the stables. Every moment, day or night, he needed something or other and would strike with his pipestem on a hanging metal plate, calling for Kara-Djula. The twins had many times, often late at night, heard blows on the metal plate, and Nura, groping the way to Kara-Djula's door, warned jestingly: "Go quickly or the plate will drive us mad."

Kara-Djula was undressing and looked at them questioningly, but in no way harshly.

"We came to see you, Kara-Djula. We didn't want to be alone," Nura said.

"Yes, yes. I was only waiting for that. I am tired and sleepy."
She sat half undressed on the cushions and, sighing, gestured to
the twins to sit down. "I don't know what to do with you. My
hands brought you up, even more than your mother's. If I tell
you, you will be horrified, and if I don't tell you, you will be
eaten up with doubts and suspicions and hatreds. Now you are
grown up and tomorrow you might get married. It is better for
you to know. Then you will understand."

And Kara-Djula told her story.

"As you have probably guessed, I am a Serb from Hercegovina.
One year—I was then thirteen, and it was my family's *slava*, the
day of the Holy Archangel—some freebooters fell upon our house
and our women. My brothers, father, and uncles were killed or
wounded. Seven of them then set fire to their homes and fled to
the Upper Morača, which had revolted earlier.

"I can remember nothing lovelier than my village. I will, I
hope, die with every stone and blade of grass before my eyes.
Close to our house, a spring burst out of the living rock. It never
dried up. In summer it was as cold as a snowflake, and in winter
tepid as a healing spa, so that we girls, when we went to fetch
water, cooled our faces or warmed our hands. Our fields were as
flat as tables and rich, and the hills around were not bare and
stony, but grassy and covered with bushes. There was always
somewhere to rest one's soul and one's eyes. And Upper Morača
was a stony desolation, a Godforsaken land, hard and hungry and
accursed, a land for exiles and the unfortunate.

"We had no one with whom to stay and nothing to live on in
the Upper Morača. But since Mina Radović had killed Hasan-
beg Mušović and raised the Lower Morača in revolt, my people
moved into a deserted serf village there.

"Even as Upper Morača was torment and misfortune, so Lower
Morača was mild and well favored; a land made for farmers and
the fortunate. But Mina could not keep his Morača, our blessed
land. The Moslems attacked Lower Morača from three sides, so
that no way out was left to us except by way of Rovci—desolation
even more accursed than the Upper Morača. Mina withdrew with
some of his band, but the people of Morača for the most part
submitted. Only those possessed by the Devil leave the good for
the worse.

"My people, too, fled with Mina to Rovci, but I was late because of the cow and the calf. I could not endure to see the children die on the rocky slopes of Rovci for lack of a drop of milk.

"The Turkish horsemen caught me on the open space below the Morača monastery, and since I seemed pretty to them—I was then fifteen—they began to quarrel about me and kill one another. But their *buljukbaša* liked the look of me and took me from them, and gave me into the charge of his groom, Rustem. Then they took a few more slaves, but more for ransom than for sale in the markets.

"Next day the submissive Morača knezes gathered there in front of the monastery, so that the Turks could fix their tribute and the men of Morača ransom the slaves. But there was no one there to ransom me, and I could hope for nothing from the Morača knezes, who did not dare to ransom Uskok and haiduk children.

"So they took me into Turkey. The groom Rustem tied me to his horse, and though he was a recent convert, I was not sorry. But I could not deceive his eyes and ears to run away or to kill either myself or him. Next day we reached Kolašin, and there the begs had a great banquet and a celebration. I did not see it; I was bound and shut up in a cabin. I only heard the singing and playing, and it tore my heart to pieces. In the evening your grandfather came into the cabin, that same Murat-beg, but young and impetuous and drunk with plum brandy, victory, and merriment, to do to me, against my will, what a husband does to his wife. I defended myself with teeth and nails and all my strength. But he whipped me till my skin and my blouse were in tatters and I lost consciousness, and he threw my plaits across the doorsill and shut the door on them. Even had I been in my right senses I could no longer have defended myself, but I remember that I asked the beg, after the shame he did to both me and himself: 'What pleasure have you got from what you took by force?' and he answered: 'None, but it seems to me that Morača is not submissive until I have conquered the women of Morača.' The beg did not touch me again that night, and I fell asleep in pain and torment.

"We remained in Kolašin three days. The beg did not come again, and we left for Plav, I bound and Rustem on horseback. I was feeling better, and later he bathed my wounds with plum brandy and put me on his horse. I no longer tried to escape. It was as if my reason had been turned upside down. Even today I do not know what came over me, but I was no longer what I had been before. I had come to terms with my slavery. Rustem understood that and kept little watch over me.

"It may have been that the change in me was due to shame over what the beg had done to me. There was no way to return to my kin or to my faith. Perhaps it was because they had already made a slave girl of me that I realized that what had happened to me had happened to all slave girls in olden times. It no longer occurred to me to take my own life, and on the third day, when we were in sight of Plav, I asked Rustem: 'Are you married?' He replied: 'I am not.' 'Would you take me, sullied as I am?' 'I would if you change your faith and if the beg agrees. You are not sullied, for you are a slave and do nothing of your own free will.'

"Murat-beg did not give me to Rustem at once, but, hiding me from his father, Husref-beg, peace be to his soul, took me to the *čardak* of his mistress at Novšić. There the lusty young begs feasted for a week and made merry with the gypsies, and the beg showed me off and made me sit beside him and he spent his nights with me. How cursed a human being can become! The beg became dear to me once I had accepted that I was to be a slave.

"But there came an end to the merrymaking of Murat-beg. One morning his father with other fathers broke in on them, drove out the gypsies, and took away their sons. I had nowhere to go except to Rustem. So I took the Turkish faith at Plav, and he took me for his wife.

"No one at Plav reproved Murat-beg for taking my virginity by force. It was considered at that time that one might do to a slave whatever one liked. Nor did anyone reproach Rustem; he had married me after I was freed. So I became reconciled to my life. In my homeland I would have had to endure shame and mockery as well as much hard work.

"With my faith, I also changed my name. From Ružica, I became Djula. Kara they added later as a nickname, because of my rough ways.

"Rustem was not handsome. His head was too big and deformed by scars, but he was good-humored and hard-working, a bit obtuse but healthy. We both served Husref-beg and his sons, and I would have had a family by him had it been so fated. But I had become pregnant by the beg at Novšić and would not bring a bastard into Rustem's house. A certain widow who did such things and lived off stillborn children procured me an abortion and injured my womb.

"From time to time Murat-beg would have periods of frenzy, and he did not calm down entirely until after he married. But he did not touch me again; it was as if there had never been anything between us. I lived in the house and looked after the beg's children and saw the death of Murat-beg's brothers and of my own Rustem; he died alongside the first brother, the one who was the standard-bearer. When the *hanum,* Murat-beg's wife, died, the beg once more turned to me, so as not to bring a second wife into the household, even though I was well advanced in years; to feed him and clothe him and warm his bed with my body, till I accompany him to the grave.

"And Izet-beg fell in love with his sister-in-law, Biba, your mother. He had been wooing her when she was still a girl, but concealed it. And he was dear to her, too, and he refused to be her escort at her marriage. But there was nothing between them; both are innocent of everything except vain longing. Omer-beg knows that. But when spite and malice overcome him, nothing pleases him so much as to taunt his brother about this, and Izet-beg is unable to defend himself. Izet-beg is himself at fault because he let his brother know; he was so tormented that he could not keep silent, but confided everything to Omer-beg. Then he enrolled for three years in the nizam, in the Sultan's spahis. And when it seemed to him that his love for his sister-in-law had burned out and was dust and ashes, the desire for his homeland drew him, and he returned and devoted himself to hunting, for which he had a passion even when he was a young boy.

"To me also, who am older and nearer the grave, my homeland comes more and more into my mind. If only I could once more wash myself in and drink from that spring. I hear that the Montenegrins have taken Nikšić, and that my family has gone back to their old lands. Perhaps some of my brothers and sisters are still alive. But there is no return for me. God's slave lives and dies where his fate takes him."

Djula's story calmed the twins for that night. But the anxiety remained, spreading and permeating everything, invisibly.

Violent quarrels broke out between Ahmet-beg and his only son, Arslan, which were pacified by the intervention of Grandfather Murat-beg and Arslan's mother. Relations between the brothers Omer-beg and Izet-beg were quite broken off. With no other way out, Izet-beg, with the agreement of Arslan, confided everything to Fatka's father. Obstinate in everything, the hodža showed himself conciliatory when it was a question of his darling. Though he had already agreed to give Fatka to Omer-beg, he withdrew his word and, fearing trouble and misfortune, sent the girl to stay with relatives at Akovo.

Depression filled Murat-beg's house. But that was better than quarrels and intolerance among women and between brothers. One could at least dream of a return to peace and good will.

Omer-beg, though the most guilty in these dissensions and misfortunes, was the weakest of all in bearing them. Driven, perhaps, by a desire to put an end to the gossip about troubles in his household and his failure to win Fatka, and also to draw Bulbul out of her isolation and Biba from her lethargy, he ordained, on the tenth day after the quarrel between the brothers, a house party for the Turkish ladies of Plav.

Grandfather Murat-beg agreed, perhaps had even put the idea into Omer-beg's head. He willingly agreed to everything that, even in appearance, would restore the brilliance of his household and the standing of his family. Izet-beg was against it, but since he could do nothing, for the party had little or nothing to do with him, he merely stated that he would spend that day hunting and that no one should on any account mention it to him.

Kara-Djula grumbled as usual, complaining about the amount of work involved, and said that the ladies of Plav were finicky gossips. But it was not clear exactly what she thought about it; she expressed an opinion only about what had happened or was happening, never about what was yet to happen.

The most important person was Biba, for her role was the most prominent. As the senior wife, she would have to introduce Bulbul to the ladies, showing that she accepted her as a blood sister, to the joy of her lord and master. For a wonder, she consented without resistance, with indifference and gentle obedience. In any case, it had to happen one day or another.

A fortnight passed between the quarrel in the garden and the party, which, as was only right, took place on a Friday. The day was a trifle too hot, but fine, and the shade of the garden was constantly enlivened by the gurgling of the stream. In the flurry about food and drink and service, in the anxiety that everything turn out so perfect that it would long be talked about, Muna and Nura again found harmony and peace of mind.

The party was timed to begin rather early in the afternoon and to last until suppertime. But it was well known that most of the ladies would not lunch at home, in order not to come already sated. Therefore, as well as sweet dishes—baklava, *kadaif*—and sweet drinks—boza, hydromel, and raspberry juice—savory dishes had been prepared: pilaff, *pita, sarma,* kebab, *kavurma,* and all kinds of fish. It seemed that there would not be enough fruit; the raspberries were over and the apples and pears still poor. But that morning two cases of early grapes arrived from Skadar. In that mountainous and roadless land, these were a great rarity and delicacy. They were carefully selected, washed, laid out in deep dishes covered with napkins, and put away in Kara-Djula's room. They were to be served last, as the greatest surprise. Relatives and neighbors had come to help with the mass of work, so that Kara-Djula, because Biba did not come out of her room all morning, became the mistress of the household, whom everyone asked for instructions and explanations and who had to see and to taste everything. She was in charge of Bešir and the other servants, who rushed wildly to the bakers to remind them not to burn the *pita*s, breads, and stews or overroast the chickens and lambs.

As soon as the dew had left the grass and the air was a little warmer, the garden began to look different. Carpets and rugs and woven woolen cushions, all of them carefully beaten, were brought out of the house. In the lower part of the garden, around the old pear tree, where Grandfather sat in the evenings, Muna and Nura covered the earth, taking care where each thing went, so as not to spoil the harmony of the garden and the cloths. Through the denseness of the natural greenery shone the flowered designs of human imagination and human hands. The garden was suddenly alive with fresh brilliance, and the coverings grew young again in the shining expanse and in the green shade. On the coverings, usually in the middle, wide metal dishes were placed, recently rubbed and polished with ashes and vinegar; on them the food would be laid out. The rims of the dishes, chased and engraved, glinted in the thousands of sunbeams which filtered through the thick branches. Not a spoon, not a dish, not a napkin dared to come from any other house, so that it could be seen that Murat-beg was a man of power and wealth despite the serf villages that had been lost and the shortages that the members of his household suffered.

All that scurrying, those piles of food and drink, the ceremonial appearance of everything, the tense care and quiet discussions—with only Kara-Djula grumbling, loudly—forced the workers to hurry, as if all eyes and all attention, all the destiny of the town, were centered on Murat-beg's house.

And to a certain extent that was true. Suppressed excitement was also to be felt in all the houses around. The ladies and their daughters were making themselves ready, bathing and perfuming themselves, choosing their newest and most beautiful dresses and belts, collars, and necklaces.

Dressed and ready by midday, Muna and Nura were trembling lest any speck or spot from the embers of the fire, from the oil or the clarified sugar and honey, some green leaf or blade of grass, should soil the bright colors of their yellow silk *salvare*, their white silk blouses, or their gold-braided velvet boleros. It seemed to them that they would never succeed in preserving the spotlessness of their clothes, for everything was not yet ready and everyone had to lend a hand, and the solemnity of the approaching occasion made them move carefully and delicately, as if the paths were scattered with unseen and perfidious dirt and thorns, which lay in wait for them alone.

"You must be more natural," Nura remarked as they went out into the courtyard.

Muna smiled. "That was just what I was going to say to you."

Nura, too, smiled. "We must be just what we are. The others will be even stiffer."

"Take care. Don't touch me," Muna warned half seriously, peering into the kitchen.

"Watch your own hands. Your palms are sweaty," Nura retorted.

Kara-Djula praised their beauty, their clothes, and their jewelry, but forgot about them a moment later and overwhelmed them with orders to carry dishes and platters into the garden.

From noon, not a single man was allowed in the house, so that the ladies and their daughters would not be exposed to the inquisitive gaze of strange men; this was a day for women only, a women's banquet. The twins regarded it as their day; since they had been recognized as young women, this was their first opportunity to show themselves to those of their own age and to the ladies of Plav. In order to mark the occasion, they had, for the first time, intentionally and by agreement, dressed differently. Nura's bolero was of red velvet and her trousers were embroidered with strange, reddish birds with swordlike blue tails, while Muna's was dark green and her trousers embroidered with wonderful greenish cats, stretched out voluptuously. The velvet for their boleros and the material for their trousers had been brought back by their father when he had brought Bulbul. He had also brought for their mother cloth woven with golden birds and flowers for her trousers, but Biba, indifferent to it, had not had it made up.

When the twins rushed to their mother to ask her to come to the garden—Kara-Djula had said that it was high time—and to rejoice in their new clothes, Biba, smiling sadly, said that they were so beautiful that she would not have recognized them, but that they still needed something more to differentiate them. She put on Nura's arm a heavy filigree bracelet with red stones, and fastened around Muna's waist a belt with a similar buckle. Both had been inherited from her mother, and were the work of Prizren filigree workers. "There, may these be a gift and something to remember me by," she said, kissing them, her eyes filled with tears.

Their mother's gifts, which she had kept not only as things of value, but also as heirlooms, made the girls weep with joy, and they ran out into the courtyard, to the sun and Kara-Djula, to see them shine and to praise them.

It was now stiflingly hot outside, and into the garden, like a fresh whirlpool, a stream of women began to pour, in silks, brocades, velvets, and morocco leather, as brightly colored as a flower garden. Biba welcomed them at the gateway into the courtyard, and Muna accompanied them to the cloths spread out around the pear tree. There they unveiled, settled themselves comfortably, and gathered into groups, but without loud talking and laughter, without noise, singing, or playing, not touching the food or peeping into the dishes under the linen napkins and silken cloths. They were waiting for the most important guest, the wife of the Plav leader, Osman-beg; for it was known, although nothing had been said, that she would come last and that only then could the feast begin.

As if she had been keeping watch—and perhaps some servant of hers had actually been doing so—after the last invited guest had arrived, Osman-begovica waited for a few moments more and then left her courtyard. But Muna was also keeping watch, in her father's room on the first floor, from which she could see, not far away, the gateway to Osman-beg's house.

As soon as the *hanum* emerged, she called to Nura in the garden, and Nura ran to tell her mother at the gateway. Holding their breath, blushing with excitement and embarrassment, Muna and Nura opened wide both wings of the gate to welcome Osman-begovica, and when she had entered, escorted by two maidservants, closed them after her.

With intentional slowness, or perhaps because she really had some difficulty, Osman-begovica raised her thin, wrinkled, transparent hand, with its dark-blue fingernails. But before it reached her face, one of the two maidservants, plump and popeyed, dark as a gypsy and young as a child, took the black silken veil from her face with a swift movement. Osman-begovica did not raise her other hand, but only moved it a little, and the other maidservant, equally dark and young, but less plump and popeyed, unbuttoned and with a single movement slipped off her mistress' *feredža*. Osman-begovica was at once transformed; this was no longer a living person, but a heavy, gold-embroidered robe embossed with gold buttons and chains, out of which peered a withered little head, hairless under the heavy velvet-and-gold headdress, with pale lips, white pointed nose, and washed-out bloodshot eyes under lashless lids. The drooping lower lids revealed bluish whites, while the upper lids hung weary and powerless; the lid of the right eye was lower than that of the left. The heavy, wide sleeves, also weighted down with gold braid, hung down her back and pulled at the thin, frail old-woman's body. In so heavy an outfit not even a strong young bride could have moved easily, and Osman-begovica could not move by herself. Muna only then noticed that the maidservants supported her under the arms.

Osman-begovica poked her little head out of her golden armor, and Biba put her face to those death's-head lips. Biba's eyes were full of tears, from pride that she had come and from the memory that she had been honored at her marriage by the presence of this distinguished guest, or from who knows what, and Osman-begovica's face crinkled, perhaps with a desire to smile. But her mouth yawned, toothless and dark as a cave, and so remained, as if she had forgotten how to close it.

"These are my daughters, *hanum*." Biba presented the twins, holding Muna by the right arm and Nura by the left. The girls curtsied and, taking the bony old woman's fingers in their fresh unwrinkled hands raised them to their lips. Muna felt that the two of them ought to burst into tears, from emotion. But of emotion there was not a trace, and she drew herself up, looking slyly at Nura. She, too, had not been moved; her eyes showed astonishment and her lips revulsion.

Biba led the way, taking care not to leave Osman-begovica behind. Muna was afraid that something terrible would happen at the wicket gate, for the servant girls could not go through it at the same time as Osman-begovica. She stopped, to cry out and warn them, but before she could do so, the dark girls cleverly maneuvered the *hanum* through the gate and led her into the garden.

A passage far wider than was needful opened before the wife of Osman-beg of Plav, as if her wide, stiff skirts burned with fire. The servant girls skillfully extracted Osman-begovica from her coat and leaned it against the pear tree; the gold dress bent as if bowing, and so remained. They took off the old woman's bolero and belt, bracelets and necklaces, even her gold-embroidered slippers, and placed them all in front of the coat, so that they looked like the showcase of a shop selling expensive goods. Then they seated Osman-begovica on the most valuable rug, but because she was not able to hold herself upright, and so that she should have something soft on which to lean, they packed her in on three sides with thick woolen cushions. Then it could be seen that Osman-begovica was somehow not living, not human, but only a pile of bones in a dried-up, hanging mantle of skin. What was more, now that she was separated from them, her clothes and ornaments found their erstwhile brilliance and beauty and came alive again.

Mother went to bring Bulbul from the *čardak,* and Nura whispered to Muna, as they were accompanying her across the garden: "Kara-Djula told me Uncle is in Father's room."

"Uncle! How could he even think of it?"

"Not Izet-beg—Smail-beg."

"Ah, that's different."

"Terrible."

"Yes, a scandal. But keep your mouth shut. Don't tell anyone."

"I'll keep quiet. But the scandal might break."

Biba took Bulbul by the left hand and then, after halting as if to take breath, went with her across the garden. On the faces of both women there was a stiff, unnatural smile, but whereas Biba's might at any moment be transformed into a stifled sob or an outbreak of tears, Bulbul's was, as ever, chill and enigmatic.

The murmur of words and rustling of silks ceased, and the gurgling of the brook could be heard. Bulbul was dressed in fine and rich, but light, clothes, and for ornament she wore only a gold bracelet and a fragile silver flower in her hair above her left temple. She moved so lightly and so smoothly, and at the same time so carefully, that Nura whispered to Muna: "As if she were rope-dancing!"

Biba led Bulbul through the guests and approached Osman-begovica. The old woman, with an effort, turned her stiff neck and peered at the newcomer with her washed-out, weary eyes. But Bulbul, either because her husband had not instructed her as he should have, or because she did not understand, or because she did not want to bow and kiss the hand of the wife of the leader of this little foreign town, remained standing, with that chill smile on her face. Biba tried to help her, pressing her hand on Bulbul's left shoulder, and even said to her: "Kneel. Kiss the *hanum*'s hand!"

But it was all in vain; the foreigner did not understand. Those ladies who knew a little Turkish either were at a loss or did not want to get involved. There was no obvious way out of this mis-understanding. Muna knew that her mother would not hold out, and just as she was about to warn Nura, though she did not know how she could be of any assistance, Biba pushed Bulbul aside and snapped, as if to herself: "Idiot!"

Bulbul did not understand that either, though Biba's actions had been sharp, even rough. Still smiling, she withdrew after a slight bow and approached a small group of ladies who were watching her inquisitively. Although Osman-begovica noticed that everything had not turned out as it should, she said nothing, but her toothless jaw quivered with disapproval.

Yet everything was quickly forgotten in the flood of gossip and young girls' songs and abundant hospitality.

Thinking that the ladies were now so busy with their amuse-ments that her absence would not be noticed, Muna rushed into the house with the vague idea of warning Uncle Smail-beg that, since he had already brought shame on the household by con-cealing himself, he should at least remain securely hidden, in order to preserve the reputation of the family and avoid any con-flict with husbands or fathers, which might end in a bloody settle-ment of accounts. She found her uncle curled up on a divan and peering through the lattice so intently that it seemed to her that his big green eyes bulged out of their sockets through the thick, crisscrossed wooden slats. She had never seen such an expression on his face, so tense and feverish, his cheeks quivering and his sparse reddish beard twitching. Even his body was changed. Of medium height and well built, though with too long a head, too big a nose, and too thick lips, he now seemed cramped, twisted, convulsed.

Uncle did not move, though he must have heard the squeak of the hinges and the patter of her slippers on the floor. Though frightened and bewildered by his appearance, she approached him and pulled at his sleeve.

He turned slowly and with an effort, as if her tug at his sleeve had separated him not only from something very attractive, but also from some task of exceptional importance to him, though he had done nothing more than sit and look. He looked at her in the same way, concentrated and intense. Only when his glance shone straight through her and began to slide down her from top to toe did Muna notice that there was something forceful, even violent, in it, which was impossible to resist. From his eyes and mouth dripped a thick, opaque mucus.

Hesitating whether to go or stay, she remembered why she had come, but all the harshness and bitterness of her imagined reproach stuck in her throat, and she uttered something quite different. "Uncle, in God's name, what are you doing?"

Her uncle was now eying her up and down with such intensity that it seemed to her that he was stroking her with some passionate, irresistible enjoyment. When his glance reached her breasts, she quivered as if he had touched them with his hands. Then he peered fixedly at her lips and muttered, as if he had not heard her words: "I never noticed how great a beauty you have grown!"

A blush began to flood Muna's cheeks. Angry at herself for not being able to stem the flood of her blushes, she retorted: "Uncle, in God's name, you will bring scandal on yourself and on us!"

"Don't be silly!" he whispered. "No one can see us here. Come and sit beside me."

But Muna did not sit. She was not afraid of her uncle, but of that something violent and irresistible in his eyes. She replied, almost collectedly: "Don't you know what might happen if they were to find you here? Take care, I implore you. So many misfortunes have already befallen us, and now a scandal like this on top of everything else!"

Uncle smiled feverishly and strangely, while that mucus seemed to ooze out of him. "What scandal or misfortune can there be if a man looks at a pretty woman?"

"But it is shameful."

"There is no shame if no one talks about it," said Smail-beg, and he stretched out his hand, with its slender, tobacco-stained fingers.

Muna retreated, but not far enough and hesitantly. He seized her by the wrist and, although she resisted, pulled her toward him, forcing her with almost painful strength to sit—not beside him, but on his knee.

Muna was uncertain what all this meant and what she ought to do. At first she wanted to tear herself away roughly and run, even if Smail-beg would be angry that she had interpreted his tenderness wrongly. But there was no likelihood that Smail-beg would let her go so easily. She did not dare to call for help; that would lead to the discovery of Smail-beg and to unheard-of scandal and misfortune. The strangest thing was that the violence in his eyes and the sweet mucus on his face suddenly no longer seemed unpleasant or strange. She understood that if she should give way, these things would become stronger in him, and that his clouded consciousness and already suspect sweetness would affect her also. He suspected or in some way noticed her emotion. Slowly setting her legs on the floor, he put his right arm around her waist, whispering in a strange and unfamiliar voice: "Come, my wild one, don't be afraid."

Realizing, for the first time since she had rolled down the staircase in her childhood, that she was losing consciousness and the power of resistance, and that now, in one way or another, something terrible would happen, she dumbly and tensely drummed on his chest with her fists. At that moment, over his shoulder she saw Nura walking across the garden and, thinking to herself, What would she do in my place? she tore herself free and shouted: "Nura, Nura, come up here!"

While she was tucking in her blouse, which had been pulled out, and smoothing the wrinkles, Uncle Smail-beg smiled with shame, but impudently, and finally remarked: "What will you think of me now? You won't let your uncle caress you."

Nura came quietly into the room, then, looking in wonder at her flushed and excited sister, asked: "What's wrong with you?"

"The heat, and my head is aching from all that rushing about," Muna replied, smiling wryly.

"Yes, it is hot. And there has been a lot of rushing about. I thought you were busy in the kitchen, and I was coming to lend a hand."

Uncle had again turned to the window. That expression and that trembling had gone from his eyes and his face. Now he seemed once again familiar and intimate, though paler and with a touch of indignation about his lips.

"Did you tell him?" Nura asked.

Muna knew what her sister meant, though they had not discussed it, and answered readily: "I did. He won't leave the room until all the women have gone."

Smail-beg was forced to listen to them, but did not say anything.

He only asked: "Which is the new one, brought from Radak this spring for the son of Simo the tinsmith?"

The twins pressed their faces to the window, close to their uncle's head, and following his glance at once picked out a slender young woman with a long white throat and a firm ruddy face quite unlike the women of the town. She was approaching Biba, accompanied by Stojna Simov. That must be the daughter-in-law of Simo the tinsmith, for Muna and Nura knew all the women in the town except this young woman. But neither of them would confirm it, Muna because she had been attacked and Nura because she was still angry with Smail-beg.

They turned to leave without saying a word. At the door, Muna noticed that her uncle was once more gazing into the garden and that his eyes and face were again suffused with that trembling violence and lust she had seen before, but so distant and weak that her sister did not notice it, though she, too, had turned around. Muna would not have to give her any explanation.

The party continued in the best possible way until, in the evening shadows, after the ladies, weary of food, had stretched out on the rugs, and the girls were sitting together in small groups, competing in singing, it occurred to someone spiteful or inquisitive among those who stammered a little Turkish to induce Bulbul, who had the reputation of playing and singing well, to entertain them.

Bulbul ran into the *čardak* and came back at once with the *šarkija* in her hand. Since the garden sloped gently down to the bank of the stream, she stopped at the first carpet, so as to be more easily seen. The ladies, reclining or sitting, moved to form a semicircle, with Osman-begovica at its center, open toward Bulbul.

Without surprise, Bulbul bowed stiffly, like a dancer in a booth. Then she raised her hand and, with a set smile, waited until the tension and the silence were stretched to breaking point, struck the *šarkija,* and in her dark, hoarse voice sang a song with incomprehensible words, but whose sounds they had all heard from early childhood, from soldiers, from traders and gypsies, and which were woven into the pattern of local song. The ladies listened to Bulbul with interest, even with enjoyment. The incomprehensibility of the words did not worry them, for the sound was comprehensible, like a skein unraveled and separated. The song spoke of the longing and sorrow of a forsaken heart wrung by loneliness.

When she had finished her song, Bulbul smiled with sad amiability and again bowed. She was awaiting applause, and some of the ladies, those who had traveled, applauded.

Encouraged by their approval, Bulbul put aside the *šarkija* and, clapping her thin hands, began to dance. At first she only moved her feet slightly, then she twisted and turned. But when some of the ladies finally began to approve her dancing, she raised her arms wide and began to make sharp and incisive movements with them, like a bird with a broken wing. Perhaps her dance, which was not much to the taste of the older women or the young ones who had never been away from Plav, would have ended in peace if she had not begun to dance also with her hips and belly.

Quelled by the looks of the appalled old women, prudish and withered, the tolerant and approving clapping of hands died. But Bulbul, carried away, either did not notice or did not understand and went on dancing, with serpentine twistings and violent contractions. The allusions to love and the allurements of love the good ladies were somehow or other able to endure, but not the act of love transformed into dance, refined indeed, but unbridled and lascivious. The overmodest, oversimple ladies were as dismayed as if they were looking at the act of love itself, which was only mentioned in bedrooms and scarcely admitted even to themselves. Their horrified glances passed from one to another, and finally slowly concentrated on Osman-begovica, who sat with wide-open, gaping jaws and staring eyes, as if attempting to say something important, but without the force to do so.

Biba was not overprudish, but could not bear dissoluteness. She was, certainly, goaded by the attitude of the older, more distinguished ladies. There boiled up in her all the bitterness she had kept in check for weeks, awaiting the moment to burst out. In the general astonishment, no one had noticed her, until, leaping from beside Osman-begovica, she flew at Bulbul, treading on the edge of a heavy silver tray as she went. The salver tilted, spun a little, scattering sweetmeats and little glasses of sugared juices, and then settled back again with a heavy clang. Leaping at Bulbul, Biba caught her foot on the edge of the rug and stretched out her hand for the *šarkija*. She snatched it and with all her strength struck it against the trunk of a plum tree. A cry rose from its rounded, shining belly as it smashed into fragments.

Bulbul stopped dancing, her smile stiff and incredulous, as if it were not clear to her whether this was some bad joke or some assault, or some custom unknown to her. Biba, holding in her hand the long thin handle of the *šarkija,* with its broken, trailing strings, threw the fragments into the brook, and then, perhaps provoked by Bulbul's questioning smile, rushed at her, beating her on the breast with her fists and screaming: "Harlot, shameless one!"

Bulbul staggered as she stood in front of Biba, who was spitting out incomprehensible words and threatening her with clenched fists. At last realizing that she was being attacked, and even slapped, Bulbul, with a bewildered and horrified look, turned toward the ladies, but finding neither support nor explanation there, turned and ran to the *čardak*. She did not run in her usual dancing manner, but as any other desolate woman, covering her face with her hands and with her delicate, rounded shoulders shaking.

The ladies began to console Biba, who was cursing and railing against Bulbul, herself, and life. Then, recovering as suddenly as she had burst out, Biba fell on her knees at the feet of Osman-begovica, either to give vent to her grief or to beg for forgiveness, or both. But the old woman did not move a finger or an eye, or even a foot, to summon her.

In the oppressive silence the gurgling of the brook could again be heard.

At last Osman-begovica raised her hand slightly, and the maid-servants lifted her by her arms and quickly and skillfully put on her ornaments and her heavy coat. Without a word, without a sign, Osman-begovica sailed off in her golden armor.

As if only waiting for her to leave, the ladies crowded around to make their farewells, consoling Biba and trying to calm her, some with false, others with sincere, words.

The garden was empty before twilight; and that was the time

when the party should have become lively with dance and song. Piles of scarcely touched food, on crumpled cloths, vainly awaited the guests. And the twins, weeping, fell into one another's arms.

The next day broke with further horrors, which the night had concealed in its darkness.

The twins had stayed awake until late, listening in their room until the early hours to the quarrel between their father and mother, now the frantic sobs of Biba, now the tearful consolations of Izet-beg, now the complaints of Murat-beg, now the grumblings of Kara-Djula.

Worn out and exhausted, Muna at first thought that she was dreaming. The dawn or the moonlight lit up the windows, and from the courtyard came the shrieks of Kara-Djula. Scared almost out of her senses, Muna wakened her sister. "Nura, Nura, wake up! Something terrible is happening!"

Nura woke in a moment, and together, barefoot and in their nightdresses, they rushed down the steps and into the courtyard, which was dewy, chill, and lit by the early dawn. In the center lay Biba, her face expressionless and pale, her head resting on the cobbles. Izet-beg was kneeling by her, his hair disheveled, weeping silently and brushing the tears away with his hands. On the right side of the motionless Biba squatted Kara-Djula, keening in the Montenegrin peasant manner. The twins had never before heard her weep, still less keen. She cursed the cruelty of fate and enumerated Biba's virtues, breaking the tense keening with short howls. She was trying, probably according to Christian custom which had suddenly come back to her mind, to cross Biba's stiff, disobedient hands across her breast.

Biba was dressed in her finest, richest robes, their gold embroidery and heavy silk making her body seem even more rigid. On them were scraps of earth and bits of straw and hay. The hay and the earth on her stockings made it seem even more incomprehensible that she could be dead. Yet she was. Uncle Izet-beg, rising early for hunting, was surprised by the whimpering of the dogs and the whinnying of the horses. He had gone into the stables and come face to face with Biba, hanging from a beam.

The courtyard quickly filled with members of the household and servants, as if the news of the misfortune had made the rounds and wakened them. Grandfather Murat-beg, in pants and shirt, wrapped in an overcoat and with slippers on his bare feet, leaned over Biba, but quickly drew back, coughing and muttering, and went and sat on his own stone by the door. Omer-beg came barefooted, his legs wet with the dew of the garden, also in pants and shirt. Suddenly, seeing the dead Biba, he covered his face with his hands and went and sat down on the stone alongside Murat-beg.

Bulbul, too, soon appeared, fully dressed and with her hair combed. She leaned over Biba, then squatted by her head as if she wanted to kiss her, but only two tears ran down her face. She remained thus for some moments, motionless, then rose without her usual litheness, said a few words in her own language, and went to the čardak.

Grandfather Murat-beg, who was hard of hearing, asked: "What did that hag say? What does she want?"

But no one replied, for only Izet-beg had heard well and understood the foreigner. He took Biba in his arms and tenderly carried her into the house. As he passed Grandfather and Omer-beg he remarked quietly: "Now it doesn't matter any more. She, Bulbul, said that today she would go back to where she came from. Here no one loves her."

Omer-beg went on sitting there, his head buried in his hands, as if he had not heard what Murat-beg had asked or what Izet-beg had answered. Mourning, with hands on hips, Kara-Djula followed Izet-beg into the house.

The twins, one beside the other, went on squatting in the courtyard, weeping as if their mother's body had not been taken away. And Izet-beg's dogs bayed softly and mournfully, gazing at the empty, whitish dawn.

PART THREE

MOMENTS
AND ETERNITIES

The Mountain Flower

It was as if Raduša were some fresh flower, more delicately perfumed than any Rade had been smelling since noon that day, filling the air with its scent, which evaporated lightly and generously, mingling with the sun's heat and the gentle mountain air.

Without Raduša, without the contact of her body, that remembered scent was weak, faint, even harsh and melancholy. Only when blended with her presence did it seem like the overnight scent of flowering limes, chilled by the frost and warmed by the fresh burgeoning of spring, like the intoxicating perfume of sun-drenched basil or the scent of autumn juniper or mint. As soon as he embraced her that scent submerged consciousness and memory in a mist of passion; it became one with her body, with her gentle resistance and compliance to his hands and lips, the shining bubbles of her half-closed hazel eyes and the sweet suffering prolonged and contracted on her suddenly pale dry lips.

Only when she withdrew from his embrace on the heap of new-mown grass did Rade find in the wave of perfume, which flooded him with a seductiveness so rich and warm that he could feel it on his face, all that he had sought and craved that morning in the stifling, overpowering scent of the new-cut grass. He had not expected, had not known, that she would come. Now, as they lay on the grass, he realized that all that morning she had been present in the sunlight, warm as her breath, in the juices of the grasses, melancholy and weak without her perfume, in the coomb, gloomy without her eyes, in himself, disheartened and desolate without her.

For the past three days, ever since his brother Akan had driven the stock to market for money to ransom their father, Rade had been cutting and stacking yew and sycamore. But when that was finished, it had occurred to him to cut the grass for his one cow and Vojin's one cow and their calves. It was senseless to drive them to distant pastures, and they would have to stay another three weeks in the *katun* and the hayfields.

There was no good pasture nearby, for the cattle had cropped all the grasses. Then he had remembered the little coomb near the *katun*, inaccessible to the cattle, in which there grew rich, not dense, but juicy grass. The coomb was hemmed in on three sides by grassy slopes studded with sharp rocks, and on the lower, wider, side it was closed by dense pine forest and broken trees, through which meandered almost impenetrable paths. Rade knew well how to get there; in the past, grass had been brought from that valley to the calves when there was no more pasture in or around the *katun*. On its western side, at the edge of the forest, there remained a snowfield from which the shepherds, pasturing their flocks on the grassy hillocks, cut triangular chunks of hardened snow and into them milked their beasts. Then, lying on their backs and throwing their heads back, they let the white liquid flow directly into their mouths in icy freshness.

Rade had not been in the coomb for a long time, and had never been in it at noon, so he was astonished at the warmth there, despite the fact that the sun shone on it for only a short time about midday. The heat obviously came from the warm stones, and it clashed with the freshness of the forest, which rose from below, patches of coolness in that overheated islet. It was perhaps just that mingling of heat and freshness, of fierce sun and snowdrifts still piled up in sheltered places, unmelted until midsummer, which encouraged the growth of all kinds of juicy grasses. The sickle collected at every stroke so thick a bouquet that one's fingers could not close around it.

Here everything dripped with fatness. The spruces grew too high, the beetles were huge and full-fed, and the snakes, sated and fat, slithered slowly among the stones. Even the chittering of the eagles that soared over the coomb seemed louder and more penetrating.

The stuffy, moist heat overcame Rade with every sweep of his sickle, with every perfumed and juicy wound in the green tapestry of the grasses. It filled him with an impersonal, male longing, which increased and was in some way melancholy. The valley breathed with the sweet seductiveness of a bed which the huge, hot sun had covered with a heavenly cloth.

He stripped to the waist, but the sweat continued to stream from every pore, dripping down his chest and back, and he was forced to find in the dense greenery a pocket of drifted snow and to detach a hunk. The snow cooled him at once, and after he had rubbed his neck with his damp hands, he went slowly back, carrying the lump on the point of his sickle.

Suddenly everything became clearer; every blade of grass and every pebble displayed its form and color. Only then did he recall Raduša, clearly and distinctly, her broad white forehead, her fine, shining, curly dark hair, the dimple in her chin, and the fine lines on either side of her freckled nose whenever she smiled. Her perfume came back to him in memory, but he did not yet connect his longing, vague and heavily oppressive, with her.

He once more turned to his work. But the sweat again overcame him, and he decided to rest until the sun went down a little. He went over to the lump of snow, which he had placed on a rock so that it would not melt. All that remained of it was a granular piece of ice. He put it in his mouth and, throwing his cloak and his shirt over his right shoulder, went into the shade of a young spruce which rose, isolated, in the open with its gray-green branches reaching the ground.

Even under the spruce it was hot, but shady and moist. He spread out his cloak and shirt and lay face downward, his hands under his face. It was as if his longing had secretly been waiting for just this moment, this hidden place and his reverie; as if the ground beneath him, soft from the thick layer of dry spruce needles, opened, alive, juicy, and warm, as a woman opens under a man, as the widow Jana had opened to him that winter, as Raduša, a girl of his own kin, might never open to him.

He soon fell asleep, and had heavy, troubled dreams, which he could not recall on waking, though he knew his longing had continued even in the dreams. The end of the valley was already in shadow; the heat had lessened, and that warm-cold current was dying away. He went on slowly cutting the grass and piling it in heaps, which he later collected in two loads at the end of the path into the forest.

He saw Raduša as he was going toward the heaps with another bundle of grass. She had come out of the forest as if out of the night, and her pale oval face and smooth, strong white throat stood out against the dark trees. She was standing between the fresh heaps of grass, a rope in her right hand, smiling uncertainly, imploringly, mischieviously.

Before he could utter a word or put down the bundle, she threw down the cord, stretched out her arms so that the grass fell about their feet, and pulled him in her embrace down on the pile of grass.

Then he realized what perfume it was that he had sought so vainly in the vertiginous medley of scents and colors. He had found her, just her, here in the coomb stifling with warmth and exuberance. He knew everything that would happen between them, and knew that it would be, must be, as if it had never happened.

Their caresses had begun in the spring, during the kolo at Roksanda's wedding. In the crowd that the dance had forced back against the wall, Raduša had found herself beside Rade. The whirl of the dance, totally unrestrained, brought them imperceptibly closer, and Raduša, as if by chance, pressed against him with the whole length of her firm young body. As the dance reached its climax, her body, with sweet pressure, melted into his, and his knees felt the soft tension of her thighs under her wide young woman's apron, his crotch the smooth roundness of her buttocks and the warm weight of her back. That more and more intense realization of her body seemed without frontiers. He knew that that mutual pressure could never be complete, that there could be no fusion of one with the other. Nonetheless, it drew him irresistibly into its sweet, intoxicating endlessness, demanding a conclusion. The low-ceilinged room was stifling with sweating bodies, and he felt a light trembling run through him, which he feared, and at the same time hoped, Raduša, too, might feel. He knew that this inexhaustible sweetness was not provoked merely by the contact of a young and desirable woman's body with his own unconsumed energy. It was because that body was hers, because it belonged to Raduša, Vojin's sister, too close a relative even by the rules of the church and much more so by the customs of the clan. Though he was sure that the pressure of her body against his was not accidental or against her will, he wanted to make certain. He moved, two or three times, away from her, but each time she again pressed against him. He had to stop this all-too-sweet and imaginary interrogation, lest others notice and lest she, should she later think it over and regret it, put it down to chance and the closeness of their kin.

The dance ended, and with it their contact, and he, suddenly ashamed, was afraid to meet her eyes. But in the half-darkness she looked openly at him, smiling at him with shy radiance, but also with regret that the pressure of their bodies had ended so quickly and inconclusively.

The dance of their bodies continued within him. He stood where Raduša had left him, where he had been standing with her, indifferent to the well-known faces around him and to the chatter of the dispersing guests. He had to keep assuring himself that he had not been mistaken, that what had happened with Raduša had really happened, and that their bodies had not come together by chance. He marveled that he had not realized earlier his own and her bodily longing; only now did he begin to remember events that had hinted at the inevitability of their coming together in this way.

The most revealing and exciting of all was that first moment, when in fact it had all begun, with those early mountain flowers, yellow and shining like wrought gold and perfumed with the first scent of spring, filled with the rising sap and the purity of the melting snowdrifts. Everything was again as it had been then, two years ago, joyful and full of hope. The war had temporarily ended, the clan was united, Raduša was burgeoning in her seventeenth year, and he, in his sixteenth year, was just becoming aware of his manhood.

He had been returning on Palm Sunday from the monastery of Dečani, where he had served the monks and learned to read. In the mountains he had plucked a bunch of the golden flowers to please his sister, Roksanda, and his sister-in-law Stamena, who, like most of the women and young people of the village, liked them better than anything else. Though they were short-lived, they smelled subtly but very strongly.

He had emerged suddenly from the thin, green forest, from its play of light and shade, its soil saturated with spring waters and thick with decayed leaves, into the bright, warm spring morning. Below he could see his village, enveloped in a cloud of bluish smoke and red and white blossoms. The path was soft and slippery, and above the fields, still moist with sprouting grass, and above the rich furrows slipped white, fleecy clouds. The sky was shining like glass, the fields smiled with tiny blue-eyed orchids, and the meadows drowsed in stifling richness. Everything was bursting forth, scented, refreshing as sweet milk and gentle as a mother's lap.

At the top of the meadow, on a broad tree stump, Raduša was sitting, tending the cattle; about fifteen lean and dirty cows were eagerly cropping the young grass. Her back was turned, and she was intent on her knitting. She did not notice him. The sight of her was joyful to him, dearer and more beautiful than he had ever expected after six months of austerity and loneliness in the service of the monks. He had missed someone fresh and young, and here was this girl, in all her youth and beauty. As children, the two of them had instinctively chosen each other as companions in their games and had often gone off on their own. Memories welled up, not of any special incident, but like a wave of warm, still-childish joy, which encompassed all his youth.

He stole up to her and, as in a childish game, covered her eyes with his hands. He knew her nature—mild, rather slow to anger. She put her knitting down in her lap and began cautiously to touch his hands and sleeves. Then, taking his hands away, she called out: "Rade! Who else!" Appraising him with happy eyes, she said: "How you've grown! But you are pale and thin—as in a song. Milk and fresh air will soon put you right again, even if Milena and Stamena don't cluck around you and feed you."

He was astonished at how much she had changed. In truth, he and the whole village had already noticed, over the past three or four years, how the thin, silent, pale, and reserved girl, with wide eyes and full lips, had become a young woman of mild and gentle temperament, with rather full, rounded breasts and soft, broad hips. Now, that change, perhaps not so great since last autumn, when he had gone to the monastery, was astonishingly new for him, as if she were some person whom, God alone knew, he had never really seen till then and whose remembered features merged only with difficulty into those he saw now. That change in her body and also, as he soon found out, in her temperament struck him with unsuspected force, as if it had taken place in himself.

It had been evident earlier that Raduša would be a girl of unique, unpeasantlike appearance. Though she had the robustness and firmness of the village girls, the rather narrow waist and broad thighs, she was soft, white, and had fine wrists and ankles. Perhaps Vojin had something to do with that. After Anto, he was the richest man in the clan and, having no children, had spoiled his only sister and spared her hard work. Vojin's wife, Jelica, was also good to her, so that Raduša did not suffer too much from the early death of her mother.

The change, however, was most fully revealed in her laugh, which was full, gurgling, and came from the depths of her chest. Before, her voice had been mild, rather deep, and without harshness, but it had not had that roundness and volume, in harmony with her firm body and smiling expression.

He noticed, too, a change in her hands and her teeth—or perhaps he only then became aware of them. Her palms were soft and her wrists dimpled, her fingers plump, with long nails and tips red as buds. Her teeth were white, rather strong and slightly protruding, which gave her quick, smothered laughter something roguish and carefree. He was at once struck by the way she threw back her head whenever she wanted to laugh or was surprised at anything. She had always done this, even as a girl, compassionate and headstrong. But now, by stressing the rounded throat, whose softness made her short plump chin seem smaller, it gave her face an expression of contentment and satisfaction.

They chatted, sitting beside one another, she of the changes in and around the village, and he of life in the monastery and its beauty, a stone vision on a hillock above the waves of the plain, at the mouth of the gorge from whose smooth white arch flowed the mountain trout stream, mingling its chill murmurings with the scented rustling of the chestnut trees and walnut groves. Rade told her what he had learned from the monks and what he himself had experienced. Dečani was somewhere between Heaven and earth, between asceticism and luxury, between the heat and fatness of the plain and the chill and purity of the mountains. He told her how the holy King Stefan, searching for a place to lay the foundations of his bequest, had stopped there to rest; the peasants had brought him lamb, wine, and bread, and he had said: "Here where these three gifts of the earth meet shall I make my bequest." The unfortunate holy king, whose father was blinded and whose son drowned, did not live to complete his bequest. It was left to his surviving son, Dušan, to create that beauty and so give his conscience peace. All that was beautiful in Serbian churches, from the sea to the Danube, was fused there at Dečani, growing below and before the hills, higher and higher and more graceful as the eyes took it in, while its cupola linked it to Heaven itself. It was as if the angels had built Dečani, Rade exclaimed suddenly, in a revelation to himself and to Raduša.

Only later did he realize that, speaking to Raduša about Dečani, he had revealed beauties and things of interest that till then had been unnoticed or forgotten. She spoke little and only rarely asked a question, encouraging him by her interest and her evident eagerness to hear more. For the first time, sitting beside her, looking down into the depths of the valley, seen indistinctly in the shadows and the heat, under a sky pure and filled with cloudlets dancing like lambs, among the fields and meadows and orchards from which came the sounds of men at work, the lowing of cattle, the clucking of poultry, the twitter of birds, the whirr of beetles, and the hum of bees, he realized with joy that he, too, was a part of this universal burgeoning and creation. Someone dear was listening to him, and the words and their meaning, his own stories and descriptions, became a part of the life around him in the boundless expanse.

They remained there together till twilight, till the time came to call the cattle, as if his own home were not longingly awaiting him. He had already divided the bouquet in half and given part to her, forgetting to tell her not to hold it in her hands, so that it would last longer. She, too, did not remember, but clutched the flowers in her hot palms and fingers, smelling them from time to time. When at last they parted, in front of her house, he noticed that the golden flowers had begun to hang their heads and that the edges of the petals had the leaden color of withering. She noticed his sorrowful expression and remarked with a smile: "No matter. Next year you will pick me fresh ones."

That night, though he went late to sleep after talking with his relatives, he awakened from a troubling dream, filled with an anxiety and remorse that did not let him sleep again until dawn.

In his dream he went with Father Vikentije, a hermit from a cave in the Dečanska Bistrica who rarely came to the monastery, to light a candle for the evening service. Suddenly they came upon many candles, lit as for the great festivals, and the whole monastery was illumined by some other, its own, brilliance, so that there were no longer any shadows or dark corners in its arched expanses. Though he knew that he had not sinned, he was filled with fear of the solemn space as he entered with Father Vikentije, who kept pressing him closer and closer with his arm, as if he suspected Rade's secret wish to run away. Just as they passed from the mild illumination and the simplicity of the portico into the nave, shining and clear to the minutest detail, Father Vikentije, as if by chance touching Rade on the cheek with the rough goatskin of his mantle, turned on him, his face filled with fury, his beard bristling, and hissed in a hoarse voice, spitting from his gap-toothed mouth: "Accursed one, you did not cross yourself!" That was all the stranger because the hermit, too, had neglected to cross himself, though he could easily have done so, because he was holding Rade with his left hand.

Crossing the smooth marble flags of the nave, Rade, overcome by fear and confusion, noticed how the swords and lances of the holy warriors on the walls moved toward him and how the hair and the beards of the saints were furiously interwoven with whips, just as with Father Vikentije. The march forward somehow stretched into eternity, and the Virgin above the altar, her face darkened by sorrow, pale palms outspread, quickly slipped away into the half-darkness, into the heavenly twilight of the altar. Rade wanted to implore the most blessed Mother of God to halt and turn her merciful eyes on him, to stretch out her suffering hands to him; he even tried to shout, but no sound came. He turned to Father Vikentije to beg him, as a priest, in Rade's and his own name, to implore the Mother of God for absolution, even though he had committed no sin. But now it was not Father Vikentije who was holding him by the hand, but an angel, that angel from the north wall of the porch, fair-haired and with pursed lips, of whom Rade—now he suddenly thought of it—had often and gladly, but with timid shame, been aware. The angel held him gently and tenderly; he could feel the warmth of the pink fingers. His wings were like those of a dove, plump and fleshy at the root, and his throat was white and rounded, like that of some girl he knew but whose name he could not remember. Ashamed because of his sinful notice of the angel's girlish features, Rade wanted to ask where he was leading him. But the angel's smile, considerate and seductive, made it impossible to say anything that might repulse or offend him, and such a question—Rade was sure of it—would both offend and repulse him. If an angel leads me, why should I be afraid? Rade took courage, striding on bare feet—yes, till then he had not noticed that he was barefoot—over the cold multicolored flags worn smooth by the knees and feet of men over hundreds of years. The angel silently led him to the Virgin's robe, entered into her circle, tapping strangely with his bare reddish soles. That was the first and only sound Rade heard in the huge and shining emptiness of the church. Even though the angel led him more and more gently, Rade stopped at the edge of the holy circle, fearing that he was being led to the judgment seat for sins he had not yet committed but would commit. Entering the circle of the Virgin, which the priest alone may enter at the most solemn moment of the liturgy, not only confirmed, but also intensified, his future sins. Though still gentle, the angel was determined and resolute. In his uncertainty, Rade, remembering that at a wedding bride and bridegroom circled around the Virgin's altar, wanted to cry out that he had not yet chosen the girl. At that moment the angel drew him powerfully into the embrace of his feathery, soft, full wings. A mortal fear, but at the same time a feeling of immeasurable bliss, seized Rade in the warm, girlish embrace of the angel in the hallowed circle. And just when he wanted to ask the angel what they were doing and in such a place, the angel disappeared and he was in the embrace of one of the sinners in Hell from the west wall of the portico, with rich, burgeoning hips and waist slenderer than in the fresco, and he was no longer in the Virgin's circle but on the same tree stump on which he had been sitting that day with Raduša. Encouraged that he had in some way, though with the aid of a sinner, extracted himself from sacrilege, Rade gave himself up fully to the quivering caresses of the smooth woman's curves and then seized her, his left arm about her waist and his right under her knees, and sat her on his lap, as he had heard from dissolute young men was the proper thing to do with women. But this was no longer the sinner from the Dečani portico, but Raduša, gentle, approachable, and pure, yet consciously and lasciviously yielding, welcoming him with softness and caresses.

He started up in passion and horror, bathed in sweat and breathing heavily, his temples beating to the rhythm of a tired, terrified, and somehow alien heart.

With that Palm Sunday and that dream his love for Raduša began.

Individual incidents had been erased from Rade's memory. The first year after that Palm Sunday and the dream, he recalled as a trembling, urgent search for intimacy with Raduša. From the time when they had sat together on the tree stump, they had begun to look especially for one another and to caress one another. Their love, always on the border between brotherly and sisterly tenderness and something else, became almost proverbial in the clan. No one opposed it; they even approved, though they regarded it as somewhat excessive. Raduša had a brother and three cousins, but she did not feel close to them, for they were much older than she; and in this relationship everyone considered that she had found a real brother.

But Rade was now aware that their love was not only their love as Radak kin, but also that other, forbidden, love, even though the frontiers between the one and the other were not yet defined. It was enough to love and to meet Raduša in kinship, secretly longing for a miracle to happen so that they could escape from the net of kinship into joy and happiness. But he knew that complete happiness could not be allied with sin; kinship could not be wiped out, nor could the real joy of passionate longing for Raduša be fulfilled without sin, without transgression against the clan.

Thus he lived for a year, in the misty, shining, and sweet dream of love and in the terrible inevitability of open sin.

His love for Raduša and their half-innocent, half-seductive caresses brought redoubled fear and remorse, not only because of the clan, but also for himself, his own existence. Once consummated, their love would mean separation from the clan, from brothers and relatives, and therefore also from the revolt, from obligations to Serbdom and faith, which were now an integral part of his life, a confirmation of his individuality, something sacred yet at the same time human in him. And those obligations, learned with his first words and with his way of life, could not be set aside for the sake of anything personal and material. Besides, the clan and his brothers had to carry out the revolt, and not only would they be unable to condone any sin between him and Raduša, but it would shatter them and turn them from the right path.

He could not know exactly what Raduša thought and felt. They never spoke to each other of their feeling, since each displayed it to the other as kinship. Nonetheless, he suspected that she, too, lived through something similar, at least insofar as ties with the clan were concerned; for her, inclined toward comforts and everyday needs, toward her future home and family, the revolt was of far less significance.

But he was mistaken. It seemed to him that he had been wrong in attributing such great significance to the bond between them, to her love for him. The next spring, a year after that Palm Sunday and the dream, a love affair began between Obrad and Raduša.

By then the war was over, even though peace had not been concluded or the frontiers marked out. The armies had withdrawn and been disbanded, and the small patrols of guards that remained were unable to stem the torrent of normal relations among men. At the gathering on Holy Trinity at the ruined church, Raduša had made the acquaintance of Obrad, a young man from Veliko, of a wealthy family and a line of chieftains. He was a tall, slender youth, with narrow shoulders and long arms, ruddy face and smooth black hair. Perhaps because of the chieftainship his father had obtained through service in the war and the insurrection, perhaps because of his wealth, but most of all because of his personal attraction, Obrad made a deep impression on the nonworking, ladylike only daughter, the more so as he always dressed smartly and rode good horses. He had a reputation as a lady-killer, and it was therefore strange that Raduša would have anything to do with him. But it was important to her, or so it seemed to Rade, to win Obrad from other girls and thereby confirm her own beauty. She knew that she was pretty, perhaps the prettiest girl in the whole district, and Rade had noticed her liking for flirtation, for easy conquests, and for risqué stories, though she took care never to promise too much to any of her suitors or to use improper words in her stories, preferring to reveal their substance by allusions, laughter, and winks.

It soon became common gossip that Obrad and Raduša liked one another; in fact, it could not be concealed. And Vojin, though he pretended to know nothing, was quite prepared to give his sister to a wealthy and famous family in which she could continue her life of ease. Raduša, in accordance with tradition and custom, did not dare to be seen with Obrad except at gatherings and festivals, but, driven by some inner madness, she refused to renounce her secret meetings with him. He courted her, made her small presents and great promises, and for days on end Raduša would walk as if spellbound, dropping objects from her hands and forgetting her household duties, besotted, looking into a quivering, enchanted world.

There were certainly women in the clan in whom Raduša could confide, but because Veliko was far from the Radak village—two hours' walk in unsettled and unsure conditions—only a man could carry messages between the lovers when their meetings were postponed. For that, Raduša turned to Rade, and he became a go-between for his first, unspoken love.

Her demand that Rade assist her in her love affair with another man, and thereby to some extent take part in it, so overwhelmed him that he went to Veliko, to Obrad, without stopping to think, suffering all the way there and back from the thought that he was doing something offensive and unnatural toward that unquenched and smoldering love within himself. Though he was

surer than ever that Raduša did not behave to him only as to a
dear relative, it was clear to him that he would never dare mention it to her, and that she would never admit anything of the sort.
He must reject Raduša and her love, confirm his apparent sinless-
ness and unselfishness, and go on taking her messages to Obrad.

He convinced himself, without conviction, that Raduša had
never had any feeling for him other than family affection, that it
must all have been the undisciplined fruit of his own imagination. For Obrad, he felt only repulsion, even hatred. He handed
over Raduša's messages and took back the replies attentively and
conscientiously, though he was sure that this braggart, this con-
ceited smiling dandy, would deceive Raduša.

Not all men are good, Rade concluded, after his first visit to
Obrad. Indeed, most of them are the same: they take, they deceive,
they kill, and they seduce. But he, Rade, was not like that, so that
those others seemed to him unnatural. He did nothing about it,
sure that she would misunderstand him, would think he was dis-
paraging Obrad for his own advantage.

So he carried their messages and even kept watch, so that no
one would catch them, convinced that time would dull his longing for her. She, meanwhile, became more and more distant, treating him not even as a relative, but as someone who for some
reason was under an obligation to serve her in her love for Obrad.
Nonetheless, from time to time she burst out in a sort of embarrassed shame, not so much because he was aware of her relation
with Obrad, but because of something else, something like a theft
or a betrayal. But she then passed this over with a jest. He ignored
it, but remained bitter, hostile, and dumb. It was a matter for
her conscience and her destiny. It was up to her to make the first
explanation.

He forgave her and understood her love for Obrad as the spell
of passion, as the desire to be married.

But there was no end to the bitterness. He had even had to help
her in her carefully considered loss of her virginity, had had to
help her give herself to Obrad.

It had happened when they were going down from the *katun* to
the autumn pastures, to the hayfields below. He remained with
the cattle. Jelica and Raduša were helping him with the milking,

for Stamena and Stanija had gone down to the village to do some other work. One evening, when the cattle were settled for the night, Obrad burst out of the forest and came to Rade's cabin. Raduša had not said that he would come, and Rade went to Vojin's cabin. Vojin was not there, but it was necessary to hide the event from Jelica; strict and old-fashioned as she was, she would never have allowed Raduša to have a secret meeting, especially at night. Rade whispered to Raduša that Obrad had come, though he suspected that that meeting by night must have some special significance.

Raduša came out of her cabin. The fires were extinguished, and the cattle were noisily chewing the cud. The nights were beginning to be chilly, and Rade could not force the lovers to spend the night in the open, nor could he stay with them. As if it had already been arranged, he carried out to the end the obligation he had undertaken; he took his felt blanket and sheet, left his cabin, and, lying down in the milking shed, prepared for sleep, even though he knew that Raduša, inexperienced and eager for pleasure, was there nearby and that the night would burn out her virginity.

But he was unable to close an eye. The moon was riding somewhere over the mountains, and the fields swelled like enigmatic green rivers under the bare crests merging with the sky. The cabins and cattle pens were small and black, dwarfed by a flood of dark, bluish brilliance, lost in the immeasurable hardness of the hills. He could hear the beating of his own insubordinate heart, while in the cabin, five or six steps away, the embers were smoldering under the ash, and he could hear the loud, occasional words of Obrad and the cooing, soft laughter of Raduša.

At last all was quiet but his heart and the sound of the spring below the cabin. He blamed himself for not protecting Raduša when she was no longer able or willing to protect herself. He wavered between useless regret for himself and blind, furious hatred for Obrad. Hopelessly lost and entangled in these extremes and contradictions, he tried to think of something else, of the monastery and the monks, of the revolt, and of his brother Grgur. But his mind kept returning to the cabin there beside him, where in the darkness, broken only by the sword thrusts of the moonlight between the slats, something fateful must have happened, fateful both for him and for Raduša. His heart and the spring would not, could not, let him find peace.

The silence lasted a long time, one, two, perhaps three, hours, until somewhere or other a cock crowed, and at the extreme edges of the sky the dawn whitened, mingling with the moonlight. He got up, shivering from cold and from his terrible vigil; it seemed to him that he was a changed man, someone unknown. Now he had to warn those two that the day was breaking. But just at that moment Obrad slunk out of the cabin, through the low door, as if afraid he would be seen. He was smirking, tired, and self-satisfied. "How quickly the night passed," he said, wrapping a red scarf around his long neck.

Then, without a farewell, he moved across the meadow with long, unhurried strides; there was no longer any reason to hide. Rade watched him without hatred or disdain until, blurred and thin, he was lost in the dark forest. He always remembered that in those moments he had been cold and emotionless, without thought or desire.

Raduša came out, settling her kerchief on her disheveled hair. She looked crumpled and worn out, shattered, Rade thought. And what was strangest and most repugnant was that in her expression, despite her weary and almost beseeching smile, was the stiff stupor of a bitch which has been led to mating. She dragged herself away without a word, really dragged herself away, twisted by the cold and exhausted by sensual pleasures. Rade went into the cabin, stifled by the sharp heavy smell of male and female, and lay down on the bed, still warm from their bodies. But he arose at once and, opening the door to air the cabin, raked the fire, threw out the ashes, and lay down again, covering his back with his jacket and turning his face toward the hearth.

The little flames flickered, dancing, and then died away, flashing with angry sparks. He fell asleep, in painful lethargy, in the warmth and play of the fire.

The bellowing of the cattle and movements in the *katun* awoke him. He got up and rubbed his eyes. His teeth ached strangely. He felt as if he had been gnashing them. He went outside and remembered that he must go to Vojin's cabin to get the pitchfork.

But he did not go, in order not to see Raduša in the bright light of day.

Raduša's love affair with Obrad continued right up to the winter. But Rade was no longer informed about it, nor did Raduša ask him for any further services.

Their love did not outlive the winter. Obrad ceased to have any connection with Raduša, using as excuse the heavy snowfalls and the skirmishes that broke out because of Ali-beg's refusal to hand over Plav and Gusinje to Montenegro. His family did not want him to marry into an undistinguished household from a village that might or might not belong to Montenegro, or perhaps he had grown tired of Raduša. On Christmas Day it was heard that he had asked for the hand of a girl from the household of a Vasojević chieftain. He did not send Raduša even a word of consolation.

In earlier times, the abandonment of a girl in this way would, more often than not, have resulted in a bloody settlement of accounts. But Vojin and his cousins, like the other Radaks, did not suspect all that had happened and believed that Raduša and Obrad had only looked favorably on one another and sent messages to one another. Furthermore, in Montenegro and the nearby districts, especially those recently liberated, relations between men and women had become freer, and by that standard Raduša's and Obrad's association, at least so far as it was known, had never overstepped the mark.

Nonetheless, by her sudden withdrawal into household tasks and isolation, into stifled desperation and dumb bitterness, which Rade alone fully understood, Raduša provoked fresh gossip among the Radaks and in the neighboring villages. They began to talk about her as a deceived and forsaken girl. Her reputation fell suddenly, and offers of betrothal and marriage ceased altogether. Now all that remained to her was marriage in accordance with her family's wishes and on the first suitable occasion.

Yet her beauty blossomed from that time onward. Her features became soft and melancholy, her body more mature and robust. Her eyes grew darker and deeper, her smile weary but brilliant. Her paleness was relieved only by the shining radiance of her hair and her large, sad eyes. The clan watched her lonely sadness with disapproval, and Rade, unable to help her and unwilling to approach her more closely, felt sorry for her.

It was she who summoned him. The spring breezes aroused the smoldering, banked-up life within her. He came across her—in fact, she had been waiting for him—as she returned from the spring with buckets from which water was splashing. It had suddenly darkened, as if a veil had been drawn across the valley, and her hands were reddened by the damp chill. He was walking behind her, so he could not see her face, but her words revealed to him the beseeching, pitiful gentleness of her smile and her eyes. "Why don't you ever come to see me?"

He replied that he had been afraid to distress her, since he knew what had happened and how much she must be suffering. "No," she said, "it doesn't hurt. It was hard for me at first; I was stunned. But I soon recovered. It was only you I wanted."

He did not know if she was inviting him as a kinsman or as a young man. But she seemed to know something he had not yet grasped, even though that winter he had spent a night with the widow Jana and had come to know the secret relations between man and woman. Unasked, she said to him as they parted, after a long silence: "It had to happen. It happens to everyone. To some before marriage and to others in marriage. The soul demands its rights, and the body, too, demands its rights."

They met the next day. But they could not revive that pure delight, which, before, had made each meeting like a new birth, a blossoming in a new, still more beautiful and carefree world. They had become mature, more prudent, and avoided talking about Obrad or about their own past together. So it remained right up to Roksanda's wedding.

After the dance he was making his way across the courtyard, in the flickering light from the kitchen fire, to look for Stamena and tell her to prepare beds for the guests who were staying the night. From the darkness Raduša's warm voice called out: "Will you see me home? Have they all gone?"

He could scarcely recognize her in her white kerchief and dark dress, fitfully lit by the flames, which the women were stirring up to get embers for the morrow's baking. As they moved out, her face became clearer to him, and, coming closer, he could see her full throat, her eyes half-shut, shining slits, and her lips, which implored even as she threw her arms around his neck, saying: "Kiss me, kiss me on both eyes!"

He kissed her without hesitation, as she wanted him to, and then, taking her hand, went with her. It was dark and chilly. Halting for a moment, they kissed each other on eyes and face, neck and lips. "I love you, love you, love you, foolish one! I have never loved anyone but you! I wanted to run away from you, escape from loving you. You are kin to me, so we daren't; it would be a scandal. And you do not know, you must not know, nobody must know!" she whispered in his ear, as though from some vast immense distance, at the same time unbuttoning her blouse, so he could bury his head in her breasts, full, not firm, yet moist and cool from the dew and the night. They smelled of that same perfume he had long remembered as hers, and it awoke with restless fire under his touch. Her body seemed strangely familiar to him. Only later, thinking it over, was he to realize the inevitability of their actions and, because of them, be filled with remorse and regret. But now everything paled and was forgotten—things and thoughts, Obrad and the clan. All that remained was the boundless joy of her full, fresh, welcoming body.

That evening, and also later when they embraced long and passionately, he was indifferent to her assertions that she loved him and him alone. He neither believed nor disbelieved her words. He knew, both then and later, that she loved him, but not that she would not be able to renounce him. She was not using him to fill the emptiness Obrad had left in her. Rade had his place and his time and, later, when she mentioned Obrad, she did so only scornfully, because of his weak-kneed obedience to his relatives and her own girlish credulity. Rade could believe, too, that she loved him more than she could ever love anyone else, but it was clear to him, from their first embrace, that her love for him was without the hesitations, the remorse, and the suffering from which he could not for a moment free himself. Her regard for the clan and her relatives she considered as something self-evident—undeniable and unchangeable. She did not lie, not consciously; she was no liar. But it was hard to believe that she was speaking the whole truth; truth, like lying, was not her weakness or her passion. She tried to embellish everything, to blunt sharpnesses and to fill chasms, to live without tormenting herself or others—so, too, with her love for him.

Thus she was dear to him, giving him all that he lacked in himself. She was always in his thoughts, from the night of their first kisses and embraces, her body responding to his uncertain, unskilled caresses, with lips and hands that absorbed him, careless of everything, with an acquiescence that asked for nothing, that bound him to nothing.

They did not search each other out intentionally after Roksanda's wedding, but they kissed and caressed whenever they met. It seemed as though she saw nothing sinful in it. It even seemed to him that she would not have thought it sinful if their caresses had gone beyond those final limits, those limits of which strumpets and whores are not ashamed, or husbands with their wives. But he always held back, perhaps less because of sin than because he was unable to see how it could end. What would he do with her and where would they go? Would he leave her, as Obrad had done, or would they run away into the wide world just at the moment of the revolt and the possible massacre of the clan and of his brothers? And what if she became pregnant? Where would she go with a child? Who could endure such disgrace?

Then came Anto's arrest—a fresh burden and a fresh temptation. Was he to couple with a girl from his own clan while his father, in torture, defended the life and destinies of that same clan?

But now, in the valley, on that heap of soft, springing grass, which welcomed them with its green freshness, his father's tortures were far away, as if they concerned someone of whom he had only heard. So it was also with the clan and his brothers and even with the revolt. There was only one worry that obsessed him: what if she became pregnant?

She neither thought nor cared about all that had happened since the dance, and still less about what was happening now. She taught him how to kiss on the mouth. Soul to soul, she said, as she had heard that they kissed in the towns, and as Obrad had taught her. She did that now, passionately fusing with him. Though Rade recalled Obrad, he, too, was far away and alien, as if he had never existed. Her lips, familiar and irresistible in surrender, pressed against his. Yet in the uncertainty, in the vagueness, of her movements he realized that she had made up her mind to leave everything to him. He was the man, and it was up to him to make the decisions.

"The grass will spoil your dress," he remarked, but she replied readily: "Everything I have on is old and dark-colored."

So you thought of that in advance! How wonderful you are, Raduša, my soul! So you had already thought of giving yourself to me, of being all mine, and concluded that you dared, you could, that we dared, we could. That was why you came. How clever of you and how noble! "Of course! You could not carry grass in a new, clean dress."

She did not reply, and he knew that he had been right: she had thought about rolling on the ground, on the grass, and so she had worn old clothes. Instead of a reply, instead of words, her scarcely moist, quivering lips suddenly became huge, able to accept him all, like a whirlpool, like the earth.

Nonetheless, I must know everything for certain before we take one another. I must hear from your own lips if you have thought of everything. I cannot be the only one to be guilty, Raduša! Let us be together in suffering, as now we are in joy! You must know, Raduša, we are the first in the clan to sin together. Behind us are hundreds and hundreds of sinless graves, and before us a progeny accursed and still unborn to bear our sin. No, Raduša, tell me. I must know. Have you really considered everything? Do you know some woman's secret and have the power not to become pregnant? "Listen, I am afraid! You will conceive!" he said loudly, after drawing his lips away from hers.

She looked him straight in the eyes, almost scornfully, as if to say, "How can you think of such things now?" and without hesitation slipped her leg under his, embracing him closely and more deeply. Without shame, she pulled her skirt up to her knees and, still lying on the grass, looked with shining, golden, happy eyes at the blue sky above the tops of the cliffs, which were still red from the sunset somewhere far away, beyond the valley and their love.

Rade, lying beside her, leaned on his left arm, and she drew his arm around her neck and began to kiss him gently and tenderly, as if she wanted him to go on questioning her. So he talked to her, stroking her hair, mixed with the grass, and kissing her eyelids, moist and salt with happy tears.

Then, running from the night, they went with their piles of grass into the darkness of the forest, moist and silent, pushing their way with difficulty through the undergrowth and over the rocks. They did not speak, panting under their burdens and feeling their way through the darkness.

When they reached the turn above the *katun* they sat down to rest. Cones and beech nuts fell from the pines and the beeches, gently tapping on the mast below, and a squirrel began feverishly to collect them.

"I really am afraid," he said, "in case you become pregnant."

"I, too, am afraid of it. But what can I do?"

"If we could only take some precautions, avoid it. And that, too, is shameful. Have you thought of all that?"

"I have. Many times. For a long time past. Ever since you gave me those flowers—do you remember?—when you came back from the monastery."

"I remember. Of course I remember! What did you think?"

"Nothing. What could I? It had to be."

So she must have said to Obrad: "It had to be!"

"One has to take risks," she added boldly in the darkness.

Now she'll say: "The soul demands its own and the body its own, too."

And that was just what she did say: "The soul demands its own and the body, too. As for pregnancy, it does not happen every time. And there are women who know how to procure abortions. Petrana knows, and Jana, also; they say she is a witch."

"How do you know?"

"The women gossip, and I listen. We women are accursed—we must always know more. And you, do you know Jana?"

"I know her. Why not—village to village."

"Not that! Have you ever had anything to do with her? She hunts young men."

He lied. He lied in order to preserve his purity before her, the purity of their love. "No, I have never had any dealings with her."

"So I am your first."

300

"Yes."

"It's your fault that you are not my first. You know that."

I ought to say to you: "It is not my fault, and if I am to blame, then you, too, are guilty."

But he did not reply, uncertain what to say, and she went on: "We are both at fault. We neither knew nor could, and so we were ashamed—the clan, our relatives."

"Yes. And now, do you feel sinful?"

"Sinful? Yes, I do feel sinful, but one must live somehow. I don't know. You don't understand me, but I know with no one except you would it have been so sweet. Whether it is because it is a sin, or because you are so dear to me, I don't know. But that is how it is. Only don't let us talk about it any longer. Kiss me. I'm cold and I'm afraid—the forest, the darkness, the silence!"

She came closer to him and began groping in the darkness to arrange the ropes on his shoulders; he had taken off his burden, but was leaning against it. At the same time she sought his lips with hers. He quickly wriggled his arms free of the ropes, took off his jacket, felt for a level place, and then, putting his arm around her waist, pulled her to him and to the ground.

He no longer thought of the clan, or the sin; or of his father, or the revolt. It was total darkness; nothing except her lips, her cool breasts, and her body, welcoming, warm, infinite.

From that moment, much was changed, not only their feeling toward one another, but also much else in Rade's viewpoint and existence.

Whereas earlier they had sought each other out, now they avoided meeting in the presence of others, especially by day. Indeed, Rade avoided her as if afraid that someone in the clan would discover their sin from their glances. Sometimes he thought that could be possible, so openly did she look at him and smile at him. He even blamed her for that, for the intimacy of her bearing and her glance, which said to him unconcealedly, unrestrainedly: "I am yours; we have been together and will be again, perhaps tonight, perhaps tomorrow night, as man and wife." She assured him that she looked at him and joked with him as before, but that he now saw it differently.

In truth, he saw many things differently. The mountain, deserted since Akan had driven off the cattle for sale, shone with a warm, vibrant splendor, and there was a strong, fresh breeze, like warm milk from snowy breasts. Everything was alive, the stones and the waters, and Rade wondered why he had not seen that earlier, or realized that he, too, was a part of that effortless, exultant existence.

He had noticed the change the morning after his meeting with Raduša in the coomb. All night he had been unable to sleep, carried away by the happiness of his union with her but also consumed with worries. When at last sleep took him unawares, he slept peacefully and deeply, until it seemed to him that someone entered the cabin with the sunlight. He turned over and opened his eyes. Raduša was squatting by his head, with a radiant smile hitherto unknown to him, bursting with stifled, satisfied joy, and the sun had spread out a shining kerchief through the open door.

"Why don't you get up, my lazy darling?" she whispered, planting a swift kiss on his eyes.

He had to pull himself together to remember all that had happened between them last night, for she was waking him as a bride does her bridegroom. He put his hand out to her. But she drew back, pulling the blanket off him. "We must be careful. I have driven your cow with mine to the pasture."

He ran out after her; she had driven away the calf and was kneeling to milk the cow. His gaze embraced her body, her body which now in the sunlight, as last night in the coomb, was his. She was kneeling, straight-backed, with slightly bent, rounded shoulders. She was barefoot, and her legs, slender, muscular in the calf, and thin in the ankle, were reddened and tense in the chill morning dew.

He glanced around at the yellowing grassy peaks and the steep slopes slipping down to the *katun*, in the pure morning mountain air. Raduša was like the mountain, a little chill yet warm, fresh and dewy and smiling, without the rich iridescence and the mockery of the open plain.

His feeling of union with the mountain that morning and later the love for the mountain within himself, as a part of his youthful, virile enjoyment, gradually subsided and was transformed into a conception of the incomparable beauty and freshness of life on the mountain. But Raduša's presence in everything, and especially in his body like a flower in full bloom, made heavier by its own sweetness, and that especial hungering, as if everything was empty as soon as he was away from her, did not lessen, not even after a night spent in sated and seductive memories.

Something strange had happened; the longer and more often he was with Raduša and the more they enjoyed one another frankly and intentionally, the more the thoughts he had had before their meeting in the coomb that she was an egoistic and dissolute little bitch became ugly and shameful. Raduša's surrender, her open, unrestrained, and slavish submission to his moods, revealed to him her hitherto unrealized devotion, loyalty, and even modesty. It was not, nor could it be, the loyalty of a wife to her husband or of a lover to a lover. Rade knew, and she did not hide it, that she might, without reference to him, be married on the first suitable occasion and to the first man who wanted her. It was a devotion and loyalty just to him, Rade, who was both kinsman and lover to her, a loyalty to their secret and sinful love. There was something in her, even in her body, that would always belong to him, belong only to him. Obrad, or some future husband, whoever it might be, could never wean her from him, for his place was quite different and was unattainable to anyone but him.

She said all that to him, awaiting him with a smile in the morning and welcoming his embraces in the night. "We grew up beside one another, for one another. I don't know what you are to me, but you are me; I cannot even in my thoughts separate you from me. When I embrace you, I know that you are male, but a male who does at every moment what I want, who is a part of me, and from whom I take nothing and demand nothing. You are not my eyes or my heart or my body—you are my very soul. I walk, I think, I live, and I will continue to live without you, but my womb and my heart will always be open to you, for they were yours even before you entered them, even as I was yours even before I was conscious of myself. Our love is sinful for everyone except me, except us. But you are different the moment you are alone; as soon as you are without me the sin in you comes alive and oppresses you. You have other things in your life—your brothers and Serbdom, your faith and the revolt. But I have not, nor have I in myself anything that is not you; I know nothing of sin when I am with you. I do not even pray to God to forgive me. There will be time enough for that when I have sinned with another. Since He has marked us out, God has permitted me to love you; let me enjoy that fully and be what I am. That I become you, my darling! Soon terrors and beliefs, duties and oaths and our own existence will keep us apart, my brother and my man!"

The thought of having to leave the mountain no longer tormented him; it had been once more revealed to him, through Raduša, as a part of his being. He knew that existence with Raduša, wherever they found themselves, must take its course and find its own banks.

It was purposeless, senseless, to remain on the mountain without the stock. But the Radak folk feared evil and would neither begin nor end any task before they were compelled to do so. They waited on the mountain until they knew for certain that all the stock had been sold. And those two, Rade and Raduša, in Anto's and Vojin's cabins, spent their days in love on the mountain.

Thus passed the ten or so days before Akan's return. Fearing robbers on the roads, Akan had separated from the rest of the band and, more by night than by day, made his way by the goat paths, the money in his belt. The following day, when the rest of the drovers arrived, it was proved that his precautions had been justified. Plunderers had stopped them on the road and stripped them to the bare skin. They had even taken the shoes from their horses, looking for the ducats. Then, after taking even the Radaks' belt buckles, they had let them pass.

Nightfall brought Akan to the cabin. Without a greeting, he whispered to Rade: "I haven't the money on me. As I agreed with Grgur, I shoved it into the stump of that beech tree from which we cleared the bees' nest last year—until I could find out what was happening in the *katun*."

He was unshaven, and his hair showed reddish in the glow from the flames of the hearth; his small, close-set teeth gleamed like those of a wild beast ready to bite. He was obviously tired and suffering from lack of sleep, but his clothes were neat and clean. He took from his belt a revolver, such as Rade had seen some of the begs wearing, but had never held in his own hands. "I had to buy it—for any emergency," Akan explained. "And it will be useful to Grgur, also. Five shots; just press the trigger and they come out one after the other. And it is easy to reload. Not like an old-fashioned *kubura*—only one shot and you can never be sure that the spark will catch. I didn't buy anything else, and I sold the cattle for more than I had hoped, seeing that it is not yet the season for market."

Though famished, he ate slowly, taking a full spoonful and asking questions between mouthfuls. "You say there is nothing new. Haven't the Turks come? Down there in Peć they say that the Turks of Skadar have formed some sort of league in the Malesia and the Metohija—what does it matter where?—to defend Plav and Gusinje. The Albanians are supporting them, and small wonder, when all their *barjaktars* have been bribed. And the Dečani monks are scared out of their lives! They sent their greetings to you; they remembered you and wondered why you had not come back to continue your schooling. They care nothing for our misfortunes. They are trying to outsmart the Turks as they have always done, to preserve the faith and the shrine and the monastery property. That is enough for them. And as far as we are concerned: have faith in yourselves and don't rely on others. If someone stronger does not stick his finger in the pie, then there is nothing left us but to become beggars."

Akan neither drank nor smoked, and was skilled in every craft, even woman's work; looking after the stock in childhood and early youth and keeping watch over them in the winter loneliness of the mountain he had learned, partly from necessity and partly to pass the time, how to knit, mix, and cook as well as the most skillful housewife. But because it was considered indecorous among the Radaks for a man to do woman's work, and because he had devoted himself to trading, he had neglected his skills, only making use of them when forced to do so. Brushing the crumbs from his lap and wiping his lips with his hand, he now devoted himself to stringing his sandals, whose laces had broken. He refused to let Rade call one of the women from the *katun*. "Let them be! It's all the better if no one knows I have come, until the money reaches its destination. They belong to the clan and are of our blood, but they still have tongues."

He refused to think of spending the night. "It only needs that! If the Albanians waylaid them on the road, and one of them in fear said that the money was on me, they could attack the cabins by night, or waylay me somewhere. No, no! Now we have lost all our stock, we must at **least** gain some advantage from it."

Plaiting the laces, he went on as if to himself: "Slinking through the mountains yesterday, I thought: Good God, what wealth is being wasted for nothing! Forests, meadows, pastures! From stock alone a man could amass uncounted treasure; he could buy animals in the spring when they are thin and feed them up on the mountains and then sell them in the autumn. Money would breed money. But in this wretched Turkey there is no security or freedom, even for the Turks! And we are so tied to this rocky wilderness, where we have been for the past thousand years—as if there were nowhere outside it! Here one can no longer live like a man, even without the Turks. How much less with them!"

As soon as he had finished lacing his sandals, he moved on. "I'm going now. I will take the money and go by the goat paths to the valley. I will tell Vojin, too, in a moment. Is he here? And when are you coming down from the mountain? Now there is nothing to stay for. Only if some of the hay has not been cut. As for the rest—cattle, small stock, and implements—it could all go tomorrow."

He took the revolver from Rade, opened the breech, and looked into the barrel in the firelight; the steel shone, outside and in. "Arms must be kept like the eyes in one's head; women and guns should never be lent."

He disappeared into the darkness, and Rade thought: Like a haiduk, yet there is nothing of the haiduk in him.

Left alone by the hearth, Rade thought things over and waited for Raduša. What if she was delayed, or Vojin came up from the village to move everything down next day? What if there was someone with her? He heaped the embers with ash and hoped she would come soon. He undressed quickly and lay down on the bed.

It was now toward the end of summer; in a day or two they would have to go down to the hayfields, where they would stay about a fortnight, until the hay was gathered and stacked.

The begs had interfered with the Radak haymaking, even though they had pastured and reaped there from time immemorial; they had to pay grass tax to the authorities and rent to the begs. In fact, the greater part of the mountain belonged to two families, Anto's and Vojin's, while the other Radaks only used it for pasture, after the hay had been mown and stacked. It was said among the Radaks that they had originally been clan pastures which Anto's ancestors had taken over and exploited, relying on the begs to whom they had given a third of their produce, as they did of everything else. Mad Grandfather Pavle had been known to say: "When something is torn from the clan, then blood is worth no more than water!" One way or another, this tangled ownership had caused bitterness within the clan and between the clan and the begs.

The pastures on the way from the *katun* to the village were not wide, but about half an hour's walk in length. They were not particularly rich, but were convenient for haymaking because of the lack of stones and the easy slope. Their special advantage was that they lay on the route from the mountain to the village, so that the cattle could stay up there for a month, or even two, before the first snowfalls.

But this year, because of the lack of stock, it was only needful to stay there until the hay was ready. Rade did not know if anyone would come from the village to help. He hoped that, despite the amount of work to be done, no one would come, so that he could be alone with Raduša for as long as possible. Those would be his last days of ecstatic isolation with her. After that, there would be the village and life under the eyes of the clan and perhaps, so he had heard, Raduša's being given in marriage, and the revolt. It was as if sentence had already been passed: this is your last and only summertime; you have sought and found one another, never to meet again.

Raduša knew what was worrying him. The door of the cabin squeaked on its hinges, and by the light of the moon, still not full, he recognized her skirt flapping about her knees, its fine, soft pleats stressing the provocative roundness of her hips.

"Are you asleep?" she asked, shutting the door and settling down somewhere near him. She loved to be with him in the dark.

"I was just drowsing," he said, and stretched out his hand in the darkness to touch her skirt and feel her thigh—both were well known to him—as if by doing so he saw all of her and held her in his arms.

"Don't," she said, pushing away his hand, which he slyly put back again, and she forgot all about it. "I came over to tell you

307

my brother is here and has agreed with Akan that we should go to the village tomorrow. He has already discussed it with Grgur, but was waiting until Akan's return. He will take your things with him and the cow. We two, you and I, must go to the hayfields and look after the ricks; they will come in a day or two. So there you are; I thought you ought to know. Don't oversleep in the morning."

She was about to go, but hesitated and, finding his lips, pressed short, moist kisses on them. He clutched her strongly and desperately around the hips, crying out: "Stay a minute—I beg you."

"No, no! I can't like this—I wasn't thinking of that. I'm not ready! You know I don't like to—on the spur of the moment."

"But, for my sake!"

"No! When it is only for your sake—you know yourself—it is not nice for you either."

She slipped away, deluding him with one last kiss. Her skirt again fluttered in the doorway, and darkness swallowed the cabin and everything in it and her, everything except one spark, solitary and forgotten.

She had cultivated their love. Passion was only a moment in it, certainly its most complete culmination, but one that, inseparable from the whole, she must prepare for. It must come of itself. Yet this attitude did not weaken or dispel her fierce desire, which, in its nakedness and savagery, reminded Rade of the coupling of mares and stallions in the pastures or bulls and heifers in the pens. In their passionate solitudes, even Raduša admitted that the coupling of animals had excited her as a girl and now drove her to seek out the most complete union with him. But her unrestrained desire never for a moment eliminated the careful, devoted tenderness and charm of her caresses. Even that savage union must be prepared for, cultivated, allowed to grow.

So now, when she shut the door of the cabin behind her, there remained on his hands in the darkness the sense of the luxuriant nakedness of her body. And just because she was not there and because he could not lull himself to sleep with satisfied desire, there awoke in him inextinguishable remorse because of his sin, the clan, his brothers, and the revolt, though it was hard now to call it sin. Having become accustomed to Raduša, to making love to her, the sin had slipped away, hidden itself, become transformed into something else.

The clan itself, he now realized, was not, at least not quite, what it was supposed to be, still less what many of its members wanted it to be. Each man—and this had been true for a long time past—lived for himself. And died for himself. Quarrels about boundary marks and trespass were no rare thing. But centuries of existence under foreign swords, under the begs' whips, harried by blood feuds, always in the same surroundings and the same way of life, had forced the Radaks into a unity and had kept them in it, had bound them together in union and loyalty. Tomorrow, when they freed themselves from the Turks and serfdom, each would look to himself, and the clan would remain only as a beautiful, far-off memory. But no one saw that; not even Grgur saw it, dared to see it. He was tearing himself apart between the revolt and the clan, between his heroism and the impossibility of fulfilling that heroism. Whatever happened, as soon as he raised his gun against the Turks someone always pushed the barrel aside. Others, too, were tearing themselves apart. Everyone—except Raduša. She, no! Why was it that she did not tear herself apart? What would she say? She would say: "I live as I must; the body demands its own and the soul its own!"

Everything was strange and clear in the total darkness. He belonged to the clan and yet the clan was breaking into pieces—even all that was great and beautiful in it, as though it were only a fairy tale.

He remembered his ancestor Radule and his grave. Radule, he who had languished on the hooks at Peć, had always been, for Rade, a person especially near, almost intimate; even their names had been, intentionally, allied. The story did not greatly embellish his death: he had begged his father and the Turks to shorten his agony. But the tale lived on, as did the grave, which the Radaks, and Rade himself when he went to Peć and Dečani, used to visit and care for.

And he had not remembered to ask Akan about the grave. It was two years since anyone had visited it, and even then it had been overgrown and the railing around it broken and fallen. Another year or so and it would be swallowed up; the grave would be dug over and finally forgotten. But would his sin with Raduša be forgotten? No, not so long as there were Radaks! Everything was entangled and turned upside down; he was ready to die for the clan, yet secretly hoped for its destruction.

Because of the sin, he, too, was on the hooks, perhaps more terrible than Radule's just because they were invisible, and there was no one whom he could implore for help. Yet perhaps there was no real sweetness without sin. If the clan did not exist, perhaps there would be no Raduša, no longing for her, no union with her. To die in the revolt, in the battle for the clan, in the sweetness and ecstasy of his sin with Raduša, or to live without one and without the other—was there really no choice?

There had been sin before in the clan. But the sin had been forgotten so that life could go on. Who had been those two in the clan who had loved and who had had to part? Him they had expelled; he had vanished without trace. Her they had married off by force; they had smashed her to powder. Something was known of everyone in the clan, but of those two nothing, not a memory, not a name, not a grave. They were erased from memory. Only in whispers was their sin mentioned, the disgrace they had brought upon the clan.

It was said that if a man confides in someone, it is easier for him. But in whom could one confide when established order and custom forbids, shame prevents, and fear holds one back lest it bring confusion and wavering even among those who are for the revolt? Perhaps he could tell Akan. He was not tied overclosely to the clan. But he was strict against womanizing, perhaps under Stanija's influence, and wrapped up in trading and the idea of getting rich. Even if he kept silent, he would hate and despise Rade. He could tell Stojan; he, too, it seemed, was living in sin, with Petrana. But that would be an association of fellow sinners, and Stojan, frank as he was, could not help telling Grgur, and perhaps Vojin. Grgur? He hadn't thought of him. He could tell him first of all, most gladly. But it would be a great blow to him; he would think that his own brother had betrayed him in his efforts to unite the clan in revolt. Even if he could not unite it, Grgur must appear exemplary in the eyes of his opponents in the purity of his family, even as he was superior to them in courage and understanding.

There was no confiding, no forgiveness. And perhaps it was better that way. Without them the sweetness of sin was implacable, without them love for Raduša was undiminished and imperishable. Perhaps it was better to be the grave of one's own secrets, to bury them within oneself.

The night passed in sleeplessness, in confused thoughts and longings.

Two days later they went down to the hayfields. Only after about ten days of heavy, strenuous work were Rade and Raduša left alone for the last two days.

But first, toward the end of the haying, everyone had gone down to the village to welcome Knez Anto Radak.

Anto had been transformed by torture and prison into a wraith, which Rade found difficult, even impossible, to identify with the picture in his memory. It was as if there had returned to the village, to Rade, not the former Knez, not his father, but a person shattered and ruined, unable to understand what was happening in the clan and therefore no longer fitted to be its leader. What was still more terrible, no one seemed able to see that, or perhaps did not want to see it—not even Raduša, with whom he talked when they returned alone to the hayfields. Of course everyone could see that Anto had grown thinner and had a livid and corpselike transparency from the prison dankness. They noticed, too, that he no longer possessed his former firm but reasonable intransigence; all his mildness and softness had come to the surface and also a sort of unreasonable and depressed retreat into irritability. He had become talkative, though before he had not been, as if in prison his words had become hungry and thirsty. Everyone considered these changes as temporary; they were the result of his tortures and imprisonment and would soon disappear. And so, at first, did Rade. Anto even preached forgiveness and nonresistance to the Turks, and therefore at once won over the opponents of the revolt, even Vojin, who did not entirely agree. The Radaks gathered around Anto's couch in the garden the afternoon after he had been brought from Plav and approved his maunderings and praised his courage and loyalty to the clan, which had already become transformed into a living folk tale.

Rade was the youngest child, and his father had always seemed distant and inaccessible to him, even had he not been knez and often occupied in affairs outside the household. Anto's children belonged to two generations: the elder, Grgur and Akan, and the younger, Roksanda and Rade. Between these generations stretched fifteen years of Milena's unfruitfulness and the death of two other children. Rade regarded Grgur, who was already a young man when Rade was born and had brought him up and taught him, as more of a father than Anto. His father's word was received by all unquestioningly, whereas it was possible to protest to and argue with Grgur; between him and Rade there was a brotherly intimacy, a companionship and understanding. There had never been any such contact between Rade and his father. It could not be denied that Anto was a loving and considerate parent and always interested himself in the troubles and misfortunes of each of his children, but, as Rade now realized, he had always done so in the manner of a knez, curtly, temperately, and irrevocably. For Rade his father was merged with the knez, and now also with the folk tales and traditions of the clan.

While his father was in prison, sympathy and grief had erased that sense of alienation and disagreement. But after his father's sermon the day before, on peace and unity, and the rallying around his sickbed of all those eager for compromise, it seemed to Rade that he would no longer be able to understand him as he had before, or even obey him as knez. Thus his relationship with his father became more complex; now he would have liked to obey him, but could not. Suljaga had lacerated for Rade that dear, incomparable being, had soiled him with blood, but had also exalted him.

This division, this split, in himself continued in still more definite form; it had begun, God knows when, with his love for Raduša, with his doubts about the traditions of the clan.

Since the work in the hayfields was almost at an end, and Vojin and Grgur were busy with the clan council, they all stayed in the village, while Rade and Raduša went back to finish the work. Rade's love, his conception of Raduša, had changed, as if the hayfields were responsible. From the village and from the valley came the scents of ripe and fruitful autumn, and from the mountain itself still came cool, summer breezes. It was strange, as if Raduša and the hayfields had something in common, a mingling of pure mountain youth and the dissolute maturity of the valley.

Raduša, too, had changed. After their first night in the hay-fields, in that same cabin before which he had kept vigil on the night of Obrad's visit—for a wonder he felt no embarrassment at this—Rade became aware of something new in her, a mature and firm self-conscious apprehension, which had ripened with the autumn. He noticed that mature fullness even in her body, in the sculptured movements of her back as she moved, in the firm whiteness of her throat, in the suppleness of her neck when she turned her head, and in the firmness of her legs when she reached up to get something.

In the morning, after their first night of love, as she was putting the cabin to rights, he enjoyed just looking at her body, which suddenly, incontestably, belonged only to him, like a field, like a house, but also as a woman created and ready to receive his seed and bear their children, his unknown and eternal life. And she was glad that he enjoyed looking at her and taking pleasure in her. It seemed as if the cabin, too, had changed, had become intimate and comfortable, a home. With her, he could, in this cabin —or so it seemed to him—pass his whole life.

He thought, and later told her, that she had certainly conceived that night. The next day and the following night he was aware of the mature passion and conscious readiness with which she awaited him. She had tried to explain it to him. "Now that we are alone and I am afraid of nothing and do not hold myself back for anyone, you are even dearer to me."

But she did not convince him so much by those words as by her natural movements, stressing those parts of her body she knew he could see and take pleasure in. Her bodily presence in everything that was his held, for him, some wider significance. Only with her was that ecstasy possible.

He had had little experience with women, though he knew all that was to be known about them, from observation, from the comments of his brothers about their wives, and from the tales of his contemporaries and older youths. He had watched girls and even been secretly in love while at Dečani with the miller's daughter from Bistrica, and prayed to God and the saints to forgive him his sinful desires in their holy house.

The only woman with whom he had been in closer contact had been Jana, a widow from the next village, with a lap as broad as a boat, breasts as tumid as swelling loaves, and legs as firm and powerful as tree trunks. She had a grown-up daughter and a little son, and she lived with her mother. Even during her husband's lifetime she had been known as a dissolute woman. But immediately after his death, she had begun almost openly to entertain strange men. For that she had a cabin, a dairy shed in which a bed, laid over the milking troughs, was ready and waiting to receive her lovers.

She was not a real whore; her lovers cost her more than anything she ever got from them. Often they would stay for meals. Nor was she one of those sick women who, so Rade had heard, ran after men in the vain hope of finding one who could satisfy them. No, she was only a healthy, still-desirable woman—she was about thirty-five—who neither concealed nor restrained her passions.

Swarthy, but not gypsylike, with a dark, ruddy face, she had dark hairs on her upper lip and dense masculine eyebrows. She was more dissolute in words than in deeds, and, though religious, did not go to confession and therefore did not take communion. She said: "The priest knows what I do, and if he is willing to absolve me, well and good, and if he won't, then God will forgive me since he made me sinful." Only toward her daughter, already ripe for marriage, was she strict, probably because from her early youth her own mother had always let her go her own way. It was always known who was Jana's lover, though she often changed them. Usually his fellow villagers knew this when they saw him in the morning, after a night spent with her, cutting wood in front of her house, for that was the only service she demanded from her lovers. She did not hide her lovers from her mother and daughter, and her mother used to greet them when they came. But she did not talk with her mother and daughter about them, and still less about love. Whenever they saw her go silently to the dairy shed after they had gone to bed, they knew that some man was there to spend the night with her.

Rade knew, from the jibes of the older men and the jokes of his contemporaries, that Jana most willingly seduced youths, and, from the vague desire to escape his bitterness and depression over Raduša's love affair with Obrad, as well as from more and more unbearable desire and irresistible curiosity to know a woman, he had thought more and more often of the dark, strong, and unprincipled widow near the stream below the Radak village. But the chance for so inexpert a lover did not appear until the end of winter.

After taking wood to the beg, he was returning with his horses from Plav about midday by a roundabout path which had been cleared of snow. He had come across Jana at the stream doing her washing. Her legs were bare to the knee, and her arms to the elbows, reddened by work and the cold. He greeted her in God's name, as was the custom, and slowed down, hoping that she would stop him for a chat. But she mocked him. "Don't slow your horses! I'm no cradle-snatcher!"

So began the conversation, which ended with an agreement that he should come that evening. Standing on the path, hands on hips, she shouted after him: "See that you are good and strong tonight, young man!"

When darkness came, the snow began to fall again, and when everyone at home was asleep and Rade slipped out, it was frosty and a blizzard was howling. Damp snow caked his eyelids and slithered down his neck. There was not a trace of the path. Nonetheless, he went, in order not to show himself a weakling in Jana's eyes and to prove to himself that he was able to forget, to stifle his memories of Raduša.

Fearing he might get lost, he moved directly downhill, which must lead him to the stream. So, in fact, it did. But the stream by day looked different from the stream by night in a blizzard, when he had to leap over holes and channels, skirt steep curves, and force his way through flooded willow beds. He trod in water, fell into pools, and stumbled over roots. Yet he reached the bank where Jana's house was. He knocked at the window of the dairy shed, and Jana, barefoot and in a nightshirt, looking still plumper, opened the door. "You are a man and a Radak," she said, "to come in such a storm. I knew you would come; you were ashamed before a woman and you are a man of your word."

She took off his clothes to dry them behind the stove, and he snuggled under the thick, hairy blankets, which smelled of lye and were warm from Jana's body. Gasping from the cold, her broad soles slapping on the earth floor, Jana leaped into bed and without a word began to kiss him with moist warm lips, pressing herself against his slender, still-immature body. In order to conceal his inexperience, he did the same to her, pressing her soft, heavy breasts with his cold chest.

It was never clear to him how Jana, asking him "Am I your first?" concluded that she was the first woman he had known intimately. He did not want to admit it, refusing with assumed pride to tell her the name of that other, nonexistent, one. "No matter," Jana assured him. "If you don't know, I'll soon teach you, and if you know something, then you will be able to teach me!"

Later, as they were resting, she said: "They lie. I am not a whore. What others do secretly or long for stupidly, I do openly. For a young man like you, I do it for love. You are sweet, you young devils, just as you are, inexperienced and uncorrupted. When I am with you, I feel as if I had only just learned what a man is. Men do not hate me, only women; many husbands would willingly lick their lips to get me, if I wanted them. You Radaks, too, though you consider yourselves the most upright of all. A good many of them have danced around me. First, your brother Grgur, when he was a young man. And Stojan—until recently. And Vojin, even after his marriage. Only Anto never turned his head toward me, though I danced around him from pure bitchiness, because he is older and a knez."

Jana was slow to passion and unselfish, but strong and inexhaustible. In the moments of ecstasy she bit him furiously. The next day revealed bruises and blood-lined tooth marks on his body, and he had to wrap a scarf around his neck and stay out of doors all day.

Raduša in no way resembled or reminded him of Jana. Even in the moments of most complete ecstasy he somehow felt that he was not merely embracing a woman, but just her, Raduša. Though he was conscious that he could be, and would be, intimate with other women, it was clear to him that this would happen only if he could not reach Raduša. Other women would come and go, even she whom he eventually would marry, but Raduša would remain; her place in his life could never be filled. All women in the future would be compared with her, measured by her, all future women, still unknown and unsuspected.

He wanted to speak to her about that, or, rather, not so much about that, for it was impossible to explain, but of their relationship to one another, of their common future, which involved her passionate readiness to accept his body, that readiness for which he would never find a substitute. But they had already spent two days alone in the hayfields, two days in which Rade remained obsessed by the sweetness of her body; and the words would not come. That tangled mass of wishes, thoughts, and hopes—for days, for years—he was unable to express clearly.

If you say that you are not my life, I will become the mourning of a mother for her first-born, the longing of the scorched grasses for the dew. If your path deviates from mine, I will be lost in the darkness. My mind will darken if your sun does not warm it. Look around at the great mountain and the yellowing valley, the sky and the earth, the link between God and man, labor and truth, breathe the mountain air and fill yourself with the sweetness of the fields and orchards; then you will realize for what I live, why and for what I love you. The monks of Dečani told me that twelve heavens can spin one around the other and that the stars never meet on their paths, but I have one heaven only—your love—and I must change the path of my star, that my star fuse into yours. My world and my life are with you; your smile charms the sun to rise before its time, and your wishes are flowery meadows spread out before me; you smell of the perfumes of the fruitful earth. I no longer fear even Hell, for you will be there with me. Not only are you my bread and wine, but it is to you I pray in my prayers.

They say that you are my sister! But I know: you are my only wife! Born for me and with me, from the same nest and under the same sun, from the same desire and the same song. Even as I had to be born and even as I shall not be able to avoid death, so is my love for you. We have trodden underfoot the law of the clan, human law. But if the law of God is the preservation of the root and branch of the human race, then we are as innocent as flowers. We want nothing but to fill God's world with joy and with our seed, the progeny of man and God.

Do not say to me: "Forget, my dear, the revolt, for my sake." I live in the revolt as I live in you. You are what you are, but the revolt is what I would wish to be. Don't rend me asunder, for, divided in two for you, for the revolt, for existence, for life, for hope, for Serfdom, for longing, I will wander through the world never to find my place in it. Whoever is forced to choose between passion and conscience, between eternity and existence, has already chosen suffering in this world. Do not force me, dearest, to choose! I have chosen you, who link eternity with my present. Let this be a moment that does not pass, my life and my soul.

In you I stifle my conscience! We are linked by existence, by faith, and by faith in existence! The falcon flies, the fish swims, the flowers blossom, the sun rises and sets, and man creates and dreams. Tell me: I am your life and your way and your sun.

But all these things remained unspoken.

So it came to the last day, the third of their stay in the hayfields. By the evening, as soon as the last of the work was done, they had to be in the village, where they could only meet casually, longing in vain.

It seemed as if she intentionally did not understand his haste. She was tired from the work and their nights of love; when it grew hot she lay down in the shade between two finished ricks and at once fell asleep on his cape spread on the ground.

He went down to the brook to find some sticks for binders. On his return he found her still sleeping. Sitting on the cloak beside her and looking at her face, he was filled with joy and intimacy toward her such as he had not felt since his distant childhood—he had not been two at the time, and his memory had, for a wonder, retained the incident—when his mother had taken him to her breast after she had already begun to wean him.

Raduša's face was paler than in the sunlight, and her high, smooth brow stressed her warm, human contentment. Innocent and serene, she seemed to him smaller and thinner, as his mother must have said compassionately about him before she finally cut him off from her milk. He had kissed those dark, soft lips so many times, even last night, with so much ecstasy that they, as well as his own, had begun to crack. And he had caressed into lethargy and inertia that body, now firmly braced by a broad woven belt, whose warm smoothness and vigor were now lost in the rough linen blouse, dirty from sweat and covered with bits of hay, the faded woolen skirt and dew-bespattered black woolen stockings. This was Raduša, unadorned, dressed for work, tired. But he saw only that other Raduša, smooth, seductive, fresh. He had kissed and would kiss again that body now so helpless and so apt to love, to work, and to give birth.

As if she felt his gaze on her and knew that he was thinking about her, Raduša opened her eyes, looked at him, and then closed them again. Then she opened her eyes fully and, coming to herself, smiled at him, raising herself on one elbow. "I have slept really well."

"Yes, you slept. Perhaps two, perhaps three, hours. I was cutting the binders—and looking at you. Did you dream something nice?"

"No, I didn't. Or perhaps I slept so well that I forgot my dreams. It's good that you have cut the binders. We will finish all the earlier."

"I thought of that. It will give us longer together."

"But we are together." She smiled.

"I didn't mean that—but alone."

"But we are alone." She smiled again, teasing him.

"Not in this way, but when we have no more work to do."

She smiled again, but this time roguishly, and, sitting up, she offered him her tired lips.

He tried to kiss her and caress her, but she lazily and firmly resisted him. "Someone might come, and anyhow I am still sleepy. I know you—you never know when to stop."

She leaped up lightly and began to climb onto the haycock. They set to work. She, on the slope of the haycock, only just managed to place and tread down the bundles of hay which he threw up to her at furious speed. He was unsparing of himself in work; finishing a job always gave him a feeling of satisfaction, especially now, when he was hurrying for reasons of his own. Every now and then he found time to tease Raduša, throwing the hay too high, so that it hit her on the breasts and face. She did not like this way of working, though she countered his jokes with feigned, good-humored anger. Even in everyday tasks, work of no special importance, she loved steady attentiveness and moderation. She tired quickly and, sweating, shouted down to him: "Take it easy. You'll kill me! Why must we hurry so much? We shall have to rest every few minutes. We will get back to the village one way or another."

They finished early, before the afternoon shadows from the forest and the brook crept up the hillside.

Stacked, fresh, pale green and sweetly scented, their summits crowned with leafy coronets of binders, three haycocks stood in the long smooth meadow on the slope above the brook like three voivodes from the ballads on the field of battle. They quickly fenced them in with stakes from last year's ricks, blackened and with splitting and peeling bark. The haycocks lost their proud enchantment and were transformed into voivodes with heavy, rusting greaves about their legs. When Rade and Raduša set out for the village, the shadows had reached halfway up the haycocks; their shining heads, with green plumes on their pointed helmets, were more beautiful and proud in the darkness, and the staves around them looked like heavy fetters.

Rade and Raduša halted when they reached the spring, a hundred paces from the hurdles at the head of the little valley which divided the meadow. Rade washed his neck and face, then drank, and, standing, splashed Raduša's still-flushed face. She was angry, but smiled and shook the water from her breast, and then she, too, began to wash. She did so slowly and noiselessly, like a cat, with a care that did not omit neck or ears or arms—no uncovered part of her body. Then she drank slowly, with small, slow sips. When she stood up, she put her wet hands on his smooth, warm chest.

He put his arm around her shoulders and led her along the path, to the point where it divided, one path leading deep into the undergrowth. Leaning close to one another, paying no heed to the path, they did not notice when their ankles brushed against the bushes on either side. They were glad because they had finished their work and were filled with passionate anticipation. Rade did not think about when or where they would stop, and Raduša was silent, plunged in thought. But when they came to the edge of the copse, where the path dipped steeply down into the cleared space, with its bare tree stumps, and then into the dense grove just above the village, they stopped and gazed at the blue abyss that opened before them.

To their left, at the edge of the clearing, there were still a few beeches and young hornbeams, and they went there together. They walked around the trees and finding, on the far side, a little dell of grass and leaves, they sat down on his cape.

"Do you love me?" he asked, looking into her eyes, cloudy with passion and the sunset.

"Why do you ask, when you know it?"

"I like to hear it."

"I like it, too. I love you more than my own soul."

"Tell me that you love me more than your life, and I will say to you, in fact I will say it now: I love you more than my own soul."

"But that is the same." She laughed, embraced him, and pulled him down on his back. "Now I want to be like your wife," she added uncompromisingly, bending over him, her half-closed eyes glinting and her red lips quivering.

Later they sat, tired and at ease, looking at the darkening but still-pellucid depths, at the varicolored, narrow fields and meadows, spread out like washing along the Lim. They could not see their own village, which was hidden by the rounded, yellowing hilltops, but knew that behind those hilltops wisps of smoke were rising from unseen houses. As always at such moments, everything, their feeling for one another and their future, seemed clearer and simpler. They would love as they had loved until now, and when difficulties arose, they would overcome them.

Her face, till then blissful, suddenly changed. Her eyes became gay, her lips mocking. "There, you see!" She pointed into the valley. "That village by the Lim, those white houses on the right, scattered under the hill! There—I did not tell you before—my brother will marry me off this autumn. I don't know which is the bridegroom's house, but that is his village. There I will live!" Then she added, pulling herself together and looking around: "The mountain and these hayfields can easily be seen from there. And this spot, too, will be visible, if only I can recognize it."

Rade did not know why he couldn't respond, why he could not find the right words. A sharp pain ran through him, but his mind sought vainly for something to get a grip on, for some way out. He remembered how his teeth had ached when Obrad was making love to her, and thought, though he did not know why, that it would happen again now.

"Why are you so silent?" she asked, throwing her arm around his shoulder.

Her arm was heavy but very dear. Nonetheless, he wriggled free and at last found words. "I have nothing to say!"

"Nothing! But that means our separation!"

"I know."

"And yet you—have nothing to say."

"No, no! Only I do not know how to tell you what I feel. Perhaps I will be able to, later. But now I can't. And you only just told me!"

"You suspected it. And I was reluctant to spoil our joy."

"Ah, you! It is different when it is put into words; it is like lightning striking from the clouds. Our joy has gone; the lightning has struck."

"My brother told me when we went down to the village to welcome Uncle Anto. They arranged through Milija that he would come to ask for my hand. I would have told you as soon as I knew but, as I said, I did not want to spoil our parting. Now there is no longer any way to put it off."

"And you agreed?"

"What right have I to agree or not agree?"

"And I? And us? What do you think about us?"

She did not reply at once, staring into the depths pensively. "I have little chance to choose, after all that has been whispered about Obrad and me. It was important for my brother to get me married, to get me betrothed as soon as possible. The suitor is somewhat older, neither handsome nor ugly. Not so bad, as they say. He is well off, and that is important for my brother. And for me, too, that is not to be sneezed at; I will be the less tormented. Whatever I may have liked, there is no other way."

"And what about me, about us?"

"I have thought much about that, though there is not much to think about. You will always be dear to me and welcome."

"That I know," he persisted, "but you will be another man's wife."

She smiled and broke off a beech twig. "I am both your wife and your sister, all that a woman can be to a man. But we have never thought or even imagined that I could ever marry you. It has been wonderful with you. Short-lived; I shall never forget. It would be still lovelier if it could last. They say: Good fortune is short-lived. We have really been happy."

She slowly stripped the leaves from the twig and threw them into the wind's eye so that they drifted down the slope. Rade did not like her fidgeting with the leaves. He was even more irritated with himself that he should be annoyed at such a time by anything so trivial. "Perhaps, perhaps some way could be found," he muttered, weeping with pity and anger. "You know, this parting has come too suddenly. Though I have thought about it continually, I have not been able to come to any conclusion."

She put her arm around his neck and began to wipe his eyes with the end of her kerchief. She was self-contained and calm, and he, strangely enough, did not blame her for it.

"Calm yourself, dear one. You knew!"

"Yes, I knew. But still . . ."

"Perhaps it is harder for me than for you. I go to one I do not love, for my whole life. But if it has to be so, I shall not complain. As for you, you will become reconciled and will find your own way."

All she was saying would have been repulsive and incomprehensible had she said it yesterday, or even before, when they were in the hayfields, but now he, calmed, began to think about it reasonably, even coldly.

She went on: "You did not, surely, think that I could marry you? Who in the clan would approve? And as we are, with whom could we live? I would not have known the sweets of love had you not been my brother. So it had to be, and so I wanted it. I want to bear our sweet torment forever. And I always knew that we would have to part. Marriage is one thing; you are another."

He took the twig from her and began to peel it. "We shall never see one another again. I mean—as lovers."

"God be with you! Shall we desire and love one another the less? Whenever you come, whenever we can, I am yours, all yours. I will not, cannot, renounce our love."

She hugged him and tried to kiss him, but he pushed her away, almost roughly. She looked at him with disbelief, with a childlike sorrow. "What else can I do? Tell me, what am I do? Shall we run away, into the wide world? But I know that you would not. I had thought that we would go wherever our footsteps led us, even if we wandered as vagabonds from bad to worse. I would feel no shame or embarrassment to be your wife. But, you know better than I, a strange land would become unbearable to us. As soon as we fled the clan and our homes, you would see in me only your madness and your sin."

"You are right," he said hesitantly. "I could not run away, because of the revolt, because of my brothers. How could I betray them? Yet perhaps revolt and betrayal are only an excuse; everywhere there is revolt and betrayal."

"So, you see," she concluded, standing up and arranging her skirt. "All that I know well. I know what I cannot and what you will not."

He, too, rose. "Everything is so terrible! The world is too small for the sinner and the renegade."

"It is not terrible. It must be so. You had to choose between me and the revolt! You had already chosen before I talked it over with you, before you even thought so yourself. You, my dear, are like that; you search for something above and alongside existence. All of you are of Anto's seed. For you the world is strait. Perhaps that is why I love you, satisfied with what I have had and with what I have."

He stroked her chin, to console her or perhaps himself. She smiled at him. Her eyes were moist and her skin under his fingers was smooth, warm, familiar.

"And who knows," she went on, "should you want it, should I be able, could I? I would risk leaving home and clan, but I am terribly afraid of poverty and even more of wandering and anxieties. That is not love, that is not life! You watch your children hungry and dying! And then for him who wants other things than home and children, some revolt may always be found. You are like that—never satisfied with anything. And I know I would quickly bore you if we lived together."

"Perhaps. But I would always love you. I am not resigned, and I will never be resigned, to losing you."

They went on, in silence, and then she suddenly ran in front of him, put her arms gently around his waist, and cried out: "I am yours, as always, whenever you come. Tell me, tell me that is so."

Throwing back her head and almost closing her eyes, she offered him her lips, stiff and dark, and he, leaning forward, took her by the shoulders and gave her a cold, passionless kiss, adding without reflection: "I will always come to you. I will never be reconciled to the idea that you are no longer mine."

In the village, unpleasant news awaited Rade. Not ten days

had passed since his father's return, and already a taxgatherer had come from Plav to apportion the sultan's tribute and the taxes due to the begs.

To the discontented, confused, and divided Radaks it was neither just nor acceptable that the same person should have the right to collect both the sultan's tribute and the tithes and other gifts due to the begs. These duties had previously always been divided, and the second of them had usually been carried out by the *sahibija-beg*, the landlord, in person. Because of this innovation, many had now joined the ranks of the insurgents.

To them this union of two different obligations was a godsend. They thought it meant fresh impositions and a consolidation of the rule of the Turkish authorities and of the begs. Till then the Radaks, at least in words, had recognized the established order; that had been the reason why Knez Anto had been released. But now, the authorities demanded that the Radaks should sign a paper that could be interpreted as evidence of their desire to remain under the Turks. Stojan Radak explained: "The begs want to prove to the foreign powers that their serfs support them."

Worst of all, this *sened*, the agreement on dues and tribute, was written in Turkish, so that no one was able to read it. The more intelligent of the Radaks feared they might be trapped into accepting obligations from which, they knew, it would be hard to free themselves once they had confirmed them by their thumbprints.

So the taxgatherer went back, his work unfulfilled, and the Radaks remained in confusion and disunity, though they had hoped that Anto's return would unite them.

Rade, returning from the hayfields, arrived in the garden just as they had finished their meeting at Anto's and were dispersing, still arguing furiously, as if no one was satisfied with what they had finally agreed. In fact, they had settled that Grgur and Vojin were to go to Plav and find out from the authorities what it was they wanted and what the Radaks could do about it, but they had bound them not to accept any fresh obligations until they had been agreed on by the clan, and, above all, not to put their thumbprints to anything. Not only was nobody satisfied with such temporary and inconclusive decisions, but Grgur's supporters were strongly against his going to Plav, considering the whole business a pretext for the authorities to lay hands on their leader.

It was dark, and the moon rose late. By the weak light of the kitchen fire, Rade would not have recognized the Radaks who were still in the courtyard had he not known them by their voices.

In the darkness Stojan was shouting angrily at Nasto, who crouched there, his arms dangling, as if afraid to go into the dark. "Enough of fine words! We know all too well! Yesterday you were saying that we could not resist the Turkish evil, and today you try to convince us that the Turks intend no evil against us. I don't know, and I don't want to know, what they think, but ever since what happened to Anto, we must think only of our own skins."

"But I am a Radak, too," Nasto insisted caustically.

"I don't say you are not. But even a Radak may change his faith! You are trying to get us to accept the *sened*, embellishing it even more than the taxgatherer did. You said it is only for a time, until conditions change. Today our conditions will not change unless we change them ourselves! Were it left to me, I would send no one at all to their discussions; they are not so strong as they make out. Grgur will not go. I will not let him. Men's lives are not for throwing away!"

Vojin, head and face lit by the flames from the kitchen, trying in his soft but powerful voice to blunt the sharpness of the disputes and smooth out the borders between light and darkness, said: "Every Radak has a right to say what he thinks. Were we stronger and were the time ripe, I, too, would agree that we should talk differently with the Turks. But force does not pray to God!"

"Every authority is from God," clucked the old man Milija from the darkness.

But Grandfather Pavle, also from the darkness, shouted him down. "Except the Turkish!"

Vojin laughed. "Indeed the Turkish is not from God, else we should have the same faith as they."

Rade could scarcely see Akan, who was leaning against the outhouse, to the right of the door. Out of the light and yet close to it, he seemed far less clear than the others, especially since he had not uttered a word or moved. Rade would have recognized him only with difficulty had not his shirt been unbuttoned, as was his custom, and had not a ray of light shone white on his chest. It seemed to him that Nasto, arguing and twisting in the firelight, was not justifying himself to Stojan and the others but to the motionless, silent, and enigmatic Akan.

Grgur came out of the house, and, overhearing the last words, said curtly: "From God is only that authority which respects the laws of God and man; in this house there is a living witness to what the Turks do!"

Stojan waved his arms. "To send them the chosen men of the clan! To let them cut them to pieces tomorrow, as they did Anto yesterday! No one in his senses would do that."

"We must go, Stojan, for the clan's sake and for Anto's," Grgur concluded, rather too loudly and bitterly.

"Yes, and Anto agrees that you should go," remarked Nasto, "to preserve peace and order."

"Turkish order—death and dishonor!" shouted Grandfather Pavle.

"Good, let us go," Vojin said, raising his staff. It was not clear where it was he thought of going—home, or to Plav—especially since he added, pointing with his staff at the house door, behind which, somewhere indoors, perhaps in even denser darkness, was Anto, "That martyr will be able to rest! Good night to you all!"

Nasto and Milija followed Vojin, and then the others. Nasto remarked conciliatingly: "Forgive me if there were hard words; we are brothers and we are men." But he commented acidly to Stojan: "As for you, don't stir up the embers; the fire does not care whom it burns. You have no title deeds for the Radaks!"

"Whether I have them or not, I will take them from you!" retorted Stojan, and then moved off, not down the garden with the others, but in the opposite direction, toward Petrana's house.

"How is he?" Rade asked Grgur when they were alone.

"Oh, so you have come back! I didn't see you in the darkness. Are you thinking of Father? As well as can be expected. He was ill, but is slowly getting better. Have you finished?"

"Yes. Early this morning."

"This morning? Where have you been till now?"

"To tell the truth, I was in no hurry. I was talking with Raduša."

"Yes, you two," retorted Grgur, not explaining himself. His words were uttered with many meanings: you two are always together, you two may well cause trouble for us, you two are an example of Radak affection, you two are hiding something. Rade could not make up his mind to ask what he meant by those words, and Grgur went on: "Go in and see Father. He asked about you twice this morning."

Anto was lying in the big room, on Grandfather Grgur's bed, the way a sick man lies, propped up by two pillows. At his feet Grandfather Grgur was sitting, coughing and smoking his pipe. Rade kissed Grandfather's cold, bony hand and then his father's, also bony, but hot.

"So you've come home," said Anto, pulling himself up in bed and smiling. "I have been thinking about you a lot. I kept fearing some misfortune, as if I were still in prison. Sit here beside me, so that I can see you." He looked at Rade carefully, tenderly, and with incredulity, as though he only now recognized him. "I have paid least heed to you, growing up; I will not be able to help you much, so young and immature. I often reproached myself about that when I was in prison. You have grown up a fine boy. Only you are rather thin. When shall we marry you off? Shall I live to see it?"

"You will, if God so wills," said Grandfather Grgur. "Wretched man always has something to make him sorry to die; as for me, I must wait till you have recovered from your tortures, till I see the Turks undergoing your tortures. Can I get you anything? Have you had supper yet?"

Grandfather Grgur's attitude toward Anto was noticeably different from what it had been before Anto's imprisonment, as if Anto had become the father and Grandfather Grgur the son. Even before, Grandfather Grgur used to refer to his son, the Radak knez, with respect. But now he behaved as a younger man obedient to the head of the household and showed a son's respect toward a father, whose word was not only of greater experience but also could not be contested.

"I'm not hungry," Anto replied. "I'll take only a bowl of warm milk. But no, I won't have that. I forgot that the cattle have been sold. Keep the milk for the children. Let Milena make me a thin soup with onions; she knows what I like."

"There is warm milk for you. You are the most important,"

Grandfather Grgur said, rising. "I'm going to tell the women, and you talk to your Benjamin."

"No, I said. Don't anger me!" Anto called out in a voice thin but sharp and uncompromising, such as Rade had only heard in moments of greatest anger.

Grandfather Grgur sat down again, discouraged.

"Rade will see to it. And mind—only soup!" Anto ordered.

"Good, if that's the way you want it," Grandfather agreed, sadly.

"You, Rade, sit a while longer. I will tell you when you should go."

His father was as uncompromising as before. His tenderness not only moved and disarmed Rade, but also aroused in him a feeling of sin and guilt, because of his secret love for Raduša and, even more, because of his ugly and unpardonable feeling that his father had become a barrier, a burden.

His father took his hand and began to stroke it as if he wanted to remember the feel of Rade's skin. Then he looked at it as tenderly and attentively as he had looked at Rade himself a few moments before, and continued: "Your hands are more like mine. And your head; your forehead is your mother's, but around the mouth and chin you have something of me." Then, as if remembering something, he said vaguely: "And Raduša? I did not see her when they brought me home. I hear that now you are like brother and sister. So it was with me; my cousin was dearer to me than a born sister. But you two will soon have to part. Vojin has told me that she has been asked for in marriage from a good house. It is high time. The girl is good and pretty, and it is a shame that all sorts of things should be gossiped about her."

When his father had taken his hand, Rade had been afraid lest it tremble and that he would not be able to explain why. When Anto began to talk of Raduša, he began to tremble inwardly and, frightened, slowly withdrew his hand.

Anto, meanwhile, frowned a little and clenched his teeth from the pain that continually oppressed him somewhere deep in his body and then suddenly began to tear at him. "It's there!" he groaned, hands on the small of his back. "There! Then it spreads to my crotch and up my back. But I won't sleep here. I don't want to be in the way of the other members of the household. Let Stamena make up a bed for me in the storeroom."

Grandfather was about to say something and started to rise, but sat back again without uttering a word.

"I am not able," Anto went on, not noticing Grandfather's movement, "even to go outside for my natural needs. It is shameful to think of that, and I am now in such a state that I am a nuisance to everyone. In the storeroom I shall at least be by myself, and they can leave me some old tub at night. That must be done at once, this very night."

It was impossible to think of what Father might do if he knew about Raduša. It might even be the last straw. Yet concealment of the truth would also be shameful and foolish when his martyred father had opened his heart to him, his son, with love and tenderness, making Rade feel for the first time completely and incontestably a part of his father's life. He must keep silent, must conceal and deceive, for his father's sake and for his own, because of his brothers and the Radaks.

His father raised himself, stifling his groans. "Not even to his own kin should a man become a nuisance; there is no beast more repulsive than man. There it is! It will pass, as everything passes. Go away now, Rade. Tell them to prepare the storeroom." Rade stood up and went.

"May God grant it will pass," whispered Grandfather Grgur, more to himself than to Anto.

To Rade now, faced with his father's suffering, with the family overwhelmed by doubts and waverings, with the divided clan, the feeling between himself and Raduša and all they had experienced—the coomb, the *katun,* and the hayfields—seemed different. On the one hand it was all more sinful, more repulsive and foolish, and on the other it appeared as a chance, silly escapade about which he must keep silent and which should be forgotten.

Outside, in front of the house, as if he were waiting for Rade to come out of the room, Grandfather Pavle leapt out of the darkness, seized Rade by the arm, eager to hold him until he had finished his tale, and showered him with words and spittle. "Evil, I suspect evil, though I do not know what evil! That dog Nasto is cooking up something! You, Rade, must tell Grgur. He will believe you. Don't think it is all madness. He is a dog which barks and bites; he barks from fear and bites from something worse."

Certainly no one took Grandfather Pavle's presentiments seriously. Vojin, in jest, referred to them as prophecies. But no one could deny that strange things often followed those presentiment prophecies. Most of them were never fulfilled and were soon forgotten, but it had happened occasionally that they came true, and with approximate accuracy. The graybeards concluded that angels and devils talk to the mad.

But Rade, preoccupied, scarcely listened. "All right, all right, Grandfather," he replied, and hurried into the kitchen to tell his mother and Stamena of Anto's wishes, as if by that he was freeing himself from a heavy burden.

Early next day, before Grgur and Vojin left for Plav, Nasto appeared before Anto's house, with unbuttoned jacket and quivering with fright, as if some great new misfortune had roused him from his bed. "Is Anto up?" he asked Grgur, without even saying good morning.

Grgur was just preparing to shave, rubbing his chin with hot water, while Rade was sharpening the razor on a stone. "Where is your good morning? Is it plague, or has the army attacked?" Grgur mocked him, going on with his rubbing. "Father has not slept all night. Perhaps he dozed a little this morning. Show me your wound at once; here is hot water that we may wash it and make it well."

"I want to see Anto; he is knez." Nasto tried to slip around Grgur and go into the house.

Grgur did not stop him, but nonetheless stretched out a leg to annoy Nasto. "Now you call him knez and are loyal to him, and in the kula you did not even recognize him."

"Not everyone is born a hero! Even a coward may be a loyal companion and a true brother," replied Nasto, but less angrily than despondently. He slipped across the threshold, and Grgur bade him farewell with the words: "Anto is in the storeroom. And a coward is no good to man or beast."

Among the Radaks, as among all peasants, shaving was a painful ceremony. They usually shaved on Sundays and feast days or for some special event, gathering together with neighbors skilled in that task. Their shaving tackle was bad; usually honed-down sickles and rough whetstones. Only in Anto's house was there a real razor and a real whetstone, and because Rade had a light hand it was usually he who shaved his brothers, his father, and his grandfathers when he was at home.

He had not finished shaving Grgur when Vojin arrived, dressed in his best clothes. "Really fine," he said after wishing them good morning, and then, leaning his staff against the kitchen door, he said: "Let Rade strip my bark from me, too. I ought not to appear before the Turks like this; not for their sakes, but for ours. I could soap myself while he is finishing Grgur."

Rade had just finished shaving Vojin, and Stamena, with a towel over her shoulder, was pouring water for him to wash, when Anto came out of the house, bare-legged and in his shirt and leaned on the doorpost. After him skipped Nasto, offering to support him. But he did not touch him, as if afraid that he would break or would spurn his help.

"Father, where are you going like that, in God's name?" shouted Grgur. "Naked and barefoot! Why didn't you call someone?"

"I can manage by myself," Anto groaned, holding the small of his back with his right hand and searching with his left for something to hold on to, until he found Grgur's hand. "Get me a chair."

Rade ran into the house, colliding with Nasto, who smelled of sweat and onions. He picked up a chair and the first cushion he set eyes on, took them out, and placed the chair a little away from the kitchen, at the top of the garden, where his father, in earlier times, had loved to sit in the evenings.

They wrapped Anto up and seated him on the chair, while he, breathing loudly and painfully, cried out: "And now this! A Radak living with his sister-in-law! Now we must put that, too, to rights. What do you two, Grgur and Vojin, know about it?"

"I've no idea what you are talking about," Vojin answered, drying himself on the towel.

"You don't know!" Grgur laughed. "Everyone knows that Stojan spends his nights with Petrana, only no one talks about it. What is there to talk about? That is his own affair—and Petrana's. Really, Father, I don't understand you. He is a bachelor; he needs someone to wash and mend for him, and Petrana has found a good man."

"I did hear something, but did not take it for evil. They are kin, so why not let him help her a bit and she him?" said Vojin in a conciliatory tone.

"What kin? No kin, for God's sake! But we are ready to leave, and you, Father, would do better to forget all about it, and let this fellow—" unable to find words, Grgur pointed to Nasto— "who on top of all your troubles pokes his nose into other people's business . . . Yesterday he was unable to stir up the mud in one way, so now he tries another!"

"But Nasto is one thing and Stojan and Petrana another," groaned Anto, as he sat pulling on his trousers.

"It's all the same," Grgur went on inflexibly and calmly. "Who is harmed if Stojan and Petrana live as man and wife? They are such distant relations that they could be married tomorrow. If the clan is worried about who sleeps with whom, we have come to a pretty pass."

"Enough! That is not the point," exploded Anto, turning red.

Father now lost his temper more easily than before. And Grgur, too, had become harder, more uncompromising. Everyone, little by little, was becoming tense. *What would Father say, what would he do, if he knew about us two? And what would Grgur do?* "Father, I ought to shave you, too," Rade said.

"Leave it for now." Anto waved his arm. "Can't you see I'm talking?"

Already some of the Radaks had clustered around—the old man Milija, Grandfather Grgur, Grandfather Pavle, some inquisitive children, and a few of the nearby householders. Seeing that something was going on, they came.

"It didn't even occur to me to follow him," Nasto began, turning to the onlookers. "Last night when I left, I saw Stojan was not going toward his own house, but in a different direction. I had been a bit angry with him, and he with me, and I knew that I would not sleep soundly because of it. So I, as bad luck would have it, went after him. And he—straight to Petrana's! He went into the house, the fire was burning on the hearth, and everything could be seen clearly. He put his arms around her from behind as if she were his wife, and she said to him: 'The children are asleep already, so you come and have supper, and we two will stay here by the fire.' And the Devil made me stay: I looked and wondered. He ate his supper, and she made up the bed; then he undressed and she undressed. Then she noticed the open door and shut it. I went up to the door and heard him say to her: 'You should have shut the door before; someone might see us.' And she: 'Why should anyone want to peer into someone else's house?' "

"She spoke well," Grgur broke in sarcastically.

"Call Stojan, Rade," Anto ordered.

"There has never been anything like this in the clan," Grandfather Grgur almost sobbed, and Grandfather Pavle quickly added: "Since we two have grown old."

Returning from Petrana's house—Stojan was already up and was whittling a broom handle in front of her door—Rade was in time to hear Nasto finish his tale. "I say nothing. It is as the clan and Anto decide. It is my duty to say what I saw. If you settle it one way, good; if another way, still good. But the rules of the clan must not be broken capriciously. At least we should know who is kin to whom."

Until then Rade had always been rather fond of Nasto. He was a chatterbox, polite, good-humored, always ready with a joke, though it was hard to laugh at his jokes, which were usually clumsy, forced, and never well timed. After he had heard of his unworthy behavior in the prison, he had despised him, and was now filled with hatred for him, so much that he felt that each succeeding wave would choke him. *What was the matter with Father? What sort of knez is he to countenance such spying? It could break up the clan! Even Father despised Nasto; he did not allow him to kiss his hand on his return from Plav. But why should I hate Nasto so? Is it because of Raduša? Is it because he might spy out something of the sort between her and me? No, it is not because of that, or not only because of that. He is a weakling, a conciliator; it was not in vain that the Turks had struck at him. But why is Grgur not saying anything? And Vojin? Men, brothers, Radaks, why are you silent? Everyone is playing blindman's buff, like a horde of children; they have known all about it for a long time past, and now they pretend to be horrified.* "Father, Stojan will come at once," Rade said aloud, and added with regret: "I have taken him from his work."

"And isn't this work?" Anto snarled at him. "Either you have all gone mad or I am no longer in my senses."

With an easy, assured step, head slightly bent forward, as always—though now it seemed to Rade that he walked with a calm, self-confident pride—Stojan entered the circle of clansmen, still holding the broom handle and the knife, ready to get on with his work if the discussion was prolonged. He greeted them all. Some did not reply, and Anto, as if he had not heard the greeting, raised himself in his chair and asked sternly: "What truth is there in this?"

"In what?"

"You and Petrana."

Without hesitation, smiling and with frank simplicity, Stojan replied. "It is true, all that they say. We are husband and wife."

There was general astonishment, not so much at what Stojan had said, for everyone knew it already, but at the frankness with which he said it, as if it were some quite everyday matter, nothing unusual. Nasto was astonished, too, perhaps he most of all. Vojin coughed two or three times and blinked, which with him was a sign of bewilderment and hesitation. Only on Anto's face nothing could be read; he had recovered the knez's calm and equilibrium which he had had before his imprisonment.

"How could you do such a thing?" he asked Stojan calmly. "Didn't you know that it is improper in the clan? Yet you told no one and asked no one's advice."

"Well, I asked her," Stojan began, bewildered by the astonishment he had created. His words, despite the continued amazement of the bystanders, raised a laugh. But he was not making a joke of it, and went on in a forcedly calm voice: "I had just made up my mind to mention it to you when they put you in prison. We two are only distant kin. I see nothing improper in it, except that we have not yet been to the priest."

Stojan wanted to say something more, but Grgur intervened, loudly and rather angrily. "He told me, since you were in prison."

This was something new, still more astonishing; the intrigue was revealing the participation of the eager supporters of the revolt in Stojan's sin, showing what they really thought about the clan and its traditions. But Anto, suspecting the danger of such a dispute, changed the subject and said to Grgur with the same restrained moderation: "And you kept silent about it?"

"I did."

"Why?"

"So as not to involve the clan in this on top of everything else—in these hard times."

"You should have told the householders," Anto said, too quickly. "No one has the right to conceal anything that might stir up trouble in the clan."

Anto was unable to finish what he wanted to say; twisted, contorted, and scowling with pain, he tried to rise. Vojin and Rade caught hold of him and raised him. But Anto, teetering on his bare feet, emaciated and blue with the cold, held on to the arm of the chair and spoke slowly: "I have not, and the clan has not, the right to pass judgment or to sentence anyone; nor, Stojan, can I judge or sentence you. So long as you obey me, I can pass judgment on trespasses and landmarks and decide when the summer migration shall take place and when we shall return from it and who shall be master of the mill. Nothing else, unless you include being your representative before the authorities and the begs. The Radak knez is not, and cannot be, a cadi. He has neither fetters nor prisons, neither has he a sword nor is he the law. But even so, it is known what is custom and order in the clan. Whoever transgresses, the clan must judge, when it can and as best it can. That has been so as long as men can remember. Let it pass judgment on you, Stojan. What is today? Wednesday. Good. Let Vojin and Grgur go to Plav. By then something will surely have been disentangled with the Turks—so on Sunday evening let us meet and discuss this. Let the matter rest, till we can think it over. Do you agree?"

Everyone obviously agreed, even if in fact they did not agree, for by postponement they gained breathing space. Anto's behavior and speech aroused the admiration of the Radaks by their calm and moderation and especially by the longed-for lost bond with an age-old life and justice.

Everything would have ended there, and the Radaks would have dispersed, had not Akan unexpectedly appeared. Akan never attended clan meetings; he had no interest in them. Now he was bareheaded, barefoot, and his hands were wet. Hearing the dispute, he had stopped washing out a trough he was preparing for the plum harvest and burst into the group. It was unusual for anyone to speak after the knez, especially someone from his own household. Akan himself seemed aware of that and remarked, as if by the way: "The clan cannot judge him. This is not a matter of trespass of land marks. It is his affair, and hers! And the church's, seeing that they are not married."

The supporters of the revolt were overjoyed at Akan's interruption, for he mixed little in clan affairs, though it was known that he supported Grgur. Furthermore, Akan, who because of his trading activities had traveled in Montenegro and the Metohija, was considered skilled in matters of law and order even outside the clan.

Rade noticed how Anto clenched his hands on the knobs of his chair, so that the veins stood out and the nails turned white. "What do you know?" Anto shouted angrily at Akan. "I said: I am not the law and have no prison! But ever since the Radaks have existed as a clan, they have themselves judged transgressions in the clan, and they will go on judging them as long as there is a clan. I do not know how much these two have transgressed or even if they have transgressed; that the clan will decide, and punish. Not with prison or the gallows, but with what it has at its disposal, with scorn and separation, as are separated lepers and the sacrilegious. Or they may be pardoned; not by absolution, not by prayers for the repentant, but by oblivion and brotherly love, as if nothing had ever happened."

Suddenly turning pale, he almost fell back into the chair. Sweat broke out on his forehead. Akan wanted to say something more, but noticing his father's weakness, shrugged his shoulders and slowly, with bowed head, went back to the brook.

The Radaks shouted: "That is so, Anto! That is so, our knez! God save you for us!"

And the old man Milija, overcome, knelt and embraced Anto's feet, wailing: "Our sun, thank God you have come back to us!"

The Radaks settled nothing on Sunday. They did not even hold the meeting, for events in and about the clan took quite another course. Grgur and Vojin were not able to meet the authorities, let alone talk with them, but were forced to go once more to Plav, and that on the very day fixed for the assembly, since the Moslems, who themselves worked on Sundays, knew that it would annoy their serfs. And that same Sunday, in the evening, a deputation came to ask for Raduša's hand.

And something even more important happened, which was whispered from ear to ear: Mitar Drndar, the Radak from Plav, sent a message to Grgur, through Roksanda, who had come to visit her father, that the people of Plav were planning some deviltry or other, and that the mudir had summoned Nasto to come and see him.

Though Nasto neither made much of this nor tried to conceal it—he even said that the mudir had summoned him in order to warn the Radaks and threaten them—the supporters of the revolt began to whisper about treason, something unheard of and unbelievable in the Radak clan. Some even insisted that they would not attend any meeting at which Nasto was present, so that the enemy would not know what they thought or what they intended to do.

At first Vojin, too, turned openly against Nasto. But after a conversation with Mitar at Plav, he said that everything was still far from clear and withdrew from the argument into the small but well-balanced circle of his supporters.

More and more the quarrel was limited to the group around Nasto and the group around Grgur, though Grgur himself, because of his father's indefinite attitude and bewilderment, withdrew into the background. But for that very reason relations between the two groups grew worse overnight and assumed terrible and hitherto unthought-of proportions, the resurrection of long-forgotten disputes and the sins and vices of their grandfathers, fights between their children and yelling matches between the women, and when the householders met, sarcastic silences replaced greetings and good wishes.

Anto, rotting inside, torn by the disputes in the clan and by his own impotencies and hopes, remained the straw to which all the Radaks clung. His reputation increased among all of them, though he was no longer able either to resolve or to decide. This was no longer respect for the knez, but for the martyr.

Everyone consulted him about everything and kissed his hand, but they did as they liked; they squabbled, quarreled, gossiped, exaggerated one another's weaknesses. Even his own sons began to work against him. Not only Grgur, but even Akan, the taciturn, reserved Akan, who till then had paid heed only to the lambing in the spring and the sale of the stock in the autumn.

Perhaps because of that Anto, on that Sunday morning when Grgur and Vojin were going to Plav, summoned his youngest son, to find some comfort for his torment and disillusion. Propped on cushions, he wailed, as if taking a deathbed farewell: "All night I have not been able to sleep. I kept seeing those criminals from the kula. My thoughts wandered, and I could not collect myself. Now I was all for peace and love and forgiveness, and now all for revolt and vengeance; now I would even forgive Suljaga, and now I would draw a knife on my own brothers! Then I calmed down a little, and the heavens opened before me. I separated good from evil, and it became clear to me what must be done. But I have no more strength, nor does anyone obey me.

"My own children do not understand me. Not even Grgur, to whom I devoted all my heart and mind and in whom I placed all my trust. I had hoped that he would replace me in my lifetime. And he—he is at odds with half the clan because of the revolt! Must every crumb of freedom be paid for in men's blood and quarrels among brothers? Akan I can no longer recognize; till yesterday peaceful, would not kill a fly, now he is aggressive and furious with everyone. He practically says: the Radaks are like anyone else! As if our graves and our blood did not blind us, as if we were not ordained to live in this wasps' nest! That Montenegrin woman backs him up in everything. Even if he is not all evil, there is enough evil with her in the household and in the clan. I do not deny that her brother was a man and a hero. But that heroism and manliness is perverse; it destroys itself and others. They are a maniac people; they go after their own fantasies and pay no heed to men or to life. Only you, Rade, remain to me, still immature, unspoiled. You will preserve all that I have suffered torture for, our clan, our home. You have a little book learning. You can represent the clan before learned men. Sit beside me and talk to me. I know and I remember; it is not easy to be a man! Don't be ashamed before me. Where were you, what were you doing when I was in slavery? What are you thinking now, what are you doing?"

Rade could not tell him; he might have told anyone else, but not his father. Ever since his return from prison, his father had been for him an inexorable judge of his sin with Raduša. Perhaps there would have been no sin had not his father returned. He had even thought that his father had called him that morning for an interrogation about Raduša, but it was only Anto's loneliness and the dissolution of everything for which he had lived and suffered torture that had driven him to seek consolation and support in Rade—sinning and a sinner. "So, Father, we just went on living. For the most part I was on the mountain, with the cattle," he at last managed to say.

"I know. You are a good man. But what did you think about, what did you talk about? Who was with you most?"

His father was not yet old. Though broken and lacerated, he still had a deep and quick understanding. If only his torment would lessen, he would become young again, wise and noble. But no one knew any longer what to say to him or what he dared not say, since there was nothing that would not cause him sadness or anger. Now he was mourning for the mountain. "The mountain, the mountain! I, too, used to talk to it when I was young. Even now I talk to it, and turn to it, in sleeplessness and in torment. I will never go there again, or drink its waters and warm myself in its sun. And what is dearest to you on the mountain? What did you do when you had driven the cattle to the market? Did you leave the mountain?"

Suddenly pain, desperation, and remorse boiled up in Rade, and he fell on his father's chest, sobbing: "I will obey you in everything, Father. All you say will be sacred for me."

"No, no!" His father rejected him in words, putting an arm around him. "I don't want that. I don't want to become something sacred! I want to be an elder brother to you, which I have never been to anyone. I was too strict with you, and with my wife and the others. I had to be, as knez, as head of the household. Now I want to be an elder brother to you, so that you can at least understand me as I am, as I have never been to anyone, not even to myself."

But Rade seemed not to have heard. "We are all unhappy, Father. We all want something, but no one knows what it is he wants," he lamented, sitting down beside his father and wiping away his tears.

"Someone must bear the burden that I have borne, someone must preserve the Radak clan, see that the Radaks are not scattered through the world, that the world does not remain without the name of Radak."

"We, too, were with you in prison. They wrought their tortures on you and on us."

"The world will go on without the Radaks, that I know. But for us Radaks, the world would not be what it is if we were to be dispersed. We would have lost our soul."

"With the Turks, Father, we cannot go on. Living with them, only evil is in store for us. Your tortures give us no peace, till we avenge them or till we die."

"This you must know and remember: happiness does not exist. There exists only spiritual peace, a clear conscience. So long as you keep that, no one can take your life from you. Do you hear, are you listening, my son?"

"Forgive me, Father, if there is something that I have not told you. I cannot wound you and harrow you, who are already in torment."

"We are our own seed; we have lived together for centuries, breathed the same air and been of the same blood. We must also be together in revolt, so that our union be tempered and our name become glorious."

"I know, Father, that I am sinful before you. Who is not sinful before his father? But a man does not even know what is sin until he appears before his father and his brothers."

"I am not against the revolt. Grgur thinks that I am. I can see that he is suspicious of my intentions and of my decisions. But I cannot and will not renounce the unity of the clan, even though I see that the clan is tearing itself apart. I am a slave to it, its every thought and every deed, my son."

"Like you, Father, I, too, am divided, between the revolt and my own sins. But once I have been torn apart and have set one part against the other there is no end to torment. I, too, suffer, Father, and sometimes it seems to me that I was ordained to suffering even before I was born."

Anto breathed heavily; reddish patches showed on his face, and a cold sweat bedewed his forehead. He went on, as if afraid that his thoughts would die unsaid: "And I thought to myself: you are the youngest, you are still unpoisoned by these dissensions, you have learned something in the monastery. You will understand me the best and will be able to take up my burden. So that all that I have done will not die with me! That everything will not have been in vain! That they do not say when I die: He was and now is no longer!"

"I want something and I cannot get it. Whatever I do does not turn out as I had hoped. Does a man live his whole life like that, always running after something unattainable?"

"Man is accursed; he will not, cannot, die! All that man does, he does to live after death, in his work or in his family. One cannot be separated from the other—his children and his work. But with me, as you see, they are divided; my sons no longer follow my path. Only you remain. You will endure all my torments, my cares, the Radak clan. You will be able to bear them, for you think least about yourself. You are young, you will become accustomed to human evil, you will learn how to avoid, and how to resist, evil."

The uncomprehended, even unheard words, of his father encouraged Rade to confess, to unburden himself. "But I, Father, am desirous and empty. Everything I wish to be seems so important to me that I neglect what I am and what I could be. I live in daydreams; my daydreams, Father, have become my dearest reality. You know how the walls rush in upon one and how one must break through them with one's head. It is hard, Father, and I have only just begun to live. Now I know how it was with you and how you feel now."

"When I look back, it is as if I had created nothing. And death is close, there just behind me. Now there is less and less hope that I will create anything. I live, I am crucified on that which was and on that which will not be!"

"Is it possible, Father, to be without sin? Is it not said: He who lives sins? Whenever I taste life as I would like it, I fall into sin. Can man not live? Are there only walls to break through?"

"Why did I not die under the tortures in the kula? When the unity of my clan seemed impregnable? Is all my life to be in vain?"

"Could I only fall asleep and wake in the world I long for, in my own world!"

"If only I had died like a beast in the kula, not to see my own destruction!"

"That I could stop living, to remain pure before you and before your hopes!"

"Be my dearest son. My hope."

"Forgive me, Father!"

Again he fell on his father's breast, absorbing with tears the penitential, imploring, and calming words, dedicating himself to his brothers and the revolt, to his conscience and his life, his father and Raduša. And his father stroked his head, imploring him to continue his task and preserve the Radak nest and Radak unity, to inherit his body and his thoughts, his suffering and his vows.

When they had calmed down a little, his father sent him away, wiping his tearstained face. "Go. You must be at Vojin's to welcome the arrival of the deputation. If need be, kill a sheep, cut wood, pour out plum brandy. And say to all: Be merry, don't give way to miseries!"

At Vojin's house all was busy as a beehive before swarming. Since he had already obtained Raduša's consent, Vojin had suggested that the betrothal be linked with an announcement of the wedding, and this had been agreed on. Vojin's departure for Plav with Grgur had left the house without a man in it, and so Anto had thought to send Rade to help.

The stir and bustle had overcome Raduša. Barefoot, her head wrapped in a scarf, she ran up as soon as she heard Rade's voice. She was embarrassed at first, and then, overjoyed, called out gaily: "What luck that you have come. I can take a rest. I am so busy I don't know whether I am on my head or on my heels!"

"Here in the house there is only woman's work," said Jelica beside the hearth. "To the woodpile! Take an ax, Rade, and get to the woodpile."

"We do need some firewood. Welcome!" Stamena called out, raising her head, all floury, from the mixing trough beside the hearth.

"Shall I go with him?" Raduša asked, turning to Jelica.

"Go, of course," said Jelica. "That's why I sent him! And collect the chips. That love of yours is excessive. How will you live without him when you go to a strange house?"

"I'll wait for him to come to me," said Raduša, laughing and running into the house to get ready.

Rade pulled the ax from the tree trunk and, waiting for Raduša to dress, began to examine the blade and handle, hoping to stifle the familiar, sweet, and spasmodic inner trembling. When Raduša came out, he sent her on ahead, so she would not notice his passionate uneasiness and turn from the excitement of the betrothal and the preparations to worry about him.

Raduša walked in front of him with a sprightliness evident from her ankles to her hips. When they were far enough from the house not to be overheard, she, offended by his gloomy lack of courtesy, turned, stopped, and roguishly yet compassionately reproached him. "Don't say anything nice to me, and make me feel guilty toward you."

"I would wish you well. But I am still thinking of Father; there is no end to his torture. And of you; we shall never be able to meet again."

"That no one knows. My village—O God, I am already calling my husband's village *my* village!—is not far. I will often come to visit my relatives, and you could often come to see me. The Lim is no great barrier, if you are not too pigheaded about something or other and do not turn from your daydreams."

"That is not what we want! After every meeting the parting will be harder."

"I think only about the times when all will be fine for us! And how is Uncle Anto?"

"What can I say? He suffers greatly. He is wasted by fever, burning, rotting. He has never been so dear to me as now, nor have I ever felt so sorry for him—as if his tortures were mine. What he has worked for and striven for all his life is falling to pieces. Perhaps it must be so. But I am sorry for him. And I am sorry that I cannot tell him everything, even about us. It seems worse to me than to lie to myself."

Raduša walked on. She moved quickly and easily, hurrying through the mild, open autumn serenity, through the pale-gold and scented melancholy of the dying leaves and grasses, through the rich, intoxicating maturity of the plowlands and the ripe orchards.

He went on talking about his father, about himself and his

troubles, not noticing if she was listening to him. Though she was mild-natured and sensitive, Raduša had a quite different attitude toward the sufferings and misfortunes of others. She thought of them as something alien, outside herself, which might command her sympathy, but which involved neither her life nor her fate. Rade, on the other hand, felt them as if they were his own, and even more deeply since he could not, by his will or by his endurance, lessen them. But he did not ask for her sympathy, either for himself or for his father. He wanted to talk, and to talk to her; he had no one nearer, and it was, as always, hard for him.

He was, in fact, searching for the lost way to her. He found it only when they reached the top of the meadow below the forest. She fell back beside him and called out, trembling and with flushed face: "Do you remember? The stump! The flowers! When you came back from the monastery!"

The stump was rotted to the core, its bark peeling. But it was still possible to sit on it, and he threw his jacket over it, making ready to sit down. "Don't," she whispered, stopping him with her hand. "Let's go somewhere else. It won't be the same for us now as it was then."

Now it was she who was talking, leading him by the hand. "Don't let's go by the flume; it is steep and we can't walk beside one another. Let's take the path, and then we can turn aside from it. When we were there, when you came with the flowers, we were mad and it was lovely; we could not, did not dare, kiss one another! And everything drew us together. It all began there. It was then that I admitted to myself that I loved you not merely as a kinsman, and it was clear to me that you loved me in that way, and not as a kinswoman. But it must have begun earlier, only we did not know. Otherwise it would not have burst out all at once. Later, we defended ourselves; you more than I. But I do not regret that we defended ourselves and fled from each other. Who knows? If we had rushed at one another at once, still untried and inexperienced, we might not have loved one another. Now you are sad and gloomy, as if frozen rain were falling from your eyes. And I am waiting for you—just now. I will not be able to meet you on the wedding day, and I know that then I shall want you most of all. Let's leave the path. I am dying to embrace you."

He embraced her, uneasily, torn asunder, unable to drive away his melancholy and distraction. But her kisses were so moistly warm and her embraces so intense that his passion suddenly revived and overcame him, still more pure and violent for the shadow of the melancholy that still clung to him.

"The ground is damp," he remarked, throwing his folded jacket into the hollow of a fat beech.

"We will warm one another," she jested, throwing back her head, cutting into him with the shining blades of her half-shut eyes and calling him with full, eager lips.

Later, with kisses and sweet whisperings and blissful smiles, their passion spent, they talked about their love and their unhappiness, becoming one with the soporific, dying scents of the damp earth and the melancholy warmth of the sun. But the words they wanted most of all they did not know how to utter.

I will take you with me, my dear, in my heart and in my life! Nothing can be, nothing can ever happen without you, my darling! My husband will make love to me on the first night, and I will not dare to say to him: Do not make love to me, for my brother is my husband! Then I will think of you, my dear, and dream that it is you who will loose my girdle. And when my husband asks me if I am faithful to him, I will swear it to him by the firmest, most binding oath. Love with you is a promise, as life is, and only to it can I be faithful.

And when I shall embrace my bride, I shall say to her: More beautifully, more fully did I embrace my sister, whose name you will never know! My bride will weep that I do not love her, and I will console her: Only once does one love as I loved her who could not be my bride. And if she says that I am sinful and that I have bound myself before God to love only her, I will drive out the godless one who doubted our love!

Love me, my dear. Find your life! Find in me your bride! Search for me in the revolt, in the sun and in the earth. You will find me everywhere—in your revolt, in your Serbdom, and in your brothers. When you have shed blood and tears for them, you will search for me and will find me. And when your life ends, you will say: "I have lived, for she was mine!" I am in your breath and in your thoughts; there will be nothing in which I have not my part. And when you doubt me and say to yourself: "She left

*me because she feared penury and wanted a rich and peaceful
life," then know that I trod down my conscience! I want you to
live, to search for happiness, and I want nothing to hinder you on
your way.*

*Forget me, dear one; sail away to sweetness and abundance! Do
not look for me in the dawn or in the fields or in your husband's
bedroom. You will search for me in vain except within yourself. I
am your life and your happiness. Wipe me from your memory, for
you will live with me and for me; calm and joy will be your life.
And you will be able to say I left you, my darling, because I
wanted struggle and the happiness of others.*

*My brother told me: "You will put on your prettiest dress for
your wedding, to be more lovely for your husband!" And I, inwardly, laughed at him. Before my dear one I have taken off all
my clothes and lain naked in his arms. My dear one did not say to
me: "You are my most beautiful one; you smell of rosemary, and
at midnight you are my sun." My dear one is wise, and I am the
only scent for him and a sun that never sets. So I said to my
brother: "I will dress for my husband."*

*I have spoken to my father, the martyr on his deathbed. "I will
obey you and be the son who will carry out your vows." But then
I said to you: "Take me in my nakedness, for we have nothing of
which to be ashamed; we have given and revealed everything to
one another; we have muddied no one's water or taken from any
man his sunlight." Speak words of love to me, dear one, so that I
will awake and hear them and rejoice in life. I am impregnable so
long as my mind remembers your words and your embraces. Say
words of love that I may hear the call of life and of immortality!
Do I hear your voice or have you, my dear one, taken my thoughts
from me? Can you hear, my darling, the beating of my heart and
my hope? We are a curse and a blessing to one another—before
we met, while we live, when we shall be no more! You are a vow
upon my conscience and to me! You are the breath of life on my
lips! Sin that does not oppress! Living that demands no obligations! Life! Sense and shamelessness! Living desperation and
hope! The world will not know itself without our love. God
would be deprived of his prayers without our love. Truth would
be drowned in lies and men in evil had we two never met. We
have united good and evil in our love.*

The Blows of Fate

It could only be Stanija, though the darkness concealed her form and the rain dripping from the roof deadened her footsteps.

Akan had been sure that she, tired out, had been asleep when he slipped through the window, for he had not dared to go out by the door, lest someone in the house, especially Anto, who was awake at all times, might hear it squeaking. But he was equally sure that she would wake and, as was her habit, put out her hand to touch her little son, Anto, and then touch him, her husband, in the darkness. If he was not there, she would lie awake until he returned.

But he had not expected her to come out of the house, wrapped in his cloak, to wait for him by the wall and then, detaching herself from her dark background, to come to meet him across the garden. It was incredible how she had been able to hear him, since he had approached as quietly as possible.

She had nagged him, encouraged him, reproached him, watched his every move, interpreted his every sentence and allusion, accompanied him and astonished him, just like that shadow which broke away from the wall and the night, crossed his path, and put its hand on his shoulder.

"Did you kill the dog?" she asked him in a low, tense whisper, so close to his face that he could feel her breath and the dark, passionate tremor in her words.

He did not reply. Not because he wanted to conceal anything from her, or because, like so many husbands, he kept his wife in ignorance of his affairs, but because he was still under the influence of what had happened only a short while before, and it seemed to him unnatural, even horrible, to talk about it to anyone. But she needed no words; it was enough for her that he remained silent. She understood. She took her hand from his shoulder, embraced him, put her smooth, thin face up to his, and said in a hoarse whisper: "My falcon!"

She had never called him that before. That term Stanija had used only for her dead brother, Vučeta. In her district, as in all Montenegro, the term "falcon" was reserved for those of incomparable courage and heroism.

Picking up the cloak, which was slipping from her shoulders, Akan, against his will, pulled Stanija to him. She took that as a sign of confidence and a wish for her support and assistance, and devotedly pressed against him. "Blessed be the hand with which you did it, in God's name!"

She shivered, not from cold, but from stifled, passionate satisfaction, as a dog shivers, overjoyed at seeing its master again after a long separation. He could not recall that she had ever shivered thus except in rare moments of sudden, still-unsatisfied desire.

He slowly approached the wall of the house, holding the cloak about her shoulders. Anto's house stood on a slope, with the upper part of the ground floor built into the hillside, so that only the three front windows were higher than a man's reach. Nearing the black rectangle of the window over the stream at the top of the garden, which came up to his shoulder, he remembered, suddenly, and asked Stanija, letting go of her: "How did you get out?"

"Like you, through the window."

"My clever one! How did you think of it?"

"Well, you left the window open. I woke up and felt around, and you weren't there. I went over to the coat stand—no yataghan and no knife. It at once flashed across my mind where you had gone. But take care now how you climb up. I will bring a block of wood, so that you do not mark the wall. Then you can give me a hand."

He would never have thought of the block of wood or of the marked wall. It was a good thing that Stanija, even though he had not discussed it with her, had always been aware of everything. She again appeared out of the darkness and softly placed some blocks, one on top of another. "In the morning I will get up early and put the blocks back in their place," she whispered in his ear.

As soon as they were in the room, she rekindled the embers in the grate and filled it with twigs and sticks. "To dry out your clothes and shoes. How muddy they are! I'll get up early in the morning to brush them, so that no one will know."

Through the open doors of the stove, the rekindled flames lit up the room indistinctly, and when the fire began to crackle, the little boy opened his eyes, raised himself for a moment, and then lay down again, turning on his other side, certainly thinking that it was getting-up time for his father and mother. "Warm your feet; you're wet," Stanija said, feeling Akan's soles.

Crawling under the bed on hands and knees, he stretched out his feet to the open flames. His wife spread his stockings on the clotheshorse behind the stove. She was smiling, her face lit by the reflection of the fire and her own inward radiance.

They were silent, and when the fire flared high enough to send out sparks, he closed the doors of the stove. Semidarkness invaded the room. Stanija rose, walked around her husband, took from the chest a jacket and trousers, and placed them beside his pillow, and then began to mend a waistcoat. "Now lie down and rest," she said, sitting beside the stove. "I will look after the fire until everything is dry."

He obeyed, though he was convinced that he would not be able to sleep; but it would be pleasant to lie there with wide-open eyes in the semidarkness until the light and the shadows were driven away. He lay on his back, stretching out his legs, his hands under his head.

It did not occur to him that Stanija would tell anyone about what had happened that night. What was more, he knew that she would never ask questions about it, though ever since Anto's return from prison, and especially since it had become known that Nasto was meeting the Turks, she had never given herself or him any peace, but was constantly urging him to kill Nasto.

The evening of the day they had brought Anto from Plav, she had said to him, excited and boiling over with fury, in that same room where the shattered Anto had then been lying: "He is a leper. He should be expelled from the clan. You Radaks have learned how to endure and how to conceal your own shame. But it is useless: everyone will say that you pampered and made much of a renegade and a coward." He had tried to pacify her. Nasto was not a traitor, but a weakling; it was no small thing to stir up trouble in the clan. But at that she had only laughed provokingly and mockingly. "What's the difference between a viper and an adder?" she had asked.

Before others she was silent, but when they were alone she overwhelmed him with her implacability so much that on two or three occasions, though the Radaks were not in the habit of beating their wives, he had had to silence her with cuffs and blows. In truth, he did so only if she impugned his manly honor and pride, or harmony within the family. She had learned that she must never interfere with such things, for such words he would not, could not, forgive. But in the case of Nasto, nothing availed. There was something in her as ineradicable and hereditary as had been her love for Vučeta, as if she suspected Akan's most secret thoughts. She touched him on the raw, and he not only was unable to defend himself but also longed for her to soothe him.

When he had told her, in this same little room, that Nasto was meeting the Turkish authorities secretly, she had hissed: "That, too! If there were among the Radaks not a hero, but even a man, he would kill him at once."

From then on she gave him no peace, not even in her dreams, which, waking him in the middle of the night, she would insist on repeating, as if to free herself from an illness or a nightmare. Those dreams of hers were dark abysses, pools of blood or turgid, swollen rivers from which she, or someone dear to her, would be rescued only at the last gasp. Her hatred for Nasto—not really hatred, but something material and inevitable as the taking of food and water or breathing or sleeping—she even introduced into her baby talk to her little son. "Grow up, little falcon! You will not rest, even though others do. Remember Vučeta; he is unavenged!" And also in her nightly caresses with her husband. "Love me, calm me, console me!"

But, however intransigent her hatred for Nasto, she would, in the end, have kept silent, he knew, had she not noticed in him a hidden desire and determination to do something that might not separate the Radaks from the Turks, but that would at least stir them up and dissociate him from the clan and those who stood for conciliation.

No one else really understood Stanija, though there was nothing false or underhanded about her. Even Anto to some extent had his suspicions about her. Not a month after she had been brought to his house, Anto had said: "It is not a woman who has been brought into the house, but a flaming sword!" To everyone, even to some extent to Akan himself, it seemed in some way strange and unnatural that she, who had been brought up in clan feeling and felt intensely about her own clan, should want to disperse the Radaks or at least alienate Akan from them. In fact, there was nothing strange in that; she only hissed against those Radaks who did not favor the revolt and who were reconciled to their status as serfs. The killing of her brother had stirred up the embers and excited that hatred within her, but she had brought it with her to the Radaks from Montenegro. If she had not cast her eye on Akan, and if the Radaks had not been a famous clan and Anto a good householder, her family would never have allowed her to go into Turkey among the *raja*. As if she were of different clay, she was sickened at the smell, was horrified at the sight, of the conciliators. She used to say, when she saw Nasto: "That Turkish toady is passing; like a red shadow across the eyes," or "How that Turkish pimp stinks! There is such a stink from him that I have to hold a kerchief over my nose."

She was especially sensitive and intransigent when there was any talk between them about the future of their little son, Anto. She wanted him to become a famous hero, whereas Akan wanted him to become a sensible and rich man. They agreed that he must have schooling; "if we have to tear it out of the rocks with our teeth," as he said, or "even if we have to beg our bread like gypsies," as she said. But she could never accept or understand that her children might have to grow up as Turks, to slave for a foreign faith and forge fetters for the Serbs. It would be better to kill oneself now by one's own hand! She threatened: "As long as Anto himself is willing to go to school, even if you do not approve, I will lead him by the hand myself and go into Montenegro. I will not rear Turkish slaves."

If Stanija was incomprehensible to the Radaks, her relationship with Akan was even more incomprehensible to them. Not even Grgur or Vojin understood that relationship, but considered that Akan was under Stanija's thumb and that he was unable to make any important decision without her. That was not true. She had a great influence on him, but more in how he would do something than what he would do.

It was something incomprehensible, fateful both for her and for him. Though from different backgrounds and with differing outlooks, the two of them agreed in essentials how to pass their lives and assure the future for their descendants. For her that meant liberation from the Turkish authorities, and for him the acquisition of wealth, and since neither one nor the other could ever be achieved under foreign rule, both looked to Montenegro and revolt. In truth, she believed that once they were liberated from the Turks all else would follow naturally, whereas for him liberation meant freedom to acquire property, to increase his stock and his lands, when he would no longer have to give the begs their third, when it would be possible to trade unhindered, when Christians would have equal rights with Moslems in taxes and customs duties, and the roads would be made safe from robbers.

But over and above that, Akan felt in her, and in a different manner in himself, some other, inexplicable, incitement. There was, both in him and in her, a sort of bitter, inconsolable dissatisfaction with life, with their surroundings, with themselves. They had never spoken to one another about it, nor was it a thing that could be put into words; he was conscious of it only rarely, vaguely, and momentarily. Even when the Radaks happened to agree about anything in opposition to the authorities, she was unable to be pleased, as if her hatred for the Turks was not really the mainspring of her existence. When they brought the tortured Anto back, Akan, that evening, had said to her reproachfully: "You don't seem pleased that we were agreed at least about his tortures."

She was silent, and it seemed to him that she was mocking him. Then she replied: "Why should I be pleased? Father Anto is not the first, nor will he be the last martyr."

"And so your brother is unique!" he retorted angrily.

She burst out in a torrent of words. "I do not undervalue Father-in-law and his tortures, or my brother's either. I wanted to say: What would you have done if it had not been for his tortures? Have not other clans had their martyrs, too? And you at once pick on Vučeta—my open wound!"

He was silent, wondering what she wanted, what caused her discontent. "Sometimes it seems to me," he said at last, "that grief for your brother is not so important to you as to have something to weep about, to be angry about."

She suddenly calmed down and said: "Perhaps there is some truth in that. He is dearer to me now than when he was alive. So, too, Anto; now he is really my father-in-law."

Stanija was not a madwoman, or even a troublemaker. In daily work and household affairs she was thrifty, moderate, and reasonable. But she was unable for a single moment to turn her mind from the revolt, from the longing for liberation. She was obsessed by them as by a madness, an infection. And Akan's plan was not cold and calculating. He was not a miser, was not even preoccupied with personal profit; he did not dream that others should work for him and that he should take his ease, but, rather, that he should work his fingers to the bone, for God created man to work. But he wanted to see advantage from his work, to profit by his own initiative and common sense, to build his house as he wanted it and to extend his lands as he wished.

An equal balance existed in their love life, though outwardly they seemed oddly matched. Slow and careful to the minutest detail, Akan was complementary to Stanija's impatient and unembarrassed abandonment. He was confident and unworried about her faithfulness. He was never unfaithful to her, though on his journeys he often came across women of unusual charm and spendthrift generosity. He was always restrained by the superstitious, terrible fear of becoming infected with some shameful disease, thereby shaming and destroying his family. But she, quick-witted and acute in everything, suspected in his undisciplined outbursts of passion for her those mad destructive lusts of his for other women, reproving him only in their moments of closest intimacy. "I cannot bear you to think of other women; that would sully me, humiliate me."

They agreed, in fact, about everything, though for different reasons, each of them holding firmly to their own. It was like some unspecified, loyal, and unbreakable life agreement, in which both he and she went on living in their own beliefs and personalities.

Thus Stanija believed in all the Radak tales and traditions, eagerly recalling them when it was needful to stress or reprove, whereas Akan did not hold to them in the least except insofar as they were, like any other tales, pleasant to listen to. For Stanija, all of them, as also those of her own clan, were as true as the very existence of the Radaks. Grgur and Rade, each in his own way, tried to discern some truth in them; that interested Akan not in the least. They were unconnected with his way of life, outside his dreams and possibilities. Of course, since he was a Radak, he sometimes called upon tradition and even repeated some of the tales—to support an argument, in sheer enjoyment of their beauty, or to amuse the children.

Above all, he and Stanija were in agreement—though he discussed the matter only curtly and grudgingly—that it was necessary to clear up the dissensions in the clan.

As was usual with him, he remained silent, waiting for the right moment, both in the clan and in himself, to begin. Stanija could not choose the moment for him; she knew only how to admonish, like a tradition, a conscience.

The moment for his intervention came just after Anto's return. Till then he had taken little interest in clan affairs and arguments. The final breaking point had been the sale of the stock. It had become only too evident that he and the clan would never be able to acquire wealth and power under Turkish rule, and that he would be unable to assist the clan as it now was, broken by discord even in peace and submission. This change Stanija felt in him the night of his return, tired from his journey and his haggling. Snuggling up to him, embracing his quivering, bony, muscular body, she whispered in his ear, with all the fire of her quick breath and obsessive thoughts: "Everything here is dead; what they want to do they cannot, and what they can do they will not!"

It had been hoped that after his tortures, which he had borne for the sake of the clan, Anto would become harsher and more intolerant of his Turkish masters and also of the waverers in the clan. Instead, he had become more tied to the clan, more submissive to its will and its weaknesses. Grgur was sufficiently strong and resolute to lead the clan, or at least its irreconcilable and resolute elements, if the occasion offered; but he was not able to make a beginning, to create the occasion, or to choose the moment himself.

And it did not occur to Akan for a long time that he himself would be able to do anything of the sort, not until that evening when the Radaks, disunited in fact, had dispersed after their agreement to send Vojin and Grgur to Plav.

In front of the kitchen, in the light from the hearth, Nasto had been slouching about, his long arms dangling, his mustaches and lips drooping, calling for unity, imploring them to avoid a clash with the Turkish authorities. It seemed to Akan in the dance of yellow light that it was not words that came from Nasto's lips, but a stream of slime, thick and sweetish. He did not listen carefully to what Nasto was saying, and did not remember his words.

Then Grandfather Pavle had begun to hurl maledictions against the waverers and to shout that he suspected evil. Only then did it occur to Akan that it would be best if he killed this chattering, snotty, flabby, twisted degenerate, who was leading half the clan astray, and thus cut short the endless skein of discussion and pierce the ulcer of faintheartedness. It was as if the maunderings of Grandfather Pavle were a summons to Akan to carry out a terrible duty, of which, it seemed, no one else in the clan was capable. No one could suspect what he was thinking, and he himself was horrified at his own thoughts. And no one could read anything in his expression as he leaned there in the darkness against the doorpost. Nonetheless, when Rade had looked at him with ingenuous curiosity, it seemed to Akan that he had given himself away, and, although indistinct in the darkness, he had closed his eyes, confused and stupefied.

He drove these thoughts from him. But they reappeared, especially the next day, when Nasto rushed to accuse Stojan before Anto of concubinage with Petrana. Akan had spoken before the clan that day under the pressure of his thoughts, in an effort to rid himself of them.

Then Grgur had sent him to Vojin, to tell him that they must go to Plav at once, and to inform him about Nasto's suspicious meetings with the Plav leaders. Later, recollecting his final decision, Akan did not attribute any special significance to that message about Nasto's intrigues. It was nothing new, nor did it add anything essential, even as Nasto himself paled into insignificance and was transformed into a motive, a means, to complete the fateful act of murder.

It was an exhausting, hot autumn afternoon, and Vojin was treading the plum vat, while Jelica and Raduša were packing the pulp into troughs. Akan made a sign to him, and the two of them, so that the women would not hear, moved to the top of the garden above the house. "What is it?" Vojin asked. Akan gave him the message briefly, and Vojin, not changing his tone or expression, retorted: "I would not be in too great a hurry to go to Plav, lest the Turks think that we are frightened. What Nasto is doing is ugly and unworthy. We must take greater care how we talk when he is present, so that he doesn't gossip about it." It was clear that Vojin wanted to get on with his work, but, noticing a vague dissatisfaction in Akan, he promised that he would, if possible before the evening, go to Grgur's. But Vojin was not scandalized by Nasto's behavior and said nothing about breaking with him, as if nothing essential had changed in his attitude toward him.

On leaving Vojin, Akan recollected that Anto, too, had not spoken of betrayal or even of Nasto's turncoat ways, but only of his cowardice and his lack of understanding. Nasto hoped that by playing up to the Turks he would achieve something, and he must be kept under surveillance because he could not keep a secret. Grgur spoke of betrayal, but cautiously, and without anger. Stojan burst out and said that Nasto should be well beaten. There were other supporters of the revolt who called Nasto a renegade and even a traitor. But no one spoke of killing, not even of expulsion from the clan, which would be impracticable if Nasto asked the authorities for their protection. Expulsion because of serious transgressions against the clan or the tribe existed only in stories of far-off times, when the authorities, so to speak, did not exist and when the individual, once outside the tribe, disappeared, losing his soul and his identity.

All those opinions and points of view led Akan inevitably toward the conclusion that Nasto must be killed, that that was the only way he could be expelled from the clan and at the same time—and more important—be silenced and used as an example.

But even so, busy with work, he managed to thrust such thoughts aside for a time, and had even forgotten his idea of murder, until just one sentence uttered by his father had finally confirmed his intention.

Anto had been sitting at the end of the garden in his favorite place, looking down the valley and gazing longingly at the heights, smiling at the Radaks and their houses and gardens around him. Wrapped in his cloak, he shivered in the fresh autumn evening breeze, coughing and gripping the arms of his chair with thin, bloodless hands and looking around him with feverish, wide-open eyes. Akan overheard his father saying to Grgur and Vojin, as though all the Radaks were gathered there: "For that the clan has no courts; at one time he would have been pushed under the sod."

His father had said that in reply to a comment by Vojin which, as far as he could judge, referred to Nasto, to the fact that even if Nasto should prove to be a traitor it would be impossible to do anything about it, since the Turkish authorities would at once take the renegade under their protection.

Akan had not, in fact, heard Vojin's preceding remark. He had gone out solely to serve them plum brandy, and all in a moment his father's words had acquired a special, long-desired significance, a summons to him to do what he had in mind, that for which, perhaps, he had been ordained.

Even while his father was speaking, Akan remembered the waste land by the stream, below the graveyard, which was called "the Barrow." He thought that the Barrow, its lower side overgrown with alders, could be seen from the top of the garden beside his father's chair. He looked down, and indeed could see the Barrow in the violet dusk of the valley, smooth as the palm of his hand.

No one remembered why that waste patch of land was so called; certainly its name had been given it in connection with some event, perhaps that thrusting under the sod his father had mentioned. But by this time no one in the clan knew anything about it. The Barrow was within the Radak boundaries, so that it was most probable that the Radaks had given it that name. But no one among them or in the neighboring clans remembered that anyone had been buried there. They remembered only the name and the tradition, especially alive in the Montenegrin mountains, that such a name was associated with some great crime. Akan remembered that not one of the Radaks would ever cut hay there, and men avoided pasturing their beasts there. When he was a child, one of the old men had told him that he should never let his stock stray into the Barrow, for it was not good. But no one ever said why it was not good.

On his way back to the house, with the bottle of plum brandy in his left hand and a glass in his right, Akan glanced two or three times through the tops of the half-naked branches at the yellowing surface of the Barrow. What was concealed behind that smooth surface and that enigmatic name? Murder, or betrayal of the clan, for which, according to tradition, men were thrust under the soil? Murder or treason; what Nasto was probably doing and what he, Akan, would certainly do! Akan thought, with trembling, of both one and the other, but most of all of the Barrow itself, which leaped out of the murk before his conscience like some ghost and like his own destiny.

As he came into the house to leave the plum brandy on the shelf in the big room, he again looked, out the middle window, toward the Barrow, framed by the tops of two plum trees as if on exhibition; and he wondered why he had never before noticed it from there. At that moment he had already, almost unknown to himself, made up his mind that he would kill Nasto.

It was clear to him now that only he could do it. He alone did not believe in the clan legends or hold to them. Even then, looking at the Barrow from the window, he remembered his disbelief, his rejection of such fairy tales, giving them as little thought as the embroidery on his shirt or the carving on the armchair. With a laugh, he thought that there was proof. He believed that the fairy tale about the Barrow meant merely that the Radaks had covered that place with stones to expunge the traces and the very memory of some sin they did not wish to remember, and thus to exterminate their shame.

From that moment the decision to murder Nasto withdrew into the background and was replaced by the careful and detailed consideration of how it was to be done. That evening, while he, wakeful in bed, imagined the most suitable moment and manner and weighed the consequences, Stanija, to whom he had spoken that day about Nasto's intrigues, awakened and embraced him with trembling arms. The strangest and most incomprehensible thing was how it had come into her head just that night that he, and no one but he, must kill Nasto, as if all his thoughts and calculations had seized her in sleep and awakened her. That was yet one more, the firmest, confirmation of the maturity and inevitability of his enterprise. Obviously, the time had come. Akan felt an inner tension and sense of readiness, as if his action were an inescapable and unavoidable part of himself.

But the murder was not easy to carry out. The actual act of murder appeared simple; you raised your arm and struck, or pressed the trigger. Akan did not think about that, sure that he would do it without hesitation or mistake when the time came. However, the murder must be done in such a way that the murderer would not be known, to avoid bitterness against specific persons, which would widen the gulf and spread terror in the clan. It was especially important that it not become known that he was the murderer, for if it was known, Anto's household, and even Anto himself, as knez, would lose all respect and influence in the clan. Also, the murderer must remain unknown so that the Turkish authorities would not be involved. In the clan the guesses would become more and more uncertain, for the Radaks would at once suspect—and that was essential—that someone in their own ranks had committed the murder. Nasto was poor and mild, and furthermore was in collusion with the Turks; no one would kill him for his money or for personal revenge.

All things considered, it was essential that the murder be committed when Nasto was returning from Plav, but not too far from the Radak village, so that it would not be suspected that anyone from another clan had done it. Nothing should be taken from him, to avoid any suspicion of murder for gain. Akan, therefore, began to dog Nasto's footsteps and to keep running into him by chance, though he had to be careful not to overdo it.

On the next afternoon, Akan, who was mending a plow under the lean-to near his house, noticed Nasto loading a pack horse with wood in front of his house, with the intention of driving it to Plav for sale, a task he did frequently.

Nasto's house was on the slope, a little aside and to the right of the path that led to the village, at the bottom of a steep field that now in autumn looked bare and dark. Akan could easily see Nasto's wife, Miluša, in a tattered skirt, helping him load the horse, while barefoot children kept leaping from the smoke-stained fences and rushing into the house. It was still not too late for Nasto to go to Plav and to return in daylight. But even if it were not for the drizzle, which would bring darkness on early, Akan banked on Nasto's not returning until after dark; he always liked to stop and chatter with acquaintances and pick up items of gossip. Perhaps Nasto even preferred to wait until dark so that he could talk with the Turks in comfort and unseen.

This was perhaps his last chance to wait in ambush for Nasto, for the next day Anto's household intended to begin brewing the plum brandy. Remembering this, Akan finally decided that he must kill Nasto that evening. He thought that the drizzle would not stop and that the night would be dark, even though—he had taken careful note of it—it was the time of the full moon.

He had already thought out what weapons he would take with him and exactly where he would lie in wait for Nasto. But when he found himself on the spot, at the crossroad where the main road continued down the right bank of the Lim and a side road branched off directly to the Radak village, everything seemed to him different and most unsuitable. His arms, a small pistol and a black-handled yataghan, were certainly all right, because Nasto never carried any arms. But they seemed to Akan almost superflu-ous, since he would not be able to use the pistol—there were houses nearby—and in the darkness he could not be sure of using the yataghan efficiently.

The arms were, in fact, unimportant, for he did not expect Nasto to resist. Nasto, nearing fifty, was weak and peaceable, whereas he, Akan, was in his prime, still youthful and energetic, only approaching thirty. But, more important, Akan felt that Nasto had no right to defend himself and therefore would not do so.

The place itself was unsuitable. The waste land was quite open, and he could not find good cover, even on a pitch-black night, and Nasto, if he should chance to notice him, might be-come frightened and slip away into the darkness. In daylight and in his mind the place had seemed quite different. About a dozen yards above the road there was a forested hill, and about thirty yards below the crossroad, amid alder thickets and reed beds, the Lim was joined by a little river which flowed down the entire valley, dividing it into two parts. When he had been considering the murder, the nearness of the forest had seemed convenient. If need be, he could hide in it. So, too, had seemed the nearness of the Lim and the stream, where he could wash off the blood, drag Nasto into the reed bed and extort his secrets from him. By night and in reality, a narrow and impassable place would appear more suitable for an ambush. But there was no such place as far as Plav. And this spot, at least, Akan knew and remembered to the smallest detail; as a young man he used to go there in the summer, on Sundays, to swim in the Lim with other youths, to jump and throw stones in competition. It was his intimate knowledge of the surroundings that had made him choose the spot.

Now, he concluded that the waste land would, nonetheless, serve his purpose, if he could only find something behind which to take cover.

As he was thinking this over by the side of the road, shifting from leg to leg, a flash of lightning cut across the darkness, lighting up a wild pear tree at the farther end of the waste ground. Its dark, strong trunk looked as if it had been made from rusted iron, and its few remaining leaves, dark and shining, seemed carved from bronze. He was astonished. How could he ever have forgotten that pear tree, when he had had it in his mind's eye on leaving home as an integral part of the waste land, just the right place to take cover? That forgetfulness seemed to him an evil omen. But the reappearance of the pear tree, suddenly revealed in its striking isolation and in all its metallic expressiveness by the lightning flash, could only be regarded as a good omen.

He hurriedly made his way to it. The rain had stopped, though from the moist air and low clouds he forecast more drizzle, and the Lim roared loudly. The pear tree was just beside the road. Not only would he easily be able to seize Nasto when he leaped out from behind it, but it would also serve to shelter him from the rain.

Leaning against the pear tree, he collected his thoughts and began to consider what he should do when Nasto appeared. But his thoughts would not remain centered on that. He kept thinking: Why am I here? What am I standing here for, under the pear tree? To get soaked and to murder a man—a man and a fellow clansman?

Those insistent thoughts did not so much question him as confirm him by their questionings. *Perhaps it is not me, but someone else, and I am lying peacefully alongside Stanija and our son, resting and sleeping peacefully, while that man who is standing under the pear tree will murder a man and his fellow clansman. Even if I am not forced to, that man who is standing under the pear tree is forced to stand where he is standing and to do what he is doing. For him that is not so terrible or so sinful, since he is forced to do it. It is a task, like any other.*

For a wonder, this alienation from himself, this incomprehension that it was just he who was now leaning against the pear tree awaiting his kinsman to murder him, did not bewilder him, but sharpened and accentuated his awareness. He could justify himself more clearly and more surely to that other Akan than to his well-known and everyday self.

He tried to judge the passing of time; it might well be between the third and fourth hour of the night. They usually went to bed at once after supper, an hour or an hour and a half after dusk, and another hour would pass before everything was quiet and Stanija went to sleep. It had taken him not more than half an hour to get ready and to find out whether Nasto had already returned, and then he had had to get here. It was still a long time before midnight. But because of the darkness and the rain, he felt the stillness of the depths of night. He—Akan began to avoid saying Nasto's name and to refer to him as an indeterminate he— must come soon. He must, for everything now was ripe and as it should be, even though he had not yet decided how to approach him and how to seize him.

He must think of that. Or should he leave it all to chance—as everything else? Couldn't he, say, leap from behind the pear tree when he reached it and fall upon him?

Just then Akan heard, about thirty yards away, the sound of a horse's hoofs on stone and soon the horse's sloshing on the muddy, puddled road. The horse stopped and snorted once, and then, as if thinking it over, snorted once more.

Here was something he had not foreseen. The beast had got the wind of him. A horse always senses an ambush, be it wolves or haiduks.

Without hesitation, Akan walked down the road toward the horse.

What if it were not he? No matter, he would disguise his voice, would not tell his name. But it must be he. Who other in such troublous times would be coming thus by night?

"Who are you?" He heard Nasto's rather hoarse, astonished voice.

Almost without thinking, considering in a flash that it would seem more natural if he did not pretend, for if he did not tell his name, Nasto would be on his guard, Akan replied, slowing his pace: "I am Akan, Anto's Akan."

The lightning lit up the nag and its rider crouched in the saddle. It was Nasto, though Akan had already recognized his voice. He asked, in a voice from which the tense hoarseness had not quite disappeared: "What ill luck drives you, Akan, out in this blackness and foul weather?"

Akan could distinguish the rough outline of the horse and rider against the murky sky and, approaching them, replied: "Really ill luck! Father is worse. I am going to Plav to tell Roksanda. He wants his only daughter to see him once more while he is still alive. And maybe the barber will know some remedy to lessen his torments, at least a little."

Nasto coughed, reining in his uneasy horse. "Our martyr! He was not so ill this morning. What ails him?"

Everything was happening differently from what Akan had expected, but even better than he had foreseen. "Everything!" Akan answered, and thought: You know that only too well. But I had better not remind him, so that I do not frighten him. He went on: "Tonight he began to choke and can hardly utter a word." Coming close up to the right side of the horse, he caught hold of the saddle pommel.

"Take the horse," Nasto proposed. "You'll get there quicker."

"That's a really good idea. But I'm sorry that you will have to go on foot on this filthy road."

Nasto began to dismount, and Akan, making a move to help him, touched a rope hanging from the saddle. Everything was going his way; that rope was a godsend—to bind him. Just as Nasto reached the ground, Akan freed the coil of rope, transferred it to his left hand and with his right seized Nasto by the jacket.

Nasto began to wriggle and tried to break free. "What's got into you, Akan, tonight?"

"Shut up! Move on!" Akan cut him short, pushing him ahead and striking him across the face with the rope's end. Only then did he become aware that he felt no hatred and had not intended to humiliate Nasto, but had acted only to arouse his own anger.

"Have you gone mad?" clucked Nasto, burying his face in his hands and trying timidly to free himself. Akan gripped him even more tightly and pushed him ahead, and Nasto whined: "What is it I find on the road tonight, and from my own brother?"

"Don't make a sound. Lie down."

"What do you want of me?"

"Lie down. Shut up!"

He again whipped Nasto across the face with the rope's end and kneed him in the small of the back. But the feeling of hatred, familiar and overwhelming, would not come. Nasto wailed: "What's come over you, Akan, brother by God and blood? How can I lie down in all this mud? And why? Come to your senses! I am your brother! I am innocent!"

By then Akan felt that hatred was not essential. He struck Nasto with measured force on the right leg just below the knee, putting all his weight on Nasto's shoulders to force him to kneel.

Nasto indeed knelt, and Akan gave him a push, so that he lay with hands and face in the mud. Without cursing him, Akan pressed him down with his knees till he gurgled, and then seized his wrists and tied them behind his back. He bound Nasto in a moment, taking care to dirty himself as little as possible.

"Akan, don't lay sin upon your soul! What do you want of me?"

"Let's go!" ordered Akan, standing up.

Nasto stumbled in the mud; it was hard for him to rise with tied hands. Akan took him by the shoulders and helped him. "Where are you taking me? To judgment?" he asked.

"What judgment?"

"Yours. You who are for the revolt. You have no right!"

"Tonight it is I who am judge—and law. Tell me all you have been saying to the Turks. What did you discuss with them? What are they going to do?"

"How should I know what the Turks are going to do?" Nasto halted in wonderment, but the rope dragged him farther along the path.

"I know that they will not tell you. Who confides in a slave? But you can guess from what they ask you."

"They ask all sorts of things."

"And you tell them everything."

"No, may God forbid! I only play up to them."

Akan laughed aloud. "Like a mouse against a cat!"

Nasto was silent, plodding along with a measured, familiar, tread.

They reached the pear tree. It seemed to Akan nearer than it had been a short while before, when he had left it to meet Nasto. He was still not quite sure how or where he would kill Nasto, even as, a moment or so before, he had not known that the rope would come in so handy to bind him.

The thought came into his mind to use his weapons for the deed, to take Nasto into the bushes and first to interrogate him and force him to confess. But on reaching the pear tree with the rope in his hand, he knew that the best thing would be to hang him. Once more the pear tree showed itself considerate, as if it were not by chance that it offered him its services.

And as soon as the idea of hanging came to him, Nasto's secrets, or obtaining his confession, suddenly lost all meaning. What if he did confess? This did not seem probable, though, for Nasto was firm and even convincing in his denials. What purpose would his confession serve? Akan would have to conceal that he was the murderer and by that fact would not be able to profit by Nasto's confession. It could have some significance only to soothe his conscience that he had not killed an innocent man. But he did not feel, or expect to feel, any remorse. In any case, it was not important if Nasto was really a traitor; he was against the revolt, and some devil had led him to intrigue with the Turks. He must be killed; in the whole clan there was no other person so suitable to serve as a warning to others, to break the chains of blood and kinship. The manner, hanging, also seemed suitable. Nasto did not deserve death by arms; there was something honorable in that, and it might be said that he had defended himself as a brave man, even as an innocent man. Furthermore, Akan would have to wash off the blood and thereby waste time. It was better without blood, which was, after all, Radak blood, even if poisoned by betrayal and faintheartedness. And the place was all that could have been wished: a crossroad. Let the others learn some sense!

The pear tree had two thick lower branches, one too low for a man to hang from, but the other quite high enough and, as if intentionally, overshadowing the road. In truth, there were also some snags, as there always are when something new has to be done; he could not reach the second, higher branch. He remembered that when he had picked pears as a child he had had first to catch hold of the lower branch, grasp the trunk with both arms, and stretch a little upward before he could grip the higher one. If he wanted to get hold of the upper branch, he would have to let go of Nasto, and Nasto might take the chance to get away; once out of Akan's grasp he might gain both courage and speed. How could he climb into the pear tree in order to throw the rope over the branch and at the same time guard Nasto?

Nasto, as if reading his thoughts, coughed and said: "We are alone. I had thought that there were more of you. No matter. I swear to you by God and the clan and the lives of my children that I am not guilty, that I have not torn even a feather from a Radak chicken, let alone betray my brothers."

Akan heard and understood, but it did not move or interest him. He was following his own line of thought: how to hang Nasto. And it was Nasto himself who, by his words and his supplications, gave Akan the idea—which confirmed not only the advantages but also the inevitability of what Akan had resolved. Nasto had said they were alone. Yes, they were alone, those two, Akan and Nasto. But it was also clear to Akan that he was not alone. Why not make use of Nasto in the execution of the sentence against him, in reaching the upper branch and throwing the rope over it? Everything suddenly became clear and simple, easy to carry out.

He quickly made a noose and put it around Nasto's neck, tightening it so that Nasto could not wriggle his head out of it, and then cut the rope to Nasto's hands, leaving them bound. At the same time he reckoned the length of rope; it was even longer than was needed. He led Nasto to the pear tree and by words and pressure on his shoulders ordered him to kneel; then, putting his left hand on the trunk, he climbed onto Nasto's shoulders and threw the rope over the branch.

"You want to hang me, to shed a brother's blood?" Nasto said, ready to weep.

"I won't shed a drop of blood," Akan mocked him.

"Don't mock me! You know very well that one says that when a brother raises his hand against his brother."

"Blood is a fluid like any other, as soon as a brother betrays his brothers. I certainly mean to hang you; you deserve a worse death." Then, after a pause, he added: "If you do not tell me all the secrets that you have told the Turks."

Nasto remained on his knees, imploring. "Don't, Akan, my brother, don't take a brother's death on your soul. What will happen to my children and my wife? Even with me they live in misery, so how much worse without me!"

"You did not think of our children when you betrayed us in the kula to save your skin." The words were harsh, but they did not arouse Akan to hatred. Angered, but more at himself than at Nasto, he shouted: "Get up! what are you whining about?" and pulled the rope, which straightened Nasto up as if the soil under his knees were red-hot.

Noticing how the tension on the rope had brought Nasto up so quickly, Akan stopped for a moment and said: "Tell, or I'll . . ." and slowly began to tighten the rope.

"I have nothing to tell! No, Akan, by the blood and the sun that warms both you and me."

Akan tightened the rope and stifled his words; only gurglings could be heard. In the darkness he could not be sure if he had lifted Nasto, so he kicked at him, and not finding the resistance of a standing body, slackened the rope. Nasto fell to the ground, groaning and choking.

"You see," Akan advised him. "So—be sensible."

"What can I tell you, brother? The Turks already know, or suspect, that something is in the wind. They say we have driven horses here laden with arms. They know that there are adherents of, and opposers to, a revolt. But all that I told you before. Anto, too, knows that; that was why they tortured him. They would like to avoid a revolt, so that the clan will not suffer, so that we can all live in peace and harmony, as we have always lived. I am not a traitor, Akan. I cannot stand evil and misfortune, and I cannot endure tortures. Let me go, brother, and let all you have done to me tonight be forgotten; not even the black earth will come to know of it."

Not even then did Akan hate him, though he knew that he must hang him; in fact, he had already begun to hang him. It was not necessary to hate him in order to hang him, though it would seem more natural to tighten the rope with hatred. But Nasto gave no occasion for hatred; his wailing importunities only made him contemptible. Nonetheless, Akan tried. "You're lying, you swine! You're lying, beast!"

"I am not lying, Akan, upon my soul—which you intend to snatch from me tonight. I go to our begs; tonight I was with them, to discuss how I could save the clan and they their serfs. I see that there is fury among the Radaks and that they might strike against the Turks. That would mean evil and would lead to bloodshed!"

"Don't lie! And who are you, to discuss with them, since the clan has not chosen you?"

"It has not chosen me; that is true. But no one can forbid me to help, if I can. And to tell the truth, most of the clan agrees with me, but they cannot show it, some from shame, some because they do not understand, and some because they are afraid of the Montenegrins, if they should come—and of people such as you. And I thought to myself: Is not peace and order dear to everyone? So do not destroy me, who am blameless. I could be your father."

Akan intentionally broke out in a fury, the more violently since he saw that Nasto was treating this conversation with him as a sign of weakening.

"Why, why then do you go to the mudir, Anto's torturer and your own?"

"I did not go to him. He summoned me. They took me to him, to frighten the Radaks. I was ashamed to speak of that, as I was ashamed that with Anto in the prison I did not hold out as I should have done. I was not born a hero, though I would be able to die for my clan and my home."

"And nothing more?"

"Nothing."

"No matter. I must hang you. The night is passing, and some-one might come."

"Don't burden your soul, Akan, without the judgment of the clan, by the justice of the one God! Don't leave orphans to curse you, hewing wood and drawing water for strangers!"

"You talk well and argue still better, yet you will not confess your treason. I must hang you."

"But, brother, I have nothing to confess. And I see that you do not care if I confess or not."

Only then did Akan become angry, but once again at himself and not Nasto. Resolved to delay no longer, he drew the rope tight, stifling Nasto's words; he had just begun to say something. Walking quickly around the pear tree, Akan tied the rope to the lower branch. Nasto gurgled weakly, jerking clumsily and spas-modically in the air.

Akan had heard how a hanged man might go on suffering for almost a quarter of an hour if his neck was not broken or the weight of his body was not great enough. Though he thought that Nasto deserved to be tortured, he decided to shorten his torments. They were of the same blood, and someone might come upon him if he took a long time dying.

He jumped up, put his arms around Nasto's shoulders and his legs around Nasto's body, so that the increased tension on the rope would strangle Nasto as quickly as possible. He hung thus, with Nasto in his embrace, until his arms began to hurt. Sud-denly, Nasto's body jerked convulsively, pressed against his, and then straightened out.

Akan jumped down on the muddy ground. Only then did he feel that he had separated from Nasto, not only in body, but also in thought and in existence. There arose in him hatred for Nasto, stifling and irrevocable, that hatred which he had summoned up in vain while he had been busy with the murder. He turned to-ward Nasto, motionless and darker than the surrounding gloom, spat at him, and cried out: "Swine, renegade, traitor!"

He looked around and listened: dank, impenetrable silence. Till then he had not realized that it was raining. Only now did he notice the horse standing quietly in the road within reach.

Akan kicked it angrily, but it scarcely shifted. As if he had discovered something important, Akan realized that the horse could not betray him; there had been no need to kick it.

He looked around again. He had forgotten nothing. Nasto was hanging voiceless and motionless. Everything had been done as it should have been; only, he had allowed Nasto to justify himself too much. He set out hurriedly toward the village, listening from time to time to avoid any chance meeting.

He moved quickly, more and more vigorously, as if a burden were falling from him. He thought he ought to hurry, in case someone in the house might by chance notice his absence, but he was also driven on by some inner impulse, to which he responded almost gaily. He was soon in a sweat, though the rain was still falling, and the warmth pleased him. He did not think much about Nasto, though that last convulsive jerk was unpleasant to him, as if he were still covering him with his body. He preoccupied himself mainly with finding his way back, pleased that he succeeded in doing so without stumbling against anything.

Suddenly, the path ceased to lead upward; he had reached the level, the Barrow.

Akan was not afraid; he had not much belief in ghosts. But he noticed a change in himself, and a shiver of apprehension passed over him, as if he had a chill. A shifting mist spread over the Barrow from all sides. Of a sudden he could hear the gurgling of the stream and countless petty murmurs; the waters flowing together and swelling into a whole. He did not turn back, but hurried along the bank toward the village, sure that if anyone came he would be able to avoid him and take refuge in the warm security of the village and of his father's house.

It crossed his mind that all this unease came from the Barrow and from the unconfirmed and terrible beliefs about it. He could not free himself from these forebodings, though he knew that nothing could happen to him. It was as if the Barrow were after him and goading him to hurry, to take refuge in the house with Stanija. And Nasto remained hanging there: a dog with a dog's death! Alone there, he no longer knew even death. Nothing drove him on or hurried him anywhere. Before morning he would be soaked through, and that he would not even notice. They would only come to know about his death in the morning.

When he reached the village, he slowed his pace, to calm down and to listen. All he could hear was the murmuring of the rivulets running down the ditches and ruts and the patter of the rain-drops on the leaves and grass.

Then Stanija had appeared from the darkness, from the wall of the house.

And now, in bed, he slowly came to himself after a short sleep. Everything in the room was just as when he had lain down; the stove burbled, breaking up the shadows, and Stanija was drying his jacket or her lap and gazing in front of her, her face lit by the flames and her own restless inner fire. The rain outside was pour-ing from the eaves, and somewhere a horse whinnied despair-ingly. He remembered: that far-off whinny, scarcely audible, had awakened him. It was that horse, Nasto's horse. He had forgotten all about the horse.

He had dreamed: he brought Nasto to the confluence of the stream and the Lim to kill him there. It was night, but clear, different from the moonlight, greenish and without a moon. Nasto, for a wonder, did not defend himself, only gently and hesi-tantly resisted—just as he had in reality. Only, then it had been different, it had been real night. They came to the bank of the Lim, and Akan pulled out his yataghan and ordered Nasto to sit. Nasto sat obediently and even more obediently stretched out his neck; he knew what Akan wanted and what he asked of him. But Akan reconsidered; I will not cut off his head. One only cuts off the heads of Turks and criminals. Nasto is not a murderer; he is a Serb, a Christian, even a clan brother, though, one might say, a traitor. He felt Nasto's left side, there where the heart is, and drove in his yataghan. But a yataghan is curved, and it went in with difficulty. Nasto went on sitting there with downcast head, though he must have died, for no one can live with a sword in his heart. Akan pulled out the blade and with its point sought for Nasto's heart. He could feel the beating of that heart right down the blade, but he could not locate it precisely. At last he grew impatient and decided to cut off Nasto's head, but he asked him: "Why don't you die once and for all?" "You have not found my heart," Nasto replied calmly. Akan angrily drew the blade out again, and blood flowed from the wound, gushing and gurgling. I won't cut off his head; he must be dead, since he has lost so much blood, however much he pretends that he is not dead. He crawled down to the Lim, greenish and transparent, to wash the blood from the blade. The water swiftly washed off the blood, and the red eddy shone like a sickle. He put the yataghan in its sheath and went back, but from the steep bank, visible under the shining sky. Nasto arose. "You have not washed your hands!" he said. It was true; his hands were bloodstained, though they must have been washed when he cleaned the blade. He began to wash them, and though the red eddy had now surged away he could not get them clean; every time he took them out of the water they were as bloody and sticky as if he had not washed them. No matter, he thought, hands are not important. What is important is that he is dead, and dead he is, although he still speaks.

Then he heard the horse whinnying. Yes, Nasto's horse. That horse had seen him murder Nasto. Why was it whinnying? He had forgotten it. He woke with a start and began to come to himself.

"You fell asleep," said Stanija.

"I was dozing. How did you know I was asleep?"

"I leaned over you." She rose, went around the bed, put the jacket in the chest, looked at the darkness of the windows, and asked: "Can you hear it?"

"What? The rain?"

"No, the horse. Did you hear the horse?"

"I did. What of it?"

"That's his horse. It has come back without its master and is waking everyone. Now his wife and children and the whole clan will be on the alert. But don't worry about it. All your things are dry and clean."

She squatted on the pillow beside him and put her hand on his head protectively. But to him her hand was embarrassing. He could not admit that just then he needed protection. He sat up, without violence, in order imperceptibly to free himself from her hand and her references to Nasto. He sat beside her and put his arms around her waist, whispering: "You are very good to me. You forget nothing that concerns me."

"I have nothing except you and the child," she said, leaning her cheek against his.

He remembered his dream and, as if unintentionally, looked at his hands, though he knew them to be clean. If they had not been, Stanija would already have noticed. He pulled her gently to him. "You are good. You see everything, know everything. It is not easy to find so loyal a comrade. With you beside me, nothing seems hard."

"I am only a true wife to my husband," she said, laughing and hugging him.

From the darkness could be heard a woman wailing and the crying of children. But Stanija no longer wanted to speak about that, about Nasto, though she listened with him.

"Let's lie down," she suggested. "If there is an alarm, let them find us in bed. The fire has already almost burned out."

She did not go to her mattress. They lay in one another's arms, unmoving, listening to the alarm which spread though the village.

As in an earthquake, the alarm whipped out of the wet darkness every living thing, with irrational but unmistakable whips. The cattle were uneasy, the dogs began to howl, and children aroused from the softness and bliss of sleep whimpered and yelled. Finally, the door of the room squeaked.

"Did you hear?" asked Stamena in a still sleepy but uneasy voice, and added: "How hot it is in here!"

"I heard. I couldn't help hearing," Akan replied as calmly as he could, and got up, unable to find an answer about the warmth of the room.

Then Stanija also got up. "Last night we stoked up a bit because of the little one; all that rain, and he's got a chill."

As he was getting dressed, Akan said: "I'll go out and see what is happening. Is Grgur up?"

"He's still in bed. He said you were to find out."

Anto called Stamena from the storeroom; she replied, half opening the door. Stanija, handing Akan his stockings, warmly pressed his right hand in the darkness. He returned the pressure.

The boy Anto began to whimper, calling his father. "Papa, papa!"

"Here I am, dear one! Mother is here; she will stay with you," Akan soothed him, putting on his belt. "Let the little one lie and sleep," he said to Stanija, opening the door.

But the child, now fully awake, called him. "Papa, I'm afraid! Have the Turks attacked?"

Outside, the downpour was less than it had seemed to Akan in the room. But he felt cold and, shaking himself, remarked to Stamena: "As soon as I have found out, I will come back to tell you." It seemed neither funny nor strange that he, who not only knew what it was all about but also had been the cause of it, now had to go and find out the reason for the commotion.

The uproar obviously came from Nasto's house, and, like the others, Akan called out: "What is it, for Heaven's sake? What's the matter?"

Nasto's son Miluš—he knew the voice—answered through the uproar, but Akan, if he had not already known what it was all about, would not have been able to distinguish the words. ". . . the horse . . . Nasto."

He called again: "What are you saying? What is it?"

This time a bass male voice, some Radak, replied: "The horse has come back without Nasto!"

Akan began to move slowly up the path to Nasto's house, angry that he had to struggle against the darkness and the weather, swearing to himself at Nasto, who even when dead did not behave like a man, but had to arouse the whole clan on a night like this.

When he came to the open space above the nearby gardens, he heard Vojin's resounding call: "Grgur! What is it? What's the matter?"

Akan replied: "I am Akan, Akan. The horse has come back without Nasto; the horse without Nasto!"

Vojin answered: "Wait for me."

Now he no longer felt cold. But he was still angry with Nasto. He had foreseen that there would be some uproar, but not like this, not so much, and certainly not before dawn. It was all the cursed nag's fault; he had not remembered to tie it to the pear tree near its master. Now, in this filthy weather, he must go out again to look for Nasto, as if he had nothing better to do. He had got used to the darkness, but the rain, the weeping, and the shouts, which were becoming more frequent, bothered him. He leaned against a plum tree, and the rain, shaken from the leaves and branches, soaked him, reminding him that he must not forget what he was doing.

Vojin appeared, unexpectedly huge under his goatskin cloak with a hood, plodding along the wet path. "What is all this, by God? I thought it was a fire or that the army had attacked."

"I don't know myself. I heard a call and someone said that his horse had come back without Nasto," Akan answered calmly, letting Vojin go ahead.

"What the devil drove him to get so involved in the night? The night has no witnesses," Vojin said slowly, feeling his way with his staff.

Through the open door feeble flames from Nasto's hearth lit up the courtyard, and the group on the slope was outlined by them. Akan, with displeasure, even with horror, recognized Nasto's wife, Miluša. Tiny, half-clothed, and barefoot, her hands tucked into her armpits, she did not notice the potbellied infant tugging at her skirt, or the rain that fell on her nakedness. What was more, she had forgotten shame; she was without a kerchief, her plaits were in disorder on her shoulders, and her short-sleeved blouse was unbuttoned. Beside her stood the horse, also indifferent to the rain. No one paid any attention to it; it was still saddled and bridled. Nor did the horse, Akan noticed, pay any attention to the newcomers, but went on munching tufts of grass from the slope. Akan pulled himself together; why should the horse pay any attention to him or to them? It was waiting to be unsaddled and taken to its stall. Once again he was angry with Nasto and swore at him silently. But he asked aloud: "For God's sake, Miluša, why set the village in an uproar? Has something bad happened?"

Other Radaks arrived as Miluša was wailing: "Good people, golden brothers, see for yourselves. His horse has come back without him, without my husband. Black is my home today! I heard the horse whinnying furiously, and my husband was not there! And I, to my shame, was dozing. In an evil moment I went out, and there was the horse—and my man nowhere. Who will feed my children, who will look after them?"

Vojin gently put a hand on her shoulder. "Don't cry, don't assume the worst! Perhaps the horse broke loose and ran away. And while we Radaks are here, don't worry about your children."

"No, no! There is no comfort in my black misfortune! Some harm has come to my man. The horse is peaceful; it's not like a horse, but a person. Help me, by God and by our common kinship! Help me; look for him, in case he is still alive." She began to pull herself together, fingering the fastenings of her blouse to cover her nakedness, and then took the children into the house.

Vojin turned to the Radaks. "We must look for him. If we do not find him, others will. But first we must tell Anto."

Accompanied by Akan, Vojin walked off with that same long, slow, steady stride with which he had come. And he went on talking. "The worst of it is that if anything has happened to him, the Turks will stick their noses in. They're only waiting for something of the sort. They would be quite capable of doing away with him themselves, just to have an excuse to involve themselves in the clan dissensions, one way or another."

In the storeroom, where Anto was, a taper was burning. Anto was lying propped up with pillows, a sheet up to his neck. As Akan and Vojin came in, he slowly pulled himself upright; the bedcover slipped off and revealed his thin, almost hairless, chest, and he asked, as much with his eyes as in words: "What has happened?"

"Who knows what may happen in these times?" Vojin said. "But, Nasto has gone."

"What do you mean, gone?"

"Just that. He is nowhere to be found, and his horse has come home without him."

Grgur came into the room in shirt and pants, and in the corner Rade rose from his couch, rubbing his eyes; he slept with his father, to be near him in his illness.

Anto pulled himself up a little more and tugged at the coverlet. "We must look for him," he concluded. "He is of our clan. You, Vojin, take a lantern and two or three others. You, Akan, are dressed. Go slowly, or you may miss him."

Vojin started to go, but Akan's opposition halted him. "I will not go, Father, to look for Turkish informers!"

But Anto was unyielding. "It is not important who likes whom, but what has to be done. Better that we look for him than that some outsider or Turk find him tomorrow. Whatever he may have been, he was our fellow clansman."

377

Akan followed Vojin and was welcomed by the shining glance of Stanija's black eyes; the glow on her face, which till then he had thought came from the red-hot stove, was more pronounced. "Wait!" she called out. "I will bring your cloak." She held his cloak while he put it on, and he felt the close, familiar, intentionally prolonged pressure of her hands on his shoulders.

At last, Vojin set out with his lantern. After him, in a group, moved the Radaks who had chanced to be there—Akan, Stojan, and the old man Milija. So they went, the whole way, investigating vague shadows, calling to one another, waiting and looking into whatever seemed to them suspicious, whatever looked like a man's body.

Such a search was bound to be slow, with frequent halts, with investigations of byways; from the darkness spread out a hitherto unnoticed network of paths and short cuts around the main road.

Akan, at first intentionally and then almost forgetting the senselessness of his participation in the search, investigated enigmatic shapes and, having reached them, called out what he had found, or ran quickly along some path, only to return, breathless, to say that there was nothing on that side either.

The behavior of the others, however, was in no way different, nor could it be seen from it what it was they were seeking. They rarely mentioned Nasto's name, but said: "He's not here!," "Why should he have gone this way?," or "But that doesn't even look like a man!"

Finally Vojin concluded: "Nothing has happened to him on our land."

Everyone knew that was important: the Turkish authorities had passed a law by which, if a murderer was not found, the village in whose parish the crime had been committed would be fined. These fines were severe, and the local authorities had added some of their own—traveling expenses, the costs of investigation, punishments for not reporting the crime in time, and whatever else came into their minds. Still in dispute with the authorities and the begs about the amount of tribute and the tithes, the Radaks, by the fact that Nasto was not to be found in their parish, were at least free from unforeseen impositions. To Akan, Vojin's conclusion seemed comical and petty. But it was a pleasure to him that he would not have to pay the Turks for Nasto;

when choosing the place for the murder, this had not occurred to him, and now all had turned out for the best despite his lack of forethought. He wanted to ask: "Why should we pay fines for a Turkish informer?" But since there was no occasion for argument and such words might draw suspicion upon him, he remarked: "Well, we must look farther. As far as I know, he was going to Plav."

Without argument they moved down the valley.

When they reached the crossroad, Vojin remarked: "He went to Plav; therefore we must look for him on this road."

That remark was superfluous, but Akan caught at it. "Where else could he be?"

Milija spoke. "Well, there could be other places. He went to all sorts of places to work. But at this time, no; Miluša, too, said that he had business in Plav."

They scattered along the road, still searching. Akan, too, searched, though the pear tree was very near. As soon as it was in sight, as thick, bronze, and ominous as when the lightning had lit it up, Akan saw the corpse, though it almost merged with the black background of the night and the tree trunk. All that could be seen were Nasto's white stockings. His face was not visible, though it was turned toward Akan. He, naturally, did not want to announce the discovery, and would have taken to his heels but for the fear that the Radaks might pass Nasto without seeing him. No one, indeed, noticed Nasto until Vojin nearly ran into him. He raised his lantern, lit up Nasto's face, and called out: "Here he is! Hanged!"

Nasto was without his cap, and Akan recalled neither he nor Nasto had noticed its disappearance. His head was turned to the left, with protruding blackened tongue and eyes staring at something indefinite and, to judge from their expression, incredibly horrifying. Now it was clear to Akan why he had not seen Nasto's face; it was completely plastered with mud, quite black. Only the eyes were still human in that face, and, for that reason, looked the more astounded.

Vojin walked slowly around the corpse and the pear tree, as if he wanted to remember every detail. "Bound," he said. "It doesn't look as if he tried to defend himself. Nowhere a scratch, and all his buttons are still there. That means there were several

379

of them. He would not have let a single man bind him. Take a look, too; we must remember everything, in case the authorities investigate."

The old man Milija crossed himself. "God have mercy on his soul! May he who took his life be accursed, whoever he may be."

The rest all kneeled, crossing themselves, Akan, too. Then, unnoticed till then, Grandfather Pavle leaped out of the darkness of the night. He, too, crossed himself, and shouted, almost gaily: "Hangs and is hanged!"

Vojin ordered: "Look for the cap, and you, Akan, or you, Stojan, hold him while I untie the rope."

Stojan went to look for the cap, and Akan put his arms around the corpse; but this time he did not have to jump, for the corpse had slipped down almost to the ground. As soon as he grasped the stiffened body he remembered, only now terrible in its vividness, Nasto's last convulsion in his arms. It seemed terribly long before Vojin cut the rope. The corpse dropped to the ground, and it was not difficult to keep it in an upright position. Akan wanted to let go of it, to free himself from the recollection of Nasto's last shudder. But he could not make up his mind to do so, fearing that if he did he would draw attention to himself and arouse suspicion. He must behave like the others. No one would let a dead brother fall into the mud. Vojin took the rope from Nasto's neck and freed his hands with a knife. Nasto's hands, as if wooden, dropped to each side and thus remained.

From the darkness Stojan called out: "Here is the cap!"

Vojin again thought and then said: "We have no stretcher. There's nothing for it but to take turns carrying him. You take him first, Akan, since you're holding him already, and we will relieve you."

"Have we really got to carry him?" asked Akan hesitantly.

"What else can we do?" Milija said stubbornly. "Surely we can't leave a brother here in the night."

Vojin helped to put the dead man on Akan's back. It was a slow job; for Akan, trying to carry him piggyback, felt Nasto's cheek against his and asked them to turn the corpse over on its back.

When at last he began carrying Nasto, Stojan, trying to put the cap on Nasto's head, asked: "Is it too heavy for you?"

"You can see for yourself that it's heavy," Akan replied, panting. "But it's more awkward than heavy."

His huge, swaying shadow, with its strange grotesque burden, strode across the fields and the hills, and Grandfather Pavle, trotting beside him, called out: "Bear it, bear it! Everyone bears what he is not proud of."

The Radaks buried Nasto and mourned him, united and unanimous, as if none of them had ever accused him of intriguing with the Turkish authorities and the begs and as if they had never been divided. Furthermore, Knez Anto decided to announce a large reward for the capture of the criminal, as had been done in olden days. But that seemed comic, even among the Radaks themselves, for though no one had as yet spoken openly about who might be the murderer, they at once began to whisper among themselves that the murder had been committed by someone in the clan.

But by the day after the funeral, sentiment had already changed. They began to think that the murder of Nasto should have been reported to the authorities before the funeral, and even that he should not have been taken down from the pear tree until the authorities had carried out an investigation. But such thoughts were infrequent, and, from the inherited Radak viewpoint, to subject the death of a clan member to outside interference was unreasonable. To the Radaks, it was unthinkable that one of their own men be left hanging at the crossroad so that men from other clans might take pleasure in their misfortune and his death.

Nonetheless, it was not possible to hide the crime from the authorities, not only because they would hear of it from those who had been at the funeral, from Nasto's relations, friends, and acquaintances from other villages, but also because they would soon begin to ask where he, a man inclined toward them, might be. It became evident that the crime must be reported. But when it was necessary to appoint someone to do this, no one wanted to do it.

Gloomy, tormenting, enigmatic fears and doubts seized all the Radaks, even the adherents of the revolt, though they, at the same time, were seized with a melancholy enthusiasm. Not one of them would consider informing the authorities about Nasto's murder, because they knew that the authorities were only waiting for an excuse to settle accounts with the Radaks. Mostly their excuse was that there was no need to involve any outsiders, especially Turks, in clan misfortunes.

Even those favorable to Nasto and inclined toward an understanding with the Turks, like the old man Milija, did not want to go to Plav to notify the authorities of the murder. They all made various excuses, and Milija even said openly: "I will not drag the Turks into our clan affairs, lest someone place the brand of traitor on me and sully my name and my family."

Least of all could it be expected that any of those who supported Vojin would go to Plav. For the most part they kept silent, a prey to terrible suspicions. Overnight, that group became the largest; it was joined by all those from the two extremist groups who, for one reason or another, were unable to free themselves from fear and insecurity and from mutual accusations. They became pessimistic, presaging evil, and prepared to defend themselves, but only if they were attacked.

The clan was finally divided, split into factions that were no longer open and sincere. No one was any longer capable of deciding anything, even concerning the everyday conduct of clan affairs. Their knez, Anto Radak, though they all without exception loved and respected him more than ever, was seized with ever greater despondency. Embittered by the Radaks and his own fate, he had said: "Some curse has fallen upon us. I will myself go to Plav, even though I am no longer able to sit on a horse." Perhaps, had he really set out for Plav, the whole clan would in a moment have rallied around him, imploring him not to do so. But his threat did not arouse anyone, nor was it able to change anything. He withdrew into himself, feeling impotent and ineffectual.

On the third day after the funeral, Mitar Drndar came into the village from Plav with bad news: the authorities already knew about Nasto's murder. They suspected that someone from the clan had done it, and on the pretext of looking for the murderer, but in fact because they feared a revolt that might lead to an attack on Plav and Gusinje by the Montenegrins, they were preparing to arrest the leaders and adherents of the revolt.

Anto called together the householders to inform them and ordered them to post guards on the side of the village that faced Plav.

That decision, even though the majority approved it, met with open resistance from the old man Milija. "Why should we provoke the Turks when among ourselves we are ready to tear out each other's eyes?" Nor was Vojin enthusiastic about it. "It is not the same as posting guards against an attack by the Rugovo clans. The Turks are the state, and we are not!"

In the evening of that day, Anto called his three sons to the storeroom to talk. This had never happened before. When it had been necessary for the head of the household to hold a discussion, all the adults of the household had been summoned, men and women; and if it was a personal matter, then only the person involved was called. This time Anto did not even call his own father, Grandfather Grgur. In and around the house people began to speak in whispers, with few words, as if someone were dying or some terrible misfortune was about to be revealed.

Sitting on the bed, buttoned to the throat in furs—he felt the cold more and more—Anto spoke quietly and slowly, as much from exhaustion as from deliberation and prudence. "The household will be handed on to you, and to one of you—I had hoped Grgur—also the clan. This is not my farewell to you, though I hope that I will not be so tormented for long and that God will have mercy and take my soul at last. I do not want to talk with you as a father. Everyone looks after me, cares for me, flatters me, but my heart is grieved. Whenever I look back, it seems to me that everything has been in vain. I see the clan falling apart, as if devils were scattering it on their horns. And I am so lonely and impotent that I no longer know whom to trust. In my depression of soul and my torment, it occurs to me that one of the Radaks must have murdered Nasto. But whenever I think of that, I think that my failing mind has deceived me. Surely so much hatred has not yet taken root in the clan. You are my sons; as sons you must obey me and tell me the truth. Who killed Nasto?"

He looked at them, one by one, and each of them lowered his eyes.

"Don't you know or won't you say?" he went on, with greater and greater persistence. "One of you must know. Even if Rade does not know, for he is young and innocent, then one of you two must. You, Grgur, are the leader of the revolt; it cannot be that you have no suspicions or that someone has not confided in you. It is not a small thing, as if it were a matter of a beast, or a criminal. A man has been killed. You have heard what Mitar says—the Turks are suspicious of the clan. What will happen if the Turks find the murderer among us? Who will then be able to keep the Radaks united, disunited as they are now? You are my sons; you must tell me the truth. I taught you that and I trust in that."

Grgur shifted about and opened his mouth to say something, but Akan stopped him. Raising his head, he said calmly: "I killed him!" The silence in a moment was charged with icy horror.

Both his brothers looked at him and moved away from him. Anto swayed as if someone had struck him. "You! What came over you? Are you dreaming? Are you in your right senses? Am I in my right senses?" he whispered, with an effort, looking around distractedly.

Akan withstood both words and looks. Standing by the door, his arms by his sides, he said quietly: "I don't understand why you are so surprised. I or someone else—what does it matter, since he had to be killed."

"What do you mean, had to be?" Grgur asked, pulling himself together.

"Just what I said—he had to be! How otherwise could we break loose from the Turks? How could we find out who was who among ourselves, among the Radaks? How could we begin anything without that? We would always have been guessing, putting things off."

"I know. But he was our fellow clansman," Grgur went on.

"And a Turkish informer."

Anto buried his face in his hands. "Had it been anyone else but my own son! Akan—the prop and stay of my household! Why must it be my family to break up the clan? Why didn't I die under the Turkish tortures?" he wailed.

"Father, father," Akan began, with the intention of saying something important and solemn and therefore not addressing Anto as Papa, as he usually did.

But Anto did not hear him. "Now I must bring my own son before the clan as a criminal. It only lacks that I claim the reward for him. Must I notify the Turks? Or hide the murderer of his brother?"

Grgur broke in curtly: "How could it ever have occurred to you?"

And Rade added despairingly: "Surely you could have spoken with him?"

Finding himself alone, faced with the accusations of his father and brothers, Akan became irritated. "Occur to me! Surely it would have occurred to any of you who are for the revolt. Only, you took the easy way and put it out of your minds, while I took it seriously and have ended it seriously. I do not think things over to no effect. As for talking it over with him, I could have talked with him and threatened him. But that would not have done any good, nor would it have been a warning to others. You, Father, I do not understand; you especially! You have just got away with your life from the Turkish tortures and yet you wonder that I have cut short a weakling and prevented a renegade from turning the clan over to the Turks."

His father and brothers looked at him as though he were a stranger, a madman. And when Akan paused for breath, Anto continued his lamenting. "What reputation will be left me when I go tomorrow to face the clan? With what words? Where are you, O heavens, that you do not break open? Why, O earth, do you not swallow me up? Nothing like this has ever been heard of among the Radaks. If it ever happened it has been erased from our memories. They have trodden us down, bruised us like flax, enslaved us, plundered us, taken our girls from us, and raped our young women; great armies and powerful clans have passed over us. They have forced us to become Turks, they have hanged us or cast us on the hooks in the market place and beheaded us on the bridges, but neither pestilence nor enemies, neither fire nor storm, has ever been able to scatter us and uproot us. And now we scatter ourselves and tear up our roots!"

He was silent, then raised his head, suddenly calm, as if he had awakened in a strange world and in the presence of strangers. "So it is! No one is lost until he destroys himself, does not die until he has dug his own grave. The time has come for the Radaks to be scattered. If only my eyes had not lived to see it!"

"But, Father," Grgur began, moved and given fresh heart by

his father's calm. "No one suspects Akan. There is no need to say anything to anyone. Nothing need happen. No one is rooted out— not even Nasto. We will take care of his children."

"No, Grgur. No, son. It has happened. And who did it? The wisest, the most chosen of the Radaks! The Radaks may be deep-rooted and stronger than they have ever been, but the Radak clan will not be—already it is not. The Radaks are now able to kill one another. How can they live in unity?"

"Nothing need be done," Grgur asserted. "Keep silent and wait!"

"No, no! Could I do that? Have I the strength for that? To deceive the Radaks! Why did I endure many tortures for them? If it were not for this accursed war and that revolt!"

He was silent, gazing in front of him, shrunken, withdrawn. The sons were silent. The whole house was silent, as if it knew what had happened. At last Anto looked up and with a painful contraction of his face said: "Let Milena come. I must talk with her. And you go—all three of you. And don't say anything. Until I have thought it over. Leave me to my misfortune."

Outside, in front of the house, Grgur turned to Akan, avoiding his eyes. "You should have discussed this with Stojan and me. We are all sinking in the same bog."

"But you would have prevented me. We must sink in it; we must all sink in it sooner or later."

"But why didn't you think of Father? After all, Nasto was a clansman. And what the devil led you to tell Father?"

"The same thing that drove me to wipe out Nasto. I can see and hear how Father torments himself, guesses, wonders. I had to put a stop to it. And how could I lie to Father? Can a man delude his own conscience?"

Grgur considered, chewing his mustache. "Yes. But it would have been easier for Father if you had said nothing. He is now tearing himself to pieces—for our tortures."

"I knew that it would pain him," Akan remarked with regret but with firmness. "But is there any sense in letting our opponents make capital out of the tortures he has endured?"

The brothers were silent, each looking away from the other into the moist darkness. Then Grgur turned slowly toward his brother. "You mentioned conscience. Does it reproach you?"

"I couldn't tell you," Akan replied, thinking it over. "On the first night, in a dream, it seemed as if he were pursuing me, but later—no! Now it's all the same to me—pangs or no pangs. I would be able to hang him again."

Grgur put a hand on his shoulder. "You are my brother, and it is as if I do not know you. Were I able, I would share your troubles with you. We must prevent Father from putting the whole matter before the clan. I do not believe that he will do it; there would be no advantage and much disorder and hatred. You must not pay too much heed to Father's words when he is excited. Then, he talks like one of the old curses or songs. Later, when he thinks it over, everything will fall into place, and he will be reasonable. Let him calm down tonight, and I will do my best to talk to him in the morning."

"As you like. We must do something. We've been thinking it over long enough."

"But you have begun already. Only I don't know what all this will come to."

"Do you think I know? If we knew for certain, perhaps I would not have begun. Who can know what the day will bring and what the night?"

Grgur went into the kitchen, and Rade, who, unnoticed and withdrawn, had been listening at the door, ran up to Akan and hugged him. "I would not do that before Father, in order not to hurt him, but you are a hero, a real hero! Even if it was sinful before God and before men, to me it was fine, so fine that I am trembling with worry, with love for you!"

Akan, moved, returned the hug and the brotherly kiss and muttered: "I am no hero. I do what I can. And what have you to worry about? What will be will be."

That night Akan was a long time getting to sleep. He confided in Stanija and resisted her urgings to flee into Montenegro, seeing that there was no longer any life for him among the Radaks. After a short but deep sleep, he got up early, before his usual time. He had to inspect the Radak guards on the hills looking toward Plav. That task he carried out the more conscientiously since he was, with reason, mistrustful of the regularity and discipline of the guards.

The chill of the clear late-autumn dawn invigorated him and

dispersed his chimeras. He set out toward the mountain pass above the village, looking toward Plav, whence alone the Turkish irregulars could attack.

The Radaks had established daily sentries on that side only, because the road up the valley could be seen from the village itself; from the mountains only the Shquiptars were likely to attack, and they were now at peace with the Radaks. On the mountaintop, which, steep and forested, swept down from the range to the Lim, there were shepherds' paths everywhere. It would be difficult for an army to cross it, but it was an easy matter for the retreat of a small group of haiduks. The undergrowth, sparse enough not to catch in their clothes, was dense enough to hide them from sight. By day the mountaintop could be kept under observation easily enough, for the passes to it from the plain or from the hillside that swept down to the Lim were visible. But if an enemy had already reached its slopes by night, discovery could only be a matter of hearing or of chance encounter.

Though Akan had not slept much, he felt rested and refreshed, even cheerful. He always liked to rise early, to await the coming of daylight, the emergence of things and places from the darkness of the night. It was, for him, a personal rejuvenation, the dearer and more beautiful in that a man was conscious of it and present in it. His cheerful mood increased as the dawn, whitish and clear, suddenly revealed the little path by which he had passed so often that he knew every stick and stone on it. The tree trunks and flaming sumac were so well known to him that he almost raised his hand in welcome to the heights, which he had been able to see even in the densest darkness. Everything was near and familiar and at the same time new, with fresh brilliance and inconceivable purity. That clarity was also due to the conviction, which only last night had flooded his mind and body after he had confessed to his father and brothers, that all he had believed would be broken down by Nasto's murder had indeed been broken down. It was as if he had not murdered anyone, but had done something inevitable, even sinless.

Reaching the pass at the same time as the first rosy, cheering rays of the sun, Akan moved along its bare spine between the juniper bushes. From there he could see the plain as far as Plav, and even farther, to Gusinje and its fields, still green even in late autumn, wedged between the great stone hills. But nowhere could he find a sentry, and that seemed to him stupid and ominous. Perhaps whoever had been keeping watch that night had gone away at daybreak without waiting for his relief. Perhaps it was something even worse. When posting the guards, Grgur and Vojin, especially Vojin, had paid no attention to what opinion the men who were picked to mount guard held about the revolt, as if it had been merely a matter of taking their turn at the mill. Earlier, certainly, no Radak, even though, like all peasants, slow and careless, would have failed to carry out his duty to preserve the clan. But now, especially after Nasto's murder, they had no liking for guard duty.

Despite that, Akan had not lost all confidence, and he was already close to the rounded summit when a bald head bobbed above the juniper bushes and he heard, first, the clopping of hoofs, and then the clink of weapons and men's voices. He knelt beside the nearest bush, gripping his rifle.

Along the saddle just below the summit above him, almost directly behind him, passed a group of Moslems, brightly dressed, led by a man of moderate height but heavily built, in a scarlet dolman and blue trousers, leading a saddled white horse. They were far away, only just in range, but Akan suspected that the heavily built man was Ibrica Buljukbaša, well known throughout the whole area as a tyrant and an undisciplined ruffian.

Ibrica Buljukbaša was a refugee, at one time from Podgorica. The Montenegrins had not driven out the Podgorica Moslems, defeated in war, from their homes and properties, and certainly there was truth in the story that Ibrica had had to fly because he had earlier terribly oppressed the local people. But nothing definite was known about him. His real name was probably Ibro, though no one ever called him that, but, rather, the diminutive, Ibrica, which, since he was a big man and of evil reputation, meant that he was so called more because of mockery and fear than good will. He always referred to himself as Ibrica, and always in the third person. "Take care not to fall into Ibrica's clutches!" "It is hard for anyone whom Ibrica catches!" "Who jokes with Ibrica harrows himself!" He had gathered around him a band of vagabonds and plunderers; he was their leader, their *buljukbaša*. So he had adopted the word *buljukbaša* as a surname and as an indication of his profession. "I'm no man of straw, but a *buljuk-bašaʼ!*" "The *buljukbaša* comes first, and then others!" "The *bu-ljukbaša* does not deceive, and whoever deceives him will learn to his cost who is the *buljukbaša!*"

His nationality was not known, either. He could have been a Shquiptar, a Serb, a real Turk, or, judging by the darkness of his skin, an Arab, but he respected the tenets of his faith so little that it was said that he would eat pork even when sober. He was one of those vagabonds and adventurers, robbers and mercenaries, whom the Turkish Empire, which was then falling to pieces, vomited on all sides, equally dependent on them and terrified of them and horrified at their actions. The Plav municipality felt under an obligation to help refugees, and helped them more than it could afford to. But it was unable to find service for Ibrica or any job other than what he had hitherto been doing, burning and arresting, beating and plundering. Certainly the Plav and Gusinje begs would quickly have blunted his horns had it not been a time of war or threatened war and if there had not been disaffection among the Serb serf villages. In such conditions he was a godsend to them, so they had attached him and his band, in which were many local vagabonds, to the *sejmeni,* the police irregulars, though he paid little heed to anyone's authority, descending upon villages and clans where he had heard that there was dissatisfaction, and not refraining from raids into Montenegro for cattle or heads. He preferred to time his attacks to coincide with *slava*s and weddings, when it was possible to be well entertained. Perhaps his reputation would not have been so terrible—he rarely murdered, probably fearing vendettas or responsibility should conditions change—had he not maltreated men and violated women, even Moslem women, especially when he was drunk. Usually obtuse and half-demented, he showed in his maltreatings and rapes, as in fighting, an astounding and hellish imagination. One serf he had thrown into a trough of manure because he had served him inferior plum brandy, and another he had stopped at harvest time when he was with his wife and ordered: "Hold my horse while I enjoy your wife!" He loved to deck himself out in finery, and his greatest enjoyment was to look on and listen as the serfs begged him for mercy when he threatened and maltreated them.

Akan had never seen Ibrica, but he realized at once that it could only be he; the legal authorities would have come by the road and by day, and they would not have been dressed in such brilliant colors or so decorated. Also the description he had heard in tales tallied with Ibrica: the white horse, the compact body and swarthy face, the enormous white turban around his red fez, such as in Plav only hodžas and hadjis wore. Akan knew all about him, and suspected that Ibrica's arrival had been carefully planned, even if the authorities had not sent him on any specific task. Or perhaps, hearing that something was cooking among the Radaks or that Nasto had been killed, he had decided to come of his own accord and fine them to his own benefit.

Astounded by the unexpected appearance of Ibrica and his band and only now angered that he had not come across any of the sentries, Akan looked to see how many men there were and at the same time considered what to do. Other than Ibrica, there were a dozen *sejmeni*. It was strange that there were so few. But that was Ibrica's way; he led only his own men, relying on surprise and the fear that his name aroused, and certainly also on the well-known lack of unity among the Radaks. But their number was still too great for the unprepared village—and Akan was alone. He could fire his long gun and perhaps kill someone, but that would not help the still-sleeping village. The *sejmeni* would attack before it realized what was happening, and in the meantime settle their accounts with him. And he could not outdistance them; he would not be able to make his way unseen through the thickets alongside the band, and if he tried to go through the forests on this side of the pass, he would arrive too late. Yet if he did nothing, not only would he be a coward, but the murder of Nasto would have been senseless, superfluous, criminal.

Above the juniper bushes, Akan could see a hand pointing toward the village. It was certainly Ibrica's, for a whip was dangling from its wrist. The little band began to split up. A group of four moved off to the left and one to the right, toward the outskirts of the village, while Ibrica, with those remaining, went straight down, toward Anto's house and the center of the clan.

Horror overwhelmed Akan. Ibrica would strike at the village, and he had given no warning. It was as if Nasto wanted to take his revenge at the most fateful moment and make all that Akan had done senseless, even the hanging itself. He wanted to shout out, to fire his gun. The needle-sharp spines of the juniper pricked his throat and chin, bringing him back to reality. He pushed aside the branch and stood up, but not suddenly, in case one of the Turks should notice, though they had already disappeared in the undergrowth. He looked around him; that shining, familiar light flooded things, and he could hear the distant, warning clop of horses' hoofs in the ravine.

He was quite alone, on the bare ridge, under a sky already blazing. What use was his anger, his memory of Nasto? He forgot that torment which he might always have to bear; now he had to do what must be done. He must consider calmly and decide according to circumstances, as he had always done and always liked to do. There were several possibilities: try to evade one of the groups and get between them; catch Ibrica and attack him from behind and thereby give the alarm; begin to fire and to shout—someone in the village would surely hear, for it was now well after dawn. But as he hurried down the hill—for in any event he would have to go toward the village—he rejected them one after the other. He had to run at top speed, though the Turks were bound to halt for discussion, since they were in a district not well known to them. He plunged into the undergrowth, and suddenly, in the semidarkness, he made up his mind. *The main thing is to make sure that the Turks do not notice me, that I surprise them and start a fight before they can surprise me. It was the same with Nasto; I crept up on him in the dark, confused him, deceived him, and mastered him.*

Almost at the same moment he remembered the stream. If not the most convenient, it was the safest way to get to the village unnoticed, perhaps before Ibrica's band, if he did not come upon some unforeseen obstacle. In the murder of Nasto, too, there had been unforeseen things, though he had thought out everything a hundred times.

Akan ran toward the stream, which came out to the right of Ibrica's group, nearer to Anto's than to Vojin's house. In summer the stream bed was dry, but now it was full of water. Akan heard its gentle gurgle and thought that was one of the advantages of his idea, for his footsteps could neither be seen nor heard.

But when he got to the stream an unpleasant surprise awaited him. Though he had been born and brought up alongside it, had splashed and bathed in it, and had herded stock in its vicinity, and thought that he knew it as well as his own house, the stream bed was filled with unexpectedly slippery stones and steep potholes. Though the stream was not deep—only in the stony pools into which the waters fell rushing was it up to his knees—he was soaked through in a few moments and streaming with sweat, jumping over rapids and clinging to wet, stony banks overgrown with moist, greenish moss. Wrestling with these difficulties, driven on by his own impatience to arrive before the *sejmeni* and justify himself to his brothers and the clan, he almost forgot why he was doing this. The stream fought against him like a terrible, unpredictable, unknown enemy. It could not be otherwise; the stream had flowed there for ages past, and he wanted to master its mysteries all at once. He must hurry, but with caution. The *sejmeni* would not be faced with these difficulties, but, on the other hand, they did not know their way. He must keep his mind on what had to be done, how to wriggle around that rounded stone, how to avoid that pool. One more thing he had always to bear in mind, and that was his weapon; he had to keep it dry because of that vague, far-off assignment and the anxiety that drove him on. Suddenly he found himself just above the waterfall, too high and too steep for him to get down, and at the same moment he thought with anger of Nasto—how he had brought him here and was now surrounding him with, immuring him in, stone. But he knew the remedy for Nasto: he must think and he must act. He examined his position and at once decided that it would be best if he went back a few paces and got out of the stream, taking care not to come into contact with the Turks.

He did this. As he was dragging himself out of a slippery stone pool, clutching at the bare roots of a hornbeam on the bank, it became clear to him how much his caution had been justified. About twenty or thirty paces from him were four pairs of human legs and the four white feet of a horse. He could not see the heads and bodies, for they were hidden by the dense screen of boughs, but he could hear their quiet conversation. He hid until the scuffling on the leaves and stones died away, then quickly skirted the waterfall and leaped again into the stream, which welcomed him more readily and courteously.

As soon as he emerged from the stream bed in sight of the open space above the houses, in well-known surroundings, everything was again filled with that gay, shining morning light and familiarity. His mind was alert; he could attack the *sejmeni* at the most suitable moment, a moment of his own choosing.

Ibrica and his men had already blockaded Anto's house, about a hundred and fifty paces from the place where Akan had emerged from the stony, dank, moist fetters of the stream. One of them, a short red-beard with a violet scarf around his neck, was trying in vain with the barrel of his rifle to push aside one of the Radak sheepdogs, who was defending the approach to the house with frantic leaps and barks. Akan took advantage of the tumult to run a few steps toward the open space, then took cover behind a thick old hornbeam, which would shelter him from bullets and hide him from sight with its hard trunk and thick cluster of branches.

Just then a second *sejmen*, tall, clean-shaven, tightly belted with a red sash, and in white Shquiptar trousers, pointed his pistol at the dog and, when it came almost up to him, fired. The dog fell back without a whimper and, before the whitish smoke of the powder had cleared from around his head, turned on his side and fell, legs stretched out. Barking could be heard from Vojin's house, followed by shouts. The *sejmeni* at the corners of the house smiled and shouted, but Ibrica, holding his reins in his left hand and brandishing his whip in his right, replied angrily. They suddenly fell silent, and two of them went quickly around the house, one into the garden on Anto's side of the house, where he took up a position behind an apple tree with his gun at the ready, watching the windows. In the courtyard remained two men and Ibrica himself, sheltered by his horse.

Noticing that he was panting and recalling that a panting marksman always misses, Akan slowly and carefully pushed his gun through the branches and then took off his black sheepskin cap and placed it under the barrel to deaden the noise of the shot.

The first to run out of the house was Stamena, bareheaded and in her shift. She started, as if she wanted to withdraw, but then, perhaps seeing the dead dog, began to scold with clenched fists. The red-haired man grabbed her by the arm and pulled her out of the shadow of the house, and Ibrica, leaping out, struck her three times on the back with his whip. She shouted, not because of the blows, but to warn the others in the house. The *sejmen* pushed her into the kitchen in front of the house, then stood across the doorway. The pistol in his right hand menaced those within, but this only seemed to awaken the angry cries of Stamena.

Grgur now rushed out of the house, also undressed and bareheaded, and the tall, young man in Shquiptar trousers pointed his pistol at him, seized him, and dragged him into the center of the courtyard. Confused and taken by surprise, Grgur made almost no resistance. But matters changed rapidly. In Ibrica's right hand shone a silver-mouthed pistol aimed at Grgur's bare breast, and in the hands of the young *sejmen* appeared a rope, with which, bending a little, he began to tie Grgur's hands behind his back.

Ibrica, till then sheltered by the horse, moved out of cover, and Akan took aim at his broad shoulders. But those shoulders kept shifting from right to left, their scarlet cloth shining. It seemed to Akan that he could even see Ibrica breathing. Grgur was standing a little to Ibrica's left; the shot might hit him. Akan did not dare to hesitate, for if they bound Grgur, then all the members of the household would be taken, and the Turks could easily kill him.

Intent on Ibrica's shoulders, Akan was deafened by his own shot, as if it had not been from his gun, as if he had heard someone else's. Ibrica tried to turn to his right, even raised his hand with the pistol, but, not finding the strength, fell full length on the trampled earth in front of the door of the house. As he fell, his horse started, but the reins were still gripped in Ibrica's hand, and it remained where it was, standing over its motionless master.

Ibrica's fall, his obvious death, changed the whole situation. Grgur and the young man who had started to bind him turned their heads toward Ibrica as if not believing that he could be dead. Grgur was the first to recover himself. He turned, gripped the young man, lifted him, and threw him to the ground, falling on him. The red-haired *sejmen* took his hands from the kitchen doorposts and pointed his pistol at Grgur, but Stamena seized him around the waist and pulled him back. At the house door, Milena, half-dressed and mumbling a prayer, snatched up the old ax that was kept behind the door. Elderly and heavy, she lifted the ax high in the air and went for the red-haired man, but from around the corner a gun appeared, certainly that of the other *sejmen,* whom Ibrica had sent to guard the other side of the house. The gleam of morning brilliance slid down the barrel as if to dull the smoke from it, and the shot made Milena sway. She stumbled two or three steps, holding the ax in the air, only to let go of it the next moment and, clutching her heavy stomach with her bare arms, twisted two or three times. She squatted suddenly and, crouching thus, turned on her left side, with her head resting on the kitchen doorstep. Stanija, fully dressed, rushed out of the house and seized the red-haired man's arms in such a way that the pistol barrel stuck out from beneath her armpit, so that the bullet could not touch her. Of all that had happened in front of the house, only that action of Stanija's did not surprise Akan. She was a Montenegrin woman and knew all about firearms. It moved him, and made her dearer to him.

Akan remembered that he must not lose sight of the man in the garden, who was still by the apple tree but had become uneasy after Akan's shot and, perhaps from the smoke, had discovered from where the first hostile shot had come. He aimed in the direction of the hornbeam. Akan slipped behind the trunk, and the shot broke off a twig above his head. It fell, twisting from branch to branch, into his hands.

He had to settle accounts with this man in order to help Grgur and the women. He stepped out from behind the hornbeam and fired his pistol.

In the courtyard Stamena had dragged the red-haired man to one side, holding him around the waist, while on the other side Stanija was struggling with him for his pistol. He finally fired the pistol wildly, dropped it, and thrust his hand into his belt, probably to take out a knife or a second pistol. But Stanija seized the pistol from the ground by the barrel and struck him on the head with it with such force that the stock broke and flew into the air. The red-haired man doubled up in Stamena's arms; she pushed him away, and he sat on the ground, legs crossed, holding his head.

Then the man behind the apple tree—Akan only then noticed that he was wearing a white skullcap, such as Albanians usually wear, and was tall and dark—leaped out of cover, drew his pistol, and aimed at Akan. They were quite close to one another, about thirty paces apart, and Akan could see two eyes, the dark eye of the pistol and the bright eye of the *sejmen,* glaring at him. Akan was convinced that he would hit him if he could fire first. But he could not; his hand was trembling, and he knew that if he fired before he was steady, he would miss and then be in a less enviable situation. The *sejmen* fired first. The smoke of the shot drifted away near Akan's left ear, and the *sejmen* rushed down the garden. Trembling because of the near miss, Akan tried to get a bead on him, but every few seconds he was masked by the trees. So he did not fire his pistol, thinking that it might be more useful later. He rushed to the courtyard.

Anto and the boy Trifun, who liked to creep into Grandfather's bed, appeared in the doorway of the house, and from around the corner another *sejmen* leaped out, probably the one who had fired at Milena, a small, bony man with enormous brown mustaches and wearing a red fez. He fired his pistol and then, seeing Akan running toward him, retreated behind the corner. The shot did not stop either Anto or the boy, and they rushed to help Grgur, who was still struggling with the other *sejmen.* The boy seized his right leg, and Anto caught hold of his right arm, but he shook himself free and pushed them away. They both fell backward.

Akan rushed up and, aiming his pistol at the man's temple, shouted: "Surrender, son of a bitch!"

As if waiting for this, the man submissively raised his hands above his head, and Akan rushed to the corner. The man in the red fez had already fled to the meadow, and with leaps too long for so small a man was running after the man in the white skullcap, shouting something to him. But the man in the white skullcap paid no attention, fleeing as fast as he could on long legs clad in thin black trousers; probably he thought that Akan or one of the Radaks was after him. He was already so far away that it would have been difficult to hit him even with a rifle, and Akan, disappointed, returned to the courtyard.

Grgur stood up, his lips broken and bloody and his shirt torn from his back. The *sejmen's* weapons, a short knife, a pistol, and a musket, had been thrown aside, and Grgur collected them, piling them on his arm like faggots. "Let's kill them with our teeth!" he remarked, spitting blood. Then he went up to Ibrica, collected his weapons, and turned him over with his foot, confirming gleefully: "Ibrica!" Straightening up, he went on: "You've turned his toes up, Akan! By God, if it hadn't been for you . . ." and only then, going over to the man the women had disarmed, who was holding his head in his hands, blood trickling through his fingers, did he notice Milena. She was trying to rise but could not do so, and struck her head dully against the doorstep. Grgur cried out: "Mother! She is wounded. Who wounded her?"

For a moment he was confused; should he run to help his mother or should he collect the weapons? But the women seemed to understand his uncertainty. Stanija stacked the red-haired man's weapons, and Stamena raised the upper part of Milena's body, sat on the doorstep, and cradled Milena's head in her lap.

"I'm wounded, too!" wailed Trifun, looking at his left foot, from which blood was oozing through the stocking. Though everyone heard the child, no one seemed surprised.

Everything seemed as it should be, even their mother's deathly pallor and trembling. There was nothing repugnant about Stamena's nakedness; her full, firm breasts thrust out from beneath her shift, from which all the buttons had been torn. And there was nothing strange about Stanija's masculine handling of the weapons. It was as if she had been handling them all her life. It was natural, too, that the *sejmeni* should be sitting alongside one another by the kitchen wall, as if that were their proper place and as if they could not behave in any other way. And it was most natural of all that it was Ibrica who was lying there, while his horse stood over him with drooping head, tapping every now and then with its hoofs but not trying to run away.

Akan noticed that Grandfather Grgur and Rade walked carefully around Ibrica, who was in their way, as they came out of the house, even as Anto and Trifun had done. This, too, seemed natural to Akan, because of the belief that whoever steps over a corpse will become a vampire, though he was not a believer and they, at that time, were not thinking about superstitions.

As might have been expected, other shots were heard—two louder and one weaker—from that part of the village where Pe-

trana's house was. And the imprecations of the two *sejmeni* who
were running away could also be heard.

"There are more of them," Grgur shouted.

"Indeed there are! Another four in each part of the village,"
Akan explained, rapidly loading his long gun.

"Then . . ." Grgur began to set out his forces. "You, Akan,
look after Vojin's side; I will help you. And you others . . ." He
paused, noticing Rade, and looked at him so questioningly that
Rade could not restrain himself and explained: "I was guarding
the windows. Grandfather Grgur told me to."

"All right, all right! I know you were not afraid. You, Rade,
and the old ones keep under cover and move slowly to help Stojan and his people. Shove these beasts"—he pointed to the
sejmeni—"into the stall." He began to distribute the arms, shouting: "My belt. Bring me my belt and some clothes."

Without a word, Akan motioned the *sejmeni* with his gun and
drove them around the house to the stall. Grandfather Pavle,
weary and unclothed, began to cackle joyously: "Aha, Turks!
Well come and well met! We've foxed you, you foxes, and now
you've been outfoxed. Did you bring them here to Grandfather
for him to grease their palms?"

"Forget it, Grandfather! Grgur ordered us to shut them up."

"Eh, well, Grandfather will escort them to their proper place.
It's a long time since we have had any beasts to shut in here."

On his return, Akan found Grgur stuffing Ibrica's pistols into
his belt, while Anto, kneeling, was covering Milena with his
leather jacket and shouting at her as if she were deaf: "Does it
hurt, my unfortunate one? Are you cold, my martyr?"

White and shadowy, suddenly thin, she looked at him with
clear, imploring eyes, trying to smile and to say something.

Grandfather Pavle shouted from above the house: "There they
are, there are the guilty ones!"

From Petrana's side of the village, along the fence at the foot of
the garden, two *sejmeni* in black cloaks and red fezes were moving stealthily. Rade ran toward them. The first, in yellow boots,
halted and raised his gun. "Lie down, Rade, lie down!" yelled
Grgur, as he knelt and took aim. Rade stopped, but did not lie
down, taking cover behind a pear tree. Akan, too, knelt and took
aim. Grgur fired. Almost at the same time, the *sejmen* fired—the

shot whistled over the house—then dropped his gun, seized his companion by the arm, and both leaped over the fence and fled downhill. Rade shot, from somewhere in the garden, and began to run after them, but Grgur shouted to him: "Come back. You're needed here."

Grgur again arranged his forces, angry at Rade. "Must everyone do as he likes! What would have happened if they had attacked us from the other side while we were defending you? Stay here. Load your gun. And take cover. You, Grandfather Pavle, are behaving like a child. You're as wide open as a sheet. Slowly now, bend down and crawl along the fence. That's it. And you, Father, wrap yourself up. First get dressed, then take a gun and guard the windows."

He arranged every position and appointed every task; not the smallest detail escaped him. He was considerate of everyone, but also inflexible, and it seemed to Akan that he could see Anto in him, but more decisive, Anto in his best days. "Take Milena into the house. Or at least cover her up. And you, Sister, tie up Ibrica's horse. Now he's our horse. Grandfather Grgur, look to Trifun's wound; bandage it and comfort him. Akan, we two must go to help Vojin."

Grgur and Akan, about five or six paces apart, moved toward Vojin's house, whence could be heard shooting and the barking of dogs. But they had scarcely managed to get out of the garden when two *sejmeni,* one in a gray surcoat reaching to the ground and the other in a jacket with a fox collar, burst out on the bank of the stream. They caught sight of Akan and Grgur about the same time as Akan and Grgur saw them. Both sides took aim. The man with the fur collar even knelt, and Grgur rested his gun on the branch of a plum tree.

Once again Akan saw two eyes, one above the other, the eye of the gun barrel and the eye of the man, seemingly huge above the spreading fur jacket and the black beard. He had no feeling of danger, as when he had taken aim at the man by the apple tree, perhaps because Grgur was there to see, at least, how he would be killed. All four guns spoke at almost the same moment, so that Akan did not know if he had shot first or last. A dull pain thrust his arm back and left it hanging by his side as if it were no longer his.

"The dog has bitten me," he shouted.

The man in the fur jacket slumped down, as if bowing; his fez fell off, and his bald head was half buried in the fur.

The other man, running, threw away his cloak and disappeared in the stream.

Grgur pulled out his pistol, the one Akan had brought with him from Peć, and moved off after the man who was still kneeling by the stream. But he, as if he had seen the movement of his adversary through his forehead, pulled out a pistol and fired before Grgur. Akan pulled out his pistol and ran, despite the pain, his wounded arm flapping. Without halting for a moment, Grgur fired once, twice, then, after jumping over the brook, a third time. But the man went on kneeling upright, looking calmly at Grgur and mumbling. Grgur came to within two paces of him. Blood was flowing from his beard, but, nonetheless, he lifted imploring hands to Heaven, turned toward the east, and bowed to the ground, praying. Grgur put his pistol to the bare skull, which the discharge turned into a bloody mess. Even then the man, shuddering, crouched in the same attitude of prayer.

"He won't die!" Grgur said angrily, pushing him with his foot.

Still crouched, the man toppled on his left side and slowly stretched out; forehead and face grew smaller and more compressed, unhappy and fretful, like a newborn child. From his chest, through his coffee-colored waistcoat with bronze, shining buttons, blood flowed from three holes.

"Shame about the jacket," Grgur remarked. "And you are bleeding badly. The bullet has smashed your shoulder. Run home and get Grandfather to bandage you. I will help Vojin."

One of the runaway *sejmeni* called out from above the village: "The *buljukbaša*, the *buljukbaša* has been killed!"

Akan made his way to the house. Blood was flowing from his sleeve down his fingers, draining all the strength from him, and every step seemed to him as if he had again been wounded, even more painfully.

The older Radaks were for the most part skilled in balms and poultices. And Anto, instead of more suitable implements, had a large penknife in which were inserted a saw, a pair of scissors, a gimlet, and an awl. This penknife, with a horn handle, he treasured as something of exceptional value. After Anto's arrest,

Grgur had inherited the penknife, always carrying it in his pocket tied to a black lanyard. On his way home Akan kept thinking of that penknife as a means of salvation, though also terrible, because of all its parts, so suitable for cutting, piercing, sawing, and probing wounds.

In the courtyard everything was again changed. Anto had turned back Milena's blouse as she lay stretched out on a coverlet in the middle of the courtyard and was washing the wound just below her breast with a rag dipped in plum brandy. She, ashamed, was trying to button her blouse, but all she could do was scrabble helplessly with her fingers. By her feet Grandfather Grgur was putting some ointment on Trifun's thigh, which had been pierced by a bullet. Stanija was squatting beside Grandfather, drawing the long blade of the penknife through a torch flame.

Akan was pleased to see the penknife. He started to express his pleasure at seeing it and to tell them about the pain from his wound, but Stamena, leaning over Milena with a cup of hydromel, interrupted him. "She wants to say something. What are you saying, Mother? Tell me."

Milena raised her head and tried to speak, but her head drooped to one side before Stamena was able to support it.

"She is dying," sobbed Anto, pushing aside the bottle and the rag. He stood up painfully, took two or three steps, and leaned with his right hand on the kitchen wall and cupped his forehead with his left.

The plum brandy gurgled from the overturned bottle. Anto mourned: "Wretched me! My martyr, my dear one!"

Trifun wailed: "Will I die, too?"

Akan noticed that something unusual was happening, far more unusual than the death of Milena. The house and the kitchen swayed, tilted, darkening the skies, while Grandfather Pavle shouted out of the darkness to someone about someone: "He is wounded. Hold, hold him, someone! He will fall, he will fall!"

It seemed to Akan that he heard voices, then recognized Grgur's and then Vojin's. That was incomprehensible, unbelievable, even comic, since only a few moments before he had left Grgur, who was going toward Vojin's house after he had been wounded. Mother had been lying in the courtyard and had died;

Father had said that she had died, and Grandfather Pavle had called out that someone was wounded and would fall. Now Grandfather Pavle was calling out from the brilliance: "He's come to! He's come to!"

Only then did Akan realize that it was he of whom they were talking. He had fainted just at the moment of his mother's death, either because of her death or from his own loss of blood. He had loved his mother, loved her more than anyone; she had been the only being whose love he had constantly been aware of ever since he had been conscious of himself as a person, not only in mind, but also in body, in everyday life. Life without that love seemed to him impossible and unthinkable. And now when that love had died, had been killed, all that remained was an empty meaningless void; everything had become dull and confused, transient and only partially intelligible.

He could follow the dispute between Grgur's voice and Vojin's.

Grgur's voice was angry. "Here there is no longer any existence for anyone!"

Then Vojin pointed out in his slow and deliberate manner: "Everyone is not like you. First of all, we must investigate everything; and send the women and children up the mountain."

"No, no! Blood has been shed! Blood! If Montenegro wins, then we shall come back. But now—summon the people; we must flee!"

Then a torrent of Radak voices burst out, furious, indistinguishable one from another.

"If they only look for the guilty ones?" "We are all guilty now." "Oh no, we're not! I am not guilty!" "You took up arms against the authorities." "What authorities? Those bandits?" "You talk as suits you best; now authorities, now bandits." "The bandits are the authorities." "Authority is from God—every authority." "They're all the same; as far as we're concerned, evil!" "The children; the most important thing is to save the children." "The men are the most important." "And how can you have men without women?" "What about us, the old ones? No one troubles about us." "Old men are of no value; they've served their term." "What about their wisdom, their common sense?" "We've spoiled ourselves; now we cannot agree about anything." "We never have been agreed." "Except in fairy tales." "And in bad times; evil has always brought us together." "And now it is bad times that divide us. In good times it is easy to agree."

Now Akan was aware that he would again be lost, that he was losing consciousness, that the voices and words around him were dying away, were being extinguished.

When he again came to himself, he heard Grgur. "Enough of this silly talk! Let's flee to Veliko! Whoever can carry a gun, step out and go to the foot of the garden."

Then Vojin: "Not there. Let us seek refuge in the mountain. Until we have looked into it. Even the authorities have had enough of this *buljukbaša.*"

"But you, Vojin, what have you to save? You don't even have children. As if you won't find enough land for someone to bury you in," Stojan jeered.

Akan thought: It's good that Stojan was not killed and that he is here. They are all here, except me. But I, too, must be here in front of the house, since I can hear them and can see the sky and the roof.

"Just because I have no children, I preserve the Radak traditions!" Vojin burst out.

Akan tried to rise and found he was able to move, though his wound kept him nailed to the spot. Someone's—Stanija's?—hand on his temples held him back. He could hear the mild tones of Grandfather Grgur: "Don't budge. It'll soon be all right."

It was not Stanija, but Rade who was bending over him, murmuring joyously: "And I would willingly have died for you. They say you will only be maimed in one arm."

"One is enough to trade with," Grandfather Pavle said in jest.

Grandfather Grgur explained to himself and the others: "The joint is undamaged. The bullet pierced his arm below the joint. I have taken out the bone splinters. And the bandage sits well. But the splints. I can't get them right; I will have to bind his arm to his body, so that he cannot wave it about."

"Is that sweat or water?" Akan asked, feeling his forehead.

"Both," Stanija replied in a low whisper, and congratulated him in the Montenegrin manner: "May your wounds be fortunate!"

"And Mother has died?" he asked.

Grandfather Grgur explained. "There was no hope for her.

The bullet hit her liver." Then he ordered him, in words and by painful flexings of his left hand: "Move your fingers a little. That's the way. Now it will be all right."

He was able to move his fingers, even though his arm had been strapped from shoulder to elbow between small boards. There were always such small boards in the house in case a sheep or a calf broke its leg.

"The nerves are healthy. It won't be as good as new, but you'll be able to use it."

"Keep quiet. That's the way it must be," Stanija explained with gentle words and still gentler caresses, though it was not clear to him what she meant, the bandaging of his wound or the division among the Radaks. But she was stroking his forehead, and her hand was pleasanter to him than Rade's had been.

Stanija was telling a story, almost excitedly. ". . . and in my district they say that Lazar Pecirep—there was no greater hero than he—was maimed in his left hand, but that did not hinder him, for when he aimed his gun he put his ramrod in the toe of his sandal. . . ."

Suddenly she was silent and blushed, aware that it was not proper for a woman to praise or exalt her husband or to talk too much before older persons, especially if they were men and especially alongside her dead mother-in-law. Akan leaned on the ground with his right arm and, with a little help from her, rose quite easily. But then it seemed to him that he would fall again, and he looked around for support. Rade took him by the hand, and Stanija held him under his elbow. Steadying himself, he pushed them away. "I can manage by myself. Go and help Grgur."

Women, children, and beasts milled around the house and the courtyard. The air was filled with wails, arguments, and threats.

Only around Milena and Ibrica was there peace and quiet. Milena was lying in the middle of the courtyard, on a coverlet, already dressed in her best clothes, a lighted candle at her head, while shawled old Radak women wept around her, keening softly. Ibrica was lying where he had fallen, but face upward and with open eyes. Petrana undressed him, saying, as if to herself, that it was a shame that such fine clothes should be buried in the earth when her children went naked. But when nothing was left on him but his pants she became embarrassed and stopped, and began to pile his clothes over her left arm. No one paid any attention; they merely walked around Ibrica's big flabby body—the only thing that seemed human about it was the huge wound in his chest—as they came in or out of the house. It did not occur to anyone to remove the body from in front of the doorstep.

This comparison of corpses, his mother's and Ibrica's, was unpleasant to Akan, who, though he could still hear movements and voices, could not orient himself in all the commotion around him. Two men—Grgur in the center of the courtyard and Vojin nearer the garden—were controlling this confusion, each in his own way and in different directions, though not hindering one another. Grgur was more excited than usual; his voice was more high-pitched and his movements abrupt. Vojin, on the other hand, was calmer than usual, slower and softer of speech. Those who wanted to stay in the village listened to him, to his reasonable arguments, while those who were getting ready to flee listened to Grgur, brusque and energetic.

What was inexplicable was that while the householders from Vojin's quarter for the most part supported him and those from Stojan's quarter followed Stojan—that is to say, Grgur—those from the center of the village, around Anto's house, for the most part wavered, choosing neither one nor the other. That division had been noticeable ever since the first rumors of the revolt, but now it had become tangible, harsh and inevitable, as if a decision between life and death, about the future, were for the most part dependent on where a man's house was situated and what land he worked.

Akan thought that this present split had its origins sometime far in the distant past, more distant than memory or tradition. No one could be certain when it had begun, and still less that it would come to a head at this time, just this clear, chilly morning. Perhaps everything had begun when the office of knez had gone to Anto's household. Or was the office of knez a consequence of some division? Perhaps the secret was in the unremembered division of the clan into three parts, in the threefold division of the meadows, pastures, and waters according to the position and quality of the land.

The disorder now came, for the most part, from the households and stock in the center of the village. It was only in Anto's quarter that no one knew who shouted what, while the dogs howled and the sheep strayed about, not sorted into flocks and without a shepherd.

There, too, wandered Mitar Drndar, the Radak from Plav, from Anto to Vojin. He had come the night before, too late to return to Plav the same evening, and had spent the night at Vojin's. Ibrica's raid had caught him by surprise, and now he did not dare go to Plav, for in Plav he would not be able to mention the name Radak. He had left his son, Mirko, there, and was worried about how to get word to him to flee.

Anto himself was undecided. Dressed in his fur jacket, he was sitting on the tree stump by the wall of the kitchen, looking furtively at Milena, as if he could not believe she was dead. To the men who asked his advice, and they were for the most part from his own quarter, he usually replied: "Ask Vojin," or "Ask Grgur," without paying the slightest attention to which faction they belonged. He was startled out of his daze by the shouting of the old man Milija. Akan, busy telling his little son, Anto, that they were making ready to go to more beautiful districts and better lands, did not know what Milija had been asking or what Anto had replied, till the old man began to scream out: "Are you knez? Or what are you? Order them! Shout at them, hit them, if need be! It doesn't concern me only, but the whole clan."

Anto shrugged his shoulders. Almost weeping, he replied: "Even my own sons are going, and they have not asked me."

"But your sons have trodden in blood, Turkish blood and who knows what other!"

Anto remained motionless, as if indecision had become his last, unassailable refuge.

Everyone was astonished at the change in Milija's sons. Having been silent, afraid of their father, they had not uttered a living sound, and now, of a sudden, they decided to go with Grgur's group. Paying no heed to the presence, still less to the lamentations, of old Milija, Stojan embraced Milija's middle-aged eldest son, Manojlo, who was known as Tokmak (Pestle) because of his great strength. "Eh, I always knew you were a hero and a brother!" Stojan clapped Tomak on the back. Clad in a strange fur jacket, which Akan felt that he had seen on someone else,

Tokmak was proudly stroking his long yellow mustaches, which reached down to his shoulders.

"Do you hear? Do you hear?" Milija shouted at Anto. "Children are divided from their father!"

"I cannot force anyone to do anything," Anto said in justification. "Have you seen Grgur and Vojin? It is as they decide."

"But even they do not agree. What shall I do? The number of mountainsides I have cleared! And now in my old age I must become a vagabond through the world—once more to clear mountainsides."

"I do not know even what I shall do myself, still less what you should do," Anto said, to pacify him, and added: "Go with your children, with your own blood, and take what God gives."

"With my children, with my blood! And when it comes to the pinch, they will leave me. Better I had scattered my seed on the wasteland!" the old man wailed.

Strutting proudly in the *sejmen*'s jacket—now Akan remembered that it was its owner who had wounded him; if it hadn't been so wide, he would perhaps have taken aim more carefully and have hit the *sejmen*—Tokmak was saying: "First they attacked Vojin; they didn't touch the rest of us. I heard Jelica crying 'Help! Help!' and ran out of the house with my shoes in my hand. I was just getting ready to go to the mill. I looked—and Vojin's house was surrounded. It was useless; our house is full of men, but we have no arms. The Turks knew that! Then, while I was wakening the others and making up my mind what to do, and they were grabbing scythes and axes, we again heard firing. I saw two Turks by Vojin's house fleeing downhill and one lying dead there above the brook. So I took his clothes, but the shoes were too tight, so I gave them to my youngest brother."

It had been quite different in Petrana's quarter, according to Stojan's account. There, Stojan had killed one *sejmen* and had seen the bloody trail left by the one Grgur had shot at when defending Rade.

Akan remembered the captured *sejmeni* and turned to Grgur. "What about those two prisoners? You've forgotten them."

"I haven't," said Grgur. "Stojan wanted to cut off their heads, but Vojin wouldn't let him. He says that he needs them to bear witness to the people of Plav that he is no rebel and has no evil in mind."

"False notes from those bagpipes!" shouted Grandfather Pavle, throwing a pile of bedcovers into the courtyard.

"Not so false," Grgur explained, not to Grandfather Pavle, but to Akan, Stojan, and Tokmak. "When we go, the Radaks who remain can put the whole blame on us. It won't matter to us."

"I wouldn't give him the prisoners," Stojan interrupted. "We must avenge our people! The wounded we can somehow or other overlook, but we must avenge Milena."

"The children into the panniers!" Grgur shouted to Stamena and Rade, who were leading the horses at the far end of the garden. "And hurry up! The Plav people won't be sitting with folded arms." Then to Stojan: "We daren't take revenge and make life harder for the other Radaks. Since they won't go, and we cannot force them, even if we wanted to, we must do what we can for them."

"Must we forgive the Turks our own mother?" Rade shouted, struggling to put a cushion on a packsaddle and at the same time leave free space for loading.

"We forgive them nothing. But we must preserve the Radak roots, even though we are tearing them up."

"What? Let the Turks . . . ? Not avenge our own mother?" Stanija whispered in astonishment to Akan, as she was bringing cooking pots from the kitchen. She uttered this with horror, as if it were a question of the most terrible sacrilege.

"Keep your mouth shut!" Akan retorted in a harsh whisper. Her mingling in family affairs always infuriated him. "She was his mother, and mine."

"You, Stojan," Grgur ordered, "muster all the armed men, and when the main body moves away, close the entrance to the valley. The horsemen are the most to be feared. They cannot get here from Plav before noon; that is until the *sejmeni* get there, and the Turks muster and decide what to do. But the Devil thinks only of evil; we must be on the move before then. I will take a dozen men and Tokmak and his brothers to break through the guards near Veliko if we should chance to meet them. When we have crossed the little river and reached the hills, you will follow

us slowly and guard our rear. If the Turks attack, you will have
nowhere to escape, among all those women and children. Greet
them with bullets. As for those two animals—I will think what to
do with them. I, too, would like to cut off their heads, just there
beside our dead mother, but I must listen to common sense. They
will be a godsend to Vojin, to wash his hands and justify himself."

"Best of all when heart and sense work together," Vojin commented gently, coming up beside Grgur. "I heard you talking
about those two and came so that we can settle the matter. I am
coming around to your opinion. Let us fly into the mountain till
we find out what will happen."

Stojan halted, Rade stopped loading the horses, and Stanija
leaped to the house door. Grgur looked at all of them, including
the dead Milena, as if he wanted to ask her, too. But because
everyone there, except the dazed Anto and the bewildered Milija,
was a supporter of the revolt, he was met only by cold, even
angry, glances. Not even Stamena wholly approved. She looked at
him, smiling slyly, as if she wanted to say: "Good, then, let it be
as you think. You cannot do otherwise. I know you!" Finally, he
scratched his head and asked Vojin: "Will you give me your word
that you will kill them if you do not come to an agreement with
the authorities?"

"I can't even promise you that," Vojin replied without hesitation. "I don't know how things will turn out. And I have heard
that even the Montenegrins, when they do not kill their prisoners
right away, have pity on them later. Perhaps it would be better to
send them away today, with a message to the begs saying that we
who have stopped here are not rebels, and asking them to protect
us from oppression. But first I must discuss it with my companions."

Grgur again looked around at his supporters, but found no
support, but also no audible disapproval. Suddenly he took off his
hat and beat it on the ground. "Bring them here. May the dogs
eat their own carrion!"

Everyone, even Stojan, went about his business. Vojin, without
a word, as if such a decision was quite comprehensible and in no
way unexpected, went to the stall to bring the prisoners.

Beating his hat, which the boy Anto had picked up and handed

410

to him, against his thigh, Grgur said angrily to himself: "It is enough that we are divided. Must we also give our blood because of Turkish blood?"

Vojin and the two prisoners, bareheaded and tottering a little, were making their way up the garden when Stanija again whispered: "Is there no one here who crosses himself in the name of the Trinity?"

Akan did not reply, for she had taken the words from his lips, and Stanija, with malignant joy on her face, went into the house to bring out her bridal dress.

The stock had already been collected in the garden, the horses loaded. But Stamena and Stanija were running to and fro bringing things out of the house and piling them on the already overladen horses, always adding something precious, necessary, essential. So, too, did the other Radak women and wives. And above the bundles, like little flowers, peeped the heads of inquisitive children.

"Get a move on with the stock," Grgur ordered, and shouted to Stanija and Stamena: "Enough! You can't take the whole house."

"Where shall I go?" the old man Milija wept.

"With your sons," yelled Grgur, and the old man tottered away, as if someone had cut the threads that held him together. "Good, good, Grgur, my son, just as you say."

Grgur was now speaking like the arbitrary and intransigent leader Anto had once been, and as every Radak was in his own family circle, some more, some less. He had finally taken over the rule of the household and the clan, becoming at one and the same time their father-confessor and their slave.

The drovers yelled more than was necessary at the obstinate animals. The bellowing of the cattle and the weeping of the women and the swearing of men mingled in a mad, despairing uproar. Stamena wrapped Vasa in a shawl, and when she was unable to calm her, slapped her little cheeks.

"Don't hit her!" Grgur yelled, and then added, quite unexpectedly: "Let the old people go with the stock. It's best they were on their way."

But Milija, when he reached the top of the garden, stopped and reconsidered. He would not go with the mass of the people and his sons' stock. He squatted on the ground, weeping and

411

beating his head. So he remained, between his past and his sons, between the clearings that had not been his and lands unknown and unpromised.

The courtyard emptied rapidly. Milena remained alone, covered to her head with a white linen cloth, alongside the naked Ibrica Buljukbaša. The candle at her head, unsheltered, had blown out; thin blue smoke rose between the house and the outbuildings. Akan felt apprehensive, overcome by grief for his mother and his own pain, and angry at having to leave Milena thus, alone under the skies beside an enemy.

Anto rose painfully and, leaning against the wall with his right hand, his left on the small of his back, said: "I will not go! I want to die as I have lived."

Grgur looked at him in astonishment, then took off his hat and beat it on the ground.

"You must come. I will not leave you to the Turks, that they boast, or to the Radaks, that they take a pride in your refusal."

"And Milena?" Anto remarked.

"We shall bury her. We will not leave her here."

"No matter! I will not go!" Anto repeated.

Grgur picked up his cap, dusted it against his thigh, and equally implacably, but more calmly, cut him short. "You must come! You are no longer knez, but our father. You dare not betray your own children, that men should reproach us, that our great-grandchildren be ashamed that we abandoned our martyr knez to the Turks to jeer at him and mock him. Here is Buljukbaša; take his horse. Let it be known who is knez, the man who under torture was a man and a Radak!"

Akan expected that his father would resist stubbornly and that Grgur's insistence would be in vain. But there was in Grgur and in Anto, in the whole Radak clan, a response to authority and rule, which Akan had never, not even now, fully understood.

As though he had already discussed it with his father, Grgur went on: "Rade, Rade, bring Buljukbaša's horse. Mount your father and get a move on. You behind Father, to be with him if he needs you. And you, Akan, go with the women and the loads; since you cannot fight, at least keep some order among them."

The uproar of the stock and the drovers had died away, and the people and the loads were gathered in the garden. Rade untethered Buljukbaša's horse and led it from the garden into the yard. The horse shifted uneasily from foot to foot, pricking its ears. Anto stopped between the horse and Milena, then turned back, knelt, and kissed Milena on the forehead. Grgur helped him to rise and led him to the horse. But Anto gently resisted and, leaning on Grgur, went toward the house. When he reached the threshold he crossed himself, knelt, spread his arms over the doorstep, and kissed it. Grgur again helped him to rise, brushing the tears from his eyes with his left hand. Stanija and Stamena sobbed, and Grandfather Grgur wailed. Akan, too, shed tears, and on Rade's cheeks the tears ran unhindered till he brushed them away in embarrassment. Only Anto did not weep.

Rade and Grgur helped him to mount, and he, taking the reins in his hands, said: "Since it is so fated, then let it be."

Grandfather Pavle ran out of the house, laughing at Heaven knows what, but, noticing that everyone was crying and realizing the misfortune, he suddenly turned serious. "I thought . . . I don't know what I thought. I didn't think anything!" And he, too, burst into tears.

"Let's get going, with God's help." said Grgur, taking off his hat and crossing himself.

"Don't forget the ikon," Anto shouted from the horse.

Stamena, through her sobs, reassured him. "We've got it, Father."

Grgur seized Buljukbaša by the legs and dragged him to the top of the garden. "Not to dishonor our threshold," he explained.

Then he and Tokmak took the corners of the coverlet on which Milena was lying. They carried it with difficulty into the garden, but the coverlet started to slip out of their hands and they had to lower it.

"We should have remembered to make a bier," Tokmak remarked. Grgur looked right and left and, noticing the hurdle used for carrying rubbish leaning against the fence below the house, went resolutely over to it, seized it by the handles, and with two or three blows shook out the rubbish that had remained on the mesh. He laid the hurdle beside Milena, and, with Tokmak's help, took the corners of the coverlet, lifted it, and placed Milena on the hurdle.

The coverlet covered the whole corpse. But Milena was so tall that her legs hung stiffly from the knee down. Had it been at any moment but this, and had it been anyone but Grgur, it would have been both ugly and horrible for a son to carry his own mother on a rubbish hurdle and with her thick legs, in black woolen stockings, hanging almost to the ground. Yet no one felt repulsion or made any comment. Like the killing of the *sejmeni* at dawn, so also this bearing of his mother on a rubbish hurdle, without mourning and without a funeral procession, seemed natural.

The group of Radaks moved off. The road led downhill and a little to the left, but the whole crowd, with the loads, moved toward the right, toward the stream, on whose banks, just below the stripped corpse of the *sejmen,* those Radaks who were not leaving the village had gathered to say farewell to their clan brothers. They had already said farewell to those who had gone with the stock. They were calm, standing there silently, as if gathering their forces for a fresh wave of weeping and despair.

Neither for the futigives nor for those who were saying farewell to them was it of any significance that the whole district was flooded with the clear blueness and weak sunlight of Indian summer. Nor did it have any significance for Akan, though he wondered that this was so. On any earlier, different occasion, everyone would have noticed the splendor and mildness of the day; the old people would have dragged themselves from the chimney corners into the sun, children would have hastened to unfinished games, and the cattle would have snatched at the patches of green grass that the sun had coaxed out of the earth. Now no one noticed, or if they had noticed, as Akan had, the joyful radiance and clarity, the pleasant sunlight and the clear skies would have clashed with what was happening, and hindered the feeling of desolation and hopelessness, grief and mourning.

The Radaks embraced one another, weeping and sobbing, and Milena remained in the center of the meadow, legs stretched out beyond the hurdle, her face still, white, severe, and terribly alone. The laden horses stopped and snatched at tufts of grass while awaiting their leaders. Only the children in the saddlebags, taken up with the ceaseless movement and the novelty of the situation, did not cry.

It seemed like an enormous and terribly inconsolable funeral procession, as if not only men were being accompanied to death, to the chill of the graveyard, but also fields and meadows, orchards and pastures, houses and stalls, and even the sky and the sun, nowhere else so clear and beneficent, so joyously awaited, as on those lonely, clear heights. Even Akan, who had long awaited a chance to get away from the village, shed tears. It was not so much sorrow for what was taking place, not even for his dead mother, toward whom he realized with shame that he was almost indifferent, but for something that had been and would never return.

Just on this meadow he had played standard-bearer and soldiers when he was a child; by that stream he had placed childish water wheels, made with his knife in his spare time while tending the cattle. And that alder, now old and rotting and covered with reddish lichen, was still there and, so it seemed to him, still lived and walked among the Radaks. Yet from it sprouted the fresh twigs from which he had at one time made pipes and whistles. Some other child would now make pipes of its green branches. And other men would till these lands. He wept as if he had never wanted this departure. But he knew that he could no longer reject it. It was inevitable. It was not a migration, like those of the birds and the nomads, who followed the sun and lived their own lives, but something quite different. They would have to change their former lives, some for one reason and some for another, even though in their new homeland it would be neither better nor more beautiful. He thought about that calmly and coldly, but the tears kept running down his cheeks as if he had not at last realized what he had always wanted, and for which he had shed his own and a brother's blood.

He could not decide who were unhappier, those who were staying or those who were going. They pitied one another equally. The one who was really dead—Milena—and those who were wounded, it seemed that no one pitied.

Tormented by pain and spasms of unconsciousness, Akan had been seeing men and things and events in fragmentary, disconnected snatches. Now, through his tears, the whole scene took form and then once again disintegrated; houses and gardens merged into red and gray spots, meadows and fields melted away and were transformed into green waters, crags and peaks fled into a shining height, and the blue sky, with its flecks of cloud, plunged down into the valley.

Stamena was weeping, silently, her face swollen—like the fields and meadows flooded by the waters. Stanija, too, wept, though Akan had not expected it of her, or of himself: from infinite distances she raised her tiny fists and struck herself on her thin chest. Grgur was weeping, like a woman, like Stanija. The contractions of his face fell into abysses of fields and gardens, and his fists seemed to be tearing down the mountains and striking them on his head. Anto did not dismount, though he, too, wept, but that was somewhere high up in the mute, dismembered heavens. He leaned down painfully so that the older men could kiss his hands, but even they had invisible and expressionless faces. Vojin wept, but, like a rock, without a movement of his dense eyebrows or his broad mustaches. The old man Milija, at the top of the garden, was wailing as if pieces were being torn out of his living flesh. Like her husband, Jelica was weeping, her face stony white, her clenched fists pressing against her breasts. Raduša wept like a living person, as she should; quiet, hunched up, wiping away her tears with her kerchief. So, too, wept Rade, head bent, wiping his tears away with his hand.

Just as the weeping and wailing had begun to slacken, Anto, who ever since he had mounted his horse and submitted to Grgur's order had found his old assurance, called out in a voice too loud and too strong for a sick and tortured man: "Let us move! Farewell, all you who remain!"

That again raised a storm of weeping and wailing. "Farewell!" "Remain and be happy!" "Good journey!" "May good luck be with you!" Thus sobbed the Radaks, separating quickly into two groups, as if driven by powerful unseen forces. Those with Anto hurriedly, as if fleeing, moved away downhill, and those with Vojin slowly, across the brook.

No one turned around, as if they feared that they would go back. Something unforgettable, eternal, had been torn from them which they could only stifle in oblivion.

But they had not moved more than a hundred paces when something unexpected happened, in full view of all the Radaks on both sides. On the slope above the stream two women stopped and followed Anto's group with their eyes. Akan did not notice them, for, like the others, he had not turned around, hastening to get as far away as possible as soon as possible from his home and his memories. Grgur dropped the end of the hurdle on which Milena was lying, and Rade dropped the halter by which he was leading Anto's horse. Both ran toward the stream. Then Akan and the others turned; and so, too, did those Radaks who had stayed with Vojin. It was not quite clear whether Jelica and Raduša had first stopped or Grgur and Rade had first run. Akan saw how the women were standing, each a little apart from the other, and how the two men rushed toward them, each also a little apart from the other. As far as Akan was able to see, it was Grgur who ran first, though he was not sure, but it was obvious, since they had run back separately, that Rade had not been following Grgur and had gone back of his own accord. He could not understand what those two intended to do, or which of the two women had first stopped and turned.

Grgur was the first to leap the stream, and, without halting, went right toward Jelica, behind whom, about a dozen paces away, stood Vojin, undecided and curious. Rade leaped the stream and went toward Raduša, who was standing about five or six paces behind Jelica. Both brothers approached the now smiling women almost at the same time.

Grgur took Jelica by the shoulders. She at first made a movement as if to take his hand and kiss it, as was the custom for young women toward men of their husband's family. Instead, perhaps because Grgur stopped her by a scarcely perceptible movement, or because she herself thought better of it, she gently took Grgur in her arms, and the two kissed on both cheeks. Rade and Raduša, however, embraced at the same time, kissing one another several times on the face, on the eyes, and, finally, on the lips. Then suddenly, as if by the blow of some invisible sword, they separated.

Grgur returned slowly, quiet and thoughtful, but with a gentle smile on his lips; that same smile and that same pensiveness, or something even stronger, hovered over Jelica's face.

Vojin continued standing there, waiting for his wife and his sister, now smiling benignly, even joyfully.

Rade went back as if he could no longer see the path before him; he stepped in the water and stumbled over a stone on the bank, bewildered, exalted, while Raduša watched him go with a bemused expression and half-closed eyes. Tears fell down her pale face. No one, by either word or movement, showed any astonishment at what they had seen, though it was unusual and in other circumstances would have seemed improper, for Grgur and Rade had already said farewell to Jelica and Raduša at the same time as all the others. Even Stamena, holding Vasa, looked on silently, smiling sadly and, like Vojin, almost good-humoredly.

Someone shouted that somebody should take the reins of Anto's horse, since it would not answer to Anto's weakened hands, and Rade, as if he had been expecting that, ran straight back to the horse, and Grgur again seized the hurdle bearing his mother's body.

All went to the graveyard; no one else halted or turned around. All walked silent and depressed down the hill. There Grgur and Tokmak stopped, with two other young men, to bury Milena. Rade and Akan joined them, to say farewell to their mother. The grandfathers stopped, too, Grandfather Grgur to choose the grave into which to lower Milena, and Grandfather Pavle in order not to miss the occasion. The others went across the little river and halted in the open space opposite the graveyard, under the slope of the hill, to wait for Grgur and the others to conduct the burial. Anto went with them, still on horseback. He did not want to be present while they dug the grave; either he feared that he would not be able to overcome a grief too great, improper for the burial of a woman, or he felt—or so he had said when telling his sons to bury their mother—that he had said his farewell to Milena when he had said farewell to the house.

"Open this grave," Grandfather Grgur ordered. "It is my wife's grave, her mother-in-law."

"Daughter-in-law and mother-in-law, even in the grave they'll be at odds and not even," broke in Grandfather Pavle.

But no one paid any heed to his words. "It is best that it be this grave," went on Grandfather Grgur. "And it is more suitable that she lie here, since there is no place for her near her own mother."

The young men struck with their pickaxes. Even though they hurried, it was perhaps half an hour before their pickaxes rang on the coffin lids. They quickly raised them, one after the other; in the grave were bones and scraps of clothing.

"That is all that is left of her!" said Grandfather Grgur, taking out a darkened skull. He shook the earth from it and kissed it.

"She was a mountain fairy!" said Grandfather Pavle, almost weeping. He snatched the skull from his brother's hand and began to kiss it.

Grgur gently took the skull from his hands, kissed it, and held it out to his brothers to do the same, then put it back in the grave.

"Shall we?" he asked.

From the far side of the brook came a cry, and Stamena ran stumbling across the planks of the little bridge. When she reached the grave, she threw herself on Milena's body, kissing her face and bathing it with her tears. "I never knew any other mother, mother mine!" she sobbed.

With his sound arm, Akan pulled Stamena away from the corpse and drew her to him. Stanija also embraced her dead mother-in-law, but without tears or sobs. Then the others began to kiss her, and finally her sons: Grgur with moist eyes, Rade quivering as with long-withheld sobs, and Akan, forgetting Stamena and his wound, though his movements tore fresh pieces of living flesh from his shoulder. Only then did he feel the sorrow which had been restrained or absent all that terrible yet so ordinary morning. It was not the cold, lifeless body of his mother that lay there, the lips that had kissed him, the eyes that had watched over him, the soft lap that had rocked him to sleep, and the plenteous life-giving breasts, tranquil and undemanding, but his whole life. Two of his children had died, but she had always been there, from the cradle. Only his mother had been innocent of everything, of past sufferings, momentary failures, and painful dreamings. Then, he had been without crimes and without hatreds, in the pure unsullied joys of a child at the breast. With his mother died not only everything by which he had lived till now, but, it now seemed to him, all the hitherto undarkened brilliance of his hopes and beliefs. "Mother mine," he sobbed, wishing to merge with her and disappear in the newly opened grave, dank and black under the gay and shining sunlight.

Grgur raised him from the grave, taking him gently under his wounded arm, so as to hurt him as little as possible. As if he could read Akan's feelings, he sighed: "What will you? We must go on

living," and took him to Stanija, who slipped under his sound
arm, putting it across her shoulders to serve as a support and at
the same time asking support and tenderness from him. He
leaned on her, tired, unhappy, aware that her shoulders skillfully
and gently relieved him of pressure, and her hands, like a nest,
like a bosom, welcomed his.

They buried Milena unwashed, without requiem, even without
lighted candles; no one paid any heed to that, though all knew
what ought to have been done. But when they placed her in the
grave and began to fix the covering, Grgur noticed that her face
was bare. He leaned over the edge and pulled the cloth across her
face. As soon as Milena was lowered into the grave, Akan calmed
down, though still desolate and, he felt, forever absorbed in the
idea of dying over his mother's body.

The grave was soon ready. They put back the marble stones at
her head and feet, as well as the bushes that had been there, so
that there should be no trace of fresh earth, and it would not be
noticed that anyone had been buried a short time before.

Grgur gave the order to move and led the way. But looking
back, before the level ground of the graveyard began to slope
down toward the little bridge, he saw Grandfather Grgur sitting
calmly, with legs crossed and the staff in his hands, on the grave
of his father or grandfather; the graves were by now almost level
with the soil, and only he remembered exactly whose it was.
"Come on, Grandfather!" Grgur shouted.

"No. I'm not coming," Grandfather Grgur replied calmly.

"What? Not coming? But you're on your way."

"Yes. I started. But I have thought it over again. I will stay
here. I cannot go away from here. . . ." He had not thought
much about what he wanted to say, so, waving both arms, he
ended: "From the graves."

"What? What's come over you? Anto is going! At home you
said nothing about it."

"Anto is different. You still need Anto. If he dies soon, he will
still live long for you. But I have nowhere else to live. I have lived
already—and I have lived too long."

From the far side of the river, urging his horse toward the
bank, Anto shouted. He had clearly understood the sense of the

conversation. "Let him be, Grgur! Let him stay! Why torment him?"

"But the Turks will put him to the torture," Grgur protested to Anto, to himself, to everyone.

"They won't. I'll hide," said Grandfather Grgur. "I'll hide with Vojin, or somebody else. And if I cannot run away, I'll defend myself. . . . I can die," and courageously, even youthfully, he slapped the pistol in his belt.

"All right, Grandfather, stay, and may luck be with you!" said Grgur. He went back and kissed his hand. Beside him, holding the rifle Akan had been carrying before he was wounded, stood Grandfather Pavle. "I'm staying, too," he shouted. "All our lives my brother and I have quarreled and taken different paths. But he is my brother. I have no one except him and these graves."

Grgur moved toward the little river, and the others after him, but Stanija, slipping from under Akan's arm, asked Rade to support him and ran back, agitated and elated. When she came to Arsenius' grave, where that summer the head of her brother Vučeta had been buried, she flung herself down on the mound, embracing the gravestone as if it were a living man.

She did not stay there long, nor did anyone hear her words or her kisses, but when she returned, with head raised and the black whips of her hair escaping from her kerchief, her tense face and dry, staring eyes shone with an ecstatic happiness and a proud sorrow.

PART FOUR

UNDER THE COLORS

Rain was falling and the armies mustering.

The rain, naturally, paid no heed to men or armies. The armies did not dare to allow each other to pay any heed to the rain.

Pouring down from the hills in streams and rivulets, the waters merged in the same river to flow peacefully down the valley to a still-larger river and thence into the sea. The armies, too, flowed down from the hills into the same valley, by squads and battalions, by clans and tribes, each flowing to meet the other, searching out weak spots in the defenses, each aiming to outwit the other or forestall the other's intentions, merging into a single wave or splitting up into countless smaller waves to attack and penetrate, to cut off and outflank that other army, transforming these rivers of living men into heaps of corpses to be left to the earth and the sky, to the birds and beasts, and to their kinsmen, if any such were left alive.

Wheresoever they flowed from, the rivers met and merged anonymously in the same sea, but the armies did not meet except in death.

It was the most unsuitable time for human gatherings and meetings. Autumn was scarcely over, and winter had not yet come, and the rain was such that no man would have left even his blood enemy outside his doors. But the armies fought despite the weather, despite everything. When it is needful, when war must be waged, it is better to fight than to rest. It is sweeter than love, more precious than any treasure, even than human life.

Under Voivode Marko Miljanov were two armies: the first made up mainly of fighters from the Kuči tribe, the second, for the most part from the Vasojević tribe. In both these armies there were also fighters from other clans and settlements, especially from those on the upper course of the Lim, where the armies had broken through. It had been agreed that the Kuči and the people from around their district should follow the right bank of the Lim, with the aim of taking the little town of Plav, at the junction of the Lim with the Plav lake, which was the most important settlement in the whole valley, while the Vasojevići and the districts around them—which were not fully mustered and had not yet reached the battlefield—should thrust up the left bank of the Lim, as the other wing of the Voivode's army. The army would then continue its advance along the valley of the Ljuča, the main inflow into the lake, until it could take Gusinje, about three hours' march from Plav, the second and last important objective in the whole Lim basin.

Marko Miljanov was commander in chief of both armies, but at the same time was in direct command of his own men from Kuči. Such a command had a distinct disadvantage, not only because it provoked the jealousy of the Vasojević leaders, but also because it meant that he could not control both armies directly. But the nature of the terrain and the battle order of the enemy, the men of Plav facing the men of Kuči and those of Gusinje facing the Vasojevići, necessitated such a division. What was more ominous, a sudden rising of the Lim was expected, and there was no bridge across it for three hours' march, the whole way from Plav to just below Murina.

Another disadvantage for both of the Voivode's armies was that they had to advance through the plain along the Lim, for the most part slightly over five hundred yards wide, which exposed them to the attacks of enemy horsemen. Though they were not numerous, the Voivode's armies had no horsemen at all. This restriction of maneuver and this danger the Montenegrins could counterbalance by the nearness of the hills and the undergrowth and possibly by the speed of their advance, upon which the Voivode was counting.

The key to the battle for both sides was Plav, because of its political and economic importance and its strategic situation at the throat of the two valleys.

The Montenegrins had also to reckon with the possibility that the Shquiptar tribes might rush to the help of the Plav and Gusinje begs, not so much because of their community of faith, and still less because they supported the Turkish Empire, but because they, too, aimed at descending into the Lim Valley. The Shquiptars knew that the begs would not give them the land, but they felt instinctively that the lordship of the begs had had its day. If the Montenegrins installed themselves there, their longing to acquire and cultivate those plentiful valleys would have to be postponed indefinitely. It was therefore of paramount importance for Marko Miljanov to take Plav before the Shquiptar clans made a move, for their army, unsupported by any permanent state organization, would withdraw and disband after such a victory.

Ali-beg Šabanagić, too, had reckoned on this. He had to hold and defend Plav at any cost until the reinforcement of the Shquiptar clans arrived. Plav itself was difficult to defend. The Montenegrins were skilled at taking stone kulas and would at once set fire to the town and raze it. Ali-beg had, therefore, to fight a battle for Plav, but in front of Plav. He knew this from earlier fighting and made his dispositions accordingly.

The Voivode's Kuči army, which had crossed the bridge below Murina, pressed onward up the right bank of the Lim without serious opposition as far as the village of Novšić, close to Plav.

His Vasojević army, which had advanced up the left bank and whose vanguard was for the most part made up of men from the upper Lim, also met with no serious resistance until it was close to Plav, at a point rather higher than where the enemy was awaiting the Kuči army. At the point where Ali-beg was awaiting the Kuči forces the Lim ran close to the hills, so that the plain was limited to a width of a little more than a hundred yards, whereas he awaited the Vasojevići at the bridge before Plav, at the outflow of the Lim from the lake. There, too, steep hills rose from the shores of the lake and the marshes around it, preventing further advance into the Gusinje plain. Ali-beg was aware that the Vasojevići, even if they should break through toward Gusinje, would not be able to threaten it as long as there was a force behind them at Plav. The key to this maneuver was the bridge, which was not difficult to defend, for the Lim was no longer fordable.

Thus the armies, the Voivode's and the Pasha's, at the beginning of December found themselves facing one another, each side holding back from a final settlement until reinforcements arrived. The Voivode's forces, before the arrival of the Shquiptars, were slightly larger, about five thousand fighting men. But since the Pasha's men were on the defensive, the forces might be considered equal, as was their will to win.

It was a clash of two worlds, but also something beyond that. It was a settlement of accounts between the Montenegrins, for whom death on the field of battle was the joy of existence, and the begs and Moslems, who had nothing left to them but a hero's death for their faith and for their lordship.

On the one side, Marko Miljanov was an incarnation of Montenegrin heroism, the fusion of Orthodox faith, the insurgent *raja,* and the Serbian myth of Kosovo. On the other side, on the frontiers of an empire in dissolution, Ali-beg Šabanagić was an incarnation of the still-vigorous mountain nobility, supported by its pride and imbued with the spirit of the youngest and most fanatic of the great religions. It was a clash between inevitable growth and power, undermined but still unwavering. Voivode Marko had defeated larger and more powerful armies, but he had never clashed with so powerful an opponent, one who was, so to speak, on his own threshold, defending his faith and his life. To Ali-beg, moreover, he was not something new or unknown. For thirty years past, Ali-beg had defended himself from the Vasojevići under Miljan Vukov, who had invaded the Lim Valley, incited the serfs to revolt, and taken from him one village after another, wiping out his faith and destroying his lordship.

It is not known what these two said to their armies, though both of them, it is recalled, encouraged their men on the eve of the battle, knowing from tradition and experience that men die most willingly for the eternal. But this is how the Voivode, Marko Miljanov Drekalović, might have spoken to his men at Novšić on the eve of the battle:

"I do not say to you: Fight heroically. Fight you must; you would not be men or Serbs if you did not fight. Therefore I say to you what I have always said: Fight well and fight worthily.

"Even God fights against the powers of darkness and against Satan, so he has ordained that all whom He has created must live in evil and amid the troubles of our life. In our narrow lands, where even a corpse has nowhere to stretch its legs, fighting is our daily bread, black and bloody, and heroism is earnest, terrible, and real. For five hundred years we have taken our communion with enemy blood, the blood of the infidel.

"Do not be deceived. War is an evil beyond all other evils. In it man defends his life and forgets the name of man. For what can be worse than to take away the life that God has given? What is uglier than to soil the human countenance with which God has divided us from the animals? But for wretched man, for you, my falcons, there is no choice. Force does not call on God! Only by force can force be resisted.

"See how God has created this lovely land for man, has linked the mountain and the fertile plain, the hills and waters, and in it wretched Serbs must conceal their faith like bondslaves, like naked beggars, and are ashamed of their name and of their faith.

"Know then! Act according to the highest law, both God's and man's, where evil is driven out by evil. For were it possible to drive out evil with good, then there would be no evil. That is the terrible destiny of man! That is the responsibility laid upon you! Blood is the only blessing on our arms; by it we bring judgment and deliverance into confusion and darkness, by it we open the way to human justice and to Serb freedom!

"But do not forget that you are men, when you are intoxicated by human blood, the blood of our brothers or of our enemies. You must be men, and when you kill, cut, and burn, then you must be more than ever men. We fight only to preserve human uprightness, the image of God in man. Respect enemy women as you would your own sisters and wives; honor the old and feed the enemy's children as if they were your own. Do not plunder and cut down your prisoners, but bandage their wounds, for their wounds are from your swords, so that your swords do not rust in inhumanity. And let your hands avoid injustice, that your grandchildren may not be shamed at your victory!

"Ali-beg and the Moslems and Turks say: 'This is our land, for we have the rule over it.' In truth, five hundred years ago they took it by their swords because of the disloyalty and greed of our own nobles. It is not their land, but Serb land, where every blade of grass has been watered by our sweat and our tears.

"Our churches and our songs tell us that we lost the empire at Kosovo because of the sins of our tsars and our nobles against justice and human freedom, against the law that binds men to God and other men. They took their lie for truth and their pleasure for the people's good. They forgot the language of their own people and trod human honor underfoot. They gave their wives and sisters to the foreigner for the shadow of power and lordship. Whoever is healthy to the marrow no storm can harm; new branches will break out from a healthy tree, even if it is broken, whereas from a rotten stump come only toadstools and lichens. They have reaped what they have sown; all trace of them has been obliterated. Had it been only they who were buried at Kosovo! But with them were buried those who were blameless—the Serb people and the Serb state.

"The Serb song was changed into lamentation, and the Serb idea was hidden in the caves.

"Now, by your arms, the Serb sings again, and Serbdom flashes from your swords to the four corners of the earth!

"Over these mountains is Kosovo. We have thrust forward to its threshold, and there will we die, to make smooth the way for our children in trouble and in hope, in the eternity of Serbdom. The martyrs of Kosovo lead you and summon you to death and glory —to immortality!

"This is not the hour of vengeance and hatred, but of justice and of truth.

"You must act worthily, die wisely, fearlessly, sparing yourselves less than the enemy, preserving your lives as the greatest treasure granted you, that you may live them out in joy and happiness, yet pour them out unhesitatingly for the good of men, for freedom, and for honor.

"Facing you is a heroic and warlike, noble and proud race, whose faith and glory you have already trodden down and whose very threshold you have reached today in order to drive it out. In the name of the Serb past you must conquer the future while they defend what is left them of their lordly existence. They know this, too; they will lose their very existence if they do not win. You cannot conquer them by heroism or by skill, or by your united heroism and skill, but only by a stronger will to live, by resolution that by your death you will found a Serb life, a more just humanity. Only those conquer who love humanity and who do not regret their own lives.

"Can you hear their horses whinnying? They are calling for new masters. Do you hear the winds blowing over the heights? Already they are singing songs about you.

"Who wants to survive must fight and suffer, that by his death a new life be born. Who does not long for immortality is not worthy even to live out his life as a man.

"For the land whose sowing we shall reap in the lives of our children! For the men who will recall our names and keep unquenched the fire of justice and of freedom! For Serbdom and for God's right!"

And Ali-beg Šabanagić might well have exhorted the begs and their Moslem brothers with these words:

"I am afraid to utter a word. For everything is so clear that words can only confuse. We are defending not only our faith and our honor, our existence and our rule, but also our hearths and our ancestors. Should we lose, our true faith, the sweetness of our existence and the sweetness of immortality, will be dragged in the mud and be transformed into suffering of body and soul. Not only shall we lose our subject villages and have to submit to our former serfs, but also our very roots, which we have planted here as warriors of the Prophet, will be torn out and our seed will be exterminated.

"The mountains will sob and the waters weep in lamentation for us, the roads will burst asunder sorrowing for the hoofbeats of our chargers, and the heavens will darken without our prayers, and of us only a memory will remain.

"Even if it were not so wherever the Montenegrins have set foot, it would be here. Here it is not a battle for power and lordship, but for life and death. Here it has always been so. It cannot be otherwise. They have already reached our threshold; they have brought dust and ashes into our houses and have raised their swords against our gates.

"We cannot be defeated, for only living men can suffer defeat. There is nothing left to us except to die for our descendants and our name! We have not even been given the choice between life and death; no one can take from us the sweetness of dying for our faith and our homes, for our bliss and our perpetuation.

"We no longer fight for what we are: few of us are left to be what we have been. We fight for immortality and for the lives of our children.

"Even if our empire has grown rotten, we have not! Let the storms devastate our gardens; from the roots fresh shoots will again break out. Nothing is more lovely or greater than life, even if man pass through it a thousand times. But death for one's line and one's faith is still greater and more beautiful. By it one lives while others rot.

"This battle will be forgotten, but our line and our world will go on living if we die for them like men, wisely and heroically. These waters and these gardens, which you have tended, and these mountains, which have rejoiced you as children and as old men in the morning and in the evening, will recall your name in song and in story as long as they last, if you consecrate to them your blood.

"A more terrible enemy has never stood before you, against the faith of the Prophet, against the human race and the sweetness of human existence.

"Can you hear how they shout?

"They are rejoicing in the evil they will wreak upon us, our čardaks and our gardens. They will make their beauty desolate and will take away the treasures our ancestors have collected and tended. They will raze the wonders and tread underfoot the wisdom the East has brought to man.

"They fight as one man and die one beside the other; only to war do they go with song. We have driven them back many times, and they have always returned. Only their dead do not return. Fight them to the last man, on the thresholds of our houses, before your terrified women and children, before your open graves.

"They have no faith but hatred of us, no joy but in our misfortunes. They are drunk with heroism and with our blood. They are an evil to those whom Allah punishes, for our sins and our redemption before the Prophet and our kin.

"Their leader is the Voivode Marko Miljanov, who has won his title by the sword and with his sword has drenched the land of Zeta with Turkish blood. He pays less heed to the Prince of Montenegro than to his own horse! He gives his all for the Serbian idea. Do not rely upon skill or courage against him. You cannot conquer him; but you can exterminate his army and yourselves.

"He will win who has the greatest will to die.

"For the land which our ancestors traced out by the sword! For the beauty and eternity of human life! For Allah and the Turkish name!"

Stirred by the exhortations of their leaders and their chiefs, their guslars and their *zurla* players, lighting fires and roasting meat, singing and amusing themselves by firing off their rifles, the two armies camped facing one another in anticipation of the morrow's combat and made their preparations for it.

The Radaks had been scattered through the Voivode's army, for the most part as guides and couriers.

They had been scattered before, as soon as they had left their former lands and fled from the Turks. On the first day they had stopped in the village of Veliko, a group of hamlets scattered through the Lim gorges up to the edge of the mountains. There had not been enough room for everyone in the same hamlet, so they had dispersed through all of them, for the most part in barns and stables, so that they were not even within earshot of one another. Even on the first day there was grumbling—not because they wanted to go back, but because they were separated and had halted so near the frontier that every skirmish might force them to leave again. They had lived too long together and in the same place to become reconciled to gypsy wandering and temporary accommodation.

But they had to resign themselves to being apart, for nowhere could they find enough free land to found a new Radak settlement. Only families had remained together, and even among brothers there was a desire to divide, to go in various directions.

In the few days before the arrival of the Voivode's army, some had begun to leave Veliko, Grgur among them, and cross to the left bank of the Lim, to settle in the villages there. But, as at Veliko, there was no free land, so they awaited the outcome of the battle between the Voivode and Ali-beg to move into land newly acquired for Montenegro. Some were preparing to go to Serbia, where there was free land in abundance. Almost every day, fami-

lies moved there from Montenegro and settled. Thus continued
the perpetual movement of the mountaineers to the plain and the
rivers, where wars and rebellions were only tides.

As soon as they had settled their families in the villages across
the Lim, Grgur and Stojan, three weeks after leaving the clan,
stole by night to the Radak village. The immediate reason was
reconnaisance and the gathering of information for the chiefs of
the Montenegrin army. But they were also drawn there by a longing for their former lands and by worry about their fellow clansmen. They had heard rumors that the Radaks had been plundered and massacred. The peasants along the Lim told them that
on the evening of the day of their flight; Radak houses had been
seen burning, and the smoke had eddied down from the hillside
to the Lim so that they could not distinguish anything, though a
few shots had been heard from behind that dense cloud.

First, they visited the graveyard. There were no new graves,
and in the moist darkness, under the clouded skies, it was not
possible to make out if any of the old graves had been dug up
again. That was the first sign that the Radaks had not been exterminated. As usual, rumor had exaggerated.

But, while they were still at the graveyard, the smell of soot,
bitter and acrid, came over them in waves. And as they crept
nearer to the village, these waves became stronger and more and
more persistent.

In the village itself there was neither the lowing of cattle nor
the barking of dogs to welcome them. If there had not been an
ever stronger smell of ashes and if they had not known every
landmark and every fruit tree even in the darkness, they would
not have known that they were approaching a human settlement,
one in which they had passed their whole life. They could dimly
make out the shapes of houses, at least those that had been whitewashed. But it seemed that some of them had been swallowed by
the night; they had disappeared like drawn teeth.

Grgur and Stojan had to move cautiously, for guards had been
posted throughout the district. They turned aside into the bed of
the stream and slowly crept along it toward Anto's house, invisible until they were quite near it. Only the ground-floor walls
remained, and those were half broken down. They groped along

the shattered walls searching for doors and doorposts, not believing the night and their own eyes. Of the kitchen, which had been built of wood, not a trace remained, and Grgur, feeling the ground soft under his feet, leaned down and picked up a handful. "Ashes!" he confirmed, as if to himself.

Stojan, too, bent down and took a handful. "Yes, ashes. Everything has been burned."

They stood silently in front of the house, which meant for Grgur his whole past—birth, youth, his love for Stamena, and the birth of his children—and for Stojan a refuge filled with brotherly love and understanding. There was a strange, painful emotion in their common silence, standing there over the pile of ashes. In that silence Stojan realized that both of them were filled not only with the same sorrow, but also with the inconsolable realization that they would never return to the clan and their native land.

It was not only the house that had been burned, but also their destiny. Tomorrow the begs would share out their lands among others, mainly serfs from other clans.

"Where are the people?" Grgur asked, recovering himself.

"That is just what I want to know," Stojan replied, though till then he had not spared a thought for them. "We must go around the whole village to see if there is anyone left alive and what has happened to the other houses."

Retreating into the orchards, they made their way to Stojan's quarter. All the houses of the fugitives had been burned; and also the stables, the haylofts, and even the dog kennels. It revealed not only furious hatred, but cold, calculating intelligence. Everything rebel had been wiped out. Grgur and Stojan, overcome by this calculated destruction, found that the sheep pens had been broken down and the haystacks burned.

Nasto's hovel and the stalls attached to it were untouched. But, as with the other unburned houses, there was nothing to show that anyone was alive. Stojan banged with his fist on the door, wondering why Grgur whispered that they should not go to Nasto's house. Stojan had always suspected that one of the Radaks had killed Nasto and that Grgur knew something about it. But he did not want to ask, leaving it to Grgur to tell him whatever he ought to know, apprehensive lest the truth be more terrible than the suspicion. Now, for the first time, it crossed his mind that Grgur had some closer link with the murder of Nasto. That thought was the more unpleasant because Stojan was on the closest terms with Grgur and believed in his frankness; here he was, going on a dangerous and deadly task, and he had no confidence in his companion. Nonetheless, he kept silent, for an uncertain light rustling could be heard within the house, then the creak of an inner door, and Miluša, Nasto's wife, asked, "Who's there? At this time of night!"

They identified themselves, almost at the same time, and she unbarred the door. Inside could be heard the weeping of children and the murmuring of a little girl reassuring them and rocking the cradle. It was scarcely possible to recognize Miluša's face, and while she talked in a hoarse voice she shivered from the cold.

She told them that as soon as the fugitives had disappeared over the brow of the hill and into the mountains, the zaptiahs had attacked the village. With them had been a certain Suljaga, a man, in Miluša's words, calm and patient, but also of mocking and malicious cruelty. Though he was not the leader, they all referred to him for everything. The two prisoners and two of the old Radak men had come out of the forest. Both the old men and the prisoners had begged that the houses should not be burned, and Suljaga had agreed not to touch the houses of those who had fled into the mountains with Vojin for fear of reprisals and who were not guilty of the killing of Buljukbaša and the *sejmeni*. Izetbeg, the son of Murat-beg Džidić, to whom the village belonged, insisted that not even the houses of the fugitive Radaks should be burned. But Suljaga mocked him and would not listen to him, and ordered that all the rebel houses should be burned. He himself set fire to the stalls and the hay.

Miluša had prepared to move out of the village, but had been of two minds, bewildered by her husband's death and overburdened by her children. But Suljaga, having been told that she was Nasto's wife, caressed the children and gave them money. He had said: "I maltreated him, and he was not to blame." He inquired who had killed Nasto, and when she shrugged her shoulders, remarked: "Grgur Radak killed him; either he did it or it was by his orders."

Stojan laughed, but Grgur remained strangely and gloomily silent, and then said: "The Turk is at his tricks again."

"So I thought," the woman agreed. "Why should brother kill brother—you especially, who are the head of the clan? I even said to Suljaga: 'I cannot think that one brother would kill another!' But he, the accursed one, did not reply, only grinned and said: 'Eh, *snaha!*' When did I become 'sister-in-law' to him, all of a sudden? Men are a perverse lot; there are things dearer to them than brother or son, or the whole world!"

Suljaga gave orders through the old men that within three days Vojin should come to Plav with the other householders to discuss matters and to make peace. But Vojin had not yet gone. The fugitive Radaks were still in the mountains and forests, only visiting the village in secret, for they had heard that the Montenegrin army would soon attack.

That same evening, Roksanda's husband, Kosta, had stolen into the desolate village to find out what had happened and to report that Drndar's son, Mirko, had been put in prison. Kosta's family, on the recommendation of some beg well disposed to them, had been preparing to leave the next day for Berane, a city founded about fifteen years before around the military cantonments, which afforded good prospects for craftsmen.

There was a pause. Grgur and Stojan were thinking what other questions to ask, and Miluša was hesitating, as if she still had something to say.

"Did you see Grandfathers Grgur and Pavle?" Grgur asked.

The woman began to breathe heavily. "Don't ask me, don't open my wounds, as well as Nasto's! Both were burned."

"How—burned?" Stojan asked.

"Burned up! The Turks set fire to them; may God set fire to them!" Miluša told them through her tears. "They defended their house. Grandfather Pavle managed to wound one of them, and the accursed ones burned them both with the house!"

There was no reason to linger in the village. They had found out all they could and all they wanted to know. But they remained, silent, undecided, thunderstruck.

The woman, too, was silent, collecting herself. At last she asked: "You come to me as *djever*s, and now I ask you as brothers. Tell me, if you know: who killed Nasto? That I can at least tell the children when they grow up. Swear to me that no one among the Radaks did it, so that the children may grow up among brothers and have no blood to avenge."

Stojan burst out: "Forget these mad thoughts, Miluša! The Turk, I can see, has raised doubts in you. Why should we swear it to you, when you know it yourself? Even though we did not agree with Nasto about many things, may God be my witness, it never crossed our minds to harm a hair of his head."

"Forget these stories, *snaha*," Grgur retorted, ill at ease, putting his hand on her shoulder.

The woman sighed and moved away, as if his hand were unpleasant to her. He put his hand into his breast, drew out a purse, and shook all the money out of it. Then, searching for Miluša's hand on the doorpost, he put the money in her hand and closed her fingers over it. "Don't worry; the other Radaks will not let your children starve. To Vojin as a pledge—let him put aside as much as he can from my land and let him give it to you and your children if we do not return."

Only then did the woman begin to sob, blessing and thanking him. "You have lifted a nightmare from me and from my children. My Nasto, in God's name, never betrayed the clan. Why should they take his soul with a rope?"

They borrowed a lighted torch from her, said farewell, and moved back across the garden toward Anto's house. Grgur went ahead, and with his body shielded the flame, whose light drew from the darkness rain-washed and, it seemed, dancing plum trees. The immense shadow of Grgur's body spread out over the moist earth and dark trees, while his head disappeared into the gloomy heights. He seemed a little bent, under the weight of the night and sorrow, and Stojan once again recalled his suspicions about Nasto's murder. "You gave all that you had to Miluša," he remarked, trying to give his words another significance, as if he were regretting Grgur's money.

Grgur halted and slowly turned toward him. "I, too, am Nasto's debtor." Then he turned right around to face Stojan. The reddish light of the torch shone on his face, drawn by misfortune and tense with emotion, while the top of his head vanished into the darkness as if growing into endlessness. "I have not spoken of this to you before. I was ashamed and thought that it might embarrass you. It was Akan who killed Nasto."

Stojan bit his lip, as always when he was overcome by astonishment. The dark, crowded tree trunks danced around him in the darkness. "I would have expected it of anyone but him. But when I think of it, he was always silent, yet when once he had made up his mind! Was Nasto really an informer?"

"It's hard to say. Yes and no, depending on how you look at it. He was against the revolt, was intriguing with the begs and—well, you know yourself. I, too, would never have suspected it of Akan! But, you see; perhaps he was mistaken, but what would not have been enough for you and me was enough for him."

"Yes, that was enough for him. Perhaps he was not mistaken. We could not go on under the Turks. But all this is terrible and at too high a price."

"Yes. Evil piled upon evil. We will talk about it another time," said Grgur, and again led the way, disappearing once more amid the darkness and the trees.

The ruins of the house appeared out of the darkness as if from ancient far-off times recalled in tales of horror; broken-down, yawning walls, with burned-out stumps in place of doors and windows. All that remained of the outhouses was a gluey heap of ash, some sort of burned horror which hissed under the rain, and fragments of earthenware where once the hearth had been. Most melancholy and terrible of all was the burned-out orchard; charred branches stretched out from still-untouched trunks like maimed hands.

They went into the ruins, the sooty walls of the house, and began to poke around in the ashes with their swords. But nowhere was there a trace of human bones—they had hoped to find the skulls of the old men, to bury them—and nowhere a trace of the goods with which the house had been packed, since only necessities had been taken. The steel now and again grazed a stone or a piece of glass, once even a rusty poker. Stojan finally struck his point against a piece of iron, half buried under a heap of stone by the front wall. It was a burned and twisted gun barrel, certainly the remains of the gun with which Grandfather Pavle had armed himself on their departure. Slowly they removed the stones and carefully brushed away the ashes and mortar around the barrel, but there was no trace of human hands or human bones.

"There's nothing," Grgur concluded, throwing away the gun barrel. It clashed unpleasantly against the wall in the stillness of the night and the ruins. "We are trying to bury corpses that do not exist! Let's go, Stojan, as quickly as possible. Can you imagine that people were living here until yesterday? That I lived here, too, until yesterday, and that you were my guest? And the grandfathers—if they were not burned here, perhaps they are still alive."

"There's nothing left for us but to go," Stojan agreed. "From ashes there is nothing but ashes! We ought not to have left them. Yet they died well, defending their home!"

Grgur threw away the dying torch, and once more they were in total darkness. They kept to the path that led them back into the valley.

"Well, we're no longer so afraid as when we came," said Stojan when they left the garden.

"I feel easier in the darkness," Grgur replied, "when I cannot see anything."

So they plunged into the dense blackness and space, silent and sad.

All night long they collected information from other hamlets and from the villages beside the Lim about the Turkish army and the defense preparations at Plav, and then, about dawn, made their way to the bridge below Murina.

Morning and the Montenegrin army awaited them there.

It was already full morning. But because the daylight penetrated slowly through the mist and the drizzle, which dripped, chill and pervading, from everything, it seemed as if it were still night and that the night had not ended but had fused into a gloomy, dense visibility, which might equally have been twilight or dawn.

Stojan and Grgur had to report to the command post, to say what they had found out and to get fresh orders. But they were hampered and bewildered by the silent throng of soldiers who, with unusual astonishment and curiosity, were watching the farther side of the bridge. They, too, unwillingly drawn by curiosity, reached the left bank of the Lim and forced their way through the silent throng.

At the edge of the bridge they were halted by a big, youthful-looking corporal with outspread arms. "Where have you sprung from?" he shouted, not severely, but authoritatively and with a strange expression. "Can't you see what's going on here? A traitor sentences himself."

They moved back a little, to a small rise, with a pair of middle-aged peasant soldiers from a nearby village. Both were of medium height, dressed in faded peasant cloth; they were distinguishable only because one was dark, with heavy eyebrows and thick mustaches, and the other of medium coloring, with thin brownish hair. They moved aside to make room for the Radaks, and the brown-haired one whispered almost gaily through his teeth: "You can see everything from here. And one hears better; on the bridge itself the roar of the river stifles everything."

From the other side of the river, five men emerged from a similar crowd and set foot on the bridge. In front was a small peasant with a big nose and thin black mustaches, streaked with gray, on a bony, oval face. He was bareheaded and had a high forehead and sparse hair. That firm, fine forehead was creased by some inner tension and overwhelming anxiety. He was, obviously, a lively, quick, and vigorous man. He kept looking around, though his gaze did not light on any particular person. His liveliness was the more strange and striking in that he was carrying a millstone, so wide that he bent forward in an effort to keep his balance. His body, indeed, could scarcely be seen, so that it looked as if the millstone were moving forward on a man's legs. That made him seem even smaller than he was. Through the hole in the millstone, a rope was drawn and tied. The other end of the rope was tied in a noose around the little man's neck. The length of the rope between the two ends, not much longer than the span of a man's arms, dangled in a loop in front of the stone. The man was carrying the stone in the best way he could, in his broad, knotted arms, hugging it against his chest. Such a manner of carrying was burdensome, but the little man skillfully avoided striking the stone against his thighs and walked well and even vigorously, though with legs widespread.

"Kostadin, the miller," the brown-haired soldier behind the Radaks volunteered, though no one had asked him. At the same moment, Stojan recognized the man and glanced at Grgur, who was watching the bridge with wide-open eyes and parted lips. Grgur was astounded at seeing that man there and in that situation. In the spring he had helped the Radaks to bring the arms from Montenegro, and they had been stacked in his house in the deep valley above the mill. The brown-haired soldier went on chattering. "A traitor! They caught a Turk from the next village through whom he passed secrets to the men of Plav. The Turk betrayed him under torture—and now he must carry out his own sentence."

Behind the little man with the millstone walked two soldiers, holding him by the arms. They did not do this to help him, but because they were afraid he might try to run away, though it would have been difficult for him to do so, seeing that the bridge was fenced in with planks and he was carrying the millstone around his neck.

Behind the soldiers, jostling one another, for the bridge was too narrow for three persons to walk abreast, came a rather older sergeant, who was stroking his yellowish mustaches and whispering to the man with the stone as if he had something important to say. The condemned man, it seemed, listened rather distractedly, preoccupied with his burden and his misfortune, though he leaned his head to one side as though listening and accepting the sergeant's advice.

After them trotted a thin, yellow monk, who, stretching out his long neck, also was trying to reach Kostadin's ears. The monk was dressed more like a peasant, and under his arm was his stole wrapped around a cross with glittering gilt tips.

When the group reached the middle of the stream, not more than twenty paces from the Radaks, and halted there, the sergeant shouted to the condemned man, putting his hand on his shoulder: "Here we are! Now be a man before all these brothers and ransom the evil you have done them."

The man looked around him uncertainly and then at the sergeant. "What am I to say? Tell me, in the name of God, brothers!"

"Repent! Tread down your pride and grind it to powder," the monk broke in, as if reading from a book.

"Just look at the son of a bitch!" the brown-haired soldier called out gaily from behind the Radaks. "Now he doesn't know what to say. He knew well enough how to betray us to the Turks! He told them how big an army had mustered, and perhaps even when it would attack. They say that he was to blame that the Turks tortured some knez or other and burned his village. Such people always know more than they say! And now he pretends not to know how to unburden his leprous soul—as if he has a soul—in repentance and as an example to the people."

"Shut up, for God's sake," the soldier with the black hair interrupted him imploringly. "Let's hear him! He, too, has a soul. Can't you see what a state he's in?"

"But I don't know what or how to say it," the condemned man excused himself with tearful impatience. "I have confessed everything. I am responsible for my own death; no one owes a blood debt for me."

"And not soil our hands with your death," broke in the sergeant.

"And not soil your hands with my death! But I have never spoken before the people. What am I to talk about—my shame and my contrition?"

"That's it! The Almighty will show you no mercy on the Day of Judgment!" the monk said.

"It's not our job to teach you. You must speak for yourself, from your own soul," the sergeant instructed him. "Is it so hard for you? You yourself know in what you have sinned. Talk as you talked to us: with a black shame have I brought shame upon myself to the ninth generation! I take my guilt upon myself so that others do not soil their hands with my blood. That's how."

The monk added, stretching out his thin neck: "Tell them how you feel now when the earth slides from under you and the sky above you is horror-struck. And how you trust in God Almighty and most merciful to pardon you, though among men you have not deserved it."

"He can, the accursed one, but he won't," shouted the brown-haired soldier, stepping forward.

But the dark soldier pulled him back, while hundreds of eyes turned toward them as if they were interrupting this most moving, most solemn moment. The sergeant on the bridge pointed with his finger to the rise on which the Radaks were standing, and the dark soldier whispered to the brown-haired one: "You bastard, didn't I tell you to keep your trap shut."

The brown-haired soldier sighed discontentedly and drew back. At that moment the condemned man looked toward the Radaks, and his eyes lighted first on Grgur and then on Stojan.

In this look, or so it seemed to Stojan, was not only shame that they had come upon him in such a situation but, even more, fear and suffering and sad entreaty. He shrugged his shoulders and wrinkled his nose, though it was not clear whether by that he was holding back his tears or was about to weep.

"All right, then," he began, turning to the sergeant and the monk, "I'll say what I must. But forgive me if I have not the words to say it as I should."

The sergeant and the monk smiled at him encouragingly. The sergeant even slapped him on the back, and the monk explained gently: "It is hard until you begin, but later the words will come of themselves, and everything will be easier for you the more you repent."

With the help of the guards, Kostadin wriggled through the railing and stood on the arch of the bridge over the rapids which, swollen and turbulent, foamed beneath him. He glanced around with that beseeching, unhappy look, which was quite out of keeping with his usual vivacity and, so Stojan remembered, his harsh, sarcastic humor. Now the guards were only gripping him firmly by the arms for fear that he slip out of their grasp and leap into the river before his time.

Watching the disheartened, broken man, Stojan thought of the sentence and remembered the depth of the rapids and the whirlpool below them.

The phrase "a millstone about his neck" was still in general use: "Let him tie a millstone around his neck and leap into the waters!" "He deserves no better than a millstone around his neck!" It was even recalled that clans and tribes had pronounced such a sentence on men guilty of serious crimes, on traitors, on berserk murderers of their kin, and on perjurers. The idea of this kind of punishment was, as in this case, twofold: that the criminal carried it out himself, so that no one in his clan or close family should be in debt for his blood, and that every trace of him be lost, so that no one would know his grave or make any due memorial to him. This was a newly liberated district, and therefore in it such crimes were usually punished by shooting. But having discovered a traitor on the very eve of an attack, the judges had decided to punish him in the way that would make the greatest impact on the people and on the soldiers. So they had taken from a phrase, from a tradition, the idea for Kostadin's execution. For the same reason they forced him to make a public confession of his grievous sin, not against clan or tribe, but against Serbdom and faith and the soldier's oath.

The guilty man had no hope of escape, for the more he tried to take the noose from his neck, the more the stone would drag him to the bottom. The place where the punishment was to be carried out had also been carefully chosen, at the crossing of several roads and two districts, between two armies on the march. The river—Stojan knew well, for he had often fished there for trout in the eddies—ran through a narrow cleft about a dozen feet deep, so that nothing would be seen of the guilty man, even if it had not been, as now, in spate and muddied. He would vanish forever in its opaque depth. And even when the body in time decomposed and the neck broke, it would be so rotten and eaten away by the waters that no one would be able to recognize it; the head, separated from the body, would sink into the sandy bottom and the bones be scattered in the eddies and on the shoals. Not a trace would remain of the body, and because his crime had been the betrayal of his brothers and the common cause, not even the closest of his kin would ever again mention his name.

The tense, awe-struck hush forced Kostadin to cry out in a thin, scared voice: "I am guilty! Guilty before my brothers more than before Merciful and Almighty God! I know that I no longer have the right to call you brothers. But I have no one except you from whom to ask forgiveness. Your justice and the justice of God have found me out. This death, and such a death, is for me a happiness and a reward which only your justice and God's all-wise judgment can afford me."

He fell more and more into a sort of trance, as if he had finally

445

found a way to free himself from all his cares and burdens. To Stojan, this change was unpleasant. And the brown-haired soldier grumbled discontentedly: "Why must he wash himself clean and give us a sermon?" But others, including Grgur and the dark soldier, listened to the condemned man and were carried away by the flood of his words.

He went on: "I have deserved to burn alive like a candle, to bear witness to my shame and my sin. And to stay bound at the crossroad, that all point their fingers at me and turn their heads from me. For the earth is too small to drown my shame in its abysses. And the sun—do you see?—has hidden itself that my treachery should not darken its face. May I be accursed until the end of time. And as this turbid water will swallow me, let all who live and all that has been mine forget forever my face and my name."

"Amen! Amen!" the throng of soldiers repeated, as did Grgur and the dark soldier.

"May my wife and children forgive me for the terrible burden I have left them to bear all their lives. They are innocent. I alone am guilty and I alone deserve my fate. The greed and evil of Satan overcame me. May my shameful torture and still more shameful death be a lesson to all those who cross themselves, who call themselves Serbs, and who have human shape. Let the hour be accursed in which I was conceived and when I first saw the light, and the hour in which I die."

The army shouted back: "Amen! Amen!"

Stojan, too, and the brown-haired soldier, repeated, "Amen! Amen!"

Kostadin leaned forward, balancing the stone on his haunches, freed his right hand and bunched his fingers to cross himself. But he did not succeed in doing so, either because the guards, realizing that he had said all he had to say, let go of his arms or because he was not able to hold the stone with one hand. The stone rocked and, dragging Kostadin with it, plunged into the abyss below. Gripping the stone, the fingers of his right hand spread out, forgetting the sign of the cross and the symbol of the Holy Trinity in which they had been bunched, the lively little man flew headfirst after the stone and, struggling weakly, disappeared into the tumultuous river.

The silence and the incredulity grew tenser, as if no one at that moment could understand the disappearance of the little man with the millstone around his neck who had so cursed and accused himself. The face of the sergeant revealed a victorious satisfaction, and that of the monk an insincere and mocking compassion. And from the far side of the river, from the hillock, rose the cries of a woman, to whose skirts clung two barefoot children. Her long thin arms rose out of the mist over the hillock and, striking her breast with her fists, she began to keen so loudly that the soldiers on both sides of the river could distinguish her words. "Woe, Kostadin! Woe to our family! Woe for the life that is lost!"

The monk unwrapped and put on his stole with hurried clumsiness, so that his cross nearly fell. Stojan only then remembered that the monk, contrary to custom, had not carried out any religious rite as he accompanied Kostadin to his death. Now he began to intone a prayer so loudly that it seemed he wished to drown the woman's keening. The dark soldier crossed himself, whispering: "May God have mercy on him."

Others crossed themselves, Grgur, too, whispering something or other. Even Stojan and the brown-haired soldier crossed themselves. But the latter remarked, coming down from the hillock: "The monk prayed only after he was sure that the devils had already carried off his soul."

The army began to break up into squads and platoons. Stojan and Grgur moved on. The monk was still intoning, smiling that insincere smile and waving the cross over emptiness, as if he were not praying for the soul of Kostadin, but entreating the river to forgive them for having to use it for the death of such a sinner.

When they reached the farther side, below the hillock on which the woman was still keening, Grgur took Stojan's arm and remarked, after bitter reflection: "So Nasto must have been innocent! Till now, I had always thought him guilty. But it's better this way; one feels better that there wasn't a traitor among the Radaks."

Stojan stopped and retorted, with a harsh sarcasm unusual for him: "I, too, you see, thought to myself: Nasto is guilty! But he was more dangerous than a common informer. He had grown up among the Turks and Turkish ways. Neither you nor I can quite cast off the Turks! And we shall never be able to cast them off

completely until we cut off our living flesh with our own hand.
You see what those men have done? They have learned that in
Montenegro; they have driven the leper from the fold. If the
Montenegrins had not acted thus, they would never have freed
themselves from the Turks. A man is neither capable nor good for
anything as long as he has mercy on his own faith and his own
blood. Akan understands that to some extent, but you and I, even
if we did understand, would never be able to do it."

At that their conversation ended and, pensive, they forced their
way through the press of soldiers to the command post.

There, though they objected, they were separated, according to
the duties assigned to each. Stojan, as a man familiar with the
lake and the country around it, was assigned to the battalion that
was to occupy the bridge at the source of the Lim, and Grgur
went with the main body along the right bank toward the village
of Novšić.

Both armies set out only about midday, under a rainy and
cloudy sky. They moved fairly quickly, one in sight of the other,
driving back almost without a fight the scouts and patrols of the
enemy.

For almost half an hour Stojan followed the battalion commander, Veliša, a man of about forty with black mustaches
twisted up at the ends. Slung across his chest was a long, slightly
curved sword in a black leather sheath, and he was wearing a
greenish waterproof overcoat, which came down to the top of his
boots. A taciturn man, his pale serious face only emerged from
under his hood when he wanted to ask about some place or local
name, or to confirm something he had heard earlier. It could not
be noticed that he took any special interest in anything; in the
same voice and almost in the same words he asked to whom such a
house belonged and about the Moslem preparations for battle.
Only questions about the Lim and the fords across it aroused his
interest a little. It seemed to Stojan, who knew every ford and
eddy and island, since he had fished there from childhood, that
Commander Veliša did not believe him when he said that now, as
always after floods, the river could not be crossed anywhere.

Without looking at the river, heavy and gray as lead through the network of bare alders and reeds, Veliša remarked: "Man can always find a way."

Miloš, Veliša's adjutant, was quite different, a twenty-year-old youth with small black mustaches and reddish, girlish lips. He was riding on a bay horse and was covered with a black raincoat, but his clothes could be seen when the coat opened; they were new and ceremonial, as if he had dressed for a wedding. They called him "Teacher," Teacher Miloš. Frank and cheerful, he inquired about everything and freely answered all questions. He was especially interested in how the men of Plav and Gusinje behaved in battle, how good their marksmen were, and how skilled their horsemen. From his talks with Miloš and the soldiers, Stojan got to know that Miloš had been to school in Serbia and had been too young to take part in the last war. Doubtless that was why he was so interested in such things; he would soon have to fight his first battle.

Commander Veliša's army was strangely, astonishingly varied. Stojan concluded from his dialect that he was from the Vasojević clan and was leading an army made up of various tribes, local men who were waiting in smaller groups for the arrival of the army and veterans whom Veliša had brought with him. There was no sort of uniformity, even in the arms or dress of this army. Among them were newcomers with a sickle or an ax over their shoulders. They for the most part did not belong to the Vasojević tribe, whose army was expected to arrive the next day and would form the right wing and the reserve of the Voivode's army.

They had crossed the undemarcated frontier at the beginning of their advance, though there was no way of telling this. There had never been any real fighting along it. Ali-beg's horsemen, who kept watch on the frontier, had fired a few shots at random and then had quickly withdrawn.

And there was nothing else to remind one of war, still less the killing of men. It looked more like a migration or a gathering at a local shrine, the more so because in this army were men of seventy and boys of fifteen, as well as women, who, with yokes and burdens or even on horseback, brought food and changes of clothing to brothers and husbands and others from their clan. Scarcely anyone spoke of the coming battle or the war, and it would have been hard for any outside observer to understand how this army, casually mustered in platoons and squads, could dare to meet in battle the well-disciplined and singlehearted army of Ali-beg.

Roughly in the center of the army, in front of Commander Veliša, a tall, good-looking youth, with fair skin and dense black eyebrows, was carrying an unfurled, bullet-riddled ragged red standard with a white cross in its center. His youth showed that he had received the standard as an inheritance, which was the custom in Montenegro. It was also the custom for five or six men to fight and die around the standard, so that no one from another clan could seize it. The raggedness of the standard showed that it had been borne in many battles. Except for that, neither standard nor standard-bearer was in any way reminiscent of war, but, rather, of a wedding.

No one paid any heed to that famous standard—a square of rain-sodden rag, each side rather more than an arm's length. The men were concerned only with what touched them more nearly— the mud, the rain, food, care of their weapons, powder, and shot, keeping dry, and their natural needs. It seemed that everyone intentionally avoided speaking of battles or of the war, but moved onward unhurriedly, without reason, but also without hesitation, toward an invisible, indeterminate goal.

On the other side of the Lim, the army moved in a similar manner, but in several ranks, which, broken up and separated by streams and hillocks, merged and mingled with one another, then sorted themselves out and again separated. From this side of the river it looked as if over there the disorder and indifference were greater; the small groups and broken ranks made it seem as if they kept no sort of order and even hindered one another. They were moving more slowly, though their standard, level with the one on the other side, slowly but surely succeeded in getting ahead, melancholy and independent.

A ruddy, beak-nosed old man, from the squad near the Commander, whose mouth stretched from ear to ear and who had sparse graying mustaches, as if aware that men laughed at him, exchanged banter with anyone he came across. He was known as Šuto (Hornless), which was certainly a nickname, though no one ever called him by any other name. On the march, Šuto liked most of all to tease his fellow fighter Mrgud (Scowler), a man of about the same age, also small of stature, but bovine, with shaggy gray eyebrows that almost covered his eyes and grizzled mustaches drooping over his lips. "And this one here is Mrgud," Šuto babbled. "That can be seen at a glance; he's always frowning. He could even make the sky cloudy. I have been through three wars with him, and I wonder that I never got killed—not from a Turkish bullet, for bullets won't touch me, but from ill-humor. I almost lose all will to live when I see him so scowling that the whole earth is darkened. But I can't do anything without him. Every silver lining has its cloud." They were never far from one another. However often other soldiers or other chance divided them, they always managed to come together again.

Mrgud was taciturn but obviously enjoyed Šuto's buffooneries, perhaps most of all those at his expense; then his mustaches would rise a little and curl at the ends like a dove's wings in the mating season. He had brought with him his grandson Sinan, a pale youth with just-sprouting mustaches, and a short peasant dress, who was always asking questions. That afforded Šuto a good occasion for mockery when he and Mrgud drank from a spring and the youth stood aside on the road waiting for them. "It should be a trough, then that calf of yours would get a drink!"

"What calf?" wondered Mrgud.

Šuto nodded toward the youth.

The boy heard them talking about him and concluded from the soldiers' laughter that it was some coarse joke at his expense. He turned aside, blushing, while Mrgud retorted almost angrily: "Don't poke fun at him. It's his first battle."

"That's just why. To stir him up so he won't be scared."

Šuto did not even leave in peace the women who waited at the roadside for the soldiers, offering them plum brandy, water, and food. To an elderly, heavily built, red-cheeked peasant woman who offered dried pears from a sieve, he said, peering at her heavy breasts: "I'd rather have those cheeses of yours; these dried pears you can give to Mrgud."

"You old devil," answered the woman, laughing. "You are old and you are going to die, and your mind is still full of such deviltries."

"Deviltries are never far from my mind! When I was young I never thought of such things. I knew that I could do them. But now I must ask myself and prove to myself—can I do them still? But, if you're willing, I'm not the one to break off. If your husband isn't home, or if you are a widow, and if your sons and their wives are out of the house, and if you are cold and lonely, I would willingly spend the night with you. There's always time for getting killed."

The woman watched him move away, her mouth wide open, laughing and embarrassed. Šuto began teasing Mrgud. "You, my poor fellow, have never known how to deal with women. You are always hesitating, holding back, thinking things over, and in the end you are left high and dry with your own flame and never know that heavenly savor and why men are alive. A woman is like plum brandy; it evaporates if you don't drink it, and they are like withered fruit if you don't enjoy them. Begin first of all to joke with a woman; if she joins in, she will join in everything else. If she is serious, then you turn serious, too; when she realizes it was all a joke, then everything else is up to you. It all depends on the sort of woman. Mountains lack fatness and sweetness, and so hill women are as bony as inaccessible peaks. But women from the plain know what good living is; they are soft and approachable, tame. Look at that old woman! She brought fruit—she was pleased that the Serbian army is coming at last and is filled with hope that someone will tumble her. Here, women love a joke and will agree to anything in fun, while with us—may God forgive me!—when you get near one it's like going to confession. Every hill woman is not only unbending, but behaves as if she were the Holy Virgin, until you roll her over in the straw or take her into the bushes."

On the march Mrgud instructed his grandson in how to behave in battle: not to be afraid of the bullet that whistles, for the danger from it is already past; how to take cover, but not too much, in case someone thinks you are afraid. But Šuto intervened, also with advice, half joking, half serious. "Don't be afraid of bullets. The one that will hit you is the one you don't hear. Think like this: Why should it hit just me, when there is so much open space all around me? Don't be afraid of horses; a horse won't trample a man. Horses are not like men; their sense does not leave them in battle. And don't be afraid of swords; but take care they don't cut your head off."

Sinan listened attentively to both old men, smiling in uncertainty at Šuto and pretending that their advice did not greatly interest him. But when they were eating pears by the roadside and lighting their pipes, Šuto finally aroused his interest, and the youth began to listen to him attentively. "You know, you are not afraid of death, but of being afraid and shaming yourself. You are thinking only of that, and for that reason you will be afraid; everyone is afraid in his first battle. So, once you know that you will be frightened, don't worry about it any more. You'll be afraid, all right, and we will tease you a little, and then you'll forget all about it. Next day you'll be the same as all the rest of us. And don't pay any attention to Mrgud; he will never admit to being afraid. I am always afraid. A man must be frightened of death. Of all living things, he alone knows that he cannot escape death. I joke in order to drive away my fear. Since this morning I have played the fool to drive away the thought of death. Don't believe anyone who tells you that he is not afraid or pretends that he is not. Learn to master your fear as a man should. Savić Radojev was reckoned among the greatest Montenegrin warriors of his time, but before battle he always stuffed his cap in his mouth so that his teeth would not chatter and frighten his companions. When the battle begins, there are few who are frightened; everyone is busy defending his life. And it is important how you behave in the battle; not before the battle—then everyone is afraid—or after the battle—then everyone begins boasting."

After a march of not quite three hours, the army halted and broke ranks in the village of Brezojevica, tucked away under the hills a short distance from Plav. Indeed, they could see the smoke-blackened roofs of the kulas and *čardak*s crouching as if from fear. As soon as the army settled down, everything began to look like a village festival. The quartermasters roasted sheep and lambs in front of the houses, and on the open space below the road in the center of the village. Around the standard, set up on the common land, the young soldiers started a kolo, in which they were joined, at first uncertainly and in embarrassment and then more and more enthusiastically, by the local girls and young women. On the opposite side of the river, at Novšić, something similar was going on, only there were several kolos around several standards.

The rain had slackened, and all the village notables and the officers and platoon commanders gathered around the commander in front of a whitewashed outbuilding made of hurdles, the property of the village knez, who, bareheaded, dark-skulled, and with hanging graying mustaches, was serving drinks. There, too, the conversation was of everyday matters, mostly jests and stories, and if anyone mentioned the war or the coming battle, it was incidental, as if it were some ordinary thing.

The old man Šuto, who spared only Veliša in his malicious teasing, attacked equally the army adjutant, Teacher Miloš, and the village knez. He aroused great laughter by asking the adjutant, in a serious voice, if he could say how many legs a Turk had. "Good heavens, you who have had so much schooling ought to be able to say how many legs a Turk has!" Then, as if casually, he asked the knez: "I have heard, but don't believe, that your clan always sews up a bride's trousers to save her from her *djever* on the first night."

Everyone looked fixedly at the knez, and he, embarrassed but understanding the joke, replied: "It was so in olden times—but in other clans."

"Everything that isn't nice always happens in other clans," Šuto concluded, and then added quite seriously: "God made Hell to prevent nasty things being done in Heaven."

After lunch they began target practice, at a white stone set up at the end of a field, as if at some festival. The shooting spread through the whole village and to the far side of the Lim. It would have sounded like the skirmishing of the advance guards had it not been for the bursts of applause when someone hit the mark and broke a white flake from the stone.

The rain began again about two o'clock in the afternoon. But that would not have dispersed the excited throng had there not been a loud burst of firing from Plav and, soon after, amid a thunder of hoofs, the arrival of a mounted messenger. He handed a letter to Veliša and stood at attention, which looked unnatural amid that devil-may-care crowd, in which the younger man scarcely greeted the older soldiers, and the older soldiers greeted no one. Everyone fell silent, goggling at Veliša, but his face, as if he knew that they wanted to guess the contents of the letter, remained unchanged.

"Nothing! There is no reply!" the inscrutable Veliša at last said. He did not give the letter to the adjutant, but folded it and put it away in the leather pouch that hung over his shoulder, taking care that it was not crushed. Then, noticing the rigid messenger, he ordered: "You can go. Tell Commander Miraš that we shall be moving."

Everyone concluded, perhaps from the self-conscious rigidity of the messenger, perhaps from his foam-flecked horse, perhaps from the fact that Veliša had said nothing, that the news was bad. Šuto even whispered to Mrgud: "If it had been good news, he would have announced it, you may be sure."

Even before Veliša's order that the platoons muster and be ready to advance, preparations for moving off began.

The young standard-bearer unfurled his standard and raised it with a sudden movement, so that it opened and flapped. Veliša mounted, and after him Miloš and all the other leaders. The army began to muster in the open space.

"Trumpeter, beside me!" shouted the Commander as he moved toward the standard.

On the far side of the Lim, too, there was movement, though somewhat slower. There were more men there, and the muster was more difficult.

The volleys from Plav did not diminish, but did not become heavier. They were irregular and uncontrolled, volley answering volley.

The old man Mrgud walked carefully around the muddy puddles, as if afraid of getting his clothes wet, while his grandson, pale and smiling, moved even more carefully, as if afraid he might tread on someone. Šuto continued to joke. "Not only the Turks are heartless, but our leaders, too. They get us out in this foul weather, and just as I was getting along fine with the knez's daughter-in-law. You'll see! There'll be a skirmish. Someone has advanced or retreated a couple of dozen yards. Or the firing has simply scared both sides. I've been fighting and raiding all my life, and I've never had the luck to fight a battle in good weather."

No one laughed any more, though there was no visible reason for such a change of mood; not even after they met the first stretchers, for these seemed to have come from some other land

and to belong to some unknown army. Certainly the soldiers congratulated the wounded on their wounds, but that was more according to Montenegrin custom than from any visible sympathy or real compassion. Not even the mourning of some sister or mother, accompanying a wounded man, who was hanging across a packsaddle with hands dangling almost to the ground, moved anyone. They got out of the way as they would for any other load and went on. Everyone was consumed by his own thoughts and worries: how to prevent the rain from running down the back of his neck, how not to lose touch with his unit, how to stop the beasts in his charge from wandering away, or how to make sure that nothing fell from his horse, if he were in charge of one.

Suddenly, around a bend, the wide Plav Valley opened before them, with its round lake, green and white under the cloudy sky, and in front of them the open space where the battle was taking place. There was nothing surprising in that. Shouts, shooting, and orders could be heard, as they had been earlier, though now more loudly. Only the extent of the open fields seemed unusual, wide and clear, despite the murky day—a huge dish with its rim in the clouds. From the road, raised on the slope of the hill, everything could be seen that was happening on the far side of the Lim.

The people of Plav, overnight, it seemed, had blocked the approaches to the town by redoubts. On the left bank of the Lim, in front of the bridge, they had set up a double palisade of beech and oak planks, behind whose pointed tops and loopholes they could fire at the enemy, who, to approach them, had to advance across an open space about four hundred paces wide, longer than a gunshot. Four or five hundred paces from there, on the road that continued toward Gusinje, they had set up a similar redoubt at the narrowest point between the lake and the cliffs. The two redoubts covered one another's flanks. It was not possible to outflank the redoubt by the bridge, while that on the Gusinje road could only be outflanked by clambering up the hillside, which also boasted a parapet and all kinds of natural cover. The bridge itself had not been destroyed, but was fortified by new, obliquely defensive strong points. It served Ali-beg as the closest link between the two parts of his army and made it possible for him to transfer units quickly in either direction. It was a wooden bridge on piles, sufficiently wide for two horses to pass, and fenced in with two rows of narrow planks. About fifty paces from the bridge on the far side, around two hillocks, between which ran the road to Plav, trenches had been dug; the freshly dug earth rose in two black semicircles. Men were still working around these trenches. They could be seen shoveling earth and setting up stakes; among them and around them were soldiers with rifles. Those trenches were to serve as a second line of defense for the bridge and for Plav itself.

There were other fortifications on the right bank, where the Voivode's army had to break through: in the gorge between the hills and the Lim; above the village of Novšić, an hour's march downstream from Plav; and still nearer Plav, about a quarter of an hour's march from it, between the two-headed hill of Skić and the Lim. From these redoubts to Plav stretched the bare uneven open ground of the Rudo Polje, on which Ali-beg could make a further defense by using his horsemen. By taking the Novšić and Skić palisades, the attackers could not only open a way through to Plav, but also make it possible to approach Plav from the rear through the hamlet of Prnjavor. Such a move would outflank the fortifications in front of the bridge. Everything was not only visible, but quite clear as to its possibilities and purposes—as if in advance the battle had lost all the element of surprise; as if it were a game in which the strongest, most skillful, and boldest would win.

Nonetheless, the redoubts surprised the Montenegrin army on both sides of the river. The army halted, scattered, and took cover behind outcrops in the fields or bushes on the hillsides. It was obvious that someone skilled in the art of fortification had hurriedly set up the defenses, for they followed the lie of the land and fitted well into the defiles. That confirmed rumors that the men of Plav and Gusinje were being led not only by their clan chieftains, but also by skilled and experienced Turkish officers, dressed in local national costume in order to conceal from the European powers their open intervention.

Firing broke out on the right bank of the Lim. Drowned by the firing on the left side, it could scarcely be distinguished by sound, but puffs of blue smoke could be seen from the palisades, from the bushes, and from behind the stone cairns in the fields, and even from the willow copses along the Lim.

Veliša was conferring with Commander Miraš, a huge, active man with black mustaches under a strong hooked nose. The Turks had been awaiting them at the bend of the road, reconnoitering with bands of horsemen. In the field, there in front of them, a wounded horse with a headless horseman still in the stirrups was trying in vain to rise on its forelegs, and about a dozen beheaded Montenegrins and Moslems, differing only in clothing, were lying. The cavalry attack had been repulsed, but two infantry groups had outflanked the Montenegrins on the hillside. There was a danger that they might come down suddenly onto the road and the open space and thus be exposed to the attack of a larger cavalry force.

"No matter! No matter. Let's flush them out," Veliša said, throwing down his cap. "Their cavalry has come from Gusinje; it cannot see our forces. Let the first platoon move uphill to relieve and reinforce the parts of your third, and the second and fourth go through the forest near them, but not let themselves be seen until I tell them."

He did not give his orders to anyone in particular, but the leaders of the platoons concerned at once turned their horses and moved back at a trot. Strangely, Veliša and Miraš calmly, even carelessly, remained where they had first met, considering and discussing the situation as a whole. There was not a single Montenegrin soldier in front of them, though there were some to their left and some behind them. Around them were the group commanders, for the most part old men, some youths, and five or six messengers.

The youths—Sinan, Teacher Miloš, and the standard-bearer— obviously felt uneasy at the thought that the Moslem cavalry might at any moment rush out from behind the Gusinje palisade. They could see them mustering behind it. Sinan clung to his grandfather, with eyes fixed on the palisade. Miloš paced up and down with pale, twisted lips, while the young standard-bearer in uncertainty now raised, now lowered the standard. To Stojan, too, the situation was uncomfortable, not so much because he was frightened, as because this carelessness confirmed his first, tormented and irritating, impression of lack of order and lack of care in the Montenegrin army. These men either cared nothing for danger or had some other sense of it, which foreshadowed and forestalled it and judged it by some other criterion than conditions of time and space, the number of their enemies, and their own abilities. They behaved as if it were not a question of war and killing, but of something simple, natural, and ordinary.

What was more, even when what Stojan had anticipated and the young men feared took place, when horsemen began to vomit out of two small openings in the Gusinje redoubt, and from above in the forest could be heard the yell of the Gusinje charge, not even then was there any marked change in the behavior of Veliša and Miraš. Veliša slowly ordered platoon leader Djuro, a smallish, middle-aged man with big mustaches, to withdraw his men into the forest above the road and behind the hurdles set up there. "Let half of them fire at the men above and the other half at the horsemen." He himself remained on the road with Miraš, Miloš, the red-faced, plump little trumpeter, Simo, Stojan, the standard-bearer, three messengers, and his groom and relative, Luka, a pale-faced undistinguished youth. He continued to question Miraš at the point where he had been interrupted. "Good! Have you tried to find a way through to the redoubt by the bridge?"

"We surely have; we have tried all ways. From the lower side it is impossible; the waters are high, and there is nowhere to cross, not even in the river itself. From above it might be possible. The Turks cross there, but the fire from the Gusinje redoubt does not let us."

"No matter! We shall see," concluded Veliša, apparently keeping a closer eye on the redoubt by the bridge than on the horsemen who were lining up in front of the Gusinje fortification.

The enemy could quite easily see the Commander's group from both redoubts. It was there in the open, although out of range. Perhaps it was that which led them to speed up the cavalry attack.

There were about sixty horsemen. They came out one by one through the two openings and formed up, from left to right, in front of the redoubt, until, finally, they blotted it out completely. All that remained was a living rampart of chargers and riders in black cloaks. Ali-beg's insistence on discipline could be seen in the efforts of each cavalry unit to appear the smartest and most uniform.

The black swaying wall of horsemen was awaiting some signal to charge, and every minute, every fraction of a minute, seemed interminably long, though nothing significant happened. Veliša raised his right hand, his whip hanging from his wrist, and pointed toward Plav. The standard-bearer shifted from foot to foot. Miloš gazed intently, now at the horsemen, now at his commander.

And still nothing happened, nothing of what might happen at any moment, nothing of what it was now inevitable should happen. The uneasiness became unbearable only to the adjutant, who impatiently urged his horse up to the Commander and asked: "Shall I tell the second platoon to hurry?" Stojan saw that Veliša, secretly and attentively, with half-closed, sharp, and cunning eyes, was watching how Miloš was behaving. He twice cut him short. Then, without another word, without a movement, but with a calm and rather pointed glance, he sent the adjutant back where he had come from.

At last, from the upper opening, a rider came out on a bay. He wore a green surcoat and was holding an unfurled green standard fixed in his left stirrup. The standard fluttered high, and, since the spear point could not be seen, it looked like an inconceivably large and brilliant green butterfly hovering above the horsemen. The standard-bearer took his place in the middle, between the ranks, but his horse would not keep still. From one of the openings rode a man in white uniform, with a white turban and on a white horse, accompanied by a group of riders on black horses. He placed himself at the head of the formation, like a beak, and the files behind him stretched outward like black wings. The standard-bearer now took up his position immediately behind him, and the green butterfly was transformed into a green crest. "These men die well," remarked Miraš, looking at the ranks of the cavalry. Then he made a sudden movement toward them with his right hand, which flashed like a sword.

Thundering, the black bird rushed across the open, and the Commander turned to the men about him and said, without looking at any one of them :"No matter! Let the trumpet sound the charge!"

The trumpeter leaped out to the road, and his face turned red as he angrily sounded his trumpet.

In truth, nothing more senseless could be imagined, for there was no one to be seen who could charge except the Commander and his few attendants. The calmness of Veliša, Miraš, and the groom Luka, who stood close to Veliša's right leg, as if ready to offer him the stirrup, and of the others, who slowly took the guns from their shoulders and knelt, each wherever he happened to be, increased the senselessness. Much more natural seemed the apprehension and the astonishment of the young men: the adjutant, Miloš, crouched on his horse as if ready at any moment to break into a gallop; the standard-bearer, moving a little above the road, so firmly gripping the raised staff that his hands had turned white and trembled from the tension, or from fear.

For whom had the trumpeter sounded the charge, when there was none of the army anywhere around? Surely not for himself and the Commander and the group about him, to rush upon the sabers which flew from unseen scabbards in silver flashes and cut distant fields and meadows to pieces. Nonetheless, the trumpeter had sounded the charge, and the horsemen, though they had to rush some four or five hundred paces and were charging at the gallop, seemed to advance intolerably slowly, devouring the yellowish space with their hoofs. With their shouts were mingled the neighing and stamping of the horses and the shots from the little wood, random and inaccurate, since none of the riders fell. Had it not been for that shooting and the flash of the sabers, which brought back reality, the charging cavalry might have been a pack of legendary dragons come screaming from the lake.

But it was no dragon. When it had charged to within fifty paces, so that individual faces could be recognized, the horsemen were no longer in the least terrifying to Stojan, who knelt on his right knee and took careful aim. The standard-bearer stuck his standard in the ground, holding it with his left hand, and took his pistol from his belt; so, too, did Miraš, Luka, who knelt by the horses' feet, and the Commander, who hung his whip on his stirrup. The adjutant had a composed, though still-tense, expression; he sat upright in his saddle and moved his horse forward alongside the Commander's. The horses were uneasy; both began to rear and quiver, though it was not clear whether they wanted to run away or to throw themselves into the avalanche roaring across the open space.

As if cut in two by the saber of their white-robed leader or carried away by the wind from the mountains behind them, the horsemen suddenly divided, the right wing along the open field by the river and the left curving in a semicircle, to surround Veliša and his group. Through the openings in both fortifications now flowed the infantry, yelling, discordantly but distinctly: *"Allah il Allah!"* And from above, in the forest, similar yells and shots could be heard. The white rider and the green standard-bearer, with a group of black followers, unexpectedly, as if faced by some invisible wall, stopped in the open, while the horses under them reared and twisted, choked back by their bits.

The white rider shouted something, opening his mouth wide beneath his black mustaches, and pointed with his saber at Veliša's group. If by that he was telling his men that the left wing should attack the group, there was no need, for they were already charging. Stojan understood from the shouts of the white rider: "Surround them! Kill them! Take them prisoner!"

Just then, from behind them, from the road and from the forest quite near, could be heard the soft padding of the infantry and the cry "Hurrah! Hurrah!" broken by shouts of "Aha, let us see who is a Montenegrin!"

It seemed natural that the clash should come just there, around Veliša. His group was the nearest, and the horsemen could see, if by nothing else but his clothes and his staff—Veliša had thrown off his raincoat and was resplendent in the red and blue cloth, embroidered in gold, of the ceremonial Montenegrin costume— that he was an important leader. It was quite evident also from the tasks both groups were carrying out, though there was nothing impatient or intense about them. The horsemen slowed down their horses so that they would not override Veliša in their rush, and Veliša's men—even the adjutant had pulled himself together and drawn his revolver—directed their fire with such care that their gun barrels moved slowly, following the actions of the riders on the uneven, rolling ground.

Having been a hunter, Stojan knew that nothing was to be gained by firing into the thick; who fires at the flock does not hit a single duck. Also, it is only possible to hit a moving target by firing in front of it, either nearer or farther, as it moves quicker or slower. Evidently many of the soldiers did not know that or had forgotten; the firing from the forest, though deafening, had not brought down a single horseman, and Luka had missed some point-blank shots. He angrily threw down his gun, stood up, seized a carbine, and leaned forward tensely as he aimed.

After the dragon had split into two wings and they in turn had broken into individual horsemen, definite faces, figures, hands, clothes, and horses became distinguishable as the mass of vague and mysterious shapes drew nearer. Clothing that had been impersonal in its uniformity was now revealed as, for the most part, worn out, threadbare, with many patches, almost all black in color, but washed out, turning gray and coffee-colored. Many of the horses were thin, others slow and untrained, so that it could be seen that they had been promoted from beasts of burden to cavalry chargers for the occasion. The majority of the riders were older peasants, worn out by labor, made poverty-stricken by wars —such poverty as Stojan, too, had known for many years. This made everything more natural and ordinary. The only incomprehensible thing was that they would begin to kill and that many of them would be killed.

It was all the same to Stojan which one he kept in his sights. Though individual, they were all as impersonal as if they were wild ducks. The difference was only in the size of the quarry and its nearness; all game except bears were quicker and smaller than a man, than these men. Therefore he simply chose whichever first came into his sights; in hunting, also, one must not waver or change one's target if one does not want to miss.

There was a youth so blond that his hair shone, under a new fez as red as a poppy, with a red sash around his slender waist and a yellow sash across his breast. He was among the first three or four, rode easily, and in his free right hand held, as lightly as a whip, a curved sword. Stojan concluded that this rider would have to turn and face him directly, so that it would not be necessary to fire before he did so. And, in fact, that was just what happened, almost unexpectedly and much more quickly than anything else had happened. The horse and rider, at about a dozen paces off, turned straight toward the road, and Stojan could see the horse's ears and its white chest. He raised his aim a little, to the middle of that yellow sash, between those ears, and pressed the trigger.

He heard the discharge of his own gun, but that did not have any special significance, even as it had not in hunting, even as the sound of the ax is of no importance in felling a tree or the whistle of the scythe when mowing. What was important was whether the game had been hit, if chips fell or the mown grass were cut, if the rider would fall or not. Surprisingly, he did not fall, but continued his rush forward, drawing his sword and raising his arm as if he wanted to catch hold of something firm in the air. That lasted only a moment. He was thrown from the saddle by some inner convulsion, fell over the horse's mane, and plunged to the ground. The horse shied, colliding with the horse next it, so that it, too, plunged to one side. It then trotted around in a semicircle of not more than a score of paces, and went back and stood beside its motionless master.

Before the horse stopped, even perhaps before the rider fell, Stojan threw away his gun, rose, and took the revolver from his belt, bending down a little as he fired.

The battle was raging around Veliša and also down on the open ground and somewhere in the forest above. Ten riders charged at Veliša's group. A thicket, black-mustachioed rider with huge knotted hands struck with his sword at the shoulder of the trumpeter, who fell on his face, his trumpet emitting a last discordant sound. Another, white-faced and black-haired, but older and tall, flew at Veliša. Luka fired at him but obviously missed, for his shot had no effect. But just as the rider slashed with his sword, Veliša lay flat on his horse, and the sword whistled above him. Veliša countered with his wide, slightly curved sword. Under the Moslem's left armpit yawned and vomited a bloody wound as wide as a man's hand, though it seemed to Stojan that Veliša had not touched him. The Moslem did not seem to feel the wound; he drove his horse at Luka, threw him to the ground, and, not being able to reach him with his sword, rushed on at Miraš. There, too, he had no luck. His sword could not reach the Commander, and Miraš leaped at him, almost touching him with his pistol, and fired two or three times. Stojan was not able to count how many because he was himself firing his revolver at a beardless youth, a former acquaintance of his, and missed at

five or six paces—he, the hunter who could bring down wild geese
in flight! He managed, however, to avoid the first blow of the
beardless youth's sword, but in such a way that he fell under his
horse's hoofs. He was sure—he even shut his eyes—that the second
stroke would hit him, despite the fact that he managed to scram-
ble to the upper side of the road. But nothing happened, and,
opening his eyes, he drew his *handžar*. The beardless youth's
horse was pulling him away, his right leg, in a black boot, tangled
in the stirrup, while the old man Mrgud, with a dagger in his
hand, was running after him. The youth, certainly wounded or
half out of his mind, was trying to prevent his head from being
crushed on the road. Suddenly his hands flowered with blood.

"Shoot at the horses, at the horses!" ordered Veliša, angry because his men did not obey him, perhaps did not even hear him.
He stood holding high a sword down whose glittering blade a
film of red oozed to a drop at the end. A somewhat older, red-
haired rider, paying no heed to the standard-bearer, who was firing his pistol at him, struck the boy down with a blow of his
sword on the neck, just as they cut down men in the national
ballads. The youth's head drooped on his chest and he collapsed,
still holding the standard, which wavered. The standard did not
fall, for, driving his horse forward, Miloš seized it by the point.
But his horse, since he had had to let go of the reins, carried him
into the midst of a group of enemy horsemen on the open ground
who were waving their swords and fighting with groups of Montenegrins.

Behind, to the left, on the stubble, like stooks thrown about by
a storm, lay a dozen or so Montenegrins, cut down in the first
mad charge of the horsemen. Stojan was astounded that he had
not seen this happen. Perhaps it had been when he had shut his
eyes, before the beardless youth had been dragged away with his
foot caught in the stirrup. He was afraid that everyone knew that
he had not seen it, that they had noticed that he had closed his
eyes when awaiting the second stroke. But no one glanced at him,
and he at once forgot his own fear and the slaughtered Montenegrins.

Around Veliša everything suddenly cleared. The horsemen,
busy repelling the newly arrived Montenegrin infantry, no longer
charged at him.

"It is most important not to run away from cavalry, but to shoot at the horses," Veliša explained, while Miraš approved. "I keep telling them, but it's no use."

Now the Montenegrins were attacking en masse, not so much according to approved military rules and in strict formation, but in groups, closely linked and working together, as if one body were controlling the scores of *handžars* and directing the scores of rifles and pistols. Few in number compared with the flood of the Montenegrin infantry, the horsemen began to retreat, brandishing their swords wildly to right and left, like cows driving away flies. The enemy infantry halted, many of them kneeling and firing, to let the retreating horsemen pass through their ranks.

"They are only dangerous on the plain and when we are in disorder," Veliša explained, spurring his horse. But the horse was obstinate and frightened and did not understand its master's wishes. Instead of moving toward the enemy, it began to rear. "Back! Back! Sound the retreat!" Veliša raged.

Even though the trumpeter had been cut down, the trumpet was heard. A grayish, mustachioed man, red in the face, sounded it.

The Montenegrin soldiers stopped, turned back, and took shelter behind the houses lining the road. Strangely, no cattle and no inhabitants of those houses could be seen. It was as if they had known in advance that the battle would take place just there and had hidden.

The adjutant, Miloš, returned, smiling and with the haft of the standard fixed in his stirrup.

But Mrgud, between the two retreating armies, was still dancing around the horse, which would not let itself be caught, and the beardless youth with his foot tangled in the stirrup, who still, yelling, beat at the earth with his bleeding fists. Mrgud's grandson, Sinan, rushed from the crowd of Montenegrins and with long, easy strides ran up to the horse and caught it by the reins. The horse stood still, and both armies, for a moment, ceased firing. Mrgud struck at the rider's leg once, twice, thrice, until he had severed it below the knee. Sinan, with a bound, leaped on the horse, but the severed leg was still hanging from the stirrup and in vain he tried to free it while the horse bore him into the thick of the enemy army. The Montenegrins again opened fire, while the Moslems fanned out to enclose horse and rider within their ranks. Mrgud shouted something, waving his *handžar*. Sinan at last mastered the horse and, despite the hail of shots directed at him, raced back to the Montenegrins. On his way, the severed leg fell from the stirrup.

Mrgud brandished his *handžar* and quickly cut off the head of the mutilated rider, who was trying to raise himself on his elbows. But as he was bringing the head back across the open ground, Mrgud stumbled and fell. He staggered a few steps and then lay flat, not letting go of the head in his left hand or the *handžar* in his right.

Šuto, hanging on to the long thick hair of the horseman Stojan had hit, noticed the wounded Mrgud just as he was raising his *handžar* and wailed: "Woe is me, my brother!" He did not stay his hand, but cut off the head and held it high for all to see. Then he wiped his knife on the sleeve of the headless corpse, put it carefully back in his belt, and urgently, not letting go of the severed head, rushed toward Mrgud. The Moslem infantry were continuing to retreat, though no one was driving them, but were still defending themselves with gunfire. Šuto paid no attention. Running up to Mrgud, he seized him by the shoulders, wriggled under his body, and carried him back, with an ease unusual for his age and strength. Both old men were carrying severed heads, and Mrgud also had his knife. Not one of the soldiers laughed or wondered, and Stojan understood that it was because the Montenegrins, despite prohibitions, still looked on severed heads as a sign that merited recognition and dedication to hatred and to heroism.

At that the battle ended. It was strange that, despite all the firing and charging on both sides, there were only a few killed and wounded—in all, about fifteen Montenegrins and somewhat fewer Moslems. Mrgud was wounded in the left thigh, and the groom Luka had a saber cut on the left shoulder. Stojan's cloak had been cut in two obliquely and from behind, though till then he had not noticed it.

The soldiers on both sides, though out of range, went on firing stray shots. And Sinan, with immeasurable pride, was still showing off his plundered horse, not paying any attention to what was happening to his grandfather.

Commander Veliša sheathed his sword, picked up his coat, and
ordered: "The second platoon will keep watch! And the standard
now to Mrgud's grandson. What is his name?" Then he turned
and, noticing the head in the old man's hand, said to Šuto:
"Radak killed that one; the head is his."

"But I cut it off!" Šuto retorted angrily, putting his wounded
comrade down on the road. Mrgud, as if only now realizing that
he was wounded, wailed softly.

"No matter! It belongs to the man who killed him," the Commander ordained.

"Surely it belongs to the one who cut it off; no one knows
where a bullet flies," grumbled the old man.

"It's all the same to me," Stojan remarked.

"No matter! Divide it!" the Commander said in judgment,
spurring his horse.

Šuto recovered his usual jesting mood. "So be it! I'll keep the
head and he can have the bottom!"

On the far side of the Lim the firing also died away. Lighting
their fires, the armies camped, one opposite the other.

Stojan settled down by the hearth of the knez with whom they
had lunched. Veliša, Miloš, Miraš, and two other leaders lay
down as soon as they had had supper, and the Commander
ordered the sentry not to wake him unless there was a message
from the Voivode or if the Turks attacked. He would waken himself if necessary. The members of the household lay in the smaller
room, whispering, so as not to waken the leaders, afraid of what
might happen to them if the Montenegrins did not win. By the
hearth remained Stojan, the new standard-bearer, Sinan, Sergeant Djuro, and Šuto, who was granted this comfort because of
his years. They lay on straw around the fire, which the sentries on
duty kept alight.

But Stojan could not fall asleep, despite, as was his habit, his
attempts to concentrate on some one picture—some landscape or
event. The pictures of the day's fighting flashed into his mind,
bloody and gruesome, just at the moment when he was about to
fall asleep. He had often been troubled by sleeplessness on the
eve of a hunt or of an important occasion. But that had been
quite different; anxiety or the imagination of future happenings.
In those tremors before hunting there had been something both

terrible and pleasant, though they were vague and disordered. Now, however, he recalled separate details, and was not able to join them together in a whole, even though he knew that the whole existed.

It was as if men and their deeds had disappeared, and only pictures of horror and of death remained. The stripping to the skin of the Moslem corpses, the more unnatural in that they were headless, was done by the women, swiftly, skillfully, and avidly, haggling over the spoil and squabbling about which corpse was whose. The weapons and the severed heads that the Montenegrins had taken were also hotly disputed. For wonder, the heads kept the expressions they had had when they were alive. Some of them Stojan recognized, from his hunting expeditions. The Montenegrins washed them carefully, combed their hair, even forced pipes into the stiffened jaws and capped them jauntily with fezes, to look better and more alive on the stakes before their billets or on poles within sight of the redoubt.

Now, at night, bloody fragments of clothing and heads of men he had known leaped into Stojan's memory, with monstrous clarity. The impersonality of the day, even of the Moslems he had shot, completely disappeared, as if the day's battle had never taken place, but only a killing of persons known to him, the cutting off and display of familiar heads and the plunder of familiar clothing. He remembered especially the beardless youth whose leg had been left hanging from the stirrup. They had known one another well. Stojan had once given him some trout caught at Grnčar, and the youth, whenever they met, had offered him milk and fruit. He came from a well-to-do peasant family, and Stojan remembered his home, his father, who had gone blind, his ten-year-old brother, and even his name—Mehmed. He was the best jumper in the Grnčar Valley. That day he had had the chance of taking Stojan's head, and he certainly would have done so had he not been wounded first. That day Stojan had been as impersonal as Mehmed. Now Mehmed's head was out there in front of the house, the object of fear and worry to the household, and for Stojan suddenly more real than Mehmed had ever been when he was alive.

Stojan wondered how he himself had been able to take part in such killing and slaughter so indifferently, even calmly. It was not that he hated the Turks any the less or was horror-stricken at the actual killing, even that he himself had carried out. No, it was a question of his skill, his deliberation, his detachment, in killing, as if he were doing any other kind of job, with the sole difference that he was more excited and inept, for his own life was in danger, though no more, perhaps even less, than when hunting bears.

He was aware of the folk belief, based on experience, that it is only hard to kill one's first man. But that referred to murder caused by personal impulses, and not to war. When Buljukbaša had attacked the Radaks, he had killed one of the *sejmeni*, but that was quite differently done, in a sort of sweet fury, in hatred and revenge. The spectacle of the incident itself—even though the man had died in torment, doubled across the fence with his entrails hanging out, and Petrana had stripped him to the bare skin—had not obsessed Stojan the night after, and still less later. It had been the same with his skirmishes with the Shquiptar clans. They had been, as was that assault by the *sejmeni*, attacks on his own life and the lives of his relatives, reckonings concerning pastures, or resistance to plunder and oppression. But here it was as if he had not been attacked personally, and it had not been his property that was involved. There was neither hatred nor fury, nothing but the normal everyday usualness of an artisan during the battle. Yet it was as if some unknown power threw him and the others, both Moslems and Montenegrins, one against the other.

Nothing in that could be changed or driven away. The normality of killing had made use of his skill in hunting, acquired, perfected, and refined over many years. And hunting was for him like a game, like love; all his personality was expressed and fulfilled in it. Now that personality, by which he had lived successfully and joyously, was fulfilled in immeasurable, blunt, and impersonal killing, as if his skill in hunting had become something stupid and cruel.

He knew that the next day he would do the same, with even greater calm and skill, not regarding the Moslems and Shquiptars as game or as definite things, but only as something that had to be removed, a task he must carry out, as when one had to buy some rough ground and sow it to obtain bread.

And no one in the course of this fighting had so much as mentioned Christianity and the Holy Cross, Serbdom or freedom, though all knew that in their name blood was spilled and men were killed. It was true, Stojan remembered, that the adjutant, Miloš, when he seized the standard and lifted it on high, had shouted: "For the Holy Cross and golden freedom!" But that had seemed unnatural, exaggerated, and pompous, even comic, amid the calm acceptance of killing and death.

About midnight Stojan, starting out of a light doze, got up to poke the fire, which the sentry had left unattended. Mrgud's grandson, Sinan, had not slept either, but was tossing and turning on the far side of the hearth. "Can't you sleep?" Stojan softly asked him.

The young man sat up, rubbing his eyes. "No. I keep thinking: I could have made a better show today. But that damned leg bothered me."

"Me, too. All sorts of bloody pictures kept passing before my eyes."

"It doesn't let me get to sleep, and yet it is not because I am afraid."

"No. It's not because of that. I am not afraid."

"Then why is it?"

"It happens to a man. Such things do not happen every day."

"That must be it," Sinan agreed, and lay down again.

The youth, tired out and reassured by Stojan's words, soon fell asleep, and Stojan went on sitting there, warming his bare feet and pulling his now dry stockings into shape. He had sat watching the fire, engrossed in his recollections, for perhaps half an hour when he was startled by the squeaking of the door, and the sentry, an unshaven, blond little man wrapped in a red shawl, entered in a cloud of steam.

"Someone is asking for you. He says he is a relative."

Outside, Stojan was surprised and pleased at the snowy whiteness all around. A fine snow drifted through the darkness, wrapping the whole landscape in its softness, numbing things, sounds, even the roar of the Lim.

"Stojan, brother!" a crouched shape greeted him, and Stojan recognized Mitar Drndar. "I have spent all day looking for you and couldn't reach you or find you. It's because of Mirko. As you know, he stayed in Plav. I can't get news to him or he to me since that morning with Buljukbaša. I am afraid; I am scarcely alive. They arrested him, as you know, on the first day, and I have been dancing around Plav as if I had no head on my shoulders. I even thought of going into Plav. I would give myself up to the authorities if it would do any good. So there you are—I came to the army. Perhaps someone might know something. Have you talked with any of the prisoners, or has anyone fled from Plav?"

Stojan told him of his visit to the village two nights before, and that Kosta, Roksanda's husband, had had nothing new to tell about Mirko. There had been no prisoners or refugees from Plav; had there been, he would certainly have known. Nor were there any other prisoners; two or three wounded men had been captured, but they had been beheaded by the Montenegrins.

"It is a bad thing that they cut off their heads. The Turks will do the same for every Serb."

"Not everyone does. But the soldiers, especially the older ones, are eager for heads; it's a Montenegrin custom. But come and lie down beside me and get some rest. We shall see tomorrow. We will even talk to the Commander."

They went into the house. Complaining about the stuffiness, about the wet weather and his ill luck, Mitar snuggled close to Stojan, turning his back to the fire, and, discouraged and worn out, soon fell asleep.

Stojan recalled that all that day he had not once thought of Mirko, and he was there in Plav, within sight, about a quarter of an hour's easy walk away, perhaps being subjected to tortures worse than Anto's. That was war; it takes everything from a man before he is aware of it. Yet sometimes he starts up, as from a nightmare, as he, Stojan, had done that night. The Moslems, too, kill calmly and indifferently, to kill as many as possible, to destroy the enemy army. Everything else was unimportant. And the Montenegrins cut off heads. They could not stop themselves. It was for them a confirmation of their heroism, and something more. Mrgud had explained that to him on the road. "We must cut off the main thing, that part which God gave to the Turks. That is what is important for us—to leave them only with what it would be shame to plunder. One cuts, no matter whom; one just cuts." Everyone cuts, even those who are sleeping here by the fire. And there's Mitar. He would cut off heads if he could, if he had the chance, if it were necessary. There is warmth from him, from a kinsman's blood, even though he is old, coughing, and worn out. Stojan dozed, there beside Mitar, beside all those head-cutters. What had been was forgotten, as well as what was to be. And in the white, chilly morning he would awake fresh and vigorous, not believing that the night before he had been unable to sleep.

Commander Veliša rose early, rested and good-humored. But as soon as he came out of the house to wash, he was met by three relatives of the standard-bearer who had been killed. One of them, a middle-aged, dark, and bull-necked man with an engraved silver knife in his belt, obviously knew Veliša well. He turned on him, paying scarcely any attention to his rank, and demanded angrily that the standard, granted the day before to Sinan, be returned to him. "While we are alive we will not permit the standard to leave our family. We are not to blame if none of us was there yesterday to seize the standard."

"Sinan did not seize it. I gave it to him, my good fellow." Veliša, too, was angry. "That is my right. So see to it today that you are near, and if Sinan is killed, then take the standard."

The man with the knife was flanked by two youths, his son and nephew, who was the younger brother of the dead man. Both were tall, good-looking, black-eyed; the first was in black peasant clothes and the other in threadbare blue Turkish trousers. Unskilled in talking with leaders, untried in battle, and moved by the death of the standard-bearer, they approved only by nods and an occasional word.

"He will take it into battle today over our dead bodies," the man with the knife grumbled. "You, Veliša, have the right to command. You can drive us all into the Lim to drown, but no one has the right to tread a man's honor underfoot, or to take from our clan what is ours. Already three of our house, the Djurkovići, have died around that standard: my uncle, my brother— his father"—he nodded toward the youth in the blue trousers— "and his brother."

"A standard cannot be without a standard-bearer," Veliša remarked in a conciliatory tone, drying himself with a towel which the knez's daughter-in-law, plump and red-faced, had been holding over her left shoulder.

"We are not to blame because we were not there beside the

standard. Miraš sent our whole squad out to scout, and no one foresaw that the battle would be just around you and the standard. Now do as you think best—but the standard is ours."

"How would it be for you to take turns?" suggested Veliša, half-jestingly. "That young man, Sinan, did well yesterday. He seized a horse from the Turks right under their noses."

"No, no! Only death can take turns with us," the older Djurković said.

"But I did not give him the standard forever," said Veliša, stroking his mustaches. "I am testing you. Do you really want it and will you be worthy to bear it? To carry the standard means certain death, sooner or later."

"Just give it." Djurković smiled, against his will. "Death is our affair."

"You will look for it because of the standard," Miraš remarked from the doorway.

"Better we look for it than anyone take it from us living."

Miraš brought out the standard. "To whom shall I give it?" he asked the Djurkovići and Veliša.

Veliša, too, looked questioningly at them, and the older Djurković crossed himself, seized the staff in his right hand and the flag in his left, and said curtly: "For the present, to me—and after me, to whichever of these two will be the better man."

He kissed the cloth, glowing with proud exaltation, and at the same moment Sinan rushed out of the house, flushed and ashamed. The commander consoled him. "I did not give you the standard forever. You have proved yourself; there will be plenty of medals."

"I will capture a Turkish one if I cannot have that one," Sinan burst out.

The old man Šuto came out of the house. He was sorry, because of his blood brother Mrgud, that Sinan could not carry the standard and began to jeer at the Commander. "Now he gives, now he takes."

Veliša cut him short. "First get a good breakfast. As for you, Šuto, draw in your horns, or somebody may blunt them." Then, glancing up at the sky, uniformly cloudy, as before a snowstorm, he asked Stojan: "Will the Lim be choked by snow?"

"It could be. If it's like this for three or four days and then freezes."

"No matter! Let's have breakfast, and then to work." He shouted to someone, and from the kitchen, as if awaiting his order, a bald, bandy-legged soldier brought a lamb on the spit, and the knez's daughter-in-law, holding its hot edges with a black cloth, carried a *pita* in a big dish.

The other two hurried into the house after the commander, and Šuto, spitting, commented: "The soup and the bones for us. It's always been like that and always will be."

While the leaders were eating, a messenger on a white horse drabbled with mud arrived from the rear guard.

No one read the message except the Commander and the leaders, but its general sense soon filtered through the army from the preparations the leaders quickly made. All the soldiers understood that the battle would begin at once and would be decisive. A sense of intimacy, even of tenderness, ruled between the leaders and the soldiers, and the taciturn and rather harsh Veliša, mounting his horse, remarked to his officers: "Don't squabble about heads, but about lives—your own and Turkish."

Two platoons set off uphill to outflank the redoubt on the Gusinje road, and one platoon, with a group of local fighters, took up position on the edge of the forest, facing the bridge. A fourth platoon, supported by a local platoon and some still-unassigned locals, under the command of Sergeant Djura and the adjutant, Miloš, prepared oak planks and fascines of reeds as cover for an attack on the redoubt, a task begun the night before in a sheltered valley nearby.

There were no changes apparent on the enemy side except that the trenches on the hillocks behind the bridge had been finished and on the higher, left-hand, side a green standard was waving. Built of planks, which from a distance merged into a white circular wall, the two fortifications looked like wider, lower kulas which some mysterious power had raised overnight.

There was nothing new downstream either, on the far side of the Lim. All that could be seen were the Voivode's units at Novšić, some of them already in movement on the hillsides and the others drawn up as if in readiness for attack. From the Lim to the hills, in full sight of the reinforced garrison in the lower redoubt, two Montenegrin files were moving slowly, one with planks and the other with fascines. It looked as though the whitish planks and the fascines, black against the snow, were dragging the men with them, one man to every plank and two to every fascine. Ali-beg's cavalry could not be seen. They were certainly behind the Plav foothills. Smoke rose from the fortifications. Somewhere in Plav drums were being beaten. A flock of wild geese cruised in wedges over the lake.

Just as Veliša and his staff were halting at the edge of the forest, a hundred or so paces from where they had fought the day before, cries for aid could be heard from the redoubt in front of the bridge. Even the words could be distinguished: "Brothers! Brothers!"

Veliša took a spyglass from a leather holster that hung from his saddlebow and calmly focused it. But because his horse would not keep still, he dismounted, handed the reins to a soldier without glancing at him, folded his raincoat, and sat down at the edge of the road.

Even without the spyglass, everything could be seen, though at first glance no one noticed anything unusual. The redoubt was about five hundred paces away, but just out of range of the rifles. In front of the palisade, on the outer edge of the redoubt, six men were bound, some four or five paces apart, and on the stakes were impaled seven severed heads.

At that distance it was difficult, almost impossible, to recognize men or heads, and no one asked if anyone knew any of the bound men or whose were the heads. At last Veliša handed the glass to Miraš, with the comments: "No matter! They have reinforced the garrison."

From behind, tottering, came Mitar Drndar, wailing: "My son! It is my son! Woe is me, my son, my all, my everlasting woe!"

Stojan took his left arm to support him and calm him, and then, glancing at the redoubt, recognized, third from the left, Mirko. The young man was wearing green Turkish-style trousers down to his ankles, such as merchants and craftsmen wore in the towns. It was by them that Stojan first recognized him. He was bareheaded, and even at that distance Stojan knew his blond hair, which reached halfway down his neck. His face was pale, as always, and on his left side could be seen a fragment of the red knitted scarf with which his hands had been bound behind him. But his characteristic attitude, head bent back and turned to the left, and his supple build confirmed that he was Mitar's son. Mitar, tugging Stojan with him, ran up to Miraš. "Sir, I implore you!"

Intent on looking through the spyglass, Miraš did not notice Mitar and, as if he had not heard him or did not know that he was being addressed, said nothing.

"Give it to him and let him take a look," ordered Veliša.

Mitar's hands were trembling, and his eyes brimming with tears. He did not know how to use the spyglass. "Calm down, first of all. Then turn until everything is quite clear," Miraš instructed him, leaning over him.

But Mitar could not be calm or handle the spyglass. "You look, sir, and tell me—it must be my son, alas!"

"Third from left, you said?" Miraš inquired. "That one has no mustaches. Blond. He has a coffee-colored cloak with dark piping. Green trousers. You can see for yourself."

Mitar fell to the ground on hands and knees and seized Veliša by the boots, like a slave, from long-forgotten far-off times, groveling before a powerful and oversevere master. His words, shrill cries that lacerated heart and senses, clashed with the reasoned hatred and considered actions of the soldier. "Woe is me, my son! Do something, sir! He is my only son. Save him, sir, masters, brothers, men!"

Finding himself in an uncomfortable position, Veliša gently pushed Mitar away with hands and words. "Ah, Uncle, I cannot decide how I am going to help my own army to defeat the Turks, so how can I help you, one man? It depends on how the battle goes, and so it must be for you."

"Why can't you do anything, sir? You can, you can do anything. You and God. Stop the battle and make an offer to the Turks." Mitar stopped, probably aware of the futility of his request.

Veliša said, half to himself and half to the absent leaders: "What is most important is what happens up there on the hill. If they do not overrun the Gusinje redoubt, then I cannot attack the bridge. Jump to it, my gray falcons, so that I will not be too

477

late to help the Voivode. God, strong and merciful, help us and support our arms and our sharp swords!"

Mitar continued calling for help, but without tears and no longer addressing anyone in particular. "He will be killed! If the Turks do not cut off his head, he will be hit by one of our own bullets. That's why the Turks put him there."

Miraš, looking at the redoubt through the spyglass, replied to Veliša: "Our men will succeed; they must succeed. It is not the main Gusinje force up there on the hill. Those men bound in front of the palisade are continually jerking about. It's cold for them there; it has been snowing."

"He'll freeze—my son! If nothing else, they will let him freeze to death. He's weakly, too thin, not yet mature!" Mitar wailed.

"As soon as the upper Gusinje redoubt falls," Veliša said, "choose a platoon and go at once along the lakeside and down the river. But spread the men out, to draw as much fire as possible and to lose as few as possible. With two other squads and with the locals—it's only fair that they bloody their breeches, too—go straight toward the bridge."

"It will mean losses, but—there's no other choice," Miraš answered. "There, you see, some gypsy has come out and is beating the bound men with a whip. Can't you hear their cries?"

It could be seen, even with the naked eye, that a man in a red fez was cracking a whip over the hands of the bound men. His movements were swift, like those made before a flogging, and the crack of the lash could be heard. Cries could also be heard, cries of anger and pain. Mitar joined in. "His eyes, they will harm his eyes, oh, light of my eyes!"

"We cannot strike until the Voivode has taken the first redoubt. The men of Plav would turn all their forces against us. Tell the men to take the best cover they can behind the planks and the fascines."

"I told them that this morning, but it was of no use. The locals pay no more heed to me than the Montenegrins. You know how it is with them; they consider it shameful to hide from a bullet."

"Send the locals ahead, and the Montenegrins after them with their yataghans."

"So I, too, thought. See, some lanky fellow has cut off a head; he certainly swore at him or called for help."

Mitar crawled on all fours toward the motionless, indifferent boots of the Commander. But before he reached them, he changed his mind, rose and ran with long strides toward the palisade. Stojan leaped up, but only he. It was as if he were driven by some unseen, mysterious power, which was urging him to stop Mitar or do something for him, but it was not clear what Mitar intended to do—to appeal to the Moslems, to make a sign to Mirko, or to go over to the enemy side and in some way try to save his son. Judging from his bearing, from the suddenness of his decision, even from his silent running—only that morning he had been complaining of shortness of breath—which was strangely swift, although clumsy, it seemed that he had not thought of anything definite to do, but was hurrying toward his only child, drawn by a summons stronger than will or reason. No one tried to call him back, though there were many men there older, wiser, and more responsible. Stojan was overcome by military reason and duty, stronger than the love and bonds of kinship. While he was considering what to do, Mitar came within the enemy's range. But no one shot at him.

The leaders continued discussing what they had to do and how to do it, but they, too, like the others, were looking at Mitar. It seemed to Stojan that both armies were watching Mitar intently. Veliša stopped his discussion and said: "The man is mad!" And Miraš replied, trying to explain: "An only son, a father—one cannot wonder at it." The spyglass passed to Veliša's hands. He went on observing the position, but from time to time watched Mitar, also.

And that was all. The silence was deeper, more oppressive. It seemed to Stojan to bring the two armies closer together, both of them in intense curiosity about what the strange little man, with his strange running, was going to do.

Mitar ran, without slowing down, until he was about thirty paces from the redoubt. There, his son could easily recognize him, and perhaps he, or someone else, shouted something to him, or perhaps he ran out of breath. He began to advance with his usual lopsided gait. Three Moslems came out to meet him; one had a white turban on his head and the other two were in black cloaks. Mitar stopped, spread out his arms, and then let them fall. The man in the white turban made a sign to him with his hand. Mitar knelt before him, bowed, but the white-turbaned Moslem pushed him with his yellow boots every time he tried to embrace his feet. Then the man with the turban again waved his hand, and the two men in black seized Mitar and fiddled with some cord about his waist. He put up no opposition, and they tied him on Mirko's right. The two men in black withdrew, and the third man, the one in a turban, stood in front of Mitar and struck him with his right hand, rocking to and fro as if he were laughing. But this did not last long. The turbaned man withdrew, and the other two approached Mitar and Mirko. One of them waved his right arm as if some invisible power had flung it from his shoulder.

"They have cut off the young man's head," Veliša remarked casually. "Now they have put the head there in the open for Uncle to look at. But what is the matter with our fellows up there? They never begin! And the Voivode's army, I see, is moving up the hill." Engrossed in speculation and expectation, he had now quite forgotten Mitar and his son.

The sun pierced through the mist. "I fear it may warm up and melt the snow, and the river will rise still more," Veliša said.

Stojan, suddenly filled with bitter emptiness, realized that the remark was addressed to him and hastened to reply. "There are no signs of a thaw. The wild geese are only stopping for a short rest. It looks like frost."

"But the water will not fall so quickly."

"The Lim is like that; it can rise two feet in an hour, and fall just as quickly."

"No matter! We shall see. That old fellow was a sort of uncle to you, wasn't he?"

"A sort of uncle."

"He doesn't know the Turks," Miraš broke in, standing up. "They are good for nothing except to think up fresh tortures."

Stojan wanted to explain that Mitar knew the Turks better than anyone, for he lived permanently among them and even collected information from them. But, since he had learned that it was not seemly to talk too much before the leaders, he kept silent. Moreover, the conversation had turned to the battle, which was beginning on the hills above Novšić, across the Lim. They could hear shouting as well as the shooting.

As if they had been awaiting this beginning, the soldiers on the near side, up on the forested hills, began sniping. Veliša stood up and crossed himself, as did the old man Šuto, who had just arrived from the rear with the information that the planks and fascines were ready. Miraš also rose, but did not cross himself. He hurried back to the platoons concealed in the ravine. The Commander's white horse pricked its ears and stamped.

It was difficult to decide from the sound of the firing which side was advancing. But old Djurković, who, with his son, never went far from the standard, as if afraid that somebody would steal it from him, could distinguish not only the sound of Moslem guns from that of Montenegrin guns, but even some individual ones. He commented, almost joyfully: "That's Djuro's; he's still shooting!"

Šuto jested: "That's just your fancy. I've heard women compared to guns—first you oil a gun, then load it; with women it's the other way around. But for anyone to tell one gun from another—only the deaf and the mad could believe that."

Djurković explained pompously and seriously: "You're jeering; you're always jeering when there's something to be done. You must know that every gun, even those of the same make, has a different voice—like a man."

"And like a woman! I'd agree with you about women; each one is different. If they weren't, all men would be faithful and all women chaste. But a gun is just a piece of old iron. The main thing is that it hits; and the main thing about a woman is that she squeals."

The squabble might have gone on had there not broken out from above, as if the summits were bursting with fury, a loud, prolonged, and savage "Hurrah! Hurrah!" The Montenegrins were charging, with drawn *handžars* and swords, and their cries filled the group around Veliša and the whole battlefield with suspense. It seemed to Stojan that even the river paused in its roaring course. Those cries were answered by the yells of the defenders, like huge, harsh waves beating on jagged, rocky shores and then sullenly withdrawing to take fresh impetus from the depths.

The expressions on all the faces, even on Veliša's, kept changing, in response to the ebb of the defenders or the flow of the assailants, apprehension and joy, hope and despair, as clouds covered or revealed the watery sun. It seemed as if these men were fighting for their own lives, though they were not directly threatened by anything, while yesterday, in the course of the battle, nothing like that, not even fear, could be read in their faces.

Veliša paced to and fro as if on him, the commander, fell the exclusive right to show anxiety, his own and everyone else's, while the others remained silent and motionless, wrapped in their own thoughts, in the echoes of the unseen battle.

Then suddenly everything was quiet, as if that savage and terrible wild beast of the charge no longer had any breath, or as if someone had sliced off its hundred heads. The sullen Djurković shouted exultantly: "Our fellows have driven them out. We have won!"

"How do you know?" asked Veliša, his pale lips twisted.

"Easy. We would have heard the Turkish shout of triumph if we had failed."

And in truth, on the bare mountainside above the Gusinje redoubt, running toward the pale, unmoving arch of the sky, could be seen the first, doubled-up fugitives, followed and beaten down by the unrestrained, exultant shouts and shots of the Montenegrins. Veliša's face shone with the joy of victory. Not waiting for the Montenegrins to leap over the palisade and cut them down, the men of Gusinje also began to run away, in small groups.

"Run to Miraš! Get a move on!" shouted Veliša. "Not you, Šuto; you are too old. Let the young fellows go." He called out to Djurković's son.

But old Djurković considered that only he should give orders to his son. "Run, but come back at once—to the standard."

On the bluff above the palisade were fairly large groups of scattered fugitives, and immediately behind them individual and then small groups of Montenegrins. The mass of fugitives quickly disappeared behind the hill, and the Montenegrins, more and more of them, appeared on the bare slope, streamed over it, and stopped, black as the desolate mountains.

Though the men of Gusinje had deserted the palisade, the Montenegrins moved toward it with caution. The majority remained on the bare mountainside and in the little copses around it. They were afraid to occupy the redoubt in larger numbers, for though out of range of the bridge, every attack from that side would threaten them, especially if it came from the lake, on whose greenish mirror now appeared two boats with about a dozen armed Moslems in each. Nonetheless, a large group gradually collected behind the redoubt and turned slowly toward the lake; it was the squad ordered to approach the redoubt at the bridge along the lakeside and down the river, from willow to willow, and thus draw a part of the Moslem fire. The files of the platoons straightened out and disappeared above the lakeside, and from the lake itself shots echoed like the merry fusillade of washerwomen's boards. The Montenegrins from the Gusinje redoubt lying on the road and their comrades invisible in the undergrowth above them returned the heavy but unco-ordinated fire, and the boats quickly began to withdraw, amid sharp, painful cries from the rowers and the wounded.

Almost at the same time, from the forest on the left, in two files, emerged rough-cut curved oaken planks, unpeeled on one side, forming into a wall and swinging toward the redoubt at the bridge. Though still out of range, men and planks combined in a solid mass against the enemy. In each of the two files there were about a hundred men, for the most part locals, reinforced by Montenegrins, who, in their small circular caps with red cloth tops and their wide trousers gathered just above the knee, could be easily distinguished from the other soldiers in undyed peasant cloth and the leaders in blue serge.

On the Plav side, in the entrenchment behind the bridge, there was movement. At first individually, then in threes and fours, men began without haste to cross the bridge in order to strengthen the forces at the palisade.

As the files of planks arranged themselves and took up their position on the open ground, Miraš, with two orderlies, forced his way through them and with long steady strides walked toward Veliša. As if waiting for the one commander to report to the other, there began to arrive, slowly, rocking and slipping on the damp earth of the forest, in files of about a dozen men wide and the same in depth, the reed fascines, each pushed by two local fighters without guns. Behind each fascine, among the local men, hopped, crouching, an armed Montenegrin. The Montenegrin caps behind the fascines were like poppies waving over dark, shapeless masses. The fascines, their countless thin tops and cut white stems sticking out on both sides, seemed to have no conceivable purpose. Impersonal, aimless, and unnatural were the men behind them, crouched and crawling along. Behind the files of fascines, in disorderly but close ranks, came the local fighters, also reinforced by Montenegrins, and finally about a hundred Montenegrins, in two irregular but compact groups.

Just as Miraš arrived from the open field, Miloš came up on horseback, waiting to give the word: "The army is ready to attack, sir!"

Veliša paid no attention to him, but turned to Miraš questioningly. "What do you think, Commander? What do you think?"

The adjutant was the only mounted man present, and, noticing the exceptional nature of his position, he dismounted, getting entangled with his stirrups and swearing. Miraš began to explain. "I think so. With the planks until I get to within fifty paces, then drop the fascines and—charge!"

"No matter! Good! But fifty paces is a lot. Thirty is enough. Have you a trumpeter? Link plank to plank, so that not even a snake can crawl between them. Not a single plank must drop out; as soon as one falls, another soldier must pick it up. The same with the fascines."

From the hills on the far side of the Lim came the sound of charges.

"What about the locals? Will they hold fast?" asked Veliša.

"They're all keyed up for battle. I made them a speech: Serbdom, the Holy Cross, Kosovo, and—the fight for their own freedom. And I explained to them: Whoever flinches from the Turkish guns will not—I swore to God—escape the Montenegrin knives. They see that they are being supported and backed up by the Montenegrins."

"No matter! As I said: Advance with the aid of God, and I will be among the Montenegrins. Be sure that your wall is firm—so that there will not be losses."

Miraš laughed, moving away. "Ah, well! As if there could be a wedding feast without meat."

He again withdrew with his orderlies between the two ranks of planks.

At his shout the planks swayed, pulled out of the ground, and the whole rank started to move off, the fascines swaying heavily and slowly behind them. The planks advanced swiftly and silently, quicker than the fastest march, as if they were flying from the tumult of the fascines. The men behind the fascines shouted in unison, as if rolling a single burden. Seen from behind, the movement of the planks looked like some dread religious procession, as for a crucifixion. But there was also something comic, even foolish, about it, and the waves of fascines, with their violent pitching and rolling, were no less ridiculous.

To Veliša their movement must have appeared slow. He turned and twisted, whistled nervously, and struck his boots with his riding whip.

To the defenders, however, it must have looked as if a superhuman power had crawled out of the forests and rivers, arisen from the earth itself, and was moving against them. They did not see men, but a living wall of planks, which inched forward irresistibly to the sound of many voices chanting like rowers or woodcutters. It advanced, revealing pointed, uneven, terrible teeth.

Their confusion and apprehension was shown by their irregular and random firing, which began as soon as the monster moved forward, even while it was out of range. But their fire became more concentrated and well ordered, like the sudden tearing of cloth, as the headless monster came nearer and revealed its wooden and its human form.

Some of the teeth fell out. Men dropped wounded, for the planks were often narrower than the men, and left hands, feet, and even shoulders quite uncovered. But as soon as a tooth fell out, as soon as a man fell, one of the Montenegrins from the fascines would push forward a local, who would run crouched to the plank, seize it, paying no need to the wounded man, and with it in front of his body fill the toothless gap, while the Montenegrin took over the rolling of the fascine until one of the locals came to relieve him.

Thus they relieved one another, fell and rose, to the shouts of the sergeants, the cries of the wounded, and the uniform, heavy, unwavering chant of the fascine-rollers. It was as if nothing could ever stop the rolling, the avalanche, linked by invisible clasps and tendons.

But, unexpectedly, it happened. When the plank-bearers were about a hundred paces away, amid the swarm of enemy bullets and the provocative and distinct threats of "Come nearer, swine,"

"Turn your arse, Vlach," "My sword is thirsty, Montenegrin," "The red cockerel will sing on thy head, *raja*," the ranks wavered, and a middle-aged little man, a bright-colored sheepskin cap falling over his eyes, threw down his plank, flung his hands up, began screaming "We've had it, brothers!" and took to his heels. There was confusion in the leading ranks; some plank-bearers fled, others half turned to do so, while others continued to advance. The fascines, meanwhile, went on rolling, pressing on the plank-bearers and creating greater confusion. Among the fascine-rollers till then there had been no wounded, and, urged on by their work and their united chanting, they had taken no interest in what was happening in front of them.

Commander Miraš drew his sword and yelled: "Stop, you bastards!"

In two or three strides he reached the little man in the sheepskin cap, grabbed him by the collar of his jacket, and struck him to the ground.

That, too, was a new and unexpected event, like the cry and the flight of the man in the sheepskin cap. The fugitives halted, and the whole army turned toward Miraš. He leaped forward and waved his sword at the little man, who at the time rose to his knees, clasping his hands. The sword seemed to hover over the whole army, over the plank-bearer waiting with clasped hands. It struck just at them; one hand fell, while the other hung from the wrist like a withered leaf. But the bloody stumps gushed sprays of blood, and the cries went on imploringly, until the Commander turned with his sword and struck the little man on the head. The two halves of his cap fell on opposite sides. It seemed that the Commander was still furious, because his sword, splitting the head down to the lower jaw, could not be withdrawn until he, whistling and grunting, pressed on the little man's chest with his foot. Commander Veliša was angry, too, and swore to himself. "Those Turkish arse-lickers want their freedom given them on a plate." Old Djurković shouted, waving his *handžar*: "That's the way, Miraš, our gray falcon!"

The defenders hurriedly concentrated their fire. Men fell dead, wounded men shrieked, but it seemed that no one saw anything else or paid any attention except to what Miraš and his aides were doing. This at once galvanized the Montenegrins, those with the planks as well as those behind the fascines. With the flat of their swords and *handžar*s they struck at the locals, driving them to pick up the planks once more and sending them back to their posts.

This lasted only a short while. Veliša and his staff had not managed to reach Miraš before the ranks of the plank-bearers had re-formed, although uneven and irregular.

"It's a good lesson; the bullet finds the fugitive," Veliša explained, pointing with a wave of his sword to about a score of dead and wounded scattered between the planks and the fascines.

Nobody paid any heed to them, and the Montenegrins looked at them with scorn, ready to vent their disgust and hatred with their knives. The slaughtered man with the sheepskin cap might never have existed. He was lying there in the open, with bare, bony stumps of arms peacefully outstretched and face split into two opposing expressions, the left, noseless, screwed up comically and monstrously deformed, and the right, with a nose, unhappy, guilty, and serious.

Urged on by a single thought, imbued with something powerful and terrible, the procession moved on together.

The defenders ceased their provocative cries, but went on firing, heavily though independently. Wounded men continued to fall, but the local fighters and the Montenegrins pressed onward exultantly and even gaily, filling the gaps with planks and their own bodies, as if death became more distant and more inaccessible the more often it took its toll.

About thirty paces from the redoubt, two openings appeared in the plank wall, to let the fascines pass, while the Montenegrins, racing up from behind, took cover behind the planks and aimed carefully at the enemy loopholes and at the heads that appeared above the teeth of the palisade.

Everything was in confusion, fascines, men, planks; they rolled onward, paying no heed to their lives, irresistibly borne onward by their own weight and impetus, by the yells and groans, as if on a flume on which there was not, could not be, any turning back.

As the first row of fascines was placed close against the enemy palisade, the trumpet sounded the charge, the Montenegrins leaped out from behind the fascines, and those behind charged forward with drawn swords and *handžar*s. They cut through the ropes that bound together the planks of the palisade, tried to tear out individual planks, thrust their gun barrels through the loopholes, and pulled at the heated enemy guns thrust between the planks. They climbed on the fascines and, seizing the tops of the planks, tried to leap over them.

The flood of attackers found the gate, at once cut the ties, and tried to force it open or throw it down. But it remained steady as a rock, reinforced by planks on the other side. "Onto the next man's shoulders, Uskoks!" shouted Veliša, waving his sword. Like the others, he was filled with red-hot, bloodthirsty enthusiasm, and yet remained cool and collected.

It all seemed like a round dance at a wedding, maddened by drink and merriment. All the slow, tedious work for the wedding was over—the food, the arrangement of the house, the welcoming of guests, the arrival of the wedding procession with its jester leader, the bringing of the bride—and now there was only food and drink and jollity. No one was frightened any more, or, it seemed, had anything to be frightened of, though men were falling dead and wounded, and screams and moans mingled with the angry and exultant cries. Still less did the corpses of the decapitated prisoners hinder that mad rejoicing. Their heads had been placed on stakes, among them Mitar's, with fierce desperation in the clenched jaws and incredulity in the half-open glassy eyes.

Yet everything was different from a wedding, from a dance. Everything was more urgent, more uncontrolled, and more infallible. No one made a mistake about anything, neither defenders nor attackers, though there was no one before whom to be ashamed. Men fell dead and wounded, and screamed from the wounds, not because of their own mistakes, but because their opponents were nimbler, stronger, or because slash or bullet came from an unexpected quarter.

Yet they heard and obeyed their leaders' orders. They climbed on one another's shoulders, and many succeeded in leaping over, clutching the points of the planks before the defenders' swords fell upon their hands or heads. Commander Miraš, too, leaped over, after standing with muddy boots on the shoulders of two men and holding his sword in his teeth.

An opening in the palisade was forced, amid joyous shouts, and the Montenegrins poured through in a mass, holding their *handžars* in the air, so as not to wound one another. Veliša stood by the opening with his sword, like a shepherd with his staff, watching what was happening on the other side, and when he considered that as many soldiers as were needed had passed through, he lowered his sword and barred the passage. He said something to an officer with huge yellow mustaches and a gold-embroidered jacket, and then passed through the opening himself.

The defenders, in disorder, crammed the bridge, crushed between two floods—the Montenegrins, who cut them down, and the Turks, who, pouring from the entrenchments on the other side of the river, pressed them back.

The fugitives from behind did not know what was happening in front of them, but, covering their heads with their hands, plunged into the crush. There was no longer anything military about them; they were more like men seeking refuge from hail or bad weather. Though it had been natural and desirable to cut down the armed enemy, to drive a stake into his entrails or a knife into his jugular or to smash his head to pieces, the slaughtering of these unarmed, fleeing, and desperately plunging enemies seemed both unnatural and senseless. The Montenegrins, for the most part, seized the fugitives by the shoulders and pushed them aside. But there were some who, with a mad enjoyment showing in their gaping jaws and dancing eyes, cut and slashed about them on all sides at the bewildered and disarmed men.

But the real clash, such as could not have been foreseen but was bound to happen, began on the bridge itself when the two armies, having cleared the avalanche of fugitives between them, met one another with every kind of knife and rifle butt, with fists, nails, and teeth. Neither side shot, for the bullets might hit their own men in the confusion. It was cutting, slashing, hand-to-hand conflict.

Commander Veliša obviously had the intention of seizing the bridge and, if possible, the entrenchments on the far side of the river, after disposing of the fugitives. But he must have been aware that he could gain little advantage from that as long as the enemy held the fortifications on the hillocks, whose fire raked the bridge. Probably because of this, he did not let more than sixty men through to exploit his victory to the full and to reconnoiter the possibilities of following up his success. He also had to do this to help those who had leaped over the palisade.

The Moslems who had rushed to defend the bridge were rather few in number, but they were encouraged by the shouts of their far more numerous comrades behind them. In their counter-charge, there was something rash and unconsidered. Even if they could drive the Montenegrins from the bridge, they would not be able to hold it, since they would be exposed to the fire of the men in the captured redoubt. Yet individually or in groups of five or six, unable to restrain their lust for battle, they leaped to the aid of their men in the struggle for the bridge.

The narrowness of the bridge at first made it impossible for more than two men at a time from each side to settle accounts. The fighters halted, looked at each other, shouted something insulting, and then fell upon one another. It seemed to each of them as though every man had a dozen hands and a hundred swords or *handžars*, but the clash would last only a moment or two, until the slit throat yawned, the slashed hand fell, or the severed ear was cast aside. Men fell rapidly, but hardly had three or four from each side come to grips when others forced their way past them. There was such a boiling torrent on the bridge that only those who were fighting could distinguish their adversaries, seeking them out not only with their eyes, but also by touch, while wrestling for their own lives with hand, tooth, or steel. Thus close-knit, the fighters used their swords less; swords and *handžars* were now too long. They fought with knives and dag-gers, throttled one another, gouged out eyes, tore at lips and mus-taches, broke necks, and slashed at throats. The bridge thundered as if a herd of horses were stampeding. The fight went on over dead men, scattered brains, and slashed guts, and the creaking rails of the bridge were decorated with hanging limbs and en-trails.

The standards moved forward, one against the other, a little bent, as were the fighters themselves. As each reached its own end of the bridge, it halted and wavered to and fro, as if considering what to do and where to go. But old Djurković shouted some-thing to his nephew and to those in front of him and forced the Montenegrin standard onward. It rose and fell and old

Djurković, stumbling over corpses, shouted from the melee: "Ha, let us see who is a Montenegrin!"

Beside the standard were his son and Sinan, one to guard it, the other to take it over should the standard-bearer be killed. At the center of the bridge, the standard and its defenders were halted by the crush, though behind them a wave of men pressed onward, guided and encouraged by the standard.

Paying no heed to those who were fighting, Sinan edged along the rail with his *handžar,* forced his way forward, and had succeeded in getting within three or four paces of the Turkish standard when Haim, the Plav butcher, a young man whom the whole district knew for his strength and his readiness for a fight, rushed at him with a cleaver. With disheveled red hair and dark face, he twisted his thick lips and swore at those in front of him demanding that they let him through. The crush was so great that neither he nor Sinan could use his weapon. Sinan tried to pierce Haim with his *handžar,* but his enemy parried with a stroke of his cleaver. Then they fought breast to breast, forcing the crowd aside and meeting at the railing. But their struggle lasted only a few moments. Pressed close against one another, they crashed into the railing. It cracked and gave way, and the two contestants fell through into the river. On the water appeared a Montenegrin cap and a fez, one beside the other, and a short while later, farther down the river, two bodies locked in mortal embrace.

As if waiting for the collapse of the railing, the fighters began to fall through it or to push one another into the turbulent abyss. On both sides men fell to throttling one another, as if their own death had become for them the sole aim and the final, fullest enjoyment. They were united by clan connections, oaths, obligations, and honor, but now even more by the joy of senseless killing and self-sacrifice.

Stojan felt as if he no longer had any personality of his own; he was without a past and without memories, filled with a lust for killing and maiming. His own ecstasy and the surge of the crowd forced him into the melee, thrusting his *handžar* into the throat of a thin, gray, lanky man, who still advanced, wheezing and sucking the blade into his body. Stojan found himself thrown down on the planks with his victim, who impotently squeezed his neck with bony fingers, as if embracing him, while he, hemmed in by bodies, legs, heads, tried in vain to rise and pull his *handžar* out of his opponent's body. Then he saw or felt the hilt of someone's sword, let go of his *handžar,* and put out his hand to seize it. But a pale, long-fingered hand snatched the hilt before he did. He pulled his hand back to grip his own *handžar,* but both the *handžar* and the hands that had been throttling him had vanished. He thought: Without a *handžar* I cannot fight! And I dare not go back without it—for the shame. He knew that such a thought was comic and stupid at such a moment, when his own life was at stake, but the thought of the shame would not leave him. It struck him that it would have been better if he had lost his gun. He heard above him old Djurković shouting: "Hold the standard! Die beneath it!" Exerting all his strength, he threw off a Moslem and a Montenegrin who were fighting hand to hand above him. They were close together, tearing at one another's face and throat with their teeth. Light appeared above him and, as if from the sun, a hand with a bloodstained knife struck at him; but the blow did not reach him. Old Djurković struck the man in the face with his *handžar,* and Stojan again found himself on his feet, pressed against the swaying railing. Only then could he see what was happening.

At one end of the bridge, Veliša was waving his sword, just as he had at the opening into the redoubt, and shouting: "Forward! Forward!" At the other end of the bridge, the Plav mudir, Isabeg, a tall, graying, thickset man in ceremonial dress, was brandishing his curved sword and shouting: "Come back! Come back!"

Djurković's nephew was bent over the railing, a *handžar* in his stomach. Stojan seized a sword from a man whose face he did not see, grasped young Djurković under the arm, and, forcing his way along the railing, took him back. The young man gripped his stomach and the blade with his hands, as if afraid that the *handžar* would fall out. Old Djurković's son, carrying the standard, went back, too. The standard flowed out behind him, still pointing at the enemy, as if it paid no heed to the retreat of the standard-bearer.

At the end of the bridge, beside Veliša, the old man Šuto wailed: "A crush like that is not for old bones," while from behind, cutting through the commotion like a sickle through grass, came Djurković's sibilant cry: "Save the standard, save it!"

Stojan did not want to look back; he knew that it was terrible on the bridge. The uproar, the killing, the cracking of the curved railing, the clashing, striking, slashing, and goring pierced him with countless fiery points. But he had to return to it, for Veliša, having handed Djurković's nephew on to Šuto, ordered: "Look to old Djurković, Radak!"

The crush was still boiling, tearing, strangling, pressing onward, and old Djurković, two or three paces from Stojan, leaning upon a *handžar* as on a staff, was wheezing and coughing, his throat pierced. Stojan lifted him and carried him back, hearing Veliša explaining as he passed him: "They nearly took my standard; because of foolish heroism."

With his moaning, bloodstained burden, Stojan withdrew behind the palisade. Someone spread out a blanket, and he put old Djurković down beside his nephew. Both were dying, there among those already dead and those wounded, some of whom were sitting on folded coats or on fascines. As a hunter and as a Radak, Stojan understood wounds. But here there were neither bandages nor salves, and anyway that was not his job. A special group was taking the wounded men back from the battlefield to the road, where women with horses took charge of them and carried them to villages behind the lines. He was sorry for young Djurković, who now grasped his stomach with his hands as if the *handžar* were still in it. The young man opened his dark eyes, filled with the reflection of the clear sky, and stifled his pain and guilt. "I wanted," he whispered, "to take the standard from Uncle, but they got me first." Paying no heed to his groans, two locals picked him up by the shoulders and knees and threw him onto a stretcher of unpeeled twigs plaited with ropes. Old Djurković made an effort to say something, but could only scrabble with his fingers at the edges of his cloak, while his son, standing above him, weakly holding the standard, wept, looking now at his father, now at Veliša by the half-closed opening in the redoubt.

It was incomprehensible that the gap should be half-closed while there were still fighters on the bridge. Stojan ran to the palisade, climbed on top of a fascine, pushing away a thickset Montenegrin, and stuck his head over the pointed tips. On the bridge there were still wounded men, about a score on each side, holding to the railings, crawling on all fours, trying to flee. But the Moslems, from the trench, and the Montenegrins, from the redoubt, aiming calmly, were shooting down everyone who tried to extricate himself from the piles of dead. They fired as if they were at target practice, applauding when they hit someone. And though the Montenegrins, as well as the local Moslems, brought up from childhood with firearms, were famous as good marksmen, they missed more often than not. They fired badly because of their impatience to score a hit, afraid that someone else would hit the same target.

Seeing what was happening to the wounded on the bridge, Stojan, too, steadied his gun, keeping close watch on the movements of the wounded Moslems. He drew a bead on a shaven head, whose owner's hands, clutching the top rail, were pulling him out of the mass, but his thickset neighbor warned him: "That one's mine."

A tall youth with a large head crawled out of a pile of Montenegrin wounded; he could not walk. A Moslem near him shook himself like a cock and then attacked him, in the hope of killing him with his bare teeth. The Montenegrins in the palisade called out encouragement to the youth, shouting to him by name, Markiša, but they could not prevent the Moslems from concentrating their fire on him. Stojan's neighbor finally fired and missed. The shaven head still moved, and the Montenegrin was dying under the enemy's jaws.

Stojan held his breath and took aim at the shaven head; now, it was his turn. He waited a moment or two, until the head was still, recalling that everything alive halts for a moment, and it is possible to fill it with lead as soon as it pauses. He pressed the trigger, and the shaven head fell like a pumpkin with its stalk cut through; the hands slipped slowly from the railing. At that moment they killed the tall Montenegrin, as he was trying to slip under the railing into the river. His hands and his long, sparse black hair vanished over the edge into the gray waters. His neighbor jogged Stojan with his elbow and, gazing at him with prominent green eyes, congratulated him enviously and asked with curiosity: "You're a good shot! Who are you?"

"I'm from this district; Radak, Stojan Radak. The shot was a near one, and I am a hunter."

"A hunter? Well, that accounts for it," the popeyed man said with satisfaction, and again took aim.

They killed all of them, to a man, on one side and the other. In truth, they were not so much killing men as aiming at every living movement, a hand that clutched, a leg that twitched, a head that rose for a moment. When there was no longer any movement, they aimed haphazardly at groans, coughs, sighs. As they did it, they freely exposed their heads, both the Montenegrins, from the palisade, and the Moslems, from the entrenchments, for they did not shoot at one another until silence and stillness covered the bridge. Only then, as if by agreement, did they begin to withdraw into cover and search for cracks to watch and gun barrels to aim at.

Then, suddenly, they all grew tired, were overcome by sleep. They stretched out, yawned, wiped away sweat, though there was no special reason for their fatigue, since there was none among them who had been fighting on the bridge. Some of them, hungry, took bread from their bags, while others filled short pipes with tobacco and kindled tinder with sparks.

Looking around for a place to sit, Stojan remembered Mitar Drndar and his son. Their heads and bodies had been taken down from the stakes and laid out on the open field, about ten paces away. The Montenegrins and locals had taken away their dead and wounded, but because the prisoners had no one of their own kin, they had only been taken down from the stakes, so as not to be a hindrance during the fighting. The heads had been laid out without order, near bodies to which they did not belong. Stojan felt sorry for Mitar and his son, not so much because they belonged to his clan, but because they had been hard-working, honest, and unfortunate men, and he felt it would be wrong if they were buried with heads that were not theirs. He went over and took Mitar's head—it was light, incredibly light for all that had been in it: the destruction of the Radaks, the horrors of the battle, despair for his son. That head had thought, discussed, looked at men and the world, had had its place among them, and now of all that there was only a memory; it was visible only until earth covered it. The same fate might well be his, Stojan's. And so it would be, one way or another, someday.

He did not mourn or, as the custom was, kiss the head. Tears and kissing were unnatural in the midst of a battle, in the vastness of death and the horror everywhere around him. Only now did he begin to realize that death and that horror, since only now did they come into his mind, mingled with almost impersonal depression and fatigue. He put the head on Mitar's body, and the head that had been on Mitar's body he put on that from which he had taken Mitar's. All the heads but one he recognized, but he did not know to which bodies they belonged.

Worn out, he went back to look again for somewhere to sit. Now at last he felt bodily fatigue; his joints ached and he felt drowsy. Seated on a fascine, leaning back against the palisade, feeling the warm, golden kiss of the sun on his face, soothing his doubts and fears, he heard through his drowsiness Veliša saying mockingly to Miloš, as if thorns were pricking at his hearing: "No matter! No matter! You philosophers . . ." The word "philosophers," which Stojan had heard before, must mean wise and learned men. Veliša uttered it with a jeer, though it was not clear why he did so. He went on: "You philosophers know nothing about war and you never will. As if it were not necessary to rush the bridge! You think that war can be measured by line and rule. For war there is no other measure than—kill, so that you yourself are not killed. Kill as many as you can. I, too, knew that we could not take that bridge. That was not our aim, but to let the men play a bit, let them put the fear of God into the Turks, let them bleed and sweat a little, let them be tempered and learn what war is. . . ."

Stojan no longer heard words or shots, only a gentle rippling of waves. He had withdrawn to the head of the lake through the reed bed, where were the secret paths and lairs of the otters, which he kept to himself, telling no one of them except Izet-beg, who did not hunt with traps. The first snow had fallen. The lake was not yet frozen over, and, trembling with pleasant fatigue in the morning chill and in the expectation of quarry, he approached the well-known dense patches of willows, whose branches in the wind kissed the greenish water with their long pale-green leaves. Otters were wary of traps, aware of even the most insignificant changes in the earth and able to sense on the buried iron the slightest traces of human scent. Nonetheless, in the little sandy cove under the willow he had caught otters. Finding, in the moist earth between the low tufts of grass and the young willows, traces of the beast's claws, he had set his trap there, taking great care to leave no traces of his own.

The change of season had aroused uneasiness among the otters, and they liked, at night, to gather and play on the snow-covered strand. He noticed that the little animals had left traces on the beach of last night's playtime. It seemed to him that he could see, in the undergrowth where the trap was, the coarse gray furry animal jerking and cowering, as if it were ashamed that it had let itself be caught. But he had not advanced more than four or five paces when, just as he was setting foot on the tiny beach, a huge trap snapped, one of those used for trapping wolves, under his right foot. Its rusty triangular teeth gripped him just below the right knee. It was inconceivable that anyone could have set a wolf trap there; a wolf would never set foot there, and there was no one in the vicinity who hunted them. Then he began to understand. *Someone has set that trap for me! But why, why? What harm have I done him? I only hunt; I take what God has offered equally to all men, and I am not to blame that I am more skillful than others. I am not to blame, I am not to blame! Yet here I am! Their trap has caught me. A wolf trap. It was no wolf that lay in wait for me, but a man, a neighbor—with a wolf trap. Why? Why?* But he knew there was little profit in his anger and his reasoning, and the trap gripped him, cut into him with its rusted, terrible teeth. With all his strength, he tried to force it open, but it once more closed on him. As soon as he thought he had succeeded—a little more, just a little more, and he would be free— his strength failed him, and the trap closed again with a terrible creaking, fracturing his bone and tearing his flesh. It did not hurt much. His terror was not so much from the pain, as from the loneliness of the place, from the injustice God had wrought on him. At the same time the lake suddenly grew rough, though there was no wind, and began to rise, though it was winter, and the waters ought to be falling. Already the waves along the beach were lapping at his feet, those distant waves which cut off his view while he, vainly, impotently, struggled in the trap. It horrified him how whoever had set the trap had known that the lake would rise and drown him. But there it was; someone had known—and in that was all the malignity and the evil. For he could, somehow or other, free himself from the trap if the waters were not rising. And as for the water; he could swim, even though the lake was cold, if the trap were not gripping him. There was no way out! He thought of calling for help. He even shouted, though his voice had not the force to make itself heard. Anyway, it was senseless to call; there was no one to hear him so early in the morning, and even if there were, no one would dare to wade or row out to him through the now turbulent and flooded lake. The water was already up to his waist, and as he bent over to struggle with the trap, it lapped at his lips, threatening to cover them. With his last reserves of strength, while mouth and chest were taking in mingled air and water, he tried to open the jaws. At last he succeeded in freeing his leg from its teeth, but when he tried to lift his leg a little, his strength failed, and he was no longer able to hold apart the yawning jaws of the trap. They once more leaped at his leg and gripped him, and the waters flowed in icy waves over his mouth, his eyes, his head. In terror, he started up and stood upright, uttering senseless cries, for which alone he still had the strength.

Someone was shaking him by the shoulders, and the voice that belonged to those bulging eyes mocked him: "You're a bit scared, my Radak. You've had a bad dream."

He came back to reality, to the field and the rested soldiers, to the clear sky and the gentle rippling of the river, and, stretching out his stiffened right leg, he remembered his dream and the throttling on the bridge. At the same time he felt intolerably hungry; from noon the day before, he had eaten nothing. He rose, stretched himself, and peered over the palisade.

Moslem women with unveiled faces were carrying their dead from the bridge. So, too, were the Montenegrin women. Holding to the custom that one did not shoot at women and that the removal of the dead from the battlefield was permitted, no one from either side shot at them. But they, in words, continued the battle. The Montenegrin women corroded the entrails of mothers with oaths and curses, turned children to stone, and poured on Plav and every house in it insults and threats, while the Moslem women, more docile, bound Heaven and earth with black lamentations, razed the Montenegrin hills, and exterminated the name and seed of the Montenegrins. A bullet, like the snap of an invisible finger, struck close to Stojan's left cheek with such force that he at once knelt, and the ubiquitous popeyed man, his short teeth showing through sparse reddish mustaches, jeered at him. "Look out, whiskers. You're not a woman. Their songs will give them no shame if they twist your neck for you."

The popeyed man, when Moslems had to be killed, was envious and mocking. But in fact he was good-humored, and gaiety shone in his puffy red face. He took out of his striped bag a fairly large maize loaf and a hunk of bacon fat. Spreading the bag out on a fascine, he offered some to Stojan. "Let's have a bite. I see that you haven't even an empty bag. With us military martyrs, it's like that. What you have to eat serves for your comrade, also; it's his, too. Share and share alike."

Stojan accepted eagerly, though concealing his hunger. The food was all the sweeter to him since there was now a lull in the battle around the bridge, except for the occasional shots of those who were still amusing themselves trying to pick out enemy caps or noses.

Time had passed much more quickly than anyone could have thought. Everything that had happened that morning, even the advance of the planks and the fascines, could be compressed into about an hour. Now, judging from the sun, it was about noon, one of those moments when armies, by tacit agreement, because of the need for food or sleep, break off fighting. Even over the battlefield on the far side of the river, there was now silence, through which flew soundlessly a flock of geese. The waves of the river splashed and gurgled, accompanied by the slow breathing of the rising lake among the reed beds. The soldiers, as if there had never been a battle or in longing to forget about it as quickly as possible, joked gaily, hospitably offered food and drink, or loudly toasted one another with flasks of plum brandy. The Montenegrins and the locals poked fun at one another because of differences in speech and habits, ways of life, or points of view.

They waited with open mouths and staring eyes for the end of Šuto's improper stories, which went well with food, drink, sun, and mutual teasing, and then burst into laughter or violent applause. One story went: "A real Asiatic Turk lay one night with a serf's wife. In the morning the serf was weeping, and his neighbors, as neighbors will, consoled him. 'It's no great matter; she's as good as ever she was. He hasn't harmed her.' And he said to them: 'It's not that I'm sorry about, brothers, but when a little Turk is born, who will be able to talk to him?' "

Then the Montenegrins began to mock at one another in rhymed couplets, by clans and tribes, and so did the locals, by villages and hamlets, exposing one another's shames and waggeries.

Still drowsy, chewing the maize bread and bacon fat with enjoyment, Stojan listened with pleasure, freeing himself from his dream, his terror, and the misfortune of Mitar Drndar, who, with his son, was still lying about ten paces away.

The battle began again with a messenger, with uneasiness. The messenger, without dismounting, whispered something to Veliša, and he to the messenger. Though the messenger went away at a gallop, the soldiers soon concluded that there was still no trace of the Vasojevići army, as far downriver as Murina.

Soon another messenger, a foot soldier, hurried across the open field with the message that the men of Gusinje were mustering behind the hill, certainly with the aim of recapturing the redoubt.

Veliša ordered Miraš to go with half a platoon and the locals toward the Gusinje redoubt, while he and his staff and half a detachment would stay at this redoubt, where they could see over the whole battlefield and make contact with the Voivode, if he was able to break through to Plav.

The men of Gusinje first charged the hillock below the redoubt. They attacked, calling on Allah and discharging their rifles, in masses, which broke up and withdrew as soon as they met stiff opposition, but re-formed again quickly. They were, for the most part, in dark clothing, but many Shquiptars, with their white skullcaps and white peasant dress, could be seen among them, as if white and black sheep were mingled together.

The Montenegrins resisted vigorously, and two or three times there was hand-to-hand fighting. Then, surrounded on three sides and watched with curiosity by the whole battlefield, they began to retreat in good order above the road.

Noticing that their right wing was threatened and that the enemy had the upper hand, the Montenegrins at the Gusinje redoubt began to retreat before they came into actual contact with the enemy. In small groups they ran across the open ground, as if avoiding encirclement, to join the right wing on the hillside.

But just as the first group was halfway across the open ground, a mass of Shquiptars fell like an avalanche on the abandoned redoubt, freed the openings, and the Gusinje cavalry, without forming into ranks, though the white horseman was again leading them, began to emerge by twos and threes, giving free rein to their horses.

"By platoons, at the double, to the hill!" shouted Veliša, mounting his horse, which had been brought to him.

It was clear to everyone, even without an order, what must be done. Retreat downriver into the woods and copses would be dangerous, for the enemy would be able to shoot at them from the other bank as easily as at a shooting gallery. The only way out was to capture the hill once again, and also the road below them where yesterday and again that same morning they had opened battle, while the horsemen were still busy cutting down the men retreating from the Gusinje redoubt. Everyone's eyes searched uneasily for the Commander. But Veliša did not leave them; he pranced around them on his horse, while Miloš rode among them, looking worriedly now at his horse's mane, now at the slaughter going on five or six hundred paces to the left. The others, too, running breathlessly, were unable to drag their eyes away from the terrifying sight, yet were forced to take care not to stumble on the uneven ground or fall into potholes.

At first the enemy riders charged into the Montenegrins individually, but meeting with resistance—three riderless horses were already straying on the open ground—they grouped into three bands of about thirty men each and charged at the last group, of about a score of Montenegrins. In the furious, indistinguishable interplay of horses' hoofs and the still-swifter and more frantic flashing of swords, all that was left of the Montenegrins in a few moments was a pandemonium of limbs, weapons, and heads, which five or six riders, dismounting, carefully divided, going from one man to another with bared swords, while the others rushed off to attack another group.

Certainly that terrible settlement of accounts lasted longer than it seemed. The group about Veliša was already halfway to the hill before the slaughter came to an end. But what was incomprehensible was that almost no one among the Montenegrins, till then brave and able fighters, defended himself; only five or six shots were heard, and no one either shouted or called for help. They died silently, in a foreign land, slaughtered by a power they did not know how to resist, while Veliša, forgetting that they could not hear him, shouted furiously: "Kill the horses, kill the horses!"

Like a single body with a hundred legs, the horsemen spurred on their horses and themselves by invocations to Allah and rushed at the second group. But this group had already reached the point where the road led upward and the open ground was cut by the stream. There the cavalry could not maneuver, and the Montenegrins could re-form their ranks and offer resistance. Among them could be seen Commander Miraš, in full ceremonial dress, mustering the men around him with waves of his hand. They quickly formed into a solid bunch, bristling with rifles. A united volley met the horsemen before they charged. The fallen horses and riders caused confusion, but they at once formed into three groups and attacked the Montenegrins from three sides.

"Shoot, shoot! Don't take aim, just shoot!" yelled Veliša to his men. But his soldiers were unwilling to shoot. They suspected that after the horsemen had dealt with the group they were now surrounding, it would be their turn next, since the group around Miraš had already reached the forest. They were afraid of being caught with rifles unloaded, and some were hurrying to retreat, taking no heed of anything. Unexpectedly, Veliša drew his revolver and, shouting, "Shoot, you sons of whores!" urged his rearing, prancing horse across the path of the fugitives.

The fugitives stopped. Others rushed after them, and then they, too, stopped. They were forced to shoot and await the horsemen's charge, for everyone suspected, was even sure, that Veliša would shoot down all who tried to flee.

There below the hill, the first ranks of the Shquiptars and the Gusinje infantry had reached that first group of Montenegrins cut down by the horsemen, and had stopped to strip and plunder the corpses. The second group of Montenegrins, which had been surrounded a short while before, was still defending itself, approaching the rise and the brook. Holding their rifles over their heads, they dashed under the swords and under the horses' hoofs, driving their *handžars* into the horses' stomachs, pulling off the riders, and rolling with them on the ground.

The fire from Veliša's group encouraged Miraš's men, who had now reached the wood and begun to shoot, though intermittently. There was confusion among the horsemen, who suddenly found themselves between three fires. Some began to retreat, others went on cutting down the stragglers from Miraš's group, while the main body, led by the white horseman, rushed toward Veliša.

From the start, Stojan had noticed in himself and others a desire to be in the center of the mass. This unrealizable general wish brought with it disorder. The main incentive was not so much the need to take shelter in the entrails of the mass, as sheer, naked personal fear before the imminence of death. As this became clear to him, his respect rose for Veliša, cunning and regardless, but also heroic, able to look death in the eyes and lead them back to face it. He knelt to take aim more surely. Others, too, did so, while still others drew their *handžars*.

He aimed and fired at a green breast, and over him passed the thunder of hoofbeats, the shouts of horsemen, and the swish of swords. He struck at the tendons of the last horse's legs. The horse fell backward, then leaped across the open space; another behind him neighed, and a voice groaned, "Mother mine!" He heard the Commander's order: "Kill the horses, kill the horses!" But there was no horse left, only a coarse red scarf and a heap of bloody entrails wrapped around a horse's hoofs. He turned around quickly, but the cavalry had retreated as swiftly as it had advanced. From the hill, Miraš and his platoons came running, urged on by the blasts of the trumpet and their own discordant but loud cries of "Hurrah, hurrah!"

Toward the hill, a youth was running, with hands over his head; that he was young could be seen by the ease and agility of his leaps. A rider on a black horse and in black clothes overtook him and struck with his curved sword at hands and head. Both groups fired at the rider, but it was too late. After felling the youth, he rode away, gaily waving his sword in the air. Looking around, Stojan saw that almost a quarter of them, about fifty men, were dead or wounded.

Taking their wounded with them, they hastily withdrew to the road below the hill, the shouts of the unseen Shquiptars drumming in their ears. They went on withdrawing, slowly, for more than a quarter of an hour. Veliša had left a rear guard at the stream, and halted in the middle of the village, once again at the knez's house. On the other side of the Lim, a battle was raging around the upper palisade at Skić.

Veliša dismounted, unbuttoned his coat, folded it, and sat down. "No matter! We shall halt here. We must. Adjutant Miloš, write!"

Taking a yellow pen and a notebook from his leather bag, Miloš remarked: "We fell into a trap."

"Rubbish! What trap? They got reinforcements while we . . . the trap is somewhere else, not with the Turks. No matter! Write!"

He spoke softly, so that the soldiers would not hear, and when the message was ready, called Stojan. "It's urgent! Can you ford the river?"

"Difficult. It's difficult to find a ford at this time."

"Can you swim across? Do you know how to swim?"

"Swim across? I know. I can. I will get across."

"Take this letter." He pulled him closer and whispered in his ear. "And if you lose the letter, tell the Voivode or his clerk, Tomo: 'We cannot hold out. The Shquiptars have attacked, and we have no reinforcements. The Vasojevići have not come, as was agreed. There is no trace of them from here to Murina and far below Murina!' Just that, nothing else!" Then, holding Stojan close to him, he went on: "I might be able to shout it to them across the river. But that would dishearten our soldiers. Then, too, the river is roaring too loudly. I don't know who would hear me or whether they would hear me right. And it is better that such things be said by letter; then it is known who said them and when."

Stojan tucked the letter into his cap and forced his cap tightly on his head. Then he took off his rifle and looked around for the old man Šuto, to leave it with him. "The old fellow was cut down," Veliša remarked. "Give the gun and everything else that

you don't need to the clerk. The water must be very cold just
now; take care you don't get cramp."

But Stojan knew what the Commander did not know: the Lim
here was as cold in summer as in winter, and no one knew when
cramp might take the breath from one. "It's never got me yet.
So—if I am lucky," he replied calmly, with a sudden pride.

"That's how it is. In all my army there's not a single swimmer.
We have grown up on the stone, in a waterless land," Veliša said.

"It's hard to find one even here. Here the waters are too cold to
learn to swim. But I had to—because of hunting."

"May God be with you!" Veliša shook him by the hand and
ordered: "Two of you go with him, even if you cannot help him.
A man is on his mettle when there are others watching him."

The Lim was a river in which Stojan had bathed joyfully from
childhood. Its transparent blueness and its golden-scaled fish were
a part of his youth. Whenever he looked back on his life, the Lim
always seemed to him different, now turbid as plowland, now
gray and hard as steel, now clear and vibrant as a girl's song in the
mountains; but always present in his breath and blood, in his life
and in his dreams. Yet now it was as if he could not recognize his
river—or himself.

He was not frightened by its turgid, twilit depths under the
shining waves. He had known it like this, and even more terrible
and mysterious, when, after the sudden melting of the snows, it
raged cloudily between its banks. The place was known to him, a
longish eddy making a white band along the main current. The
willows on the undercut, sandy banks now hung over it with reddish young branches, yellowed by new-washed snail tracks. Everything was familiar, every pebble known and dear, but at the same
time alien, wilder. He himself was no longer as he had been yesterday, before the battle. It was not that his conscience reproached him for the Moslems he had killed; once he was in the
battle, that had to be. But the fighting itself, his participation in
it, had in the course of a night and half a day changed both him
and everything about him. His conception of himself and of his
world had changed. He did not know how, did not even try, to
explain to himself what that change was and how it had taken
place. But it was evident; another Stojan wriggled out of the shell
of that former and familiar Stojan, revealing a merciless hardness,

first toward himself and then toward everything else, and by that fact alien to himself. Would he have been able, until yesterday, to eat and joke so sweetly alongside the decapitated Mitar and his son? Would he have been able to take aim so carefully at men, even though they were enemies? Would he have been trapped in a dream? Would he, finally, without words or without argument, even with a secret joy, have risked being drowned in the chill and swollen river?

The Lim flowed unseen and vibrant, nearer and dearer than all rivers, than all houses, than all persons. But it seemed to him as if the fair, thin boy Stojan Radak, a lively and leggy youth, had never before stood beside it, nor had the pensive and quick-witted forty-year-old who, until a short time before, had been so entranced by mountains and waters that he had neglected to get married and found his own household. The man standing there now was a man and a soldier like any other, obsessed by the thought of cramp and shivering with cold on the sandy spit. The link that till then had existed between Stojan and his beloved river had been broken; he and the river now lived, now flowed, separately.

He crossed himself and prayed to God, as a man must before undertaking a new and dangerous task, and he prayed, too, to the Lim, his river, to return to him, to accept him, that they might flow and live inseparably.

He undressed quickly, tied his clothes, sword, and pistol in a bundle on his head, and then, turning to his companions, who were watching him with pity, remarked: "Perhaps we could have found a calmer and narrower place farther down—but it doesn't matter."

He first splashed himself and rubbed his body with the water to get accustomed to the cold, and then stepped in. The water came up to his waist and carried him away. He swam slowly, to prevent the bundle on his head from getting wet.

This was nothing that he had not done before, but nonetheless he was afraid of the depths, the rapids, and the cramp, of something indefinite that he had never feared before. His breath came short, and his heart seemed to swell within him. But the farther he went, the more the river, with its chill clouded depths, responded, though not completely or willingly, to his silent calls for help. Gradually it merged with his body and his memories; it washed away all doubts, all terrors, and alienation.

At last his foot touched the smooth pebbles at the bottom, and almost at the same time he caught hold of a willow branch that danced above the turbulent waters. With an effort he dragged himself onto the undercut bank, for the bundle on his head got tangled with the slender branch and forced him back like a spring. As he climbed out, his chest and haunches covered with sand, he looked back at the river and at his companions. They were still standing on the bank, waving gaily to him, and the river, once more his, flowed on unceasingly and with no return. He laughed, waved his hand, and rubbed his smarting skin while jumping from foot to foot.

As he made his way through the thickets, he could hear heavy firing from the direction of Plav. It even seemed to him that he could hear the cries of the men. But in the undergrowth there was no trace of man or beast. The men were disputing the battle-fields, and the beasts lay hidden in their lairs.

When he came out from the whiteness and quiet of the under-growth, just below the Novšić entrenchments, he found, in a little narrow meadow, a heap of headless corpses, which the Moslem women from the nearby villages were stacking neatly on the road below the hill. The Montenegrins had not, as was their custom, taken away the severed heads to boast of them and preen themselves before their clans or companies, probably because there were too many of them and their own villages were too far away. Two Moslem women had collected the heads in a huge basket, which they carried between them, and then—just as the Montenegrins and locals had done with the heads of the prisoners from the redoubt—placed them on the stumpy, twisted necks, paying no heed to, or not knowing, to which body each head belonged.

These were the victims of yesterday's battle. The dead Monte-negrins had already been carried downstream last night to Veliko, and, judging from the remains here, the dead men had for the most part been Moslem peasants from the neighborhood. Someone from the Montenegrin command had certainly ordered or permitted the Moslem women to collect their dead, and they carried out their task with the meticulous zeal of a peasant woman on her own land, though this work was in no way reminiscent of harvesting or haymaking.

Counting those carried away and those still lying on the field, there must have been up to two hundred who had died in this short, narrow meadow, not wider than a hundred paces and not longer than three hundred paces. They proved that the conflict must have been sudden and fierce. Some of the bodies had been hastily thrown in front of the still-unfinished redoubt to make a barrier toward Plav.

Strangely enough, none of this fighting had been visible the day before from the farther side of the river. It must have taken place at the same time as the skirmish under Commander Veliša. Stojan looked across the Lim. The ranks of Veliša's army could be seen retreating, while the field between the bridge and the hill was being slowly blackened and whitened by the disordered masses of the Shquiptars. Where until yesterday there had been houses and outbuildings in which Veliša's troops had taken refuge, a pall of sooty smoke shot through with red and yellow flames eddied and billowed downriver and seemed to lick the snow-covered sides of the mountains.

On the road before him, beside the rows of corpses, an old man with a rounded, soot-blackened white beard, wearing a white turban, and bent over a staff, was throwing stones with childish clumsiness at a yellow shepherd dog, which deliberately ignored him and went on sniffing around the corpses.

Recognizing the old hodža Mehmed, Stojan wondered how he had dared to await the coming of the Montenegrins. Though he was known as a mild and peaceable man, he was nonetheless exposed to the danger that some fanatic might cut off his head in order to boast of having won the head of a member of a famous house, or just for the pleasure of killing a Moslem hodža. Even if there were no danger to him from the Montenegrins, the local peasants might have remembered him with hatred and revenge, especially those from Veliko, still longing to avenge the eighty-year-old priest whose head the Plav Moslems had cut off twenty or more years ago. The hodža must have known this, but nonetheless had elected to remain to bury the dead and comfort those women and children who had not fled; as if he were outside all that was happening, outside war and death.

Stojan leaned down to pick up a stone. The dog, seeing him do so, began to run away down the road before he was able to throw it. Thinking that the dog might be looking for its master, Stojan did not throw the stone, but greeted the hodža in the name of God, and the old man, perhaps astonished at a greeting from an enemy soldier, quickly explained: "It would be a sin to let the dogs gnaw them."

"Perhaps the dog is only looking for its master?" Stojan remarked.

The old man recognized Stojan and smiled at him with toothless gums and waxen cheeks. "Perhaps," he agreed. "I, too, thought of that. But how could I, who am almost blind, tell? There was a whole pack here, but only this one stayed." Then he added as if to justify himself: "And I, you see, keep watch over the dead—both yours and ours."

Stojan wished him good fortune and set off down the road toward the hodža's *čardak*, not far away at the foot of the hill, at the upper end of the village.

In front of the *čardak* about a dozen horses were tied to a wattle fence. To right and left of it were two other houses, belonging to the hodža's relatives. A wide alley between the buildings led to a wider courtyard, on the left side of which, against the wall of the *čardak*, was a kitchen.

In the courtyard, on and around the woodpile, about six Montenegrins were sitting, eating, and telling stories. On a tree trunk by the kitchen, apart and alone, sat a dark Montenegrin. He had a rather long face, deeply wrinkled about the eyes and on the forehead, and with thin mustaches hanging downward but curled at the tips like a dandy's. He might have been about thirty-five, and, though of moderate height, was powerful and thickset, with a broad chest, sinewy limbs, and long yellow teeth. He was gnawing a roast leg of mutton. From time to time he pulled off with unbroken clawlike nails the best bits and offered them to a black-eyed little boy in a tiny greasy fez who was standing in front of him, rubbing his bare legs against one another. The whites of the Montenegrin's eyes were yellowish as if he were ill, though he was a knot of powerful muscles and tendons. Alongside him was a jug of plum brandy, from which he drank in long gulps, pouring it straight down his throat as he held it in the air. His clothes were neat and almost dandified, but in the peasant manner, and on the left side of his white jacket he wore two medals, one silver and the other gold, and a black cross trimmed with white. Montenegrins liked to wear medals, but not with such obvious pride; and on no one else did they look so striking and so picturesque, perhaps because of the width of his chest and the whiteness of his clothes. His medals were sewn close together, but they clinked only when he made a sudden movement.

From the kitchen came smoke, chattering, and the smell of food. The men around the woodpile were eating meat and wheat bread. It was lunchtime, Stojan recollected, as the Montenegrin talked to the boy, exhorting him. "Lucky for you that you are so small and are not . . . I'd soon have had your head off!" The child was silent and serious, eating ravenously.

In the course of that day and night, and also later, sometimes from the tales of others and sometimes from the man himself—for he was talkative, though he knew how and when to keep silent— Stojan came to know all that was important about that dark Montenegrin with the medals.

His real name was Gorčin Popović, but he was often called Goro Kršinoga (Broken Leg). Nicknames were common in Montenegro, and Goro had come by his when, in some scuffle, he had struck a Turk who was kneeling and had cried out: "Ha, he has broken his legs." Goro was not known by his family name, only by his exploits and his personality, which others regarded as exceptional and in which he, too, gloried.

He was one of the best-known heroes in the Voivode's army. From the age of seventeen, he had continually raided the Turks, paying no attention to the prohibitions of the tribal leaders or the disapproval of the authorities at Cetinje. Ever since he had become conscious of himself, so it was said, he had been consumed by a flame for Serbdom, a hatred of the Turks. And since he was poor, he had to live from raiding. He plundered sheep, took merchants prisoner, attacked kulas and čardaks in the Zeta plain and, not infrequently, in Podgorica itself. "I'm off on a raid," he would say, as others said, "I'm off to the vineyards." He did not know how many Moslems he had killed, and if anyone asked, he would reply in his typical jesting manner, mocking himself as much as others: "That only the Turks know! All that interests me is how many of them are still alive who must be killed." Other numbers, too, had no sort of meaning for him; he paid no heed to how many sheep he took or how much money he plundered, but spent while it lasted, and when there was no more, or a new raiding party was being formed, he again went raiding. He was no mere plunderer; he took only from the enemy, and considered such booty a part of the warfare that from time to time was stilled by armistice but that never entirely ceased. When they asked him, at the end of the last war, what he would live from, now that Montenegro and Turkey were at peace and the frontiers settled, he answered calmly: "Surely Montenegro will have some enemies. If it were not for Turkey there would be no Montenegro."

Gorčin kept not only the great, traditional, and recognized rules not to molest children, women, or the weak, as did most Montenegrins, but also some indeterminate law and order of his own, which paid little or no attention to the wishes of his superiors. Thus it happened that he often did not carry out orders if they dictated an end to the struggle or mild behavior toward the enemy.

In the spring, they had ordered him to suppress the attacks of the Moslem refugees in the newly won districts of Zeta, and to discover who their sympathizers were. When Voivode Marko Miljanov, visiting his district, asked what he was doing, he replied: "I am maltreating the people."

"Why the people?" the Voivode burst out in anger.

"They are renegades, shelterers of evildoers. There are many like that," he replied. "But to catch one like that I must plunder and smash a hundred or so others."

The Voivode, they said, thought that over and, considering that it was better not to catch the renegades than to maltreat the people, ordered a more humane procedure.

Everyone jested readily with Goro, teased him; he, too, jested readily, though he rarely smiled, as if to say: "A man must jest, but his fate is not something to laugh at; it is a serious matter." Most frequently they teased him because to him, a man of the old heroic mold, were born only daughters; he already had six. Once one of his friends called from one hillside to another to inform him of the birth of a daughter, the fifth. Gorčin retorted: "There was no need to yell at me to tell me that, no!" He was able to say:

"It's better that they are all daughters; I needn't worry if they don't turn out to be heroes," or "When they are all married off, I will at least have my house to myself." But behind these jests could be discerned a bitterness that his line would be cut short and his name extinguished, a belief, perhaps, that it was a curse upon him for the evil he did, that he had to do.

He never talked about his war exploits; warfare was a way of life for him like any other. Why talk about plowing or vine cutting? He said: "One must fight, one must live." Without boasting or telling tall stories, he was convinced that there was not a Montenegrin, and perhaps not a human being, who would display greater audacity and presence of mind in war than he. When the first medals came from Russia to be distributed among the Montenegrins, the chiefs had for some reason passed him by. At that time, he had been commander of a detachment, and, taking advantage of the absence of his chiefs, he had mustered all the medal holders from the battalion and led them in a mad charge in full view of the whole army. "Let us see who is a bastard, who prizes his life more than a medal!" Many died and many fled, revealing that many had received their medals because of their kinship or connections.

He had the rank of platoon commander and led the flying squad, which served the Voivode in all sorts of ways, mainly for stopping unexpected enemy breakthroughs or keeping order behind the lines. Now, he had just returned from escorting the wounded to Veliko.

Considering what to do next, where he should go and to whom he should report, Stojan stood in front of the kitchen watching the dark man who was tearing off and devouring pieces of meat with enjoyment and at the same time both frightening and feeding the Moslem boy. Gorčin, watching him between mouthfuls, turned toward him and, in a deep, harsh voice, interrupted by the random, furious volleys from Plav, asked: "Who are you? Where did you come from? What do you want? You are not from our army."

"I am Radak, Stojan Radak. A local. I have a letter from Commander Veliša."

"The Voivode is at the front. But there is someone here who can take letters and messages for him. How is it with you?"

"Soso. The Shquiptars are attacking."

"Did you run away?"

"We have withdrawn a little."

"A little? Till you're out of range! Come with me to the clerk, Tomo."

He threw away the bone, wiped his hands and mouth with a huge kerchief, which he stuffed back into his pocket, and then moved toward the *čardak*, talking all the while, as if to himself. "I'm afraid that this morning that Moslem lass from one of these houses put a spell on Voivode Marko. His boots were wet and tight, so he took them off to rest and to dry them, and she said to him: 'Put on your old boots—while you have time!' The Voivode laughed heartily at that, but let's hope his laughter doesn't change to mourning for us and for him."

Stojan smiled as he followed this extraordinary man.

The upper story of the *čardak* was built into the hillside, and level with the ground there was a big anteroom with a fireplace, where the soldiers were drying themselves. Gorčin led Stojan through the anteroom into a large hall, with divans along the walls. Its comfort, order, and color contrasted strongly with the war devastation and the winter cold which had seeped into everything. On one of the divans, in the left-hand corner under the window, was sleeping a bony, graying man in muddy boots. His wide brownish mustaches rose and fell over his lips. The muddy boots on the clean covers and the sleeper still in his clothes, with his weapons stacked on the floor near his head, reminded Stojan that even here the war had found its way. A second leader, small, thin, and pale, with huge bristling mustaches, which made his face seem still smaller, bonier, and older, was sitting beneath the middle window, reading a thin book. The reading and the book contradicted the impression of everything around—the soldiers, chilled and hungry, in disorderly and miscellaneous clothes, things scattered everywhere and moved from their usual places, and the deep silence in which nothing could be heard but scraps of incomprehensible conversations and the dripping of melting snow from the eaves.

The room belonged to the old man Stojan had met tending the dead. It seemed that he, broken and old, and furthermore a hodža, was unable to leave not only the poor and weak of his village, but also his precious possessions and comforts, though his brother and nephews had fled with their families and livestock, carrying off all that they could.

The little man rose from the divan, stuck a pencil in his book, and looked questioningly at Stojan and Gorčin.

"A letter from Commander Veliša," Gorčin explained, and added as if to himself: "It looks to me as if they are retreating; as if we had all become blind and deaf."

The little man quickly turned the pages of the letter, put it in the book, and the book into a leather bag. Then, listening to the shooting outside, he shouted: "A horse, let them get a horse ready!"

He began to stuff his weapons into his belt, inquiring: "Not so good over there with you? The Albanians?"

Gorčin went out, and Stojan replied: "They are attacking. The bastards are coming from all sides."

"Too late—or a bit too early!" said the little man to himself, putting on a greenish waterproof like the one worn by Veliša and the other leaders.

Stojan had no reason to stand there any longer. But, since he had not been ordered to go and had been told nothing of what would happen to the letter, he went on waiting. The little man noticed his hesitation. "I will take the letter to the Voivode. In any case, I must go to him; I am his clerk."

They went out together. The clerk leaped on the horse as easily and lithely as he had risen from the divan, and, paying no attention to the two horsemen who were to accompany him, shouted to Gorčin: "And you, get a move on with your fellows," then he spurred his horse with short, slender legs.

"Too learned," Gorčin explained mockingly. "To dig would kill him. What good is all his learning when a Turk could knock his block off with one hand?" Then he added, pityingly, as they went toward the kitchen: "But the Voivode is like that; he loves and cares for learned men. Like this Tomo. One might think he was his son." On the threshold of the kitchen he remembered something. "There's a Radak here, too. A fine young man, slightly wounded. Is he of your kin?"

"There are no Radaks on our side of the river, and all we Radaks are kin," Stojan replied, hurrying into the kitchen.

From the smoke and obscurity emerged Rade, strained, yet smiling. "They told me one of ours had come," he said, embracing Stojan. "They got me; but only a scratch—in the arm." He was almost exalted, but with a tinge of melancholy, rather than pride, in having been wounded.

He told Stojan that Grgur and one or two of the Radaks had gone the day before to their village. He, too, had wanted to go, but had overslept, and they had not wanted to wake him because of his wound. "And what for? There, it was all desolation," he added looking away.

He had been wounded in yesterday's battle, on the open ground from which the women had been dragging the corpses. He had seen the Voivode when he had left for the battlefield the day before. The Voivode's horse, an Albanian bay, had held its head so high that he could only see part of the Voivode himself. He had been dressed in rich clothing, serge and gold, but in everything else he had been simple. He was severe only toward cowards and plunderers. "One of his mustaches is white and the other black," Rade added with wondering admiration, "so when you look at his face from one side he looks like a youth and from the other like an old man."

The battle the day before had begun, by his account, in the same way as on the other side of the river. As they moved up the Lim they had met scouts on the road, exchanged a few shots, and had then withdrawn to tell the eager soldiers and leaders what they had seen. The left wing of the army had taken to the hills and advanced slowly along the road, meeting with no serious resistance right up to the Novšić fields and meadows. Even then, when they finally clashed with the enemy, there was much random firing, and only two men had been wounded, by stray bullets. Seeing the Moslems retreating, the Montenegrins had pressed after them, though their leaders had warned them not to be in too much of a hurry. So they had come upon the cavalry and had begun to flee, some uphill, others into the undergrowth. Rade had fled madly uphill, and only when he had sat down to rest had he noticed that he was wounded in the arm. The two armies had met on the open field below, and he, paying no attention to his wound and ashamed because he had run away, hurried back. Concealed by a beech overhanging the road he could see below

515

him the Plav horsemen and infantry as they passed but none of them stopped or went after him, though he was firing all the time. Then, there in front of him, there had been an engagement. They had slashed, throttled, and trodden men underfoot, but it had not seemed to him in any way terrible. It was as if it were not being done seriously, though he was seeing it all with his own eyes.

"So the battle is still going on," he concluded, "and I cannot forgive myself that I left it yesterday. I don't believe that I killed even one Turk. Somehow I felt confused; Gorčin says that always happens the first time. And my arm hurt, though it is only a scratch. Plav might fall without me. I get none of the luck!"

At Gorčin's call from the courtyard that he should go to the front, for the Voivode might have need of him there, Stojan embraced Rade and called out: "I'll look in when I come back."

But the youth shouted, rushing into the kitchen: "I'm coming, too. Just let me get my gun and my bag."

Gorčin went with him and also Gorčin's assistant, Stanoje, a handsome man of medium height, with shining black hair, pale cheeks, full red lips, and even, glistening teeth. He was taciturn, but kept smiling to himself for no apparent reason. He was kin to Gorčin, married to a relative of his, and therefore behaved toward him not only as toward his leader, but also as toward an older friend. Gorčin evidently paid little heed to the first and still less to the second. He gave him orders simply and without insistence, but brooked no argument, like a strict parent or a master to a servant, and Stanoje obeyed them, not renouncing for a single moment his sense of kinship or his military rights. "Good, Goro, since you say so. I will, sir, since you order me."

They had not gone more than five hundred paces along the muddy but drying road when they met a group of prisoners. There were five of them, two officers in Turkish uniforms and three men from Plav—Ahmet-beg and his son, Arslan, who was leading his horse, and Sali-aga Kokot, a merchant, paunchy, fat, and flabby, whom only the exceptional circumstances and the severity of Ali-beg could ever have driven onto a battlefield.

Stojan learned later that Ahmet-beg's horse had been killed and, in falling, had crushed and broken his right leg, so that the

Montenegrins had caught him and also his son, who had been trying to get him away. Sali-aga, however, had been captured with his horse; heavy and slow-moving, he rode a clumsy and always quiet nag. Now Ahmet-beg was riding his fat, yellow horse, while he, stumbling and gasping from fatigue and fear, tottered along on short, fat legs, barefoot and blue with the cold.

Two soldiers and a sergeant were to take the group to Novšić, where, by the Voivode's order, the prisoners were gathered. But Gorčin halted the whole group, blocking their path, with his hand on his *handžar.* "Those, you say, are Turkish officers? They do not know our language?" He turned to the sergeant, jovial and tubby, with sparse brown mustaches and irregular teeth, and at once went on, as if delivering sentence: "Even though we never asked for them, they had to come. They are serving their sultan. They are prisoners of the state—the Prince's and the Voivode's. Those others hand over to me. They are of our people, turned Turk. I will take care of them."

"I was ordered . . ." the sergeant protested.

"Bind them—and get a move on!" Gorčin cut him short.

The sergeant, who obviously knew of Gorčin and his peremptory and implacable nature, tried his best to avoid trouble. "I can't, just like that. Orders! I will be held responsible. And then there is the horse," he protested.

"You can take the horse. And you, get off. Dismount!" Gorčin pronounced.

"He can't. His leg is broken," the sergeant explained.

"Are you a Turkish groom?" Gorčin snapped at him, and softly, almost tenderly, added: "He'll manage, quite well."

Arslan helped his father to dismount, clenching his teeth as he dragged his father's crushed leg. His father leaned on him even more than he had need.

"All right, since you insist." The sergeant gave way. "But the responsibility is yours. There are witnesses."

"On your way! As for responsibility . . ." Gorčin said curtly. "You, Stanoje, help the young man to carry the beg."

"As you say," Stanoje agreed, and took Ahmet-beg's right arm.

"Direction—the ditch," ordered Gorčin, pointing to a wooded hollow above the road.

"I won't. I am not guilty, I am a merchant. They forced me to go to battle," Sali-aga began to protest.

"I, too, am forcing you to go," Gorčin jested harshly, putting a hand on his shoulder and turning him in the direction of the ditch.

"You are going to kill us?" The merchant stared, popeyed, pale, and quivering.

Gorčin said nothing, prodding him with his gun to hurry. Finally, thinking it over, he remarked: "You will die by a hero's hand!"

"But I won't. I am not guilty. I have never muddied anyone's water. What does it matter to me who is a hero? I am a trader. Is there no justice for men?" the merchant wailed.

"By a hero's hand," Gorčin repeated, paying no attention to his words or his tears.

The merchant suddenly turned and knelt in the muddy snow, falling on hands and knees at Gorčin's feet.

"Don't you know what human mercy is? Don't you know what is God's justice? To whom, with what, shall my wife and children be left? Were I even guilty, had I even muddied anyone's water!"

Gorčin pulled him to his feet angrily. "Eh, when someone begins to whine, I begin to lose all respect even for my own life. I tell you: I don't know in what way, but you will die by a hero's hand!"

They went into the ditch.

"Stop, Stanoje!" Gorčin ordered after they had gone about twenty paces.

The group halted. Ahmet-beg turned, leaning on a tree. "I am Kapetanović, Ahmet-beg Kapetanović," he began. "If you have not heard about me, you have certainly heard of my house . . . we have held the captaincy for more than two hundred years. . . ."

"Be quick. I am in a hurry," Gorčin interrupted him. "I am glad that you are of noble stock. I've cut the heads off too many poor fellows. And to tell you the truth, I am fed to the teeth with captains, even in Montenegro."

"I will be quick, hero. This is my son. Is there any way for me to save him? I will give you all that I have and my own head to boot."

"I have got your head already, and I am not interested in money."

"He is my only son. Don't wipe out my seed."

Gorčin thought it over.

"Grant the youth his life," Stanoje pleaded. "It won't turn your seed to males."

But it was just that which made Gorčin decide more quickly. "You keep your mouth shut, Stanoje. What has been born to me has been born to me. And you, Beg, have cut down plenty of only sons."

"It is true; we have. But this time forgive, forget . . . it will not turn out well; it will not stop the hatred between our faiths."

"I cannot, Beg. I would have no peace if I were to forgive him. The weeping of the Montenegrin widows would give me no peace."

"At least do this much for me—kill me first!"

Gorčin did not reply; he had already drawn his *handžar* and ordered the merchant to kneel. The merchant knelt and clasped his hands, but before he could utter any sort of entreaty, Gorčin struck him on the neck. Sali-aga fell forward, rolled over on his side, and spouts of blood whistled from the severed arteries.

Ahmet-beg at last realized that entreaties and requests would be of no avail. He looked around with chill indifference. "Be a man, since you are a hero," he said at last. "Kill me first."

Gorčin did not seem to have heard. "Finish cutting off the merchant's head," he ordered Stanoje. "I don't want to leave work unfinished." Then suddenly, his upper lip twisted in anger, as if he were disgusted, and he said to Arslan: "Now you, young man, bend your neck."

"Run, run, son!" shouted Ahmet-beg, and tried to get in Gorčin's way, but Stanoje pushed him, and he fell.

"How can I leave you, Father?" Arslan shouted, his eyes filled with tears. He turned to Gorčin, standing erect. "I will not kneel. Cut as I am."

Gorčin struck him on the neck so powerfully that he almost cut off his head at a single blow. Arslan fell forward, and his head, held only by the skin of the throat, was turned around on his neck, eyes staring with unextinguished brilliance and unshed tears. Ahmet-beg shrieked and crawled toward his son. Gorčin struck him on the back and shouted harshly: "I will not sweeten your torments, Beg." And with two blows cut off his head and kicked it away.

His pale face set in a stiff, terrible grimace, he now turned his fury against Stanoje, who was still fiddling with the merchant's head. "How many times have I told you, in vain; the first blow above the great vertebra on the neck. The great vertebra itself is too low and difficult to cut through. Then afterward—stiffen the tendons and strike sharply and shortly."

But they did not completely sever Arslan's head, and so it remained turned around the wrong way on his neck.

Stanoje went through their pockets, but the prisoners had already been plundered, and the group went on its way. Gorčin's face calmed, though he remained silent, while Stanoje, from behind, cursed and swore at the soldiers who had plundered the merchant and the begs.

Not listening to him, Gorčin strode onward with long, firm strides, talking to himself. "It would have been better to have cut off their heads at some crossroad and put them up where everyone could see them, as used to be done, so that they might fill the Turks with fear and hearten our fellows. But the Voivode would be angry, and so I do it this way. It's better than nothing."

They had come out of the ditch when Stojan felt someone touch him on the shoulder. He turned, noticed Rade, and realized with horror that he had forgotten all about him. Pale, with twisted lips and staring, shining eyes, the youth whispered: "What a hero! How easily and quickly he did all that."

Gorčin stopped on the road, legs spread wide apart. "What did the boy say?"

"Nothing," Stojan retorted, forcing himself to indifference. "He wondered at your heroism and the ease with which you did all that."

"Oh, that!" Gorčin smiled. "You seem to find it hard to find the right word. I do that just because of such boys; let them learn. When you cut, the most important thing is . . . eh, only now I see that he is wounded in his right arm. You haven't a splint, by any chance? Pity! And you, Radak, act as if *that*," he stressed the word mockingly, "was unusual."

"Well, it's war—and such things must be," Stojan replied mildly, walking beside Gorčin.

"War or no war, such things must be. I tell you, that is a revenge for our prisoners and our serfs whose heads they cut off yesterday. I know; because of that I have no peace as long as I leave a Turkish renegade alive. Man is born to take the lives of men."

Gorčin also tried to take over the next, much larger, group of prisoners. But he was prevented by the arrival of the Veliko leader, a tall, mustachioed man, with a coat of arms on his Montenegrin cap, but in local dress. He pulled up his sweating bay and shouted angrily: "I know who you are and what you want! But you will go back to Montenegro, and the men of Plav will make us pay for every head of theirs with ten of ours."

"We have come to stay," shouted Gorčin. "But you, even after you are liberated, will still be bound to the Turks and the begs."

"Bound or not bound, let the prisoners alone. I know what the Voivode thinks and what he has ordered. And this district is under my control, if you want to know."

Gorčin laughed. "All right. Don't get so worked up about five or six mangy Turkish heads. Tell me, where is the Voivode?"

The chief leaned over to Gorčin and, though his anger had not yet left him, whispered: "Where? Nowhere, like you and me. The redoubt and both Veliki Skić and Mali Skić have fallen. The Voivode is almost ready to strike at Plav. The main body has moved beyond Skić, through Prnjavor, and driven the Shquiptars from the Metohija and the Malesi, down the Meteh and Ječmište. Can't you hear what sort of a battle they are fighting down there? The Voivode is there; where else should he be? I am hurrying to head off the men of Veliko, so that they do not come down from the Čakor and cut Veliko off."

From the river valleys, in front of them to the left, echoed a muffled uproar and deep groaning sobs, as if the plain itself were wounded. "So that's it!" remarked Gorčin, chewing his lower lip. "Do you know anything about my group? They're usually with the Voivode."

"No, I don't know. The Voivode was in the redoubt below Skić, whence he thought to strike at Plav when the main body came around by Prnjavor. Then, when the Shquiptars attacked, he went at high speed to the Meteh. The main body must have gone that way. Perhaps your men were holding the newly taken redoubt, so that the Plav men cannot strike at the Voivode from the rear."

The man from Veliko put spurs to his horse, and Gorčin, with the others, remained in gloomy silence on the muddy road.

As far as the palisaded entrenchment above Skić they kept meeting groups of dead and wounded, for the most part piled up in clumsy carts with wooden wheels. There were few prisoners— in all, only two more smaller groups, which confirmed the fierceness of the encounter.

The real battle had taken place in front of and around the redoubt. But on the main battlefield, on the Novšić heights, most of those among the dead were agas and begs, whose green, red, blue, and violet serge cloaks and trousers, piped with gold or silks and braids, quivered like bouquets among the dark, dirty peasant coats on the muddy, trampled, bloodstained fields and meadows. On the open ground before the redoubt itself, there had apparently been no peasants. The flowering agas and begs, with their chargers, the fascines of reeds, heavier and deader than the corpses, the planks split and bloodstained, filled almost the whole plain, about three hundred paces long and wide.

On these fields and meadows walked and squatted Montenegrin women, black and gray, like ravens and crows, searching for their dead and wounded, going through the begs' pockets, and stripping the enemy dead. They did not weep or mourn, restraining themselves in face of the enemy and also because of the impossibility and inconvenience of keening, an age-old custom, purer than the everyday and profitable habit of plundering the corpses, which they carried out from tradition and from poverty.

Stopping to look back at the battlefield, Gorčin remarked with jovial mockery: "Really, they have not been sparing of their meat for death's banquet. And the Voivode sent me to escort the wounded instead of dancing the kolo here, as a man should! But I notice something: look how quickly the women are stripping the dead. They are hurrying. They suspect that our army will not stay here long. Hurry up, Stanoje, if you are hoping to swipe a copper button or two."

Stanoje smiled, his face lit up by his shining teeth. "Such things belong to no one, Goro. But these women are cleaning up the dead more quickly than the lice from the heads of their own children. I do not collect trinkets, as you know well, sir."

Gorčin, as if he had not heard, went on with calm preoccupation: "This, too, has occurred to me. A certain Bogdan Hašanin turned up behind our lines from God knows where, a thief and a vagabond, who can charm a gypsy woman with his tales and lure her children away from her. He lives the life of a dog, yet he is happier than we who avenge Kosovo and establish humanity. The whole world is his playground, like a bird on a branch. They say that he was in prison with your Radak knez, the one they tortured in Plav this summer with tortures the mind can scarcely conceive. Yesterday, at Novšić, he did not let a Turk fall to the ground before he went through his pockets and his belt. And today I don't see him. If he has been here, he must already have passed over to the other side, to the Turks. A bad sign! It seems as if some higher power whispers to plunderers which army will lose, so they gaily move over to the army that will win."

Falling silent, he waved his hand to go on, and then, with an unconcealed sigh, cried out: "How the flower of manhood has been mown down here!"

In truth, it was here that Ali-beg had thrown down his best, his most prized men to close the way to Plav. Old men with long white beards sticky with blood and boys with still-unsprouted mustaches lay beside one another and on top of one another, pressed down by horses, severed heads and arms, scattered entrails, and smashed chests and skulls. Horses' hoofs with shining horseshoes were scattered unnaturally here and there, roughly cast aside.

Nonetheless that passage had been forced. When Gorčin and Stojan crossed the redoubt, Plav was so near that they could see women with swaddled children in their arms leaving the town. Red, sooty tongues of flame licked from the shingles and windows of the stone houses in the center of the town, left burning through carelessness or despair. No one was putting out the fires, and nothing living could be seen near them. With the smell came also a dull groan, the stifled crying of children, wailing of women, and bellowing of cattle. It was in no way reminiscent of that dark sobbing of the hills which they had heard a short while before at their meeting with the leader from Veliko; here, in the open, the sounds of pain and desperation were clearer, more evident, and more pitiful.

No army could be seen in or around Plav, though in the strong kulas and around them there was an uneasy coming and going. The surviving people of Plav, it seemed, were preparing for resistance or death on their own thresholds. A thin, black line of fighters, to the left below the hills, was slowly withdrawing toward the little town, wriggling like an earthworm around the shore of the lake. There were not many of them, three or four hundred at the most. They might be detachments of the men of Gusinje, Ali-beg's last force. Around the two little redoubts at the bridge there were fewer men than yesterday, but on the far side of the bridge, where Veliša's army had been fighting the day before, there was a movement of foot soldiers and horsemen. Now they were turned in a different direction—toward the bridge and Plav, and not toward the Montenegrins, who had retreated down the Lim. At first it seemed unusual to Stojan, though he had grown accustomed to the thought that in battle everything changed and was turned inside out just when it seemed clearest. Were they not themselves at a redoubt captured from the enemy only a couple of hours before?

Because of this changed, upside-down position, it became at once clear why yesterday's vain victory by Veliša and the defeated evacuation of the position around the bridge had been of fateful importance. The men of Gusinje, reinforced by the Shquiptars from Malesia, were now almost on the flanks of the Voivode's army. Even had it not been for the Shquiptar charge from Meteh, about which the Veliko leader had spoken, the Montenegrin army had to reckon seriously with the enemy around the bridge and on the left bank. Now the enemy threatened not only to recapture the redoubt at Mali Skić, the one on which Gorčin and Stojan were standing, but also to decimate the Voivode's army on the left bank, should the Shquiptars manage to cut them off from their Vasojevići support and drive them from the hills into the narrow plain along the river.

This, which seemed clear and terrible to Stojan, then happened. He and Gorčin were still watching Plav and the army movements around it when Stanoje whispered to them, grinning senselessly: "A man has only to expect evil and it happens. A messenger has come to say that the Shquiptars have broken through below Novšić and cut off the retreat of our army." Instead of being victorious, the Voivode's army suddenly found itself faced with disaster, transformed into a force surrounded and driven down to the narrow belt of plain about an hour's march in length, without reserves of food and ammunition, with the hills and the Shquiptar mountains on one side and the swollen Lim on the other, and with enemy armies on all sides.

The position of the army had by now become abundantly clear to every soldier. There was not a man among them who knew how they would get out of it. But they did not think of it, even forbade themselves to think of it. They were still in their units, under arms and with their leaders. Therefore, although they were afraid as individuals, as an army, or as parts of an army, they did not feel frightened or insecure. They were filled with a sort of gay disdain. At ease in their units, they were singing army songs in defiance of the nearby enemy.

Imperceptibly, relations between the soldiers and their leaders, which had till then been a mixture of familiar cordiality and strict harshness, became close, warm, considerate. The leaders asked, rather than commanded, and the soldiers rushed to carry out their orders.

The attitude toward the wounded also changed. Now they were given the best food, and the soldiers silently relinquished to them the choicest titbits. They were filled with an inexplicable yet firm sense of brotherhood; they heard only tender, honeyed words, stressing pardon and renunciation. Even those branded as cowardly and greedy—Gorčin pointed out some of them and jested with them—were now nourished on heroism and unselfishness.

Stojan was not frightened either, though to him, who knew the area and the relative strength of the two armies, the hopelessness of the position of the Voivode's army was clearer than to most of the others. Gorčin and Rade, however, knew it well.

Moving away from the palisade, Gorčin remarked, rubbing eyes which were watering from intense concentration: "It will be a tug of war. No one can win all the time. This is the first time

Voivode Marko has fought in a land he does not know and he has had to rely on an army from other tribes."

Rade drew Stojan aside and whispered: "I understand now that Plav will not be taken. We shall have to leave our lands forever. I cannot tell you how sorry I am about that, though I was glad when we left them. But I am not at all frightened—with Gorčin, with the Voivode, and with so great and brave an army."

"There's no need to be frightened," Stojan agreed. "But it really seems that for the present there is no hope of taking Plav, or of our return."

Only then did Stojan look around, at his own position. It was about three in the afternoon. The dark summits of the Prokletije were wrapped in monotonous gray turbans of cloud, announcing snow. The sunny appearance of the whole valley suddenly darkened. The river was chained in heavy unending fetters, rushing with them down the valley.

Gorčin's platoon had been broken into three sections: one at Skić, one around the redoubt, and one above the banks of the Lim. The three parts were near one another, so that Gorčin was still able to command them by shouting.

No one had yet attacked them. But defense would be, obviously, difficult. Gorčin, pacing up and down, began to look around, evidently thinking with effort and gnawing his lower lip.

First he ordered Stanoje to hurry to Veliki Skić with another detachment as a reinforcement. "You can go to Plav with your heads cut off, but no living man may leave here on his own two legs until I give the order. If they take the hills, they will have the Voivode's army by the throat, and we shall have to run away from here with our tails between our legs. Get a move on, and use your common sense."

Then he again began to pace up and down. Apparently he was afraid of his own impetuosity. He was a man of action, one who carried out what others decided, cool and ingenious once battle was joined. He turned to Stojan in uncertainty. "What do you say, Radak? You know the country and the men of Plav well."

Stojan had noted and remembered many things from yesterday's battle and from that morning, and had thought over what ought to have been done and the mistakes that had been made. Though they had charged the fortifications with skill and daring, the Montenegrins had taken practically no thought of how to take cover and fortify their own positions. Courageous and enterprising, they often surprised the enemy and created confusion even among the men of Plav and Gusinje. But if a determined opponent surprised them—and now they were faced by such a one—they easily degenerated into disorder and flight.

Certainly, the defense of the redoubt was important; it was on the flank and defended the passage of the rear guard to Skić. From the left bank of the Lim, which the enemy held, the upper part of the redoubt was scarcely within rifle range. But those nearer the water would not be able to hold out if it occurred to the Gusinje men to roll the fascines left by the Voivode's men down to the bank and to take cover behind them. That would afford an opportunity to the men of Plav to outflank the indefensible lower part of the redoubt, and thereby the whole position, from the ditches and willow copses along the Lim. If the enemy had not yet thought of this, he would certainly do so as soon as he joined battle, for fighters in a battle quickly realize every possible advantage.

There is nothing so dangerous for an army at war than to sit still and do nothing; and Stojan recollected that Veliša's army was always doing something, even when resting and eating. So now he had merely to point out the dangers and the possibilities, bearing in mind Gorčin's vanity and reputation, so that everything would appear to be Gorčin's own opinion, to enable him to get his men moving and keep them busy.

As if they had been waiting for a war cry and a command, the soldiers jumped to their tasks.

Some, in groups of three or four, began rolling fascines toward the Lim bank, shouting gaily in unison, while individuals brought planks to strengthen the palisade and extend it downriver on the right wing, working silently but with easy haste and care.

But this was being done in full view of the enemy soldiers and could only encourage them to roll down fascines from the open ground, shouting in the same way as the Montenegrins on the opposite bank.

Nonetheless, the enemy soldiers fell back and soon ceased their work. They realized that they had a wider space to cover, and

Gorčin's marksmen, already behind fascines on the bank, forced them to take cover from their flanking fire.

Finally, the fascine-rollers found themselves facing one another, while the work of strengthening the palisade went on. Having started, the soldiers, faced with battle, could no longer be held back.

Once again, the Montenegrins began. At first they hurled insults at the Moslems, shouting and calling on them to jump on top of their fascines and not skulk behind them like a pack of bastards, and promising that they would do the same. They were not far from one another, about two hundred paces, for at that point the Lim was not divided into backwaters or islands, and the two sides could hear one another despite the roar of the river.

But Gorčin was getting bored with empty confrontation and shouted with jesting provocation: "Stop shouting like women across an alley, or at least let those who want to, do so standing up."

A tall young Montenegrin in white peasant clothes, with a red-rimmed Montenegrin cap, leaped onto a fascine. "Better someone else; that fellow is too easy to hit," Gorčin grumbled.

On the opposite side, in silence, a man of middle height, who seemed very broad, probably because of his unbuttoned black jacket, stood up. "They are more sensible; a smaller man in a big jacket—easy to miss," Gorčin remarked.

The young man looked right and left at his comrades, who were telling him how to fire. He even looked behind him, smiling eagerly, his face white and his lips red under black mustaches. "Let him alone; don't hinder him!" Gorčin shouted.

But the broad man fired, the youth's cap flew away like a plucked flower, and he swayed and tottered. But he gathered his strength, strove to stand upright, and, raising his rifle with difficulty, like a huge and hideous burden, took aim slowly, to the tense expectation of both sides, at the broad man, standing motionless as a haystack. The youth swayed, clutching his rifle in his right hand and his stomach with his left. The broad man on the other side stood a little longer, as if he wanted to watch, calmly awaiting his opponent's fire. Then he whooped madly and victoriously, as shepherds do on the heights when they shout for joy, not knowing themselves at what—the mountains, the sky, the limitless expanse, or their own joy in living—before he quietly slipped down behind his fascine.

Another Montenegrin at once leaped up, a tall, robust man with white hair and mustaches. "His uncle," Gorčin said to Stojan.

They shouted from the other side that they wanted a young man and that they would give a young man in return, and the old man discontentedly and unwillingly fell back to let his place be taken by an upstanding youth with curled black mustaches. He fired first and brought down a fair youth on the other side. He shouted: "Whose turn next?" But his fellows dragged him back by the legs, and in his place rose a thickset young man with a black fur cap on his head. He, too, had good luck, hitting a slender, tight-belted antagonist. "Enough!" Gorčin shouted halfheartedly. "They breed like caddis worms."

The soldiers heard Gorčin's order. But it was neither definite nor final, for neither he nor they could stop this senseless killing. By doing so, they would admit to faintheartedness and perhaps, even more, to the superiority of the enemy in disdaining death, which was, in a way, a confirmation of their will for life, for victory. Even Stojan, who had been busy strengthening the palisade, though the whole thing had at first seemed to him senseless and pointless, was seized with a terrible, yet irresistible, impulse to join in, to rush to the fascines and expose himself to the enemy's fire. But he went on with his job, knowing that Gorčin would never allow him to join in; as someone who knew the district and its conditions, he was necessary to Gorčin.

The soldiers on both sides were seized with exaltation, as if in a game; they urged on their champions, especially if the enemy's fall was dramatic, if he fell as though mown down or with arms widespread in the air. Those who fell on the opposing side drew applause and shouts of joy.

Three or four more men fell on both sides, and Stojan, temporarily occupied with driving in a plank, heard Gorčin yelling to him: "I thought that young man of yours had had enough . . ." But he did not hear him to the end, astonished at the sight of Rade on a fascine.

He rushed toward the bank. He wanted to shout: "No, Rade, no!" But he remembered that he might embarrass the youth and spoil his aim. He kept wondering as he ran, without worrying whether those on the far side might shoot at him, if he could drag Rade under cover before he fired. But what should he do if Rade fired before he got there? Should he drag him back, shaming both Rade and himself before the Montenegrins and the men of Gusinje and before Gorčin?

He was still about twenty paces away from the fascines when two rifles spoke almost simultaneously, raising echoes from the hills on both sides of the river. Rade swayed, as if he wanted to turn, and then, letting go of his rifle, knelt and toppled over backward.

Stojan did not look to see what had happened to Rade's antagonist and did not know whether this side or that one or both shouted in approval. He grabbed Rade by the shoulders and legs and, slithering in his haste, carried him away. No one fired at him; both sides tacitly permitted the carrying-away of dead and wounded from this bizarre and intoxicating duel. Driven by sorrow and guilt, he scarcely thought of danger. All he was aware of was the feverish trembling of the youth in his arms.

He placed Rade on the damp earth, putting his head on a haversack. Gorčin, not looking at Stojan or at the wounded boy, said: "He is too young for that—but war is no respecter of persons."

Stojan unbuttoned Rade's jacket to bandage him. The bullet had struck low down, below his chest. He tried to find the opening of the wound, and his palm was at once flooded with blood and scraps of liver. He refused to accept what he knew for certain: there was no hope for the youth. But he did all that he could, that he must. He quickly cut away Rade's shirt and plugged the wound with it. The young man threw his arms around Stojan's neck, and when Stojan again laid him down, his arms continued to embrace him, unwilling and unable to let a kinsman go. Stojan was confirmed in the knowledge that Rade would die. He tenderly removed the arms from his neck and stood back, holding Rade's hands in his.

Rade looked at him darkly, with a gloomy interrogation in his eyes. Stojan smiled at him, forcing himself to show hope, yet convinced that he was unable to conceal the truth. Groaning, his whole body convulsed, and with a shadowy darkness in his eyes, Rade, with an effort, whispered: "It's nothing, it's nothing!"

His hands slipped out of Stojan's and his fingers scrabbled on the cold, damp earth, searching for support, and transferring to it his pain and suffering. He clenched his teeth and shut his eyes, and when the next moment he opened them again, they gazed fixedly past Stojan into some sort of heaven. His lips opened, and his head fell to one side.

"Woe is me! Woe, my own kin!" Stojan moaned, striking himself on the head. "Where have I brought you, to whom must I leave you?"

Someone shook him by the shoulders. Stojan looked around and stood up, insulted in his pain and sorrow. Without looking at him, Gorčin said roughly: "You are a soldier and on the battlefield. Mourn at home. Yesterday, my nephew was killed. I have no other son, but I left him, to mourn for him in an empty house."

Stojan pulled himself together, uncertain whether to thank Gorčin or to curse him. He had to cross Rade's hands and close his eyes.

Down by the river, that suicidal game had been broken off; oaths and curses were hissed. The Moslems either had not held out or were angered because someone important among them had been killed. They had mown down an older, broad-shouldered soldier with a volley.

"Bastards!" shouted Gorčin, with sharp, intense fury. "Bastards! Is it thus you keep faith? Where is your bastard of a leader, that he and I may stand on the mark? Do you hear, bastards and sons of whores!"

His mad outburst could scarcely be heard at such a distance. He again began to pace up and down, then stopped and shouted, slowly, calmly and clearly: "Oh, Turks! Let your leader, if some whore has borne him, come out to match me on the mark. Your leader, if the whore his mother has borne him!"

But on the far side they were silent and, despite the grief that flowed over him from Rade's still-warm hands, Stojan was filled with pride and joy that the enemy had not won, that they were horror-stricken and ashamed.

Stojan rose and went to Gorčin to ask him what he could do

with Rade, for by now the dead were no longer being taken to Novšić and no one had yet dug a grave. The women had been ordered to withdraw because of the nearness of the battle, and the soldiers, to the last man, were at their posts on the redoubt. But Gorčin cut in first. "You cannot take him with you now. He is here among his comrades. I will order a mass grave to be dug."

Stojan chose a rise above the road and, with the help of ten soldiers, set to digging.

They had dug a grave ten paces long when to their left, from behind an outcrop of the hill, appeared a group of men, Montenegrins and captured Moslems.

Sitting on a fascine and stuffing green tobacco into his pipe, Gorčin shouted: "You've come at the right time." A sharp, acrid smell rose from his tobacco as the group reached the road.

There were three soldiers and four Moslems. Among them Stojan at once recognized Izet-beg Džidić, who, leaning on a rough wooden pitchfork, could hardly walk. He was supported by his house servant Bešir, more lopsided and hunchbacked than ever, crouching on his short bandy legs. The other two were a beg and his servant; Stojan knew who the beg was, though he did not know him personally. Elaborately dressed, he was young and slender, with a white face and black brows and mustaches. His dumpy manservant, with small pox-pitted face and almost without brows or mustaches, was supporting the beg, almost carrying him. Twenty paces away, Stojan realized that Izet-beg had been wounded in the chest; his green dolman was soaked with blood, and his right side was dark and sticky with it; his body was stiff and bent to the left. The young beg had a wide sword cut on his left shoulder, stanched by a bundle of bloody rags, and a wound in the right leg. He groaned at every step, writhing with pain, his lips blue and dry, and he leaned on his servant with all his weight.

As they approached the gravediggers and turned down the road, Gorčin leaped up from his fascine, took his pipe out of his mouth, and ran to meet them, shouting: "Where are you taking these fellows?"

"To the command post, with the prisoners," replied a soldier with heavy eyebrows and graying mustaches, frowning with embarrassment. "That is the order. We found them in a hollow in

532

that thicket. They must have hidden there after the killing at the redoubt."

"Don't keep me waiting," Gorčin shouted, "but get back to your post. This is no time to waste men—we need them." Then he muttered to himself, grinning ferociously: "So this is my army! It's enough to make a man cross himself with his left hand. They have heard about some order two or three days old, and yet a few moments ago—their bodies are not yet cold—the Turks wiped out five or six of my comrades."

"We heard that the order was strict, from the Voivode himself," the soldier said. "And we did not take them in battle; nor did they resist."

"Get out of my sight!" shouted Gorčin. "Here, both for them and for you, I am God and Voivode."

The soldiers stood aside, and Gorčin waved the prisoners on to the open space below the road, on which were lying Rade and his four dead comrades. When the prisoners had gone on, carefully avoiding the dead men, Gorčin strode after them and called out: "Oh, Turks! Oh, Turks! These are yours, yours!" Then he turned to the gravediggers, who had stopped their work and were watching with curiosity, hands on their spades, and called, almost tenderly: "Come here, Radak. Do you recognize them?"

The enemy on the far side of the river could easily see, without Gorčin's taunts, that the prisoners were Moslems. Three of them were wearing red fezes. There could have been no doubt even about the loutish servant, though he was wearing a blackish felt cap such as smiths wear. Gorčin had called to the enemy only so that they should watch carefully while he wreaked his vengeance on their fellows.

Stojan went to the open field, and only then did his eyes meet Izet-beg's, though Izet-beg did not make any sign of recognition. He kept silent, breathing heavily and painfully and leaning all his weight on the pitchfork.

"Do you know them?" Gorčin turned to Stojan.

"I know them. Except one."

"Who are they? That I know with whom I have to deal."

Stojan looked again at Izet-beg. As when their eyes had met a few moments before, both looked away as if ashamed at such a meeting. Izet-beg was looking at Stojan with painful earnestness, with that entreating warmth typical of him, especially when he had missed his quarry or was unable to settle some domestic dispute. Stojan was afraid that tears would come to his eyes, from stifled sorrow for Rade or from sorrow for Izet-beg. He looked away and pronounced the name Izet-beg, adding, as a sort of compensation, "And that is his house servant, Bešir, a half-witted and irresponsible creature."

He fell silent, scarcely aware of the place and the circumstances. He could no longer bring himself to look at Izet-beg, though he did not know exactly why. An endless, brilliantly colored series of memories flooded over him and disturbed him, bearing him away somewhere where war and blood and death became unreal and inconceivable. Only when Gorčin pointed at him with his pipe did he remember that he had not explained who the young beg was.

Once again he was deep in that reverie of memories and dreams when Gorčin asked him, puffing a ring of bitter smoke from his pipe: "Radak, do you want to get even with Izet-beg?"

Stojan realized that it was just this question that he had feared, and tried to avoid an answer. It seemed to him that he needed to make a tremendous effort to reply. But when he said "He is a good, peaceable man," everything became clear and easy, as if he were justifying both himself and the beg.

"Peaceable! We are all peaceable! But he is an enemy, a Turk. If I do not kill him today, tomorrow he will kill me, or my brother. So you will not ease your sorrow for your kinsman?"

Stojan was silent. It was useless to explain anything to Gorčin, whose cheeks were livid, trembling violently, though his movements were measured and reasonable. Nonetheless, Stojan felt that he must explain his real reason and put an end to this misunderstanding. "We are friends. We were friends. Among us, the cutting off of heads is not a custom. And I do not believe that by doing so I would lessen my grief."

Gorčin laughed tensely, his face quivering and his lips pale. "How could you be friends? You a Serb and he a Turk, you a serf and he a beg, yet—friends! I do not understand you Serbs who are not from Montenegro. Now you revolt against the Turks and now you are friends with them!"

"So it is. We know one another from hunting; we are both

hunters. We live here differently from you in Montenegro, though we are one with you."

Involuntarily, Stojan glanced at Izet-beg, who returned his glance pityingly, as if excusing himself for bringing Stojan into such an awkward situation, as if imploring him to cut short a useless conversation, so that everything would be over as quickly as possible. Unexpectedly, he said in a tense, hoarse voice: "Let it be as it has been fated, Stojan. But implore his mercy for Bešir. You know that he does not bear arms, but only looks after my horse."

Stojan was about to promise him when Gorčin suddenly drew his *handžar*, waved Bešir aside, and ordered Izet-beg: "Kneel! Bow your head!"

Izet-beg, instead, painfully straightened himself up and, smiling sorrowfully, looked around at the river and the mountains with a dewy compassionate glance.

"Good," Gorčin concluded, and with a single stroke cut off Izet-beg's head, still holding his pipe in his left hand. Then he stuck the head on the point of his *handžar*, raised it on high to show it to those across the river, whistled and shouted as though in a kolo, and then called across the river: "This is for your breach of faith, your breach of faith!"

Then he stuck his unfinished pipe in his belt and knelt to wipe his *handžar* on Izet-beg's dolman, explaining: "A man's blood is not like an animal's. It has some kind of salt in it, so that if a blade is not wiped clean at once, spots will remain on it that cannot be washed off."

"Gorčin," Stojan said boldly, remembering Izet-beg's request, "let the servant go. He is half-witted, foolish."

"Yes, lord, I am half-witted," Bešir confirmed through his tears.

Gorčin stood up, put his *handžar* into its sheath, pulled his pipe out of his belt, and, puffing strong smoke, said, with calm smiling face: "This is the first time I have heard anyone say of himself that he has little sense. But since he is not a fighter and is half-witted, and since you beg for his life—let him go! Someone must tell the living how their brothers and comrades have fared. As for those two, cut off their heads and put all three heads on staves."

Gorčin's men at once cut off the heads of the other two, before they were able to plead for their lives. There were tears on the young beg's face. As the severed heads were being put on staves, Bešir wriggled through between the planks and ran clumsily across the open ground upriver, wiping away his tears and not looking around. Perhaps he was afraid of meeting the glassy eyes of the master he had forsaken. Gorčin sat down again on his fascine, knocking the ashes out of his pipe. The valley and the mountains were filled with a deathly silence, which rose from the earth and the waters up to the darkened sky, and Stojan felt suddenly overcome by some sort of inner peace and quiet, despite the blood that still flowed from the headless trunks on the muddy soil.

The gravediggers competed with the darkness, and with the drizzle seeping from the low mist, to finish the grave and bury the dead. Soaked with sweat and the chill drizzle, muddy and exhausted by the horrors of the still-unfinished day, Stojan could not shake off his dismay that Rade would have to be buried outside his own village and the graveyard of his ancestors, quite near the place where, only recently, Akan had hanged Nasto, as if in that there were some fearful omen of the destruction and scattering of his clan and his seed throughout the world.

He had not time to dwell on his sorrow or to place Rade with his own hands in the grave before a messenger came to say that he and Gorčin must go at top speed to Novšić for an important task that could not be postponed.

It was dark when they arrived at that same house where Stojan had first met Gorčin. Everything, however, had changed.

The Moslem corpses still lay in rows along the roadside, but below them lay the Montenegrin dead, an interminable row in the darkness. Below Novšič and in the hills above, there had been fighting all afternoon, and even now occasional shots were to be heard. Around them soldiers passed to and fro; leaders shouted overloud orders; horses, unfed, tied to fruit trees and willows, neighed and stamped with chilled, stiffened hoofs. Continually, men brought more dead and wounded out of the darkness, laid them on the road, went away, and then brought more. Fences had been torn up and houses demolished to feed the fires the soldiers had lighted everywhere, and sheep and whole oxen were

536

turning on spits. Heads of maize were hurled from the broken lattices of the storage barns by the *čardak,* and a hairy white horse, without saddle or bridle, chewed the cobs with long teeth, while the old hodža, Mehmed, calmly gathered bits of wood and twigs into a bundle as if he had nowhere to warm himself and nothing with which to start a fire. Everything smelled of spilled plum brandy, potatoes just roasted at the fires, and corpses—a sour, melancholy, inescapable smell, which, since the day before, neither the wind nor any other smell had been able to overcome, from which there was no hiding place, either in the houses or in the fields, or in sleep itself.

Gorčin went into the *čardak* to get his orders, and Stojan, hungry and chilled through, went into the kitchen. There he came upon Grgur. The locals had gathered around the command post in case they might be needed as pathfinders or messengers, for it was not yet known what Voivode Marko intended to do.

Grgur, devouring hot, ashy potatoes and hard local cheese, first asked Stojan if he had seen Rade anywhere or knew anything of him. Stojan avoided giving a direct answer. "He was here today. He had a slight wound in the arm, but set out for the positions facing Plav with some of the leaders."

"I heard he had been wounded; that's why I asked. In the arm, you say? Then it cannot have been broken if he left for the front line."

As he gave Stojan something to eat, he told him what had been happening to him. He had set out that morning with two other Radaks for their native village, but at their house there were Shquiptars, who had fired on them and tried to take them prisoner. They had driven them as far as the outflow into the Lim Valley, where the Montenegrins, retreating from Plav, had intercepted their assailants. They were the advance guard of the Albanian tribes, and by the afternoon the main mass had rushed in, so that Voivode Marko had had to send reinforcements. "And neither sight nor sound of the other Radaks. They are somewhere in flight, and winter has already come."

Eager for news of the scattered clan, and considering in what way and at what moment to tell Grgur about Rade's death, Stojan forgot his hunger and fatigue and called his kinsman to leave the overcrowded hut so that they could talk in peace outside. He was in no hurry to tell him of misfortunes; since he did not know what task he was expected to carry out, it might be that he would have to leave Grgur mourning. On the other hand, he was encouraged because Grgur did not seem greatly worried about the Radaks and the village. The war had already chilled and weakened Grgur's former anxiety about the clan, war in which men in a moment become accustomed to everything and indifferent to all misfortunes and catastrophes.

In the darkness and near the light of the campfires, Stojan took heart, aware of his affinity with Grgur. The rain and the firing had ceased, and everywhere in the dark immensity fires burst out like stars, as if there had never been any war, any killing or misfortune. The fitful, broken darkness, the murmur of conversation, and the clinking of dishes reminded them of the life they had led before the flight. Stojan could anticipate Grgur's words and thoughts before he uttered them, aware that Grgur could do the same with him. The moment to tell him of Rade's death drew nearer, though he knew that it would destroy Grgur's calm in this night that covered everything except living men and their needs. He waited for Grgur to finish his worried, not particularly sorrowful, account of Stamena's message that his father, Knez Anto, was worse and that he ought to return to his own people as soon as possible. "How can we go back? Even were I able, the reports say we are surrounded on all sides. How could I leave the army?"

He was unable to finish, and Stojan was unable to speak, for Gorčin and Tomo came out of the house. Gorčin shouted: "Have you had something to eat? We must be off at once."

"Well, I've had a little. I can go at once—if I must."

"We must. But first we must eat something. I am as hungry as a wolf. I'll get something ready."

Tomo waved to Stojan and, following Gorčin, stopped at the corner of the *čardak* and whispered: "Eat as soon as you can. Tonight we must go to the other side, through the Shquiptars. Keep quiet about this. Who is that, Radak?"

"That is my kinsman. He is reliable; he was the leader of the Radaks who fled. Couldn't he come with us? He could lead you, if it is something important."

"It's very important. He'll be welcome."

"Only, I beg you. His brother was killed today, and he does not know it yet. We must not talk about it, so as not to upset him, at least until all this is over."

"I don't talk to whom I can, but to whom I must," Gorčin said jestingly. "But you enjoy yourself with him while I extract some supper from the leaders."

He and Tomo went into the *čardak*, and Stojan went back to Grgur, who standing in the darkness waiting for him. "You'll come with me," Stojan said, taking him by the arm. "We'll get through somehow. It's a matter of importance, and you know the paths."

The conversation turned to the war and the task that lay ahead of them, as though there were no longer any family or clan worries. The former intimacy of clansmen was replaced by a different intimacy, new to Stojan but already familiar, the comradeship of soldiers devoted to pain and death. Now he should be able to tell Grgur everything, but just for that reason he did not want to tell him about Rade's death. A soldier must be fully in control of himself, untouched by emotion.

Tomo came out weighed down with weapons, small as he was, and after him Gorčin, with a basket piled high with food—dried pork, half a huge wheat loaf baked in the ashes, local cheese, and the inevitable flask of plum brandy. Half in jest and half seriously, he swore at the war and the army and the accursed soldier's life and went back again to bring out a cloth, which he slung roughly across his shoulders.

Stojan ran to him and took the cloth, searching in the garden below the *čardak* for a clear space where there was some light, since all the windows were brilliantly illuminated, throwing on the earth quivering yellowish patches of light. They all sat down on the cloth except Grgur, who, uninvited, remained in the courtyard. "What is your kinsman's name?" Gorčin asked, breaking the bread.

"Grgur. Grgur Radak."

"Call him over to eat. We shouldn't be separate at supper when we are all going to die together."

Stojan called Grgur over and added: "We have already eaten a little, and as for you two, it's better not to overload your stomachs."

"And why not?" asked Gorčin mockingly.

"Well, it's better on not too full a stomach. The mind is clearer, and wounds are less dangerous. Above all, one mustn't drink."

"Listen to him, Grgur!" Gorčin turned to Grgur, who was sitting on the edge of the cloth. "How wise your kinsman is! He has learned all that from his hunting. But hunting is not war. I should be sorry to be killed while still hungry. As for drinking, I am always the same, drink or no drink."

"I think so, too," the clerk cut in with restrained humor.

Gorčin laughed, noiselessly and slyly, like one who has been the butt of a jest but has no intention of remaining so for long. He raised the flask and poured a stream of plum brandy straight into his mouth, as he had done that morning. When he had drunk his fill, and wiped his mustaches, he seized the pork, but before he began to cut it he pointed it at the clerk. "He, Radak, can't wait to obey you. He eats like a bird. Ever since I set out with this wretched army I haven't seen him take anything but a drop of milk; he feeds on air and water. He worries about every detail and believes that one sings better for a little hunger. I have heard that Bishop Rade was like that. Bishop Rade, with all his worries about the beastliness of the Montenegrins and his singing of songs—wailing, rather than singing, I call it—caught the wasting sickness and drove himself too young into the grave. But I see, Radak, that your kinsman does not follow your advice, but keeps himself to himself. He is a robust fellow, while you—you are too peaceable for conditions like these, though today, they tell me, you stretched out two or three of them."

Gorčin enjoyed his eating and drinking and the sound of his own voice until supper ended. Then, when he was ready, filling his pipe, he said to Stojan: "Since you haven't enough sense to eat as much as you can, pick up the rest and take it to the soldiers in the kitchen. They don't get food like this unless they either plunder or steal it." But before Stojan had gathered up the food, Gorčin wrapped a large chunk of bread and some meat in a towel, stuffed it into his bag, and sighed, rather overloudly: "Pity I can't take the flask; but perhaps we shall find a mug with the Vasojevići if all goes well."

They went down to the road, silently, kept apart by the darkness and the need to take cover. Stojan went ahead in the gloom, lithely and a little bent, alert in eye, nose, bearing, and thought, toward an unknown quarry. After him went the clerk, then Grgur, and finally Gorčin. They turned down the road, between the rows of corpses—on the right Montenegrin and on the left Moslem—impersonal and forgotten in the darkness. No one uttered a word until they had passed them, as though the dead could hear, as though they should not talk in their presence. Then Stojan stopped. "What do you think? Where shall we break through?"

"But I thought you knew," Tomo said softly.

"I know. Certainly I know. I know every smallest path. But what do you think? There are many ways."

"And you, what do you think yourself?" the clerk asked hesitantly.

"I would go by the water. The surest way would be for us to swim across, then slowly downstream through the undergrowth. They won't be expecting us there. There will be no sentries."

"I won't go into the water," Gorčin objected. "I am afraid of nothing except water. I don't know how to swim. I'm shivering already at what you said, from the very thought." He became talkative. "And I won't go back. If you go by the water, then I will go straight through the Shqiptars, and will survive—or die. But I will not let that inhuman power in the water drown me; nor will I go back to the Voivode for him to cut off all my badges in front of the whole army."

"Nor am I a very good swimmer," remarked Tomo. "But if it has to be . . ."

"No, no! It hasn't to be," Gorčin whispered. "Who says that we must drown ourselves? We need not! If we must die—then let it be. But to let water drown us—that, no! Not while I am alive!"

"So what do you think? Over the hills?" Grgur said, turning to Stojan.

Stojan answered quickly; he had been thinking that himself. "No. That would not be so bad, but it is very dark and we could easily lose one another in the darkness and the ravines. And if anything should happen to us two, you two would lose your way. We must find a way we can all go."

"That's what I like to hear," Gorčin said, for he had not lost his sense of humor. "But not water. You locals are different. You are fish, frogs grown up beside the river and lake. And we are from the Prokletije, from the bare stone."

"The level ground is narrow and open," Stojan commented, "on the one side the water and on the other the hills. What if we strike along the water, and keep in the undergrowth? But there is one narrow place, where the banks are near one another and the river comes right up to the open fields; there will be a guard there."

"That's what I like to hear; along the water but not in the water," Gorčin agreed jestingly, encouraged.

"If we get through that neck and reach the undergrowth again we'll be all right. But there is the gap, the narrows."

Everyone finally agreed to go that way, and Tomo said: "I have the letter, in my jacket. It must not fall into Turkish hands. You ought to know what it is all about. The Voivode will wait until midday for help from the Vasojevići on this side of the Lim, and will then begin his breakthrough. He dares not wait longer. He might even do it tonight, if the army is mustered and rested."

They went on, in the same order, in Indian file. Stojan considered it his duty to go ahead, not only because he knew the paths best and, as a hunter, was the most skillful, but also because he was prepared, ready to do what he would never have allowed the others to do, had they been in front of him. None of them could lose their way; they had only to keep close to the riverbank, and, though the moon was behind the clouds, it was still light enough to insure that a man would not stumble down the steep bank. But it was not wholly a question of losing the way. They might easily come across scouts or sentries. Stojan was confident in his eyes, his nose, and his legs, sure that he would see before he was seen, could scent the presence of man and would sense branches or twigs before stepping on them. All his powers were concentrated and controlled, especially that instinct by which he found his way in the darkness and the forests, aware of dangers before his senses detected them. The whole path, the whole area over which they must pass, with all its details, was clear in his mind, and in his thoughts he set up and avoided ambushes, skirted obstacles, took short cuts, and leaped over ditches and barriers.

Following the boundaries between the fields, they quickly

reached the river and turned downstream. The dangers suddenly lessened, as if the noisy roar of the river, darker than the night, had swallowed them up. They passed through the Montenegrin guards, who were warming themselves and did not even notice them. That encouraged them; perhaps the enemy would be equally haphazard and careless. Stojan noted this and sent Grgur back to tell them of their passage and warn them to keep on the alert.

"It's a good thing that the water roars," Gorčin remarked. "It will be harder for them to hear us."

"There's some good even in water," Stojan jested, with a sudden sense of companionship for this rough, frank, and upright man. "But no sort of roar is going to help us if we do not ourselves take care. See that steel does not clink on steel or a gun butt scrape on the ground. When a man is alone on guard he becomes a wild beast, hears a hundred times better, sees through the blackness, and can tell the difference between the rustling of the wind and the rustling caused by some living being."

Grgur returned, smiling. "They say that the Turks are having supper, just as they are doing."

All smiled at the soldiers' carefree indifference. And, indeed, except for the countless fires at the foot of the hillsides, at the frontiers of the visible world, and the roar of the river rushing on from darkness into darkness, the valley breathed in quiet obscurity and peace.

They set out once more, but more lightly and carefully, letting Stojan go a little ahead, stopping when he stopped, lying down when he lay down. It was hard to figure how long they went on this way, for their progress was broken by halts, listening and watching. But it must have been for more than an hour. Even those behind saw that the river turned sharply toward the hills, straight toward the campfires, more and more directly. Stojan moved onward more slowly and cautiously, ever more frequently stopping and crouching on the damp earth. They might have guessed, and Grgur knew, that they were entering the narrows about which Stojan had spoken. They approached to within two hundred paces, then a hundred and fifty, and then to a hundred paces, and they could see black and shining human figures pass-

ing in front of them and sitting around the campfires. But they
humbly and obediently followed Stojan, trusting in his exceptional powers.

Stojan again crouched, but for longer than usual. They realized that he was watching and listening, searching for a way
through. But they did wonder when, signing to them to retreat as
carefully as possible, he rose and went silently back toward
Grgur. Slowly, obediently, they went back until, after about
thirty paces, he stopped them.

"Wait for me here. I must investigate," he whispered. "It seems
there is a guard on the bank."

He left his rifle and sword behind, leaped to the edge of the
bank, went back a few steps, and looked around him. His three
companions watched him carefully and attentively, and he went
on, unheard, into the night which lay in wait for life and death.

Stojan was quite sure that a human form had disappeared behind the screen of boughs that ran from the bank down toward
the river. He wanted to confirm this, knowing that eyes can deceive when a man is tense, transforming a thing into a living
being and into a phantasm. He was afraid of making a fool of
himself before the others, especially Gorčin, though he did not
know why. He felt him there behind him, invisible, somewhere in
the darkness, like a thought, like his conscience.

He decided after a few steps to take cover near the bank, in the
copse of nut and willow trees, his movements masked by the roar
of the river. He did not dare, nor would it have been honorable,
to take the slightest risk. This was not a hunt. Men were involved, Serbs and a clansman, as well as a great and exceptional
task, such as would never again fall upon his shoulders, for which,
it seemed to him, he had been preparing all his life.

As soon as he slipped into the bushes, he realized that, should a
rotten branch or broken twig crack, they might betray his presence, even though they now hid him from sight, from prying eyes.
The slope down to the river was slippery with moisture and rotting leaves. He had to be sure of his foothold, to find some trunk
or branch on which to rely before crawling farther. He dug his
fingers into the cold, sandy earth, weighing every movement,
throwing his whole weight on his toes, on his fingers, as in hunting, but with greater effort, tenser and more cautious. Twigs

whipped his face and eyes, branches struck him in the chest, slipped under his feet, but he always removed them or skirted them noiselessly.

When he reached the top of the bank, the undergrowth prevented him from seeing, but by cautiously turning his head to left and right, he was able to distinguish the black outlines of the branches and twigs from the grayer, more even, empty background.

His progress was, he knew, slow when compared with a normal walking pace. But time was no longer of any importance. Time did not exist; only little things, the branches he pushed aside or suspected, the earth against which he pressed his body and into which he dug his fingers, and his hopes, his heart drumming in his breast while he listened, holding his breath. He enjoyed sniffing like a roebuck, lying in wait like a cat, crawling like a snake, confident that he was making no mistake, that he was craftier than any living thing—except a man.

Thoughts kept coming into his mind. What if that man, too, were a hunter? What if he were even more skillful? What if he were younger, more robust? Perhaps he had not lived through so terrible a day? Perhaps he, too, scented danger and was even now slipping away from the bank or running to get help?

He did not consider what he would have to do. As in hunting, when he saw, then he made up his mind. But this was not hunting, he reminded himself.

Time dragged on. He thought that those who had remained behind might grow uneasy and do something silly, might begin to look for him. But Grgur was there; he knew him and had trust in him. He would hold the others back. Those fears, he knew, came from impatience and uncertainty.

He sat down, only then feeling that he could breathe, and rested, looking to see where he was and how far he had gone. There was the bend in the river, the narrows about which he had warned his comrades. He knew that from the familiar gurgling of the whirlpool below him, from its stony breath, which he could feel, and the lighter, yellowish color, which he could see before him. Nonetheless, he felt that in some way he must confirm this. Squatting down, he slowly lifted his head. He had not been mistaken; he could see that by the light of the two campfires about sixty paces from him. Beyond them was unbroken darkness, in which there was no war and no enemy.

Just then he heard above the roar of the river a gentle padding, and from the darkness a black, somewhat bent, human form was coming straight toward him. Muttering from boredom or from fear, the sentry came so close that Stojan, had he leaned forward, could have seized him by the ankle and hurled him down the steep bank into the river. But such a course would have been senseless and purposeless. The sentry might shout or his gun strike loudly against something. Furthermore, Stojan had to assess his strength, the circumstances, his behavior. The sentry had been strolling along and was now standing there, within reach, shifting from one foot to the other, looking into the darkness, at the fires, God knows where. Voices and the clinking of cooking pots could be heard around the fires. Perhaps the sentry was interested in them. Perhaps they reminded him of his home and family. He remained standing there while a man could count five, terribly long it seemed to Stojan, and then went back again, stamping, already familiar with the path.

Stojan knew that he would come back and would stand in the same place, or somewhere else quite near him. Among men, habits are more regular than among beasts. By that time he must know what to do; he must do what he must.

There was no sense in going back, for his friends could not help him. Probably, almost certainly, one of them would make some sudden noise and spoil everything. His big knife, like his gun, he had left behind, so as not to hamper him. But he could not use the big knife, even though a man cut through the neck makes no sound. For that man had a scarf around his neck, and it was by no means sure that in the darkness he would find the right spot, below the nape of the neck and above the great vertebra, as Gorčin had taught him that same day. He had his pistol, but he could not think of using that; the discharge would betray him. He could rely only on using the little knife, single-bladed, with silver-encrusted hilt and curved point of dark-blue tempered steel, which Izet-beg had given him. Yes, the little knife, Izet-beg's knife. Only that would do.

Stojan used that knife every day. His hand knew all its qualities, had grown sure and infallible in its use. With it he had killed many beasts, wounded deer and wild goats. Wild animals, and also cattle, make no sound if their throats are cut at a single stroke. They only kick for a time, till the spinal cord is cut. It must be the same for a man, for a man is like every other animal —he eats, breeds, dies.

The sentry began once again to pad along and take shape. He was a short, rather bent man, bowlegged, like a horseman or a peasant brought up on the land, perhaps a Moslem peasant from the villages on the plain, who for the most part are short and slow-moving. He once more came close to Stojan, halted, looked up the road, and then began in a thin whistle to recall from memory some familiar song. He also looked toward the campfires, rather longer than before, as if awaiting something—supper, a comrade —and then started back again.

Stojan leaped swiftly and silently, closing the man's mouth with his left hand and at the same time plunging the knife into his throat, cutting the windpipe. The sentry tried to shout and raised his arms, but his voice was stifled by Stojan's hand and the welling up of his own blood. He collapsed beside Stojan, who, kneeling on his left knee, deftly and skillfully supported his weight.

The little man twisted convulsively, his throat bubbling. Stojan pulled back his head, and after two cuts the knife reached the spine. But it stuck there, grinding, and the blood, thick, warm, and darker than the night, covered Stojan's hands and spattered his face. He must find the joint. He found it, thrust in the point of the knife, and, twisting it to right and left, cut the spinal cord.

He hastened back, not forgetting to move as noiselessly as possible. His comrades were standing on the bank.

"I have your gun and sword," Grgur whispered to him.

"Follow me. But as silently as you can."

They ran along the riverbank and, one after the other, leaped over the twisted, motionless corpse on the path. When they had passed the campfires, Stojan halted, waved to his companions, and plunged down the steep bank to the river. They tumbled after him, hurrying through the undergrowth, through the thickets, over islets and marshes, waiting for one another and keeping in contact by low whistles.

They stopped in the bushes on a sandy clearing, trembling and out of breath.

"The worst is over. Here we are safe; we can take a rest," Stojan whispered.

"High time, too. I have never run away like that when no one was after me," Gorčin jested, sitting down and clearing his throat.

"And I'm going to wash this off," Stojan added.

"What?" asked the clerk.

"Blood."

"You can never cleanse yourself of that," Gorčin remarked, and it was not clear if he were jesting or speaking seriously.

"I must. I am not a wolf. And the knife, too."

"Sometimes it would be better if one could be a wolf," Tomo breathed heavily, and sighed.

Gorčin was surprised, hearing Stojan splashing himself, that the river was so near. "I'll never get away from that cursed water."

Stojan, washing his hands, knife, and face with water from the dark river, cleaning off the blood, which had not yet congealed, recalled the man whose throat he had just cut as someone distant, almost not within his experience. His fatigue and tension had lessened, washed away with the blood, carried away by the dear, familiar river, whose other bank could scarcely be seen.

As from a limitless and unknown distance, shots broke out, and there were shouts in a foreign language, there behind them, by the dead sentry, some two or three hundred paces away. There were five or six shots, and an uproar of cries and calls.

"They've found him," Grgur said.

Gorčin added, as if to himself: "So, you locals know well enough how to cut a throat. And I used to think it was solely a Montenegrin trick, and that it was too much for you even to kill a chicken."

They were silent, each thinking his own thoughts, amid the uproar and the shooting, which spread along the base of the hills and was answered by the Montenegrin army.

"Now our people are wondering if all this commotion is because of us," the clerk commented.

Even as the uproar and the shooting had suddenly burst out, so, too, it suddenly died down. The two armies lay down to rest, to be ready for the battle the following day.

They went on slowly through the icy drizzle and the still-icier blows of the twigs, down through the undergrowth, until Stojan, after a few hundred more paces, emerged onto the open fields.

"We must give them the agreed signal that we have got through," Tomo said.

Stojan led them silently toward a paling around a haystack. Gorčin set fire to it, and the others, lighting handfuls of hay, fired the other three sides of the stack.

As they were going away, Grgur asked: "Whose hay was that?"

But not even Stojan knew, and Gorčin, in his half-serious manner, commented: "Now it's ours."

Behind them flamed a gigantic torch, which defied the night and the hillsides with its tongues of red flame and clouds of white smoke.

By the Murina bridge they met the scouts of Voivode Todor Miljanov's army, and when they got to the village the clerk and Gorčin went to look for the Commander.

In the cottage where Anto's family was housed, a gentle murmur met Stojan and Grgur from around the candle above the dead face of Anto, serious and worried, as in life.

The children were asleep in the corner around Akan, but Stamena and Stanija were keeping vigil, with some old women from the village.

"Tonight; he died tonight. Just as it was getting dark." Stamena wept, falling on Grgur's breast.

With dry eyes and compressed lips, Stanija added: "He was in agony and also it was very cold. He has been ill ever since we fled. But we did not expect him to die, until yesterday morning, when he became delirious."

Akan woke up and said unemotionally but with grief-stricken face: "He asked for you, Grgur, when he came to his senses about noon. And for the other Radaks. We said, for so we had heard, that our village was free, that you were there with the army, and that you would soon return. But it seemed to me that he did not believe it."

Forgetting to cross himself, Grgur fell beside his dead father, keening.

Morning dawned with fierce attacks by the battalions of Todor Miljanov's army against the Shquiptars on the right bank.

In the darkness the army dragged its way along the muddy road by the darkened river, driven on by the snow and wind, by the Shquiptar infantry and Ali-beg's cavalry, proud of the defeat for which it felt it was not to blame, proud of the wounded it carried with it and of the dead it left behind, furious at God the unmerciful and the gospodar who did not send help in time, yet ready to fight and to die once again.

In the twilight, following the army, the Radaks moved, leading their dead knez on the horse taken from the oppressor Buljuk-baša. When they left the village for the bare, stony gorge, Stanija lamented, her moans louder than the roar of the iron river. She called upon the dead comrades of the exhausted soldiers and fugitives and linked their unrecorded sufferings and sacrifices with the horror, shame, and suffering of the day. From defeat, from vagabondage, hunger, and great effort arose the immortality of human endurance and compassion.

The dead walked alongside the living, and reality and tradition were fused in tears. In the midst of the invisible, nonexistent heavens rose a huge black sun, and rivers of blood flowed up the hillsides.

The life of the Serbs and of the human race, imagined as it was and as it would be after the grave, followed in the wake of the footsteps of the wounded fighters and glittered with hope in the eyes of the fugitives.

Stanija mourned for her father-in-law, the clan knez, and still more for the Serbian defeat and for human suffering, for the scattered army of the Voivode.

In prison at Sremska Mitrovica
August 1962–May 1963

Glossary

GLOSSARY

(Words originally Turkish are given in their local, Slavic form.)

aga: sir; citizen of good standing. Sometimes denotes military rank. Often merely an honorific. Exclusively Moslem.

barjaktar: from *barjak,* a standard. In Montenegro a standard-bearer; in Albania a clan chieftain.

beg: a noble. Often merely an honorific. Always Moslem. The feminine form, in Slavic, is *begovica.*

begler-beg: title of supreme military authority in a large area or province.

bes (Albanian): "given word." Almost equivalent to "honor." One of the highest moral obligations of an Albanian.

Branković: Vuk Branković, who, according to Serbian tradition, though the episode is unhistorical, at the Battle of Kosovo (*q.v.*) betrayed Knez Lazar, leader of the Serbian army that was defeated by the Turks. His family name is often used in popular speech as a synonym for "traitor."

bula (plural: *bule*): Moslem woman.

buljukbaša: military rank, roughly equivalent to platoon commander. In the medieval Turkish army, a *buljuk* (band or platoon) numbered about a hundred men. In the time of this book, a *buljuk* was much smaller and was usually composed of irregulars.

Bušatli: Albanian noble family from the village of Bušatli. For about two hundred years they were hereditary viziers of Skadar and ruled over northern Albania and parts of Montenegro. According to Montenegrin tradition, they were descended from the last Christian princes of Zeta, the Crnojevići. They were deprived of their vizierate in 1831.

cadi, kadi: Moslem judge.

Čakor: mountain pass between Dečani and Montenegro. The present road did not exist at the time of this story.

captaincy: civil and military local rank, taken by the Turks from the Venetians and used mainly in Bosnia. From it comes the family name Kapetanović.

čardak: fine, usually two-story, house surrounded by gardens; or a decorated balcony.

Glossary

ćatib (Turkish): clerk or civil servant. His tasks and duties were indeterminate.

ćevabčići: small skinless sausages of mixed meat cooked on a charcoal grill; a Serbian specialty.

čitluk, čifluk: beg's feudal property or estate.

čoček: Turkish dancing girl. Often used in a pejorative sense.

Crnojević (plural: Crnojevići): last medieval Serbian Christian rulers of Montenegro, in the fifteenth century. The most famous was Prince Ivan Crnojević. One of his sons was converted to Islam and became the first sanjakbeg of Montenegro.

Danilo, Prince: *see* Petrović, Danilo.

Dečani: Serbian monastery near Peć, built between 1327 and 1335 by the Serbian King Stefan, of the Nemanja family, who became known as Dečanski and the Holy King. Under Turkish rule it remained a Serbian Orthodox monastery.

dervish: Moslem monk; member of a dervish order.

dimije: wide Turkish trousers worn by women, for which over six yards of material are needed.

djever: brother-in-law. Other meanings denote close kinship. Often used rather loosely, as among the Radaks.

Djurdjevi Stubovi: great Serbian monastery, now a ruin, founded by the Grand Župan Stefan Nemanja (1170–1196).

Drekalović, Marko Miljanov: voivode of the Kuči tribe, general, hero, and author (1833–1901).

Dušan: son of King Stefan; king 1331–1346; tsar 1346–1355.

džezva: long-handled copper pot used for making Turkish coffee.

feredža (Turkish): enveloping cloak, usually black, worn by Moslem women when they went into the streets. Worn with the *jašmak* (veil), which for long journeys on horseback was replaced by the *peča.*

fildžan (Turkish): handleless cup for Turkish coffee.

fis (Albanian): tribe or clan.

ghazi, gazi (Turkish): hero or conqueror.

gusle: Montenegrin musical instrument played with a bow and having one string, or occasionally two. Heroic ballads are chanted to its somewhat monotonous accompaniment. The player is a guslar.

hadji (Moslem): one who has made the pilgrimage to Mecca.

haiduk (Serbian): brigand or outlaw. Since many Montenegrins and Serbs became outlaws after quarrels with or oppression by the Turkish authorities, the haiduks were regarded almost as national heroes, and there are many ballads about their exploits.

handžar: long Montenegrin knife, equivalent to a short sword.

Glossary

hanum (Turkish): "my lady"; feminine equivalent of effendi (sir). Usually used only for women of a certain social standing.

Hatti-humayun: decree of Sultan Abdul-Medjid, February 18, 1856, which guaranteed, among other things, freedom of worship to Christians in the Turkish Empire, abolition of physical punishments, private ownership, and the establishment of mixed Moslem-Christian courts. It was honored more in the breach than in the observance.

hodža: Moslem priest. The family name Hodžić indicates descent from a hodža. In Suljaga's case, it is a translation from the Orthodox Popović, indicating descent from a *pop* (priest).

kajmak (Turkish): cream. In Yugoslavia, a sort of light cream cheese.

kajmekam (Turkish): district administrator; representative of the vali or vizier.

katun (Montenegrin): mountain herdsmen's village, inhabited only in summer. There are various names for such villages in other parts of Yugoslavia.

kmet: Christian Orthodox householder.

knez: local Christian village or district headman, always elected, though there was a tendency for the knezship to remain in one family. His powers were limited. The area under his control was a knežina.

kolo: round dance.

Kosovo: district in southwest Serbia where a battle took place between Serbs and Turks in 1389 that, in popular tradition, confirmed Turkish conquest of the medieval Serb state. Ballads about it are still much alive.

Krusi: village in Montenegro where a battle took place in 1796 between the Montenegrins and the Vizier of Skadar, Mahmut-pasha, who was killed. His death put an end to the pretensions of the Skadar viziers to exercise dominion over Montenegro.

kubura: old-fashioned pistol.

Kuč, Ilija: mid-nineteenth-century outlaw from the Metohija renowned for his resistance to torture.

Kuči: Montenegrin tribe on the Albanian frontier.

kula: part of a fortress, equivalent to a donjon or keep; a stone house.

kum (feminine: *kuma*): special relationship, sometimes equivalent to godparent. *Kumstvo* is a close tie between individuals, often closer than blood relationship.

Malesia, Malisori: district and tribal group in northern Albania, mainly Moslem, who live in a patriarchal manner and are fiercely independent.

Malezez (Albanian): the Black Mountain: hence, Montenegro.

Glossary

Metohija: district around Peć and Dečani, now with a large Albanian minority. The word means "monastery estate."

mudir: Turkish administrative official, roughly equivalent to mayor.

Nikola, Prince: *see* Petrović, Nikola.

nizam: Turkish regular army, established in 1826; a soldier of that army.

oka: Turkish measure equivalent to 2¾ pounds or 1.35 liquid quarts.

oro: Montenegrin dance for two persons.

Pavlović, Peko: Montenegrin hero and leader of the revolt in Hercegovina, 1875–1877.

Pecirep, Lazar: Montenegrin hero mentioned in traditional eighteenth-century stories who continued insulting the Turks after being impaled at Plevlje.

Petrović, Danilo: Prince of Montenegro, 1851–1860.

Petrović, Nikola: Prince of Montenegro, 1860–1910; king, 1910–1918.

Piletić, Jole: Montenegrin hero of the mid-nineteenth century.

pita: pastry with either sweet or savory filling.

Prokletije: mountain range along the present Montenegrin-Albanian frontier.

Rade: Petar II Petrović Njegoš, Prince-Bishop of Montenegro 1830–1851, and the greatest Serbian poet. His masterpiece is *The Mountain Wreath (Gorski Vijenac)*.

Radović, Mina: early nineteenth-century hero and insurgent from Morača.

raja: infidel, mainly Christian, subjects of the Turkish Empire. Often used insultingly as equivalent to serf.

sahibija (Turkish): feudal landlord.

salvara (plural: *salvare*): wide Turkish trousers worn by women and older men.

šarkija: Turkish musical instrument.

sejmen (plural: *sejmeni*): guard, policeman; usually an irregular. Originally a rank among the Janissaries.

sened (Turkish): written assessment of tithes, feudal dues, etc.

sherbet: sweet nonalcoholic drink.

Shquiptar (Albanian): an Albanian. The country is Shquipnie or Shquiperie.

sirdar, serdar: high military rank among the Montenegrins.

slava: patronal clan or family feast.

snaha: sister-in-law. Familiar way to address young women.

tooth money: money extorted by Turkish irregulars for the wear of their teeth in eating food provided by Christian serfs.

trim (Albanian): hero.

Glossary

Uskok: literally, "one who jumps over." In this case, a man who has fled from Turkey into the liberated Christian districts.

vali (Turkish): governor of a district or province.

Vasojević (plural: Vasojevići): largest of the Montenegrin clans, living around the headwaters of the Lim and Tara rivers.

Vešović, Miljan Vukov: voivode of the Vasojević tribe who raised a rebellion against the Turkish authorities and liberated the lands of his tribe and the districts between the upper courses of the Lim and the Tara. He died in 1886.

voivode: marshal or war leader; highest rank in the prewar Yugoslav army.

Vuković, Todor Miljanov: voivode and brigadier; son of Miljan Vukov Vešović. When he died suddenly, while relatively young, it was rumored that he had been poisoned, with the connivance of the court at Cetinje, because he was in favor of the union of Montenegro and Serbia.

zadušnica (plural: zadušnice) (Serbian): "for the good of the soul." Often the bequest of a church or monastery. Also a feast for the souls of the dead.

zaptiah (Turkish): policeman.

Zeta: medieval name for Montenegro, now generally applied to the districts, especially the plain, at the head of the Lake of Skadar and around Podgorica (present-day Titograd).

zurla (plural: zurle): Oriental wind instrument, similar to a primitive oboe.